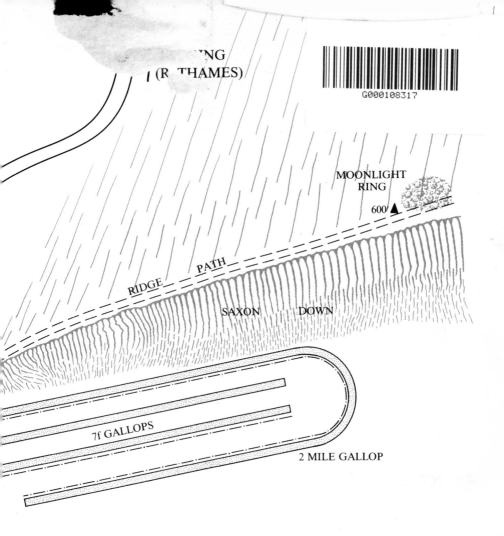

NG
(R THAMES)

G000108317

MOONLIGHT
RING

600

RIDGE ___ PATH

SAXON   DOWN

7f GALLOPS

2 MILE GALLOP

EW

UND

– o SAND TRACK

SAXON
COURT
TRAINING
GROUNDS

THE BLUE RIBAND

DEREK NICHOLLS

THE BLUE RIBAND

Hodder & Stoughton

LONDON SYDNEY AUCKLAND TORONTO

British Library Cataloguing in Publication Data

Nicholls, Derek
  The blue riband.
  I. Title
  823'.914[F]

ISBN 0-340-41699-8

Published by Hodder and Stoughton,
a division of Hodder and Stoughton Ltd,
Mill Road, Dunton Green, Sevenoaks, Kent TN13 2YA
Editorial Office: 47 Bedford Square, London WC1B 3DP

Photoset by Rowland Phototypesetting Ltd,
Bury St Edmunds, Suffolk

Printed in Great Britain by Mackays of Chatham plc,
Chatham, Kent

ACKNOWLEDGEMENTS

All the human beings and most of the horses in this book are imaginary. However, a few great horses of the past are mentioned, most particularly my own hero, Mill Reef, winner of ten of his twelve races, including the 1971 Derby.

Mill Reef was trained at Kingsclere in Hampshire by Ian Balding, to whom I wish to express my very deep gratitude for help in writing *The Blue Riband*. Mr Balding allowed me to spend several days wandering round his superb stable. I saw everything, and had all my questions – however stupid – answered either by Ian Balding himself, or members of his dedicated staff. Any errors in stable routine or training methods are all my own work; they did not originate at Park House, Kingsclere.

My thanks also go to Henry Cecil who answered some very detailed questions for me shortly after training Mill Reef's son Reference Point to win the 1987 Derby.

Finally, my editor, Nick Sayers, provided unfailing support and made many invaluable suggestions.

Derek Nicholls

PROLOGUE

On the evening of 14 May 1779, Edward Stanley, twelfth Earl of Derby gave a dinner at his house in Epsom. The occasion was to commemorate the first running of the Oaks, the Classic race for fillies named after Stanley's Epsom residence, and won that day by his own Bridget. The dinner was a glittering event with Richard Brinsley Sheridan and Charles James Fox among the many famous guests. At some stage it was suggested that an important race for three-year-old colts should be organised for the following year.

Agreement on the need for the race as a means of testing and improving bloodstock lines was swift and unanimous. What to call it was another matter. A clutch of eminent men wanted their name used. After a heated argument well into the small hours of the following morning, there was a short list of two, 'Bunbury' and 'Derby'. Sir Charles Bunbury, the undisputed leader of the Jockey Club, the man whose zeal to rid racing of sharp practice was to cause him to make Newmarket untenable for the Prince of Wales, felt very strongly that the honour should be his.

Eventually the matter was decided by the toss of a coin which came down in Stanley's favour. Almost twelve months later, on 4 May 1780, the first Derby was run on Epsom Downs and Sir Charles Bunbury's colt, Diomed, was the winner.

The race rapidly gained the prestige its founders had wished for. By 1847, Parliament had voted itself a holiday on Derby Day, and all London clogged every road to Epsom. On the day after the 1848 race, Benjamin Disraeli encountered his good friend Lord George Bentinck in the House of Commons and demanded to know the reason for Bentinck's obvious misery. Bentinck explained that he had once owned Surplice, the previous day's victor, but had sold him some eighteen months previously. This was the culmination of what was to be a tragically short life devoted to winning what was already the world's premier race.

"However, I suppose you have no idea what the Derby is," Bentinck said to the future Prime Minister.

"Most certainly I do, sir," Disraeli replied. "Why, it is the Blue Riband of the Turf."

He was using the accepted name for the blue sash worn to signify the Order of the Garter of which he was an immensely proud owner.

Melbourne staged the Victoria Derby in 1855, the first of dozens of races the world over to appropriate the name as a symbol of local excellence.

James Henry Manning first went to Epsom in 1933, the year that the diminutive Hyperion performed the annual miracle.

In 1971, his grandson Edward was kicking his heels in Cambridge, waiting the results of his final examinations. Edward jumped at the old man's invitation to accompany him, and persuaded his lifelong friend Richard Stewart to tear himself away from the bank to join them.

That year it was the magnificent Mill Reef with his distinctive sheepskin noseband who came up the hill in peerless fashion to the rapturous acclaim of the tens of thousands who had come to see him do it. After his defeat by Brigadier Gerard in the Two Thousand Guineas, there had been doubts about Mill Reef, but that day his stamina and courage were placed permanently beyond the doubts of mere mortals. As in all his races, he did it in style, and this time he seemed to be wearing a top hat at a jaunty angle. His immense fan club loved it.

As James Henry wandered off to sympathise with a bookmaker or two, Richard realised that Edward was overcome by emotion. When he spoke, his voice was tight.

"I'd like to do that some day," he said.

James Henry had always wanted to train a Derby winner but was the first to recognise that his ambition was a source of affectionate amusement to those who knew and loved him.

This was different. Richard saw that Edward's face was white with determination. He wasn't joking.

CHAPTER I

The fifty-five members of staff were still filing back into the common room after the final assembly of term as Horace Merritt produced a bottle of sherry from his locker. Edward Manning wasted no time in joining him to accept a 'tincture' from one of his ludicrously effete glasses.

"All the very best, old cock," Horace said, raising his glass. Edward inclined his head in thanks tinged with mock gravity. He was going to miss Horace, Head of Chemistry, self-made reprobate and one of King Henry's School's most outstanding characters. The portly protagonist of evil-smelling mayhem and proud owner of an infinite number of silk bow ties had been a vivid feature of his life for as long as he could remember. When the eleven-year-old Manning, E. J. had become a pupil at King Henry's in 1961, Horace had been the only ray of light in a daunting world. Once Edward achieved the lordly status of the VIth Form, they discovered an affinity for the less serious aspects of learning that survived Edward's departure to Cambridge to read Physics. "I have entertained the highest hopes of you, my boy," Horace had declared, "but Physics! My God!"

Despite his professed horror at the ruination of a promising career, Horace provided every support when Edward returned to teach five years later. Full of advice on what he called "the near-maintenance of good order and discipline while keeping things bright", he had nevertheless warned of the perils of too close an association with his circle of free-thinkers. "They on high don't like it," he counselled. "You'll never get to be an ink monitor if you stick too close to me."

Realising his very deep concern, Edward had taken Horace into his confidence and explained that teaching was not to be his chosen vocation. Whenever the call came from his grandfather, he would disappear as soon as possible. Vastly impressed, Horace had kept the secret even from his wife.

James Henry Manning made his decision that summer and Edward saw the Headmaster on the first day of term to tender his resignation. Edmund Weaver had mellowed a little as retirement approached but he was still incapable of comprehending what was put before him that day.

"You're going to train racehorses?" he said when Edward had finished speaking.

"Yes, Headmaster."

9

"You are taking over from your grandfather – in Ireland?"

"Yes, Headmaster."

"Good gracious me!" Edmund Weaver was clearly trying to think of something to say. When he got it, Edward found keeping a straight face was not easy. "But your father is a banker."

"He works for a bank."

"In a most senior and respected capacity." Edmund Weaver always knew things like that yet even he seemed to recognise the dubious relevance of the fact in this context. "It presents me with a problem – you will not be easy to replace."

"It's kind of you to say so, Headmaster."

"I've always felt that you had such a promising future with us. It seems a trifle strange that you should have come to this decision so late in life."

"I'm only twenty-eight."

"Oh quite – absolutely. What I meant was that if that sort of thing were in the blood – as it were – then it might be expected to emerge sooner rather than later."

"It did, Headmaster. This has been on the cards for ten years or more." Edmund Weaver's eyebrows rose and Edward hastened to explain. "Grandfather has wanted me to join him for some time but I had to wait until he was ready to retire because we could never work together – we're both far too self-opinionated for that. So I had to find a sort of temporary job. This was the obvious choice and I think I've made a contribution."

"Yes indeed." But Edmund Weaver had sounded most uneasy and his demeanour as he came into the common room to make the presentation was a replica of that difficult occasion three months ago. Refusing another of Horace's tinctures, Edward concentrated on looking suitably serious as the Headmaster made a mercifully short speech. There were references to "a surprising new career" and "unsuspected talents" – what Horace called "getting his two penn'orth in" – and it was all over. A handshake, a thin smile and Edmund Weaver was gone.

As relaxation enveloped the occupants of the common room, Edward took off his relatively new gown and handed it to Horace. "There you are, you old rogue, that should keep you going until they pension you off," he said.

Discarding the disreputable rag that had long since given up the struggle against chemicals, Horace donned his new acquisition, beamed happily and said, "Cor! Don't I look a toff? His Majestic Importance might give me Brownie points for this next term."

There were cries of "Rubbish!" and someone said, "Can't you take him with you, Edward? Go on. Please. We'll have another whip round if you do."

"What would I do with him?" Edward asked.

"Anything! Just take him away."

Half an hour later, with all the goodbyes said, Horace accompanied Edward to the car park and smiled wryly as his young friend took what was so obviously a last ceremonial look round. "Miss us a bit?" he asked.

"Yes, I will – I really will." Edward was surprised. The present site of King Henry's dated only from the mid-thirties, with many post-war additions, but the sense of a history going back well over four centuries was definitely there. It would have been easy to become sentimental so he turned to Horace and grasped his hand. "Cheerio, Horace – thanks for everything – always."

"Cheerio, old cock. Try and keep in touch."

"I will."

"Good luck." For a moment there was a flash of something more serious than anything that had ever passed between them before, until Horace dispersed it with one of his facetiously portentous remarks. "I shall follow your future progress with great interest, young Manning. I might even start glancing at the racing pages."

Horace Merritt had been the first memory that Edward ever had of King Henry's School and seventeen years later, he was the last. Looking in the mirror as he drove out through the main gates, he saw him standing quite still, his new gown wrapped tightly round his rotund form, an almost wistful expression on his face.

Edmund Weaver was by no means the first person to be taken aback by James Henry Manning. After war service that had ended in a Japanese prisoner-of-war camp, his son Frank was demobbed in 1946 and applied for a job in a bank. On the very day that he learned his interview had been successful, James Henry announced that he had herewith ceased to be a stockbroker and was going to be a trainer of racehorses. Because everything in post-war England looked so bleakly unpromising, the venture was to be launched in Ireland and Frank was invited to join in. Innately cautious and searching for comfortable stability after the war, Frank declined the offer.

As he made his last journey into Worcestershire from King Henry's on the south-western outskirts of Birmingham, Edward thought about it for the umpteenth time and, as usual, smiled to himself. Poor dad! What a facer it must have been – but he surely knew the score. No one who had spent more than five minutes in James Henry's company had any excuse for supposing that he was anything other than totally remarkable. Frank had said that it was the sheer suddenness of it all that had been so shocking, although hindsight had enabled him to appreciate the causes and reasons. James Henry's war was thoroughly miserable;

he was forty-one when it started and thus unable to take part. He was devoid of any talent for sitting around while other people did things – mostly badly in his view. Bitterness replaced frustration when his beloved wife Hester was killed in the notorious air-raid on Coventry while visiting her sister and this was followed by a further grievous blow when James, Frank's elder brother, was lost in a bombing raid over Germany. For James Henry, peace was utterly negated by the result of the 1945 General Election, a topic upon which he could still be awesome thirty-three years later. Given his method of thinking, the move to Ireland was perfectly logical.

Before he went, he gave Frank the house. Edward stopped the car in the gateway and studied it, a beautifully restored country house built around 1900. The garden of over an acre was looking rather sorry for itself now but for nine months of the year it was a riot of colour and interest thanks to his mother's efforts. There were six bedrooms, three bathrooms and goodness knows what else, making up a considerable residence even for the Regional Manager of a major clearing bank – but how the devil had a trainee cashier coped with it? The vision of his father camping out in the smallest bedroom and kitchen had always been irresistible and funny.

Ann Manning was baking. As ever, she looked cool, efficient and ten years younger than her age.

"All over?" she asked.

"Yes."

"Did it go all right?"

"Yes." He filled a kettle to make tea. "Edmund Weaver had his little dig, as forecast by Horace – it was fine apart from that. I shall miss the place."

"You sound surprised."

"I am. I thought I wouldn't mind all that much, but I did. Still, after seventeen years, man and boy, it was bound to happen. I shall concentrate on becoming an illustrious old boy."

"Surely not, dear. They'll never recognise what you're going to do."

"Don't be pessimistic. Edmund Weaver is retiring in two years. The betting is that the governors will go for something very different. You can take me to the airport tomorrow?"

"Of course." His mother was used to his sudden changes of manner. The instant transition from small-talk to serious business was a characteristic Edward had inherited or acquired from James Henry. She had often thought that it would have been nice if she and Frank had been able to match his grandfather's influence, but Frank was always content to let things develop their own way. "I expect you'll be seeing Susan tonight?" she asked.

12

"No mother, she's away in London. In any case, we had a long chat last week."

The finality was unmistakable and Ann Manning found that she was struggling to control exasperation. Susan Watts had been the last hope that the madcap scheme would fall through. A year ago the relationship seemed to have become serious and she sensed that the girl not only shared her disquiet at the proposed adventure but might be in a position to exert a calming influence. Unfortunately, the last few months had seen history repeating itself as Susan had gradually drifted into the obscurity that was the inevitable fate of all Edward's girl friends. Having convinced herself that this urge to get mixed up with horses and what must be a horde of undesirable hangers-on represented a dreadful watershed, Ann felt her chances of ever having a grandchild becoming more remote.

She dismissed these thoughts in favour of a brave face, especially over dinner. The results of her efforts in the kitchen were always first rate but she had excelled herself for the occasion and the meal engendered an extremely pleasant atmosphere. Frank asked Edward several questions about his last morning at school and his son appeared to find them increasingly amusing. "I knew it would happen," he said. "Any minute now you're going to ask me if I'm absolutely certain I'm doing the right thing."

"I most certainly am not," Frank replied in the tone of mild reproof he might have used to someone at work who was threatening to step out of line. "I merely think it's a strange course of action for a physicist to take. Now what are you laughing at?"

"You sound just like Edmund Weaver." Frank pulled a face; he was well aware of his son's opinion of his ex-Headmaster. "I'm not a *real* physicist, dad. Teaching kids is a very far cry from pushing the frontiers of science forward."

"I know. I also know that the chances of total failure if you follow James Henry's example and advice are pretty slim – if you're that way inclined."

While Edward was laughing at the sting in the tail, Ann perceived one of the root causes of what she had always seen as a problem. Whenever anyone talked of him, it was always 'James Henry' – never 'Father' or 'Grandfather' or 'Mr Manning'. She was a great admirer of the old man, readily recognising that he had made a success of the amazing life he had embarked upon at about the time she first met Frank – yet surely there was no need to refer to him in this unusual, special way? She constantly half-expected that one day someone would change 'James Henry' into 'the Great Man' and that it would be accepted as perfectly natural.

"Don't worry, dad, I intend carrying on from where James Henry leaves off. I shall be a household name."

13

"That's what I'm afraid of," Frank smiled. "Once I've got this early retirement in the bag you can do what you like – but go steady until then."

"How long will that be?"

"Two years should do it – and then look out. It's about time I came up with something earth-shattering. And it's no good looking like that – I just might break the habit of a lifetime. Good old predictable Frank could disappear overnight."

Edward smiled fondly. He knew that whatever his father had said – or more usually implied – over the years, he was immensely proud of James Henry.

They made their formal farewell shortly after eight o'clock the following morning in the depressing gloom of an outstandingly nasty shortest day. "You know, I've always detested this time of year," Frank said as he fastened his seat belt. "Never mind, the days start getting longer now." Then he did a very surprising thing. He extended his right hand through the open window. "Good luck," he said as Edward grasped it. "I know you're going to be up to your eyes in it but don't forget to let us know how things are going. We'll come over for our summer holidays."

"Make sure you do." Edward found the moment unexpectedly emotional; it was the first time his father had ever shaken his hand. It had very nearly happened when he won the scholarship to Cambridge and again when he graduated. Today, Frank had not withdrawn at the last moment.

Just before she set off to the airport with Edward, Ann found it necessary to conceal her feelings again. He was carrying only one small bag that would qualify as cabin luggage on the aircraft. Everything else that he wanted had been packed up and sent on ahead two weeks ago. At some stage she would have to do something about all the things that weren't wanted and had been left behind. She would wait a year. That would give him a chance to change his mind. He dealt a death-blow to such thoughts as he eased the car down the drive. "Remember to sell this car for me, mother. You've got all the papers?"

"Yes."

"There's no point in leaving it around doing nothing. They start rotting very quickly."

"All right."

For the rest of the journey she forced the conversation to be inconsequential and he was glad of it. He sensed her mood and diagnosed it perfectly. She knew precisely where he was going; she had been there many times and said how much she liked it. She also knew that he was going to be surrounded by capable people who were anxious that he succeed. Even allowing for the car journeys at either end it was no more than three hours away. And yet she felt that he was leaving home for the first time to go to a hostile environment on the other side of the world. So it was a relief to hear about all the Christmas shopping she still had to do and the mince pies she had promised to make for her sister.

He gave her a big hug outside the check-in hall at Birmingham Airport. "Don't worry," he ordered. "I'm going to be perfectly all right – and you'll be able to see for yourself when you come over."

"Yes. Take care."

"I will."

He watched, waving, as she drove away, then headed briskly for the check-in counter. Once or twice in the early days he had gone over by train and boat but it had usually been by air with a return ticket. Now he had a single and the pretty Irish girl commented on the fact when she gave him his boarding card. Perhaps even he had been cherishing a tenuous notion that it was nothing more than a short escapade, that he would be coming back fairly soon and none of it really mattered. There was no room for that now. It did matter. Before long, he would be on a path so dramatically different that it was scarcely conceivable.

At last, after eight years, he was taking the first step towards the dream of winning the Derby.

As the Aer Lingus jet climbed through the cloud over Birmingham en route for Dublin, Edward closed his eyes and tried to compose his thoughts. He had under an hour in which to prepare for a completely new way of life. After ten minutes he gave up and recalled what had led up to this journey. His first recollection of Avoca House, James Henry's stable near Newbridge, County Kildare, went back twenty years. During a two-week holiday there with his parents, he had fallen head over heels in love with the place and the twenty horses it housed. Because his mother was so clearly uneasy at the bond between himself and James Henry, it had taken two years of scheming and persuasion to get back. Then, he went for the whole of his summer holiday from school, travelled both ways on his own and learned to ride on a mare called Drogheda's Daughter who was amiable enough for such a task and talented enough to have won races. After that, every holiday, Christmas, Easter and summer, had been spent there. So how many trips was that? Three a year for eighteen years – fifty-four. There had been exceptions; he had spent three Christmasses at home and sacrificed the Easter before his final exams at Cambridge. So that was a nice round fifty during which he had probably gained five or six years experience of handling horses and now he was going to take charge of it all. And things had changed a good deal since the eight-year-old had been bowled over; the yard had been enlarged and currently had forty-five horses.

The weather forecast had held out the prospect of clearer weather moving in from the west and sure enough, towards the end of the short flight, the Irish Sea appeared through breaks in the cloud. By the time he walked down the aircraft steps at Dublin, there was hardly a cloud in the sky although it was much colder. Customs were not interested in his small bag and Edward walked into the arrivals area to be met by Finoula.

Her nature was unashamedly uninhibited and exuberant. "When you're greeted by Finoula, you know all about it," they said and she was in outstandingly fine form this morning. With a whoop of delight that turned heads hundreds of feet away, she launched herself at him and ended with her arms round his neck and her feet clear of the ground. He managed to stay upright by taking a vaguely controlled pace backwards; he also gasped as an awful lot of breath was knocked out of him.

"And how's yourself?" she asked when she had let go of him and was standing on her own feet again. "You're looking peaky. That's what you get being stuck in a mouldy owd school." As ever when she was excited, she sounded very, very Irish.

"You, however, are looking wonderful," he told her.

She always did. Finoula was the archetypal Irish beauty, shining black hair, green eyes and a challenging, quizzical set to her head. At eighteen, she was in full bloom, her face glowing with a colour no cosmetic could ever achieve.

"I see you've been working," he said as they made for the exit.

She had come for him just as she was, well-worn riding breeches, roll-neck sweater and quilted waistcoat.

"Sure I have. Time and horses wait for no man."

"Is that a fact?"

"It is so," she retorted before realising he was teasing her. "Edward Manning, you're as bad as your grandfather."

"Now there's a compliment. How is he?"

"He's very well – but here, wait till I tell you, the owd devil is looking forward to retirement – no, he really is."

"I don't believe it!"

"You'll see. He's become very relaxed this last month – and he talks about you all the time. As a matter of fact, to tell you the God's honest truth, we're sick of hearing about you. I'm sorry about this." She was apologising for the battered Land Rover. "I wanted to bring something decent but he said you'd got to get used to roughing it now you're one of us."

Once in the vehicle, Edward braced himself. Finoula's driving was as exhilarating as her approach to everything else and was composed of naked vigour laced with bursts of creativity. When he realised that she intended avoiding the centre of Dublin in favour of lanes and back streets in order to reach the main road to Naas and the Curragh, he resigned himself to fireworks. Her concentration, never good, was much impaired by her insistence on giving him a report on virtually every horse in the yard. Since Finoula was incapable of conducting a conversation without masses of eye contact, she spent much less than half the time looking at the road and he found it impossible to take much notice of what she was saying. However, when he saw that she was missing things by wider margins than usual, he paid attention; these were *his* horses she was talking about.

On the mercifully deserted trunk road to the west, comparative serenity descended despite the speed and she told him all about people. Edward let it all wash over him, secure in the knowledge that there was no bad news and it would do him good to find out everything for himself in his own time. When she was in this mood, bubbling with happiness, he could listen to her for hours for the sheer pleasure of her voice and because, apart from James Henry himself, she was the person who typified Avoca House best for him. She had been born there during his first proper visit when he was ten. Her father was Declan Kelly, now head lad, her mother Mary was housekeeper. Her adoration of horses had also emerged early, and it had never occurred to anyone that she would do anything other than spend her life with them. For the last year, as the prospect of taking over Avoca House became a reality, Edward had assumed that he could rely on her knowledge and flair to help him through what was surely going to be a difficult period.

At Newbridge, she turned on to a minor road without reducing speed and laughed at the look on his face. "You really will have to learn to live a bit," she said.

"That's precisely what I want to do."

"You'll improve now we've got you away from that school," she said, understanding his meaning perfectly.

After three hair-raising miles, she turned into the lane that led only to Avoca House and, as usual, her driving underwent a dramatic transformation with speed reduced to a gentle walking pace. To the uninitiated, it would have been incomprehensible but they had not travelled far before the reason appeared – six horses on walking exercise were returning home. Only three had riders; the others, without saddles but with James Henry's distinctive pale grey and royal blue rugs over their backs were being led. "That's Liam Corrigan on Murgatroyd in front," Finoula explained, making no attempt to pass them. "He's only wearing that helmet to impress you."

"He can carry on impressing me that way," Edward said quietly but firmly, aware that Liam normally refused to wear one. For once, Finoula's attention was fully on the road as she kept a safe distance from the last pair but she shot a quick glance at him. His mood had changed as he leaned forward to study the horses. In no doubt that she had just heard the first utterance of Avoca House's new master, Finoula realised that her own habits with headgear would have to change.

When the horses had reached the safety of the yard, she swung the Land Rover in front of the house, abandoned it with the engine still running and scampered off. Everyone would be in the yard at this time of day and Edward came close to feeling sorry for her. Of course she was excited and bursting to release the news of his arrival but even she had to observe the fundamental rule that excitement was forbidden in front of horses who could behave disastrously in the face of raised voices and jumping about. The prospect of Finoula doing her best to walk quietly up to someone and say, "Himself is here," in a normal voice was quite amusing. Edward studied the rather nondescript front of Avoca House with new eyes. Built some time just before 1800 and much messed about with since, it could never be called attractive. It was doubtful whether the dirty grey stone could be improved by cleaning and a particularly dire shade of blackish slate had been used on the roof. Now it was both home and work-place.

Turning at the sound of footsteps on the gravel, he saw James Henry and Declan approaching with Finoula jigging up and down beside them. It was impossible to believe that James Henry had celebrated his eightieth birthday two months ago. He was just over six feet tall and ramrod upright, towering over a diminutive Declan. His handsome features belonged to a healthy sixty-year-old and the mop of once-golden hair was still luxuriant although it had whitened since he passed seventy. His firm handshake was accompanied by an impish grin and the question, "How's your father?"

"He's OK. Mother took it fairly badly though – she's going to need a bit of time to get used to it."

"Only to be expected – give Frank something useful to do. May I present your head lad, Mr Kelly."

"Hello, Declan," Edward said, smiling at the old man's facetiousness.

"You're very welcome, sor," Declan said and touched his cap.

Well, that was that and Edward had trouble keeping his equilibrium. Declan Kelly had called him just about everything over the years but never had anything remotely approaching 'sir' been used. Gazing into the pale blue eyes in the bony face, he found nothing but respect and trust. He had arrived and this was the deep end. Declan, well known as a man of few words, had never done a better job in his life; lesser souls could have spoken for hours and still not conveyed the same sense of the responsibility he was assuming.

"A quick look round the yard," James Henry said, "and then Fin's got a surprise for you."

It was a quadrangle with one side missing. The original brick-built stable block with twenty boxes faced the back of the house. The newer wooden boxes had been added in two lines at right-angles to it – fifteen on one side, ten on the other. Beyond the shorter line was the feed shed with the tack room above it, an assortment of brick and wooden buildings, an American barn, the hostel block where the lads lived and Declan's splendid modern bungalow. In many respects it looked nothing like the popular conception of a racing stable or the better-class English establishments but Edward knew that it was effective and easily worked.

A group of lads who were putting the six horses from the lane into their boxes stiffened expectantly when they saw Edward but James Henry called, "Get on with it!" to them. "You've all seen him before and you'll be sick of the sight of him within a month." As they carried on, he said to Edward, "I'd be happy to believe that was the very last order I gave round here." It was said quietly; not even Declan heard it.

Edward gave him a look which said, "Do you *really* mean that?" and the old man nodded decisively.

"I'm getting tired at last," he said and they strolled towards the back door of the house in deep conversation. Declan felt well satisfied as he watched them. He had been with James Henry for over thirty years and had long approved of his chosen successor. Now, with the burden already settling on him, Edward looked more like a chip off the old block than ever. Their looks were very similar, they had the same way of walking, many of the gestures were identical and they thought alike – almost telepathically sometimes.

Inside the back door, they passed the office, currently deserted but tidier and more efficient-looking than Edward had ever seen it. He made a mental note to ask about it. At the end of the passage, they found Finoula and her mother Mary in the huge kitchen that did service as a snack bar to all and sundry between early morning and late afternoon. Finoula's looks and vivacity came straight from Mary who, flushed with happiness, looked little older than her daughter. She was forty, twelve years younger than her wiry, ageless husband and managed to do even better than Finoula by taking Edward's hand, kissing him on the cheek, executing a sort of curtsy and bursting into a voluble speech of welcome – all at more or less the same time.

"Thank you very much, Mary," Edward said when she finally paused for breath. "It's wonderful to be here."

"Wait until you see what Fin's got for you," James Henry said. "Go on girl, show him before you blow up."

Finoula grabbed Edward's hand and pulled him into the main entrance hall towards the staircase. The stairs were the house's finest feature, although James Henry loathed them. Edward had always envisaged them as the ideal setting for beautiful women in fine gowns on their way to a ball. On the landing, Finoula guided him to the left towards a group of rooms that were dowdy and rarely used. But the state of the corridor indicated that things had changed. It was freshly decorated with new carpet and light fittings and three of the four doors that had opened into rooms at the back of the house had vanished. "Your suite, my lord," Finoula said as she flung the remaining door open and pushed him in.

"It's magnificent," he said five minutes later when he had completed his first inspection. "Your idea?"

"Yes. I told himself that we ought to put on a bit of the owd style for you – because the place wasn't fit to live in – and he said to get on with it."

It was impossible to recall what had been there before. Now there was a lounge-cum-study in which most of the things he had sent over in advance were already arranged, a bedroom, a bathroom straight out of the glossiest magazine, and a tiny kitchen. The windows had views of the yard, the decor and furnishings were impeccable. "It really is wonderful," he said. "Did you choose this lot?" He waved a hand to encompass carpet, curtains and furniture.

"I did. I thought it wasn't bad."

"What about the knocking down and putting back?"

"Ah . . . I had to have some help with that," she admitted. "That was Flanagan from Kilcullen. Terrible man. You should see the mess he made. It was drastic."

Over lunch in the kitchen Edward asked, "Who's taking care of the office? I've never seen it looking so tidy."

"That's Siobhan," James Henry said.

"Is she doing the job permanently now?"

"I thought so – you might want to change it."

"Not on your life! That looks perfect – just what I want. Where is she by the way?"

"She's away to Dublin with Dooley," Mary told him. "There's business with Mrs Malahide."

Edward nodded. Mrs Malahide was the owner of eight of the horses and Paddy Dooley, the yard's odd-job man would have gone simply to do the driving. Siobhan was Mary's younger daughter who had left school in the summer aged sixteen. She was not old enough to drive herself to Dublin but she was more than capable of doing the business once Dooley got her there.

When she returned, Edward spent most of the afternoon with her in the office. Siobhan was very nearly the precise opposite of Finoula, though she too was pretty in a restrained, subtle way. She had her father's pale blue eyes and colouring – happily his sandy hair had become blonde for her. Also like her father, she was careful of thought and sparing with words but she was prepared to use her soft, musical voice rather more than Declan. "It really is first class," Edward told her. "The whole thing was a shambles back in summer."

"Mrs O'Keefe hadn't been very well," she said quietly and he smiled to himself. Mrs O'Keefe was an incompetent harridan whom he had come to suspect had an evil hold over James Henry.

"She's gone for good, has she?" he asked.

"Oh yes. She had to give it up because of her chest."

"Right, I want you to carry on. Is there anything we can get to make life easier for you?"

"No. I don't think so." As always with Siobhan, it was a scrupulously considered statement.

"Don't you think an electric typewriter would be useful?"

"Yes. I suppose it would."

"Get Dooley to drive you somewhere tomorrow and buy one – and if you have any ideas for improvements, let me know at once. There's plenty of money for essentials. That goes for everything – the yard as well. We're going to see if we can do a bit better."

Her smile told him that she understood.

Stepping out of the office, he heard James Henry and Mary gossiping in the kitchen. Instead of joining them, he went into the yard. It was almost five o'clock and quite dark and most of the boxes had lights on inside them. He found Declan with Ocean Lady, a nice mare who had won three decent races for Mrs Malahide during the past season. He sensed at once that something was wrong but waited to be told. Declan was standing close to the mare, an arm over her withers, watching her half-hearted attempts to eat.

"She's not right, sor," Declan said.

"How's her temperature?"

"It's high."

"How long?"

"This is the third day."

Edward ran a hand down the mare's neck and looked closely at her listless eyes. "Right, we'll have the vet tomorrow morning."

Declan nodded. "Will you do evening stables?" he asked.

The question came as something of a shock. Evening stables was a ritualistic amalgam of commanding officer's inspection and alchemy. It was the last and most formal check of the day on the horses' well-being and a chance for each of the lads to exchange a few words with the 'guv'nor'. During the racing season, the questions and answers about each horse played an important part in formulating the campaign plan and the training programme to achieve it. In winter, it was largely a question of making sure that the horses were in good health and reasonably fit. Fully aware that evening stables was to be one of his most important functions and a key to setting his style on Avoca House, Edward decided to take the responsibility at once. "Yes, I'll do it," he said.

As they stepped out of Ocean Lady's box, Declan called out, "Evening stables!" producing a disciplined flurry of activity as the lads ran to their posts. James Henry always went round the yard anti-clockwise and Edward automatically walked to the appropriate starting point.

The routine was the same in each box. The lad who looked after or 'did' the horse stood at the head of his charge. After giving the animal a handful of horse nuts from the bucket carried round by Declan, Edward stooped to feel the legs, running his hand from just below the knee or hock down to the ankle. This was to test the complex arrangement of ligaments and tendons, ever vulnerable to strain. The first sign of trouble was usually heat, readily detectable by hand. When Edward had first come to Avoca House, he had been fascinated by the constant obsession with the horses' legs and had often tried to observe the number of times the check was carried out each day. It was an impossible task; although it had been fairly easy to see Declan and James Henry doing it, the lads would also do it before and after each piece of exercise and at any other time that occurred to them. He had given up, bemused and frustrated but certain that it was at least a dozen times a day for every horse. He had soon learned to take the procedure very seriously indeed. "A racehorse needs legs and lungs," James Henry drilled into him. "The only way you can be sure of his lungs is to work him hard. But before you do that, make sure his legs are right."

Once he was satisfied with the legs, Edward ran his hand along the horse's back and studied his coat, looking for unusual marks or blemishes. Finally he said, "Round we go," and the lad persuaded the horse to move in a half-circle to prove his mobility. There were questions about how the horse was eating and drinking, then it was on to the next box. Each lad did two horses, so as Edward and Declan departed, a rug was thrown over the horse they had just seen and the lad hurried away to be ready for them in his other box.

Even during the racing season when decisions had to be made about work programmes and race entries, James Henry went round in no more than forty minutes. Edward took over an hour as he began to build his knowledge of the horses and lads. Declan looked on approvingly as the new master of Avoca House began to assimilate fine detail and show the beginnings of a new style of authority. When they had finished and all the boxes were shut up for the night, Declan walked as far as the back door with Edward.

"What time ought we to start in the morning?" Edward asked.

"Half eight. That's plenty early enough at this time of year."

"Right. Good night, Declan."

"Good night, sor." He touched his cap, had a last look round the yard and went off towards his bungalow.

Edward found Siobhan still at work in the office and he put his head

22

round the door to ask her to organise the vet for Ocean Lady. He also told her to finish off for the night but doubted whether she would for at least another half an hour. Then he went upstairs and began making himself at home in the suite of which Finoula was so justly proud.

Later, James Henry and Edward had a simple meal together in the kitchen, quiet now that everyone had gone for the evening. Their conversation was full of the sparkle that had drawn them so close. Serious issues were ignored until they were washing up.

"Declan's started calling me 'sir'," Edward said.

"Of course he has."

"There's no 'of course' about it. I'm going to tell him to stop it."

"You'll do no such thing!"

"Why not?" Edward was nonplussed by the vehemence of James Henry's reaction.

"Look, understand this if you do nothing else. Declan Kelly left school at fourteen with no hope of anything. His mother was dead and his father was a feckless wastrel. Luckily he got himself taken on in a stable – except that it wasn't too great a slice of luck because the bastard in charge was an incompetent sadist. There were still some right wrong 'uns around in those days. Declan got in such a state that he asked me for a job. Me! A joker barely off the boat from good old England who'd just about learned which end of a horse was which. Declan's done well, very well because he bloody well deserves to – but he firmly believes it's all down to me. You and I know different, but he thinks I'm God almighty. I'm godfather to his daughters and his wife still flirts with me something rotten but he's always called me 'sir' because I'm supposed to be the one with all the responsibility and all the answers. Now it's your turn. If you start pulling any fancy tricks, you'll destroy his belief in the system and that will be your loss. Declan Kelly is the best and you need him – just as he is. You're going to do big things and this place is probably only a jumping-off point – but whatever you do, Declan will be with you all the way if you treat him right. So you get used to being called 'sir' and make damned sure you live up to it. Am I making myself plain?"

Edward said, "Yes," in a rather small voice.

He still had one more lesson. A few minutes later, he saw a light moving round the yard.

"There's someone out there with a torch," he said.

"Then it's half past nine," James Henry replied. "Declan always does a round at half past nine."

"Should I go out?"

"No, you should not! Let the poor man do his job in peace."

It had been an amazing day and Edward was very tired. However, before he fell asleep, he rang his mother from his bedside telephone.

23

She had been hoping that he would and a short chat left her feeling much better.

Next morning, Declan was waiting by the rose garden as he always had done for James Henry. As ever, the major features of his dapper appearance were spotlessly clean riding breeches and boots and a very smart check cap. He stiffened to attention when he saw Edward and raised the handle of his riding crop to the peak of the cap. "Good morning, sor. Everything's in order."

"Good morning, Declan. Thank you." Edward knew that absolute faith could be placed in Declan's judgement that all was well. He would have been in the yard since seven o'clock and gone over everything with a fine-tooth comb.

"Will you have them out for exercise?" Declan asked.

"Yes. How's the ground?"

"It's fine. We've not had much rain."

"We'll use the gallop then and save the barn for when it gets really bad."

"Make the first lot ready," Declan said, slightly louder than normal so that his voice carried to every corner of the yard and the expectant stillness gave way to bustle. With two horses per lad, exercise and work was carried out in two parts, each group of horses being known as a 'lot'.

"Will you have the mare?" Declan asked and Edward nodded. He intended riding out with his horses whenever possible both to set an example and to keep fit. He would start as he intended carrying on. As he turned to fetch a riding helmet from the tack room, his eye caught a garish flash of colour at a bedroom window. James Henry, clad in an appalling silk dressing-gown was drinking a cup of tea. He raised it in salute and winked horribly.

"Don't you dare come down here in that thing," Edward said to him through the open window that had obviously been used for eaves-dropping. "You'll frighten the horses."

Declan brought Daisy Chain, a retired hunter into the yard, saddled and ready for Edward; he was also leading his own horse, a big, elegant bay gelding who had won a dozen races in his time. Taking a last look round before mounting, Edward saw a bare-headed Liam Corrigan. "The helmet, Liam," he said quietly. To the astonishment of the onlookers, Liam showed signs of objecting but Edward reacted swiftly. "Liam, I've come here to produce winners not widows," he said, still quiet but with an unequivocal edge in his voice. Liam meekly took a helmet from a lad who was staying behind and avoided looking at his young wife Kathleen who had stopped helping Mary in the kitchen to watch them go. She was blatantly triumphant; Declan's approval was concealed but equally strong.

Edward led the string past the sheds and barn and into the huge hundred-acre field that contained the gallop. Most of the L-shaped mile-and-a-half track that was used for the fast work was shrouded in the damp December mist that would not lift until a gale or rain shifted it. Unconcerned, Edward headed for the cantering track, a well-used elliptical circuit of about two furlongs. All trace of grass had long since disappeared from the narrow strip into which sawdust and peat had been trodden to give a good surface in all but the coldest and wettest weather. As Edward guided Daisy Chain into the centre of the loop, the other horses filed on to the track and settled down to walk.

Declan was the first to catch his eye. He was a superb natural horseman with an innate style that was streets ahead of all the other lads and many jockeys and this was obvious even at the walk. After they had gone round twice, the horses were warmed up and sent on at the trot. Declan's stylistic supremacy was now more apparent and Edward noted with amusement that Liam Corrigan was doing his best to imitate him. There was no need for it; Liam, like all the others, was a perfectly good rider in his own right, it was just that Declan was so much better.

There was much to be learned from the way a horse moved whether walking, trotting, cantering or galloping. Any signs of ungainliness could point to hitherto undiscovered ailments and exceptional talent might be indicated by quality of movement. Secure in the knowledge that the rest of his working life would involve thousands of hours of close scrutiny of horses at exercise, Edward happily settled himself to the task. He had done it many times with James Henry, now the responsibility for observation, decision and action was his.

On Christmas Day, Edward introduced a new custom to Avoca House by helping to serve dinner in the lads' hostel and making sure that everyone had their meal there. The magnificent spread, cooked by Mary and Kathleen Corrigan was eaten in the evening after the day's work was finished and was a splendid success. A bemused James Henry watched his grandson's idea work like a charm and whispered, "He seems to know what he's doing," to Declan.

"He's going to be very good."

"Good grief, Declan, do you know what you're saying?"

"Yes."

"By the way, what was that kerfuffle in the yard this afternoon? I was trying to have a nap." He saw no need to mention that his drowsiness had been induced by a substantial foretaste of the Christmas dinner.

"We were making changes. Moving horses around."

"Why?"

"The guv'nor wanted it. We put Sybil next to that thing of yours."

James Henry knew that Declan was referring to Murgatroyd whom he owned. "Why?" he asked.

"He cheers her up. We should have spotted it months ago."

"So you think he knows what he's doing?"

"Haven't I just told you?"

New Year's Day 1979 was a normal working day. The weather was mild, there had been no heavy rain and all the horses cantered a few furlongs in the morning. When he returned with the second lot, Edward found a very familiar Rolls-Royce parked between the rose garden and the back of the house. Attracted by the sound of hooves on cobbles, three generations of Stewarts spilled out of the back door by the office. They were Sir Nicholas, the eleventh Baronet, a great friend of James Henry, his son Richard, who was a year older than Edward and a friend of eighteen years, and his son, young Nicholas.

"Happy New Year," they called.

Edward returned the greeting, adding, "I thought it was about time we had the bailiffs in."

"We thought we should give you time to get your feet under the table and see Christmas off," Sir Nick said.

"My feet haven't touched the ground yet," Edward replied, dismounting and handing his mare over to one of the lads. He went through the firmly established procedure of shaking hands with them – rather respectfully with Sir Nick, very warmly with Richard, solemnly with young Nicholas. In the kitchen, Sir Nick's wife Julia and Richard's wife Imogen were drinking sherry and laughing at something James Henry had said while Mary and Finoula bustled around preparing lunch. As Edward was kissing Julia, of whom he was very fond, and Imogen, who mostly frightened the life out of him, Finoula told him that the Stewarts were staying for a meal.

When James Henry arrived in Dublin in 1946, he had one piece of incredibly good luck. Within forty-eight hours he had met and established a friendship with Sir Nicholas Stewart who had just succeeded to both the title and chairmanship of the family merchant bank. That their paths had ever crossed at all was quite remarkable for Sir Nick spent hardly any time in Dublin; his working life was in London at the offices of Stewart's the bank, and he went to Belfields, his County Kildare estate at weekends. The fateful meeting had taken place at a blood-stock sale in Ballsbridge where Sir Nick was fruitlessly looking for a miraculous bargain and James Henry was simply looking. It might have been the common ground of their financial backgrounds that had drawn them together – although Edward had always doubted that – but for whatever reason, they had lunch together and learned a great deal about each other. Sir Nick had a few horses in a stable on his estate but the place was very run down and his somewhat untalented and indifferent trainer had recently drunk himself to death. The Jockey Club were not prepared to grant a licence to either of the two men who were interested and the place was barely ticking over with a skeleton staff who did no more than feed the horses and keep them reasonably clean. The first time James Henry saw Avoca House, it was filthy, leaking like a sieve, infested with vermin and had nine horses in what passed for a yard. Sir Nick had been very apologetic, saying that it was his fault the place had got into such a state, that he should have taken more interest. But he had been in the war from the start, had come back to find problems at the bank which were followed by the untimely death of his father and his taking charge of a complicated, esoteric business about which he knew next to nothing. And in any case, horses were only a hobby.

James Henry took the place on and worked fifteen hours a day at everything from mucking out and teaching himself to ride to helping the builders while he waited for a licence. The fact that he insisted on a decent roof for the original stable block before the leaks in his own bedroom were put right had entered the folklore of Avoca House. Six months after the licence appeared, Sir Nick had his first winner. It was in a mile handicap at Thurles and the prize-money was eighty-seven pounds and a few shillings. Twelve months later, James Henry and Declan had found one another in a seedy bar near the Curragh.

In the same way that Sir Nick and James Henry had become very close, Edward and Richard had grown up to be the firmest of friends. Edward had been best man at Richard's wedding and was godfather to four-year-old young Nicholas. Both were aware that the time would come when they had to take charge of Avoca House and had already sketched out a general plan by the time they were twenty. Richard shared his father's fondness for racing but, in his case, an interest had come close to a passion. In James Henry's thirty-two years, Avoca House had turned out nearly a thousand winners, a remarkable achievement for an ex-stockbroker who had not taken up training until he was nearly fifty, and the number of successes was increasing each year. Richard made no bones about wanting more, not just for himself but for other owners too so that the the strength and prestige of the stable could be seen to grow. He was also adamant about the need to win better-class races with the ultimate objective of having horses who were useful at stud. Three years ago, he had started a small farm at Belfields; it was almost literally a shoe-string operation in the back garden and served no useful purpose other than to amuse Sir Nick. However, both Richard and Edward were confident that it would lead to something.

During a lull in the conversation in the kitchen, Richard picked up a slim leather document case that he had left on the table and looked meaningfully at James Henry.

"Ah yes! Come on." The old man beckoned to Edward. "We've got some business to transact. It looks as though we're going to have to deal with the junior staff of this blasted bank."

Richard smiled. He was Managing Director of Stewart's.

They went to what James Henry – with a hint of self-irony – always called the library. Certainly there were a few hundred books, a handful of them not connected with racing, but they comprised a very small proportion of the wall space. Once they were seated round a cheerful log fire, Richard began.

"A domestic matter first," he said to Edward. "In my capacity as Chief Executive of the Belfields Estate, I'm very pleased to be able to tell you that we shall be offering you a contract to carry on the business of training racehorses here at Avoca House with no increase in rent above what your grandfather has been paying."

Edward inclined his head in thanks.

"Right!" James Henry said, "Let's sort the main business out." He looked hard at Edward. "You've got to have my money."

Edward tried to protest. The subject had been discussed in August. "Look here, grandfather, we agreed . . ." He was cut short.

"We agreed nothing of the sort – whatever you think it was. You are going to have my money *now* and that's an end to it."

"What about father?"

"What about him?"

"He's your son and heir."

"*You* are my heir as far as this place is concerned and the money goes with it. What the devil does Frank want money for?" Edward could think of nothing to say that was not trite. "He's got a house worth well over a hundred thousand, he's earning twenty thousand and he's heading for an inflation-proofed pension of twelve thousand for which he's never paid a penny."

"How do you know that?" Edward asked lamely.

"Because I rang him up and asked him," James Henry said triumphantly and Richard hid his smile behind a sheaf of papers. "All right, Richard, get on with it."

Richard cleared his throat, and, making a tremendous effort to be serious said, "Mr Manning, we at Stewart's have had the privilege of looking after your grandfather's affairs for over thirty years. We would be delighted and honoured if you felt able to place the same confidence in us."

"I do," Edward said, raising his right hand.

"Thank you. Would you be kind enough to sign this where marked please."

Richard passed across a piece of paper that had the texture and weight of parchment and was mostly covered with embossed, copper-plate printing although Edward's name and address had been added in violet ink. He signed it and returned it to Richard who put it and the other papers back in the document case.

"Is that it?" Edward asked, feeling slightly cheated by the simplicity of it all.

"Yes. That was a request to open a personal account with us. As you know, we don't have many such clients but you have passed the stringent acceptance procedure. James Henry's instructions have already been made clear and the totality of his account will be transferred to you at start of business tomorrow. For technical reasons, the transfer will take place via a subsidiary in Zürich. Think of it as a deposit account attracting fairly favourable interest and you'll have a good idea of the mechanism. For your information, the account stood at a little over four hundred and thirty-five when we closed for Christmas."

"Four hundred and thirty-five?" Edward echoed, unaware of what his friend meant.

"Thousand," Richard added crisply.

Edward gaped at him then stared at James Henry who was fast losing interest in the proceedings. "That's every penny you've got I presume," he said when he had collected a few of his thoughts.

"Yes."

"Well . . ." Edward groped for words. ". . . what happens if *you* need money?"

James Henry gave him the famous pitying look that he reserved for those he considered weak in the head. "You give it me, of course," he said wearily.

———

Musetta arrived at Avoca House at lunchtime on a blustery Sunday at the end of February. Paddy Dooley drove the horse van into the yard with the fierce concentration of a man in charge of a ton of loose eggs. As he sat hunched over the wheel, the determined set of his face was rather spoiled by the tip of his tongue protruding through clenched teeth. Beside him, Richard grinned like a schoolboy. When the tail-gate was down, Declan, who had travelled with the filly from Brendan O'Sullivan's place at Blessington, led her out with undisguised pride. Those who had not seen her before fell in love with her at once. As she took stock of her new surroundings, James Henry recognised her bold intelligence and murmured, "Now that *is* class." When Declan walked her round, he added, "Yes, most definitely, she's class."

Back in November, Richard had spent ten days in Boston on business.

29

Over the weekend involved in the trip, he had taken a break, gone to Lexington in Kentucky and paid the equivalent of thirty-five thousand pounds for the yearling filly. "I think she might be useful," he told Edward. "Her dam's a Welsh Pageant mare."

"What about her sire?"

"Ah yes . . . he never quite made it on the racecourse. But the line is good. The chap who sold her thought she was a thoroughly good sort."

"Well he would do, wouldn't he!"

But Edward's scepticism disappeared the moment he saw her. After her flight across the Atlantic, she had gone straight to Brendan O'Sullivan, a friend of Richard who specialised in the schooling of young horses that was necessary before training. Edward had visited Blessington with Richard and Declan and was won over instantly. Declan took longer; he watched her moving round on a lungeing rein for five minutes before pronouncing her, "Fine."

"She's the best we've had so far I think," Richard said.

"No doubt of it," Edward agreed. "What are you going to call her?"

"I thought 'Musetta'."

"That's nice – as in *La Bohème*?"

"Yes. Finding decent names for horses is a devil of a job so I thought we'd have a go at opera."

"Good idea – gives us a sort of trademark as well."

Like all horses, Musetta's birthday was reckoned to be 1 January, so she was now two and ready to start her racing career.

All the other horses had their heads out as Declan led her on two complete circuits of the yard and many of them made welcoming noises which Musetta accepted in her regal stride. When Declan took her to the box that had been prepared for her and she went in without any trace of nervousness, James Henry, Edward and Richard went into the kitchen where Richard collapsed into a chair and gratefully accepted the drink that Mary offered him.

"Thank God that's over," he said. "I've had ten sorts of kittens over getting her here in one piece and worrying whether she'd take to it."

"No problems," James Henry said as though he had personally been magnificently responsible for every inch of the way from Lexington. "You've done well there, Richard. She's going to raise the class a notch or two."

"I thought we might get a couple of decent Stakes races out of her," Richard said.

"Should do if she's handled right." James Henry gave Edward a hard stare. "She might even be the first step towards Epsom."

Edward and Richard exchanged knowing glances. "Be fair, he hasn't mentioned it for some time," Richard said with simulated tolerance and Edward nodded.

The main reason why James Henry had taken up training was because he wanted to win the Derby. The great race had always been at the centre of his interest in racing. As a young man, he had adopted Fred Darling of Beckhampton as his hero and was not to be disappointed; Fred trained seven winners of the race, ending his brilliant career by breeding the famous Pinza. In 1933, James Henry took a day off, drove to Epsom Downs and saw his first Derby. He was never the same again. "My dear, it quite turned his head, you know," Edward's grandmother used to tell people subsequently and she was right. By the time Richard and Edward had come under his influence, the mile and a half on the first Wednesday in June had assumed a near-mystic significance. James Henry drew a series of diagrams to explain every nuance of the testing switchback of a course with its two left-handed bends, sharp descent to Tattenham Corner and straight run-in of less than four furlongs, the last furlong steeply uphill. At sixteen, Richard had christened it 'the north face of racing' and likened James Henry to an old mountaineer gripped by dreams of glory totally beyond his grasp. It was unkind but true, for as the years passed, Avoca House was never to see a horse that could possibly justify the cost of transport to Epsom let alone be considered to have a serious chance in the race. However, when they listened to the old man's pronouncements, they always had the kindness not to voice such thoughts.

Edward and Richard thought of Mill Reef in 1971. Reading their minds, James Henry gave them a look that defied them to argue with him.

An anxious-looking Siobhan hurried in and was immediately conscious of the atmosphere. She was in her Sunday best for mass and was clutching the spiral notebook that was becoming her constant companion.

"I'm sorry to interrupt you, Edward, but there's something I forgot to tell you," she said. "Mr Tuomey is coming tomorrow. I told him between one and two would be your best time."

"Who's Mr Tuomey?" Edward asked.

"The tailor. From Dublin. He's very good. The best."

"Why do I want a tailor, Siobhan?"

"It's the morning suits. You need two. We always go to Royal Ascot, do you see?"

Edward smiled at the collective 'we'. He was certain that the wildest horses wouldn't succeed in dragging Siobhan anywhere near Royal Ascot.

"And there's the fittings as well so we need to do it before you start getting busy," she added. "Mr Tuomey will come here for that as well – you don't have to bother."

"Right. Thank you, Siobhan."

"There's Epsom, too," she said as she left. "I believe it's morning dress there for certain things."

"'Before you get busy,'" James Henry chuckled. "That girl is a dream."

CHAPTER 2

"So you're ready to start?" Richard asked.

"Yes. Murgatroyd will go at Thurles a week on Tuesday." Edward was moderately successful at sounding calmly in control of himself.

"What are the prospects?"

"He must have a good chance. He's been working well and he's coming up to peak condition. Declan tells me the opposition isn't likely to be all that sharp."

"And James Henry?"

"Monumentally indifferent!"

Richard laughed. Were it true, James Henry would be the first owner in the history of the sport to have achieved such a happy state. So far, the four-year-old gelding had run seven times. He had never disgraced himself and always appeared completely genuine, yet had never finished closer than third in company that was considered moderate. Now, he was to have the distinction of being Avoca House's first runner under its new trainer.

It was the afternoon of Easter Sunday and they were nearing the end of a post-lunch walk round Belfields. After two hours of fairly brisk exercise they had still covered only a small part of the two thousand five hundred acres, confining themselves to Edward's favourite haunts, the special places he had first loved as a child. Twenty years ago this huge park, with its lush woods concealing places of infinite variety and excitement, had been second only to James Henry and Avoca House in his affections. He and Richard had wandered for whole days from sunrise to sunset in their own private world with nothing to constrain the fantasies of their games.

They halted as they cleared a beech wood and saw the front of the house half a mile away. "Do you know, I'm not at all sure whether I like that or not," Richard said. "Absolute heresy of course and not to be bandied around – but don't you think it's a bit ugly?"

Edward studied it. The part of the house visible from where they were standing had been built around 1730 by a pupil of Nicholas Hawksmoor. It was in the Palladian style with nine bays, the middle five articulated by plain cylindrical Corinthian columns. There were three storeys. "Looks all right," he said. "I've always liked it."

"H'm." Richard looked and sounded unconvinced. "The proportions

33

seem all wrong to me. The top windows are squat and that ledge just below the roof is far too massive."

"So what are you going to do about it?" Edward asked.

Richard laughed and started to walk again. "I could do what the Stewarts have always done and build a bit more," he replied.

Extending the house had become an obsessive hobby with Richard's forebears about 1820 and had continued more or less unabated until the outbreak of war in 1939. The original front had acquired two wings which had finally been joined by an outrageous Victorian Gothic cloister to form a quadrangle. Beyond the cloisters there was an elaborate maze of outbuildings, some of them of greater grandeur and quality than the house itself. The stables, built by Richard's great-grandfather in 1895 were particularly fine, had found their way into a couple of books on architecture and were currently used by Julia, Sir Nick's wife, as a mushroom farm. With a strange logic that was a feature of the two-hundred-and-fifty-year Stewart occupation of Belfields, this dictated that the handful of brood mares that constituted Richard's budding stud farm were housed in the old dairy.

Near the end of their walk they met Imogen who seemed to be surrounded by dozens of dogs. Richard sensed Edward's discomfort as she approached. He was well aware of his friend's discomfort with most women of about his own age, and realised that this disquiet frequently reached its peak with Imogen.

"Edward's sending out his first runner soon, darling," Richard said.

"Is he really?" She favoured Edward with a gaze that was undoubtedly meant to be friendly but, as so often, seemed haughty. Imogen was formidably good-looking – perhaps more handsome than pretty – and belonged to a family that Edward felt sure must have arrived with William the Conqueror and had been asserting itself ever since. Her eyes were the most arresting feature of her aristocratic, strong-jawed face, and they fixed him now, pale blue, piercing, very disconcerting.

"Who's it to be?" she asked.

"Murgatroyd."

"Ah, yes. A sound fellow, I believe. Doesn't show a lot of class, though, does he?"

"He never has done, but I fancy he's been undervalued. Liam reckons he's found some new tactics that will suit him better and I've been talking to him."

"What, to Liam?"

"No!" Edward laughed. "To Murgatroyd."

Imogen stared at him in silence for a few moments, then said, "Do you know, I rather think you'd better explain."

So Edward did. Richard smiled secretly at his enthusiasm which swept all signs of nervousness away. For nearly an hour Edward explained exactly how Murgatroyd was being got ready for the race and Imogen loved it.

―――――――――

"I shall go and support Murgatroyd," Imogen told Richard as they were getting ready for bed that night.

"Fine. But go easy on Edward. Don't give him the jitters."

"You really do get hold of the most fanciful ideas, my sweet," Imogen said with a passable imitation of wide-eyed innocence. "I wouldn't hurt a fly."

"Come off it! You can send stronger men than Edward into a terminal decline when you put your mind to it."

She nodded understandingly. "But look at how he was this afternoon. Much more relaxed. I think he's starting to realise that I don't actually devour my young for breakfast." She was suddenly thoughtful. "You might have to keep a careful eye on him."

"Whatever for?" Richard looked startled.

"He's going to get married one of these days . . . yes, he is. Underneath all that shyness he's jolly fond of women."

"So, what's the problem?"

"It will be interesting to see what he chooses. She might be *totally* unsuitable."

Richard did not know whether to be dismayed or amused. At twenty-seven, Imogen often assumed an attitude that seemed to give a strong indication of the *grande dame* she would like to be in forty years time. "You can be the most awful snob when you put your mind to it," he said at last.

"No I can't," she replied with complete equanimity. "If Edward married the wrong sort there would be problems – and well you know it."

―――――――――

Murgatroyd's engagement at Thurles was in a race worth about eight hundred pounds to the winner. It was for horses of all ages and was a handicap in which the contestants were allocated the weight they had to carry according to the official judgement of their ability based on past performance. For the connections – the owners and trainers – this was the most modest form of the sport, especially when the prize-money was so small. Handicaps were, however, the backbone of what was effectively an industry and never failed to attract droves of eager punters, all convinced that their system or insight had enabled them to spot the horse and then give him a tickle. He'll go all right once he sees you mean it."

Sean nodded, Edward helped him to mount and they went out of the yard towards the gallop. Murgatroyd's partners were to be the filly Sybil who had come on tremendously since being put in the box next to him and a big chestnut gelding called Arquebus who had never done anything outstanding but had developed an interesting rivalry with Sybil. Finoula rode the filly, Liam Corrigan was up on Arquebus. Edward invited James Henry to watch.

"That's very decent of you, my boy," the old man said grandly. "We has-beens are very grateful for these morsels of comfort."

"I always knew you were good at it, but you really have been excelling yourself lately," Edward told him.

"Good at what?"

"Being pig-headed."

"I told you I wouldn't interfere."

"Does that extend to wanting a gilt-edged invitation to watch your horse do a gallop?"

"I don't want to be a nuisance."

"Are you coming to the race on Tuesday?"

"Ah yes, I'm entitled to that. I'm the owner."

Declan, walking beside them, remained completely impassive.

They watched the three horses go to the mile start on the gallop, walking at first with Sean Gillespie listening to Finoula, who, judging by the continuous and often dramatic gesticulation of her left hand, had even more than usual to say for herself. When the horses were warmed up, they eased into a gentle canter for the last three furlongs. Edward noticed that despite his protestations of surprise at being asked to watch the gallop, James Henry had not forgotten to bring his binoculars with him and wasted no time in using them.

The start, which Edward presumed was organised by Finoula, was briskly done and the horses soon settled into a steady gallop. They ran shoulder to shoulder for the arranged six furlongs with Murgatroyd in the middle. When Sean Gillespie asked him to go, he surged forward eagerly and it seemed to be over. However, Finoula started riding Sybil hard and managed to get in front for a few strides before Sean Gillespie persuaded Murgatroyd to give of his best and he won by a length. Arquebus, not feeling like meeting Sybil's challenge this time, was a long way behind.

"H'm – no better than he needs to be," James Henry said, trying to sound unimpressed.

"It wasn't bad at all," Edward retorted, showing him the time on his stop-watch.

"You can't tell anything from those things!" James Henry seemed to find the idea that any reliance could be placed on the time-piece quite laughable. Edward and Declan exchanged looks.

Sean Gillespie was not displeased. "Yes. He's improved," he said and drove off without bothering with the breakfast that was customary on such occasions.

Tuesday dawned fine with a good weather forecast. A blustery south-east wind was driving large fleecy clouds across a dazzling blue sky with the assurance that there would be no rain. Wanting to be on the course before lunchtime, Edward had decreed that the sixty-five mile journey to Thurles should begin at nine o'clock which gave him time to watch the first lot before leaving. Paddy Dooley was driving the horse van, Liam Corrigan was travelling with Murgatroyd, and Finoula, assuming that she would be needed, had donned a pretty pink and white dress. They were ready to go, Liam Corrigan in the back with Murgatroyd, Finoula and Edward jammed in the cab with Dooley, when Siobhan came rushing out of the office brandishing a large paper bag from which she produced a brown trilby hat.

"Your hat," she gasped, thrusting it at Edward. "You can't go without it. All the trainers have them. Mr Tuomey sent it down yesterday. It's the right size."

Edward put it on, producing shrieks of laughter from Finoula while Siobhan looked satisfied.

"Where's himself?" Finoula asked as Dooley eased the van into the lane.

"God knows. I haven't seen him this morning." Edward was trying to gauge the effect of the hat by leaning out of the window and peering into the wing mirror.

"Is he coming?"

"Oh yes. It was a positive threat."

"So how's he getting there?"

"How should I know? Imogen said she was coming as well but I expect she's forgotten all about it."

"Are you excited?"

"I suppose so . . . more nervous actually." Edward saw no point in attempting to deny it.

"Murgatroyd knows what to do."

"I know. It's me I'm worried about, not him."

Paddy Dooley, slumped in his customary posture which made it seem that he was using the steering wheel to prop himself up said, "Don't worry, sor. We'll see you right." Edward kept his smile to himself. Other than getting them to Thurles in one piece, it was difficult to see what Dooley could do. Nevertheless, the simple comment betokened a loyalty that was deep and widespread. There had been some tensely expectant faces in the yard when they left and Declan, that expert purveyor of nods, had produced the most meaningful specimen yet.

38

During the journey, Edward's spirits lifted. Finoula's constant chatter was an effective deterrent to serious thought and he enjoyed studying the countryside. This was his first trip of any length since taking over Avoca House and he enjoyed being reminded of the hundred subtle ways in which Ireland looked so different from England. Apart from the additional myriad shades of green, he noticed that each of the towns they passed through was fairly compact, with no sprawling suburbs. There was a strong sense of community evidenced by the groups, particularly of men, in earnest conversation at every strategic point. One or two of them always waved at Dooley and he waved back with the dignity of an important personage on a tour of inspection. Edward attached no special importance to the greetings in Kildare and Monaster-evin, since these two bustling market towns were relatively close to Avoca House. But it kept happening – at Port Laoise, Abbeyleix, and every village along the road. In Twomileborris, sixty miles from home, there were only two men and they both waved.

"Who were those chaps, Paddy?" Edward asked, doing his best to sound casual.

"The fellah in the cap is Seamus Doyle's brother-in-law and the other is his wife's cousin from Waterford. He'll be here for the wedding."

Edward stared straight ahead, not daring to look at Finoula; it was bad enough to feel her shaking with silent laughter.

Upon arrival at the racecourse, Edward went through the procedure in which he had already participated many times on James Henry's behalf. Murgatroyd was brought out of the van, obviously intrigued by the journey and knowing that something was expected of him. He was put in a box in the stables provided for the runners and while Liam Corrigan was giving him the extra special grooming that horses received before a race, an official came to check Murgatroyd's papers. Every horse had what was known as a passport, containing, among other things, a detailed description of the animal so that the unscrupulous were not able to make substitutions. It so happened that the official knew Murgatroyd well, and when he heard that he was Edward's very first runner, took him to be introduced to the Stewards of the meeting.

When all the formalities were out of the way and Paddy Dooley had disappeared, presumably to find some cronies, Edward and Finoula went for lunch in the room reserved for owners and trainers. The facilities were spartan compared to grander, more famous courses and Edward, suspicious of the menu, settled for a sandwich and a cup of tea. It was interesting to renew and make new acquaintances with his fellow trainers, seeing them now with the critical eye of the insider rather than as a representative of his grandfather. There were all sorts. Some were affable, devoid of ambition and simply loved working with horses; others were blatantly anxious to succeed and patently mistrustful of virtually everyone while one or two had given up and were consoling themselves with drink. They displayed every attitude about horses from knowledgeable enthusiasm to something dangerously close to indifference. Edward concluded that they were the typical cross-section of any profession.

Murgatroyd's race was third on the card at half past two; carrying out Edward's instructions, Liam Corrigan was walking him round the pre-parade paddock by the stables an hour before this. He was saddled with one of Avoca House's new rugs over his back; Edward had kept the distinctive pale grey with a royal blue border and black initials – EM now instead of JHM. He and Finoula leaned on the rail and watched Murgatroyd go round, giving them a bright look of recognition every time he passed them.

"He looks well enough," Edward said.

"He's grand. He's come on even better these last few days."

"What are his chances?"

Finoula looked at her race card and told him everything she knew about the other eleven horses. They came to the conclusion that at eight stone they were in with a fair chance and were so engrossed in their deliberations that they missed the second race. Just before they followed Murgatroyd into the paddock, Edward realised that James Henry was nowhere to be seen. "Do you suppose something's gone wrong?" he asked.

"No, he's just having a bit of fun and keeping out of your way."

"I'd much rather have him where I can see him," Edward muttered, betraying his first signs of real nervousness. Then, realising that he was still carrying his hat, he slapped it on his head with a pretence at bravado.

Finoula burst out laughing. "God, you look drastic in that thing!" she chortled. At once, his nerves steadied, he laughed with her and they walked to the centre of the paddock together. To Edward's relief, they were met by the smiling face of Charles Rooney who trained near the Curragh and was a great friend of James Henry.

"Welcome to the lunatic asylum, my boy," he said, shaking Edward's hand and allowing Finoula to kiss him on the cheek. "This is your debut, I believe?"

"Yes, it is."

"Don't worry, it's only the first ten years that are really bad. Mind you, your horse looks damned well. Where's the proud owner?"

"I don't know. He is supposed to be here."

"Ah – the man himself!" Charles Rooney cried and Edward turned to see his grandfather strolling into the paddock with Imogen on his arm.

Finoula nudged him in the ribs. "Raise your hat," she whispered. "That's what it's for. And look pleased."

40

who was so favourably loaded that he or she would romp home in effortless glory at thirty-three to one.

James Henry watched the preparation of his horse with great amusement which he kept well concealed. He had made a most solemn promise to himself that he would not even comment on the work of the yard, let alone interfere once Edward had taken over. But it was extremely hard not to be facetious about the attention that Edward, aided and abetted by Finoula and Liam Corrigan gave to Murgatroyd.

On Easter Monday, the old man stood by the back door and pretended not to be looking at his horse who was being inspected by Edward and Finoula after returning from work on the gallop. The examination was minute, they listened carefully to all that Liam, who had been riding him, had to say, and Edward seemed to be taking account of Murgatroyd's views, a thing he was rumoured to do because of the long periods he spent sitting in the animal's box. Declan approached James Henry on his way to the office and the two stood looking at each other, reading each other's minds.

"I take it he does know that horse is only going to Thurles not Epsom," James Henry said.

Declan gave him a scathing look. "You had your first runner once," he said.

"I did indeed – and I was very relaxed about it."

"And where did it end up?"

"Last but one," James Henry admitted.

Declan nodded and went into the office to collect the feed schedules.

Three days before the race, Murgatroyd had his last serious gallop for which he was partnered by the jockey who would ride him on the day. For the past three years, James Henry had been using Sean Gillespie who was working as a freelance in Ireland after an apprenticeship in Newmarket that had failed to launch an English career. Having checked, Edward knew that Gillespie was only twenty-four, although his taciturn, almost sour, attitude could give the impression that he was twice that age. He arrived at seven o'clock on Saturday morning in a battered old car but he was correctly and immaculately turned out.

"He's got plenty of condition," he announced after running an apparently jaundiced eye over his mount. Edward decided to take this as a compliment despite the fact that it was no more than the plain truth. Murgatroyd was in tremendous form, on his toes without being unruly, very bright and alert and with a good sheen on his coat.

"You should find he's come on a good deal since you rode him at Limerick last September," Edward said. Sean Gillespie's mouth moved fractionally, indicating that he realised the new master of Avoca House had been doing his homework. "We think that a mile is his ideal distance and we've found he likes company so hold him up for six furlongs

Quite unable to understand why Edward was making a fuss, James Henry blandly explained what he had been doing. "Imogen was kind enough to offer me a lift and of course I accepted. We had lunch at a very nice place in . . . where was it, my dear?"

"Abbeyleix," Imogen said.

"Yes, that's right, Abbeyleix. Do you know, it really was awfully good – as a matter of fact, the roast beef was the best I've had in a long time – but don't you dare tell Mary that."

"It was first rate," Imogen confirmed in her most upper-class manner. For the first time, Edward saw that she, too, was under the old man's spell and was playing up to him.

James Henry's obvious intention to give a full account of the meal was cut mercifully short by the arrival of the jockeys. Sean Gillespie, looking grimmer than ever, marched up to them and raised a forefinger to the peak of the silk cap he wore over his protective helmet. It was a greeting intended for all of them, it looked like all they were going to get and it caused Edward a moment of near panic. He felt sure they ought to launch into a significant conversation about the tactics of the imminent race but he had nothing to say. Imogen came serenely to the rescue in a startling way.

"Good afternoon, Mr Gillespie. How's your mother?"

"She's fine, ma'am," Sean replied, and before Edward's disbelieving eyes, his face lit up. He stopped just short of actually smiling but the effect was still dramatic. "That pillow you sent her is great. She sleeps wonderfully well now."

"Yes, they're very good. My aunt Hermione Bradshawe had the same problem until we got her sorted out with one of those. And how's the knee?"

Sean Gillespie shuffled and looked uncomfortable. "She doesn't want to see the doctor about it," he mumbled.

"That won't do at all!"

People rarely demonstrated much resistance when Imogen adopted that tone and Sean Gillespie was no exception. He wilted visibly.

"If she won't toe the line, I shall take her to see my man in Dublin. Make sure you tell her that."

"Yes ma'am." Sean Gillespie touched his cap again.

James Henry, savouring the expression on Edward's face, gave him a villainous wink and looked smug. Further possible revelations were cut short by the ringing of the bell signalling that it was time for the jockeys to mount. Liam Corrigan brought Murgatroyd to them, Finoula pulled the rug off his back, Edward let the stirrups down and gave Sean a leg up. He felt relieved to see that his jockey's composure had returned and that the mask was in place once more as Liam led Murgatroyd out of the paddock towards the course.

Seeing that Imogen and Finoula were in conversation some distance away, Edward asked his grandfather, "What's wrong with Sean Gillespie's mother?"

"Spondylitis – and a bad knee by the sound of things."

"What the devil's spondulitis?"

"Trouble at the top of the spine that causes nasty pains in the neck. Stops you getting a decent night's sleep among other things."

"And how did Imogen get mixed up with Sean's mother?"

"I never ask questions like that and you'd do well to follow my example. Now if you'll excuse me, there's someone I want Imogen to meet." He strode off, taking Imogen with him.

Finoula showed Edward an almost deserted vantage point where they would have a reasonable view of the last half of the race. "Are you going to watch?" she asked with a fair idea of what his answer was going to be.

"No," he said. "I don't think I'm up to that yet."

"Well give me those then," she said and helped herself to the binoculars hanging from his shoulder. She soon found a position from which she could see the start and told him what was going on. "They're putting them in the stalls now," she said and named half a dozen horses as they went in. "Well now, would you look at that – our fella's just walked in on his own as calm as you please." She chatted on until there was only one left and it was painfully obvious to Edward that he was going to be troublesome and pose the threat of unsettling the others. For an agonisingly long three minutes, Finoula kept him informed of the comings and goings with constant assurances that Murgatroyd was maintaining his composure. "Here we go," she said at last. "There's the flag – they're away!" Her statement was a noticeable couple of seconds ahead of the public commentary on which they now had to rely until the turn into the home straight. Edward was able to deduce that the early leaders were setting a very moderate pace and that Murgatroyd was cruising along at the back with two horses that Finoula had earlier dismissed as no-hopers.

"Sean's taken him very wide," she announced as the field came into her view and her voice had an edge that made him apprehensive. "Now what's happening?"

"Well?" Edward asked impatiently when no information was forth-coming.

"He's going past them all," she said with astonishing lack of emotion as though she did not really believe it.

"He can't be."

"He is."

"It's too soon."

"Well, he is, I tell you!"

And the loudspeakers confirmed it: "Two furlongs to run and it's Murgatroyd taking it up from Monahan Spring and Castle Keep."

"Sean's let him off the bit now," Finoula said, still calm. Her voice rose as the truth dawned on her. "They aren't going to catch him – they've nothing left. Will you look at that! He's won it."

Edward forced himself to look and came to the conclusion that Finoula was probably right. Passing the furlong marker, Murgatroyd was enjoying himself immensely and going further away with every stride. For the twelve seconds that it took his horse to cover that last furlong, Edward had the strange feeling that he was another person watching it in slow motion. Fifty yards from the winning post, Sean Gillespie glanced over his shoulder and, with a look that was a mixture of satisfaction with his horse and contempt for the opposition, began pulling Murgatroyd up. The winning distance was three lengths and Edward was vaguely aware that the few thousand spectators seemed quite pleased by the result.

Finoula's reaction was, by her standards, fairly subdued, possibly because of a responsibility she felt for Edward. "Come on, me laddo," she said, "you've got a job to do." She took his hand and steered him towards the gate on to the course where Liam Corrigan was hovering, waiting for Sean Gillespie to bring Murgatroyd back. When Liam did retrieve him, he handed the reins to Edward and said, "There you are, sor – you'll be wanting this fellah." He was grinning broadly.

James Henry, looking very pleased, materialised at his side. "Will you take him?" Edward asked.

"Dear me, no! You only get one first winner. You make the most of it."

As Edward led a very satisfied-looking Murgatroyd towards the winner's enclosure, he became aware that he was passing through a crowd of happy people, many of whom patted him on the back. In front of him, walking backwards with utter aplomb, Imogen made liberal use of a camera she had produced from her handbag. Now that she had played her part as a stabilising influence, Finoula felt entitled to give vent to her feelings and found plenty of willing listeners among the onlookers, most of whom she appeared to know. Edward had a quiet word with Sean Gillespie as he was taking his saddle off Murgatroyd.

"Thank you, Sean," he said. "That meant a great deal to me."

"Like you said, he's come on a lot. That was easy."

"Do you think we can move him up a class – or two?"

"Yes."

"I've got him entered for Ascot."

"The Hunt Cup?"

"Yes."

"Worth a try."

"Will you ride him for me?"

"I'm your man."

"Thanks." Edward patted him on the shoulder and added, "Give me a ring this evening. I'll have some more for you next week."

Even Sean Gillespie betrayed relief at the knowledge that he was to continue working for Avoca House. However, as he headed for the weighing room, Imogen called out to him, "Remember to tell your mother what I said, Mr Gillespie," and he looked less happy.

There were no formalities and Edward was soon walking alongside Murgatroyd as Liam Corrigan led him back to the stables, with Imogen still taking photographs and capturing on film what looked for all the world like an earnest conversation between Murgatroyd and his trainer. On the way, they passed Finoula in a phone box; she was jumping up and down, waving her free hand about and making absolutely certain that Siobhan understood what had happened. In the stables, Edward held Murgatroyd while Liam sluiced him down with a hose-pipe, then set about brushing him dry and Imogen used up the last of the film. Edward was just about to ask if she knew where James Henry was when he ambled into view looking positively smug. One of his jacket pockets was bulging untidily and he provided an immediate explanation by pulling out a bundle of bank notes.

"Yours was a fiver, wasn't it, my dear?" he said to Imogen, who nodded and held her hand out. "There you are, I got six to one about him so it's thirty for you." While he was counting the notes out, Paddy Dooley appeared from nowhere and the old man chuckled. "Amazing thing about Dooley," he explained to Imogen. "He goes missing the minute you get him on a racecourse but as soon as it's divvy-up time, he crawls out of the woodwork. Six to one in ponies, you old rogue – and it was my brilliance that got that. He ended up five to two favourite."

"How on earth did that happen?" asked Edward, who gaped as James Henry counted one hundred and fifty pounds into Dooley's palm.

"What else can you expect in a place like this when some joker rolls up and sticks five hundred on at six to one?"

"Who did that?"

"Me," said James Henry angelically. "Then all the punters started piling in." He laughed at the look on Edward's face. "I must tell you," he said to Imogen, "that we have a chap here who has never bet on a horse in his life. It's worse than that, because I've a feeling he never will."

"Did you have that much confidence in him?" Edward asked.

"Of course I did. He's been working like a dream for you."

"You've never seen him – not until the other day."

"It's high time you had a look out of my bedroom window," James Henry said. "Splendid view of the gallop."

"Well I'm damned!"

"Oh I don't think so – in fact you could have a promising career ahead of you with a bit more attention to detail. Shall we think about getting back, my dear? We must be there in good time to greet the conquering heroes."

Paddy Dooley brought the van up and they loaded Murgatroyd, eager for the well-deserved feed that Liam had ready for him. Finoula excelled herself in recounting Siobhan's reaction to their news and Paddy Dooley continued to receive waves from the bystanders, some of whom greeted their passage with great enthusiasm; there were broad smiles, thumbs held on high and one or two members of the old school raised their hats. After twenty miles of this, an idea formed in Edward's mind.

"Do you suppose that any of these chaps had a bet on today, Paddy?" he asked.

"They usually do, sor."

"Might they have had a go on Murgatroyd?"

Dooley mulled this over for a fair time. "I would say there was a definite possibility of that," was his eventual considered opinion.

"Why's that?"

"Oh he was strongly fancied, very strongly fancied."

"Was he indeed?" Edward was no longer bothering to keep a straight face.

"Oh yes, he was strongly fancied. And you'll be very popular. Doing the business like that – first time an' all – is very good, d'you see."

There was no doubting the warmth of the reception at Avoca House. When they arrived, the yard was full of people, some of whom Edward had never seen before and Declan was smiling; Edward looked twice to make sure and it was true, he really was smiling.

"What about that, Declan?" he asked as he climbed down from the van.

"Very good indeed, sor. It's a fine omen."

"Marvellous!" James Henry agreed. "It's a wonderful beginning. Well done. And that was where I had my first winner, you know."

"I do indeed." Edward had hardly dared hope for such a thing but he had come close to praying for it.

"And how long did it take you?" Declan asked James Henry.

"Six months. There's two things you have to remember though."

"Yes?"

"I didn't have *me* to pave the way and I didn't have *you* to help me."

Declan sniffed, sensed the truth of this and went off to Murgatroyd's box to make sure he had come to no harm.

When Edward and James Henry went into the house, they found the kitchen in a state of near uproar as Finoula told the tale of all the men who had waved at Paddy Dooley and Edward's reaction to it. As soon as Siobhan saw Edward, she anticipated his most pressing need and poured him a pint mug of tea.

Sitting down beside her, he collected his thoughts then said, "We got four of those new blankets with my initials on, didn't we, Siobhan?"

"We did."

"There's something I'd like you to do for me. That one we used today is special – I want it marked so that it doesn't get mixed up with the others. Can you do that for me?"

"I can sew a piece of tape inside it."

"Good. And make sure you keep an eye on it – I don't want it getting lost or hidden away."

"I will." Eager as ever, Siobhan went to attend to it at once.

"So we're getting superstitious already?" James Henry said and there was a strong hint of reproof.

"Will you listen to the man!" Mary said and James Henry was instantly less sure of himself. "You're a fine one to be accusing folks of being superstitious! Who was it used to have bunches of lucky white heather all over the place? Who was it used to throw a pinch of salt over his shoulder before every race?"

While James Henry was wondering whether to bother denying it, Imogen sailed in with even more damning information. "I've heard some pretty rum tales from Nicholas," she said. "Wasn't there some palaver about walking horses three times round the yard in the light of a new moon? And I understand it had to be done anti-clockwise to be completely efficacious." The old man looked sheepishly guilty. "I'd say that having a lucky blanket was pretty mild compared to that," Imogen concluded.

Edward received two phone calls that evening. The first was from Sean Gillespie to make arrangements for future races. Then it was Richard in London who had already spoken to Imogen and was offering fulsome congratulations. After that, Edward telephoned his mother and father and was gratified to discover how pleased they were by his news – although Ann hinted that Murgatroyd's victory had been accomplished in a race that was not very important in a place she'd never heard of. He knew that she would fabricate a piece of logic from this to suggest that he would soon return to a 'proper' job. He would have liked to ease her learning process but knew there was nothing he could do.

Edward was acutely conscious of the need to avoid euphoria; it was good that the first winner had come so quickly, now it was imperative to produce some more. Strategically, there was only one option open to him, that of firing enough shots in the hope of hitting something. The idea had grown during January and February when he had spent many hours with Siobhan planning race entries. With all the horses fit, he was in the happy position of being able to put this plan into operation. To Sean Gillespie's disgust, neither of his next two rides for Edward amounted to anything. However, the following week saw a second and two more winners. Travelling to Navan, north-west of Dublin and in the opposite direction to Thurles, Paddy Dooley yet again attracted considerable attention from passers-by. It was obviously a natural phenomenon for which no simple explanation would ever be found and Edward resolved to stop worrying about it.

Among the next batch of runners was Ocean Lady, the mare who had been unwell when Edward took over the stable. Long since fully recovered and with a month of solid work behind her, she made an almost effortless return to her winning ways in a good class handicap at the Curragh and gave Edward as much satisfaction as Murgatroyd had done. Ocean Lady had been owned by T. P. Malahide, who, after Sir Nick, was James Henry's longest standing and most loyal owner. 'T.P.', as he was always known, had built a haulage business from scratch and sold it for a great deal of money ten years previously when he had surprised his friends by acquiring a wife over thirty years younger than himself. T.P. and Valerie had enjoyed nine very happy years together before his death almost twelve months ago. Retired and very wealthy, T.P. had indulged his life-long passion for the turf without ever paying more than five thousand pounds for a horse and had been guided into unpretentious sponsorship of the arts by his wife. Valerie Malahide had taken over the ownership of her late husband's horses, was making earnest efforts to understand it all and was talking of buying horses herself.

After Ocean Lady's win, Edward had no hesitation in accepting an out-of-the-blue invitation to dinner with Valerie Malahide; because he had known her for so long, he was at ease with her. She was only four years older than him and attractive in a quietly elegant way, yet he was always comfortable with her. As they sat on the balcony of her house at Howth and admired the view across Dublin Bay on a perfect May evening, he started to experience the first sensations of belonging and achievement.

"I don't think Ocean Lady has ever run as well as she did this afternoon," Valerie Malahide said. "What have you been doing with her?"

"We've found a new feed mixture she seems to like," Edward said, "and I've played around with her work programme quite a lot."

"I'd heard you were an inveterate experimenter," she said. "Never the same two days running. I believe you even take them for different walks so they get a change of scenery."

"My goodness, you are well informed. Who's been leaking all my secrets?"

"Siobhan. I had a long chat with her on the phone yesterday. She seemed very impressed by what you're doing."

"You must never let a horse get bored," Edward explained. "If you lose their interest, you've had it. They won't work, won't eat and it's time to pack up and go back to sweeping roads."

"Or teaching Physics?"

"Never!"

"You must tell me all about it. I'd love to know as much about horses as T.P. did."

Edward laughed. "So would I," he said, "so would I!"

CHAPTER 3

From his earliest days at Avoca House, James Henry had always attended Royal Ascot, often staying in England longer than the four days of the meeting in order to visit friends. Essentially it was a holiday with a little of the pilgrimage about it. In 1960, the stable had a horse good enough to be worth a try in the Gold Cup, and although he did not earn a place in the first three, Pundit by no means disgraced himself and founded something of a tradition. After that, at least one Avoca House horse had gone to Ascot every year. Nowadays the tendency to linger in England had faded away; many of James Henry's friends were dead and he viewed the state of the country with dismay, claiming that it vindicated his 1946 decision to leave it.

However, he still relished his visit to the Royal meeting and was pleased by Edward's intention to continue the tradition. There had been the exciting prospect that Musetta would make her debut at Ascot but she had not come on at all well. Apart from failing to settle to the idea of regular work and feeding, she behaved disastrously in, or sometimes simply near, starting stalls. Edward decided that Royal Ascot was the last place to risk an outburst of her nerves and Richard was in full agreement once he had seen the problem for himself. Having been disappointed by this, James Henry was then taken aback by Edward's insistence that Murgatroyd should run in the Royal Hunt Cup.

"He's never good enough for that," James Henry protested.

"You should have more faith in your horse," Mary Kelly told him, not pausing in rolling out the pastry for a vast steak and kidney pie. The discussion was taking place in the kitchen where Edward was having a cup of tea after working with the second lot.

"Not to mention your trainer," Edward said mildly.

"Well of course I have faith," James Henry said, bridling at the suggestion. "But Murgatroyd isn't up to it."

"Since when did that stop this stable sending a horse to Ascot?" Edward asked.

"You impudent young devil!"

"I know. But come on now, tell me all about the great horses you've sent over."

"Well . . ." James Henry presented the most unusual spectacle of unease ". . . there was Pundit."

"Yes."

49

"And Cistercian."

"There was indeed . . . he came fourth in the Wokingham in 'sixty-three."

"'Sixty-four," James Henry said and glowered.

"Sorry. Right. Go on."

"Nick's horse ran well in the Gold Cup in 'seventy-one."

"Belfields Major – yes he did."

James Henry frowned into his mug and said, "And that's about it," rather forlornly.

"But you enjoyed yourselves."

"We did!"

"Well you're going to do it again, so get the mothballs out of your tails. Whatever else he does, Murgatroyd won't disgrace himself or us."

"And that's you told," Mary said to James Henry as Edward went back to the yard.

He nodded and pushed his mug across the table for a refill. "He may have a point," he admitted. "The horse has been working awfully well – he's come on a lot since that race at Thurles."

"Have you been up to your tricks at that bedroom window again?" Mary asked.

James Henry grinned. "I've been out on the gallop quite a bit – honoured guest and all that. I can't see the extra weight doing him any harm." The official handicapper had given Murgatroyd an additional five pounds to carry at Ascot as a 'penalty' for his win at Thurles.

"He's going to be all right, isn't he?" Mary asked.

James Henry stared hard at her, fully aware that she was talking about Edward, not Murgatroyd. "Yes he is," he said. "He would never have come here in the first place if there'd been any doubt about that."

The arrangements – or logistics as James Henry grandly called them – for going to Ascot were mercifully short-winded and so well established as to be semi-automatic once Siobhan had made the necessary phone calls. The only disruption to Edward's schedules of work stemmed from Finoula's decision that, for the first time, she would go to Ascot. This meant a trip to Dublin in search of 'a decent frock and hat'. Edward was mildly annoyed when she took off without telling him and had to bite back irritation when she returned after a full day with nothing to show for it but sore feet. Two days later she went back with Mary, this time returning with some very expensive-looking parcels, the contents of which were to be kept secret until the great day. Declan was part of the audience who heard all about it in the kitchen and sustained Edward with several looks of a soothing nature. "It's the ladies, d'you see," he said as they went out for evening stables, summing it up rather nicely and making Edward smile.

The Royal Hunt Cup was run on Wednesday, the second day of the meeting, so they travelled on the Tuesday. The party consisted of Murgatroyd, James Henry, Finoula, Liam Corrigan, Edward and, of course, Paddy Dooley. The first leg of the journey was the twelve miles to Brendan O'Sullivan's place at Blessington. One of the many services provided by O'Sullivan to the racing stables in the vicinity of the Curragh was air transport, and the 'flying horse box', a high-wing, propeller-driven aircraft, was waiting for them. Murgatroyd boarded it as though he had been doing it all his life and was soon comfortably wedged in the tight, padded stall that had been provided for him. On the other side of a bulkhead, Edward and his companions sat in conventional airline seats and fastened their safety belts – all except Liam Corrigan, who insisted on being with his horse and was allowed to do so by the pilot.

During the seventy-five-minute flight to Gatwick, Paddy Dooley remained strapped in his seat, clutched his canvas holdall to his chest and gave the impression of being petrified. James Henry laughed at the concern Edward expressed about it while they were checking that the totally unmoved Murgatroyd had no problems.

"Don't you believe it," he said. "He's enjoying every minute of it."

"He looks frightened to death."

"That's to make us think he *is* frightened."

"Why should he want us to do that?"

"This is his big annual treat – but he suspects that we wouldn't bring him with us if we realised that. Quite simple."

"So who would drive the box?"

"I would."

"Oh no you wouldn't!"

"That's official is it?"

"It is."

James Henry nodded. "But you see, Dooley doesn't know that," he said, unleashing his ace.

A hired horse van was waiting for them at Gatwick and after Liam had walked Murgatroyd for a few minutes to ease boredom and possible stiffness, they put him into it. The van, part of Siobhan's impeccable organisation, had a second, very comfortable cab behind the driver into which James Henry, Finoula, Edward and their luggage fitted easily and they set off, Dooley negotiating his way out of the airport as though he had been doing it every day for years. Once they were on the main road to Guildford, Edward began looking around with an almost apprehensive air and Finoula started to giggle at him.

"What's the matter?" James Henry asked.

"He's looking for Dooley's friends," Finoula whispered.

51

"What friends?"

"The ones that wave at him."

"Every-damned-where we go," Edward said.

"Oh those chaps – you won't find any round here," James Henry said airily. "At least not on the busy main roads. There might be a few on the way to the course tomorrow."

The look on Edward's face reduced Finoula to tears of laughter, while James Henry asked Dooley how he was getting on and was told that power-assisted steering was a fine thing.

The Royal Ascot ritual revolved around the Walgraves and their house 'The Elms' near Bagshot, only a few miles from the course. Visitors from Avoca House, both human and equine, had stayed there since the first sortie in 1960.

This had originally been under the auspices of Desmond Walgrave, an exact contemporary of James Henry. They were school friends and comrades-in-arms in The Great War. Afterwards, while James Henry started to dabble in finance, Desmond Walgrave set up a small engineering business in Birmingham, and each had been best man at the other's wedding. Desmond's enterprise had come close to disaster twice; on both occasions, James Henry had come to the rescue with a substantial interest-free loan. Shortly before Desmond's death in 1969 he had moved his operation to a big new factory in rural Surrey. Walgrave Precision, now presided over by his son Simon, was a fully mature prestige organisation employing over two hundred highly skilled staff.

Whoever had owned The Elms before Desmond Walgrave had hunted and maintained what was left of the Victorian stables so that there were four very good horse boxes at the back of the house. One had been prepared for Murgatroyd with ample supplies of the sawdust that Edward favoured instead of straw for bedding and the horse was soon comfortably at home and waiting for Liam to unpack the feed he had brought from Avoca House.

Simon Walgrave was a widower who seemed content to live virtually alone in the large house, secretly relieved that his son Mark and his young wife Sarah had always found good reasons for refusing his occasional half-hearted suggestions that they should join him. Domestic arrangements were in the capable hands of a middle-aged couple who lived in; as Mr Hargreaves showed them to their rooms, he told James Henry that Simon would unfortunately be late home that evening since he was attending a function of his professional institution in London. However, young Mr Mark and his wife would be coming to dine with

52

them and his demeanour brightened visibly as he made the announcement.

Edward spent most of the afternoon with Murgatroyd, satisfying himself that the flight had produced no ill-effects and double checking every item of equipment – James Henry's racing silks, the saddle cloth and above all, the lucky rug. On three separate occasions, he interrupted a task to check that the rug they had brought was indeed the one marked by Siobhan. At half past six, Finoula came out to remind him that it was time to think about getting cleaned up for dinner and to report that Sean Gillespie had telephoned to say that his first day at Ascot, riding two horses for another trainer, had been unsuccessful, that he was back in his lodgings and would see them on the course the following day.

Dinner was a happy affair and ironically, it made Edward feel uncomfortable. From the moment they had landed at Gatwick, his nerves had been playing tricks on him and he would have preferred a light meal on his own rather than be forced to pretend he was without care. James Henry and Mark Walgrave always had a robustly humorous conversation while Finoula and Sarah Walgrave, meeting for the first time, shared a boisterous *joie de vivre*. Edward was relieved when Simon Walgrave arrived, rather earlier than anyone had expected. Simon was as courteous as ever and genuinely pleased to see them but his natural gravity dampened the proceedings and Edward was able to slip away and be in bed by ten o'clock without being missed.

He woke soon after five o'clock and decided at once that any further attempt at sleep was pointless. While dressing in his working clothes, he saw that it was already a fine morning with the promise of a glorious day to come. Using the back stairs, Edward was confident that he had managed to get out of the house without waking anyone, yet he was not the first to be up and about. Liam Corrigan was already grooming Murgatroyd.

"Good morning, sor. It's a grand day for us."

"Good morning, Liam. It is. How is he?"

"He's grand."

"Did he eat up last night?"

"He did." Liam indicated the empty hay rack. Edward ran a hand over Murgatroyd's glossy back and nodded with satisfaction.

The Elms had no near neighbours so there was no one to be disturbed when they took Murgatroyd out and set off down the grass verge of the heavily wooded lane. After ten minutes they were passed by a postman who was cycling to work. Greetings were exchanged and the man looked at the handsome horse in the cellular travelling rug with great interest. Apart from the postman they were alone and unseen.

"Do you think we've a chance, sor?" Liam asked eventually, slightly uneasy at breaking the silence.

"I think so," Edward replied. "He's a good horse and we've got him as right as he ever will be. But it's one hell of a race, you know." He suddenly felt the need to say more. "I've come to the conclusion that it's a very fortunate thing to have a horse in this condition on the day of a race. I know it's exactly what we're supposed to do but I wonder how many times we shall pull it off? There's one thing we can be sure of – he'll do his best."

Liam nodded sagely and they walked on, deep in thought while Murgatroyd watched new scenery unfold with lively interest.

Edward never knew how the morning passed. He concentrated on keeping out of everyone's way and derived a certain grim pride from *not* doing certain things. Once Murgatroyd was back in his box and having a light feed, he did not pester Liam. He did not telephone Declan to ask how things were at Avoca House or hope for last-minute pearls of wisdom – although he did look longingly at the instrument at about nine o'clock when he knew Declan would be having a short break between the first and second lots. And above all else, he did not run to James Henry for answers to non-existent problems. When it was time to get ready, he shaved slowly and carefully and put on the morning suit which, thanks to Siobhan's packing, was in perfect condition.

Paddy Dooley had performed one of his famous reappearing acts. Within minutes of reaching The Elms the previous afternoon, he and the hired horse van had vanished without trace. Edward was approaching the stable as the miracle happened and Dooley brought the van in within a minute or two of Liam's completing Murgatroyd's preparation. Like Liam, Dooley was also wearing a suit, although, unlike Liam's, the outfit was a double-breasted museum piece that clashed horribly with the new cap and adventurous silk tie. Edward was diverted from trying to find out where he had spent the night by the arrival of James Henry, immaculate, urbane and clearly ready for a most enjoyable afternoon. Whereas Edward had chosen an all-grey suit and hat, James Henry wore the traditional black coat with striped trousers. With his gleaming black hat at a jaunty angle, a venerable tan leather binocular case swinging at his hip, a rose in his buttonhole and an eager gleam in his eye, the old man radiated an air of rakish Edwardian elegance. He raised his eyebrows in injured innocence when Edward burst out laughing.

"What's tickled your fancy?" he asked.

"You, you old devil! You've got it on you."

"Is that the way to talk to one of your owners?"

"It's the only way to talk to you when you're in this mood."

"My dear boy . . ." the manner became lordly ". . . this is my big treat of the year. You surely don't begrudge an old man this one simple pleasure?"

"Certainly not!"

"Well, there you are then. Allow me to wish you good luck in your endeavours this afternoon."

"And to you too, sir." Edward bowed grandly and doffed his hat as they shook hands.

For a reason that he was unable to understand at the time, much of Edward's feeling of well-being evaporated with the ebullient appearance of Finoula, excitedly displaying the outfit that, he sourly reflected, had cost so much in time and probably money as well.

"My word, that's an exciting sort of get-up," James Henry said approvingly, but Edward was unable to share his enthusiasm. Seeing the look on his face, his grandfather poked his chest and whispered, "Stop that! None of your starchiness today, thank you. The girl's out to enjoy herself."

Edward saw the justice of the comments and asked himself how else Finoula might have been expected to react to her first visit to Royal Ascot. She looked quite striking in a matching hat and dress of crimson and emerald green that was a complement to her natural colouring and temperament. Perhaps if the hat had been smaller and the back of the dress had not plunged quite so much he would have been happier. Without showing any of these misgivings, he helped her into the rear cab of the horse van and with Murgatroyd safely aboard, they set off.

"Imagine being all dressed up like this and going to the races in a horse box," Finoula said, making a half-serious complaint that caused James Henry to chuckle.

"I think it's a great wheeze," he said. "These little eccentricities are one of the compensations of age. Any fool can hire a Rolls but a van is serious stuff. The hoi-polloi can sneer as much as they like but it puts us several notches up on them."

"How so?" Finoula asked.

"It's the ultimate status symbol round here, my dear child. It means we've got a horse running."

"Ah yes." She smiled happily and was content.

To Edward's relief, they reached the course without anyone waving at Paddy Dooley, even though they saw several likely-looking groups of men. As with Gatwick Airport, Dooley knew exactly which way to go to avoid the huge build-up of traffic and get them to the right entrance. When he had looked at Murgatroyd and seen that he was all right, James Henry, treating Finoula like a favourite grand-daughter, took her away. "Come along, my dear," he said, "let's leave the experts to it and have some lunch. I've got a couple of tickets for one of the posh places and we might meet somebody decent."

Edward went to carry out the official formalities of declaring a runner, acutely conscious that he was doing it for himself this time, not acting on James Henry's behalf. He met Sean Gillespie, who reported that the course had been riding exactly the way Murgatroyd liked it the previous day and that nothing had happened to change that. All that remained was to wait, and he went back to Liam to share a lunch of sandwiches and a flask of tea. Dooley had been swallowed up into the crowd but he had left the van in the approved park and they made themselves comfortable in the cab.

At the appropriate time, Edward found a good vantage point on the rails and watched the Royal Procession, rather surprising himself at the pleasure he obtained from raising his hat at the passage of the first carriage carrying Her Majesty. Then he wandered aimlessly for ten minutes, not knowing anyone but perfectly content to take in the scene and study the crowd. As ever, it was a colourful and spirited gathering, from which he felt set apart. From their attitude and snatches of overheard conversation, Edward decided that many people were not in the least interested in horses or racing and had come simply to be *seen*, many of the women apparently finding it necessary to look outrageous or downright silly to aid this objective. He reminded himself that he was never an admirer of the latest fashions in ladies' clothes even when the designs were held within what he regarded as reasonable bounds, and watched the first race from the grandstand before returning to Liam and Murgatroyd.

There was another race to come, then, in fifty minutes or so, the Royal Hunt Cup would be run and it was time to think about getting Murgatroyd into the exercise paddock before he went into the main paddock to be scrutinised by race-goers and TV cameras. Liam had him ready, saddled and as smart as a new pin. Edward looked at his horse and felt very proud of him. There was only one problem – the afternoon was far too hot to require a blanket over the saddle. If they had used it, even the equable Murgatroyd would be sweating and distressed within a couple of minutes. Edward compromised by passing the lucky blanket briefly over the horse's back while Liam kept a very straight face and the few stable hands who saw it gaped in amazement.

Once in the main paddock with all thirty-three runners parading and the connections – owners, trainers and specially invited friends – forming quite a crowd, Edward caught the overwhelming sense of occasion and fell prey to his nerves again. By contrast, James Henry, who had lunched well, and Finoula, who had been introduced to some very exciting people, were in fine form.

"I must say, our horse is looking exceptionally well," James Henry said. "You've done wonders for him, Edward." The TV commentators were saying almost the same thing; a hundred miles away in Worcestershire, Edward's mother had stopped gardening and was having a cup of tea while she watched it.

Edward did his best to make polite conversation while keeping an eye

56

on the clock, willing the minutes away until it was time for the jockeys to mount. He gave Sean Gillespie a leg up and received a dour nod once their roles had been reversed and the five-foot-three jockey suddenly towered over him. As the horses left the paddock, Edward became aware of the women in his immediate vicinity. Without exception, they were dressed in quiet elegance; the dominant colours were cream or subdued pastels, the hats were modest and there were no lurid, eye-catching accessories. He knew it was unjust to expect Finoula at only eighteen to match such taste and experience – they were mostly the wives of owners and trainers – but as a representative of Avoca House, she might have tried.

Waiting for the horses to canter down to the start a mile away and for all thirty-three of them to be put in the starting stalls was an interminable time for Edward and he knew that he would see next to nothing of the race unless he went up into the grandstand – which he was unwilling to do. Ann Manning, however, had a splendid view of it on her TV screen. As soon as the horses burst from the start in front of the gates leading to Windsor Castle, a furious cavalry charge of a race developed for one of the most prestigious handicap prizes of the year. At the half-way point, all the horses seemed to be galloping in a straight line abreast but as they hit the rising ground that extended almost to the winning post, the field spread out as the less able horses fell back. With under a furlong to go, only a dozen horses remained in serious contention and the number dwindled as the blistering pace took its toll. In the mounting fervour of the TV commentary, Ann was constantly reminded that Murgatroyd was going well on the stands side.

Deafened by the roar of the crowd, Edward could not hear the loudspeaker commentary. He had a view of the winning post but the angle was dreadful and when he saw Murgatroyd pass it, Sean Gillespie's face set grimly as he rode for all he was worth, there was no way of knowing how he had fared in relation to the group on the far side of the course. Armed with the pictures and commentary of TV, Ann Manning was in no doubt about the outcome; the Royal Hunt Cup had been won by Murgatroyd, owned by Mr James Henry Manning, trained in Ireland by Edward Manning and ridden by Sean Gillespie. She turned the set off with a mixture of pleasure and sadness. Any hope that Edward might change his mind and come back home was gone for good; in three months he had done what his remarkable grandfather had failed to achieve in over thirty years. There would be no looking back now.

Edward was one of the last people to realise what had happened. Throughout the race, James Henry had never taken his eyes off Liam Corrigan who was positioned on the rails, fifty yards past the winning post. Liam had received the signal from Sean Gillespie and promptly gone into a dervish-like jig of delight which James Henry had no difficulty interpreting. "He's won it. By God, he's won it!" he shouted and sent Finoula into near hysteria. It was actually Edward who reached the gate on to the course first and took Murgatroyd from Liam who was grinning fit to split his face. James Henry had difficulty getting through the dense crowd and when he reached his horse, Edward removed his hat and gave him the reins.

"There you are, sir," Edward said, finding that he had difficulty controlling his voice, "lead in your horse."

"Really?"

"Yes."

"Oh . . . I say," James Henry said quietly. For a moment, his man-of-the-world mask slipped and there was a tear in the corner of his eye. "I hope they watched that back home," he said, getting his feelings under control.

"They will have done. Come on. Chin up and look pleased."

"No trouble with that." James Henry squared his shoulders and set off towards the winner's enclosure. Edward fell in step beside him and a press photographer got a nice picture of them smiling at one another in a very special way. It appeared in a popular newspaper the following day with the caption:

OK GRAND-DAD?

Edward and Liam escaped with Murgatroyd at the earliest opportunity leaving James Henry to talk to the press. Edward had seen them hovering and knew that the day would come when he would have to deal with them; as yet he was not ready, whereas James Henry was, and deserved every last scrap of pleasure he would derive from the occasion. While Liam was washing Murgatroyd down and Edward was preparing his feed, a breathless Finoula arrived. She was carrying her hat, which had been trampled on after she had thrown it into the air, and was still incoherent with joy.

"Congratulations, Liam," Edward said when he was satisfied that Murgatroyd was settling down to his feed. "You did well to get him that right. Very well done."

"I had some help from yourself, sor. Declan's quite right."

"What about?"

"He says you're going to be a wizard when you get going."

Edward was flabbergasted. Assuming that Liam was telling the truth, the best thing to do with this astonishing piece of information was to forget it. Declan would be furious if he ever discovered that his statement had been repeated. Liam's excuse was his excitement; apart from the pleasure of seeing his horse win so bravely, he was three hundred and forty pounds richer. As winning owner, James Henry would receive a prize of seventeen thousand pounds; four per cent of this went to the staff of the yard. Following a ballot of the lads some years ago, the lad who did the horse got two per cent while the other two per cent went into the communal kitty for equal distribution.

James Henry did not stint himself in his moment of triumph and it was long after the last race when he came to the van where they had been waiting patiently for some time. No one complained – although Dooley looked as though he would have liked to. As they moved off, Finoula gave James Henry a huge kiss, regained the power of speech and launched into a ten-minute account of Murgatroyd's famous victory.

"How did you do, Liam?" James Henry asked when she finally paused for breath and inspiration.

"Not too bad, sor. I got twelve to one about him."

"What about you, Paddy?"

"I was unavoidably detained," Dooley grumbled. "I met O'Byrne from Ballybrophy. Consequent upon this, I was too bloody late to get anything better than ten to one."

"My God, you're losing your grip," James Henry said sadly. "I got twenties." Liam whistled in admiration while Dooley slumped more morosely than ever over the steering wheel. "So what we're going to do tonight," James Henry announced, "is to go out and have one hell of a meal – and I know just the place. We'll rope in young Mark and Sarah and let our hair down. Is it any good asking you, Dooley?"

"No thank you, sor. That's very kind but I have a prior engagement."

"You'll come, Liam?"

"Thank you very much, sor."

Edward was torn between the need for two pieces of information. On balance, he thought it unlikely that Dooley would reveal any details about his 'prior engagement', so he turned to James Henry. "Excuse me, how much did you put on this horse of yours – you know, the one you didn't think had a snowball's chance in hell?"

"Only a hundred." James Henry pulled the resultant two thousand pounds out of his trouser pocket and smiled. Edward stared into space wondering whether to laugh or cry. His eyes gradually focussed on three men at a crossroads ahead and he was overwhelmed by an appalling conviction that he knew what was going to happen. It did. They waved and gave the thumbs-up sign.

Murgatroyd and his entourage were safely back home at Avoca House for a late lunch the following day. Mary had appointed herself leader of the welcoming party and was delightfully eloquent, especially after Finoula had given her a mass of detail, some of it actually real, some owing a great deal to the imaginations that had run riot over a most

59

convivial celebration dinner. Edward was gratified to see that everyone was very pleased and to learn that warm congratulations had arrived from dozens of people. However, after an hour or so, he left James Henry and Finoula holding court in the kitchen while he went to the office to plan out the next few weeks with Declan and Siobhan.

"We've some more racing coming up, haven't we?" Edward asked.

"Yes, you're taking two to Naas on Saturday," Siobhan replied, checking her book with the wall-chart. "Sybil and Glendalough. First and last races."

"How are they, Declan?"

"Fine. They did their last work this morning. Sean Gillespie was pleased."

Edward reflected on the arduous life of a jockey; Sean had no more rides at Ascot after Murgatroyd and had flown back to Ireland in search of his next job within two hours of his Royal Hunt Cup victory. There had been no time for him to celebrate and he had been at Avoca House for ride work at seven that morning.

"There is a problem about Saturday," Siobhan pointed out. "Your mother and father are coming over for two weeks, Edward. They've to be met at the airport at two o'clock."

"That's all right. James Henry can do that. I'll sort him out."

"And there's this." The English newspapers reached Avoca House about midday and Siobhan had taken a great liking to the picture with the "OK GRAND-DAD?" caption.

"Ah yes." Edward smiled. "I saw that at Gatwick. What do you think, Declan?"

"It's a good picture."

"Isn't it? Siobhan, can you ring somebody up and get a nice big print of that." She made a note. "That might be worth framing, don't you think?"

"Yes." Declan was quite definite.

"Are you going to start a collection?" Siobhan asked.

"I very much hope so. Now then, Declan, what the devil are we going to do about this filly?"

Siobhan listened, notebook and pencil ready in case notes were necessary, while Edward and Declan discussed Musetta. Declan had no new ideas for making her more consistent and Edward had to confess that nothing had occurred to him either. But he made it absolutely clear that he did not regard himself as beaten – far from it in fact. "I believe she's good," he declared. "She might be very good and it's up to us to find a way of releasing that potential. That filly has class, she looks good and she moves well once she decides to. Don't ask me how we're going to get through to her but if we have to stand on our heads and recite Latin verse to make her perform, we'll do it."

Both Declan and Siobhan noticed the subtle change that had come over Edward as a result of his trip to Ascot. He had shouldered authority and responsibility from the start. Now he was strengthened by confidence.

This was very much in evidence when he returned from racing at Naas on Saturday after Sybil had won and Glendalough had performed much better than expected to come third in the hotly contested finish of an exceptionally competitive race. Edward's mother and father were in the yard with James Henry as Declan deputised for Edward at evening stables and Ann detected the difference in her son immediately.

"You look like the cat that's scoffed the cream," James Henry said.

Edward greeted his parents, then explained his self-satisfaction. "They made Sybil favourite," he said. "She started at five to two and got backed down to even money."

"Ah . . . that explains why Dooley's looking so downright bloody miserable, does it?"

"Yes, he did go on about it a bit. The thing is, they're starting to take me seriously."

"I see your point. Yes, very good."

Edward had arranged for Mary to cook dinner for them that evening and she did them proud, earning the unstinting praise of Ann. The four Mannings were joined by Sir Nick, Julia, Richard and Imogen in what was, as Richard pointed out, an unprecedented gathering of the two families. For a great part of the meal, the conversation was naturally concerned with Murgatroyd and Royal Ascot. James Henry praised Edward for spotting the horse's potential and preparing him so well. "And it's all very apt really," he went on. "It's a wonderful thing to have a winner at Royal Ascot, but the Hunt Cup is only a handicap when all is said and done, so it was right for me. I've always wanted greater things but that's up to these two." He indicated Edward and Richard.

Ann listened very carefully to the conversation, especially the comments of Richard and Imogen whom she had scarcely known previously. It soon became clear to her that she had taken a wildly pessimistic view of Edward's move to Ireland. He had not fallen among thieves and was unlikely ever to do so; on the contrary, he was surrounded and influenced by good people. Sir Nick insisted that she and Frank must visit Belfields, spending a few nights there to have a good look round and Imogen was full of suggestions of places they might visit. Next morning, the seal was set on Ann's peace of mind when Edward took her on a detailed tour of inspection of the yard. Because it was Sunday, half the lads had a day off, the horses did no work and only the essential routines of mucking out, feeding and medical inspection were carried out. Ann was a little chary of the horses at first as she always had been, but, guided by her son, she soon fell under their spell. She gave the hero of Royal Ascot a carrot and had her hand nibbled by his gentle, rubbery lips.

"Aren't they all *beautiful*," Ann said, looking round the yard. "They don't look this good on the telly."

Edward laughed. "Does anything?" he asked.

Ann made a point of getting up very early on Monday. She and Frank were leaving for a three-day tour round the Ring of Kerry during the morning, but first, she was anxious to see the horses exercise and work. Delighted that his daughter-in-law had been so smitten, James Henry took her out to the gallop with the first lot and explained what was going on. After they had cantered several circuits of the ellipse, the horses were walked six furlongs down the gallop and all except two came back in pairs at speed, about a hundred yards separating each pair. The other two went to the mile start and then returned very fast indeed. James Henry told Ann that as far as he knew both horses were racing within the next few days and this would be their last serious piece of preparation work. He also pointed out that the rider of the bay with the white blaze was none other than Sean Gillespie who was now visiting Avoca House three mornings a week to do ride work.

Watching the scene in the yard as the first lot filed back, Ann was not at all sure that she was not witnessing a scene of barely controlled chaos. "Oh no," James Henry assured her, "they all know what they're doing – in fact that son of yours has tightened things up. He's a bit of a stickler, you know. What happens is they sponge the first lot down, give them a feed, then the lads go and have their breakfast. The second lot will be out in three-quarters of an hour."

"What about that?" Ann pointed to a group consisting of Edward, Declan and Finoula who had gathered round Musetta and her lad.

"That's Musetta, the problem child."

"What's wrong with her?"

"Nothing you can put your finger on. She won't work or eat consistently and she usually goes berserk when she sees starting stalls. It's basically a question of temperament."

"What's the answer?"

"God knows!"

But by the time Ann and Frank came back from Killarney on Wednesday evening, Edward was well on the way to finding it.

"You've never ridden the filly, have you?" he asked Finoula on an impulse.

"No."

"Or done anything with her – never given her a feed on a Sunday for example?"

"Never."

"I wonder . . ."

"What?"

"Whether she needs a woman's touch."

"Do you think it might help?"

"I don't know, but we'll give it a go. We'll start off with you riding her tomorrow morning."

Edward explained carefully to Cathal O'Brien, Musetta's lad, what he was proposing to try, making sure that the earnest eighteen-year-old appreciated that it was no reflection on his abilities. "You know what an awkward so-and-so she is, Cathal, and we must try and do something with her for Mr Stewart's sake. She cost a lot of money and we want to see her give us a decent run for it at least."

Cathal understood. He had been expecting it.

Edward and Declan watched the experiment very closely.

"What do you think?" Edward asked, when Musetta had cantered three times round the ellipse.

"Very nice," Declan said.

"Better?"

"Yes. Her action's much freer."

"I thought so, too."

They were even more pleased with the gallop over five furlongs. Musetta went about her work with a stylish determination that she had demonstrated only fleetingly in the past months.

"That looks promising," Edward told Finoula as he rode back to the yard with her. "By the way, I've never noticed before just how good you are on a horse. You'll be as good as your father in a few years."

"Thank you!" She was naturally pleased by the compliment although the full extent of her flushed pleasure escaped Edward.

"I'd like you to give her feed to her," he said. "She often doesn't eat properly even after she's worked well."

This time, Musetta ate up and seemed to be suggesting that she would have liked more when her pail was empty.

"All right, let's go the whole hog," Edward said. "Will you take her over for a week, Finoula, do everything and give her plenty of love and encouragement. We'll see how she takes to that."

"I will so. I think she's beautiful." Finoula rubbed noses with the filly.

"This leaves you short of work, Cathal," Edward said to young O'Brien. "I'm sure we'll be able to find something for you." Declan nodded firmly.

The following day proved that the first favourable results had not been a fluke; Musetta did what was expected of her and showed considerable zest for her work and the progress continued. At the end of the first week of their holiday, Ann and Frank saw what Ann immediately recognised as an unusual sight. As they returned from an after-lunch stroll round the grounds of Avoca House, Edward on Daisy Chain and Finoula on Musetta were riding past the barn and heading for the gallop.

"I thought you didn't do anything with the horses in the afternoon,"

Ann said to James Henry whom they met in furtive pursuit of the two riders, his binoculars at the ready.

"*I* never did," he grumbled, "but this chap makes the rules up as he goes along. It's all down to a lax upbringing you know." Frank smiled secretly. He knew how proud of Edward James Henry was; the old man had admitted to him that he was very taken by his grandson's innovative approach.

"What are they doing?" Ann asked.

"We shall have to wait and see." James Henry was lurking behind a clump of bushes and beckoned them to join him. "Come on! Don't let them see us."

Edward and Finoula were, however, completely oblivious to anything that was going on three hundred yards behind them. They were in no hurry to do whatever it was they had in mind. The horses walked down the gallop with Finoula's left arm indicating that she and Edward were having an animated conversation.

"They aren't doing anything," Ann said as they rounded the bend at the half-way point of the gallop. "He's just taken her out for a walk."

"Don't you believe it." James Henry emerged from the bushes and used the binoculars. Several minutes passed, then he grunted with satisfaction. "Yes, of course, the starting stalls. I saw them being shifted this morning."

On Edward's instructions, Paddy Dooley had taken the Land-Rover across the field and towed the twin stall unit to the far end of the gallop. Musetta had now reached the device, had not panicked and was having a good look at it. Edward dismounted, tethered Daisy Chain to a rail, and opened both front and rear gates of the stalls. Then he waited patiently while Musetta circled round the contraption that had caused her so much anxiety. Watching through the binoculars, James Henry was pleased when he saw that Edward was in no hurry; it would take as long as it took and that was that. Eventually, as Ann was becoming restive, Finoula brought the filly to a halt behind the stalls and allowed her to take a last look before, with very little urging, she walked straight through them. She was still hesitant and unsure, but there was no trace of the agitation that had bedevilled her earlier encounters.

"That's it," James Henry said, lowering the binoculars. "They'll have that sorted in a couple of days. Let's go and see if we can find a cup of tea."

Edward and Finoula did not return to the yard for over two hours. They had strolled back, leading the horses and were looking very pleased with themselves.

"Finoula's turning into a nice girl," Ann said as she watched them. "Very pretty too. She's a bit young for him although I don't think that matters all that much."

"You surely don't think . . .?" Frank left the question unfinished.

"It's obvious she thinks the world of him."

"Yes." Frank sighed. "I suspect that Edward is one of the few people who haven't realised that."

Ann had come to Avoca House with mixed feelings and expectations. After two weeks of agreeable surprises, she was sorry when the day of their departure came. Fortunately, there was one more piece of good news before she left. On the most beautiful morning of all the fine days she and Frank had enjoyed, they watched Musetta do a wonderful gallop in which she left her older, more experienced, companion Sybil trailing hopelessly when asked to do so. They had started from the stalls and, with Edward's heart in his mouth and fingers crossed, Musetta had been ridden by Cathal O'Brien.

"Terrific!" was Edward's happy verdict. "She's starting to learn what it's about. We'll get Sean Gillespie on her next week and really find out how she's doing." Ann was disappointed by his decision to keep Finoula in charge of the filly and tried to share Cathal O'Brien's calmly philosophical outlook.

Since he was not racing that day, Edward was able to drive his parents to the airport. He knew that the fortnight had been a great success; Frank was looking relaxed and well and his mother would be a lot happier without the misgivings that had burdened her for six months. "So you don't think I've gone to the dogs?" he asked her.

"No, you seem to be in good hands. Just make sure you let me know how that beautiful filly gets on."

They parted lovingly, Frank concealing his relief at piloting Ann away from Edward and into the departure formalities before she could think of a way of mentioning Finoula.

On the way home, Edward called in at Belfields to see Richard about Musetta.

"What do you think then?" Richard asked after he had heard about her improvement and subsequent progress.

"She's entered for the Curragh next Saturday if we want it," Edward said. "I've arranged for Sean Gillespie to ride her on Monday morning and we should let her run unless that's a disaster. It's high time she had a race, whatever happens."

"Right." Richard was consulting his diary. "I shan't be there, I'm afraid – I've got to go to Bonn for the weekend."

"Big stuff?"

"Could be – we're in negotiation with the Bundesbank for a very nice piece of business. No doubt you have some plans for her beyond next Saturday?"

Smiling, Edward pulled a piece of paper from his pocket. "She's down for the Phoenix Park in August and the Curragh again in September."

"That last one's a bit classy, isn't it?"

"Yes, the Clare Castle Stakes – Group Three."

Richard whistled. Pattern races, graded Group One, Two and Three in descending order of prestige, prize-money and supposed excellence of the contenders were the cream of the Racing Calendar. A high proportion of them were for horses of the same age, all carrying the same weight, although fillies received a three-pound allowance when competing against colts. The race that Edward had mentioned was for fillies only and had a first prize of nearly twenty thousand Irish pounds.

"Ambitious," Richard said.

"I was always taught to aim high. It's easy enough to lower your sights if you miss."

"James Henry?"

"No, that's not one of his, actually. That came from Horace Merritt, a mate at school."

"Very sensible advice. Any ideas about next year?"

Edward knew that the question was deliberately facetious since there was no sensible foundation for speculation so far ahead on an unraced two-year-old. "She's entered for the Newmarket Guineas, isn't she?" he asked.

"Yes."

"It won't do any harm to leave her in for the time being."

Monday's gallop went as well as Edward had hoped so Musetta duly made the short journey to the Curragh on Saturday, accompanied by Edward, Finoula and Imogen. Musetta's race was five furlongs of rapidly alternating anticipation, despair and excitement. It took a fraction over sixty-two seconds and was the longest, most nerve-racking minute that Edward had ever lived through. She was actually reluctant to leave the stalls and when she did come out, spent nearly half the race prancing about in the rear of the field giving Sean Gillespie a terrible time. Once he settled her, however, she devoured the ground and set the crowd alight as she got up to win by a neck. Momentarily drained of feeling, Edward found that he was hanging on to Finoula for support.

Sean Gillespie's report was terse and to the point. "She's a bitch – but she's going to be good," he said and strode off to the weighing room.

To the detriment of Edward's blood pressure, he and Finoula had enjoyed a good view of the race and when they sat down to compare their impressions, they agreed that Musetta had shown a truly sensational turn of speed over the last two furlongs. Intuitively, Edward had always known that the filly was good but there was now the distinct possibility that she might be very good indeed and it was necessary to plan accordingly. Although he hated the idea of having a 'special' horse in the yard, it was inevitable that Musetta should receive more, if not better, attention than the other horses. As a result of all the thinking, talking

66

and work on the gallop, Edward and Finoula became virtually inseparable throughout each working day – of which there were seven in a week. They were apart only when he took horses to the races. This was often a rewarding experience as the number of winners mounted steadily, yet he always looked forward to getting back to Avoca House where Finoula would run to meet him with her latest idea.

Five weeks after her debut, Musetta raced again at the Phoenix Park, the attractive course in the western suburbs of Dublin where a fine summer Saturday always brought families out to enjoy themselves. Richard was present to watch her and she did not disappoint, although she made an over-exciting meal of the job again, causing Richard, Edward and Finoula to die a thousand deaths while Imogen looked on with bland indifference. "Sean Gillespie said that animal was going to be good and I think he's right," she said afterwards.

"Perhaps I'm being unreasonable, but I'd like her to do it a little more conventionally," Richard said as his presence of mind returned.

"How very boring!" Imogen declared and moved off to waylay Sean Gillespie about his mother's knee.

Edward and Finoula increased their efforts with Musetta to the point where the yard staff began to make up jokes about the treatment the filly was getting. All the stories were affectionate and were, Edward suspected, fuelled by James Henry. Now that it was plain to all that Edward was very much his own man, James Henry was making frequent appearances in the yard and revelling in the role of elder statesman. He was almost certainly responsible for the idea that Musetta was receiving illustrated lectures on the basic principles of racing, and it was he who produced the biggest laugh by meeting the first lot on their return from work one morning with a glass of water on a silver tray for Musetta.

On the last Saturday in September, Edward was mildly surprised to see James Henry, wearing his best race-going suit, joining Richard and Imogen in their car as they set out for the Curragh. "Nice to see you taking an interest," he said in the tone of warm sarcasm that was a hallmark of their relationship.

But the old man was in a very businesslike mood. "My sources tell me that there's a damned good chance this stable is going to win its first Group race today," he said. "You just try and keep me away."

Musetta had improved and ran a very different race. She was out of the stalls keenly, got all the antics out of her system within the first furlong and then settled down to give Sean Gillespie the option of running the race how *he* wanted it. He unleashed her acceleration at the furlong marker and was easing her as she passed the post, three lengths clear of the rest. Everyone was delighted. James Henry congratulated Richard on his American purchase, adding, "And it looks very much as though your trainer is getting the hang of the job." Edward and Finoula, their arms round one another, were almost beside themselves with joy and although Imogen and Sean Gillespie were poker-faced, they too were pleased. Only Paddy Dooley had grounds for complaint. Bookmakers and punters had taken Musetta and her trainer very seriously indeed and sent her off as favourite at eleven to eight, so that Dooley's twenty-pound stake had yielded winnings of less than sixteen pounds. Whenever he moaned about short odds, James Henry told him that it was a damned sight better than the Post Office Savings Bank.

Two weeks later, the admirable Murgatroyd provided what Edward knew would be the last win of the season. The following day, Edward and Siobhan spent several hours in the office compiling the summary of his first year. They had won thirty-six races from one hundred and seventy-six attempts and the winners total was only two less than James Henry's best-ever score. Thanks to Murgatroyd and Musetta, total prize-money was over a hundred thousand pounds, double the previous best. Prospects for next year were good and morale in the yard was high.

"Not bad," Edward said. "It will do for a start."

"It's very good indeed," Siobhan said. As he smiled at her, Edward did not realise she suspected that Finoula had fallen head-over-heels in love with him and was dreading the possible consequences.

CHAPTER 4

Siobhan called Edward from the yard on a wet, early-November afternoon to take a phone call. It was Imogen.

"Nicholas has had a heart attack," she announced calmly. "They believe he's going to be all right."

"Good God! Where is he?"

She gave the name of a respected hospital in Kildare, and went on to explain when it happened. Although she did not say so, Edward formed the impression that Imogen had almost certainly played a major part in saving Sir Nick's life. "I'm expecting Richard at any minute," she concluded. "He landed at Dublin forty minutes ago."

"Can we go and see him?" Edward asked.

"Yes. I think he would like to see James Henry."

Edward understood. He found his grandfather in the library, poring over a book about great horses of the past, and was careful to emphasise that Sir Nick was expected to be all right. James Henry took a little time to assimilate the news, then he put the book away and went for his overcoat. "He's never been right since that bloody war," he said bitterly. "He had a terrible time. And that bank's worried him sick more often than not."

At the hospital, a nun took them to the small ward that was Sir Nick's temporary home. Before anything else registered, Edward was shocked to see that although Sir Nick was obviously very ill, he also contrived to look worried. Julia sat at the bedside; Richard, straight from his London office and impeccably attired as a merchant banker, stood opposite his mother, looking grave and relieved simultaneously. There was no sign of Imogen. Sir Nick's face lit up when he saw James Henry, and as their hands came together in a warm clasp, he said the one word, "Jimmy!" This unique form of address, never used by anyone else as far as Edward knew, was a summation of the very special friendship between them.

"What have you been up to, you silly devil?" James Henry demanded, and Sir Nick smiled weakly. Before he could think of a suitably humorous reply, Richard moved towards the door, signalling Edward to accompany him.

"We'll leave them for a while," Richard said as they strolled down the corridor towards a group of chairs. "They'd like that." After a slight pause, he added, "That seems to have been a damned close thing. He might have gone if it hadn't been for Imogen. I didn't know she was an expert at resuscitation."

"I suspect she may be an expert at all sorts of things we don't know about," Edward said.

"Yes." They sat down, and Edward waited while Richard collected his thoughts. "This is going to make quite a difference," he said at last.

"Why?"

"He's said he wants me to take over as Chairman at Stewart's," Richard replied, "and I shall carry on as Managing Director. I'm going to be busy . . . very busy."

"I thought the Chairman didn't do all that much," Edward said.

"Father hasn't – but we've always known things would have to change. He was intending to step down soon anyway."

"What needs doing?"

"We ought to recognise the twentieth century. Our practices are pretty archaic and some of the underlying attitudes are unbelievable. We're still not awfully happy doing business with someone unless he went to the 'right' school and we knew his father."

"Really? I thought it was all dynamic cut and thrust in the City nowadays."

"It is in most places. Father's always indicated that he wouldn't want change and I've gone along with him – although I haven't had all that much choice to be honest. A majority of the existing Board think the same way."

"Existing?" Edward picked on the key word.

"Yes. Attitudes as deeply entrenched as ours can only be changed by new faces."

"Is that likely to be messy?"

"Not all of it. There will be some trouble. I'll handle it." Richard's tone was determined. "There have been several big deals in the last year that were ours for the asking, but they weren't considered 'quite the right sort of thing'." The sneer in his voice as he quoted was unmistakable.

"Good luck with that!" Edward said, profoundly glad that such matters were nothing to do with him, yet suspecting that Richard would confront the task with relish. "And what about Sir Nick?"

"I had a long talk with the doctor, and he's going to be all right. They'll keep him here until they're sure, then he can go back to Belfields. Mother will make sure he does as he's told."

"And you?"

"I'm going to be stuck in London for quite a while."

"Imogen won't like that."

"True. We shall manage."

After a week in hospital, Sir Nick went home to Belfields and the loving care of Julia. A few days later, considering that her duty lay in London with Richard, Imogen left, taking young Nicholas with her. James Henry fell easily into the habit of visiting Sir Nick every afternoon; a car came to collect him at two o'clock, and he returned to Avoca House at six. They reminisced, played dominoes or simply sat together. Around four o'clock, Julia brought a tea tray into what was both sitting room and bedroom for her husband and stayed with them for half an hour. One apparent consequence of these visits caused Edward some concern. Perhaps by coincidence, but more probably as a result of events, James Henry's age seemed suddenly to have laid a heavy hand on him. As if Sir Nick's heart attack had reminded him of his own mortality, he became noticeably slower and showed signs of tiredness.

Edward himself was gloomy and restive. This time of year always rendered him vulnerable to depression as the days became shorter and the weather worsened. There was the added disadvantage of having very little to do; for the next three months at least, the work of the yard would be no more demanding than mere routine to keep the horses healthy and reasonably fit. Throughout his first season as a trainer, he had been accustomed to working long hours, and with time on his hands, Edward realised that the single-minded confines of Avoca House were claustrophobic. Much as he enjoyed Finoula's company, he would have liked to do many other things instead of listening to her endless enthusiasm for Musetta. He regretted his limited circle of acquaintances; in England, he had enjoyed a varied social life by virtue of his association with King Henry's School, whereas in Ireland, he knew no one outside the limited circle of Avoca House and Belfields.

It was Valerie Malahide who rescued him. She telephoned to announce her intention of attending a bloodstock sale in Dublin and asking for help in selecting a purchase. Near the end of a pleasant afternoon Edward made his recommendation and a handsome, if rather diffident, colt changed hands for fifteen thousand pounds. Pleased with the purchase, and feeling almost elated after a few hours in convivial company, Edward suggested a drink in a nearby bar, and Valerie Malahide promptly agreed.

"This is much more like it," he said when they were comfortably settled.

She smiled at his boyish delight in what was a simple thing. "What on earth have you been doing with yourself?" she asked.

"Having a terrible time!" He told her about Sir Nick's heart attack, of James Henry's daily visits to him, of Richard's prolonged absence in London and his boredom with life. "The place is like a prison sometimes," he said.

"You need to get out and about."

"That's why I was so pleased about this afternoon. You see it's horses,

horses, horses, nothing but horses. Much as I love them, I wish people would stop talking about them for five minutes."

She laughed. "So I haven't been much use to you then?"

"No, that's different," he assured her. "Different horses, different surroundings – and we did talk about other things. This filly of Richard's is an absolute cracker, and I think the world of her, but according to all the talk I've had to put up with, she's already won every race of any value in next year's calendar."

"I believe you're running her in the Guineas at Newmarket?"

"That's the plan if she gets through the winter all right. I'm desperately anxious for her to do well – but there are other things in life. I've been living in this country for nearly a year now and I still don't know the name of the Prime Minister."

"You've missed nothing."

"Possibly – I still ought to know about these things."

"I've an idea," she said after a moment's thought.

"Go on."

"We're both at a loose end socially . . . Yes I am," she insisted when she saw his surprise. "I've lots of friends, but they don't seem to know what to do about me. All the decent men fight shy of propositioning T.P.'s widow, so I don't even get invited to dinner parties. We could team up."

Edward nodded. "Yes, I'd like that."

"Good. Do you like the theatre?"

"Yes I do. Haven't been for ages."

"Neither have I. Let's go to the Abbey tomorrow evening."

"What's on?"

"I haven't the faintest idea!"

"All right. Why not?"

"I'll take care of the tickets, you just get yourself up here."

At breakfast the following morning, Edward was cheerful again. "There's no need to leave a meal for me tonight, Mary," he said. "I'm going to the theatre in Dublin with Mrs Malahide."

"That's nice. What about himself?"

"He can have a meal at Belfields with Sir Nick and Lady Stewart," he said. "I'll fix that and you can have an early night."

Siobhan, eating breakfast with her usual quiet concentration, noticed the scowl on Finoula's face.

It was a very enjoyable evening. The play was a revival of *Lovers* by Brian Friel, a contrasting double bill full of humour, sadness and the poetry that only the Irish can distil. It was beautifully performed to an appreciative audience and Edward had a spring in his step as they went to Finnegan's for supper afterwards. Talking over the meal, they discovered a mutual interest in music that quickly gave rise to their next arrangement to meet. Valerie Malahide had taken up the cause of four young musicians who had formed a string quartet and were struggling to make the first steps towards recognition. She had hired a small, fashionable hall for them to give a concert the following week and invited around a hundred influential people to come and listen. Edward assured her he would be pleased to accompany her.

"I wish them every success," he said, and the doubt in his voice was evident.

"And what does that mean?" she asked.

"Well . . . Dublin isn't exactly the centre of the universe is it, musical or otherwise?"

"No, but we're getting rid of the bog-trotting image. *Messiah* was first performed here and it doesn't seem to have come to any harm."

"I never knew that."

"See – you live and learn."

Finoula was edgy with pent-up feelings at breakfast. "And what time did you get home last night?" she asked Edward in none too pleasant a tone.

"It was nearly half past one this morning," he admitted. "The traffic coming out of Dublin was fearsome. Is it always like that at midnight?"

"I'm sure I wouldn't know," Finoula snapped, and this time, Edward did notice that something was wrong. Finoula caught Siobhan's eye and thought better of saying any more. She snatched up her mug of tea and marched out into the yard. Staring after her, Edward did not see Declan and Siobhan exchange a brief glance that was almost, but not totally, devoid of meaning.

The chamber concert was a great success. The quartet received a very good reception and three bookings, while Edward met a man who seemed to have no interest in music, but gave the impression of being quite serious about wanting to own a racehorse or two. They chatted for a while and Edward left him with his card. Another non-music-lover made a nuisance of himself with Valerie until she moved smoothly across the room, took proprietorial possession of Edward and used him to deter attentions that were blatantly lecherous.

"There," she said after the man had retreated in a huff, "see how useful you can be!"

"Where on earth did he come from?"

"God knows! I don't have to worry now I've got you."

Edward found that he enjoyed being Valerie Malahide's guardian, and, as their meetings became more frequent, he derived satisfaction from the wildly inaccurate assumptions that people began to make about them. His depression dispelled, he was able to take a vigorous interest in what little was happening in the yard, and spent many hours in the office with Siobhan, making plans for next season. His one concern was

73

James Henry. Although he looked forward to his visits to Belfields, and had taken to staying overnight when Edward saw Valerie, the old man always came back looking slightly more depressed and weary. When he was at Avoca House, he had breakfast in bed and rarely got up before eleven. Twinges of rheumatism, which Edward felt sure were fairly mild, made him excessively sorry for himself, and even caused bouts of utterly uncharacteristic cantankerousness.

Finoula's attitude was increasingly difficult to understand, and Edward soon adopted his usual policy when a woman was being what he considered awkward or behaving inconsistently. He ignored the problem and acted as though everything were normal. With the horses on minimal work, their daily conferences on everything in general and Musetta in particular were no longer necessary, and she avoided him for days on end. Inasmuch as he took any notice of her during these periods, she always seemed to be in a fairly black mood. Then, without reason, she would seek him out and be her old, effervescent self. Finoula herself was acutely aware of her moods, but was unable to exert any control over them. After Edward had seen Valerie Malahide, her temper was filthy, yet within two or three days, she calmed down and simply wanted to be with him.

Everyone was happy at Christmas. Richard and Imogen returned to Belfields for a few days and were at Avoca House for Christmas lunch. Edward took the opportunity to have a few words in private with Richard about the progress he was making at the bank.

"So far, so good," Richard said. "It's costing a small fortune in golden handshakes, and there has been the odd spot of nastiness – but we're getting there. Two more to go and I shall have a comfortable majority."

"Well done!"

"I've had a lot of help. Imogen's been absolutely marvellous. She hasn't stood for any nonsense from the old guard and she's wooed the new men like nobody's business. I actually caught her fluttering her eyelashes at one chap."

"Good grief!" Edward was impressed, and slightly sceptical.

"And I've found an ally I never knew I had," Richard went on. "Fellow called Edwin Fforbes. He's been around a fair time and always seemed to be one of them, but as soon as the shooting started, he came to see me, said he was as fed up with things as I was, and could he join in."

"That is good news."

"Yes." Richard was much more at ease than when Edward had last seen him. "How have things been here?"

"Very quiet. Rather dull actually."

"I hear you've been seeing a great deal of Valerie Malahide."

"How did you know that?"

"How do you think? Imogen wanted all the news the minute we reached Belfields. Mother had been talking to James Henry."

"We get on jolly well together. She's a very nice lady."

"Attractive and wealthy too," Richard said, realising even before he received Edward's pained look, that the remark had been unworthy and irrelevant.

On New Year's Day 1980, James Henry had the symptoms of a cold, so Mary insisted on him staying in bed, and lit a fire in his room to supplement the central heating. The following day was bitterly cold with a leaden sky threatening snow. Edward sat with his grandfather while he ate a bowl of soup and an omelette for lunch, leaving when he began to feel sleepy.

It was a miserable afternoon in the yard, with lads and horses acutely conscious of the freezing wind. Edward spent an hour helping Declan with a mare who had damaged a knee against the door of her box. Before using an antiseptic cream and a lint-packed rubber knee-cap, it was necessary to bathe the wound thoroughly and at great length with plenty of cold water. By the time the job was finished, Edward's hands and wrists were turning blue and almost devoid of feeling. Seeing his plight, Declan told him to get inside for a mug of tea while he finished the job.

It was Mary's afternoon off, and Liam Corrigan's pretty wife was taking care of the kitchen. A little excited by the opportunity of having Edward all to herself, she prattled on excitedly about everything she could think of, producing a deluge of words that washed over him without making any impact. He was starting to wonder how long Declan would be when something happened that shut Kathleen up in the middle of a sentence and brought him to his feet. The door from the kitchen to the main entrance hall was slightly ajar, and through it came the sound of a sickening thud, followed by a cry of anguish and two more horrible thumps. Edward and Kathleen froze, staring wide-eyed at one another across the table; then Edward led the dash into the hall.

James Henry was sitting at the foot of the main stairs with his legs splayed out and a look of total bewilderment on his face. The brightly-patterned silk dressing-gown over his pyjamas heightened the impression that he had turned into a rag doll. He sat quite still and showed no inclination to move.

"What happened?" Edward asked as he crouched down beside him.

"Fell downstairs." The effort of speaking made him gasp with pain and despite the chill in the cavernous hall, beads of perspiration appeared on his brow.

"Where are you hurt?"

75

"Pretty much all over I think." He paused for breath. "My chest hurts. That arm's broken." He used his right hand to point at his left arm. "I've always said these stairs were no damned good." Then he fainted.

"Kathleen, get Siobhan to telephone for an ambulance and fetch Declan," Edward said quietly. She was in a trance, and he had to repeat it, turning it into an order to shock her to action. She fled, white-faced with fear, and undoubtedly did what he asked as quickly as possible, yet it still seemed an age before Declan arrived. He assessed the situation calmly and knelt down on the other side of James Henry, opposite Edward.

"He's fallen downstairs," Edward explained. "He's broken his left arm and there's a pain in his chest. He's passed out. God knows what he thought he was doing." Declan looked as though that question was of no importance whatsoever. "Siobhan's organising an ambulance?"

"She's done it."

James Henry regained consciousness fairly quickly, and speaking with tremendous difficulty, explained that he had wanted a cup of tea. He tried to give further vent to his feelings on the stairs, but pain prevented him muttering more than a few incoherent phrases. He grumbled sporadically until Siobhan hurried through from the office to open the rarely-used front door for the ambulancemen. They eased him onto the stretcher with great tenderness. Once that was done, Declan shuffled and decided to go back to the yard. Reading his thoughts, Edward caught him by the arm. "You're coming with me, Declan," he said. "He'll be glad to see you once they've fixed him up."

They sat for no more than an hour in the hospital waiting room, given constant up-to-date information, yet Edward still chafed nervously. Within twenty minutes they knew that the X-rays were complete and no serious damage had been found. As James Henry had said, his left arm was broken. The X-ray plates also revealed two cracked ribs, and this was the relatively harmless explanation of the pain in his chest. Then came the news that his arm had been set and put in plaster, that his ribs were being strapped, and they would soon be able to see him.

James Henry looked amazingly well when they went into his ward, and Edward was reminded that, despite his apparent decline since Sir Nick's heart attack, he did have an iron constitution. He had been given a pain-killing drug and was drowsy, but he was very pleased with his left arm, neatly encased in plaster from elbow to shoulder, and the wide band of strapping round his chest.

"Not at all bad," he said in reply to Edward's anxious question. "Mind you, I haven't had that cup of tea yet."

"Ah yes . . ." Edward explained to Declan ". . . he woke up, wanted a drink and fell downstairs trying to get it. I bet he was half asleep."

76

"I was not!" James Henry was outraged by the suggestion.

"You're a silly owd fool," Declan pronounced after due consideration of the facts. "You ought to be more careful. You've no right to go round frightening folks like that."

James Henry's face cracked into a broad grin. "Do you know, Declan, that must be one of the longest utterances you've ever made. I believe you were slightly more verbose when O'Gorman's mare got loose at the Phoenix Park." Declan sniffed and stared hard at him. "Now then, look here," James Henry said to Edward in a businesslike manner, "I don't want to stay in here a minute longer than I have to."

"We shall have to wait and see what they say," Edward protested.

"Let's not have any argument, there's a good lad," James Henry said in a long-suffering tone. "Just listen to what I've got to say. I don't like hospitals. You leave me here any length of time, and I've had it. Fitzgerald can look after me well enough."

Doctor Fitzgerald, a youthful seventy-year-old, had always been the Avoca House 'medicine man'; he looked after everyone, had brought Finoula and Siobhan into the world, was implicitly trusted by James Henry, and had even treated horses in moments of crisis. Unsure of how he should react, Edward looked instinctively to Declan for guidance, and received a firm nod.

"All right, I'll see what I can do," he said. "But I'm not going to start ignoring sound medical advice."

"No. Do your best."

Edward did not raise the matter with the hospital staff that day. He felt that the doctors and nurses should have time to form a proper opinion before he made his request. Back at Avoca House, Declan set about spreading calm and assurance while Edward went up to his rooms and started making phone calls. Although he was careful to present the news as no more than a minor problem, his father sounded extremely worried. "A bad fall like that could be very nasty at his age," Frank said. "Do you think I ought to come over?"

"No, leave it," Edward replied firmly. "He'll get fed up and nervous if people start panicking. Wait until he's feeling better and we'll make it look as though you were coming over anyway."

Richard, to whom he spoke next, was much more distressed than he had expected.

"Are you absolutely certain he's not in any danger?" he asked repeatedly.

"Yes, I am. He's given himself a bad fright but he's got away with it very lightly."

"You don't think I should come over?"

"No! Father was all for jumping on the next plane. You'll scare him out of his wits if you all start rallying round and looking serious."

"All right, if you're sure . . . But you will keep me posted?"

"I will. I promise."

At breakfast the following morning, Edward took advantage of having Mary, Finoula, Siobhan and Kathleen Corrigan all together in the kitchen to tackle an important issue. First, he gave them the latest news from the hospital, which was good. "He wants to come home," he said, "and the sooner the better as far as he's concerned."

"Of course he does," Mary said. "We'll be getting ready for him this morning." The others nodded in whole-hearted agreement.

"Just a minute." Edward raised a hand. "That's all very well, but he's going to need looking after."

"Well of course he is!" Mary looked at him as though he had said something of quite outstanding stupidity.

"I thought I'd better mention it," he said lamely. "Things might be difficult for a few days."

"I expect so. He's been difficult for as long as I've known him and this business won't have helped."

"It would never do for him to stay in hospital," Siobhan said quietly.

"You don't think he should, do you?" Finoula demanded.

"Certainly not! I'm worried about the extra work."

"You worry about your horses and we'll look after himself," Mary said, and Edward recognised the end of the conversation.

Edward arrived at the hospital shortly after lunch to find Doctor Fitzgerald sitting by James Henry's bed. They were enjoying a joke, James Henry's ribs causing his laughter to be mixed with wincing.

"Ah, there y'are," the doctor said. "I've fixed it with the powers that be for him to come home tomorrow. It's a fine hospital and no mistake at all about that – but it's not a place for a man of his calibre."

Edward had to agree.

Enlisting help from the yard, Mary had brought James Henry's bed downstairs and installed it in the library. It had always been his favourite room and was handy for the kitchen. By getting rid of some unnecessary furniture and borrowing a pair of standard lamps from other rooms, she made it thoroughly welcoming, the more so with a log fire blazing. Edward allowed himself to be hauled off by Finoula to inspect it and agreed that it was a good idea. He noticed that she was in high spirits and was thankful for this without bothering to ask himself why. He would have been appalled to learn that Finoula had decided James Henry's accident might not be a completely bad thing if it kept Edward at Avoca House and away from Valerie Malahide.

Edward was busy in the yard the following morning, assuming that a way of bringing James Henry back would be organised. He noticed Paddy Dooley and two of the lads set off with the horse van and thought nothing of it; he presumed Declan had given them a job to do, and he never questioned that sort of thing. It was not until they were having their mid-morning break that he discovered Declan knew nothing about Dooley's mission, and had been assuming that *he* had sent them off. Fortunately, they did not have long to wait; fifteen minutes later, Dooley brought the van into the yard. He was all alone in the cab. There was no sign of the two lads who had gone with him.

All was revealed when the tail-gate came down. The lads were in the back of the van with a wheelchair holding a jaunty James Henry. He was wrapped in blankets and had one of his own monogrammed horse rugs round his shoulders. Edward looked surprised, then displeased, and finally burst out laughing.

"I thought that might brighten the place up a bit," James Henry said as the lads eased the wheelchair down the ramp.

"Where did you get that chair from?" Edward asked.

James Henry looked accusingly at Dooley who scratched the back of his neck and became decidedly sheepish. "We borrowed it from the hospital, sor. We felt entitled to it in a manner of speaking."

"How's that?"

"All the trouble and expense we saved them by bringing himself back home ourselves."

Edward nodded, feeling that he was beginning to get a grasp on whatever it was Dooley used for logic. "Make sure it goes back – soon!" he ordered. "Apart from anything else, I don't want my yard looking like a geriatric ward."

James Henry smiled at him proudly.

The old man was delighted with the library and settled into it with an ease that showed Edward how tired he was beneath the brave front he was presenting. Numerous bruises of various hues, reminders of the dreadful fall he had taken, were now appearing all over his body, and a delayed shock reaction set in. Unhappily, this was at its worst when Frank arrived for the weekend; after spending half an hour with James Henry, he returned to Edward in a very sombre mood.

"He may not have done much obvious damage to himself, but it didn't half knock him about," he said.

"Yes. Remember he's pretty good for his age though," Edward replied. "There's every chance that he'll make a full recovery. He may have to accept the fact that he's an old man, but he'll be all right."

"I don't suppose you're ready to lose him yet, are you?" Frank asked after a few moments of deep thought.

"No, not really." Edward was surprised by his father's insight and candour, suddenly seeing them as qualities he must always have had yet rarely demonstrated. He was probably different at work. "I've survived my first season and I've got some new ideas for the one that's coming up, but I'm a long way from being ready to go solo."

"He told me you never asked him for advice. He seemed very pleased about that."

Edward smiled. "There's no need to. It's enough just having him around."

Deep in thought, Frank's face had a faraway, sad look. "Father and I have always been the very best of friends," he said. "We've never quarrelled and we've had plenty of good times. The one thing I've missed is never being able to get close enough to his *greatness* to enjoy it. Jimmy did." Frank mentioned his long-dead brother with visible sadness. "And you did from the day you first came here. How old were you?"

"About eight, wasn't it?"

"Yes. And you've been like a part of him ever since."

On Sunday afternoon, Edward drove Frank to Dublin for his return flight to Birmingham. Hardly a word was spoken on the journey, Frank wanting to do nothing except stare at the passing countryside which was drab under an overcast sky. Edward was certain that something of very great significance had passed between him and James Henry. At lunch, Frank had been quite cheerful, then, after a long talk with the old man in the library, he had reappeared looking very downcast. When he thanked Mary for looking after him and made his farewells, his voice betrayed a level of emotion that Edward had never heard before. At the airport, they observed an instinctive protocol, saying all the right things with great sincerity while ensuring that the parting was dealt with as quickly as possible.

The effect of shock on James Henry worsened. On Monday, he was unable to get up. By Wednesday, Doctor Fitzgerald was concerned, and Edward saw that he was keeping a close watch on James Henry's temperature. He also eased the strapping round his chest. "We've to make sure he keeps breathing normally," he said. "There's nasty things can happen here if we're not careful."

"Pneumonia?" Edward asked.

"Aye, that's the fellah I'm worried about."

"Ought he to go back to hospital?"

Doctor Fitzgerald grimaced. "Are you going to ask him that, or are you suggesting that I might like to volunteer?"

"No, I'll do it."

Edward explained his fears to James Henry.

"Yes, I can understand all that," he said, "and I wouldn't expect you to be anything but worried. But there's something very important for you to understand. I've always promised myself that when the time comes, I'm going to die here, in this house. That's if I got the choice, and it looks as though I have."

"I see."

"Do you?"

80

"Yes. It's a question of dignity."

"And I belong here."

"You won't find anyone arguing with that."

Edward knew that James Henry now needed something very close to twenty-four-hour-a-day attention, if only to monitor his temperature and administer drugs at the correct times. While he was still casting around for the faintest idea as to how this might be achieved, Mary presented him with the solution, complete, all tied up, and with no room for argument. Mary herself would be responsible for the twelve hours from seven in the morning every day; the night shift would be taken in rotation by Finoula, Siobhan and Kathleen Corrigan, who would be excused from other work for whatever time was needed for them to catch up on their sleep after each spell of duty. Siobhan took the first turn, and after satisfying himself that she was happy with her task, Edward telephoned Valerie Malahide and was invited to share her dinner.

"Yes, I know it's very trying," Valerie said after he had told her everything, "but it's perfectly natural. T.P. was just the same. He had cancer and there was nothing they could do. As soon as they told him, he discharged himself and came here. This place meant a great deal to him – he'd sweated blood to get here from a not very nice part of Dublin. He loved it. And me of course." She made this last statement with an unaffected simplicity that would have convinced the most hardened cynic. "And James Henry feels just the same about Avoca House. Do you know, that place was a shambles when he moved in. It was a disgrace."

"So I understand."

"T.P. used to say that no decent man in his right mind would have sent a horse there but for one thing – James Henry Manning!" She said the name with relish, giving it a stirring resonance.

"I suppose I'm being very selfish about it – I'm plain terrified of not having him there."

"You'll manage."

"You sound very confident."

"I am. If you weren't the man for the job, he wouldn't have picked you. Come on, let's see how that casserole's getting on, I'm starving."

For two days, James Henry seemed to hold his own. After that, it was clear that the drugs were only partially effective and that pneumonia was taking a grip. When Edward rang his father, Frank seemed perfectly resigned to the news and made no suggestion that he should come over. Richard, however, whom Edward contacted at the bank during working hours, was very anxious.

"Do you think he's in immediate danger?" he asked.

"No. He's still got the constitution of an ox."

"All right. I'm bringing Imogen and Nicholas back to Belfields this weekend and having a bit of a break. Everything is sorted out here, by the way."

"Well done. Does that mean Imogen will be staying at Belfields now?"

"Yes, and she can't wait. Tell James Henry I'll be there to see him on Friday evening."

Edward passed the news on at once and James Henry was pleased. "By the way," he said casually, "how are you and Mrs Malahide getting along?"

"Very well indeed. As a matter of fact, we're going to a concert this evening."

"She's a good woman."

"Yes."

"She was a wonderful wife to old T.P." Edward was uncertain whether the pause that followed was intended to be significant or was the consequence of breathing difficulties. "I reckon she'll do the same again one day for some lucky chap."

"Possibly."

There was no mistaking the function of the pause this time. "I don't suppose you've had any ideas in that direction?"

"Certainly not!"

"All right, all right, keep your shirt on." James Henry raised his right hand in a mollifying gesture. "You'll need to be careful about choosing the right woman to marry."

"I fully intend to be," Edward said stiffly.

James Henry ignored the remark and what it was intended to convey. "Very difficult finding a decent wife in the horse game," he said with the assurance of someone propounding a universal truth. "You need a woman who's hooked on the business. I've seen some terrible messes. Do you remember Vernon Dalby – used to be in Tim Barry's place on the Curragh?"

"I've heard you and Sir Nick talk about him."

"Awful foul-up! He showed a great deal of promise – and he was getting people putting the right sort of horses in his yard. He won the Guineas in '69 or '70 with a good filly called Philomena. Then he married the owner's daughter. She was an absolute corker! Had *the* most magnificent legs." He chuckled fondly at the memory. "But she didn't know the first thing about horses, and didn't much care either. I believe she was quite upset when she found out what a 'nuisance' they were – you know, the wretched things had to be looked after all the time. She cleared off with a Hungarian tennis player and Vernon was on the bottle and bankrupt within two years."

"I'll bear it in mind."

"You do that." James Henry gave him a long, hard look. "You're operating in a closed community and it doesn't do to hanker after anything outside it."

At eight o'clock, Avoca House was still and quiet on a cold, starlit night. It was Siobhan's turn for night duty again. Rather than waste her time with knitting or a book, she was working on the stable accounts, and had them spread out all over the kitchen table. Deeply engrossed, she was not particularly pleased when Finoula appeared.

"Is Edward in?" Finoula asked.

"No." Siobhan half hoped that the curt, uninformative reply would shut her sister up, or, better still, send her home. She was disappointed.

"Mrs Malahide again, is it?"

"I believe so."

"Jesus, Mary and Joseph!" Finoula flung herself into a chair, then bounced up again. "How can he keep seeing that woman with himself at death's door?"

"He's not, Fin! Don't be so silly."

"Well he's not very well now, is he?"

"No. But Edward's fully entitled to some relaxation."

"Relaxation! With that owd bag? He's out of his mind."

"Fin, she's a very nice lady – and she's not at all old."

Finoula glowered at her, painfully and fully aware that she was right. "I love him crazy," she said in a small, pathetic voice.

"I know, and you shouldn't." Siobhan was distressed. "It cannot do any good, and it might do a lot of harm. Surely he'd have said something by now if he was interested in you – in that way."

"I wouldn't be too sure about that," Finoula said. "He's very shy." Siobhan saw that an idea had occurred to her. "He is! He's drastic shy! That's what it is. I shall have to think of a way to make it easy for him."

"Be careful," Siobhan urged. "You know what you can be like when you get these ideas."

"I shall be as careful as a little, frightened pussycat," Finoula said, mimicking the way she had talked as a child. "I'm going to go and think about it."

Siobhan stared after her with misgiving. She recognised the signs; the probability was that Finoula had already made up her mind. All that remained to be done was to hope and pray that it was not one of her wilder schemes. Before returning to her figures, Siobhan went to the library and checked that James Henry was comfortable. He was reading the inevitable racing book, looked fairly cheerful, and asked for a cup of hot milk at his usual time.

Finoula returned to the bungalow, made tea for Declan and Mary and watched television with them until their bedtime at ten o'clock. She went to her room when they did, followed the normal ritual and bade her parents good night. But instead of getting into bed, she remained fully clothed, and read a book, glancing at the alarm clock from time to time. At half past eleven, she laid the book aside, turned the light out, carefully opened the window, and climbed out. The stillness of the night was so profound that she fancied she could hear her own heart beating, and she had to move with extreme caution over paths of noisy gravel. At last she reached the kitchen window, uncurtained and brightly lit. Peering in, she found the room empty. The ever-conscientious Siobhan was with James Henry, watching over him, and, Finoula thought, probably still doing those blasted books. With agonising care, she opened the heavy back door, glad that Edward had made Dooley fix it. She removed her shoes outside the office and carried them into the hall. To her immense relief, the library door was fully closed. She ran up the solid, unyielding stairs.

An hour later, Edward arrived back. He left his car at the side of the house, walked quietly into the yard and stood listening, his head cocked for any unusual sounds from the boxes. Satisfied, he went in, finding Siobhan in the kitchen, refilling a water jug.

"How is he?" he asked.

"All right. A bit restless."

"Shall I go and see him?"

"No, I think he's dropping off now. I gave him a tablet."

"Good night then."

Siobhan stood at the library door and watched him go up the stairs. She was certain that he was not having an affair with Mrs Malahide and wished she could convince Finoula of that.

―――――――

Edward found Finoula in the sitting room of his flat. She was curled up in an armchair, wearing his bathrobe. Her feet and what he could see of her legs were bare. Instinctively, he knew that she was naked beneath the robe.

They stared at one another throughout a silence that seemed interminable.

At last she said, "You're not too late tonight." She looked and sounded completely at ease.

Willing himself to be calm, Edward sat down opposite her. He chose the chair that put the greatest possible distance between them. "Finoula, what are you doing here at this time of night?" he asked.

"I've come to show you how much I love you," she said. There was a fierce simplicity in it.

"Love me?" It was difficult to convey astonishment, embarrassment and even a hint of anger in a near-whisper meant to be inaudible in the rest of the house, but he came close to it.

"Yes. I love you ten times more than Mrs Malahide does . . . and I'll be much better for you."

Edward struggled to order his thoughts coherently. "Finoula, Mrs Malahide does *not* love me . . . and I don't love her. We're friends. Very good friends. That's all."

"Are you really certain sure?"

"Yes. Of course I am."

"Ah well . . . that's all right then." She smiled happily.

"No, Finoula, it is *not* all right. Just because there's nothing between Mrs Malahide and me doesn't mean I'm in love with you."

"Ah, come on," she cajoled him. "I don't think you know what you're talking about. How can you tell until you've tried it?"

He had no excuse now for misunderstanding her intentions. "Finoula, we're great friends. We make a fine team and we have a lot of laughs. But that doesn't mean we have to start getting silly." He felt he ought to make the point forcefully. "That's an outrageous idea . . . stupid . . . out of the question."

He remembered afterwards that he thought he'd overdone it, that her silence was probably dangerous.

"You don't think I'm good enough!" She sounded angry, but the bravado that had got her this far was evaporating rapidly.

"You're quite wrong, my dear. Do you think I don't know how very fond we've always been of each other? If we were right for one another, I'd have asked you to marry me some time ago."

Her face showed the thought that had occurred to her. "You actually thought about it?" she asked.

"Yes." He ran a hand through his hair. "Yes, as a matter of fact, I did."

"When?"

"Last year."

"Hell!" Finoula scowled. "I've made an eejut of myself."

"No you haven't. This won't change anything."

"Maybe not for you! It's different for me. I *am* an eejut."

"It'll be all right, I promise you. Come on, let's get you out of here."

He stood up decisively. Catching his mood, Finoula did the same. Her movement was too precipitate and the bathrobe fell open. Several very tangible seconds passed before she bothered drawing it round her again. She spent the time studying the look on Edward's face.

"You nearly wanted me then, didn't you?" she said, both defiance and sadness mixed in her voice.

"You're very beautiful," he replied. He felt light-headed. The perfection of her body had come as a shock to him.

When she returned, fully dressed, from his bedroom a few minutes

85

later, Edward gave the impression of being his normal self again. "I take it your mother and father know nothing about this?" he said.

"They do not! Give me some credit."

He nodded. "Make sure you get back in without disturbing them, and they never will."

Preceding Finoula, he stood by the library door as she crept downstairs. He had wild, utterly impractical notions of creating some sort of diversion if Siobhan came out, but it was not necessary. The house remained still. At the back door, he supported Finoula with an arm as she put her shoes on, then drew her quickly to him and kissed her. "Remember, this never happened," he whispered.

She nodded and slipped into the darkness.

Back upstairs, Edward collapsed into a chair, closed his eyes and went over it all again. She had seemed to agree with him, it had never happened. That, he suspected, was a forlorn hope. Whatever Finoula had indicated in her anxiety to escape, to go away and hide, there were bound to be repercussions.

But in one respect, she had been right. He *had* wanted her. And he had gone close to taking advantage of her.

James Henry was better than he had been for some time on the Friday evening that Richard and Imogen arrived, bringing Sir Nick and Julia with them. He asked to see Sir Nick and Julia first, just the three of them alone. No one thought this strange; during the forty-minute conversation between James Henry and his two dear friends, Richard told Edward of the latest developments in bank politics while Imogen asked Siobhan about some new cushion covers she was contemplating. Among her many accomplishments, Siobhan was an expert needle-woman, and was frequently consulted on changes to the furnishings at Belfields. More often than not, it also fell to her to play a major role in implementing Imogen's schemes.

When Imogen, Richard and Edward went into the library after Sir Nick and Julia had come out, they found James Henry looking eager and alert. He was weak and in great discomfort, but he seemed to have gained immense spiritual stature. Edward felt that he had an aura of radiance and afterwards, Richard and Imogen said they had experienced the same sensation. Imogen sat at his right side and grasped his good hand, Richard and Edward sat opposite her.

"You're looking very well," James Henry told Imogen, then he peered very closely at her. "I do believe you're in foal again," he said.

"As a matter of fact, I am," she replied happily. "It was confirmed yesterday."

"Thought so. You've got that same look about you as when you were carrying young Nicholas. I take it you're pleased?"

"Very."

"So am I, my dear, so am I. What about you?" James Henry turned his attention to Richard who was looking slightly bashful and rather smug at the same time.

"Very pleased indeed," Richard said.

"Good. I hope you'll do something useful with this one instead of stuffing him into that blasted bank."

"Possibly he'll get mixed up in your side of the business," Richard said.

"That's up to him," James Henry said, indicating Edward. "Now listen, you two, I want you to make me a promise." Richard and Edward waited while he eased into a more comfortable position. "You know I've always wanted to win the Derby – and you've been pretty decent about it. You haven't made too much fun of me. Silly, isn't it? The greatest race in the world, and I wanted to win it!" He chuckled at his own impertinent ambition. "They call it 'The Blue Riband', you know. It's had that title for a long time . . . long before those chaps on the transatlantic liners pinched it. It's the greatest honour and accolade there is on the Turf and I want you to win it. Do you understand that? You're to win it!" They both nodded as he paused for breath. "And something else . . . don't get one of these multi-million-dollar 'super horses' . . . they're mostly duds anyway. I want you to win it with a decent, honest horse, a brave horse, the sort of horse that any owner could have had if he was prepared to spend a bit . . . but not millions. I want you to win it with a horse that will restore people's faith in their dreams. Will you try and do that for me?"

Both Richard and Edward said, "Yes."

"I'll make sure they do," Imogen said in a way more gentle than Edward would have believed had he not heard it for himself. She squeezed James Henry's hand reassuringly.

He closed his eyes which had been very bright and animated. When he reopened them, the light had gone and he was a very old man, spent and tired. They talked for a while about ordinary things – the changes that Richard had made at the bank and Imogen's immense relief at escaping from London and returning to Belfields. When it became obvious that he was drifting into sleep, they left him and went back to the kitchen where Sir Nick and Julia were sitting quietly with Declan. There was a long silence which Edward finally broke. "I don't think it's going to be very much longer," he said. "He's changed a lot today. He was very bright, but now . . ." There was no need for him to finish.

"I'm afraid you're right," Julia said. She exchanged a glance with Sir Nick before adding, "He said goodbye to us."

87

Edward had the strange feeling that the four Stewarts looked far more upset than he felt. He thought that perhaps he was already being taken over by practical considerations.

In the morning, Kathleen Corrigan reported that James Henry had slept extremely well, without any sign of distress and was eating a good breakfast. An hour later, he insisted on being helped to get up, summoned Edward and demanded to see the yard. Edward offered no resistance. A somewhat furtive Paddy Dooley admitted that the wheelchair had not been returned to the hospital, and when James Henry was wrapped in blankets, Edward wheeled him out. Declan and a small group of the lads watched, taut-faced, doing their best to conceal their feelings. James Henry had a good look at Musetta and nodded approvingly, then he pointed to Murgatroyd who was watching with sad-eyed curiosity. Edward pushed the chair right into Murgatroyd's box, and they stayed there for several minutes, Murgatroyd nuzzling James Henry's face, while the old man whispered a few breathless words to him.

By six o'clock that evening, James Henry's condition was critical. Doctor Fitzgerald shook his head after examining him, and for once, could think of nothing cheerful to say. Edward resolved to stay with his grandfather for the night, and telephoned both Valerie Malahide and his father. They reacted almost identically to his news. "He's done wonderfully well," Frank said, and Edward knew he was talking about the past fifty years, not just the last two weeks. "Make sure *you're* with him. He'd like that."

To Edward's relief, it was Siobhan's turn for night duty. Between eight and midnight, he sat in the library alone while Siobhan worked in the office. When she joined him, she brought a tea tray and a sheaf of papers for him to read and sign. The fact that she was clearly thinking along the same lines as he, gave him strength. Life would have to go on. There were over forty horses in the yard who would need looking after whatever happened, and the old man in the bed would have been the first to insist upon that principle. They did not speak, and for most of the time remained quite still; Edward attended to the fire several times, and Siobhan made another drink at four o'clock. On the occasions when Edward looked at her, she seemed completely relaxed. She watched James Henry with a calm intensity, her pale face in the dim light reminiscent of a medieval portrayal of a saint. They were oblivious to time.

When he thought that James Henry's breathing had stopped, Edward was certain that it was an aberration caused by his own concentration. Nevertheless, he leaned forward to check. Perhaps it was his breath on James Henry's cheek, or the slight movement of the bed when he leaned against it; the old man opened his eyes and grasped Edward's hand. They stared at one another for what seemed like an eternity. In reality, it was only a few seconds before James Henry spoke.

"It's been good," he said. "I've been very lucky. Don't forget . . . you promised."

His eyes closed and Edward felt the life slip from him as the grip of his hand faded into mere contact.

"That's it. He's gone," Edward said, surprised at the steadiness of his voice. Siobhan knelt down beside the bed, crossed herself, and bowed her head in prayer. Edward left her, wandered into the office and looked at the clock on the wall. It was twenty minutes to seven, the long night was nearly over. He telephoned Doctor Fitzgerald. Then, without knowing why, he took one of Siobhan's felt-tipped pens and put a thick black ring round the date on the calendar – Sunday, January the twentieth. He was in the kitchen, filling the huge kettle that Mary kept simmering all day, when Declan came in.

"It's all over," Edward told him.

"When?"

"Just now – about ten minutes ago."

Declan sat down and took his cap off. Edward had never seen him do that before. Nothing more was said until Siobhan joined them. Most of her composure was gone and she was close to tears. Declan stood up and put his arms round her, and she buried her face in his shoulder. The love between them was palpable, yet Declan still preserved his dignified frugality of emotion. "He was *the* most wonderful man," Siobhan said and the tears came. Suddenly realising that he was unshaven and still wearing yesterday's clothes, Edward had the perfect excuse to leave them and go up to his rooms. However, it was some time before he got as far as the bathroom; as soon as he was safely shut away, he, too, wept.

Richard and Imogen arrived just after breakfast. Richard had something to say, and did so at the first opportunity. "If you haven't any definite plans of your own, we want to suggest that you might like to bury James Henry in our family plot," he said to Edward.

"I agree with that," Imogen said in the way she always used to make something completely official. "So do Nicholas and Julia."

Edward was taken aback. He had not considered the matter, and was at a loss for words. There was a small Protestant church on the southern boundary of the Belfields estate. Generations of Stewarts were buried in a reserved corner of the churchyard, although there were other names on a few of the headstones. Edward thought that Imogen might have an explanation, and he was right.

"It's always been the custom to offer places to very good friends of the family," she said. "You've seen Miles Bulstrode's grave?" Edward nodded. "He was a servant of the bank who died preventing a robbery on a train in 1855. We were shipping bullion to Dover for Paris – all to do with the Crimean War." In happier circumstances, Edward would have smiled at her use of the word 'we'; she made it sound as though she had been personally responsible.

"It's very kind of you," Edward said, still at a loss. "I'm sure he would have liked that . . . in fact he would have been jolly proud."

"Right! That's settled then," Imogen said. "I'll start having words with people." She was into the office and busy on the telephone before Edward had time for second thoughts.

When Edward collected his mother and father from Dublin Airport that afternoon, he was surprised to discover that far from being upset, they were almost cheerful. "I was sorted out the last time I saw him," Frank said. "You remember, when I spoke to him after lunch. He told me what was going to happen and ordered me to get a grip on myself. 'Don't start acting like a bloody wet weekend' were his precise words."

"True to form," Edward said, and felt no need to hide his smile. "He managed to die as he lived – not many get to do that. In fact he achieved every ambition except one."

"What was that?"

"The Derby."

"Oh yes." Frank sounded gently dismissive.

"And I'm going to do that for him."

———————

The day of the funeral was cold, bright and sunny. Edward was astonished by the size of the congregation that packed the small church. There were over three hundred. He was inclined to wonder whether Paddy Dooley's communications system had been at work, but discovered that it was Sir Nick who had ensured that all James Henry's friends of the past thirty years were present. Six of the lads, led by Declan, acted as pall bearers, and at Frank's insistence, Edward was chief mourner. After he had thrown the first handfuls of earth on to the coffin, he looked up and saw Finoula on the other side of the grave. She was staring stony-faced at Valerie Malahide who stood just behind his left shoulder. He forced himself to ignore the fact that there was much more in her look than the occasion demanded.

Afterwards, Avoca House played host to an old-fashioned wake of increasing jollity and happiness. Mary, Kathleen Corrigan and a girl from the Belfields kitchens had provided a sumptuous spread of food and there was no shortage of drink. Mark and Sarah Walgrave had come over from Bagshot, and after a chat with them, Edward met dozens of people whom James Henry had helped to a greater or lesser extent, and who spoke fondly of him. As darkness fell and they drifted unwillingly away, Edward was given a stream of addresses and telephone numbers to contact whenever he needed a favour.

"That was amazing," he said to Valerie as he drove to Belfields where they were to have dinner with Richard and Imogen. "That wasn't a funeral, it was an absolute knees-up."

"No . . . it was a thanksgiving," she said quietly. "And he deserved every minute of it."

Two days later, Edward spent the afternoon in the library, now returned to its former state. He had decided to use it himself and had half-formed notions of making slight changes to the furniture and layout, but was side-tracked by a book on the history of racing. When he eventually tore himself away from it and returned it to the shelf, he walked past a window that overlooked the front of the house, and caught a brief glimpse of something unusual out of the corner of his eye. Looking properly, he saw a boy standing at the gate. He wore blue jeans and a grey anorak and was carrying a bright blue bag of the type used for sports gear. Edward judged him to be about sixteen although he was quite small. The boy's stance was a fascinating mixture of wariness, doubt and resolution.

Walking down the drive towards him, Edward found that the lad was familiar, but he did not know why. The flicker of recognition in his face encouraged the boy to come forward to meet him.

"Hello. Where have I seen you before?" Edward asked.

"King Henry's, sir – but you never taught my form. I'm Lane, sir, Robin Lane."

"What on earth are you doing here?"

"I've come to ask you for a job, sir. Actually, I've sort of run away from home . . . not that anyone will mind."

Edward saw that Robin Lane was tired, cold and hungry. "Come on," he said, "let's have you inside and get to the bottom of all this."

Mary produced a steaming mug of tea without batting an eyelid, then set about spiriting up bacon, egg, sausage and beans in little more time than it took Murgatroyd to cover a mile. Edward sat and listened to the boy's story, disjointed by mouthfuls of food. He prompted and sought clarification where necessary.

Robin Lane had taken his O-Levels the previous summer. The results had been disastrous, prohibiting any hope of passage into the VIth form, and making it very unlikely that he would find a job. Because such abysmal results were most unusual at King Henry's, Edward probed the background. Robin's parents had divorced two years ago, his father apparently handing over virtually everything to his mother and disappearing to the Middle East. Mrs Lane had installed another man almost immediately, but had not yet seen fit to marry him. With what seemed to have been very bad grace, she had agreed to pay for another term so that Robin could attempt a re-take. The results had come a week ago and showed no improvement. The only thing that Robin knew or cared about that might fit him for a job was horses; his father had encouraged him to ride from an early age, and he clearly adored the animals. "I don't want to be a jockey or anything brilliant, sir," he said, "I just want to work with horses."

"Whatever made you come here?"

"Well everyone talks about you at King Henry's – especially after Ascot – and I spoke to Mr Merritt. He said I should write to you, but I came instead."

Dear old Horace! Robin had travelled on the night boat from Holyhead to Dun Laoghaire, caught a train to Dublin, then Naas, and wandered around for nearly five hours looking for Avoca House. Edward extracted his home telephone number from him and shut himself in the office while Mary produced a massive helping of apple pie and custard.

The woman who answered the phone made her brittle insincerity felt simply by announcing her number.

"Mrs Lane?"

"Speaking."

"My name is Edward Manning. I used to teach at King Henry's, but now I train horses in Ireland. I . . ."

She cut him short. "I was wondering if he was there."

Edward did his best to avoid reacting to her tone. "If you mean your son, Mrs Lane, yes, he is here. He arrived about half an hour ago."

"Looking for a job, I suppose?"

"Yes, he is."

"Stupid little fool! I'm sorry you've been troubled, but one really doesn't have eyes in the back of one's head and he is old enough to know better. Can you put him on a boat, or a plane – or something?"

He was fairly certain that she had been drinking. "Would you have any objection to my offering Robin a job, Mrs Lane?" he asked.

"Er . . . no." She was clearly thrown totally off balance by the question. "He's got to do *something*. Do you think you'll be able to?"

"It depends on his ability, Mrs Lane. If he's up to the mark, I can certainly use him. He seems a very decent young man to me."

"Oh." She was groping for words now. "No, I wouldn't mind that. You'll let me know, will you?"

"I will indeed. In the meantime, you may rest assured that he is being looked after."

Robin listened wide-eyed as Edward told him about it. Waving his gratitude aside, Edward moved on. "First things first," he said. "We must find you a bed and I bet you could do with a bath. What shall we do with him, Mary?"

"Kathleen and Liam Corrigan have got a good spare room," she said. "He'll be very comfortable there."

"Just the ticket," Edward said. "I'll take you to meet them in a while. Tomorrow morning, we'll find out what you can do. Is that all right?"

"Oh yes, sir."

The Corrigans had a cosy little cottage about ten minutes walk from the yard. James Henry had done it up for them when they married, a few months before Edward moved to Avoca House. Robin was set down in front of a cheerful fire and Edward explained the bare essentials of the situation to Kathleen and Liam. Then, while Kathleen went upstairs to make the spare bed, he took Liam into the kitchen and told him the full story. Liam was disgusted to hear about Robin's mother, and promised to make the boy feel at home.

After twelve hours' sleep, Robin looked both eager and anxious when Liam brought him into the yard the following morning. Edward had already told Declan all about it, and indicated that he was keen to give the boy a chance. They watched while Robin mucked out and groomed Murgatroyd under Liam's direction, Edward noting that Robin and Liam had already struck up a happy relationship based on the well-known fact that Liam was a genius. When half the horses went out walking, Liam allowed Robin to ride Murgatroyd, and the boy could hardly contain his feelings at being up on the hero of Royal Ascot. It was obvious that Robin sat on a horse well, and had natural talent as a horseman. When they were back in the yard, Edward did some office work while Declan gave Robin a verbal grilling.

"He's all right," was Declan's verdict when he came in for his mug of tea.

"Right, we'll have him!"

Edward derived enormous pleasure from telephoning Mrs Lane. At first, she was stunned by the news that anyone should consider her son worth employing; then she betrayed her relief at having him off her hands. Promising to write her a letter, Edward left her to the gin bottle.

Looking into the yard as he left the office, he saw Robin listening with attentive awe to Liam who was making a world-shattering point with much waving of arms. At Edward's approach, however, he became much more statesmanlike.

"How do you feel about it?" Edward asked Robin.

"It's wonderful, sir, it really is."

"Do you think you'd like it here?"

"Oh yes!"

"All right, you're on."

The boy blinked several times in disbelief, and when he finally managed to say, "Thank you, sir, thank you very much," Edward was sure that the sparkle in his eyes was brightened by tears.

That afternoon, Edward and Declan watched Liam giving Robin the full tour of the yard.

"Do you know, Declan, I've a feeling that lad is going to be worth his weight in gold," Edward said. "Would the old man have approved?"

Declan thought about it. "Yes," he said. "But it's your opinion that counts."

Edward smiled ruefully at him. As long as Declan was around, he would never have an excuse for forgetting his responsibilities.

CHAPTER 5

Siobhan was the first person to see the change in Edward's attitude to his profession. In February, three weeks after James Henry's death, they spent several days in the office, planning the coming season in detail. Edward's intention to contest better-class races was immediately apparent, and as the English race entries grew, she realised that the flying horse box was going to be in great demand.

Musetta was the spearhead of the campaign. With the end of the winter in sight, it was safe to start assuming that she had come through it well, and Edward was able to reaffirm his resolve to send her to Newmarket for the One Thousand Guineas at the end of April. His choice of a preparation race was surprising; rather than obviously suitable races at the Curragh or the Phoenix Park, he selected the Nell Gwyn Stakes at Newmarket, run on the first day of the Craven Meeting, sixteen days before the One Thousand Guineas.

"I want her to get used to travelling, and the Nell Gwyn will give her a look at Newmarket," Edward explained. "Much as I love her, I sometimes wonder if we shall ever be able to relax with that temperament of hers."

Siobhan understood. From the information in front of her, she could see that the Nell Gwyn was run over the last seven furlongs of the famous Rowley Mile course that was used for the Guineas. She knew that Edward had never been to Newmarket, the Mecca of racing, but was certain that he had found out everything he needed to know about the place.

Ten of the previous season's horses had left Avoca House, some to start a new career in hurdling or chasing, others to enter an honourable retirement. To replace them, ten new two-year-olds had come into the yard, and Edward attached very special importance to them even before they arrived. These were the first batch that were unquestionably *his*; he had helped to pick most of them, and whatever they achieved would be his responsibility alone.

Without any justification other than intuition and a leavening of prejudice, Edward decided that the best of the bunch were two more of Richard's Kentucky acquisitions and the colt he had helped Valerie Malahide buy for fifteen thousand pounds. Richard's pair, a colt and filly, had been named Radames and Leonora respectively, continuing the operatic theme established by Musetta. Valerie Malahide had an idea

95

what she wanted to call hers, but had been uncertain about it until Edward provided the necessary encouragement, and the colt was registered as T. P. Malahide. Like the others, the trio had come to Avoca House via Brendan O'Sullivan's where they had been schooled. Edward wasted no time in entering them for Ascot, where they would be joined by Murgatroyd for a second attempt on the Royal Hunt Cup.

T. P. Malahide was allocated to Robin Lane, who would only be doing one horse until he was fully settled in and knew the ropes. The boy was delighted to be given such an important assignment straight away, and went about his work in a manner that showed he was determined to succeed. Both Leonora and Radames were given to Cathal O'Brien who had emerged from the winter as a close friend of Robin. There were good grounds for the choice. Edward had seen that Cathal's considerable talent was based on a tender patience that was ideally suited to young horses. He was secretly glad to have such a sound reason to make amends for the disappointment with Musetta that Cathal had borne so well.

March began with what Declan, in a rare display of feeling, called 'Musetta weather' and the phrase caught on. After a mild, wet February that saturated the gallop, March did indeed come in like a lion. For three days, a fierce gale raged without respite. There was some rain, but the skies were mostly blue and the drying effect of the strong wind on the gallop was miraculous. By the end of the week, Declan pronounced the ground fit, and Musetta started cantering. Edward and Finoula, who had avoided each other since the day of James Henry's funeral, were back in close contact. Musetta soon proved that she had indeed wintered well and was eager to work. Taking her duties very seriously, Finoula was immediately getting the best from her and a great weight was lifted from Edward's mind.

"We're in business," he said to Finoula after the filly had cantered five furlongs and shown that her action was, if anything, better than last year. "We can start where we left off."

"Looks like it," was all he got as an unsmiling reply. Declan at his most dour would have been hard pressed to beat it; he was, in any case, incapable of such bad grace.

Edward sensed that there was not much point in hoping for an improvement, and he was right. Not even the practice air trip at the beginning of April caused Finoula's attitude to change. In order to discover whether Musetta would have any problems travelling by air, Edward chartered the flying horse box for a morning and they took her on a joy-ride. From Blessington, the flight path was straight across Ireland to Galway Bay. The sky was clear, they flew at no more than two thousand feet, and Musetta was unconcerned, but still Finoula said no more than was strictly necessary. Turning south towards the mouth of the Shannon, they passed between the Aran Islands and the awesome Cliffs of Moher. The view was stunning, one of the most memorable sights that Edward had ever seen, and he said so at fulsome length. Finoula nodded and said "Yes" occasionally. Edward gave up. She was doing her job and he supposed he had no right to expect anything else. He had no idea what he could do about it, and froze the problem out of his mind.

Preparing Musetta for her first visit to Newmarket, Edward discussed strategy with Declan.

"Am I right in thinking I don't want her *too* ready for this one, Declan?" he asked.

"You are. We want something to work on when she gets back."

"So we want her almost right, but needing the race."

"We do. And it's best if she doesn't have too hard a race."

This was achieved by omitting two of the pieces of work that Musetta would have been given if she were being fully prepared. She was cantered and walked long distances each day, and a week before they travelled to Newmarket, Sean Gillespie rode her and said she would do. He was in more of a hurry than ever, waved aside offers of breakfast, and hurtled off to do more ride work for another of his trainers. That afternoon, he rode in all six races at Navan, a sign of his improving fortune, and appropriately, one of those rides was a winner for Avoca House, the stable that had brought him to prominence the previous year. Sybil had made good, early progress in her work, and beat a moderate field without a great deal of effort.

For Newmarket, Edward made use of facilities that had been offered to him at James Henry's funeral by a man called Gordon Chapman. Since Chapman, who was aged about sixty, had never been in Ireland, it was difficult to deduce how his and James Henry's paths could ever have crossed, and Chapman did not volunteer the information. However, one thing was quite certain: for whatever reason, Gordon Chapman had thought very highly indeed of the old man, and felt a powerful duty to repay favours that must have been substantial. Chapman was prepared to make available accommodation similar to that at The Elms, the difference being that he was a trainer himself. As a stranger to Newmarket, and somewhat daunted by the prospects it held out, Edward was glad to accept.

Like so many trainers' quarters in Newmarket, Chapman's place was quite small, and not at all grand. His compact yard alongside the Limekilns on the Bury Road, had twenty boxes, only fifteen of which were occupied. For reasons of economy and space, trainers at the headquarters of racing did not have their own gallops, but used communal land to exercise their horses, observing locations and schedules laid down by the Jockey Club. The Limekilns was one of several grounds used for this purpose.

The Nell Gwyn Stakes, a Group Three race, was run on the first day of the Craven Meeting, a Tuesday. Musetta, Edward, Finoula and Dooley travelled on Sunday afternoon to allow a full day in Newmarket before the race. They flew to Cambridge where a horse van was waiting, and at the end of the short drive Dooley got lost in Newmarket and had to ask the way. Edward did not allow himself to be too pleased about this, realising it was a momentary aberration caused by the simple fact that Dooley had never been to Newmarket before. As Musetta was being introduced to her temporary quarters, Dooley and the van disappeared, and Edward knew that within hours the whole of Newmarket would be an open book to him.

Gordon Chapman drove Edward and Finoula round on a sightseeing tour that evening. They saw very little apart from dozens of imposing buildings including the Jockey Club and National Stud. The complete lack of activity was disappointing. Edward knew that Avoca House would be quiet and closed up for the night, but somehow, he had expected Newmarket to be different. It was a frustrating and almost eerie experience to pause outside the more famous stables, and see nothing except well-manicured lawns and big houses, one or two of them in a riotous Victorian style that would have appealed to those of Richard's ancestors who had added to Belfields.

Things were very different next morning. The world seemed full of horses, hundreds, perhaps thousands of them. Musetta cantered on the Limekilns with Chapman's first – and only – lot, and Edward was amused by the crowded bustle. Order soon emerged from the apparent chaos. It was rather like a busy airport, with the gallops being used as though they were runways. They were about to go back, Edward satisfied with Musetta, when his attention was caught by a huge string of horses moving on to the exercise ground from the Bury Road.

"That's a pretty imposing sight," he said to Chapman.

"Isn't it just! That's Bernard Dalrymple – wonder boy." Chapman's tone was bantering, but the underlying hint of sour grapes was clear. The name was very familiar to Edward; Dalrymple was in the top flight of trainers, consistently very successful, and only about five years older than himself.

"How many horses has he got there, for goodness' sake?" Edward asked.

"Nigh on a hundred. Not bad for a first lot, is it? And just look at that gang at the back. He's got more assistants than he knows what to do with."

At the end of the string, Dalrymple himself was mounted on a good-looking brown hunter. With him were six men and one woman, all obviously part of what he called his 'management team'.

Gordon Chapman laughed at the look on Edward's face and said, "Makes you feel very humble, doesn't it?"

Edward was far from sure. The overall impact was one of quality; he felt a little like a tramp steamer watching a glittering luxury liner pass. Asking himself whether he would ever achieve anything remotely like it seemed pointless, a flight of pure fancy. Finoula's interest was avid and noticeable; for the first time in weeks, her face displayed genuine animation. A child might have viewed a fabulous caravan on the road to Samarkand with similar wonderment. When she turned Musetta to follow Chapman's horses back to his small yard, the magic went, and her expression resumed the strained look of discontent that had been normal since that dreadful night in January.

Although fairly certain that there would be nothing for him to do or celebrate, Richard left London for the afternoon, and came to Newmarket to see Musetta race. Edward was grateful for his company and moral support, without which his first appearance at the focal point of world racing would have been a nerve-racking and lonely experience. They were both glad of Gordon Chapman's guidance through the preliminary formalities, and explanation of the important features of what was not one but two racecourses combined.

Sean Gillespie was also making his debut at Newmarket and knew that the outing was as much for his benefit as Musetta's. During the preceding few weeks, he had studied over fifty films and video-recordings of races run over the Rowley Mile, the straight, undulating course that took its name from the favourite horse and nickname of King Charles II. There was, however, no substitute for riding it, and in the race named after the most famous of Charles II's mistresses, he and Musetta acquitted themselves well. Musetta had matured and steadied during the winter, and her display of antics on leaving the stalls was minimal. She settled quickly, and did exactly what Sean Gillespie wanted of her. The pace, although not particularly sharp, was good enough for Edward's purpose; as instructed, his filly was given an easy time, was discouraged from a final effort, and finished with the main group of six about four lengths behind the winner.

"Very smooth. You should be able to do something with that in two weeks," Sean Gillespie said and went to weigh in.

Edward and Richard stayed chatting with Gordon Chapman, while Finoula took Musetta away to prepare her for the journey back to Ireland. Eventually they parted, Richard to drive back to London, Chapman going home, after promising to have everything ready for Edward in two weeks when he returned for the Guineas. It did not take Edward long to spot Dooley, materialising on cue to manoeuvre the van into position ready for Musetta. He was surprised to see that Finoula was talking to a somewhat suave young man, and seeming to enjoy herself a great deal. They stopped as he approached, the man holding out his right hand.

"How do you do, Mr Manning," he said, far too smoothly, "I'm Alexander Abercrombie, Mr Dalrymple's chief assistant. I've just been admiring your filly."

There was something so intensely irritating about Abercrombie that Edward very nearly said, "Which one?" Instead, he forced what he hoped was a careless smile to his face. "Yes, she's nice, isn't she? We think a lot of her," he said.

"She's already won her Group race, I believe?" Abercrombie drawled, in an accent that had to be pure affectation. He was apparently supporting the cynical theory that a filly needed to win only one decent race in order to attract value as a brood mare. Edward was having none of it.

"She's won *one*," he replied, "but it was only Group Three."

His meaning was obvious even to the self-opinionated Abercrombie who went off in search of his colleagues.

The journey back to Avoca House was uneventful. Finoula made a point of talking incessantly to Sean Gillespie who had cadged a lift with them, and Edward was content to leave them to it. After taking off from Cambridge Airport, there was a good aerial view of the city. He picked out his old college and smiled wryly. What would they think of him now? At Blessington, Sean Gillespie made a dash for a bus to Dublin and Finoula reverted to straight-faced silence. Resigned, Edward accepted it. The only topic of conversation he had the slightest inclination to raise was Alexander Abercrombie, and he had no intention of giving her that satisfaction.

Musetta had two days of light exercise to recover from the Nell Gwyn Stakes, then work began in earnest to prepare her for the One Thousand Guineas. As though sensing that something very important was afoot, she began to display a gusto for galloping that lifted Edward's hopes and inspired Finoula to greater heights in her work, although her general demeanour did not improve. For five consecutive days, Edward took horses racing every afternoon, having two winners and a near miss to show for it. The weather was exceptionally fine for late April, and in company with the other horses, Musetta spent each afternoon in the paddock at Avoca House, enjoying the powerful twin benefits of sun and lush spring grass. "A horse is no good until he's had the sun on his back," James Henry had always preached, and when Edward looked at Musetta each evening, he saw that this was right. She threw off the last signs of winter when she came quickly into her summer coat with a fine silken sheen.

Richard watched her last hard gallop on the Saturday morning, five days before the race. "She looks wonderful," he said. "I've no way of telling whether she *is* right, but she certainly looks it. By the way, we shall all be there on Thursday."

"Oh, is Imogen coming?" Edward asked.

"And mother and father."

"Really? Will Sir Nick be all right?"

Richard shrugged helplessly. "I asked him, of course. He said he'd got two choices!"

"That's a typical James Henry remark."

"Just what I thought. But he won't be put off. He's determined to see Newmarket and he wants to do a few things in the bank and round London. He and mother are flying to London with me on Monday morning. Imogen's coming over on Wednesday."

This time, Edward considered that the day before the race was sufficiently early to take Musetta over. Despite the nature of the occasion, Edward felt far more relaxed than he had done two weeks previously; he knew his filly was in the best condition attainable and Newmarket had no hidden fears for him.

When they arrived, Dooley delayed his disappearing act to ask a vital question. "What are the expectations, sor?"

Edward laughed. To Dooley's disgust, there had been an embargo on betting for the Nell Gwyn Stakes. Being wise after the event did little to mollify him and he was visibly fretting, eager for action.

"If I were a betting man Paddy, I would be investing in her," Edward said.

Dooley's face lit up. "Thank you, sor! Thank you very much."

"Each way," Edward cautioned, secure in the knowledge that he was almost certainly wasting his breath.

On the day of the race, Edward had lunch on the racecourse with Sir Nick, Julia, Richard and Imogen. It was a cheerful affair with an atmosphere that reminded Edward of the last day at school before a holiday. Sir Nick looked extremely well and behaved like one of the schoolboys about to be let out, clearly delighted at seeing the family's racing colours making their first appearance in a Classic race. Edward was a little sad that James Henry had not lived to enhance the occasion, and he suspected that Richard was having similar thoughts. The old man would have been at the peak of his form on a day like this, an event tailor-made for him.

When Edward went to the stables to saddle Musetta, he was annoyed to find Alexander Abercrombie talking to Finoula. The two aspects of the scene that most displeased him were Abercrombie's air of languid superiority and Finoula's wide-eyed attention to his every word. As a representative of the yard that was fielding the firm favourite, Abercrombie was entitled to his confidence, but Edward wished that he would go somewhere else and do it. When he saw Edward approaching, he did precisely that, strolling casually as if to deny any suggestion that he had been put to flight. To Edward's surprise, her conversation with Abercrombie had left Finoula very cheerful and she seemed to go out of her way to afford him some of the respect that trainers usually received from their staff. It was she who suggested that, since it was a fairly cool afternoon, Musetta could go into the parade ring with the lucky blanket.

In the paddock, Edward discovered that he was enjoying himself. Albeit for a short space of time, he was an important person, the man responsible for a reasonably fancied contender for the One Thousand Guineas. Imogen, who had been keeping an eye on the betting, told him that Musetta was third favourite after Bernard Dalrymple's Duchess of Malfi and the French filly Montparnasse. When the jockeys came out, Edward suddenly realised how very distinguished were the colours that Richard had developed from those handed down by Sir Nick. The azure blue jacket had a gold Cross of Jerusalem front and back while the blue cap had a golden tassel, added by Richard and heartily endorsed by Edward. Sean Gillespie stood with arms folded, pale, intense and silent, listening to Imogen venting her wrath about a tradesman who had failed to deliver two new chairs to Belfields on time, profoundly grateful that, for today at least, his mother seemed to be forgotten.

Edward watched the race. It was the first time he had ever done it from start to finish, and he used James Henry's old, but very powerful binoculars to do so. Musetta launched herself boldly from the stalls and was rock-steady within three strides. Inside the first half furlong, Sean Gillespie had her exactly where he wanted her, nicely covered up in the middle of the fourteen-horse field. That was where she stayed until the race began with a vengeance, a little more than two furlongs from home. As was often the case on the Rowley Mile, this happened as they passed 'The Bushes', a clump of stunted trees that would have been utterly nondescript anywhere but in the otherwise featureless vastness of Newmarket Heath. Before the furlong marker, Duchess of Malfi, Montparnasse and a rank outsider called Princess Iona were fighting it out furiously and drawing relentlessly clear of the rest.

The instant at which Sean Gillespie made his decision could be seen clearly through the binoculars. Musetta responded immediately and surged forward into the electrifying acceleration that she had not been asked for since last September at the Curragh. In less than a hundred yards, she had the three leaders stone cold and was opening daylight between herself and them. Sean Gillespie did not let up until he was safely well past the winning post; Musetta was very important indeed for the Stewarts and Edward, but she was also *his* first Classic winner. She beat Montparnasse by two lengths as Bernard Dalrymple's Duchess of Malfi faded badly to leave Princess Iona in third place.

There was a long, perfectly calm silence between Richard and Edward.

"That was pretty bloody good," Richard said at last.

"Hell of a shame James Henry missed it."

"Yes. But he saw Royal Ascot and her Group race. He knew the way things were going."

"I hope so." Edward sounded as though he desperately wanted to believe it. Then they laughed and shook hands.

"Come on," Richard said, "we've things to do."

Imogen was busy with her camera as Richard and Edward led Musetta in. A visibly cheerful Sean Gillespie asked Edward, "All right?" from his commanding height.

"Yes. Thank you very much. That was a lovely ride you gave her."

"I told you she was good." Sean allowed a flash of pleasure to cross his face as he dismounted, collected the saddle and bolted for the weighing room before Imogen could catch him.

Ann Manning, watching it all on TV, was thrilled. She still knew next to nothing about racing, and would continue to cherish her ignorance, but she understood full well that the filly of whom she was so fond had achieved a notable feat, and that Edward had shown considerable skill in preparing her for it.

After Finoula had taken Musetta away, Edward was surrounded by racing journalists, eager for information. They wanted to know all about the unknown, who, only four weeks into his second season as a trainer, had snatched a rich prize from the best that England and France had to offer. As a result of what Edward told them, James Henry received more coverage on the following day's racing pages than he had ever dreamed of in his lifetime. Then they wanted to know about the plans for Musetta: was she going to Epsom for the Oaks? Edward said that he had yet to make up his mind; he wanted to give her a few days to settle down after this race before deciding about her next engagement. Edward was pleased and relieved to have come unscathed through his first major encounter with the press. The subsequent reporting was fair and favourable, although there was emphasis on this being another 'lucky Irish' occurrence. One paper was more thoughtful. Musetta's connections weren't Irish at all, it pointed out. The owner was the wealthy managing director of a merchant bank, and the trainer had, until fairly recently, been a physics master at a prestige English school. They were both young, had a close partnership, and clearly meant business. Much more was likely to be heard of them.

Rejoining the Stewarts, Edward was astonished to see Imogen in the process of handing a bundle of ten-pound notes to a very happy Sir Nick. Seeing Edward's look, Sir Nick was momentarily sheepish, then rallied strongly. "I had a bet," he said. "First time in my life. And she won!"

"What on earth got into you?" Edward asked, precariously balanced between disapproval and pleasure.

"I was told to!" Sir Nick replied defiantly.

"Who by?"

"Jimmy." He automatically used his special name for James Henry. "He said she'd win if you got her right – and you wouldn't send her otherwise. He gave me two hundred pounds to put on for him and told me to have a bet while I was about it."

Edward's jaw sagged.

Richard laughed. "Well there you are," he said. "Argue with that if you dare! The old man *did* know."

Shaking his head in disbelief, Edward set off for the stables to check on his filly. She was untroubled, relatively fresh and was being doted on by Paddy Dooley, whom Edward had never imagined capable of such joyous affection. Even more surprisingly, he removed his cap when he saw Edward.

"My felicitations, sor," he said. "That was grand!"

Where on earth did Dooley get these words from, Edward wondered. "Thank you, Paddy," he said, keeping a very straight face. "It was a team effort, remember."

"Ah yes, sor – but you're the one with the *ideas*, d'you see?"

"Thank you. I suppose you had a bit on?"

"Five hundred, sor – and I got ten to one about her."

"Five hundred!" Edward was flabbergasted.

Dooley produced a grin that Liam Corrigan would have admired. "That was a team effort as well, sor." He explained who had contributed to the vast stake; the seemingly endless list included Siobhan and Robin Lane, both of whom had provided five pounds.

Edward was still assessing this huge vote of confidence when Finoula appeared. She was carrying her suitcase and was very keyed up.

"Well done, Finoula," he said to her. "She did you proud. You'll simply have to have the two per cent of this one." She had refused her 'lad's' share of Musetta's previous winnings, insisting that it went into the communal kitty.

"Thank you," she said, anxious to change the subject. "I'm going to stay here for a few days. It's a good opportunity to have a look at everything. You don't mind, do you? You won't want me while she's resting. And you can get her back by yourself, can't you?" The words came out in a well-rehearsed rush.

He said the first thing that came into his head. "Where will you stay?"

"I'll find a small hotel. Spend some of my winnings. Treat myself." She smiled weakly.

He did not believe her. She came very close indeed to seeing precisely what passed through his mind: the sequence of expressions on his face was plain enough. Should he tell her not to be so damned silly and come home? No, she was perfectly capable of starting a public row in response to that one. There was nothing he could do at the moment. "Yes, all right," he said. "Have a nice time."

"Thanks."

Before he had the chance to think of anything else to say, she was gone.

Sean Gillespie looked decidedly uneasy when Imogen, smitten with her homing instinct and anxious to be back at Belfields, hitched a lift on the flying horse box, leaving Richard and his parents to go back to London. But he had no need to worry. With her pregnancy starting to show, and a poor night's sleep in an hotel behind her, she wanted nothing more than to put her feet up and relax. She asked about Finoula, raising her eyebrows when Edward told her what had happened.

"Now that *is* interesting," she said.

"What do you mean?"

"I fancy your problems in that direction will soon be over," she replied.

"I don't understand."

"Oh yes you do!" She may have been weary, but she was still capable of producing a formidably hard stare.

Because of Finoula, Edward arrived back at Avoca House with mixed feelings. To his immense relief, Mary waved aside his hesitant attempt at an explanation of her daughter's absence. "She rang while you were on your way," she said. "It might do her good to stay there for a few days."

With that out of the way, Edward was able to sit back and enjoy the acclaim. Declan told him that they had all piled into the recreation room in the lads' hostel to watch the race on TV. Edward received a very vivid picture of the excitement that had begun to build up while Musetta was still walking round the parade ring, and the pandemonium that had broken loose when she began her winning run must have come close to raising the roof.

When he rode out with the first lot the following morning, Edward was pleased to see that the effect of Musetta's great victory was very plain. Avoca House had always been a happy and efficient place, but this had usually gone hand-in-hand with an acceptance of its modest status within the world of racing. No stable cared for its horses better, they always looked well and won their share of races. They were, however, unspectacular, bread-and-butter races, constrained by the calibre of the raw material with which they were working. Last year had provided the first hopeful signs of greater things to come: now, they had turned out the winner of the One Thousand Guineas Stakes, a Group One race and an English Classic. The lads seemed smarter, more alert, showing more pride, and the horses quickly picked it up. There was a certain swagger about the proceedings, as though a bunch of gifted amateurs had suddenly discovered they were a company of top-flight professionals.

"Musetta seems to have worked wonders for us," Edward said to Declan.

"We've moved up a notch or two," Declan declared. There was a gleam in his eye that suggested he did more than simply approve – he *liked* it.

Siobhan and Edward were in the office for the afternoon when the telephone rang. After she had answered it, Siobhan's face showed surprise and awe as she listened. "It's Bernard Dalrymple from Newmarket," she said, putting her hand over the mouthpiece. "He's asking for you."

Edward nodded and took the instrument from her. "Good afternoon, Mr Dalrymple," he said, determined to play the part.

"Good afternoon, Mr Manning. Congratulations on your win yesterday. She's a very good filly."

"Thank you." Edward reflected that Bernard Dalrymple sounded perfectly decent and sensible, nothing at all like Abercrombie.

"I have a problem, Mr Manning," Dalrymple went on. "Finoula Kelly has been to see me – young Abercrombie brought her in. Not to beat about the bush, she's asked me for a job – begged me, in fact. It so happens that I could use her. One of my assistants is going off to New Zealand to see what he can do. Clearly I had to speak to you before I even thought of making a move."

"That's good of you."

"Not at all. If we don't do things the right way, this business can get unpleasant and impossible. Tell me, do you think she's just acting on impulse?"

"Well, she is an impulsive person as you've obviously spotted – but I've a strong idea that this isn't like that. She's probably been thinking of a move for some months. I know she was very taken with Newmarket when we came over for the Craven Meeting and I imagine she's carried on from there."

"I see. Would you mind me offering her a post?"

Edward took a deep breath. "I don't want to lose her," he said, "but I think there are powerful reasons why I can't or shouldn't keep her. So I wouldn't object."

"That's good of you. Presumably you can vouch for her?"

"Absolutely. She's done well for me and my grandfather."

"She tells me she did most of the preparation work with your filly that won the Guineas. Is that correct?"

"Quite true."

They chatted socially for a couple of minutes or so, then ended the call with mutual good wishes. Edward looked at Siobhan, whose face was very grave. "I need to talk to your mother and father," he said, standing up. "You'd better come too."

Declan and Mary were having tea in the kitchen of their bungalow, and as Mary found two more cups, she told Edward that they already knew. Finoula had rung an hour ago.

"And there's something Mr Dalrymple won't have told you," Declan said and looked at Mary.

Even the forthright Mary found it difficult. "She wants to start over there right away. She doesn't want to come back here at all. She says she couldn't bear it."

There was a long silence.

"This is a devil of a shaker," Edward said at last.

"It is," Declan agreed. "But it's the best thing."

Mary and Siobhan nodded agreement.

"We know how things are," Mary said.

While Edward was wondering what she meant, Siobhan explained. "Fin told me about that night. The night she went up to your rooms."

"Oh." Edward stared at the table.

"She's a fool." Declan made it sound like a statement of fact, not an opinion. "Give it a year and things will be right."

"We'll have to pack her things up and send them," Siobhan said forlornly as a new aspect of the affair dawned on her.

"Oh no, we can't have that," Edward said forcefully. He racked his brains and came up with the answer. "Mary, you'll want to see she's properly settled and everything, won't you?"

"It would be nice."

"It's essential. You must go over and sort her out. Stay as long as you like."

"How will you all manage?"

"Don't be silly! Kathleen Corrigan can cope and if the worse did come to the worst, I could always get help from Belfields."

Mary looked doubtfully at Declan, but did not need much convincing. "All right then," she said.

"And don't worry about what it costs," Edward told her firmly.

Mary was away for eight days. By the time she returned, satisfied that Finoula was safely settled, Edward and Declan knew they had an acute problem that was going to cause crushing disappointment. Without Finoula, Musetta would either eat or work, but not both. She had reverted to her state of the previous summer. They tried everything. Edward started by putting Cathal O'Brien back on her. She worked reasonably well but refused to eat anything like the quantities needed to maintain her condition. Liam Corrigan could get her to do neither. Every one of the yard's twenty-three lads had a go with her, and all failed, although Edward noticed that Robin Lane got the best out of her on the gallop. Trying to pursue the original idea of the woman's touch, both Siobhan and Kathleen Corrigan attempted to get her to eat, while Robin Lane looked after her work. It was all to no avail.

Edward's mother was the first person outside Avoca House to hear anything like the full story, and, with the aid of the impersonal nature of the telephone, just managed to conceal the extent of her dismay. It was not necessary to labour the point that the problem was caused by Finoula's sudden departure. Ann suspected that most people, including Finoula's parents, would have judged her to be at fault; she was certain that she knew differently. Frank had to spend two evenings listening to Ann's theory that Finoula, far from being silly and headstrong, was the latest example of what she called "Edward's girl friend disasters".

When Richard spent a Saturday morning at Avoca House towards the end of May, it did not take him long to make up his mind about Musetta. "It's a great pity," he said, "but she's untrainable like that."

"It's more than a pity," Edward retorted grimly. Despite his calm statement to the press after she had won the Guineas, he had been building ambitious ideas round her, believing that a worthwhile attempt at the Oaks was within his grasp.

"Never mind. It was a wonderful achievement to get her this far after the problems we had with her last year. And she doesn't owe us anything, you know."

It was quite true. Musetta had recouped her original cost more than twice over and covered all the expenses of her training and racing. "So what happens now?" Edward asked.

"We'll breed from her, of course. I'll send her to a decent stallion next season. What do you think we ought to do with her in the meantime? Is there any point in keeping her here?"

"No, not really." It hurt Edward very much to say it, but he knew that Musetta was simply wasting the yard's time. There was also the risk that she might disrupt the routine of other horses.

"Right, we'll have her at Belfields," Richard said.

"She'll be very happy there," Imogen told Edward. Having correctly interpreted the expression on his face, she thought it was high time she said something. "We have quite generous visiting hours." Edward smiled. "And remember what I told you," she went on, "this is a good thing. I know it's a terrible disappointment, but the alternative would have been an absolute mess."

Returning her searching stare, Edward began to realise that she knew a great deal about practically everything.

Paddy Dooley took Musetta to Belfields the following afternoon. He and everyone else looked thoroughly miserable about it. Later, just before evening stables, Edward stood in the yard and looked at Sybil and Murgatroyd. As was so often the case, the two good friends had their heads out of their boxes and were nodding at one another. A possible conversation between them suddenly sprang into Edward's mind.

"Here Murgatroyd, where's that Musetta gone?"

"Belfields."

"Why's that then?"

"Idle bitch wouldn't work, would she?"

"So what they going to do with her?"

"I heard Mr Stewart tell the guv'nor they was going to breed from her."

"Cor! Some people have all the luck, don't they? Mind you, Murgatroyd, knowing her, I wouldn't be a bit surprised if she refused to have anything to do with a stallion."

"True, very true. On the other hand, my dear, she may produce something quite exceptional."

Edward found the thought so funny, yet so perfectly feasible from the behaviour of the two horses, that he smiled. Liam Corrigan saw him and said, "That's right, sor, we'll get some more as good as her."

Throughout the excitement and tribulations of Musetta, Edward had been keeping a close watch on the two-year-olds. They had all settled well to stable life and were showing signs that they were ready to race. The one exception was Radames who had proved to be an extrovert character with a wildly extravagant action that Edward doubted would ever be fully controllable. He made his debut at the Curragh two days after Musetta went to Belfields, finishing a stylish last after making all the running for the first four furlongs, then losing interest. In the jargon, he ran 'too freely'. This was an understatement; he virtually bolted from the stalls, became bored, and then expected a prize for doing it.

In the same week, Leonora came third in a decent race at Navan and T. P. Malahide went to Thurles with Murgatroyd. The happy combination of Robin Lane, the lucky blanket and the course where both James Henry and Edward had enjoyed their first successes, gave Valerie Malahide her first winner in her own right. In the very next race, Murgatroyd, better than ever, strolled home, but at odds so short that Dooley was curdled for a week, and blind to the passage of another important milestone. It was the first time that Avoca House had produced a double, two winners on the same day.

Edward and Siobhan spent hours on the final dispositions for Royal Ascot. Murgatroyd's entry for the Royal Hunt Cup was allowed to stand without question. Leonora and T. P. Malahide, however, kept them busy for a long time as they considered the strength of the likely opposition in the three races for which they were eligible. Eventually, they concluded that Leonora should go in the Queen Mary Stakes which was for fillies only, and that T. P. Malahide would take his chance in the highly competitive Coventry Stakes, both races being classified as Group Three. Once the decisions had been made, Siobhan was able to set about making the arrangements.

This year, with horses competing on the first two days of the Royal Meeting, the stay with the Walgraves at The Elms needed to be over three nights. Siobhan discovered that Simon was to be in America on business that week, but Mark and Sarah would be in residence to officiate. When Edward spoke to Mark, mentioning that Valerie Malahide wanted to come over to see her horse run, Mark insisted that she too must stay at The Elms rather than attempt to find an hotel. When the flying horse box left Blessington on Monday morning, it was loaded almost to capacity with Edward, Valerie Malahide, Sean Gillespie, Liam Corrigan, Cathal O'Brien, Robin Lane, the three horses and Paddy Dooley, clutching his holdall and concentrating hard on looking terrified. However, his demeanour improved dramatically when he discovered that the hired horse van was more like a luxury coach than ever, with technology that made even power-assisted steering seem like old hat.

The first race of the meeting was won very convincingly by one of Bernard Dalrymple's horses. To Edward's relief, neither Finoula nor Alexander Abercrombie appeared to be on the course although the stable had at least one runner in every race. Edward and Valerie Malahide watched proceedings in the winner's enclosure, and when they were over, Bernard Dalrymple came over to them. He and Edward shook hands, and Edward introduced "Mrs Malahide, one of my owners."

"Thank you very much for Finoula Kelly," Dalrymple said. "She's doing very well indeed."

"I knew she would," Edward said. "I'd rate her as especially good with young horses."

"She is. I've got her overseeing thirty juveniles and they're all coming along very nicely."

"I'm pleased."

"You're having another go at the Hunt Cup with Murgatroyd I believe."

"That's right."

"Good luck. Miss Kelly speaks very highly of him."

"He seems a very decent chap," Valerie said after he had gone.

"Yes, he is. But it's 'Miss Kelly' now, you notice. She's taken a real step up in the world."

"Good for her!" Valerie Malahide knew nothing of the circumstances leading up to Finoula's departure from Avoca House and was being allowed to assume that she had moved on to further her career.

The first day ended with the Coventry Stakes, a six-furlong race for two-year-old colts and fillies. First run in 1890, the race had acquired the reputation of being one of the first pointers to next season's Classic three-year-olds. As ever, the competition was stiff and the pace fierce, but for one or two heart-stopping moments during the last furlong, it really did seem that T. P. Malahide was in with a chance. However, there were two better horses, and he finished third, by no means disgraced, and pleasing Edward enormously.

"Did you see his ears?" he asked Valerie Malahide.

"No," she replied, mystified by his question.

"When the going got really tough at the end, his ears went loppy – all over the place like Bugs Bunny." She nodded in comprehension. "That's a good sign. It means he's thoroughly gutsy and genuine. He's going to win a decent race before any of us are much older."

The next day, Richard and Imogen were there to watch Leonora. To conceal her burgeoning pregnancy, Imogen wore a dress that she disparagingly dismissed as a "bell tent". Edward felt that many of the women present would have done well to copy its simple elegance. The Queen Mary Stakes, five furlongs for two-year-old fillies, showed Edward what an exceptionally good jockey Sean Gillespie was becoming. He nursed Leonora along very gently for most of the race before unleashing a back-stabbing charge on the leaders when they were powerless to do anything about it.

"This is getting to be a habit," Richard said as they stood at Leonora's head in the winner's enclosure.

"Are you complaining?" Edward asked.

"Certainly not!"

"Well shut up and smile for the cameras."

But it was the next race that provided the high spot of the afternoon. For his second attempt on the Royal Hunt Cup, Murgatroyd had been given the heavy weight of nine stones two pounds. This time, he seemed to have acquired a massive fan club who were not deterred by the weight and backed him heavily, causing him to start favourite. Nor did Murgatroyd allow himself to be deterred; he produced a tour de force of a performance that had the crowd roaring. Carrying the colours that had once belonged to James Henry, Murgatroyd was now Edward's horse, so he, like his grandfather a year before, made his first visit to the winner's enclosure at Royal Ascot.

From that point in mid-June, Edward had to learn a series of hard lessons as the remainder of the season became something of an anti-climax. The winners kept coming, and nothing disastrous occurred, but the three two-year-olds from whom he had expected so much were unable to produce their best efforts when it mattered. Radames was particularly infuriating. In an effort to teach him some common sense, he was raced regularly, every ten days or so. He showed some improvement, but was unable to get closer than fourth in very moderate company. Leonora suffered a damaged ankle while working on the gallop and was out of action for the whole of July. When Edward and Cathal O'Brien did get her right, she lacked the sparkle of Royal Ascot, finishing third in both her subsequent races. Most disappointing of all, it was not possible to find a race for T. P. Malahide to win. He went to the Curragh twice and then the Phoenix Park, coming second, third and second again. In something close to desperation, Edward took him back to Ascot in September; yet again, he finished second.

"That horse has won over ten thousand pounds by coming second and third," Richard pointed out when Edward complained bitterly about T. P. Malahide's bad luck.

"I know that. But I like coming first."

Richard laughed. "James Henry always said you'd be far worse than him once you got going," he said. "You're going to have to learn to take the rough with the smooth, my boy."

"I know, I know. I'm just not all that keen on that part of the job."

Imogen's baby, another son, was born on the last day of September. Having established that mother and child were both well, Edward plunged into the last hectic phase of the season with eleven runners in four days. James Henry had always carried on racing until the very end of the season in November, but Edward had already decided that there was nothing to be gained by going on beyond the end of the first week in October. The prize-money on offer did not, in his view, justify keeping horses and lads fully wound up for a few extra weeks of dubious weather. He returned from the Phoenix Park at the end of the four days, reasonably well satisfied, and intending to go to Belfields within the hour. It was time he had a look at the latest member of the Stewart family; the baby, called Richard, was to be his second godson.

Siobhan dashed into the yard to meet Edward as soon as he and Dooley arrived, jumping frantically on to the running board of the horse van while it was still moving. "Sir Nick's had another heart attack," she gasped.

"How is he?"

"He's dead."

"Dead?"

"Yes."

"Are you sure?"

"Positive."

"God!"

Edward and Dooley sat staring at one another for a very long time. Eventually, the two lads in the back of the van started shouting to remind them that they and their horses wanted letting out.

"When did this happen?" Edward asked Siobhan as they hurried towards the office and a telephone.

"I don't know exactly. This morning, I think. Richard . . ." She stopped, thought, and corrected herself. "Sir Richard rang at about one o'clock."

Edward drove straight to Belfields and found Imogen in total command of the situation. Richard, now the twelfth Baronet, was with his mother who was resting. "Julia was with him," Imogen explained. "They went for a walk. Apparently Nicholas suddenly said 'Oh dear', and that was that. He collapsed and died at her feet."

Edward gazed dumbly at her, and Imogen realised that he was on the verge of tears. "You'll stay to dinner of course," she said briskly. "It's likely to be a pretty scratch affair, I'm afraid. Now then, come and admire my son – he's absolutely gorgeous."

Sir Nick was buried five days later in a plot only yards away from James Henry. Many of those who came were from the world of banking. Some of them were very important indeed, and for the first time, Edward became aware of the tensions in Ireland stemming from the Ulster issue. There was a police presence both at Belfields and in the church yard. It was discreet, but the Garda were there, some in uniform trying to look nonchalant, others in civilian clothes were very hard-faced and alert.

The funeral proved to be the occasion when Edward finally became a full member of the Stewart family circle. Richard spent most of the time they were on show at his mother's side. Imogen's father and two brothers had come over from England; however, as they all left the house, she chose Edward as her escort, and they remained together until after they had returned from the service and interment. For more than ten years, Edward had realised, and happily accepted, that his life would probably be bound up with the Stewarts. When Imogen took his arm and piloted him towards the limousine immediately behind the hearse, he knew that the bond had finally become indissoluble.

Edward stayed at Belfields long after all the other mourners and guests had gone. When he did decide it was time to go home, Julia walked with him to his car. She looked tired and drawn; her behaviour during the day had elicited a great deal of admiration, but the effort of maintaining such brave dignity had drained her. "Thank you for all your support and help, Edward," she said. "You've been marvellous."

"Not at all," he replied, embarrassed by her thanks. "I was only doing what I wanted to."

"I know, my dear, and it was much appreciated. I would like you to come to dinner on Sunday."

"Of course. Anything special?"

"In a way. There'll be just the four of us." As if to confirm the new, close ties, she kissed him on the cheek. "Good night."

Sunday evening brought a pleasant meal that was eaten in a quiet, relaxed atmosphere in the elegant dining room of the flat in the east wing that Sir Nick and Julia had enjoyed for so many years. It was not until after the meal, when they had settled in Julia's sitting room, that she addressed the issue that had caused her to call the gathering.

"I have decided that there is something you should know, Edward," she said. "Goodness only knows whether you *ought* to know about it, but I think you *should*. Richard and Imogen agree with me." Sensing the seriousness of what was to come, Edward looked at them; they both nodded. "Now, before I tell you about it, you ought to appreciate the background . . . it's a sort of historical perspective, I suppose. Imogen, you're the expert on that, could you explain, please?"

"Certainly. As you probably know, the Baronetcy was conferred by Charles II in 1661. I assume this was Restoration gratitude for services rendered by the family before and during the Commonwealth. As far as I can see, the first four holders of the title were complete and utter rogues. This estate was acquired and built up by some very dubious activities. Apart from skulduggery, they seem to have been very good at living for a long time and procreating. The four criminal Stewarts lasted nearly a hundred and forty years and never had any problems about coming up with an heir. Then everything changed. William, the fifth Baronet, was every bit as atrocious as the rest, but I imagine he was a coward and had delusions of grandeur – so he founded the bank in 1801." Richard smiled at this assessment of Stewart's illustrious founder. "From then on, heirs became much more important. The bank had to be kept in the family. It was always very firmly understood that no bunch of fearful outsiders would ever get their grubby hands anywhere near a controlling interest. The fact that the bank is still in private hands is a remarkable achievement and I'm not altogether sure that I would approve of *some* of the ways in which it was done. But it's most important to understand this obsession with handing it on . . . of having someone to hand it on to." She stopped and glanced at Julia.

"Thank you, dear," Julia said. "Nick and I married during the war, Edward, in 1943. We had some time together, then Nick went over on D-Day and was wounded. We didn't really start our marriage until the latter part of 1945. We were both very eager to have a child, but after two years, we began to suspect that something was awfully wrong. We both had tests." She paused. "That was a distressing business. I believe these things are handled much more sympathetically nowadays. The outcome of it all was that Nick was shown to be sterile. It was a terrible disappointment for us personally and an absolute disaster for the bank.

Nick had a younger brother, but he was killed at Arnhem. We thought there might be other Stewarts dotted about the world. When we talked about it, it seemed so awful to have some stranger from America or Australia coming in to run the bank after Nick." She paused and took a sip of coffee. "It was all my idea. After a few months, I plucked up the courage to tell Nick about it. The solution had to be for me to conceive a child by another man and for it to be brought up as our own . . . as a Stewart." A wan smile spread across her pale face as she saw Edward stiffen in a combination of shock and expectation. "It couldn't have been just *anyone* of course. We both had to like and trust him. Ideally, we wanted a man with fair hair and blue eyes like the Stewarts – although the genetics of that could have misfired. And he simply had to have the right blood group so that no one would ever be able to come along and prove that my child *couldn't* have been Nick's. So you see, we were looking for a remarkable man. It was a question of saying, 'Look here, you've got the right colour eyes and hair, would you mind having a blood test. If that comes out right, could you please give me a child?'" She paused to smile at the idea. "We were very fortunate. He was living virtually on the doorstep."

Edward looked at her, dumbfounded. "James Henry?" he managed to ask at last.

"That's right."

He slumped back in his chair and gaped at her. Richard and Imogen, their faces expressionless, remained silent. "We got it right first time," Julia said, with a trace of something like pride. "I had a son."

Edward found himself curbing a stupid urge to ask her where she and James Henry had gone to conceive Richard. Gradually, shapes came out of the fog in his mind. He saw why everyone, especially Richard, had been so upset when James Henry had died; he saw something of the very special relationship between Sir Nick and 'Jimmy', the man who had sired his son; he perceived why James Henry had always been so fond of Imogen and young Nicholas, his other daughter-in-law and grandson, and his delight at learning, just in time, of Imogen's second pregnancy; and he understood why James Henry had been buried in the Stewart family plot.

"You knew about this?" he asked Richard.

"Yes. Father told me when I came of age." Richard's use of his habitual, respectful form of address for Sir Nick was noticeable. It was well deserved. There had always been a powerful love between Sir Nick and Richard.

Edward suddenly saw a humorous side to the revelation. "So you're some sort of uncle to me," he said to Richard.

"Something like that," Richard replied and they laughed.

"Well I am completely and utterly damned, blow me if I'm not," Edward said. "The old devil!"

"He had considerable encouragement," Julia said.

Once more, Edward gaped at her, far from sure that he would ever understand it. Imogen had an opinion.

"If you and Richard were horses," she said to Edward, "we should all have certain expectations of you – and I'm fairly certain that James Henry did. You're the real 'chip-off-the-old-block', Edward – which often happens, doesn't it? A horse frequently has more affinity with his grand-sire than his sire." Edward and Richard greeted this latest display of her hidden knowledge with amazement. "But you can see a lot of the traits in Richard as well. The pair of you together must be strong favourites to do what he wanted."

"He actually said something along those lines about a year before he died," Julia said. "He'd watched you two very closely over the years and come to the conclusion that you could do it."

"Together though," Imogen said to Julia. "They wouldn't be any good on their own."

Edward smiled at the way she made the point, as though he and Richard simply weren't there.

They talked until after midnight, and Edward was still staggered. As he was leaving, Imogen walked to the door with him. "There you are," she said. "Now you know. I think you took it very well."

She gave him one of her very special smiles. It was the first time that he had been a recipient rather than a mere observer.

CHAPTER 6

In February 1981, Edward spent a long weekend with his parents in Worcestershire. The visit was motivated partly from a sense of duty, since he had not been back for more than two years, and partly from a desire to see old friends, particularly Horace. When she heard of the trip, Valerie Malahide asked to go with him. Their winter friendship had easily resumed the closeness of the previous year, and there was nothing unusual in the request, to which Edward had readily agreed. Quite simply, Valerie had nothing else to do that weekend, was frankly curious to learn something of Edward's background, and wanted to see a part of England she had never visited. Ann realised immediately that Valerie was nothing like any of her son's previous women friends, jumped to the wrong conclusion, and made her very welcome.

The hopes that Edward had for the trip were soon badly shaken. On the first evening, he and Valerie went to see Horace and his wife for a meal. Horace was in tremendous form and captivated Valerie within minutes of their meeting, while she impressed Horace by her svelte good looks and intelligence. However, when Edward encouraged Horace to talk about King Henry's, he was surprised to find that his interest in what his old friend had to say was very low indeed. Edmund Weaver had retired and been replaced. Unfortunately, the new man was adjudged a complete disaster. Two days after his arrival, he had suggested that girls should be admitted to the school. While most people were still reeling from this shock, he had declared the curriculum to be too inflexible, and launched an investigation into ways of remedying the defect. Naturally, this had caused political factions to form among both staff and governors, and Edward was totally bemused by Horace's account of the subsequent in-fighting. Little more than two years ago, he would have been involved in all this. Now it was largely incomprehensible and pointless. "Of course, that weird bugger Wilson thinks it's all quite spiffing," Horace said, and Edward had to rack his brains to remember who Wilson was.

When the conversation turned to Avoca House, Robin Lane was the first topic; Horace was very pleased to hear that the boy was doing so well and showing promise of being very good indeed when he had more experience under his belt. But once Edward tried to explain a little of how horses were looked after and trained, they were in trouble. Horace had no feeling for any sort of animal, let alone one as sensitively clever as a horse, and the jargon that was now an integral part of Edward's life was double-Dutch to him. "She completely lost her action," Edward said, speaking of the filly Leonora, "and when we let her down again, she was all arms and legs." Horace dissolved into irreverent mirth, and Edward gave up.

Later, when Edward and Horace were alone in the kitchen, turning washing-up into a laboriously complex operation, Horace broached a topic that was intriguing him. "Mrs Malahide seems a most pleasant lady," he said casually. Somewhat mockingly, he used the formal mode of address that Edward habitually employed when talking to or about his owners in the presence of 'outsiders'.

"Yes, she is. Her late husband had horses with James Henry for a good many years and she's continuing the tradition."

"You and she seem very good friends," Horace said.

"We are. We get on tremendously well together. As a matter of fact, she keeps me sane during the winter when there isn't all that much to do apart from sit around and worry."

Horace nodded sympathetically. There was a slight pause before he asked, "Are you two ... er...?" and left the question hanging suggestively.

"Are we what?" Edward asked, not having the faintest idea what Horace meant.

"Thinking of getting married ... or anything."

"Good heavens, no," Edward replied. "And certainly not *anything*," he added forcibly.

It was just the same with other friends. On the last afternoon of their stay, Edward cancelled a visit to King Henry's itself, which he was certain would have made him feel like a fish out of water and left Valerie exposed to his mother's cross-examination and suggestions for several hours. Instead, he and Valerie went off in search of places associated with Edward Elgar. Starting with the birthplace at Broadheath, they went to Malvern where they stood at the graveside in a biting east wind and finally drove on to Hereford. Over tea and toast in front of a blazing fire Edward told Valerie how profoundly glad he would be to get back home to Avoca House.

She smiled at his ill humour. "It may not be agreeable," she said, "but it isn't in the least surprising. You were bound to grow away from the life you had over here."

"I suppose so," he said, still baffled that he and his one-time friends now spoke virtually different languages. "And the assumptions that people make about us are starting to get on my nerves."

"Oh? What assumptions are they?" Valerie was well aware of the answer. Mischievously, she decided to cause him a little discomfort.

"Well ... they assume we're either thinking of getting married ... or up to something."

"Up to something?" she asked with a pretence at naïvety.

"Yes!" There was a good deal of truculence in the short, sharp reply, indicating unwillingness to say any more.

"Actually, it's a natural enough mistake for people to make," Valerie said. "I believe we make what is known as 'a nice couple'."

He stared at her, assimilating the idea. "Do you suppose we ought to?" he asked.

"Ought to what?"

"Be up to something?"

Valerie collapsed into helpless laughter, startling the waitress who was clearing an adjacent table. "Oh Edward, you really are priceless," she said when she was able to speak. "You might know a thing or two about horses, but you aren't really fit to be let out in other respects sometimes. No, it isn't compulsory. We don't have to start cavorting round bedrooms if we don't want to."

Edward's natural inclination to say nothing was reinforced by the look on the waitress's face.

Shortly after lunch the following day, Siobhan smiled at his uninhibited delight at being back home. However, she had a message for him that he was in a mood to find irritating.

"Sir Richard rang on Sunday," she told him. "He wants you to go to dinner at Belfields on Saturday. And you're to take Mrs Malahide with you."

"God, has he started as well?" Edward demanded rhetorically.

"Started what?"

"Assuming that Mrs Malahide and I are some sort of . . ." He cast around for a suitable phrase to express his annoyance ". . . mating pair!"

Siobhan regarded him with the steady, sombre expression she always used to calm him down. "It's easy enough to get that impression," she said.

"I know." Edward subsided. "Mrs Malahide herself said almost exactly the same thing the other day."

One of the features of the entrance hall at Belfields was a huge mirror, extending from floor to ceiling and some fifteen feet wide. Normally, it was covered by a curtain, but on Saturday evening, some of it was exposed, giving Edward a glimpse of Valerie and himself as they crossed the hall on the way to the west wing and Richard's flat. He stopped to study their reflection. Valerie smiled, reading his thoughts with total accuracy. "See what I mean?" she asked quietly, and he nodded his agreement. As usual on these occasions, he was wearing a dinner jacket and black tie, while Valerie's auburn colouring was beautifully set off by a simple, full-length pale green dress.

Julia joined them for dinner, and despite the convivial air of relaxation, Edward sensed that Richard had something of great importance he wanted to tackle when the time was right. It would, he knew, be a little while before Richard was ready, and the first topic that came up was one guaranteed to give Edward nothing but pleasure.

"Can I borrow Dooley and the van for a couple of hours on Thursday?" Richard asked.

Edward consulted the slim, leather notebook he took everywhere. "Of course – that's March the fifth – we aren't doing anything that day. What's happening?"

"Musetta's going to Blessington to catch the flying horse box."

"Ah – where's she going?"

"Newmarket – the National Stud."

"Great! Who's she going to?"

"Mill Reef."

Edward blinked several times. "You're joking," he said.

"I am not. It's taken several months to organise, but she's considered worthy of the great man, so off she goes."

"How much is that costing?"

"Twenty-five thousand."

"No foal, no fee?"

"Not quite." Edward saw that Richard was not keen to elaborate on the financial arrangements. "I take it you wouldn't mind attempting to do something with the outcome of the union?" Richard asked.

"Just try and stop me!"

"James Henry would have liked that," Valerie said. "What wouldn't he have given to have an animal that well bred?"

Conversation for the rest of the meal was centred on Edward's hopes for the coming season. His immediate concern was to find out how Leonora and T. P. Malahide had wintered, but Richard was surprised to learn that the wayward Radames was also scheduled for a great deal of attention.

"I thought he was a bit of a dud," he said.

Edward shook his head vigorously. "Far from it! *Physically* he's a very good horse. His big problem has been his idiotic mentality. Cathal O'Brien and Robin Lane have spent a lot of time with him these last few months, and they reckon he's grown up quite a bit. They're confident he's got a fairly respectable brain more or less functional now."

"You rate that pair pretty highly, don't you?"

"Definitely. The others have started calling them 'The Theory Merchants'. They're always reading books and suggesting new things."

"Oh yes, I can see that appealing to you," Imogen said. Although she still professed total ignorance of what went on at Avoca House, she knew of Edward's reputation as a dyed-in-the-wool experimenter.

"As a matter of fact," Edward said, smiling at Imogen for what he knew was a compliment, "Robin's become our resident horse psychiatrist. He's spent a great deal of time talking to Radames."

"More than you?" Imogen asked.

"Yes, much more."

"Good God!"

When they went to the sitting room at the end of the meal, there was a change of atmosphere. Julia and Richard were manifestly a little on edge and even Imogen displayed unnecessary and uncharacteristic fussiness in pouring coffee and handing the cups round.

Edward took the bull by the horns. "All right," he said to Richard. "Let's get on with it."

Richard smiled ruefully. "You're getting far too good at mind-reading," he said. There was a slight pause while he composed himself. "As you know, I've never been all that keen on Belfields," he began, and Edward nodded. "As a matter of fact, that's putting it rather mildly. I think the place is a confounded nuisance. It's also an anachronism. It might have been perfectly splendid a hundred and fifty years ago, but it's no use at all to a family involved with running a modern banking operation in London. We've been talking things over a great deal since father died." He glanced briefly at Julia and Imogen, both of whom were looking earnest and supportive. "I want to spend much more time with Imogen and the boys. I appreciate her views on London, and I wouldn't dream of asking her to live there. So what do I do? Get a place within easy daily commuting distance of the office, of course. But what happens to Belfields?"

"It's a bit much for a holiday home," Edward said.

"Quite. Now we've been through an immense amount of soul-searching and the conclusion is that we should up sticks and go to England. We would very much like it if you came with us – in fact, we think you should."

Edward was caught off balance. He had expected nothing remotely like this. For a moment or two, it seemed that he was about to react extremely negatively. Then he exchanged looks with Valerie and calmed down. "Why do you think that?" he asked Richard.

"Well, apart from the fact that we would like you to be near us, Avoca House isn't big enough and it's short on facilities. We could fill that yard twice over as a result of what you've achieved already."

"I doubt it. I haven't had would-be owners clamouring at the door."

"You should try spending a day in my office in London," Richard said. "People sit up and take notice when you win the Guineas and have a couple at Royal Ascot. I've had colleagues and clients making enquiries."

"Really?" Edward was surprised and flattered.

"Yes, really. I'm telling them to hang on until we get more space and better facilities – but I don't want to have to do that too much longer. Now we could add twenty more boxes to Avoca House at a pinch – and where would that get us? The exercise barn is hardly big enough as it is, the gallop needs a fortune spending on it, and you could do with a covered ride."

"I'd like a good-sized swimming pool as well," Edward admitted. He had been reading about the beneficial effects that swimming had on horses and was eager to give it a try.

"Remember that James Henry always said you'd want a bigger place," Richard went on. "The more horses you have, the more good ones there are. More space and better facilities inevitably means a much bigger operation than Avoca House could ever handle. You must think of costs as well. If you're going to race in England, you want to be there, not paying heavy transport charges."

"I can't disagree with that," Edward said.

Richard paused and became more serious. "There is another point we have to consider. Whether we like it or not, we have to recognise that Ireland is no longer *safe* for people like us. Do you remember the security at father's funeral? That was at the insistence of the Government in Dublin. They had ten sorts of kittens when they saw the guest list. There were at least thirty people on that list that were prime targets, and I don't mean for outright murder. The IRA and the INLA and God knows who else are after money – lots of it. Ransom is becoming an attractive proposition, and in that respect I'm very vulnerable." Edward nodded, seeing the possibilities that a terrorist might envisage in Julia, Imogen and the two boys. "And I don't think it has to stop with the immediate family," Richard added. "What happens if some gang of thugs grab you, or Siobhan . . . or one of the horses for that matter? I'll tell you. My first and continuing reaction would be to pay up. The powers that be would disapprove of that and actively do their damnedest to stop me – and we'd all go through hell! This isn't alarmist fantasy by the way. I've taken the opinion of a firm of internationally respected security consultants that we use at the bank."

Edward considered the problem. "All right, I take your point," he said.

Richard appeared to ignore the comment. "It's going to be a hell of a wrench, of course," he went on. "The family's been here a long time. It isn't the sort of thing to do lightly."

"We shall be all right," Julia said. "You must think of the staff, though, my dear."

"Oh, yes, of course." Richard nodded vigorously. "I'm hoping a lot of them will want to come with us."

"And the others?"

"They'll be well looked after, don't worry."

Seeing that Julia seemed satisfied by Richard's assurances, Edward made another attempt to discover what Richard had in mind.

"So, what are you proposing?" he asked.

"Well, this isn't all pie in the sky," Richard admitted. "I have some definite ideas in mind."

"I see." Edward's attitude changed markedly.

"Just listen," Richard said. "And bear in mind that you have a free choice at the end of the day. The starting point is that I've had a very good offer for Belfields – with or without Avoca House. International Digital want it."

"Really?" Edward was impressed. ID was an American-based multi-national corporation with a large share of the world market in computer and telecommunications networks.

"Apparently Belfields is just what they've always wanted for a European Management Staff College – or some such grandiose thing."

"How far has it gone?" Edward asked guardedly.

"It hasn't. Their offer has effectively been on the table for six weeks now, but I told them that I wouldn't make a move until I'd seen what I wanted in England and spoken to you."

"Is there anything going in England?"

"Yes – just this week. They're both still under wraps and haven't gone on to the open market yet – and that's how it's going to stay if I have anything to do with it. I think I would like the new Stewart 'family seat' to be at Widney Cheyne Manor."

"Where's that?" Edward asked.

"South Oxfordshire – near a place called Easton Bagpuize."

"Lovely name," Imogen said with relish and obvious approval.

"Nice piece of architecture according to the photographs," Richard said. "There are excellent facilities for a proper stud and around three hundred acres of first-class parkland. Two and a half million for a quick sale."

Edward whistled and tried to comprehend the figure.

"Seems awfully handy," Imogen commented. "I shall be able to drive the lord and master to Didcot each morning and collect him in the evening. Only thirty-two minutes from Paddington on a decent train."

"Sounds just the job," Edward said drily. "You implied there were two properties. Where would I be?"

"Saxon Court," Richard replied, doing his best to sound as though he were saying something quite ordinary.

Valerie Malahide had to remind herself that this was a most serious business, otherwise she would surely have burst out laughing at the expression on Edward's face. She sympathised with him. Still doing her best to learn about the rudiments of racing, even she had heard of Saxon Court. It was one of the oldest and most famous of English racing stables, situated on the Berkshire Downs between Newbury and Oxford.

"You've gone completely mad," Edward eventually managed to tell Richard.

"I have not," Richard replied, quietly but firmly. "It's available, it's right, and we may as well have it."

"Cyril Brookes-Smith trains there, doesn't he?" Edward asked.

"He does. He's been there twenty-five years or so, although he's never really managed to do a great deal with it. I wouldn't say he's been a failure, but the place was absolutely top-flight before him. His wife died a couple of years ago and I understand he took it very badly. My information is that his own health isn't too good and he wants out – he's had enough. We'd have to do things to it, but the basics are good. The yard has a hundred boxes and you'd have over fifteen hundred acres for your gallops."

"Don't tell me, let me guess," Edward said flippantly. "It's all going for a song for a quick sale."

"I believe that to be the case," Richard said in his best merchant banker tone.

"How much?"

"Brookes-Smith and his agent are talking about three and a half. That will come down to three if we move fast enough."

"Three what?"

"Million of course."

It was Imogen who cut Edward's scornful laughter short. "As I understand it, the whole thing is perfectly feasible," she said. "Mind you, I'm only a director of a merchant bank." Her snippet of news disconcerted Edward, which was precisely what she had intended. Richard, who had appointed her the previous day, smiled proudly at her. "International Digital's offer for Belfields will more than cover the cost of both Widney Cheyne and Saxon Court. There'll be some left over for improvements and we might all get a weekend in Bognor Regis out of the change."

Edward looked long and hard at Richard. "You really are serious," he said at last. It was a statement, not a question.

"I am."

"Look here, Richard, I can't take on a place like that."

"Why not?"

"I'm not up to it. I'm just not good enough." Edward watched as Richard cupped his hand to his ear and listened. "What are you doing?" he asked.

"I was wondering if I could hear James Henry turning in his grave," Richard replied, and Edward had the grace to look slightly ashamed.

"You've been bold enough so far," Valerie told Edward. "You didn't mess about with Royal Ascot, did you? James Henry would never have thought of running Murgatroyd like you did – he told me."

"And Newmarket," Julia added. "That probably took a lot of guts."

Edward looked at each of them in turn, and found that their faces all told the same story. "I'd need to take as many as possible of the Avoca House crew with me," he said.

"If you decide to go, you dictate the terms," Richard assured him.

"And I can stay here if I want to?"

"Yes. I can keep Avoca House and all the land round it back from the sale. But I have to tell you that you'll be a pain in the neck if you do stay."

"That's rather harsh, Richard," Julia said.

"No it isn't, mother. If I want to see my horses work, I don't want to have to fly over here occasionally when I can find the time."

Edward mulled it over. "Right," he said, appearing to reach some sort of decision. "Where do we start?"

"We go and have a look at it."

"You must, Edward," Valerie said, seeing that he was hesitating, looking for a way out.

"Yes, all right. You'll organise it I suppose, Richard?"

"As quickly as possible."

Later, when Richard and Imogen were alone, Richard said, "Edward took that a good deal better than I thought he would. I can see his point about Saxon Court. It is a bit daunting for a relatively inexperienced chap."

"Valerie Malahide," Imogen replied. "I told you she'd be a help."

"Yes, you did, and I think you're right. Beats me how or why though. You say they aren't having an affair?"

"Quite definitely not! But she does seem to steady him up a great deal. As a matter of fact, *not* having an affair with Valerie is a very sensible thing."

"Really?"

"Oh yes. They aren't at all right for one another."

"I thought they were."

"Only superficially. Edward needs someone with much more of a cutting edge."

Richard retreated to the bathroom, completely baffled.

Although it was Sunday, Richard telephoned Edward at eleven o'clock the following morning to say that he had already spoken to Cyril Brookes-Smith at Saxon Court. "He's asked us to go and have a good look at the place whenever we like," Richard reported. "The earliest I can manage is next Monday – a week tomorrow. Is that all right for you?"

"Yes." Edward saw that Siobhan's wall-chart had nothing on it for the whole of that week.

"He's invited us to stay with him, but I thought not," Richard said. "It's best to keep it strictly on a business footing at this stage. My secretary can find us an hotel in Newbury or Reading."

"Will I see you before we go?" Edward asked.

"Yes. I'll pop over to Avoca House some time next weekend."

Edward had just put the phone down, and was staring into space with fierce concentration, when Siobhan looked into the office. She always did on her way back from Mass to see if there was anything to do.

"Is anything wrong?" she asked when she saw the look on his face.

"No, not really," he replied vaguely and without conviction. She waited, and was duly rewarded as he made his mind up. "I'd like to talk to you and your father, Siobhan," he said. "Do you think you could go and find him, please?"

It did not take her long. Sunday or no Sunday, Declan was never far away. His one concession to the sabbath was a 'best' cap. Curiously, he always took his cap off in the office, while leaving it on in any other part of the house, and he did so now before sitting down beside Siobhan.

"We may have something pretty important coming up, and I thought you should know about it straightaway," Edward said. "I was over at Belfields last night with Sir Richard. There's every chance that the Stewarts are selling up and moving to England. They want me to go with them. I haven't begun to think about it seriously yet, but I've already said I won't consider going unless everyone here comes with me – everyone who wanted to, that is."

Declan nodded. "Where might we be going?" he asked.

"Sir Richard is talking of buying Saxon Court," Edward said.

Siobhan gasped, then quickly put a hand over her mouth.

"Is he now?" Declan said, and Edward was surprised to see emotion register on his face. There was a glint in his eyes.

"What would you say to that, Declan?" Edward asked.

"I'd say that was good, sor, very good indeed."

"Really?"

"Yes."

"You'd come with me – as head lad, of course."

"Like a flash."

"What about Mary?"

"I think she'd love it," Siobhan said. "There'd have to be a church with a good priest."

"Do you think many of the others would want to come?" Edward asked.

"All of them," Declan replied firmly.

"What about leaving Ireland?"

"We work in your stable, not a country."

Edward was stunned by the remark. He had been expecting and half-hoping for difficulties, and was almost disappointed at the reaction he was receiving. "It's going to be a hell of a decision to make, Declan," he warned.

"Oh yes, I can see that. But we could do the business with a place like that." There was enthusiasm in Declan's face and tone. "And it can't be more than forty miles to Epsom," he added, hammering the point home with typical economy.

"Sir Richard and I are going over to have a look at it next week," Edward said. "I imagine we shall be gone a few days. I don't want to start making announcements yet, and I certainly don't want all sorts of rumours flying around and upsetting people."

"We can say you've gone to look at some horses," Siobhan suggested.

"Yes, that's very good, Siobhan."

The conversation left Edward with the uneasy feeling that he might be drawn into a trap. He would have bet on Declan being opposed to any suggestion of a move, even to a better stable on the other side of the Curragh, let alone across the water in England. Instead, he had given the strong impression that he could hardly wait. The feeling of unease persisted all week, improved neither by the weather nor Richard's visit the following Sunday morning with detailed plans of Saxon Court. When Edward tried to study them, he was unable to progress beyond the impression that the place was big, probably very imposing and altogether too much for him to handle.

Richard and Edward flew from Dublin to London on a mid-morning flight, and collected a hired car at Heathrow Airport. Edward drove, heading west along the M4 motorway until Richard told him to take an exit on to a road from Oxford to Newbury. They went north, towards Oxford. The day was fine and clear with no frost. Ahead of them was the continuous arc of downs that ran for almost thirty miles between Reading and Swindon.

"Here we are," Richard said after about four miles, "this must be the turning."

It was. Compton Norris was the first of four village names listed on the sign. The road was little more than a narrow lane. Edward had to negotiate a path past a tractor travelling in the opposite direction, then a bus that caused Richard to curse good-humouredly. "I bet there's only one a week, and we have to meet it," he said, but Edward remained tensely unresponsive.

The village of Compton Norris was an unspoiled delight. No new housing was visible from the main street, which seemed to have been assembled around 1800 and not touched since. There was a magnificent late-fourteenth-century church, a school so traditional that it hardly seemed real, three pubs and a good selection of unobtrusive shops. The two representatives of the outside world, both banks, had gone to pains to merge into the surroundings, abandoning the eye-catching posturing that was usual for the urban high street. The village hall was set in the centre of a large green, complete with massive oak trees and a duck pond. The houses that were visible, either in clusters around the green or down side streets, were characterised by pantiles and bow windows. "This place must look like a chocolate box in summer," Richard said, but again there was no response from Edward.

Beyond the village, the road twisted through several tortuous bends and rose steeply. Then it fell into a valley before starting its long climb over the downs towards the River Thames. The view from the brow of the hill was magnificent, and caused Edward to draw into a convenient lay-by. His eyes were held on the horizon by the aesthetically satisfying, inevitable sweep of the downs. Then he saw the equally arresting foreground. Saxon Court was about four hundred yards away and a hundred feet below them.

"Good grief!" Edward said when he had finished struggling with his first impression.

"You should be able to do something with that, don't you think?" Richard said in a deliberately neutral voice.

Engrossed in having a longer look, Edward did not reply. He could see virtually everything, laid out like a plan come to life, although the view would be very different in summer. Along Saxon Court's considerable frontage and its southern flank was an L-shaped yew hedge and tree screen that would render the place virtually invisible when the trees were in leaf. It seemed to be an incomprehensible jumble of buildings, albeit of matching mellow brick and tile, occupying about ten acres. Immense purpose was given to the scene by the stable block, a huge, narrow rectangle that acted as the establishment's backbone. The main outside walls of the stable were unbroken except for gated arches that seemed to provide a way straight through. The arches, not quite in the centre of the yard, were surmounted on the side nearest the house and other buildings by an elegant superstructure supporting a clock-tower.

"Just look at that stable block," Edward said quietly.

"You won't find anything better architecturally," Richard said. "As you saw from the plans, it's just over two hundred yards long."

Edward had seen nothing of the sort, and was totally unprepared for his first sighting of Saxon Court's justly famous feature. Behind the stables was the covered ride, rather like an athletics stadium, then a poplar-lined avenue leading to open downland.

"And there," Richard said, following Edward's gaze, "you have one thousand five hundred acres of prime gallop. Shall we go and get on with it?"

As he turned into the drive, Edward found that the clock-tower was directly ahead of him. To his left, there were three well-separated houses surrounded by lawns and gardens, to the right was Saxon Court itself, an imposing yet pretty house built in 1820 with bricks of a warm ochre colour that had become the standard for all subsequent construction. A single-storey extension had been added at the rear of the house, it had a side door marked *Office*, and they headed towards it.

Cyril Brookes-Smith came out to meet them, clutching a mug of soup that was his interrupted lunch. He was a big man in his early sixties. He had not yet gone to seed, but his once-fine features were in blurred decline, and he bore an air of pain and weariness.

"Sir Richard Stewart? Mr Manning? I'm Brookes-Smith. Good of you to come. You're a bit early. No matter." They shook hands. "I expect you'd like a quick look round? Get your bearings."

Without waiting for comment, Brookes-Smith was heading towards the stables, still with his mug of soup. It was about a hundred yards from the office to the imposing rounded arch that was the entry to the yard. On one side, in the area behind the house, the space was taken up by a huge lawn of the finest quality with a substantial rose garden in the far corner. On the other side, they passed the entrance of a roadway leading to a group of buildings that seemed to disappear into the distance. Then there was the gable end of a two-storey building with numerous windows down its long side walls.

"Lads' hostel," Brookes-Smith said in response to Edward's questioning look. "It's got all the communal facilities. The girls live over there." He waved a hand vaguely.

As they approached the clock-tower, Edward saw that the clock did not work, and that the gilt hands and numerals were badly tarnished. However, all critical thoughts were wiped from his mind as they passed through the arch into a closed, magical world. They were in a massive square. There was another arch straight ahead, also with gates; on either side, slightly smaller arches gave access to the two halves of the yard.

Brookes-Smith smiled at the look on Edward's face. "Yes, it's very grand, isn't it?" he said. "Much better than those wretched sheds they use nowadays." Edward and Richard followed him through the arch on the right into the smaller of the two yards. "This is called the 'Old Yard'," Brookes-Smith said. He did not explain why, and sipped at his soup while Edward walked into the centre and looked round. There were forty boxes in all, seventeen down one side, seven across the end, and sixteen down the other side with the symmetry completed by a feed store in the near right-hand corner. To Edward's surprise, all the boxes were empty and bare. The strong smell of disinfectant, and small pools of milky water lying in hollows indicated that cleansing and scrubbing had taken place during the morning.

"Where are your horses?" Edward asked Brookes-Smith.

"Mostly still in winter quarters. There are a few in the New Yard."

"Where do you send them?"

"Anywhere that's comfortable and cheap. Owners can make their own arrangements if they prefer."

"I see. You don't like to have them working by now?" Richard was uneasy at the edge of censure in Edward's voice, but if Brookes-Smith detected it, he ignored it.

"Not in this weather. Don't see the point in running up costs with no hope of a return. I don't have a full complement of staff until the end of March. Might not bother with that this year."

"You lay staff off in winter?"

"Oh yes."

"What do they do?"

"No idea. A lot of them do six months and never come back so the question never arises."

Richard knew this was one way of running a stable; he also knew it would never be Edward's. To forestall any critical comment that Edward might choose to make, Richard strolled towards the other, larger part of the yard, and was relieved when Edward and Brookes-Smith followed him. The 'New Yard' accommodated sixty horses, twenty were in residence, and the signs of activity suspended for lunch indicated that more were expected. Several huge bales of straw for bedding were stacked in the middle of the yard with forks and other implements much in evidence. While Richard and Brookes-Smith indulged in the affected small-talk of two men who might be preparing to do business, Edward inspected the horses. They were a decent enough bunch, but he would have been most unhappy if his own charges had looked so insipid. After five months off work and with a dull winter coat, any horse looked far below its mid-season best; however, most of these had a disheartened, listless demeanour. Edward judged them to be four-year-olds and upwards who were only too well accustomed to life at Saxon Court.

Eventually, he rejoined Richard and Brookes-Smith who were chatting in the centre of the four arches. "I like it very much," he said. "It certainly puts Avoca House to shame."

Brookes-Smith nodded, obviously considering the remark justified. "We'll go and have a look at the house now," he said. "And I suppose you'll have a few questions . . . ah . . . here's my daughter."

Edward, standing with his back to the clock-tower, turned. His impression of the arched courtyard had been that it suggested a cathedral transept, and that was entirely appropriate. As the sun caught her golden hair, the sensation of magnificence was totally overwhelming. She was five feet seven inches tall and carried her head high, with a slightly imperious tilt to the chin. But in that very first instant, Edward knew that she often threw her head back even further in laughter. She had deep blue eyes, a broad brow that reinforced the intelligent frankness of the eyes, and cheekbones to give her beauty into old age. As Brookes-Smith was saying, "My daughter, Caroline . . ." Richard saw Edward blink and sway slightly as though he were momentarily dazed.

"How do you do, Sir Richard?" Her voice had music in it despite its confidence.

"Hello, Mr Manning." As she and Edward shook hands, Richard felt certain that something passed between them. However fanciful it seemed, it was as if they recognised one another. The moment was swept away as Caroline caught sight of the mug in Brookes-Smith's hand.

"Oh really, father! Haven't you had a proper meal? And you, gentlemen? You flew over this morning, didn't you? Come along, you must have something."

As Edward fell in beside her, Richard knew that he had not been mistaken. Caroline Brookes-Smith, beautiful, confident and probably immensely self-willed, had not frightened Edward: if anything, she had produced precisely the reverse effect. As they strode away, they were in deep conversation, and he heard Edward laugh.

The Saxon Court kitchen was very similar to that at Avoca House, although, Edward thought, not used by so many people as an important meeting place. Caroline tossed her faded blue denim jacket across the back of a chair, and set to with practised vigour. With the aid of a microwave cooker, she produced an appetising snack within five minutes. While Richard and Brookes-Smith returned to the stilted conventions of small-talk, Caroline and Edward sat apart from them at the other end of the table. They said very little, but Richard had a strong feeling that they were *together*. At the end of the meal, Caroline stood up and put her jacket back on. She took command of the situation and abandoned formality at a stroke. "Come along, Edward, let me give you the *proper* guided tour," she said. "Sir Richard and father can surely find something to talk about."

As they came out of the side door of the office, Edward was looking directly at the three houses opposite. "Miss Brookes-Smith . . ." he began.

"Caroline," she told him.

". . . Caroline, what are those houses?"

"The two at the front are head lad and second head lad," she replied. "Our head lad is retiring, and the deputy is leaving – it's a pity he didn't do it two years ago. He hasn't been one of father's better choices. The house at the back is for the travelling head lad. He went to Canada last autumn and we haven't bothered to replace him. If we ever do have any more runners, I can take them to the course." There was regret and sorrow in her voice.

"I do that myself at the moment," Edward said.

"You wouldn't be able to here."

"I know. It's hard enough sometimes doing it for my few. I suppose you've been very much involved here, have you?"

"Yes. I've been running the place to all intents and purposes for the last four years. I'm twenty-five by the way."

Edward was so startled by her frank answer to a question that he had indeed been asking himself that he said, "I'm thirty-one."

"And you've done jolly well in two years."

"I've had some very good luck."

"Winning the Guineas wasn't luck. That filly was beautifully prepared. I was at Newmarket that day."

"Oh." They were walking between the gardens of the head lads' houses and the hostel.

"This is the Colour Room," Caroline said as they approached a building rather like a small bungalow. "It's also a bit of a museum, but we've been neglecting it – like a lot of other things."

Going in, Edward discovered that the whole building consisted of only one room with a polished oak floor and the roof beams left exposed and stained. He was torn between the display of racing colours and saddlecloths along the wall facing the door, and Caroline, heading purposefully towards the far wall which had a display of framed photographs. He went to her side and looked up at a portrait of a rather ethereal-looking man whose eyes had the languid glaze of the dilettante. "That's Ollie Derwent," she said. The Honourable Oliver Derwent, fourth son of the Earl of Andover, had owned Saxon Court from 1884 to 1918, and elevated it to pre-eminence from a relatively humble beginning. "Ollie built the Old Yard," Caroline explained. "When he came here, there were only ten boxes just round the corner – we use them for hacks now. As you know, Ollie won the Derby three times." She moved a little to the right. "Then this character came along." Edward found himself looking at a gaunt-faced man with quite the most formidable chin he had ever seen, and eyes that pierced him even from the lifelessness of a photograph.

"Ah – Joshua Fielding," Edward said.

"The man himself. He was here from 1918 until father came in 1956. He built the New Yard. Apparently he scoured England to get bricks to match the Old Yard – nearly a hundred thousand of them."

"He looks like the sort of man who would," Edward said.

"He turned out six Derby winners – and over four thousand other winners."

"Did he build the clock-tower?"

"Yes. Do you like it?"

"Very much."

"Me too. I've tried to get father to do it up, but he always says it isn't worth it. I'm afraid he's lost interest since mother died and his heart started to play up." She was lost in thought for a few moments. "Actually, that's making excuses," she said. "After Ollie Derwent and Joshua Fielding, this place must have found us very disappointing."

"That can't be true," Edward said.

"Oh yes it is! We didn't win a single Group race last year, and only one the year before. It's hard to believe that a place like this could do so badly."

"You probably didn't have the right horses."

"We didn't, and that's a chicken-and-egg business, isn't it? If we'd done better the year before, we might have got some decent two-year-olds."

Sensing the bitter disappointment that she was concealing, Edward did not attempt to pursue the subject, and allowed her to carry on the tour. They looked at the original small yard, now home of four hacks used by Caroline and the head lad for riding out to supervise work. "We can take a couple of these tomorrow morning and go on Saxon Down," Caroline said. "You'll get a much better idea of the gallops from up there." They looked briefly at the girls' hostel, and beyond that, screened by trees, the four isolation boxes that could be used for horses with contagious diseases. Last, they had a thorough look over the lads' hostel. The bedrooms and bathrooms were upstairs, the ground floor had facilities that were shared by the girls, a dining room and kitchen, TV room, a lounge and two games rooms. It was all adequate, but Edward thought that renovation and improvements were necessary.

It was nearly six o'clock when Edward and Richard left Saxon Court to drive to Newbury and the hotel that had been booked for them. Once he had established that Edward was very impressed indeed by what he had seen, Richard was careful to avoid asking questions, making sure that he applied no pressure towards a decision. After Edward had talked at length over dinner about his plans for the horses at Avoca House, they went to their rooms, Edward to sleep, Richard to catch up on work from the bank.

Caroline was waiting for them outside the office the following morning, and since Richard was driving, Edward was out of the car in a flash to greet her. She was dressed for riding, cream roll-neck sweater and navy-blue breeches, and was carrying a padded anorak. Her long hair was fastened back by a bow at the nape of the neck. In the small yard, one of the lads had two horses, a pair of big geldings, saddled and ready for them. Edward guessed the lad's age at around sixty, and noticed that there was weary disinterest beneath his outward show of respectfulness.

Caroline showed that she already understood his facial expressions. "An awful lot of them are very near retirement," she explained as they rode past the lads' hostel. "And they've been pretty fed up these last few years. It hasn't been all that exciting, and the winnings pool has been fairly miserable. Fortunately, there's a very good pension fund. I believe father set it up the day he moved in here. There's over a million pounds in it, and I imagine all the old hands will want a share of it."

They passed under the clock-tower and straight through the opposite arch, outside which several well-worn tracks began. One went to the covered ride, and Edward accepted Caroline's suggestion that they go in. "This looks to be very nearly a furlong," he said as their horses walked round the track.

"It is. And usable all year round, of course. We could have done something with this." Today, the tone was matter-of-fact, with no suggestion of regret.

The downs were reached from a straight track lined with mature poplar trees. Edward needed no telling that the four-hundred-yard avenue would be lovely in summer, and looked at the five cottages in an enclosure behind the trees. None were inhabited, and they were in various stages of disrepair. Caroline read his thoughts again. "They're part of the estate," she said. "It wouldn't take all that much to turn them into good homes."

At the end of the Avenue, the two lines of poplars flared out like the mouth of a funnel, and Edward had his first sight of the seemingly vast expanse of the gallops. On his left, to the north, the great bulk of Saxon Down swept up, reaching its highest point about a mile away. Straight ahead of them was a large U-shaped gallop with a white fence to accustom horses to racecourse conditions. The U was two miles round, with a pair of seven-furlong straights in its centre. One of these gallops also had a white fence.

"Over here," Caroline said, and urged her horse on to a track towards the higher ground. "This is called the Ridge Path. There's a wonderful view from the top."

The total rise was no more than three hundred feet, comfortably spread over a mile, and the horses ambled up it without exertion in fifteen minutes. However, they had started at slightly over three hundred feet above sea level, and Caroline was right, the view was tremendous. Edward's attention was immediately drawn to the glint of sunlight on the River Thames five miles away. Caroline laughed when he asked about the great clump of tall trees that dominated the top of the down. "That's Moonlight Ring," she said. "It's supposed to be very, very old – Ancient Britons and all that – and it's smothered in folklore. There might have been something there from the old days, but my theory is that some joker planted this lot around 1750, say. Ever since then, he's been laughing his socks off at all the old wives' tales."

They had a commanding view of the gallops, and Caroline explained that they were by no means flat. "That big U is like a switchback," she said. "You can simulate almost anything on that, depending on where you start and which way you go round it. Popular belief has it that Ollie Derwent designed it to resemble Epsom. I don't know whether that's true or not, but he and old Joshua did all right with it. And there's over seven hundred acres going to waste down there. You could have at least one all-weather gallop and a track for two-year-olds on that."

Dismounting, they walked back down the hill, leading the horses. Their progress was very leisurely, and it was lunchtime when they returned the horses to their boxes. On the way down, Edward had told Caroline the story of James Henry, and learned something about her life which had been almost completely tied up with Saxon Court and her mother, whom she had adored. He stopped to take a closer look at the cottages on the avenue, and they saw another four horses arrive in the New Yard.

"I don't think there are going to be many more," Caroline said. "To be frank, I can't imagine what we're supposed to do about this lot. I'm sure father hasn't the slightest intention of working them or trying to race them."

"I would have thought the owners might have had other ideas," Edward said.

"They may not know what's going on. Father's always dealt with them, and it's never been a very communicative business. Four years ago, we had a winner at Ascot. All very nice, apart from one thing."

"What was that?"

"The owner didn't know his horse was running until he saw the morning paper."

"God, I bet he was pleased!"

"Very! He was on a plane to Stockholm at the time."

During his morning with the present owner of Saxon Court, Richard's initial impressions had been confirmed. Brookes-Smith was desperately anxious to be rid of his property; there was no question of a quick sale at any price, but for the life of him, Brookes-Smith could not understand why anyone should have to take more than an hour to make up their minds about such a desirable establishment. When the inescapable question came, Richard saw Edward's face show exactly what he had expected, dismay, indecision, then truculence. It was Caroline who sailed in to the rescue.

"Don't be absurd, father! Edward can't possibly be expected to reach a decision that quickly. You'd spend more time choosing a yearling, let alone something like this."

Abashed, Brookes-Smith shut up. Richard was intrigued. Caroline's intervention had defused a potentially difficult situation most effectively;

but although her statement had been no more than obvious common sense, there was much more to it. Richard found it easy to believe that Caroline was adopting a protective attitude towards Edward.

When they had finished lunch, Caroline insisted that her father, who was looking tired and unwell, should go to his room and rest. Sensing that Caroline and Edward were about to become deeply involved in looking at something else, and anxious not to interfere with the process, Richard asked if he might have the use of a telephone. "I really ought to find out what's happening at the bank," he said.

"Of course. Let's see if we can make you comfortable in the office," Caroline said. "This place is a disgrace!" she said angrily as they went into the big, airy room. Privately, Edward agreed with her. It was in a far worse mess than the office at Avoca House had been in the bad old days before Siobhan. With its large bow window that looked across the lawn to the clock-tower, the room could easily have been made an elegant and pleasing place in which to work. Edward noticed the window-seat, piled high with magazines, newspapers and racing-form books, all months, if not years, out of date; he had an image of himself sitting in the window on a beautiful summer evening, well content with the day's work. It had a powerful appeal.

Caroline gathered an armful of papers from the desk and dumped them on the floor. "There you are, Sir Richard," she said. "It isn't exactly perfect, but you should be all right there. Now, Edward, you haven't seen round the house yet – come along." Richard looked bemused as Edward did as he was told and followed her.

Richard discovered that something of importance had cropped up at the bank. Edwin Fforbes wanted to give him a full account of it, and out of consideration for Brookes-Smith's telephone bill, rang back to do so. The possibility of a substantial piece of business with an Anglo-German engineering consortium had come to fruition much earlier than anticipated, and a firm proposal had to be assembled within days. Richard said that he would be back in the office the following afternoon; however, they still discussed the matter at length so that Edwin Fforbes could begin work on a draft. The conversation lasted well over an hour, and when Richard replaced the phone, he was immediately conscious of the house's total silence. There was a passage outside the office that ran the whole length of the building, and Richard walked carefully along it, peeping through the open doors of rooms as he went. There was no sign of Caroline and Edward, and he assumed that they had gone out to have another look at something. Before going to find them, he took a pair of binoculars which were hanging on the pegs among an assortment of waterproof coats at the side door.

Outside, the stillness and lack of activity had strong overtones of neglect. Richard was well aware that mid-afternoon was a time of quiescence in any racing stable; he also knew that near the start of a racing season, there should be a sense of purpose that was tangible even when no obvious activity was in progress. The noise of a radio came from the lads' hostel; apart from that, there was no trace of life. Richard suspected that Edward, only recently fully settled at Avoca House, would be looking for excuses not to move. Saxon Court's air of aimless indifference was an obvious encouragement to such an attitude.

When he received his first sight of Saxon Down and the gallops at the end of the avenue, Richard's pleasure at the view was quickly replaced by exasperation when he failed to see Caroline and Edward. "Where the hell have they got to?" he said to himself in an unusual burst of petulance. He was about to go back to the house when his attention was caught by a bright flash of yellow a long way down the main U-shaped gallop. Using the binoculars, he saw that it was Caroline who had turned to show the bright facings on an otherwise green anorak. She and Edward had been leaning on the rail, and were now walking back, deep in conversation. Richard kept the binoculars trained on them and watched, what he saw making him believe that his gloom was unjustified.

They walked slowly, close together, their shoulders touching. First, Caroline had something to say. It was long and probably complex. Edward listened carefully. Then she shut up, and it was his turn. Her attention was as complete as his had been to her. The binoculars were powerful enough to reveal that she weighed every word he said, and that her eyes never left his face. In order to make a point in her reply, Caroline stopped, her hands became eloquent and Edward nodded. As they moved on again, he said something that caused her to laugh uproariously, then seriousness returned. Fascinated, Richard watched for ten minutes before slipping away to return to the house where he waited for them in the office. He had no idea what they had been talking about, but there was only one other person with whom Edward had ever enjoyed such rapport. An utterly fantastic concept entered Richard's mind: was this self-assured, exciting and attractive woman a possible successor to James Henry? Once that notion had taken root, the suggestion that she could give Edward even more than his grandfather had done seemed quite natural.

Cyril Brookes-Smith was still asleep upstairs when Richard and Edward left. Richard thanked Caroline profusely and promised that he would be in touch with her father as soon as a decision had been made. After he had walked briskly to the car and got into the driving seat, he saw that Caroline and Edward were grabbing a last chance to exchange a few words. They parted with great reluctance, and she stood waving as they drove out into the lane to Compton Norris.

"Lovely girl," Richard said, feeling duty bound to state the completely obvious and have done with it.

"Yes." Edward's reply was flatly neutral, and there was no way of telling whether that was by accident or design.

Richard was painfully aware of the fact that he had no alternative than to raise the all-important topic over dinner. Edward's suspicions at his failure to do so would have been more damaging than his resentfulness at being forced to discuss it.

"Yes, I agree, it's a wonderful place," Edward said. "Whether it's right for me is another question."

"What's your problem?"

"It's too big. I don't know if I could cope with it. And where do we find the owners to fill a yard that size? Brookes-Smith isn't going to leave anything worth having."

"Leave that to me," Richard said.

"What about the three million?"

"You can leave that to me as well. It's a good investment. And there's the Derby winner, remember."

"What difference does he make?"

"His stud fees would pay for it in less than four years."

As their conversation developed, Richard saw Edward's thoughts were not as negative as his first statements had suggested. Beneath the reservations concerning his inability to handle such a large establishment, and his worries about the cost, he was strongly attracted to the project. He could not conceal his admiration for the facilities offered by Saxon Court, and agreed that its potential was enormous.

"The gallops are marvellous," he said. "And there's enough room to lay several all-weather strips. It's a damned shame that Brookes-Smith has done so little with it – Ollie Derwent and Joshua Fielding did. I know he's had problems, but even so . . ."

It was clear that Edward *wanted* Saxon Court, and Richard decided to leave him alone for the time being to work things out for himself.

Next morning, Edward would much rather have retreated with his thoughts to the safety of Ireland and Avoca House. Instead, he dutifully drove thirty miles north with Richard from their hotel in Newbury to Easton Bagpuize in Oxfordshire. There was no difficulty in finding Widney Cheyne Manor, a late Georgian building in brick and tile, similar in hue to Saxon Court. The house, well-concealed from the road by a winding drive was smaller than Belfields and less imposing, but it was much more attractive, and Richard began to talk definitely of buying it as soon as he saw it. For a complicated reason that Edward had not bothered to understand, the owners had already left to join their son in Australia, and it was being looked after by a resident caretaker.

While realising that it was all very pleasant, Edward absorbed very little during the three-hour tour. Richard kept a careful watch on him. Edward wandered round Widney Cheyne in a state of great abstraction, looking at things without seeing them. He was, Richard appreciated, thinking very hard about Saxon Court, struggling to reconcile prudence with ambition. But there was more than that in his attitude. Richard was rapidly coming to terms with ideas that he would have dismissed out of hand as capricious only forty-eight hours ago; today, Edward was giving the impression of a man who was lonely. Briefly, there were flashes of something much deeper: he was bereft.

"I'll get Imogen to have a look at this," Richard said when they had finished the inspection. "If she likes it, I'll buy it."

Edward accepted the inevitable with a nod.

They parted outside the front door of the Manor. A car driven by a uniformed chauffeur had come to whisk Richard back to his office in London. Edward drove to Heathrow, gave up the hired car, and flew to Dublin where he was surprised to be met by Declan. After he had telephoned Siobhan, he assumed that either she, with her recently-won driving licence, or Dooley would come for him. Declan's presence was the clearest possible indication of his eagerness to know all about Saxon Court, and they stopped for a drink in a pub as soon as they were clear of Dublin.

Declan listened in attentive silence as Edward did his best to relay all the relevant facts and his impressions. After ten minutes, Declan had an almost complete picture. Saxon Court was a truly splendid establishment with facilities that were first-rate; some improvements might be necessary, but these could be accomplished easily without spoiling what was already there. And the magnificently unique stable block had a clock-tower. Declan came close to showing his amusement at Edward's frequent enthusiastic references to this feature.

Back at Avoca House, and enveloped by a feeling of being at home and safe, Edward went over it all again with Siobhan, who listened patiently without expressing an opinion. After inviting herself to dinner, Imogen felt no such restraint.

"Sounds ideal," she said. "You ought not to be too long making up your mind over that. Richard seems very impressed by this Widney Cheyne place. I'm going over to see it next week."

"It was nice," Edward said. "In some ways I could jump at Saxon Court. In other ways it frightens me to death."

"You need to get a grip," was Imogen's brisk judgement. "It really would be a shame if we were separated now," she added in a much softer tone.

The following day, Edward packed all the Avoca House staff into the TV room in the hostel, and told them where he had been and what his opinions were. He stressed that as a business enterprise, Saxon Court was run down to the point of collapse, needing both staff and horses. Thus, if he did decide to move, most of the horses would go with him and there would be jobs for everyone who wanted to come. Liam Corrigan became verbosely excited at the prospect of working in such a famous stable and stirred up what proved to be a useful discussion, at the end of which virtually everyone had said that they would like to go. It was also made plain to Edward that they would support him whatever he decided to do.

During the following four days, Edward raked over the problem with anyone who was likely to be involved or seemed relevant. Sean Gillespie gave his blessing; Valerie Malahide thought it was far too good an opportunity to miss, as did Edward's parents to whom he spoke at great and exorbitantly expensive length on the telephone. When Richard returned to Belfields for the weekend, he happily sat through several hours of Edward's soul-searching, listening and offering occasional guidance. Edward went over all aspects of Saxon Court, including the difficulties that might arise if and when it was time to start moving everything.

To no one, however, did he ever mention Caroline.

CHAPTER 7

For three days, Edward thought of nothing but Saxon Court. Fearing that it was going to be impossible to make a decision, he embraced what appeared to be the perfect excuse for putting off the evil day. The horses had to be prepared for the season ahead, but this time there was no 'Musetta weather' to make it easy. Although there were fleeting hours of respite, the weather during the last week of March and the first few days of April consisted largely of torrential rain, usually made infinitely more unpleasant by harsh, driving winds. No one had any great desire for work. Only Declan and Paddy Dooley escaped catching a streaming head cold that turned everyone else into useless miseries for several days, and the horses took most unkindly to the abysmal conditions. Even the stalwart Murgatroyd was less than willing to set foot outside his box during the worst of it.

They were reduced to exercising horses in the barn, walking and trotting them in small groups of ten, Edward trying to make himself believe that it was doing some good, and keeping close to a plentiful supply of paper handkerchiefs. The thought of the very useful covered ride at Saxon Court inevitably suggested itself. For the first time in Declan's experience, the gallop became very soft indeed, and about four hundred yards of it degenerated into a quagmire at the first attempt to canter horses over it. Responding to Edward's vehemently expressed frustration, Declan gently commented on the need for an all-weather gallop, fully aware that in so doing he was applying pressure in favour of the move.

Exhibiting marked signs of sheer pig-headedness, Edward insisted on taking Leonora to Newmarket for the One Thousand Guineas. She had done only one serious piece of work, was looking substantially below her best and there was no question of a prep race. As her owner, Richard could have stopped it by the simple expedient of refusing to sanction the costs of the trip, but he decided to carry on with the waiting game for a little longer. On the flight over, Edward found that he was forced to admit to himself that he was being rather stupid. Dooley's disgust at being associated with a no-hoper was monumental enough to make him forget his alleged fear of flying, and Cathal O'Brien was clearly uneasy at the prospect of making his first appearance at a big race under such inauspicious conditions.

Arrival in Newmarket brought nothing except the prospect of a thoroughly miserable pre-race evening. Gordon Chapman was on hand to welcome him and make sure that everything was all right, but said he had to go out and was not expecting to be back before midnight. Around seven o'clock, Edward looked at Leonora, who seemed happy enough, checked that Cathal O'Brien had eaten and had a comfortable bed, and then wandered out of the yard with absolutely no idea what to do next. He was just standing, hands in pockets and looking frankly lost when a sports car stopped on the other side of the road. It was a perfectly ordinary, mass-produced car and was far from new, so it failed to register with him at first. Only when Finoula got out and walked towards him did his attention focus.

There was conscious bravery in the way she approached him. "Hiya!" she said. "I thought I might find you here. How're you doing?"

"I'm fine," he replied and took a good look at her. "You look very well."

"I am, thanks." There was a pause that threatened to become uncomfortable. "Look, I'm sorry . . . walking out on you like that."

"That's all right. They say these things are supposed to happen for the best."

"That's what they say." She kicked at a tuft of grass, and watched it with bogus concentration. "It was my fault you couldn't do a thing with Musetta, wasn't it?"

"Well . . ." Edward would have given a lot to be able to evade the question.

"It was so! Mother tells me that father's still calling me everything. He's only spoken to me once . . . that was to tell me not to bother going home for Christmas."

"Oh dear."

"How is she?"

"Who?" Preoccupied with thoughts of Declan's unexpected severity, Edward had no idea who she was talking about.

"Musetta!"

"Oh . . . yes . . . she's very well. We're keeping our fingers crossed and hoping she's in foal to Mill Reef."

"Hey, that's great! What are you doing standing around like a lost soul?"

"Precisely that, I suppose. I've nothing to do."

"You can buy me a meal."

"All right."

"There's a good place at Bury St Edmunds," she said as they crossed the road to her car.

"So how are you getting on?" Edward asked once they were on the way, and travelling in her usual hectic style.

"Very well. Mr Dalrymple's a marvellous boss. I'm in charge of thirty two-year-olds and it's great."

"Good people to work with?"

"Oh yes. I was worried at first in case they might be a bit stuck up, but they're not at all like that. Sure, half of them are Irish anyway!"

After they had ordered their meal, she had a confession to make. "You were right that night. I was such an eejut."

"Don't worry about it," he said. "You'll find the right man one of these days."

"I think I have done." Her attitude told Edward that she was very serious. "He works for Mr Dalrymple as well."

"Not Alexander Abercrombie?" he asked suspiciously.

"Good God, no!" She glared at him furiously. "He was a right dose! Drastic! He's left. Gone to Canada. He told us all that he'd had a marvellous offer, but my man reckons Mr Dalrymple told him to go. He's called Patrick Prendegast by the way."

"Who is?"

"My man! He's from Cork. He's lovely."

"I hope it turns out all right for you."

"Thanks. Now tell me about this Saxon Court business."

Surprised, Edward almost reacted by asking her how she knew; then he realised that she and Mary probably talked on the telephone at least twice a week. "Richard's selling Belfields and moving over here," he said. "He wants to buy Saxon Court. That's all there is to it really."

"You must be over the moon. Imagine getting a place like that."

"Well, it is a very exciting prospect, but I haven't made my mind up about it yet."

"Why not? What are you messing about for?"

"I've only just started to get the hang of Avoca House," he replied, and wondered what to say next.

Finoula did it for him. "And you don't know if you can make a go of a big place."

Edward was startled to see how well she knew him.

They talked it over until she dropped him off at Gordon Chapman's yard two hours later. "You'd better decide soon," Finoula told him. "And make sure you get it right. Father won't be very pleased if you don't go."

"I see. That's official is it?"

"It is so! Think about it." She kissed him with a return of the sisterly affection that had been the foundation of their friendship before things had gone wrong, and he stood waving as she roared off towards Tewkesbury Lodge, Bernard Dalrymple's huge stable that was twice the size of Saxon Court.

For the sake of appearances, and to celebrate the anniversary of Musetta's triumph, Richard travelled to Newmarket for the One Thousand Guineas. In the parade ring before the race, Edward behaved as though everything was exactly as it should be; secretly, however, he loathed every second of it, and promised himself that he would never again race such a poorly prepared horse. When Leonora left the paddock and went down to the start, Edward came close to being afraid of what was likely to happen. Fortunately, Sean Gillespie had the answer. In the absence of any instructions as to how to ride the race, he treated it like a stiff piece of work at home, and although Leonora posed no threat to the first three, she covered the final two furlongs in very fine style.

"She'll be better for that," Sean Gillespie told Edward afterwards. "You want to start training her now. She'll come good for Ascot. I think she wants more than a mile."

Edward accepted the advice gratefully, and turned to face Richard, having a very good idea what was coming.

"I need a decision," Richard said.

"When?"

"Soon. International Digital are getting impatient about Belfields. They've decided they want Avoca House – yes, I know, they didn't originally, but these things change. On top of this, Brookes-Smith is talking about putting Saxon Court up for auction. That would attract all sorts of attention, and the price might go sky-high."

This was the point that Edward had been dreading. He was trapped.

"Will Monday be soon enough?" he asked, without a single constructive idea as to what he was going to do with the intervening three days.

"Yes. But no later than lunchtime. I must be able to say something to ID in New York when they open for business."

They walked to the now-deserted paddock rail in silence. "I can understand and sympathise with your misgivings, Edward," Richard said when he was sure they could not be overheard. "What you seem determined not to grasp is that you will not be *allowed* to fail."

"I know that. I want to feel I can do it on my own."

"All right, but let's not have too many mock heroics. Have you ever wondered what happens if you get one of these terrible bugs in the yard – either at Avoca House or anywhere else? What happens if you can't send a horse near a racecourse for a year or more?" He cited a current, well-known example. "Look at the mess Ralph Lewis is in. You need help. Everybody needs help all the time. If it weren't for your grandfather, I wouldn't even *be* here, God alone knows what would have happened to the bank and the family money, and you'd still be teaching. There's one racing certainty I can give you – we stand more chance of flying to the moon by flapping our arms than we do of winning the Derby from Avoca House. You've got to make your mind up about whether you

144

really are going to carry on where James Henry left off, or just muck around playing the dilettante."

Dooley's morose misery in the flying horse box on the way home suited Edward's mood perfectly. Richard had not exactly lost his temper, but Edward was in no doubt that he had been given a severe ticking-off by someone who was used to authority as well as being a son of James Henry.

As usual, Declan was waiting to make his report on the yard. Having done so, he hung around instead of going home to Mary.

"Yes, Declan?" Edward asked.

"I believe you saw the girl last night, sor."

The efficiency of the bush telegraph caused Edward to smile for the first time that day. "Yes I did, Declan. She was in good form. She's looking very well and I reckon she's doing all right. There aren't any hard feelings between her and me, and I suggest you might like to take the same view." Declan shuffled his feet and cleared his throat unnecessarily. "For your information," Edward continued, "she thinks I'm a fool for not jumping at Saxon Court, and Sir Richard gave me a fair old ear-bashing on the same topic at Newmarket this afternoon."

After a rather guilty-looking Declan had gone, Edward stayed in the office. Siobhan usually left him a file of papers when he had been away overnight; he found it and started to work through it. There were letters for signature, questions to be answered and things that Siobhan thought he should know about. When it was done, he sat and thought about what Richard had said. It had been tantamount to an ultimatum, no doubt sparked off by frustration at what Richard now saw as downright indecision, probably based on something dangerously close to cowardice. After five minutes of contemplating this unpalatable fact, he was startled by the ringing of the telephone.

"Avoca House, Edward Manning."

"Hello, Edward, it's Caroline. How are you?"

"All right, thanks." He was surprised to find how excited he was to hear her voice.

"Just back from Newmarket?"

"About an hour ago."

"I watched it on TV. Presumably that filly of yours wasn't meant to do any better?"

"She certainly needed the race."

"I thought she wanted a longer trip. She was going on nicely at the end. Why don't you try her over ten furlongs?"

"That's more or less what Sean Gillespie said."

"There you are then. Now look, Edward, there's a bit of a flap on. Father's getting fed up because he thinks you aren't serious about having this place. He's talking about putting it up for auction."

"I know. Richard Stewart told me this afternoon."

"Are you going to have it?"

Edward felt that it was a very good thing she could not see him wince at the question. "I don't know," he replied.

"I don't want it going up for grabs if it can possibly be avoided," Caroline said, mercifully appearing to ignore him. "Do you think it would be helpful if you came and had another look at it?"

"Yes, I think it would."

"When?"

"Soon! I've promised Richard a decision by Monday."

"Tomorrow then?"

"Yes." This time, Edward did not bother to look at the wall-chart.

"Can you get here by lunchtime – about the same as before?"

"Yes. I'll let you know if I can't get on to one of the morning flights and there's any delay."

"Right. And don't bother about an hotel. This place is full of spare rooms."

With elation at the prospect of seeing her again pushing everything else far into the background, Edward rang Richard at his London flat.

"That sounds like a good idea," Richard said after Edward had explained.

"I think so. This should sort it out one way or the other."

"Good. Look, I'm going to be stuck here all weekend working on a proposal. Get in touch if you want any help or advice."

"I will."

"I'm sorry I got steamed up this afternoon."

"Don't worry about that. I expect I've deserved it."

Edward had never bothered Declan at home so late, but he was made welcome and listened to very attentively.

"I can get you a reservation now," Siobhan said, and hurried off to use the office telephone.

"I shall need to have a look at this place, you know," Mary told Edward. "There's the measuring up for curtains and things to be looked into."

"Hang on, Mary," Edward laughed. "I still haven't decided anything. I'm only going to have another look."

"Well, let me tell you this," Mary said, "if you stay here, you can have him all to yourself," she indicated Declan, "because he won't be fit to live with."

Declan's expression of contrived innocence suggested that Mary was not exaggerating all that much.

Following Siobhan's early-morning drive to Dublin Airport that enabled him to catch the first flight, Edward drove slowly from Heathrow to Saxon Court in the hired car to avoid arriving too early. Caroline waved to him from the office when he did get there, and he went in to find that she had very nearly finished clearing the place out: the last few piles of paper disappeared into sacks as he watched. She made coffee and explained the present state of the yard. In the end, only forty horses had come back after the winter, and all but two or three of these would either go to other stables or drift out of racing altogether. If anything, the staff position was even worse. Bill Morris who had been head lad for all of Cyril Brookes-Smith's twenty-five years, and had worked for Joshua Fielding before that, had decided to retire. He and his wife May were, at that moment, in Devon, finalising the purchase of a cottage overlooking the sea. All but twelve of the lads had either left or opted for retirement. "So you see," Caroline concluded, "things are in a fair old mess."

"And your father's utterly fed up with it all," Edward prompted.

"Oh yes. He's told me to get on and sort it all out. He's had enough. He isn't here by the way."

"Oh."

"I've packed him off to hospital for a few days. There are some tests that need doing – the doctor thinks he might have a condition that can be treated. I should have made him do it a year ago."

They sat and talked until lunch, Caroline making certain that Edward was under no illusions about the state of the business. "It all boils down to this," she told him, "there isn't any 'goodwill'. Whoever takes this place over gets no horses and virtually no staff to go with it."

"What about the twelve lads who aren't fixed up with anything?" Edward asked.

"Two lads and ten girls actually," she said. "All fairly young."

"Are they any good?"

"I hired them and trained them myself."

After a snack lunch, they took two of the hacks and rode out on to Saxon Down. Several days of warm, sunny weather had made some amends for the dismal start to the spring, and most of the trees were coming into leaf. In two more weeks, Edward thought, it would all be looking quite lovely; given activity and a sense of purpose instead of its present aimless lethargy, Saxon Court was the place of his dreams.

They stayed out all afternoon, and for most of the time, Caroline conducted a gentle, very subtle cross-examination of Edward. He was so happy talking to her that he failed to notice how much she was systematically learning about him. She had already heard a great deal about James Henry and his ambition to win the Derby; now, she conducted a detailed scrutiny of Edward's entire life, from his early schooldays, through university, back to King Henry's as a teacher and the well-calculated end of his teaching career. Edward was unaware that he was telling her anything other than a series of obvious facts, not realising that he was revealing opinions, beliefs and full details of the people who had been close to him. From time to time she asked harmless-sounding questions that made him go into greater detail on a specific point. For over three hours, she listened, ending with a picture of Edward that he would have found devastating in its completeness had he taken the trouble to work out what she had been doing.

When they returned to the yard, Edward was pleased to see considerable activity as the skeleton staff went through the preparations for evening stables. "There may not be all that much point in it, but I'm trying to keep *some* routine going," Caroline said. One of the girls detached herself from the bustle and followed them to take their horses. "Thanks, Alison," Caroline said as she dismounted. "This is Mr Manning. He's having another look round. Alison Bairstow, Edward."

"How do you do, sir?"

Edward thought she was seventeen or eighteen, attractive in a breezy, no-nonsense way, and he took an instant liking to her forthright demeanour. She surveyed him with a mixture of respect, frank appraisal and sheer curiosity.

"She's good," Caroline said as they walked past the Colour Room towards the house. "She's only been here about eighteen months, poor kid. I took a horse to Thirsk, and she just marched up to me and asked for a job."

They had a quick cup of tea, then Caroline stretched, feigning weariness. "I'd better do a quick round," she said. "Would you like to come with me?"

"I'd love to."

"Come on then. It might cheer them up a bit to have a *real* trainer take an interest." As they headed towards the clock-tower, she amplified what had seemed a bitter, graceless remark. "Father was very good – although he never had much luck. He's lost interest these last two years, we've hardly had a decent horse in the place, and that's all this bunch have ever known."

"I understand."

All the horses were in the Old Yard. Caroline went round fairly briskly, checking only that there was nothing wrong. Even so, Edward had time to appreciate that they were a pretty moderate collection. The two lads and ten girls kept popping up, trying to be everywhere at once, all eager for a good look at the ex-schoolmaster who had done so well in his first two years as a trainer working from an obscure base in Ireland. Edward sensed that they were all on their best behaviour and every bit as anxious as Richard and Declan to know what was going to happen.

In the last box, Alison Bairstow was waiting with a good-looking chestnut colt. He had a white blaze, and would almost certainly have been condemned as 'too flashy' by the purists, but he was a substantial cut above the rest, and Edward was immediately taken by him. "This fellow looks all right," he said, advancing into the box. "He's got a very good eye – nice and bold."

"The only trouble is, he's a bit of an idiot, sir," Alison Bairstow said, very pleased that one of her horses had been singled out.

"Really?" Edward smiled at her and patted the horse's neck. "I've got one like him at home."

"What do you do with him?"

"Despair!" They laughed. "No, seriously, it's a hell of a problem, but one of my lads reckons he's talked some sense into him over the winter. He might win something this year."

"That's one of the horses that's staying," Caroline said as they left the yard.

"Who's the owner?"

"The Duke of Dorchester. He's always had a few here. To be perfectly honest, I don't think His Grace knows the first thing about horses, which is probably why that one's staying. My guess is that they've forgotten all about him!"

Edward was about to suggest that they might go out to eat when Caroline pre-empted him. "I could murder a decent meal," she said. "But I'm not going to cook and I don't fancy going out."

"So what do we do?" Edward asked.

"Aha! Meals on wheels!" She laughed at his puzzled look. "The Fortescue Arms – that's the best of the pubs in the village – has a good restaurant. I can ring up and ask them to deliver. Their roast lamb is usually pretty good."

"That's fine by me."

Caroline telephoned the order, then showed him up to his room. It was at the back of the house with a view of the yard and Saxon Down. "Bathroom down there to the left," she said. "Take your time and come down to the kitchen when you're ready."

Half an hour later there was no sign of her, so he went into the office and made himself comfortable on the window-seat. The evening sun was on the west-facing wall of the yard, giving the bricks a warm, orange glow, and making the clock-tower especially distinctive.

While Edward was basking in the view, the conversation over the evening meal in the lads' hostel reflected the fever pitch of interest in his visit.

"Do you think he'll have the place?"

"Bound to."

"Don't be so sure. Old Cyril's asking a hell of a price."

"How much?"

"Oh, millions and millions."

"Mr Manning's got a bank behind him."

"Will he keep us on?"

"Shouldn't think so. Who'd want a load of deadbeats like us?"

"Speak for yourself, pig-face! I'm the greatest!"

"Look, we ain't even *seen* a winner since we come here, let alone trained one of the bleeders!"

Alison intervened. "I think he's a good bloke," she said. "If he does take the place, we'll be all right."

"Ah go on! You're only saying that 'cos he's dishy."

"No I'm not." Alison thought about it. "But he has got a lovely smile," she had to admit to a chorus of cat-calls.

The Fortescue Arms meal was a great success. After Caroline had reappeared in a simple white blouse and a pair of beautifully tailored navy blue slacks, Edward would have enjoyed it even if it had been rubbish. In the event, it was a very good meal indeed; they ate in the kitchen, then went into the pretty and stylish sitting-room at the front of the house. Caroline put a couple of lamps on to combat the deepening twilight, and turned briskly to business.

"Well, are you going to take it?"

"I'm almost convinced."

"What's stopping you?"

"I've got this niggling idea that I'd make a mess of it. Haven't you thought of having a go yourself?"

"Yes, and it's out of the question. There's no chance of me getting the financial backing, and I'd struggle for owners. Our owners have always been a fairly mediocre bunch. Pretty mean mostly – they've wanted champagne on a beer budget. So I'd have to look elsewhere, compete in the rat-race. I'm a woman, which is a tremendous disadvantage despite what people say, and the Brookes-Smith reputation doesn't exactly glitter."

"You've looked into it?"

"Of course."

Edward fell silent. Although Caroline had made herself comfortable in an armchair, he was still standing; he wandered restlessly into the huge bow window dominating one wall, extending from floor to ceiling. He pretended to be admiring the view across the downs towards Lambourn, whereas the late-evening gloom prevented him seeing further than the flower bed in the middle of the lawn.

"There is a suggestion I'd like to make," Caroline said, and he turned to face her to signal his willingness to listen. "If you tried to run this place without an assistant, you almost certainly would fail. Once the yard is full, there's far too much for one person to do. If you were foolish enough to try it, you'd run yourself into the ground in a week. The question is, of course, where do you find somebody who can do the job and is reliable. Actually, reliability is putting it very mildly – you'd need loyalty."

Edward nodded.

"I also have a problem," Caroline went on. "I love this place very much indeed. I was born here and I've never lived anywhere else. To be perfectly frank with you, I haven't the vaguest idea what's going to happen to me when this is all over. I'm dreading it. Father's made a few suggestions, but they're rather silly really and none of them are appealing. Some friends have offered me a job and a flat in Gloucestershire – sounds fine except that it doesn't amount to more than looking after a few hunters. I've been working in that yard since I was ten, and I reckon I'm worth a bit more than that. You wouldn't do much better than me for an assistant."

"Well, yes . . . I'm sure you're right." Edward could hardly believe what he had heard.

"So how does that strike you?" she asked when she realised that he was not going to say any more.

"You want to be my assistant?"

"Yes, in a manner of speaking. I've thought it all out, and I've come to the conclusion that we could make a first-class job of running this place. We'd have to make the proper arrangements of course – put the thing on the right footing."

"Yes . . . naturally . . . of course . . . er . . . what would you suggest?"

"I think we should get married."

He found that she was staring at him quite calmly. She had her chin up and was utterly determined not to give any sign that she had said something quite extraordinary. The room was very quiet; through the partially open door, the ticking of the grandfather clock on the upstairs landing was clearly audible.

"You'd better sit down," she said at last, and gave him time to compose himself. "I think that's a very good idea. Don't you?"

"Well, yes, I do," he said.

"So?"

"I . . . you see . . . well . . ."

"My dear Edward, whatever is the matter?" she asked, and smiled encouragingly.

"I just don't know what to say."

"Why? Was it such a ludicrous suggestion?"

"Oh no . . . definitely not."

"What then?"

"I can't believe what you said."

"I meant it." To Edward's greater discomfort, Caroline studied him carefully, her head cocked to one side. A number of ideas occurred to her, but she decided to keep them to herself. "I don't think that we exactly hate the sight of one another," she said gently.

"No! Definitely not!" Edward agreed with her almost passionately, and then subsided, painfully conscious that he ought to be able to think of something else to say. She came to his rescue.

"As a matter of fact, I believe we rather like each other," she said.

Edward cleared his throat nervously and said, "Yes." Caroline thought that he was going to seize up again, then the truth came out in a rush. "Actually, I thought you were absolutely marvellous the minute I saw you, and the way we get on is . . . well . . . wonderful."

"Yes, I know," she said calmly. "And the feeling was mutual – *and* it was noticed."

"Really?"

"Oh yes. Father mentioned it once or twice." There was a mischievous twinkle in her eyes to indicate that Cyril Brookes-Smith had spoken at great length on the subject. "I imagine your friend Richard spotted it too."

"Good heavens!"

"Although I think he was rather baffled and didn't know what to make of it."

"I can't think straight."

"Look, you need a top-class stable – yes, you do!" She squashed the argument before it started. "If you want to produce a Derby winner, you've got to have the best of everything. The days of a small yard coming up with a fairytale ending are over. That's one side of it, right?" He nodded. "The other side is even more simple. I don't want to leave here. I didn't have much hope of achieving this until you turned up, and I found out how we were with one another. You may never train a Derby winner, Edward, but I believe we'd be very happy trying to do it together." The blue eyes became startlingly intense. "Very happy indeed," she emphasised, "and from what I've seen of life, it's wrong to chuck opportunities like that away."

Edward stood up and began prowling round the room. "Are you sure about this?" he asked.

"Absolutely positive!"

He saw that she was. After two complete circuits of the coffee table and an armchair, he stopped, and made his decision.

"Yes – you are right! Will you marry me, Caroline?"

"Yes, Edward, I will."

She stood up and walked towards him purposefully. For an insane moment, Caroline thought he was going to shake her hand. Until she put her arms round him, that had been Edward's intention; when he did pluck up the courage to embrace his wife-to-be, she reacted enthusiastically, and he was engulfed by the sweetest excitement he had ever known.

"That was nice," Caroline said when she reluctantly decided that she had to breathe. Studying him carefully, she wrinkled her nose, a trait that Edward had noticed several times; it seemed to happen when she was perplexed or amused. "You're a bit of an idiot really, aren't you?" she said, rubbing her nose against his cheek.

"Yes . . . I suppose I am."

"H'm. We shall have to do something about that before we're much older."

"I shall look forward to it."

It was after midnight when Caroline insisted that she was too tired to go on talking, and that they had made quite enough plans to be going on with. "Come on, we've got a busy few days ahead of us," she said. "And I start looking like a hag if I don't get my beauty sleep."

"Impossible!"

Caroline laughed. "That is precisely the sort of loyalty I'm looking for," she said. "It's very sweet of you – and totally misplaced."

Although the stairs were not as grand as those at Avoca House, they were wide enough for them to walk up side-by-side, with their arms round each other. "Sleep tight," she said after a last kiss outside her bedroom door, and she gave him a smile of surpassing beauty, a smile that dispelled every fear he had ever known.

When he was in bed, Edward assembled the events of a day even more momentous than the one on which he had taken over Avoca House. No sooner had he done so, and was preparing to relish his staggering good fortune with Caroline, than he fell asleep. He slept better and longer than he had done for many years.

The sound of a cup of tea being placed on the bedside table woke him a fraction of a second before Caroline sat on the edge of his bed and kissed him.

"What time is it?" he asked, searching for his watch.

"Past eight o'clock. The day's half over!" She was dressed in working clothes and was brightly cheerful.

"What have you been doing?" Edward struggled to sit up and reached for the tea.

"Motivating the staff – no, it's all right, I haven't said a word. You can do that."

She watched while he drank his tea, taking in his slightly puzzled look; he appeared to be contemplating something profound and complex. "What's up?" she asked.

"Are we in love?"

The nose wrinkled furiously. "I don't know. Mind you, I've no idea what that means anyway. I've always thought that people bandy it around far too much because they can't think of anything better – it's a convenient form of short-hand, I suppose. I *do* know I've never felt this way about anybody before, and I'm convinced that we're going to be all right."

"Me too."

"Right. Hurry up. There are things to do."

After a quick breakfast, they went into the office, and Edward sat down with a piece of paper. "Richard first," he said, "and then I must let them know at home. Presumably I should talk to your staff after that?"

"I think so." Caroline stood behind him, watching as he made quick notes, an arm resting lightly across his shoulders.

"I'm going to offer them all jobs – OK?"

"Yes."

"What shall we do after that?"

"Go and see father."

"Of course. Where is he?"

"At a place on the other side of Reading."

"Right!" He reached for the telephone. "Let's get on with it."

Richard was sitting at the desk in the study of his London flat, and answered immediately.

"I've got your decision," Edward said, cutting through his pleasantries. "I'll take Saxon Court on."

"Marvellous! I'm very pleased. I'll talk to Brookes-Smith as soon as we've finished."

"No you won't, he's in hospital . . . no, it's all right, he's only there for observation and tests. He'll be out . . . when? . . ." Caroline whispered, "Monday or Tuesday," and Edward passed it on. "I'll be seeing him later. He might want to ring you. Are you in all day?"

"Yes. I expect I shall nip out for a bite to eat this evening. When are you going back to Ireland?"

"I don't know yet. Not before Tuesday, I imagine. There are things to do. I want to get a builder and see about those cottages on the Avenue."

"Do what you want, and I'll pay. Have you told them at Avoca House yet?"

"No, you're the first. I'll call Siobhan next, and then talk to the people here. I'm offering them all jobs."

"You sound very pleased with yourself."

"I am!"

"So am I. And Edwin Fforbes will be as well – he can hardly wait to become an owner. Is there anything else I need to know?"

"No, I think that's it for the moment . . . no, hang on, Caroline and I are getting married."

"You mean Caroline Brookes-Smith?" Richard asked in a voice that sounded rather strangled.

"Yes."

"Bloody hell!" Richard said, and he sounded appalled.

"Very nice! Thank you!" Edward replied, wondering what on earth could have produced such a reaction.

"No, sorry, warmest congratulations and all that," Richard said hurriedly. "I expect I shall soon be very happy for you. But you have dropped me in it from the most lavatorial height."

"How?"

"I didn't tell Imogen about Caroline. As a matter of fact, I never even mentioned her."

"Oh dear," Edward chuckled. "You *do* have problems."

"She's going to go off her trolley!"

"Very possibly!" Edward thought it was very funny. "It seems to have been a bit remiss of you – Caroline tells me that you may have spotted a certain something between us."

"Well of course I did, I'm not blind."

"You should have told Imogen then."

"I never imagined for a minute that you'd actually have the guts to do anything about it."

"Ah! Yes. I must tell you about that some time."

Before ringing Avoca House, Edward tried to explain Richard's predicament. He sketched Imogen well enough for Caroline to be amused, though not, he noticed, apprehensive at the prospect of meeting her. Then he spoke to both Declan and Siobhan, telling them of his decision about Saxon Court, and asking if they could keep going without him until Tuesday. Declan's answer was a masterpiece. Edward judged that this was not the time to complicate their excitement by introducing Caroline.

"Now your staff," Edward said as he replaced the phone.

Caroline looked at the clock. "Yes. We should catch them at breakfast."

As they walked across the open space to the lads' hostel, Caroline took Edward's hand. It seemed the most natural thing in the world, and they were still hand-in-hand when they entered the hostel dining room, immediately causing an expectant silence. The twelve looked rather like refugees in a corner of a room that could accommodate fifty with ease, most of them heightening that impression by looking tense at the sudden interruption. Not so Alison Bairstow; Caroline and Edward's closeness told her everything.

"I know you've all been having a worrying time," Edward began at once, "and I expect you all know that I've been looking at Saxon Court with a view to taking it over. Well, I've decided to do that. Sir Richard Stewart, who's Chairman of a merchant bank and one of my owners, is going to buy the place from Mr Brookes-Smith, and I shall be training and living here. I'll tell you here and now that I want to train a Derby winner, and that is one of the reasons why I shall be coming to Saxon Court. Now I have a very good staff in Ireland, and I'm hoping that every one of them will come here with me, but Avoca House is only a forty-five box yard, so I shall need more people. There are jobs for any of you who want them." The twelve faces in front of him looked much happier. "Incidentally, my contract terms are full-time, all the year round. I don't lay staff off in the winter. Yes?" A dark-haired girl had put her hand up.

"When do you expect to be moving in and getting things going, sir?"

"Susan Hicks," Caroline said quietly.

"I don't know yet, Susan. The decision was only taken yesterday evening, and I haven't got round to the details yet. But it's going to be as soon as possible, and if any of you want to work for me, I'll take you on to my pay-roll the minute you stop working for Mr Brookes-Smith. I shall be here until Tuesday, so have a think about it, and come and see me if you want a job. Any more questions?" There were none, so with a broad smile, Edward delivered his parting shot. "And to show you that I really do mean business, Miss Brookes-Smith and I are getting married."

The news was greeted by gasps, and a fevered buzz of conversation broke out before Caroline and Edward were out of ear shot.

"I think we deserve a cup of coffee," Caroline said, and they went back to the house.

"Is there a decent builder in the area?" Edward asked as they drank their coffee in the kitchen.

"There's Eli Roberts and Sons in the village."

"Are they any good, do you know?"

"Oh yes. George Roberts is the fifth generation. His great-grandfather built the Old Yard for Ollie Derwent."

Edward smiled. "And his grandfather built the New Yard?"

"Correct!"

"He was the one that had to find the bricks?"

"That's right."

"Sounds good enough."

"Do you want me to get George up here?"

"Yes, please. Monday would be ideal."

Caroline went to the office to telephone, but came back at once. "You'd better deal with this lot while I talk to George," she said. Following her, Edward saw the two lads and ten girls in a huddle outside the office window. When he opened the side door and went out to them, it was Alison Bairstow who came forward as spokeswoman.

"We all want to work for you, please, sir," she said.

It was still barely eleven o'clock when they left Saxon Court, with

Caroline under the impression that they were going to find somewhere to have lunch before visiting her father.

"We shall be able to retire next year if we carry on at this rate," she said flippantly.

"I don't think so," Edward said. "I don't remember saying we were only going to win the Derby *once*."

She smiled at him. It was fascinating watching the change in his attitude as he realised what had happened to him, and his confidence grew. "I see. We're going to do better than Joshua Fielding, are we?"

"It gives us a target to aim at, doesn't it?"

Caroline soon realised that Edward was driving towards Newbury rather than Reading.

"I'm going to buy something," he said in response to her question. "My hunch is that Newbury is the best place to find it."

"What do you want?"

"Wait and see."

In Newbury, they walked down three streets before Edward saw what he was looking for, and hauled Caroline across the road without too much regard for traffic. "Well?" she asked, finding herself outside a jeweller's shop, but she still had to wait until they were inside.

"We want an engagement ring," Edward said to the owner of the shop. His eye was caught by a flash of brilliant blue from a tray of rings on display. "That's the idea, that one there – that blue stone."

"Sapphires, sir," the man said.

"Right! Match your eyes," Edward explained to Caroline. "Beautiful!" She was slightly bemused, half-smiling, and Edward took advantage of it to draw the owner aside. "I'm looking for something better than those," he said, indicating all the rings under the glass counter, and dismissing them at a stroke. The man nodded, studied Caroline for a moment, and went into the back of the shop. At once Caroline started to protest, only to find herself silenced by a kiss.

The man returned with six rings on a velvet pad. Three of them fitted perfectly, and by a happy chance, they were the ones that Caroline liked best. The selection process lasted more than half an hour; while it was going on, several other customers came in with items for repair or to make small purchases. For most of the time, the owner of the shop left them to their own devices, and Edward guided Caroline towards the ring for which he had formed an instant liking. With four perfect sapphires set in a diamond shape, it somehow possessed the style and élan that was quintessentially Caroline, and it looked magnificent on her hand. As if sensing that it was by far the most expensive of the three, at over four thousand pounds, Caroline professed to like another, much cheaper one. However, after enough persuasion, Edward clinched the matter by the simple expedient of insisting on his choice. He had always rather disapproved of the internationally reputable charge card that Richard urged him to have, and had never used it. Because of it, however, the transaction was completed satisfactorily within minutes, and Caroline was able to wear the ring as they left the shop.

They had walked some way along the street before she realised that she had not thanked him. As the fervour of her kiss passed its peak, Edward regained consciousness of his surroundings, and saw that scores of people were looking at them. His instinctive embarrassment faded when he realised that they were all smiling, not at something humorous, but as though they were happy, uplifted by the sight of an attractive couple behaving like a pair of love-struck teenagers. Caroline caught a fleeting glimpse of the scene before it unfroze and evaporated into the bustle of Saturday shopping.

"There you are," she said. "They think we're all right."

"I'm not arguing," Edward pointed out.

Caroline's father was in a private hospital on the southern outskirts of Reading. They found him dressed, relaxing on a verandah overlooking pleasant gardens. He looked much better than when Edward had last seen him, and his face brightened when they appeared. Then, as a sunbeam caught the sapphires on Caroline's left hand, and he saw the myriad flashes of cornflower blue, he smiled.

"How are you feeling?" Caroline asked, bending to kiss him.

"Much better. That doctor chap reckons he's found something with one of those gadgets of his. Been giving me some new pills since Thursday evening. They seem to be all right. Haven't had that pain."

"Marvellous! Edward and I have got everything fixed up."

"So I see. Let's have a look at it." Caroline held out her hand, and Cyril Brookes-Smith peered closely at her ring, turning it on her finger so that it caught the light. "Very good," he said to Edward. "Must have cost a shilling or two."

"Worth every penny, sir!"

"Anyway, jolly well done. Congratulations." He extended a hand, and Edward shook it warmly.

"Richard Stewart would like to get in touch with you about Saxon Court as soon as possible," Edward told his future father-in-law. "He's spending the weekend at his flat in London if you'd like to ring him."

"I'll do that. But tell me all about it first."

Caroline and Edward drew up chairs to sit on either side of him, and Edward was quite content to let Caroline do most of the talking. Her account of the past twenty-four hours was concise but graphic, and contained every vital detail. "*You* proposed marriage?" her father asked at the appropriate time, looking as though he did not believe her.

"Oh yes. It was the only way, otherwise we'd have been messing about for ages."

Still unsure, Brookes-Smith looked at Edward and received a nod.

"Well if this doesn't beat everything," he said. "I've always known you had a mind of your own, my dear, but this . . ."

"How else was I to stay at Saxon Court?" Caroline asked, apparently seriously; her father relaxed as he intercepted the wink she gave Edward. A few minutes later, Caroline went off in search of the doctor who was looking after her father, and Brookes-Smith seized the chance to talk to Edward alone.

"You will look after her, won't you?" he said so earnestly that it came close to desperation.

"Yes, I will."

"It's been difficult for her. I know she's been disappointed with the way things have gone at Saxon Court. And her mother dying – very sudden, awful shock. They were very close indeed."

"Don't worry, we're going to be very happy, and I think we might do something with the yard."

"That's the ticket! She'd love that."

Caroline was completely satisfied with whatever the doctor told her, making a point of repeating his instructions to her father so that he had no excuse for not knowing what was expected of him. "So that's how things are," she concluded. "With these pills, the right diet and plenty of rest, you're going to be good for a long time. Now let's go and ring Sir Richard."

Cyril Brookes-Smith and Richard had a long chat during which it was agreed that the sale of Saxon Court would be finalised within days. At the end, however, Caroline saw her father's relief at having his problems resolved turn towards despondency.

"What's wrong?" she asked.

"Just dawned on me. I'll have to look for somewhere to live. Imagine that – got this far and haven't given it a thought."

Caroline glanced at Edward, who responded at once. "There's going to be absolutely no pressure for you to leave Saxon Court," he said. "In fact, to be honest, it would be to my advantage if you stayed for a while. The next few months are going to be murder, and you could probably help out."

"Really?"

"Yes. I've no idea yet how we're going to handle the move, but I imagine that I shall be running things down at Avoca House while Caroline looks after this end. Does that sound about right, darling?" His first ever use of the word came effortlessly, and she nodded. "We shall need all the help we can get, and you'll be able to contribute just by *being* here, so do as the doctor says. Look after yourself and don't worry about a thing."

When they left him, Cyril Brookes-Smith was very happy.

"Any idea what he'll do?" Edward asked Caroline as he drove them back to Saxon Court.

"Yes. Torquay."

"Are you going to tell me any more?" he asked after a long pause during which she did her best to look obtuse.

"No. All very confidential. I imagine the poor dear thinks I don't know. Worry not! All will be revealed."

When they reached Saxon Court, there was a man at work in the garden of the first house.

"That's Bill Morris," Caroline said. "Come and meet him."

Bill Morris had enjoyed almost every minute of his life with horses, had thrived on hard work, and looked much younger than his sixty-five years. He was respectful, but as they shook hands, Edward felt himself being assessed by very shrewd eyes, and realised that Bill Morris and Caroline had been close allies in trying to do something with Saxon Court. There was convincing proof of this in Bill's reaction to Caroline's account of what had been decided while he had been away in Devon. His relief and pleasure that Saxon Court was passing into good hands, and that Caroline had found the perfect solution to her difficulties was plain to see.

"And how did you get on with the cottage?" Caroline asked.

"Oh, all right."

Caroline pounced on his obvious unease. "What's wrong?" she demanded.

"Well, it's all signed and sealed, but it's going to be a long time before we can move in. The old lady who's sold it to us is having trouble with her new place and we didn't like to make a fuss about it."

"How long?" Caroline asked.

"Anything up to three months," Bill Morris replied unhappily. Caroline looked at Edward.

"That's a tremendous piece of luck for me," he said. "You can stay here until your place is available. In fact I'll pay you to do it."

"Is that a fact, sir?" Bill Morris began to look more cheerful.

"It is! You can help Miss Brookes-Smith keep an eye on things when I start bringing horses in here."

"That would be a great help, sir. May was getting very worried about it – well, we both were. We thought we'd have to find digs."

"Of course you won't. All I need to do is have your house decorated for my head lad."

"We can camp out in one of the others while you do that."

"We'll see. There's certainly no need for you to worry about it. Now, will you be around tomorrow?"

"Yes sir. I'm going to start getting the garden right."

"I'd like you to keep an eye on the place. Miss Brookes-Smith and I shall be away for most of the day."

"I'll do that, sir."

Caroline looked questioningly at Edward, but said nothing. He explained later over a meal, this time in the Fortescue Arms itself, where Edward was warmly welcomed by the proprietor and his wife as Caroline made the introductions. "We're going to see my mother and father," he said. "My mother has waited a long time for you."

As soon as he saw the weather the following morning and heard the forecast, Edward felt certain that there was no need to telephone a warning to his parents. Like Bill Morris, his mother would be working in the garden in such glorious weather, and even if he had avoided being dragooned into helping, his father would not be far away. Armed with the element of surprise, Caroline and Edward left Saxon Court before nine o'clock, with Caroline gleefully aware of the secondary purpose of the visit. After an effortless seventy miles over deserted roads, they arrived to find Ann and Frank in the front garden. Frank was still drinking his habitual post-breakfast cup of coffee, and looking rather worried at what Ann was proposing for a rockery. The expressions on their faces were ample rewards for Edward's prank; surprise at his unannounced arrival was replaced by mystification when they saw that he was accompanied by an attractive stranger. Finally, as she got out of the car, and they were able to see exactly how attractive she was, they looked stupefied.

Edward grasped the opportunity of his mother's speechlessness, and sailed in. "Hello, you two. I'm over to have another look at Saxon Court, so I thought I'd come and see you while I was so close. And I can give you the news in person."

"News?" his mother echoed, unable to take her eyes off Caroline, and getting perilously close to rudeness in the process.

"Yes. This is Caroline. She's the daughter of Cyril Brookes-Smith who owns Saxon Court. I've decided to go ahead with the stable and Richard is buying it."

"Oh, good," Ann said. "Very nice to meet you, Caroline."

Edward delivered his *coup de grâce* while his mother was shaking hands with Caroline. "We're getting married."

They laughed about it a good deal afterwards. At the time, it took Ann nearly ten minutes to come to terms with Edward's sensational surprise, while Frank fidgeted nervously and made surreptitious attempts to smarten himself up. Ann's ecstatic admiration of Caroline's engagement ring was cut short by Edward who wanted a cup of coffee. As they all walked round to the back of the house, Frank dawdled with Edward so that Ann and Caroline drew well ahead of them. Finally Frank stopped altogether and gave his verdict. "She's gorgeous," he said. "In fact, she's a proper humdinger!"

161

"Where the devil did you learn language like that?" Edward laughed.

"You'd be amazed! Wherever did you find the courage? Out of a bottle?"

"No, there was no need to. She decided that we ought to get married and told me all about it. Quite simple really."

"When was this?"

"The other evening – Thursday – no, Friday." The hectic events of the last few days were starting to have a disorientating effect on Edward.

"Well I'm damned." Frank stared at him in disbelief. "I'll say one thing – it's shut your mother up."

"But not for long, I'll bet."

Edward insisted on taking them to an hotel for lunch, and by the time they were seated at the table, Ann had regained all her faculties and speech. She bombarded Caroline and Edward with a constant stream of questions, allowing no time for answers. When was Edward going to move from Avoca House to Saxon Court? She assumed that it would be no more complicated than moving house, would be all over in a day or two and made suggestions as to the best way to go about it. And what about the wedding? When and where was it to be? She was horrified to discover that they had yet to think about this vital problem.

"I suppose it will have to be towards the end of the season," Edward said. "We shan't have time before then."

"That sounds about right," Caroline agreed.

"So when might it be?" Ann asked.

"Mid-October," Edward suggested. "We should be straight by then."

"That's a long time," Ann complained. She gave the impression that she wanted to see it happen within the next few days.

"It isn't all that long, mother," Edward told her. "You'll need that length of time to find something decent to wear."

Appalled at the thought, Frank nodded gloomily.

On the way back to Saxon Court, Caroline and Edward talked and laughed a great deal about Ann. "Say what you like, I think she's very sweet," was Caroline's final verdict. "And she is very happy about it all."

"More relieved, I'd say," Edward replied. "I have been a sore trial to her."

"I'm quite glad about that."

"Oh, why?"

"What would have become of me if you'd married someone else? It seems that Eileen Wilcox was the odds-on favourite for a long time."

Edward laughed. "God! Did you get the story about that? That was nearly ten years ago. Anyway, you only want me for one thing."

"What's that?"

"Saxon Court, of course."

"Of course!"

They exchanged a look indicating that there were even more important things at stake.

The Compton Norris builder arrived at eight o'clock on Monday morning, and Edward saw at once that his requirements would be in good hands. George Roberts conveyed assured professionalism and a deep concern for the rightness of things simply by standing at the office door, raising a forefinger to the brim of his dusty old trilby hat and saying, "Good morning, sir."

They went to the lads' hostel first, deserted now that Bill Morris had the small staff working with an enthusiasm that the yard had not known for several years. When they went upstairs, George Roberts solved the problem of the two antiquated dormitories at a stroke.

"There's too much space," he announced. "Place looks like a barn. Mind you, that's a good thing. Means we got plenty of scope for anything you like."

"Could we turn it into individual rooms?" Edward asked.

"How many do you want?"

"Forty." Edward plucked a figure out of the air as the number of male staff he would eventually need at full strength.

"No. That wouldn't work. It's the windows is your problem. Not enough to go round, and we don't want to start knocking the outside about. Spoil things, that would. And we might want some more of them bricks." He chuckled at the thought of the folklore surrounding his grandfather's search on behalf of Joshua Fielding. "No, with what we got here, I can do you twenty very nice twin rooms. They'd be about eighteen foot by eight with a corridor down the middle." He demonstrated what he meant by walking around and waving his pencil. It was surprisingly lucid.

"That sounds about right," Edward said. "What about these awful bathrooms?"

"Rip 'em out! You see – you've got the same thing here, all this space wasted. We can increase the facilities and make it nicer – more private. I like a good bit of privacy for the ablutions."

Downstairs, there was no need to be quite so severe. With the exception of the kitchen, things could be left as they were, provided that complete redecoration was carried out. But George Roberts was damning about the kitchen. "Oh no! You can't have this," he said. "Won't do at all!"

"No?"

"Oh no. You'd never get a certificate for this lot. Best have it all out and start again. You need some proper tackle in here – sinks, waste-disposal, work-surfaces, ceramic hobs. Just look at that cooker. That'll be the one my granddad put in for Mr Fielding."

Edward doubted that it was quite that old, but agreed with the idea.

"Now then, Miss Caroline said you wanted them cottages fixing," George Roberts said when he had finished writing in his notebook.

As they approached the clock-tower on the way down to the avenue, George Roberts gave it a withering look, reminding Edward of what was, in many ways, the highest priority job.

"I want that sorted," he said.

"Not before time," George Roberts growled, and set to work on his notebook again. Edward noted that he had a rare talent: while walking, and with the notebook held at an awkward angle, George Roberts was producing flowing copperplate writing with a pencil that showed no inclination to go blunt. "I'll have to get an expert in to look at the apparatus and the gilt," he said.

"Do you know one?"

"Oh yes! Ernie Blagrave down Devizes way – he's the boy for paraphernalia like that."

Edward had to suppress a smile. Although his Berkshire accent was as mellow as his grandfather's brickwork, George Roberts was starting to sound awfully like Paddy Dooley.

Edward was dismayed to discover that the run-down exterior of the cottages flattered them. Inside, ceilings were sagging, plaster had fallen from walls to reveal bricks and laths, and woodwork was disintegrating with what appeared to be every known form of rot. However, George Roberts did not hold with crisis, and carried out his inspection quite calmly, with no more than an occasional grunt as comment.

"Well, I'll tell you what," he said at last. "'Tis a straightforward enough job. There's no piddling about with this lot, and that's for sure. We'll just gut it and start again."

"But will it be all right?"

"Don't you fear! You see, the walls and roofs are sound. Hardly want touching. They was built right." He winked and smiled, to himself rather than Edward.

Back in the house, Edward and George Roberts sat at the kitchen table while Caroline, just in from the yard, made coffee.

"I want this work done," Edward said. "I want it done well, and I must have it done pretty quickly, George. I'd like this place all fettled up by the end of August."

George Roberts nodded. "I can put men on it today," he said. "Unless you want to bother with estimates and screeds of paper."

164

"I don't think so. It isn't necessary, is it?"

"Not for me! Pain in the backside – begging your pardon, miss. Some folks like it. But I'll see you right without it – and I won't rob you."

"I believe that."

They shook hands. Caroline began to explain something that she wanted doing in the house, and once more, the notebook was in action. While searching through a document case for his English cheque-book, Edward learned that he and Caroline were going to use her bedroom at the front of the house after they were married, and that an adjoining smaller room was to be converted into an *en suite* bathroom. As Caroline sketched in the details of what she wanted, Edward wrote a cheque for ten thousand pounds which he passed to George Roberts. "Let me know when you need some more," he said.

When Edward left on Tuesday morning to return to Ireland, he and Caroline were surprised to find how unhappy they were at separating, even for what was expected to be a short time. Assuming that her father's progress towards better health continued, Caroline was to pay her first visit to Avoca House on Friday, only three days later. Nevertheless, their parting was prolonged and emotional, and the final stages by the car were watched by Alison Bairstow, who, in a state of mind made up of excitement and apprehension, was going with Edward. Caroline had agreed whole-heartedly with his suggestion that one of the Saxon Court lads should spend some time at Avoca House to get to know the staff and their working methods, and Alison had been quick to step forward when a volunteer was called for. At first, Alison sat still and quiet beside Edward as he drove towards London Airport, but she soon felt compelled to say something about his depression.

"Cheer up, sir. It'll soon be Friday."

He smiled self-consciously. "Is it that obvious?" he asked.

"Afraid so! But it's nice, and we're all very happy about it. I mean it's good having a job after all the worry and uncertainty, but everybody's ever so pleased about you and Miss Brookes-Smith."

Encouraged by Edward, Alison chatted freely from then on until Siobhan met them at Dublin. Then she shut up, determined to listen, look and learn. Calmly and systematically, Siobhan gave a concise account of the commotion that the news about Saxon Court had caused, how much everyone was looking forward to it, and how Dooley had already worked out the most incredibly complex way of moving the horses. "Of course, Dooley's delighted after Saturday," she said, "so there's no holding him."

"What about Saturday?" Edward asked, suddenly fearing that Dooley's information service had told him about Caroline's engagement ring.

"Sybil won, of course."

"Good Lord, did she? I'd completely forgotten she was going."

"You were busy," Siobhan said. She was doing her best to be sympathetic, but Edward detected that she did not approve of his lapse.

"I hadn't expected her to do that well," he said.

"No one did. She started at twelve to one."

"Hence Dooley's delight?"

"That's right."

Declan and Mary were all agog for news, but rather than tell them the sort of things they were expecting to hear, Edward thought it was time to take Caroline off the secret list. Still uneasy about the Finoula débâcle, he was gratified to find that the news was extremely well received.

"What's she like?" Mary asked.

"Er ... very nice," Edward replied, completely unbalanced by the question. "She's coming over on Friday, so you'll be able to see for yourself."

"Actually, she's wonderful," Alison said, deciding it was time she made a contribution. "She's very attractive, she's a wonderful person and she knows all about horses."

Mary immediately decided that it was time to take Alison away to settle her into Finoula's old room which was to be her home for the duration of her stay. While Mary was fact-finding on Caroline, Edward, Declan and Siobhan set about making a policy for moving to Saxon Court.

"Everybody wants to come – if you'll have them," Declan said.

"Of course I will. You did say *everybody*?"

"Yes."

"Including Dooley?"

"*Especially* Dooley," Siobhan said, smiling.

"Oh dear!"

"Why, don't you want him to?"

"Oh yes. It's just that I'm worried that he should be so keen. It makes me wonder what he knows."

"It's easy," Declan said. "He reckons you'll have to buy a decent van for a place like that."

"And he must have a garden," Siobhan added.

"He's well in there," Edward said. "The big house has a huge garden and lawns for him to look after, and the cottages all have decent-sized plots."

Edward told them all that had happened, including the renovations that George Roberts was doing. He gave Siobhan the names of the two lads and ten girls so that they could have a formal letter offering them a job, and explained to Declan the part that Bill Morris could play until

166

he and his wife were able to move into their cottage in Devon. Then they started to think about a possible timetable.

"I think we might send a few horses out of Saxon Court this season," Edward said. "Let's start with Royal Ascot. We're going to be taking horses and staff over, and we may as well leave them there afterwards. So what's that? About six weeks, isn't it?"

"Royal Ascot starts six weeks today," Siobhan confirmed after a look at her wall-chart.

"That sounds about right. Now I suggest that you and Mary ought to come over with us, Declan." When he saw the look on Declan's face, Edward hastened to explain. "It's all right, I don't want you to go to the races, but you'll need to have a look at your new home." Declan relaxed. His aversion to going anywhere near a racecourse was legendary. According to rumour, he had done it under protest in the early days with James Henry, but like most head lads, he preferred to be at home with his horses. Since Musetta's One Thousand Guineas victory, he had apparently become more amenable to watching racing on TV.

Totally engrossed, they talked until Siobhan reminded them that it was time for evening stables. Edward got up eagerly, anxious for the routine he had missed since before Leonora's visit to Newmarket which now seemed years ago instead of last week. Siobhan had to run after him with a piece of news she had forgotten in all the excitement.

"There was a message," she said, trotting to keep up with Edward. "Yesterday. From Belfields. It's Musetta. She's confirmed in foal to Mill Reef."

Edward stopped dead and beamed at her. "That's great!" he said. "Absolutely marvellous. What about that, Declan?"

"It's very good."

Edward's eye was always at its keenest as he surveyed the yard before evening stables, and he spotted Alison Bairstow immediately, even though she was inside one of the boxes and partially hidden by the horse. Pleased that she was involved so quickly, he saw that she was with Robin Lane and engaged in animated debate.

"Ah – you two have met," he said when he reached the box. "Will you see that Alison gets to know everything, Robin?"

"Yes, sir."

"And this is Mr Kelly, Alison. He's my head lad. He will be taking over from Mr Morris at Saxon Court." Declan made sure that Alison, who was obviously getting on very well with the guv'nor, found him totally forbidding.

Until it was time to go and meet Caroline on Friday, Edward prayed that Imogen would not telephone him, or, worse still, descend on Avoca

House. His prayers were answered. Richard rang several times, finally to confirm that he now owned Saxon Court, but of Imogen there was mercifully neither sight nor word.

He introduced Caroline to Avoca House with considerable diffidence, worried about what she would think of it, and fretful to know what everyone thought of her. Very soon after she arrived, he felt ashamed of his faint-heartedness. Caroline said that the yard looked splendid, and within minutes, people were queueing up to meet her.

As ever, Mary was uninhibited. "Oh, but you're beautiful," she told Caroline, "absolutely beautiful." Mary stood back a little, as though admiring a picture. "Whatever has he done to deserve you?"

Caroline laughed. "Thank you very much, Mary. You're very kind."

There was great disappointment in the yard when Caroline did not make an appearance at evening stables, but she was out first thing the following morning. Wearing a pair of maroon riding breeches that were tailored to fit extremely well, she was the focus of attention. Later, Edward came to suspect that this was probably the occasion when Liam Corrigan first pronounced that, "The guv'nor's lady is a fine-looking woman to be sure!"

Caroline and Liam fell into conversation, and Edward approached them to be greeted with one of her most dazzling smiles.

"I was wondering if I could ride something for you," she said. "Liam has suggested Murgatroyd."

"Fine. Let's see how good you are."

As Edward gave her a leg up, he noticed that Murgatroyd seemed conscious of the honour being bestowed on him.

Among the first lot, Alison Bairstow was riding Radames. Edward commented on it to Declan as they moved to the centre of the cantering circuit on their hacks.

"Robin Lane's idea," Declan said. "He's got a theory."

Edward laughed. "That horse has been the subject of more theories than I've had hot dinners," he said, but he was very pleased that Declan was paying Robin the respect of listening to him.

Caroline and Murgatroyd were elegantly balanced as they went three times round the track at a good pace.

"Your lady can ride, sor," Declan declared.

"And look at Alison," Edward said. "You can see who taught her to ride – although she's nowhere near as good. Do you think Radames looks more settled? He strikes me as being a bit less flashy."

"We'll see," Declan said. "They're going to work him over a mile now."

"T. P. Malahide looks very good," Edward said afterwards. "We'll run him at Ascot, I think. And Radames looks much more like a racehorse. We might have to start taking notice of some of these theories, Declan."

They found Richard in the yard when they got back. He broke away from Siobhan and Mary, and walked over to meet them, reaching up to shake hands with Caroline. "He's put you to work already then?" he joked.

"Yes, I'm nothing but a skivvy."

"And that's your girl Alison on my useless article?"

"It is. He's just worked very well, as a matter of fact."

"Very good. By the way, I was speaking to your father yesterday evening, and it's all finalised now. The money will be transferred to him on Monday."

"That will be a tremendous weight off his mind."

"Will you come to dinner this evening?" Richard asked Edward who had dismounted and joined them. "We're going to celebrate Saxon Court and your betrothal." He used the 'Imogen word' with a grandiose flourish. "By the way, Caroline, are you sure you know what you're doing? It isn't too late."

"Yes!" she said with total assurance.

"So there!" Edward said, looking happier than Richard had ever seen him. "Usual time this evening?"

"Yes. Valerie Malahide's coming too. She's every bit as bad as Imogen and my mother," Richard said to Caroline. "She's dying to meet you and find out all about it."

Caroline had complied with Edward's suggestion that she should bring 'some posh clothes' with her. That evening, he stood in the hall of Avoca House and gazed up the stairs in wonder as she came down. She wore a white blouse with lace cuffs and bodice adorned with a beautiful cameo that had belonged to her mother, and a long, flowing skirt of royal blue silk, matched by the bow to hold her hair at the nape of her neck. She had added the merest touch of cosmetic colour to her cheeks, serving to enhance the startling beauty of her bone structure.

"You look smashing," he told her.

"Thank you, kind sir. You don't look so bad yourself now you've got some decent clothes on."

"This is nothing. You should see me when I'm dolled up for Ascot."

"I will," she reminded him. "Quite soon."

Caroline never appreciated it, but they were late arriving at Belfields as a result of deliberate engineering by Edward. Richard, looking at his watch every thirty seconds, was waiting at the door for them. When she saw the entrance hall at Belfields, Caroline took Edward's hand for moral support and tilted her chin up. As they crossed the threshold, Imogen and Valerie Malahide emerged from a side room at the other end of the hall. Even at sixty feet, the sight of Caroline and Edward stopped them dead in their tracks.

"Blimey!" Imogen whispered.

"Now *that* is a nice couple," Valerie Malahide said quietly. "A very nice couple indeed."

CHAPTER 8

After his engagement to Caroline, Edward did not visit Saxon Court again until he went with the advance party for Ascot on the Saturday before the meeting. He spoke to Caroline on the telephone at least once a day, and soon reached the stage of being sceptical of her reports on the progress of the renovations. Deciding that it was going well, but not nearly as well as Caroline was saying, he concentrated on preparing horses and working with Declan and Siobhan to plan the move. However, when Dooley nursed the big van into the drive for the first time, Edward saw that the clock, with numerals and hands gleaming, was telling the right time. Later, he discovered that the lads' hostel was nearly finished, and the avenue cottages had been gutted, the carpenters had done their work and that they were ready for internal plastering.

The only disappointment was the absence of Murgatroyd. Edward had wanted him to make a third assault on the Royal Hunt Cup, but he had picked up a foot infection three weeks previously. Although it was now cured, two weeks of vital work had been missed. Despite Sean Gillespie's insistence that Murgatroyd was capable of taking his chance, the fiasco of Leonora and the One Thousand Guineas had scarred Edward, and Murgatroyd stayed at home. Leonora, now fully prepared, was first out of the van. Then came T. P. Malahide and Radames. There was no doubt that Edward's favourite idiot was fit and well; it remained to be seen whether Robin Lane and Alison were right about his vastly improved mentality. The three horses were taken into the Old Yard where they joined the only two that remained and were staying.

"I suppose we have to start somewhere," Edward said to Caroline. As they looked at the five horses, seemingly lost in the huge spaces of Ollie Derwent's splendid structure, Edward was doing his best not to think of the sixty empty boxes in the New Yard.

"Isn't it awful," Caroline said, mocking his apprehension. "You've done the wrong thing, and we're all going to be murdered in our beds! Come on, let's try and make the best of a bad job."

Edward and Dooley had been accompanied by Siobhan, Alison Bairstow and Robin Lane. While Alison took Robin to the hostel, and then for a full tour, Siobhan simply stood, gazing at her surroundings with joyous amazement.

"Oh yes," she said, when Edward asked her, "this is beautiful. It's really pretty. Father's going to like it!"

Edward realised that she had put a finger on a very important feature; especially now that midsummer had arrived, Saxon Court was indeed very *pretty*.

That evening Edward set about imprinting his style on the place. With the exception of Caroline's father, who was dining with friends in Compton Norris, everyone had their evening meal in the newly-decorated dining room of the lads' hostel. There was a party atmosphere. Dooley, told by Edward not to disappear on pain of death, did his best to appear his usual uneasy, slightly miserable self. He had come to the conclusion that Saxon Court was going to be all right; he liked the look of the place, and had been much taken with the avenue cottage that was going to be his. The large garden was ideal for his twin passions of lupins and brussels sprouts, but it was the news about the horse van that made his conversion complete. Bill Morris had met the flying horse box at Gatwick with the most magnificent specimen that Dooley had yet seen, its facilities including a bed, TV and shower. Mysteriously, it appeared to be absolutely new, and Edward looked pleased with himself when the fact was mentioned.

"That's because it *is* new, Paddy," he said. "It's ours. We bought it the other day."

Siobhan confirmed that Dooley had never looked so happy.

Bill Morris's wife, May, and one of the girls were operating in the splendid new kitchen, and they produced a meal fit for a king.

At the other end of the table, Alison Bairstow was telling a group of Saxon Court girls what she had learned during her six weeks at Avoca House. As the conversation between Caroline, Bill Morris and himself suddenly dried up, Edward heard Alison's final summary.

"The most important thing with the guv'nor is *horses*," she said. "He really cares about them. Every one is an individual to him. If your horse isn't right, you tell him – at once. It doesn't matter how small the problem is, tell him. You'll never go wrong doing that, but he'll have your guts if you don't."

Caroline and Edward exchanged a look.

The following day, Sunday, Dooley set off with 'his' van to make another collection from the flying horse box. Mary, all dressed up and excited was first off the aircraft, whereas Declan was determined to take everything in his stride; he expected to be working and was dressed accordingly. His main concern was that there was neither a Manning nor a Kelly at Avoca House for the first time in thirty years. Liam Corrigan was looking after the yard, while Imogen had insisted on showing what she could do with the office. The passenger list was completed by Cathal O'Brien and another lad, Michael Doyle, who had come to familiarise themselves with Saxon Court as part of Edward's 'cross fertilisation' programme. He had used the phrase only half-seriously, and had soon resigned himself to the fact that it was a rich source of merriment.

Declan found it very difficult indeed to maintain his poker face when he saw Saxon Court. As Mary plunged into domestic sightseeing, Edward took him down to the yard. The clock-tower registered, and Declan saw the point of Edward's incessant eulogies. His face started to crack as they entered the courtyard surrounded by arches. After a brief look at the deserted New Yard, he walked into the Old Yard, scrutinised it carefully and smiled.

"Well?" Edward was torn between anxiety and impatience. "What do you think?"

"It's very good, sor. Very good indeed."

"Do you suppose you can do something with it?"

"*We* will!" Before leaving the yard, he took another look round. "Oh yes, we'll do something with this," he said, and there was a triumphant gleam in his eye.

"Tell me something, Declan," Edward said as they walked back under the clock-tower. "Have you always wanted a place like this?"

"Yes, sor, I have. This is what I call a proper yard."

Declan wanted to ride out and inspect the gallops, but Mary insisted that he looked at what was going to be their house. Built in 1920 in the aftermath of the Great War, the house had a spaciousness and style that was redolent of the assertive optimism of Saxon Court under Joshua Fielding rather than the jittery introspection of the era. For Mary, the four bedrooms and splendidly equipped kitchen were the outstanding features, and she had a very great deal to say about the spotless condition of the walls and paintwork, while Bill and May Morris looked on, embarrassed but pleased.

"You needn't bother with this," Mary informed Edward. "We can move straight in when Bill and May have got fixed up. Dooley can give it a lick of paint."

Edward never ceased to be amazed at the multifarious range of jobs that Mary and Siobhan could persuade Dooley to undertake. He grumbled, and never seemed to do anything, but the results were always highly professional.

On Monday, Sean Gillespie arrived, and Edward drove to Heathrow Airport to collect Valerie Malahide. Sean Gillespie inspected Saxon Court like a cat prospecting a new home, and seemed to find it to his liking, especially after he had taken one of the hacks and ridden over the gallops. Edward was careful to leave him to his own devices; he wanted Sean to be stable jockey, and had it in mind to help him buy a house in the area, but thought it best to let him make his own decision. Dooley, already very comfortable in one of the new rooms in the lads' hostel, settled Sean in as his next-door neighbour, and charmed the girl who was acting as cook into looking after his special diet.

Valerie Malahide's excitement over Saxon Court calmed down only when Edward mentioned Caroline. "She's absolutely marvellous – just right for you," she said, and her intense seriousness made the point very forcibly. "Everyone's so happy for you. Imogen can't stop talking about her."

"Really?" Edward was surprised.

"Oh yes. It took her a bit of a time to get over the shock – you know, the night you came to dinner. Now, she always calls her 'the veritable cat's whisker' or 'her gorgeous highness'."

Edward laughed at Valerie's reasonably successful attempt to imitate Imogen.

For Caroline and Edward, the first day of Royal Ascot meant Radames and his involvement in the Prince of Wales Stakes. Edward discovered that Alison Bairstow was to go with the horse and lead him round the parade ring, and that for some obscure reason, Robin Lane had to accompany them. No sooner were they on the course and surveying the scene in the paddock before the arrival of the Royal Party than Bernard Dalrymple approached them.

"Many congratulations, Mr Manning," he said. "Saxon Court *and* the fair Caroline. Well done!"

"Thank you, Mr Dalrymple." Edward looked suitably grave as they shook hands.

"My best wishes for your future." Bernard Dalrymple paused to look more closely at Caroline. "You look quite superb, my dear," he announced.

She did. Wearing a simple white dress trimmed with pink and with a matching hat of classic style and proportions, she looked a picture.

"Gosh!" Caroline said in mock awe after Bernard Dalrymple had passed on his way. "Fancy him knowing that I exist! Whatever next?"

"Aha! You're moving in exalted circles now, darling," Edward told her. "Well now, look at that!"

Following his gaze, Caroline spotted her father with a rather chic lady on his arm. A casual observer would never have guessed that she was nearing her fiftieth birthday.

"Torquay," Caroline said.

"Eh?"

"Mrs Elspeth Cheshire. A very dear friend of mother's. She was widowed just before mother died."

"And she lives at Torquay?"

"Correct!"

"I see."

"Don't jump to conclusions!"

Caroline took Edward towards them to introduce him to Elspeth Cheshire.

At about four o'clock, Saxon Court was almost quiet on a brilliantly sunny afternoon. The only sound was that of a TV from an open window of the lads' hostel. Declan and Bill Morris were walking slowly back from the yard. As they approached the hostel, the TV commentary of a race was drowned by an increasing buzz from the watchers, and a girl shouted, "He's going to win it! He is. Look at him!" There was a burst of near-hysterical speech from the TV, then pandemonium erupted in the hostel. Amidst shouting, cheering and screaming, it sounded as though someone was jumping up and down on a table. To Declan's astonishment, Mary flung another window open and waved at him.

"Radames has won!" she called.

As a general rule, neither Declan nor Bill Morris ever ran anywhere. They did now, arriving in the TV room in time to see the replay. Sean Gillespie had Radames well placed all through the final two furlongs, and this time, the colt was living up to his full potential, travelling extremely fast and concentrating hard on the job in hand. With fifty yards to go, Sean hurled one of his increasingly famous back-stabbing challenges into the fray, and Radames won it by a neck.

They watched Richard lead his horse in. He was looking very pleased with himself, and Edward could not conceal his delighted disbelief. Richard was speaking to Alison, and it was possible to lip-read the word 'theory' before they both burst out laughing. Declan and Bill Morris had decided that there was nothing else to see, and were on their way out when someone called out, "Look! They're going to interview the guv'nor and Miss Caroline."

Wesley Davies, who had been fostering an image of himself as the doyen of racing observers for years, had rounded up Caroline and Edward.

"Congratulations, Edward," he began, as though they were old friends. "I understand Radames has been spending a few days at your new place, Saxon Court."

"Yes, we brought him over on Saturday."

"He certainly seems to like it here. He's never shown much form before this, has he?"

"No, he's been quite an awkward customer. I was thinking of entering him for a village idiot competition last year, but he's come on quite a bit over the winter. One of my lads at Avoca House has done a good deal with him, and there's a girl at Saxon Court who seems to have done him some good. She insisted on coming with him today, and I'm glad I didn't argue."

"A good omen?"

"I hope so."

"When will you be fully operational at Saxon Court?"

"September, I hope."

"And you're getting married to Caroline as well?"

The remainder of the interview was watched in rapt silence by those in the TV room. Ann Manning in Worcestershire, and Imogen, starting to organise the move from Belfields, were both amazed by the natural ease with which Edward handled his first interview for TV.

The return of Radames to Saxon Court that evening produced astonishing scenes: Edward had to remind himself that less than twenty people made up the reception committee, not twenty thousand as it seemed at first. Although he had only just arrived, Radames was now a Saxon Court horse, and he had gone out to win a Group race. Moreover, as the new guv'nor had been quick to point out, it was more than likely that Alison Bairstow had played a significant part in the first major victory that the stable had seen for a very long time. Certainly Richard thought so, for he had given Alison a hundred pounds in notes on the spot. It had to be a portent of much better times to come.

Radames had put Saxon Court back on the map, and the following day Leonora turned the spotlight on it when she won the Coronation Stakes. Contrary to the advice of both Caroline and Sean Gillespie, Edward had kept the filly to a mile and was rewarded with a handsome three-lengths victory. On Thursday, however, T. P. Malahide failed miserably in the King George V Stakes, and Edward needed no telling that he had got the distance wrong in this case. At ten furlongs the colt was going well, but a mile and a half was too far for him. Edward, who would cheerfully have sacrificed the victories of Radames and Leonora for the sake of giving Valerie Malahide a good winner, was very disappointed.

"Two out of three isn't bad," Richard said.

"Especially when they're *your* two," Edward replied, not at all certain that he wanted to be cheered up.

"Look at it this way," Valerie Malahide said. "It won't be all that long before you're bringing a dozen runners to this meeting. If you maintain this success rate, we'll all be happy."

Before returning to Ireland, Edward spent a day at Saxon Court planning the future. During the morning he was with Siobhan, deciding how the office would be set up and function, then, with Declan and Bill Morris, he discussed the working of the yard. As they did so, Edward was conscious of the lads and girls, all going about their work busily, but watching his every move and gesture. They were expecting miracles, and the realisation of this gave him his first real sensation of responsibility for his new stable. Around midday, Cyril Brookes-Smith and Elspeth Cheshire passed through to have a quick look; although mildly interested in horses, Mrs Cheshire was intimidated by them. She and Brookes-Smith clearly had other things on their minds, they disappeared as quickly as they had come, and over lunch Caroline said they had driven down to spend a few days at Torquay.

The afternoon was devoted to George Roberts, an appraisal of the work done so far, and debate of what was to come.

"You've done us proud, George," Edward said. "We couldn't have managed this week without you."

"It helps to have the place decent," George agreed. "Mind you, 'tis handy to have some decent horses and a particle of aptitude. Leastways, that's what my granddad always said about old Joshua."

Alison Bairstow and Robin Lane stayed at Saxon Court when Edward and the others went back to Ireland. As soon as Edward reached Avoca House, he telephoned Caroline to tell her that he missed her badly and would be glad when it was all over and they were together.

That feeling grew stronger, reaching a peak at the end of June when Imogen and Richard left Belfields for good and moved to Widney Cheyne. Edward had a busy week's racing immediately before the move, but was kept informed of developments by Mary, who spent a great deal of time helping out at Belfields. Although the impression given by Mary was of total chaos, Edward was certain that Imogen knew exactly what was in each lorry and container, and that every member of the vast workforce deployed by the contractors had been told what was expected of him. When Imogen, Richard, their two sons and most of the staff finally left, Edward was acutely conscious of a void.

Throughout July, Dooley made two trips a week to Saxon Court. He went in the flying horse box with three horses and a lad, was met by Bill Morris with the van at Gatwick, and returned by a scheduled flight from London to Dublin the following day.

At the end of the month, with only fifteen horses left at Avoca House, Edward spent a long weekend at Saxon Court. He and Caroline visited Widney Cheyne to find an embattled Imogen, surrounded by tea chests, and camping out with the children in what was eventually going to be Richard's study. Richard himself was using the flat in London.

"The bloody decorators let us down," Imogen explained. "It's quite pointless trying to do anything with this lot until it's all been done."

"So what happens?" Caroline asked, surveying a vast expanse of anarchy with dismay.

"I've found some new chaps. They've promised to start on Monday, and they know what happens if they don't."

"What?" Edward asked.

"I have faithfully, and with total sincerity, promised to castrate each and every one of them with the bread knife," Imogen replied with tremendous enthusiasm.

"Why the bread knife?" Edward asked.

Imogen glared at him with impotent fury. "Because it's the only vaguely suitable implement I can find at the moment," she snarled.

Back at Saxon Court, Edward told Caroline that he now had a date from the Jockey Club from which his licence to train would be valid at his new yard. "We can start on September the first," he said. "Here are a list of race entries we've made. Those with the ticks are the ones I'm really keen on."

She smiled as she saw the first tick, right at the top of the list. T. P. Malahide was entered for a ten-furlong Group race at Newbury, their local course, on September the fifth. "You'd like me to start work on these?" she asked.

"Yes, please. Try Alison with T.P. He's ready to be brought on a bit. She might do the trick."

"Right. I see we've nothing after October the seventh."

"No. I'm not keen on racing much after that anyway, and we've got to get married some time."

"Oh, that reminds me! I shall be away for a couple of days next week. Bill Morris can cope."

Edward looked at her closely. "Let me guess," he said. "Torquay?"

"Right! And for sixty-four thousand dollars?"

"Your father and Mrs Cheshire are getting married?"

"Right again!"

"What happens then?"

"He stays there with her. Elspeth's got a very nice house which father likes and she doesn't want to leave."

By the middle of August, everyone but Edward, Declan, Mary, Liam and Kathleen Corrigan and Dooley had left Avoca House. Siobhan had been gone a week, already had the office at Saxon Court set up the way she wanted it, and was tidying up her future home. May Morris and all her furniture had gone down to the cottage of her dreams in Devon, and Bill Morris was using the second head lad's house while he fulfilled his promise to stay on until Declan arrived. There were only three horses left at Avoca House, and they were there for a very special reason. Sybil and Ocean Lady were keeping their friend Murgatroyd company, and on Saturday, August the fifteenth, he went to the Phoenix Park as Avoca House's last runner. Prepared to perfection, and looking ready for anything, he made light work of the race. Sean Gillespie let him get on with it his way, and he ran out the four-lengths winner of a good handicap.

They were much later than usual leaving the course. As well as James Henry's old cronies, Edward had made many friends of his own among the racing fraternity during his three seasons in Ireland, and most of them had turned up to say farewell and wish him luck. The gathering took over one of the racecourse bars where Edward drank his customary mineral water, and listened to increasingly fanciful speculation as to what might become of him in a renowned English stable. After a quart of the best stout had been sent to be mixed with Murgatroyd's post-race feed, and as the shadows began to lengthen, they went back to Avoca House for the last time. There was a good turn out of Dooley's fan club, the men who stood and waved. To Edward, they seemed to convey their sorrow at his departure and good wishes for the future in the eloquent, dignified manner that the Irish have at such times. He knew he would miss them.

The following day, Murgatroyd and his two companions went to Saxon Court, accompanied by Liam Corrigan and Dooley, and the business of packing up began. The same removal contractors who had taken Imogen and Richard from Belfields to Widney Cheyne were used, and they did very well, but it was still a sad, eerie business with no horses and so few people around the place. Most of the furniture in Avoca House was going into a disposal sale. All that Edward wanted was the old roll-top desk that James Henry had bought for two pounds from a Dublin junk shop the day after he arrived in Ireland. Mary and Declan were encouraged to select everything they liked to furnish their much larger new house, and the agent's man went round sticking labels on everything else.

They used the flying horse box to go; it was not all that much more expensive than the alternative, and it enabled them to take massive quantities of personal belongings with them rather than have them buried by the removal men for several days. Brendan O'Sullivan himself came to pick them up with a van, and made a diversion through Kildare so that Edward could leave the keys at the agent's office and sign a couple of documents. "That's it then," he said and lapsed into a tight-lipped silence. Not until they were airborne, and Mary took his hand, did he relax.

"You're not leaving the old man," she said. "You're going to do what he wanted."

As soon as he reached Saxon Court, Edward looked at the horses, saw they were all right, and set off with great purpose to organise himself rudimentary accommodation in one of Mary's spare bedrooms. Caroline was vastly amused, and decided to tackle him about it as they ate their meal that evening.

"You've done it for the sake of appearance," she said challengingly. His reaction surprised her.

"Of course I have! That sort of thing is very important."

"Why?"

"We have to set standards." Caroline had her mouth open to tell him not to be so priggish, but she was not permitted to interrupt. "Have you never thought what a most peculiar situation we live and work in?" he asked.

"No, I haven't. It's very pleasant."

"I agree – but it's also very dicey. We rely utterly on the integrity and loyalty of the staff. Just imagine the mayhem that one of the lads could cause in five minutes in that yard. I could lose my licence and our livelihood just like that." He snapped a thumb and index finger together. "Now we both think that we've got a very good bunch – and we have. But it's a lot easier for them to respect us if they see us doing the right thing."

Caroline saw that his conviction was rock-solid and respected it.

"I'll be in that bedroom of yours fast enough when the right time comes," he promised.

"You will indeed!" she replied and smiled.

Two weeks later, Dooley and Alison Bairstow took T. P. Malahide to Newbury in the splendid new van, while Caroline and Edward followed in a car. They had Valerie Malahide, who had obeyed what was virtually an order to come over from Dublin, with them. Edward was as excited and nervous as the day he had gone to Thurles with Murgatroyd, but this time there was no fear of the unknown. Both the distance and the course were precisely to the colt's liking, and after he was shaken up at the furlong distance, he went forward boldly, ears all over the place, and won much more convincingly than the official two-lengths verdict suggested.

"There y'are," Sean Gillespie said to Valerie in the winner's enclosure. "I told you he'd be all right!"

"He did too," Valerie said as he headed for the weighing room. "He rang me up the other evening and said I wasn't to worry."

"Good grief!" Edward stared after his jockey in disbelief. "He must be going soft in the head."

There were three more runners before Edward's early end to the season. Sybil came up at Salisbury and one of Valerie Malahide's two-year-olds won a nice race at Newmarket. The surprise was a horse that Edward had frankly forgotten. Caroline had made an entry for the Duke of Dorchester's flashy colt Hohenzollern at Bath, and after receiving the 'Radames treatment' from Alison Bairstow, helped this time by Cathal O'Brien, he duly won. "That horse is starting to look useful," Edward said to Caroline after they had watched the race.

"He'll be more than useful if he jogs His Grace's memory," Caroline replied.

Edward spent twelve or more hours each day in the yard or out on the gallops. He acted as though he were starting training all over again; every last detail was examined and changed if necessary after he had chewed it over with Murgatroyd. Some of the original Saxon Court staff found it difficult to adjust to the monologues that often issued from Murgatroyd's box, although they accepted that Edward was perfectly sound in the head. Caroline was often at his side, offering advice, pointing out things that he might have missed, but she was also deeply involved in planning their wedding on a date largely determined by Richard. He had arranged to visit his friends in Kentucky to buy yearlings for himself and Edwin Fforbes; there were to be three days on the stud farm, followed by a week of business in New York and Washington. When Caroline discovered that Imogen was accompanying Richard, she decided that a few days in Kentucky would be a splendid start to her honeymoon, and fixed the date of the wedding for the Saturday before Richard's planned departure to the USA. While Edward was conducting his microscopic examination of the yard, the cake was ordered, invitations sent out and the Fortescue Arms told to prepare for the largest function it had seen for a long time.

"That sounds marvellous," Edward said when Caroline decided it was time he was put in the picture. "What shall we do after Kentucky?"

"I haven't the faintest idea," Caroline replied. "Perhaps you'd like to organise that bit."

"You want a surprise?"

"That would be nice."

"We can go *anywhere*?"

"Anywhere you like – except the North Pole. I'd like some sun."

The organist of St Matthew and All Saints Church, Compton Norris, liked to do things with style, but seldom had the chance. Caroline's big day was a gift from the gods which he grasped eagerly. He had already enjoyed himself enormously during the preliminaries, and when the signal was given, he launched into 'Here Comes the Bride' with considerable bravura. Edward stood up, turned to Richard at his side for reassurance, and looked down the aisle. Cyril Brookes-Smith had every reason to look proud. Caroline was magnificent, and the golden October sun streaming through the large fourteenth-century windows to play on her veil and the flowers in her hair gave her a magical halo. The dress was of gleaming white silk with tulle facings on the bodice, the design simple and timelessly elegant. Behind Caroline and her father, her sixteen-year-old cousin was acting as bridesmaid, and following her were young Nicholas and Imogen's niece Clarissa Benbow. They were dressed in perfect replicas of early-nineteenth-century costume and came close to stealing the show several times during the ceremony and wedding breakfast.

Even as he signed the register in the vestry, Edward found that he could remember very little of the service, apart from the fact that Caroline's left hand had looked startlingly bare without her sapphire ring, and he was glad to see her transfer it to its rightful place from her right hand before they walked back down the aisle together. Passing through a crowded sea of smiling faces and good wishes, they came out into the sunshine, and the bells started ringing. They were astonished and touched to see that most of the villagers, about two hundred of them, were waiting outside, raising a cheer as they appeared.

"Saxon Court is very important to them," Caroline said softly as she waved.

"So I see," Edward replied. "We must do our best not to let them down."

The 'official' photographer got to work, but soon found that as well as the usual difficulties of weddings, he had to contend with Imogen, who brought two cameras into play, and had her own ideas as to how the groups should be formed and posed. Progress was slow, and not always sure. Caroline and Edward introduced some order to the confusion by insisting upon starting with young Nicholas and Clarissa Benbow. After that, it was parents, and Ann Manning was in her element. Her outfit, fully approved in advance by Edward, would have graced a Buckingham Palace garden party, she looked younger than ever and was ridiculously happy. Although Frank was just as pleased, he sometimes appeared to be in danger of letting her down; he was always uneasy at such large, festive gatherings, and allowed himself to be unnerved by insignificant things. Today, he was concerned that the slightly imperfect fit of his morning suit betrayed that unlike all the others, his was hired.

The photographer had decided that he had more or less finished when Liam Corrigan created a sensational diversion by bringing Murgatroyd up to the church yard gate. Edward had noticed Liam slipping out at the end of the service, and had thought he looked like a man with a mission. Among the buzz of interest and excitement from guests and villagers, Caroline and Edward walked to the gate, to greet the yard's elder statesman. He was turned out impeccably, as though he were going racing with his lucky rug, but was unsaddled.

"I wondered what you were up to, Liam," Edward said, as he rubbed his horse's nose.

"Well, it's like this, sor – you've to have a horseshoe for luck, and we thought you'd like four of them."

"We?"

"Dooley and me, sor. It was Dooley suggested that you'd appreciate it better if they was on the hoof."

"Thank you, Liam. It was very thoughtful of you." Edward kept a straight face, and turned to Caroline. "How would you like a ride across to the Fortescue, darling?"

"What a smashing idea!" she replied.

They achieved perfect synchronisation between Caroline's jump and Edward's lift. Without sacrificing an iota of grace, Caroline was perched quite comfortably and safely sideways on Murgatroyd's back. She smiled and waved at the acclaim of the onlookers, and, as cameras began to click furiously, Edward guided Murgatroyd across the road and over the green towards the Fortescue Arms. When she had finally run out of film, Imogen took a long, hard look at the scene.

"He won't lead in a better winner than that," she said to Mary. "Ever!"

It was several years since the Fortescue Arms had hosted such an important function, and deeply appreciative of Caroline's wish for a village celebration, management and staff provided a sumptuous wedding breakfast for the two hundred guests. The room was perfect, with french windows along two sides overlooking attractive gardens and woods bathed in the orange and golden tints of autumn. Throughout the meal, each and every guest occasionally broke off conversation with neighbours to glance towards the top table. They saw what Richard had observed in the kitchen of Saxon Court within minutes of Caroline and Edward first meeting. Whether they were talking to their immediate companions, exchanging shouted jokes with people at other tables, chatting to one another, or simply eating, they were *together*, belonging to each other.

Richard's speech as best man was a well-ordered masterpiece that blended the past with the present, and voiced the hopes of everyone there for the future. He ended with a roof-raiser. "I can reveal to you, that the honeymoon will commence on a stud farm." He blinked innocently at the cheerful uproar this created. "I don't know how long we shall have to wait for an outcome, but I'm certain there will be one, either in the winner's enclosure at Ascot, or another trip across the road for a christening." When the laughter had subsided, he raised his glass high. "Ladies and gentlemen, Caroline and Edward Manning!"

Before Edward performed his traditional duty of thanking everyone, he had a very important matter to get off his chest. "I want to say something about my wife. I doubt very much if any of us will ever see a more beautiful bride in such a lovely dress." There were murmurs of agreement and Caroline wrinkled her nose. "As some of you know, I have what I believe are regarded as peculiar views when it comes to ladies' fashions, but I couldn't have wished for a nicer dress. By the way, you might like to know that I'm turned out in my working clothes." He tugged at the lapel of his jacket. "This suit has been to Royal Ascot a few times. I know it's the bride who's supposed to have something old . . ."

During the subsequent laughter, Imogen clouted the table with a dessert spoon and said, "Hear, hear!" very loudly. What amazed Edward, was that she actually had the grace to look ever so slightly embarrassed about it.

After Caroline and Edward had spoken to all their guests individually, Richard gave them a lift back to Saxon Court in the new Rolls-Royce that Imogen had thought Widney Cheyne deserved. As he was turning into the drive, they saw the gathering. Apart from two unfortunates who had drawn the lots to stay in the yard to look after the horses, all the lads and girls had been in the church and at the Fortescue Arms. Now they had come together for their own private greeting, to welcome their newly-wed master and mistress home.

"This all looks a bit feudal to me," Richard said, as he and Edward helped Caroline and her dress out of the car. "I'm clearing off. I'll pick you up on Tuesday morning. Have fun!"

Because he had not expected it, Edward was bewildered by what happened next, but he was also touched by the immense depth of feeling displayed. There was a burst of applause; everyone started clapping their hands. As Caroline walked towards them, more confetti was thrown and another batch of cameras went into action. Edward watched Caroline move among them like a princess, unable to believe that she was his. He was especially pleased to see that Finoula and Patrick Prendegast, now engaged, had come back, and presumed they were staying overnight with Declan and Mary. After ten minutes of being overwhelmed with good wishes, Edward made a move towards the house, and Caroline caught his hand to steer him away from the office entrance.

"The front door," she whispered. "We always use it for special occasions."

"Oh – that's a nice idea."

"In any case, you'd probably ruin my dress carrying me across the office threshold," she said.

As they reached the front door, with everyone following, Mary who had been waiting for them in the house, flung both halves of it open. When Edward picked Caroline up and set off up the steps, the cameras clicked yet again and Declan asked, "Are we having evening stables today, sor?"

Caroline smiled sweetly at him over Edward's shoulder. "No, Declan, not today, thank you," she said, and waved with regal assurance as her husband carried her into what had always been her home.

After Mary had gone, Caroline locked the door after her, then went into the office and disconnected both the business and private telephone lines. She turned to Edward, her arms held wide. "Thank you, sweetheart," she said, embracing him, and laying her cheek against his. "That was all perfectly lovely."

"I thought so, too."

"Everyone was so happy!"

"Marvellous, wasn't it?" He suddenly remembered a tiny incident. "What were you and your father arguing about?"

"When?"

"Just before we left the Fortescue – while Dooley was dancing a jig with Imogen."

"Oh yes!" She remembered. "Oh, that was nothing. I just said it was a pity Nigel wasn't able to get here."

"Ah!"

Caroline's brother Nigel was serving with the Army in Germany. Edward had assumed that he would be at the wedding, and had been surprised by his absence. Cyril Brookes-Smith made no bones about regarding his son as an utter ne'er-do-well, and became angry whenever his name was mentioned, but Caroline was fiercely and protectively fond of him. "I suppose he must have been very busy – we'll see him soon, I expect."

The moment passed. She kissed him in what seemed an almost perfunctory fashion, and appeared to become businesslike. "There's something we must attend to," she said. "Come with me, my boy."

Edward had not seen what was now their bedroom with its *en suite* bathroom since George Roberts had finished it, and he wanted to stand and stare at it. There was much to admire, but Caroline had other ideas. "Help me with this dress," she said, after she had kicked her shoes off and given a little sigh of relief. He found the zip at the back and pulled it down gingerly. "Those are your wardrobes over there," she said as she picked the dress up and shook it, scattering confetti. Edward studiously removed his jacket and hung it up, finding that his capacious cupboards were already equipped with highly polished wooden coat-hangers.

"And the waistcoat," Caroline instructed.

Without turning, Edward did as he was told, adding his tie for good measure. When he did look at his wife, he caught his breath. Sitting on the end of the bed, she was pulling off her tights, and was now wearing only a pretty bra and briefs set.

"What's the matter?" she asked quietly.

"Nothing . . . nothing at all. I was boggling at you."

"All right?"

"Yes."

"You don't want your money back?"

"Oh no. You're wonderful, absolutely wonderful."

She laughed, stood up, displaying her flawless body to even better advantage and walked into his arms. Instantly, he was aware of a new, vibrant willingness in her, and their kiss became impetuous.

"I'm going to have a shower," she said, eventually slipping out of his embrace. "You need one, too," she added as she disappeared into the bathroom. When he followed her, his attention was caught first by George Roberts' masterpiece, the sunken bath that looked big enough for three or four people, but the lure of the shower soon proved much more powerful. Shedding the last of his clothes, Edward joined Caroline.

"Now then, that isn't totally beastly, is it?" she asked, sliding soapy hands down his back.

"No. I think I could get to like this in time," he replied.

"Good." She rubbed her breasts across his smooth chest. "I'm glad you aren't hairy – and your legs are much better than I thought. I reckon I've done all right here."

"I certainly have!"

"We can't do it in here, can we?" he said a few minutes later.

"It has been known, apparently. We'd better use the bed while we're learning."

For the second time that afternoon, he took her in his arms and carried her. This time she was wrapped in a soft bath sheet, and he placed her carefully on the bed. Another wave of disbelief came over him as he stared down at her. "I don't know whether to worship you or make love to you," he said.

"Let's save the worship until later," she said. "Your needs seem to be even greater than mine."

He was totally unprepared for the electrifying sensation of her flesh. "God, you feel as good as you look!" he gasped.

She laughed, and squirmed luxuriously in the embrace that he had meant to be gentle until her body galvanised him. "Just relax and take it steady," she said. "We'll soon get the hang of it."

"But nothing seems to fit properly," he complained, only to be shaken about as she dissolved into a gale of laughter.

"Oh dear, I'm sorry, sweetheart," she said when she saw his pained look. "Just remember one thing, will you?" She was suddenly serious. "They say that the good Lord invented sex as a joke, but when no one laughed, he turned it into a sin and made everybody desperate. Let's make sure we laugh, eh?"

"Where did you get that from?" Edward asked, intrigued.

"I believe it's an old Irish saying actually. Now, like this look . . . let's try that . . . that might be it."

Afterwards, Edward lay on his back and stared at the ceiling while Caroline waited patiently for the doom-laden pronouncement that she felt sure was on its way.

"That wasn't much good for you, was it?" he said at last.

She chose her words carefully. "I understand it can be better," she replied. "But there's nothing to get upset about. Have you ever made love before?"

"No," he admitted, not knowing whether he was proud or guilty.

"Neither have I. As you will have noticed, I wasn't *virgo intacta* . . ." Edward tried to look as though he had. ". . . but that's what riding horses does to a girl. I was fully entitled to that white dress! I'd say that was pretty good for a first attempt by two inexperienced incompetents."

He started to smile. "So, what do we do about it?"

"What did you do about Radames?" she asked.

"Kept trying."

"Exactly!"

"Lots of practice?" he asked, his smile broadening.

"Lots and lots," she replied, taking one of his hands and placing it on her breast. "Let's start there, shall we? I rather like that."

Imogen had a very great deal to say about it, but for the last stage of the twelve-hour journey from Saxon Court to Lexington, Kentucky, Caroline and Edward were fast asleep, leaving Richard the sole beneficiary. The two-hour wait for a connecting flight in New York had failed to impress Imogen, and she wanted to know why they couldn't have done it at a more 'civilised' location such as Washington or Boston. Richard's attempts to explain the rudiments of American air travel to his wife were doomed from the start, and he philosophically endured castigation at twenty-nine thousand feet over the states of Pennsylvania and Ohio. Yet as soon as she caught her first breath of Kentucky air and saw the pleasantness of the surroundings, Imogen began to soften. Caroline and Edward were captivated at once. They had left Saxon Court at eight o'clock on a damp, miserable morning; after twelve hours, it was now three o'clock in the north-east Kentucky afternoon, and they were cheered up by what they saw.

When they had cleared the arrival formalities at Lexington's Blue Grass Airport, Richard led the way through the last barrier to be greeted like an old friend by a handsomely attractive girl with chestnut hair, brown eyes and a calmly poised air of assurance. "This is Nancy

Bloomfield," Richard said, introducing her to Imogen first. "Nancy is the reason I know so much about bloodstock."

"Now I know what the attraction in Kentucky is," Imogen said. "How d'you do, Nancy?"

"I'm very pleased to meet you, Lady Stewart." Nancy had a soft voice coloured by an agreeable accent. As ever when anyone used her title, Imogen seemed to glow.

"And this is Edward Manning who does the training, and his brand-new wife, Caroline."

"You trained Musetta?" Nancy asked as she shook hands with Edward.

"I did. She was marvellous."

"I knew she would be. How is she?"

"Very well indeed. She's in foal to Mill Reef."

"Hey! That could be something."

"We're hoping so," Richard said. "Edward's the genius. He mutters things in their ears and they perform. He even made sense of that useless colt you sold me last time. We won a Group race at Ascot with him."

"Now, c'mon," Nancy Bloomfield protested. "Don't blame me for that guy! I told you he was questionable, and you went right ahead and bought him!"

"And I was right," Richard said. "Have you got anything good for us this time?"

"Yes, we have." They had been walking towards the car park, but she stopped to look at him very earnestly. "We've got a very, very nice Northern Dancer colt, but it's going to cost you two hundred thousand dollars to keep him out of the ring. Mr Drury wants to put him in the Keeneland sale next month."

Richard nodded, and they walked on until they stopped alongside the biggest car that Edward had ever seen. As the porter loaded their luggage into the enormous boot, Richard laughed at the look on his friend's face. "Dooley would like this," he said. "It's got power-assisted steering!"

Leaving the airport site, they were almost immediately on a broad, perfectly straight road heading north-east. "This is the Paris Pike," Nancy said. "A lot of the big farms are up ahead. We'll go left soon up Route 64."

Sat in the back of the car, and holding hands like a pair of moonstruck teenagers, Caroline and Edward giggled as Richard explained to Imogen that in this context, 'Pike' was short for 'Turnpike Road' and had nothing to do with fish. When they had controlled their humour, they settled down to watch the passage of the lush, rolling landscape with childlike fascination. Without a shadow of a doubt, this was horse country; even when they could not see the animals sunning themselves in the paddocks, there were the diversely elegant barns and stables and mile upon mile of white board fences. Among the stately groves of trees, there were frequent glimpses of magnificent houses, mostly gleaming white with column-decorated front elevations. And there were the signs with the farm names: Double L, Domino, Dixiana, Plum Lane, Flying C and Spendthrift.

"We're nearly there now," Nancy announced for the benefit of all but Richard as she turned north-west on to Route 75, which went to Cincinnati and then up through the eastern side of Ohio and Michigan to the Canadian border. After about ten miles, a sign to the left said 'Tornado Stud' and Nancy turned the huge Chevrolet into a narrow, tree-lined lane as Caroline was seized by another fit of giggling.

"I should have warned you about that," Richard admitted.

The house was less grand than many they had passed, but the welcome was massive. No sooner had Nancy stopped the car than all two hundred pounds of Elmer Drury was greeting them. Edward judged him to be in his late fifties, and in rude health, despite his weight. He affected the style and manners of a backwoodsman, with a loud check shirt, the sleeves of which were rolled back to reveal brawny forearms, and trousers that looked literally home-spun supported by both scarlet braces and a matching belt like a saddle girth. His eyes, however, were very shrewd. When the introductions were made, and Richard had indicated the sort of business he had in mind, Elmer Drury whistled.

"You want fifteen hosses?" he asked.

"At least," Richard replied. "We're stocking a new stable and we have a new owner who wants to make a start in the game. He wants quantity rather than absolute quality and I need at least two good colts."

"That's some order, Sir Richard."

"It is indeed, Elmer, but I'm sure you can fill it."

"OK. Let's get you folks fixed up. We're gonna have dinner at seven – that all right with you?" They all agreed. "Right Nance, take 'em to the chalets."

The Tornado Stud was relatively small by Lexington standards, covering only two thousand acres. In the far corner of its paddocks and woods, there was a four-acre site with five vacation homes, hired by tired New Yorkers in spring and summer, empty for the rest of the year except for visiting customers. The chalets were very-high-quality log cabins with all the facilities of a luxury house. Imogen had paid scant attention when Richard had extolled their virtues, but her eyes opened wide once she was inside one.

Caroline was equally impressed. "Come and look at this bathroom," she called to Edward.

Obeying her summons, he found that the bathroom was indeed worth looking at, and so was Caroline. She was naked.

"What are you trying to do to me?" he asked plaintively.

"Nothing at all," she replied. "I am merely getting ready for a much-needed shower. However, should you wish to avail yourself of the superb amenities . . ."

A wonderful steak put the finishing touches to what had been a long and extremely tiring day, and they collapsed into bed just after nine o'clock, Edward pointing out with his last breath that it was really two o'clock in the morning, and they had travelled several thousand miles.

They slept for ten hours, made their own breakfast, and were ready at half past eight when Nancy came to collect them. Without explaining why, she drove to a paddock containing five advanced yearling colts and left them to it.

"I wonder what these are supposed to be," Richard said.

"The best!" Caroline and Edward replied in unison.

"And that one is the pick of the bunch by twenty lengths," Caroline announced firmly, pointing at a brown colt who was cropping grass slightly apart from the others. As she did so, the colt raised his head and regarded her boldly. "He is bee-yoo-tiful!" Caroline said. "I want to see him move."

The colt snorted, pawed the ground, nodded his head several times with great vigour, then launched himself into a gallop. His acceleration and the speed he attained very rapidly were breathtaking, but equally noticeable was the style with which he unleashed and handled his tremendous power. "Have you ever seen one move like that before?" Caroline asked in a hushed voice.

"No, I most certainly have not," Edward said, his eyes fixed on the colt.

"Even I can see he's good," Imogen said.

"He is brilliant," Caroline breathed.

After two circuits round an imaginary boundary known only to him, the colt came to rest at almost exactly the point from which he had started. Again, he surveyed Caroline.

"Come here!" she called to him.

He did. Quite deliberately, and with no time for anyone else, he approached Caroline. After the initial contact had been made, she climbed up to sit astride the fence where she could pat his neck and tug gently at his ears.

"This is the one," she said. "He's going to be a corker. You can win anything you like with this chap."

"The Derby?" Richard asked flippantly.

"I'd need to know a bit more about him first," Caroline said. "But with that action he's got to be a winner. And just look at his eye! Lovely!"

"Amazing temperament," Edward said.

"He's a sweetie," Caroline agreed. She now had an arm round the colt's neck and was rubbing her cheek against his nose.

"You could do something with him?" Richard asked Edward.

"I'd have to recommend you find another trainer if I couldn't. You know what the old man would have said about him, don't you?"

Richard clasped his hands behind his back and struck a James Henry pose. "That's class that is, real *class*," he said, in a very good imitation.

"Now we shall find out," Edward said. "Here's Nancy Bloomfield."

She was smiling as she climbed out of the battered old runabout. "You've found him then?" she said.

"This is the two-hundred-thousand-dollar Northern Dancer?" Richard asked.

"Yes. Nice, isn't he?"

"You'd recommend him?"

"Of course. The only problem you have with him is keeping him out of the ring."

"I might know how to do that," Richard smiled. "Should I be interested in anything else?"

"Yes. See that one on the right . . . the bay with the white star? He's a Northern Dancer as well. On paper he isn't anywhere near as good as the other one . . . dam's line isn't too good actually. I think he might win a race or two, but I wouldn't buy him for that."

"No?"

Edward could see that Richard was very interested.

"I'd want him as a stallion."

"Really?"

"My hunch is that he'll be good – brilliant even. If you study the Northern Dancers, you find that a lot of the best breeders come from fairly moderate dams . . ."

Nancy Bloomfield and Richard moved away, Richard hanging on her every word, asking the occasional question.

Elmer Drury kept out of the way during the morning.

"Playing hard to get, do you think?" Caroline asked Edward.

"Probably. I don't blame him for trying, but he'll need a damned sight more than tactics with Richard."

"He's good, is he?"

"Must be! You can't run a merchant bank by being as nice as he is with us."

"Good point! Have you ever seen him at it?"

"No, and I don't think I want to."

By the time they had lunch with Elmer Drury and a rather improbable young woman who seemed to enjoy some sort of special relationship with him, Richard had spotted a dozen yearlings that he thought might give Edwin Fforbes a good start as an owner. Elmer produced a stubby pencil, and wrote figures down on a scrap of paper as Nancy described the animals in which Richard had expressed an interest.

191

"They're a good bunch of hosses," he said, nodding sagaciously. "Gonna break my heart parting with some of them."

"And there were two you thought Valerie Malahide might like?" Richard said to Edward.

Elmer added some more figures to his list. "That's best part of six hundred grand, Sir Richard," he announced happily.

"And there's a Northern Dancer colt I want," Richard said. Caroline and Edward held their breath, and Elmer Drury seemed to tense. "The bay with the white star wasn't it, Nancy?" Richard added after a slight pause, and Elmer grinned broadly.

"Good hoss," he said, "very good hoss." He went through the motions of thinking hard. "I can let you have him for a hundred and twenty grand."

Richard smiled, shrugged in what looked like philosophical acceptance, and changed the subject. There was no mention of the brown colt.

After lunch, Elmer suggested an outing. "My buddy Rick Teshemacher over at Spiral Reach sure would be honoured if you folks had a look round his place," he said. "He's got some really great stallions up there."

"That sounds nice!" Imogen said brightly. Pleading continuing tiredness after the journey of the previous day, Caroline and Edward stayed behind. As soon as Elmer had driven Imogen and Richard away, they went with Nancy to have another look at the brown colt. Again he came to the fence of his paddock when he saw Caroline, and they spent nearly an hour talking to and about him.

"I think he's absolutely brilliant," was Caroline's repeated assertion.

"Could be," Nancy agreed. "He's basically bred for middle distances. I believe that a mile and a half could be his ideal distance – and he might not be too useful below that."

Edward was impressed by the careful seriousness of her thought processes. There was another glimpse of what lay beneath the bland surface she presented to the world as she walked part of the way back to the chalet with them. Elmer's lady friend tore past them in a station wagon from which the sounds of Country and Western music blared almost painfully. Nancy Bloomfield stared into the trailing dust cloud with a flash of unconcealed distaste.

Caroline thoroughly enjoyed the next forty-eight hours. They saw the whole of Tornado Stud with its one hundred and thirty brood mares. Imogen had to be told that the mares visited stallions on other farms for a few days each year, and then came back to Tornado to await the birth of their foals. Once she had understood this, Imogen quickly cottoned on to the financial possibilities of such an operation. "So if Elmer Drury can clear as little as two thousand on each foal, he's making a quarter of a million a year?" she said.

192

"That's right," Richard agreed.

"Be jolly good if we can do that in the back garden at Widney Cheyne."

"That's the idea. The real money is with stallions, of course. Even with a small operation like this, Elmer's probably paying about two million a year for stallion services."

Caroline and Edward spent much of the two days in total relaxation for the first time in many months. The chalet and its idyllic surroundings were very conducive to doing nothing except love-making, and Caroline was happy to report real improvement in their performance.

"You will let me know when I get it really right?" Edward asked anxiously.

"I don't think you'll have any difficulty spotting that for yourself," she replied with the straightest face she could muster.

The only thing that worried her was Richard's failure to raise the question of the brown colt with Elmer Drury. She did her best to believe Edward's hourly reassurances that Richard knew what he was doing.

It came during dinner on the last evening. The main dish was burgoo, a game-meat casserole that was as special to Kentucky as the cold mint juleps that had also impressed Imogen. After she had extracted the recipe, Elmer Drury beamed at Richard. "I believe we have a deal, Sir Richard," he said.

"We do indeed," Richard said, and laid his cheque-book on the table. "Just one small addition. I've decided that I rather like the brown Northern Dancer colt – the one in with the bay. I'll take him as well, please."

There was a slight pause before Elmer shook his head sadly. "I'm sure as hell sorry, Sir Richard, but you can't have that guy."

"Oh? Why?"

"I'm going to put him in the ring at Keeneland next month. That boy will fetch three hundred grand."

"I see." Richard pursed his lips. "That much, you think."

"Sure – give or take."

"I'll give you two hundred thousand for him."

Elmer looked baffled, then he laughed. "That's some joke, Sir Richard," he said.

"No joke, Elmer. Two hundred thousand, on the table, here and now, no auctioneer commission."

Elmer wavered. "No, I can't do it," he said. "Hell! That's one of the best hosses I ever had."

"Shame," Richard said quietly, and picked up his cheque-book. After slipping it into his pocket, he carried on eating his burgoo, as if completely unaware of the stupefied silence around him and the fact that Elmer was open-mouthed.

"Hey! What about our deal?" Elmer asked.

"What deal?" Richard asked with devastating innocence.

"Those fifteen hosses. Seven hundred and twenty thousand dollars."

"Elmer, it's *sixteen* horses at nine hundred and twenty thousand or nothing," Richard said quietly, but with implacable firmness.

"Quite right!" Imogen said. "Nine hundred thousand for cash."

Caroline's stomach turned over.

"I think you're probably doing the right thing, Elmer," Richard said. "Put the whole lot through the ring, and you might do much better."

Elmer Drury mulled it over. At first he seemed defiant, then he was calculating, assessing risks and probabilities. He took a long time over it, but the end was swift, his face splitting into a huge grin. "OK, you got yourself a deal."

Richard reached across the table to shake hands on it. "And we'll have the usual arrangement for delivery," he said.

"Goddamit, you'll have the shirt off my back," Elmer said, and roared with laughter. "That's a good piece of business there, c'mon, let's have some more drinks to celebrate."

An hour later, Caroline, Edward, Imogen and Richard walked back to their chalets, all arm-in-arm, through a delightful autumn evening.

"My God, that was nerve-racking," Caroline said.

"Wasn't it just?" Richard agreed.

"Fiddlesticks!" Imogen said firmly. "The man who wants something is always stronger than the man who doesn't want him to have it."

"I'm horrified at the price," Edward said.

"No need to be. I'd say two hundred thousand was pretty fair."

"No, I mean for all of them. You've paid an average of forty thousand each for the Edwin Fforbes bunch."

"True, but my guess is that in three or four years, we'd be paying up to five times that."

"Why?"

"The Arabs are coming! It isn't going to be all that long before *everything* with four decent legs goes through the auction ring and fetches ludicrous prices."

"By which time, we shall be breeding our own," Imogen said triumphantly.

"This is a lovely place," Caroline said as they reached the chalets and stopped. "I've really enjoyed it here."

"And it's the great unknown tomorrow," Imogen said.

"Come on, you can tell us now," Richard said to Edward. "Where are you going?"

"No, I don't want to know!" Caroline protested.

Edward took Richard to one side and whispered directly into his ear. Richard burst out laughing.

"I thought so," Imogen said. "You're going for a conducted tour of Newmarket!"

Edward had to divulge that the flight he and Caroline were booked on left Lexington twenty minutes before Imogen and Richard were due to go to Washington. Nancy Bloomfield drove them all to the airport. After she had wished the honeymooners well and said goodbye to Imogen, Richard spoke to Nancy privately. There was no doubting the seriousness of the conversation; Nancy was nodding earnestly, Richard took very special notice of what she had to say, and gave her one of his visiting cards as they parted. Studying Imogen, Edward had the fleeting impression that she knew what it was all about. After Nancy had gone, they chatted until a flight to Miami was called.

"That's ours," Edward told Caroline.

"Really? I wouldn't have thought that was your style at all," she said. "Far too flashy, surely?"

"Worry not, that's a mere staging post," Richard assured her.

"That's right," Edward agreed. "As a matter of fact, this could be an epic journey. We'd better enjoy it for Siobhan's sake – she went to a great deal of trouble organising it. And you very nearly made it impossible by dashing in and out of the office every five minutes, darling."

"Sorry about that. Yes, I'll do my best to enjoy it, just as long as arriving is better than travelling hopefully."

"It will be!"

Imogen and Richard waved and watched as Caroline and Edward went through the departure gates and disappeared from view. "There's no need to worry," Imogen said. "He's in good hands. She's a gift from the gods."

Richard looked at her quizzically. "That's strong language, my dear," he said.

"I know. Perfectly justified, though."

Two hours later when they reached Miami, Caroline waited patiently for fifteen minutes before asking where they were going next.

"Puerto Rico," Edward replied.

"Another stepping stone?"

"Yes."

"How long do we have here?"

"An hour."

"Right, shan't be long." She wandered nonchalantly into a bookshop that had caught her eye, and disappeared among a crowd. When she came out, she was carrying a large book that had been ostentatiously gift-wrapped, and was looking pleased with herself.

"What's that?" Edward asked.

"Get on with your surprise and let me hatch mine."

After another two-hour flight, Caroline decreed that they should have a meal at San Juan Airport when they reached Puerto Rico and she found there was another hour to wait.

"We can't really call this lunch," she said, looking at her watch and finding that it was two-thirty. "Have we gone into another time zone?"

"Yes. It's half past three local time."

Laughing, she made the change. "You're trying to confuse me so that I'm powerless in your evil grasp."

"I'm sorry about this." Dreadfully serious, Edward had still to realise that they were alone and about to begin their life together.

"Where next?" she enquired.

"This is the last bit. We're going to Antigua."

The cottage, its verandah only twenty yards from high water, was on Half Moon Bay. It was perfect.

After she had inspected it, Caroline took stock of the unbelievably beautiful location, shading her eyes against the glare of the sun on the near-white sand.

"This is marvellous, sweetheart," she said. "Really marvellous. Where are we?"

"Antigua."

"I know that, you idiot! What's the name of that place over there?" She pointed to a group of houses appearing to make up a village across the bay.

"What, that place there?"

"Yes."

"That's Mill Reef."

She looked at him and said, "Mill Reef?" very quietly.

"That's right."

"Uh-huh." She traced a pattern in the sand with a toe. "Is this, by any chance, the place your hero was named after?"

"Er . . . yes, it is."

Her look actually convinced him that she was somehow displeased. Then she laughed, flung her arms round his neck and said, "You're priceless, my boy! Who else would bring me to a Derby winner for my honeymoon?"

When they woke up to their first morning at Half Moon Bay, Caroline and Edward fell into a pattern that was to last for the whole of their holiday. They swam in the sea, had breakfast, talked, explored the woods and beach, swam again and thought about lunch. As they ate a selection of the local delicacies, Caroline retrieved the book she had bought at Miami Airport. When she unceremoniously tore off the garish wrapping paper, Edward came close to choking on a prawn croquette at the sight of the title:

Sexual Fulfilment: Your Complete, Personalised Guide.

"From what I saw of it in the shop, that's going to be very useful," Caroline said as she passed it to him. "Twenty-five dollars well spent, I'd say."

Edward inspected the book as though he were expecting it to blow up or bite him. There were fifty pages of detailed explanatory text at the front, and he discovered that it seemed to be carefully thought out and well written, without any suggestion of mechanistic performance. Then, in the main body of the book, an attractive couple showed how it should be done in two hundred pages of colour photographs. He found that his initial shock soon turned to curiosity, then excitement.

"Why did they make such a production of gift-wrapping it?" he asked, suddenly realising that a hectically busy airport bookshop would not normally take such trouble.

"I've no idea," she said, her smile destroying all pretence at innocence.

"What did you say to them?"

"Very little really – I *might* have mentioned that I was on honeymoon. I can't remember."

He nodded knowingly. The combination of Caroline's looks and direct, friendly manner was usually irresistible. His fond contemplation of this phenomenon was shattered by one of the photographs towards the end of the book. "Good grief!" he said, and his face registered a mixture of disbelief and admiration. Caroline got up to look over his shoulder, and laughed.

"The neighbours wouldn't care for that," she said.

"We haven't got any."

"True." She studied the picture carefully. "I think we'd have to go into strict training for it."

"Do you think so?" He sounded disappointed.

"Yes – and our wardrobes are far too high. There's lots of easier stuff to get stuck into, and it's high time we did."

A week of marriage to Caroline had already given Edward's inhibitions a battering from which he hoped they would never recover. The secret world of their bungalow, the beach and the incomparable views across the bay continued the process, and the culmination came on the third day. At breakfast, Edward found that he was looking at Caroline with new eyes. He savoured the nascent awareness that this beautiful woman really was *his*, appreciating for the first time the powerful attractive force produced by the combination of her mind and body. As ever, she detected precisely what he was thinking, and a hitherto unknown seriousness enveloped them. The morning was still full of laughter, but there were interludes of great intensity that appeared quite suddenly in the middle of a perfectly ordinary conversation. Their eyes held each other for longer than usual, and physical contact between them increased. From the beginning, Caroline had habitually touched Edward when making an important point; generally, she would grasp his arm above the elbow, now she placed both hands on his shoulders.

By unspoken consent, they let the forceful new emotion between them build up, actively stifling anything that might dissipate it. In the afternoon, there was an increasingly unbearable aura of sexual tension between them which gradually paralysed conversation. It was Edward who finally snapped, grabbing Caroline, carrying her into the bedroom, dumping her on the bed and ripping off her flimsy bikini. From the instant their bodies coalesced, they sensed that it was going to be totally different. Their passion produced a frenetic energy and purpose in both of them that they had only glimpsed fleetingly before. Just before the end, Caroline muttered, "God Almighty!" Although it was little more than a whisper, Edward was alarmed by the thought that she was in distress or pain, but as she embraced the final ecstasy by arching her body against his with immense force, he knew they were tumbling into oblivion together.

For five minutes or more they were too exhausted and preoccupied with their innermost thoughts to speak. When they did look at one another, it was with an almost wild wonder.

Caroline wrinkled her nose and smiled with a luminosity he had never seen before. "That was glorious," she said. "That was abso-bloody-lutely glorious!" She was still slightly breathless.

"Was that it? Was that the one you said I'd know about?"

"I reckon that was it. You're improving, my boy."

"I had some help!"

"Yes, I think I did get a bit carried away. Hey! Where do you think you're going?" She threw a restraining arm round him.

"To get some orange juice."

"All right. Don't be long. We need to make sure that wasn't a fluke."

It wasn't. As they drank a cup of tea in bed the following morning, Caroline looked almost bewildered. "Did we ever get anything to eat last night?" she asked.

"We had a snack about ten."

"Oh yes, that's right. What time did we go to sleep?"

"I think it was two o'clock when you finally wore me out."

She remembered and chuckled. "Am I insatiable?"

"Looks like it."

"What are you going to do about it?"

"Do you want to swim before or after?" She found that he answered the question for her.

Afterwards, she was lost in thoughts that clearly amused her.

"What are you thinking about?" he asked.

"Tornado Stud."

"What about it?"

"I think it might be a good name for you."

"That really appealed to you, didn't it?"

"Yes. So do you."

The process that had begun on the day they first met had reached its ultimate conclusion. The mental and emotional ties that were often close enough to produce something like telepathy were now augmented by a physical union that was, by turn, companionable and searingly beautiful. They were a complete whole.

On the last day, they acquired a very special remembrance of their time in paradise. Edward discovered a large conch shell of exceptional shape and translucence on the beach, and shouted, "Look at this, Caro."

"I like that," she said when she had come out of the sea and joined him. She was ignoring the shell.

"What?"

"*Caro* . . . you called me 'Caro'."

"Sorry. I wasn't thinking."

"Don't be sorry – it's nice."

"You like it?"

"Yes!"

Edward thought about it. "So do I," he said firmly. "Very much!"

It was settled. From that point on, she was 'Caro'.

She was visibly sad as they took off on the long non-stop flight to London, and held Edward's hand tightly until they had climbed high into the cloudless early evening sky. Then, when heaven and sea had merged into an azure orb, darkening as they flew towards the night, she relaxed and smiled.

"It couldn't have been better," she said.

After dinner which was served by a happy group of West Indian stewardesses, they reclined their seats and prepared for sleep.

"Shall we go back next year?" Caroline asked.

"Oh yes!"

"And every year after that?"

"Yes."

She was quiet for a few minutes, and he thought she had gone to sleep.

"We're very lucky," Caroline said without opening her eyes.

"We are."

"I suppose hundreds of couples must have had honeymoons as good as ours."

"Thousands and thousands."

"But they didn't have what we've got to look forward to."

She opened her eyes then, and stared at him with burning intensity. He had forgotten just how very blue they were.

CHAPTER 9

"I don't know why you're so surprised. I told you they wouldn't mess about. And if you want paying during the winter, you'll have to work for it!"

Thus did Alison Bairstow acquaint one of the less stout-hearted girls with the facts of life as she saw them.

"Bloody hell, Alison! It is November, and they've only just come back from honeymoon. You'd think they could take it easy for a bit."

"This job's important. It's got to be done before the weather gets cold after Christmas."

The job was the construction of two five-furlong all-weather gallops and a one-mile sand track for two-year-olds. The site chosen was the one pointed out by Caroline from Moonlight Ring when she and Edward had first ridden up to the summit of Saxon Down in March. Most of the work was being done by men that George Roberts had brought in, and they were armed with farming equipment and a pair of bull-dozers.

Each of the strips was ten feet wide, and the construction was begun by digging out two feet of earth and the laying of drains. A seemingly endless procession of lorries then brought loads of carefully graded stone to fill in the first part of the long, shallow trenches, and a polythene membrane was laid on top. For the two all-weather gallops, the final layer consisted of a mixture of peat and wood shavings; on the two-year-old track, a good dressing of sand went over the peat. Despite mechanisation, some of the work, such as stretching the polythene sheets into place, did require people to bend their backs, and it was this task that caused Linda Brown to complain, and incur Alison's displeasure.

When Edward was not supervising work on the New Ground, his major preoccupation was with the swimming pool. This was to be at the north end of the yard on a piece of ground that had been a half-hearted lawn, weed patch or quagmire depending on the whims of Caroline's father and the weather. The first discussions with George Roberts were rendered confused by Edward's failure to mention that the pool was for horses, not human beings. When the point was eventually made, a slow, happy smile spread over George's face.

"Do you know, I couldn't for the life of me work it out," he said. "I was wondering what you wanted such a damned great thing stuck in this funny old corner for."

Edward smiled at the misunderstanding. "Sorry about that, George. Yes, it's for horses."

"Ah, 'tis elementary then. What we want is a bloody great hole lined with concrete."

"That's it. There has to be a ramp in one corner, and we want rubber mats on it."

George Roberts was happy again, especially when he calculated that the pool would hold about a quarter of a million gallons of water, and that a way of filling and emptying it had to be found. The completely successful solution to this was forthcoming from an outlandish individual who answered to the names of Arthur or Percy according to his mood, and appeared to play an enigmatic part-time role in the workings of Didcot power station.

At the end of November, the sixteen yearlings from Tornado arrived in England, and were taken for schooling to a stable kept by friends of Caroline near Newbury. Caroline visited them at least twice a week, often taking Alison Bairstow and Robin Lane with her. Shortly before Christmas, Edward went with them, found that the horses all looked extremely well, and that most of them were making good progress in their lessons. Caroline's Northern Dancer colt was proving to be as exceptional as she had prophesied, and the immediate bond between them that had been so striking in Kentucky had strengthened. As soon as Caroline appeared on the scene, he had eyes for no one else, his bearing became prouder, and he accepted her affection with a gentle fondness that was touching in a creature of his size and power.

On Boxing Day, Imogen, Richard and the children came to Saxon Court, and Caroline wasted no time in raising a topic very close to her heart. "This Northern Dancer of yours," she said to Richard.

"Which one?" he asked, meeting her determination with merchant banker urbanity.

"The brown one."

"Yes."

"It's time he had a name."

"Yes – we must register him."

"I don't think he should have one of your operatic names."

Richard smiled. "Did you have anything in mind?"

"Yes. James Henry!"

It came as a total surprise to Edward.

Richard thought about it and smiled. "I would find that very difficult to argue with," he said.

"What do you think, sweetheart?" Caroline asked Edward.

"It's a lovely idea."

"Right, Siobhan can send his papers off. What about the other one?"

"He's going to be called Parsifal," Richard replied.

"That's Wagner," Imogen explained. "Some concoction about the Knights of the Round Table and the Holy Grail as far as I can see. Sounds a complete farce!"

"Parsifal was the 'perfect fool' of mythology," Richard explained.

"That's all we need," Edward laughed. "He'll turn out to be worse than Radames."

"Oh no." Caroline was quietly firm. "He's going to be useful. Alison Bairstow and Robin Lane think so too."

"Ah, well, that's it then."

Having been gently mocking about Caroline's infallible and apparently inseparable pair of experts, Richard turned to the mild-mannered man he had brought with him. "What about your bunch, Edwin?"

Edwin Fforbes, Richard's colleague and friend from the bank, was paying his first visit to Saxon Court, and was slightly overawed, despite the relaxed, festive atmosphere. About forty-five years old, and still mourning his wife who had died five years ago, he was a shy man, slightly ill at ease when not operating in his professional capacity; he always took time to adapt to new surroundings and people.

"Well . . . I rather like your idea, Richard . . . I'll stick with opera, I think."

"Aha!" Richard produced a large sheet of paper with a flourish. "Take your pick from that lot," he said, and handed it across.

"I'll help you choose," Caroline said to Edwin Fforbes. "Come with me to see them next week and we can christen them. They're all having a birthday on Tuesday so we can go then." Edwin Fforbes smiled gratefully, then looked at Edward, as though seeking confirmation that this was the thing to do.

"Quite right," Edward told him. "Go with Caro, and she'll sort it all out for you."

"Isn't he a sweetie?" Caroline said after Edwin Fforbes had gone back to Widney Cheyne with Imogen and Richard.

"He certainly looks like being a model owner."

"My God, yes. Father could have used a dozen like him!"

In the first days of 1982, Edward had turned his attention to the important question of a travelling head lad. The man appointed would be responsible for taking horses racing, a duty that was particularly onerous when it was necessary to spend one or more nights away from home. Loyalty and discretion, often in the face of substantial temptation, were imperative, and Edward had already consulted Declan. Mercifully, he had a suggestion.

"You need 'Freezer'," he said.

"Who?"

"Graeme Frost. They call him 'Freezer'."

It seemed that Graeme Frost was fifty-one or -two. Thirty-five years ago he had served an apprenticeship at a good stable in Newmarket, then gone to Ireland in search of a career as a jockey. For ten years, he had ridden for James Henry, always struggling to make a living. As other trainers upon whom he relied for work had either retired or died, matters had gradually reached the stage where he had been forced back to England. His old guv'nor at Newmarket had used him for ride work and recommended him to others, but it was always a precarious business, and now that he was too old for the rigours of the gallops, he was reduced to freelance odd-jobbing.

"He's as straight as they come," Declan declared. "Even with her."

Edward discovered that the 'her' of this cryptically scathing comment was Freezer's ex-wife. At its most charitable, Declan's opinion of her was that she had been 'unsuitable', her extravagance had made anything that Freezer could earn look like chickenfeed, yet he had never gambled, let alone resorted to other pressures.

"He had a terrible time," Declan said grimly. "She led him a right old dance. Spending his money before he got it – and she went mad when that plastic stuff came out. His luck finally turned about five years ago. Some fool ran off with her. I understand he's repaid all the debts – every last penny."

Edward was vastly impressed by Declan's tirade, and was certain it rivalled his verbosity on the legendary occasion that O'Gorman's mare had got loose at the Phoenix Park. "He's rid of her now?" he asked.

"Oh yes."

"Could you have a chat with him and sound him out please, Declan."

"He's interested," was the report, two days later.

"Really?"

"He'd jump at it," Declan admitted.

"Good. Suggest that he comes and talks to me."

On the appointed day, he arrived late because his old car had broken down, and he looked worried sick. Both the kitchen and the office were crowded, so Edward took him into the sitting-room. Initially, Graeme Frost was ill at ease in surroundings he considered far too grand for him, but after Caroline had brought some sandwiches and tea in, and given him one of her smiles, he began to look more at home.

"You rode Muckley Corner for my grandfather, Mr Frost," Edward began.

"Yes, sir. Five times."

"And he won all of them?"

"Yes, sir. He was a very good horse."

"So I understand. I think he was probably the best that Avoca House had before Murgatroyd came along."

"Yes, sir – but Hammerwich was good as well, sir."

Edward smiled. "Yes, you're right. I'd forgotten about him." He was pleased to see that his little bit of research had paid dividends: Graeme Frost was relaxing.

"Now, Mr Frost, I need a travelling head lad, and Declan Kelly tells me that you're the man for the job."

"That's very kind of him, sir."

They talked for over an hour. In his anxiety to please, Graeme Frost held nothing back, and Edward learned virtually everything he needed to know. His knowledge of horses was great; equally important, his love of them was profound and sincere. He spoke of one famous Classic-winning filly he had ridden at work with the same tenderness as an old man might use when talking of a lovely girl of long ago, lost, but never forgotten. His wide-ranging interests included literature and painting; somewhat shamefacedly, he confessed that during the last two years, he had been boosting his meagre and uncertain income by selling a few water-colours.

Declan took him on the tour of the yard, and when they came back, Graeme Frost was very pleased but nervous. Edward understood at once. He had seen the promised land, and was terrified of being pitched out of it.

"Well, what did you think of it, Mr Frost?" Edward asked as Declan brought him into the office which was empty now.

"It's very nice, sir. Well, actually, it's magnificent."

"Would you like it here?"

"Oh yes, sir!"

"Right, you can be my travelling head lad." Edward named a salary that caused Graeme Frost's face to flush. "And there's the house as well. You'd want that?"

"Yes please, sir."

"So, what do you think?"

"I'll take it, and thank you very much, sir." As they shook hands on the deal, he added, "Everyone calls me Freezer, sir."

Edward smiled and nodded. "You can start as soon as you like," he said. "Have you got much sorting out to do?"

"No, sir. The only thing is, I'm getting married next week." Freezer said it as though he did not quite believe it himself. "This will be a marvellous place for a honeymoon." He meant it. To him and his wife-to-be, Saxon Court and the hopes it inspired were the ambition that had been written off ten unhappy years ago.

Edward decided that it was best to say nothing. Instead, he went to the safe, and took out one of the bundles of five hundred pounds that Siobhan always checked carefully, even though they came direct from the bank in sealed packets.

"Here you are, Freezer," he said, tossing the wad across, "that's an advance on your share of our first season's kitty. Get your car fixed, and buy your wife something nice for her wedding day."

Freezer found speech difficult. He tried to say, "Thank you," but failed. In the end he managed, "I won't let you down, sir," and went out. Edward was pleased to see that he went to see Mary and Declan before he set off back to Newmarket.

When Caroline came into the office a few minutes later, she found Edward in the window-seat. He was very thoughtful, almost sad, she thought.

"Was he all right?" she asked.

"Very much so. He's starting as soon as possible."

"What's the matter then?"

"Oh, nothing. Yes, damn it, there is! He's not just a good man, he's a *very* good man."

"And you've hired him."

"Yes, I know. But he was on the scrap-heap, and if it hadn't been for us and Declan, he'd have stayed there. It can be a bloody awful life when it wants to be."

She walked over to him, knelt down beside him and rested her arms on his knees. "I told you that," she said quietly. "Remember? I said we ought to do something about it."

"Yes, you did. And I had the incredibly good sense to take your advice."

"Well, it was more of an order really, wasn't it?" she asked, and wrinkled her nose.

He ran his fingertips along the line of one of her fascinating cheek-bones. "Have I told you how beautiful you are?" he asked.

"Not today."

"Well you are, very beautiful."

Two days later, on a Saturday afternoon, Mark and Sarah Walgrave arrived at Saxon Court unexpectedly. Mark's principal news was that his father had retired on medical advice, and surprised everyone by severing all links with Walgrave Precision and moving to a villa near Antibes.

"He actually told me that he'd hated every minute of working for the firm," Mark said, still hardly able to believe something that had happened several weeks ago. "He'd always wanted to play the piano!"

"Can he?" Edward asked.

"No, that's the funny part of it. I believe he's having lessons now, and he seems to have started lotus eating."

"That's a turn-up for the book!" Edward said. "So, presumably you're running the company?"

"I am. And making a splendid job of it!"

"And we've sold our house and moved into the dreaded Elms," Sarah said. "Mind you, we're having the place put right – you know, modified slightly."

"It's a bit of a demolition job really," Mark confessed. "We've come to grief over the bathroom. Her ladyship wants it *en suite* to a new master bedroom."

"What's the difficulty?" Caroline asked.

"According to our 'expert', it can't be done."

"Rubbish! Come and have a look at ours."

After they had gone, Mark wandered round the kitchen making fatuous small-talk until he got on Edward's nerves.

"Mark! What on earth's the matter with you?"

Mark stopped dead in his tracks and looked sheepish. "Well, the fact is, I've bought eight horses."

"You've done what?"

"I've bought eight horses."

"Racehorses?"

"Yes – well, they're supposed to be."

"When? Where?"

"Last week. There was a disposal sale of Willoughby Stanton's stuff down at Broadbridge, his place in Sussex."

"Yes, I read about that."

"So I went down – just to see what it was like, really."

"And you bought eight?"

"Yes."

"How much?"

"Twenty-seven thousand."

"Each?"

"No, for the lot."

"How old are they?"

"Two."

"What, this year or last year?"

"Oh, last year."

"Why didn't you ask me to come with you?"

"You wouldn't have let me buy anything."

"You're probably right!"

Edward stared at him, not knowing whether to laugh or cry. In the end, he had difficulty keeping a straight face.

"They're very good," Mark protested. "Two of them are entered for the Derby."

"My God, Bernard Dalrymple must be losing sleep!"

"Who's Bernard Dalrymple?"

"He's the chap who's probably going to win it. I was looking at the list this morning. He's got *nine* horses entered at the moment. He'll only run one, of course, and I think I know which one it will be, but I'd give my eye teeth to have any one of them in my yard."

"Oh." Mark looked crestfallen. "I was hoping you'd train them for me."

Edward grinned. "Of course I will. Where are they at the moment?"

"Still at Broadbridge."

"We'd better get them out of there. They won't be looked after any too well now they're sold. You do realise that this is going to cost money?"

"Oh yes." Mark was dreadfully eager.

Although it was a Saturday afternoon, Siobhan was busy in the office. Edward explained Mark's position to her. "We shall have to get Mr Walgrave registered," he said, "and you need to select your racing colours, Mark."

"Sarah's got some ideas about that," Mark replied, and pulled a piece of paper out of a pocket.

"She's keen, is she?" Edward asked, taking the paper and passing it straight to Siobhan.

"Yes, very."

"Good." There were unlikely to be problems stemming from domestic disharmony: Edward was pleased by the unexpected windfall of eight horses, but recognised that they might disappear as quickly as they had come. "I hope Sarah won't be disappointed if she can't have these colours. They might be very close to someone else's – or the Jockey Club could decide they don't like them."

"She'll understand."

"Whatever happens, we'll see you fixed up with something decent. Now then, let me explain what I can do for you. I shall have a look at these animals of yours, give them some work, and decide what they're good for. Then I shall enter them for races where I think they might be in with a chance. In big races with an experienced owner like Richard Stewart or Valerie Malahide, I'd consult the owner before declaring the horse to run. I'd prefer not to do that with you."

Mark nodded agreement. "You'd be much better without me confusing the issue," he said. "You will let me know when you're going to run one, won't you? We'd like to be there."

"Don't worry, you shall go to the ball," Edward promised.

February the twenty-first saw two momentous events. The first took place at Widney Cheyne in the small hours of the morning, and those at Saxon Court were unaware of it until late afternoon.

At eight o'clock, the colts James Henry and Parsifal arrived at their permanent home. They had finished schooling and were ready for training. Everyone turned out to see them, including Mary, who abandoned her breakfast preparations for a few minutes. She and Kathleen Corrigan stood on either side of Rosie Frost, Freezer's wife of a few weeks. Rosie was fortyish, pretty, plump, and a bundle of bustling activity whom Mary had taken to her heart at once. The moment Rosie arrived, she was looking for work, and ways of helping. She had gained instantaneous acceptance and popularity, and Edward insisted on paying her for all she did. Now Rosie was witnessing her first major event at Saxon Court, with Mary and Kathleen making sure that she was one of the family.

Robin Lane led Parsifal from the van first. The colt stood for a few moments, assessing his surroundings and the semi-circle of nearly fifty people who had come to see him. Once he had decided that all was well, Robin walked him round in a circle and murmurs of approval rippled through the onlookers. When Caroline brought James Henry out, he was at home immediately, apparently regarding the admiring crowd as no more than his entitlement.

"Come on, Freezer," Caroline said. "You've got to get to know this fellow. Walk him round." Rosie felt honoured as Freezer made friends with Caroline's pride and joy.

Edward was reminded of the day Musetta had arrived at Avoca House. "Now that *is* class," James Henry had said, and everyone present had agreed with him. Now, three years later almost to the day, the same sentiments were expressed about his namesake. "He's lovely," Siobhan said. Normally she would have refrained from expressing an opinion because she was convinced that she knew nothing about horses; on this occasion, her comment was a spontaneous reaction to a superb animal.

While the two colts were taken into the New Yard to inspect their boxes, Dooley set off to fetch some more of the Kentucky acquisitions, and the crowd dispersed. Nothing was said, no one made an announcement or voiced a hunch, but two hours later, they all gathered again. After a short wait, they were rewarded by the sound of hooves on the cobbles inside the arches as Caroline and Robin Lane rode James Henry and Parsifal out.

"They're going to baptise one of the all-weather gallops," Edward told Freezer. "Nothing too serious, but they have been working quite hard at school, and we may as well keep them up to the mark."

Everyone trooped through the arches, following the two colts to the point at which the path divided, straight on to the Avenue and Saxon Down, right for the New Ground. Approaching the start of the newly-laid gallops, they saw Declan riding back along them on a hack, and Edward hurried forward to speak to him.

"It's all right," Declan declared. "Very nice surface. Do you want to go with them?"

"Yes, please," Edward replied. Declan got down off the hack, and gave him a leg-up.

They set off at a walk, James Henry and Parsifal side by side, Edward keeping a good distance behind them to watch the way they moved. After two furlongs with no sign of problems, they moved on to a trot, and again, everything was as it should be.

"All right, Caro?" Edward asked when they reached the end of the all-weather strip. "How does he feel?"

"Wonderful!"

"Robin?"

"He's very good indeed, sir."

Edward looked the horses over, pleased with the way they had behaved so far. "They've been well schooled," he said.

"Hugh and Celia Massingham know what they're doing," Caroline replied.

"All right, let's give them a canter back."

Caroline smiled reassuringly at the slight anxiety he betrayed. "Robin and I have ridden this pair several times already," she said. "I never told you, but we've been on them for over three weeks."

"I should have worked that out," Edward replied. He had noticed that Robin had been going with her almost every day. "And I suppose Alison and Cathal O'Brien have been up on the others?"

"They have."

Parsifal had a clean, workmanlike action reminiscent of Murgatroyd, whereas James Henry immediately demonstrated that he was in a class of his own. He wanted to go off at a tremendous pace, and Caroline had a struggle to settle him. When he did calm down from his initial excitement, he moved like a dream, revelling in the sense of his own power, eating up the ground with a long stride that seemed almost nonchalant; his elegance was controlled, as if he knew all about it, and was seeking ways to make it even better.

"I've never seen one that good," Rosie Frost said.

"Nor me," Freezer agreed. "And I'll tell you something else, love. Mrs Manning can't half ride."

"Don't they make a picture!"

Rosie was the first to comment upon a sight that was destined to become widely admired. Edward noticed it too. Caroline and her colt seemed to be part of one another. Caroline had enlivened the occasion with a small item of dress. As usual in such doubtful weather, she was wearing a dark-green waterproof boiler-suit: the safety helmet was the bane of her life. Unadorned, she thought it ludicrous and ugly. Normally, she covered hers with a woolly hat, but today she was using one of

Richard's silk racing caps, and the golden tassel streamed out over James Henry for the first time. When the colts were pulled up, there was a burst of applause from the crowd, and Edward saw dozens of happy smiles as his hack ambled up, a good many lengths behind them.

"Well?" he asked Declan.

"Yes. He's useful."

"They both are."

"The other's not bad."

Several busy hours followed as Dooley and Liam Corrigan fetched the other new two-year-olds from school, and it was four-thirty before they were at ease in the office with a cup of tea. Siobhan picked the phone up when it rang. "Lady Stewart," she said, passing it to Edward.

"Musetta foaled this morning," Imogen announced. "Five o'clock apparently. Mother and child both doing splendidly."

"Wonderful! What's he like?"

"*She* is lovely."

"Oh!"

"Richard said you'd be cheesed off if it was a girl."

Edward laughed at Imogen's choice of words, coloured by her habitual pronunciation of 'off' as 'orf'. "No, I'm delighted," he assured her. "I take it they're both being looked after?"

"I assume so. Damn it, you chose the staff!"

It was true. As yet, there were only two middle-aged men working in the stud at Widney Cheyne, and Edward had helped Richard pick both of them. "I must get over to see them."

"Come to lunch on Sunday."

Inevitably, Caroline became quite sentimental over the foal, and Edward, who had never seen one so young before, was also affected. "She's all legs," he said. "And she seems to have more of them than she can cope with at the moment."

"Those legs are going to be all right," Richard said with an air of the proud father about him. "She's going to win the Guineas like her mother."

"She's gorgeous," Caroline said for the thirty-seventh time. "What are you going to call her, Richard?"

"Rhinemaiden," he replied firmly.

"We *really* are into Wagner this year," Imogen said gloomily.

"So I see," Edward chuckled. He was fussing Musetta, who was always pleased to see him.

"It's all very well for you," Imogen complained. "You only have to train the consequences. I actually have to *listen* to the wretched stuff. We even have it in the car on the way to the station in the morning!"

Richard produced a surprise as they sat down to lunch. "I was talking to one of your owners the other day," he said.

Edward was mystified. "Who?"

"His Grace the Duke of Dorchester."

"I've never seen him or heard from him – he pays his bill of course. How did you come to meet him?"

"He's a client of the bank," Richard said. "He comes for a chat once a year. We have lunch, put the world to rights, and talk a little business. Very civilised!" There was a pause as he debated a point with himself. "He isn't in a financial pickle like so many of the aristocracy – rather the reverse in fact."

"As I understand it, he's in trade, isn't he?" Imogen said.

Caroline, who was learning to know her, started to giggle.

"That's something of an over-simplification, my dear," Richard said mildly. "The Duke has two major estates, both of several thousand acres. There's one in Norfolk that's arable farm as far as the eye can see – you can imagine what that could mean with Common Market subsidies the way they are. The other one in Scotland has the lot – forestry, game, every sort of fishing, a couple of distilleries, two hotels and now time-sharing holiday apartments. It's all very well managed by the heir."

"Gerald, Marquess of Saxmundham," Imogen explained. "Married Ariadne Baverstock's dreadful daughter. He's a frightening merchant."

"That's the Harvard Business School for you," Richard said. "He's very good indeed."

"Why does he lurk in some Scottish forest?" Imogen demanded.

"I believe he likes it there. I know he's got strange eyebrows, my dear, but he does turn in a very handy profit. I know of a dozen so-called blue-chip companies that could use Gerald to their advantage."

"He'd have to change some of his habits if he got himself a proper job," Imogen muttered.

Richard addressed himself to Edward in order to return to the point. "The Duke and I came to the conclusion that he has some capital that could be gainfully employed rather than letting the Revenue have it."

"How much?" Edward asked, forgetting himself.

"Are we going to become a tax fiddle?" Caroline asked.

"Now, children," Richard said with mock-severity. "At this rate you won't get any pudding. His Grace intimated that he would like to put it to 'sporting' use. Naturally I suggested bloodstock."

"There you are," Caroline said. "I told you!"

"He said he'd think about it," Richard said, and gave up.

Frederick Algernon de Vere Lawson-Grey, ninth Duke of Dorchester and Earl of Ballater, lived near Marlborough, only twenty miles from Saxon Court, so it was easy for him to drive over one morning. Caroline and Edward were in the covered ride watching the second lot warm up before they went out to the gallops, when Siobhan dashed up to them.

"The Duke of Dorchester's here," she gasped. "Arrived! Just like that."

Edward at least had Richard's warning to be thankful for. Telling Declan to carry on, he grabbed Caroline's hand, and they hurried through the arches towards the house. They found the Duke in the kitchen, happily puffing away at a pipe, and chatting to Rosie Frost who was placing a cup of coffee in front of him. In his mid-sixties, and dressed in comfortable casual clothes that must have cost a fortune ten years ago when new, he had the benignly relaxed air that Edward felt should always accompany wealth and position. He glowed with health.

"My dear chap, sorry to burst in on you like this," he said, standing up and holding out his hand.

"That's perfectly all right, Your Grace," Edward managed to say. "You know my wife, don't you?"

"Yes, indeed. Hello, Caroline, my dear." He kissed her hand with great gallantry, and stood back to admire her. "By God, you're lovelier than ever," he said. "Marriage agrees with you. You're a lucky fellow, Manning."

"I know, sir."

"Right!" The Duke sat down and sipped his coffee. "I wasn't 'just passing' as they say – I came especially. Had a chat with Richard Stewart the other day."

"Yes, sir, he mentioned it."

"Good! Sit down! Have some coffee!" They did as they were told, Edward glad to see Caroline's nose wrinkle; she too found the Duke's attitude hilarious. "I've chewed over what young Stewart told me, and I've decided to take racing rather more seriously. As a matter of fact, I'd rather like to win the Derby, you know."

Edward gaped, then struggled for words. "Er . . . that's a nice idea," he said. "It's likely to be expensive."

"Ha! That's the least of the problems from what Stewart said. It seems that after one's shelled out the spondulicks, the blasted animals go lame, or start coughing or generally don't feel like it. That right?"

"It can happen, sir. I believe patience is the main thing, not money."

"All right, well said! I've got the money. You got the patience?"

"I'm in the wrong business if I haven't."

"You game to have a go?"

"The principal objective of this place is to train a Derby winner."

"Splendid! Where do we start?"

Caroline and Edward spent nearly an hour explaining the fundamentals, dismaying the Duke with the news that it would be at least eight months before any worthwhile yearlings came on to the market, and another eight months until any of them could reasonably expect to see a racecourse.

"Can't we start now?" he asked.

"No reason why not," Edward replied. "Presumably you don't mind winning other races?"

"What – have a sort of practice, do you mean?" The Duke laughed at the idea.

"You could put it like that."

"All right. I'll get some horses."

"That might not be easy at this time of year," Caroline warned. "Anything being sold now could well be suspect."

"Don't worry, m'dear! I can smell a rat at two thousand paces. Now then, lunch. That pub in the village is pretty fair, isn't it?"

It was nearly two o'clock when the Duke brought them back in his thirty-year-old sports car. The lunch-time crowd in the public bar of the Fortescue Arms had vastly enjoyed the entertaining company of the old boy who was clearly a bit of a toff, until Edward had called him "Your Grace". Things had quietened down a bit after that, and the Duke acted swiftly to prevent further similar discomfort. "Look here, we can't have this," he said. "If we're going to work together, you'd better call me 'Freddie' – everyone does – and I'll call you 'Manning'. That should preserve the social order, don't you think?" Guffawing, he unleashed his car and roared off.

"There doesn't seem to be a lot wrong with him," Edward said, quite bemused by the whole business.

"I never realised he was such a card," Caroline said reflectively. "Nor did I know he was so wealthy. I told you father used to handle owners badly. Sad, isn't it?" Her mood changed completely. "Sit down! Have some coffee!" she barked in imitation of the Duke, and they fell about laughing, holding on to one another for support. Mary saw them from one of her front windows, and smiled to herself. Rosie had told her all about the Duke's unheralded arrival, and what they had been discussing. It had clearly gone well.

Edward went into the office, flopped down in the window-seat and told Siobhan all about it.

"So we're going to get some more horses?" she said.

An important thought suddenly struck Edward. "Siobhan, I want James Henry and Parsifal entered in the Guineas and the Derby for next year," he said. "Could you do that at the appropriate time, please?"

Caroline kissed Edward's forehead. "There you are, we're in business," she said.

"Well, we've done the easy bit. Now we've got to look after them and train them."

They stayed in the office mulling over plans for the approaching season. At four thirty, Sean Gillespie came in. He was actually looking pleased with himself.

"I've bought that house," he announced.

"Very good!" Edward had started to fear that Sean's interest in the cottage near the village green had waned. He had seemed perfectly happy with a makeshift arrangement, first in the lads' hostel, then with Dooley, but this manifestation of a desire for permanency was most welcome. "Can you afford it?" Edward asked.

"Just about." It was the first time Edward had ever seen Sean Gillespie look uneasy.

"Let me know if you want any help. How about furniture and things?"

"Lady Stewart's helping out. I must go and have a look at his lordship."

"He's been in and out of the yard an awful lot," Caroline said after he had gone.

"He's very smitten with your colt," Edward replied. This was perfectly true. Like everyone else, Sean Gillespie had taken one look at James Henry, and been won over. He had already ridden him several times, pronounced him to be the best horse he had ever sat on, and always called him 'his lordship'.

"I have a feeling there's more to it than that," Caroline said thoughtfully.

Fine weather throughout March and the early part of April pleased everyone except Edward. "Typical, isn't it!" he grumbled to Declan. "We've got the covered ride and the all-weather tracks so that we can handle everything, and look at it! There'll be a drought if this goes on much longer."

"The perversity of nature, sor."

"I'd call it something else!"

The first runner, one of Mark Walgrave's horses, went out to Newmarket in the middle of April. It was Freezer's debut as travelling head lad, and among the kit he took with him was a sheepskin noseband, one of a brand new batch of twenty. The great Mill Reef had always worn one when he raced, and Edward had decided that his horses would do the same. It was something he had never quite got round to at Avoca House, but Siobhan had seen to it during the winter. Mark's filly Heliotrope was the first to wear the new Saxon Court insignia in public, but even with this and the lucky blanket, she still ran indifferently and finished among the stragglers. Over the next two weeks, nine horses went out, they all failed to get anywhere, and Dooley's patience was wearing thin.

Edward's answer was successful, although it failed to please Dooley.

"He should give you something to smile at," Edward told Freezer as

215

Murgatroyd was loaded for the long journey to Catterick. He did; unfortunately for Dooley, the northern bookmakers saw him coming as soon as he left Berkshire and had him at odds on from the moment betting started. After that, there was another disappointing two weeks, with horses racing nearly every day, and coming home with nothing to show for it. As one or two worried faces began to appear in the yard, three winners came in two days. Then, T. P. Malahide consolidated his victory at Newbury, by making a good field of nine horses look very moderate in a Group Three race at Sandown Park. Freezer and Dooley came back from that one looking very happy, although for different reasons. That evening, Edward spent an hour in the office after evening stables. After a careful study of the coming week's races, he rang Mark Walgrave.

"I'm going to run that filly Heliotrope at Bath next Tuesday," he said.

"So soon?"

"That last race seems to have done her a lot of good. She's been looking very well since, and her work's improving all the time."

"Oh. That's good."

"I think you should be there if possible."

"Do you think she's going to win?" Mark's excitement was sudden and overwhelming.

"I believe she'll run well."

Edward went to Bath to keep Mark company, and they were duly rewarded. Sean Gillespie held Heliotrope back until Mark was certain that all was lost, and even Edward was having doubts; everyone was surprised by Heliotrope's barnstorming finish, especially the jockey of another horse, who was convinced he was heading for the winner's enclosure. Mark had won a prize of a little under one thousand pounds, and had a brief moment of glory leading his first winner in. He was so pleased that he did not realise that hardly anyone took any notice of him or the filly who had ensured his future enthusiasm for the sport. A group of racing journalists gathered round Edward, but they wanted to talk about everything except Heliotrope. When he had finished with them, Edward set about explaining to Mark that he now had to give quite appreciable slices of his prize-money to a number of deserving causes such as Sean Gillespie and the yard kitty.

With seventy horses in the yard, and all the lads fully employed with two horses each, the first weeks of the season saw the establishment of a sacrosanct routine at Saxon Court. Everything revolved round ten o'clock in the morning. This was inviolate. It was the time by which runners for the following day had to be declared. Siobhan usually made the important telephone call; on the rare occasions when she was unavailable, Caroline did it. The day began at six o'clock when Declan went round all the horses to check that the night had not brought problems. Unless he had travelled away for an overnight stay with a horse that was racing, Freezer usually joined Declan for this first inspection. The lads were in the yard at seven for mucking out and making ready, and the first lot went out on the stroke of eight with Caroline or Edward accompanying them to supervise the work. Mary or Rosie had breakfast ready for nine-thirty. Over the meal, Caroline, Edward, Declan, Freezer and Sean Gillespie made any decisions necessary for the ten o'clock phone call and considered future plans. The second lot went out at ten-thirty and were back by twelve. From twelve until one, the horses were fed and groomed, and Edward worked in the office with Siobhan. Officially, nothing happened in the yard until evening stables at five-thirty, but Declan was generally around, keeping an eye on horses with strained ligaments or other minor injuries. When evening stables had finished at about six-thirty, the lads went to supper, and the yard settled down for the night. Declan did a round at nine, and was always on hand to deal with horses coming back late from racing.

Things were slightly different if Edward had to go racing, but, because of Freezer, the need for this dropped sharply.

Caroline soon found a use for those afternoons that were totally free between a late lunch and evening stables. "We can go and have a little lie-down," she said. "There are lots of things in that book we haven't tried yet. In any case, you need all the relaxation you can get." Edward needed little persuading, and the 'siesta' became a regular feature. The framework of their relationship was rock-solid, based on their respect for each other and their work together, and the telepathic bond between them often made it seem that they had been together for twenty years or more. Against this backcloth, a constant stream of new excitement unfolded. Caroline's afternoons, which she invested with a sense of the illicit, were a major part of this.

"It's after dark you're supposed to do it, you know," Edward told her after one exhaustingly satisfying bout of love-making.

"Do what?"

"Turn into a raving nymphomaniac."

"No, I've decided to be different. Bigger and better orgasms in broad daylight is the new motto. Is this a complaint, by the way?"

"Oh no, but I think I shall need to review the situation from time to time."

"How often?"

"Every ten years or so."

They always had a pot of tea afterwards. This was the time when, completely at peace with the world, Edward usually had the best ideas for future strategy. After he and Caroline had knocked his first thoughts into shape, they would be discussed at a breakfast meeting.

"That colt of yours is ready for a race," he said one afternoon.

"He's going to Ascot presumably?"

"Yes. But I fancy giving him a run first – something nice and gentle to get him used to the idea."

"And you've got something in mind?"

"I'm going to take him to Wolverhampton next week."

"Oh!" Caroline was surprised. Her father had never sent a runner to the Midland course, and inasmuch as she had thought about it, she had assumed that James Henry would make a more spectacular debut.

"I don't like pitching young horses in at the deep end," Edward explained. "A lot of people expect too much of two-year-olds. We want something to work on for next year. That fellow of yours is pretty good, and I reckon he can take care of himself, but I'd like to set him off with a good experience. He should walk all over them if he's as good as we think he is."

"When is it?"

"Thursday."

"A good gallop tomorrow then?"

"Yes. Sean had better ride him. I'll talk to him later."

"And then Ascot?"

"Oh yes!"

"What else are we sending to Ascot?"

"I don't know yet. They're all doing well, so we can take our pick when the time comes."

Caroline nodded. They had over twenty entries for the meeting, some horses in more than one race. There was no need to think of final plans until four days before each of the races, with the final decision coming at ten o'clock the day before.

"I'll tell you what, though," Edward went on. "I think I'm going to give Murgatroyd another go at the Hunt Cup."

She laughed. "Isn't he marvellous!"

"Better than ever. Do you know, I was wondering if he might have been over the hill, but these two-year-olds have really brightened him up."

Ridden as ever by Liam Corrigan, Murgatroyd had been showing the Kentucky youngsters the way on the new sand track. Every Wednesday and Saturday morning, they worked a brisk five furlongs in groups of three about fifty yards apart, with Murgatroyd leading the way, enjoying himself enormously. James Henry and Parsifal had started off in the group, but had been taken out after two weeks to tackle more challenging work.

As Caroline moved across the room to refill their cups, Edward indulged in one of his favourite pastimes, admiring her legs. She smiled at the seriousness he brought to bear on the activity.

"I can never work out if your interest is personal or professional," she said.

"Sorry, I'm not with you."

"When you look at me like that, is it lust, or are you checking for spavins and strains?"

"Oh, it's pure lust – likely to become applied as soon as I can get hold of you."

"Pure and applied lust!" Caroline chortled at the idea. "You never taught that at King Henry's, I'll bet."

"I did! Three times a day."

"H'm . . . so you are going off then. Here, talking of lust, what were you doing with Alison this morning?"

"My hands never left my arms, your honour!"

"You were closeted in the tack room for an awfully long time."

"T. P. Malahide," he said. Since Robin Lane was now looking after James Henry and Parsifal, Alison Bairstow had taken over T. P. Malahide and Radames. "We were deciding what to do with him."

"And?"

"I think we're going to give him a crack at the Eclipse."

"Really?" Her eyes widened in surprise. Named after a legendary horse of around 1770, the Eclipse Stakes, run at Sandown Park in early July, was a prestigious event for horses aged three and upwards. Classified as Group One, it sometimes saw the defeat of the winner of the Derby by an older horse. "Is he good enough?"

"There's only one way to find out," Edward replied. "I think he might be. Ten furlongs is his trip, and he's starting to turn into a really good horse."

"That's patience for you," Caroline said.

"Alison's brought him on a lot. He used to be a bit timid. She's put a stop to that."

"You said she would!"

Edward telephoned Widney Cheyne that evening to speak to Richard. "He's not here," Imogen told him. "He's swanning around America again."

"Oh . . . when did he go?"

"Last Wednesday. Due back on Sunday."

"Business, presumably."

"Some of it is – but I can smell horses as well. Did you want him for something important?"

"Yes. I'm going to give James Henry his first outing next Thursday."

"He'll be interested in that. Where is it?"

"Wolverhampton."

"Wolverhampton?" Imogen's tone was a mixture of disbelief and horror.

"That's right."

"Good God!"

James Henry set off for the Midlands the day before the race, accompanied by Freezer and Robin Lane. Edward had a word with Dooley as he climbed into the cab of the van. "You'll find he isn't worth having a bet on, Paddy," he warned.

Dooley nodded mournfully. "I thought that would be the case, sor. Bookmakers have no finer feelings."

"That may be true – although my grandfather claimed to have known some very nice ones. However, they are not mugs!"

Leaving Saxon Court after the second lot had come back, Caroline and Edward arrived on the course an hour before the race, and promptly spotted Richard among the smallish crowd. Edward was surprised to see that Richard had a woman with him, and was staggered when she turned round and he recognised her. "That's Nancy Bloomfield," he said. "What the hell's she doing here?"

"Perhaps she's come to see how her yearling's getting on," Caroline suggested. She knew it was a far-fetched notion, and sounded unconvinced by it.

"What, four thousand miles to see him deal with this bunch?"

Richard laughed at the expressions on their faces. "It's only Nancy," he said. "You look as though you've seen a ghost."

"We're very surprised," Edward said, shaking hands with Nancy. "Hello, Nancy. You must be the last person I expected to see here."

She always smiled slowly. It took a little time to achieve its full effect, but eventually, the whole of her face and brown eyes were lit up. "I had to see how my fella was getting on," she said. "It's a big day for him."

"It's lovely to see you," Caroline said. "What a way to come, though!"

"Ah, well . . ." Nancy allowed them to make the most of their assumptions. Not until Caroline and Richard had gone to check on James Henry while he was in the exercise ring by the racecourse stables, did she reveal the truth to Edward.

"Actually, I'm working for Sir Richard now," she said.

"You mean here, in England?"

"Yeah. I'm going to be the stud manager."

"At Widney Cheyne?"

She smiled and nodded. "He's fixing me up with a house and everything."

"I'm very pleased," Edward said. "My word, this is a shaker! When did all this happen?"

"Last week. I came over from the States with him. But we've talked about it for some time. Sir Richard knew I wanted a move away from Tornado. I thought it was time I got some more experience, saw some proper racing, as well. And Marylou had gotten up my nose." She said it with her customary quietness, yet invested it with immense feeling.

"Marylou?" Edward was lost.

"Elmer Drury's woman."

"Ah! Yes." He recalled the blonde of indeterminate age who had said very little, drunk rather a lot and needed a permanent supply of Country and Western music. "There were problems?"

"Oh yes, there were problems. So I thought, 'What the hell? Let's have a complete change of scene.' I guess that was just before you came over, last fall. So here I am!"

Edward had often thought about the last private, and very earnest-looking conversation that Richard and Nancy had had at Lexington Airport. Now, he found himself wondering if an unhappy love affair had prompted Nancy; had she and Elmer Drury been close before Marylou turned up? Surely not! "What did Elmer have to say about you clearing off?" he asked.

"Not much. He was as glad to be rid of me as I was to be out of it. Anyhow, how're you making out with your new place?"

"Very well. We've been getting the winners, all the horses are fine, and I think we might be seeing some real action soon."

"You've got Ascot coming up?" He was charmed by her pronunciation of it: two quite distinct syllables – "Ass-cart".

"Yes, in two weeks."

"I'm hoping to see some of that."

"You certainly will! You'll be our guest."

"Will I get to wear one of those hats?"

"It's up to you – anything you like."

Caroline and Richard reappeared as the horses came into the paddock.

"Have you found out?" Caroline asked Edward.

"Yes." Edward looked at Richard, who was rather pleased with himself. "How long have you been hiding her?" he asked.

"Only three days – she's been jet-lagged and trying to understand Imogen for most of the time."

After knowing Richard for twenty years, Edward was used to his tricks, and this had been a prime example of his favourite, the *fait accompli* cloaked in secrecy to be produced when it would have maximum effect. It was rather like the way Sean Gillespie sometimes rode a race, and it was, Edward supposed, a useful technique in the world of merchant banking.

"Hey! Look at him," Nancy said as Robin Lane brought James Henry into the paddock, and her face glowed. He had grown a good deal since she had last seen him, and although he had looked well at Tornado, he was magnificent now that he was in training and approaching his peak.

"Good, isn't he?" Edward said proudly.

"I've never seen one in that condition," Nancy said. "And that sheepskin's a knock-out."

The noseband looked particularly well on a horse of outstanding class, who habitually carried his head high.

"That's his lad, Robin Lane leading him," Edward explained. "Poor Robin doesn't ride him very often. Caro does that."

Before they went into the centre of the paddock, James Henry passed them while they were still outside, leaning on the rail. He recognised Nancy at once, and wanted to stop. However, he showed his equable temperament and appreciation that something serious was afoot by moving on smartly the instant Robin spoke to him. Nancy's chance to greet him came a few minutes later as Edward gave Sean Gillespie a leg-up.

The Wheaton Aston Maiden Stakes had been in existence for about thirty years as a race for two-year-old colts and fillies who had not won previously. Over the years, its value to the winner had increased from a hundred and eight to eight hundred and seventy pounds, and fourteen of the fifteen runners reflected the modesty of this figure. As the horses went down to the start, James Henry stood out dominantly.

"My word, he does move well," Richard said admiringly.

"Let's see if he comes back like that," Edward replied, cautious in spite of his convictions.

The point was not lost on the real experts among the spectators. "Just look at that thing with the sheepskin noseband," a hardbitten racing journalist from Birmingham said to a couple of London cronies. "What *does* Manning think he's doing here?"

"Easy debut. Just running him in," one of the London men suggested, and the other nodded agreement. "That's a bloody good horse, that is. And they know it! Look at the mob that's turned out to watch him. That's the Saxon Court first team."

"Who's the bird with Stewart?"

"Seems she's a Yank. Charlie Onions reckons she worked for the breeder of the horse. Stewart's got her now. Brought her over the other day. Fair looker."

"Not as easy on the eye as the luscious Caroline!"

"Each to his own, Nocker, each to his own."

The man from Birmingham had another look through his binoculars. "He moves like a Rolls, I'll say that for him. But a golden bloody tassel on his hat as well . . . I ask you!"

There were problems at the start with two horses who responded adversely to the occasion; one of them refused point-blank to enter the stalls, and was withdrawn. James Henry remained perfectly calm, in fact the jockeys in the compartments on either side of him thought he was sedated to the eyeballs, and were crass enough to voice this opinion to an unresponsive Sean Gillespie. The moment the gates opened, they knew they had been wrong. James Henry propelled himself out of the stalls like a bullet, and set off for home along the perfectly straight and level five furlongs.

"Do you suppose he's going to keep this up?" Richard asked Edward after James Henry had covered two furlongs with five or six lengths between himself and the rest of the field.

"Should do. This is how he is at home. The object of this exercise is to find out how he takes to racing."

"I'd say he'd more or less got the hang of it," Richard said, managing to keep the excitement out of his voice, and hiding most of his face behind binoculars.

"Looks like it." As they passed the furlong post, Edward added, "Oh dear!" in a small voice.

"What's wrong?" Richard demanded anxiously.

"Sean Gillespie's going to start riding him," Edward replied. "This may be embarrassing."

So far, Sean Gillespie had done nothing more than sit on James Henry's back like a reasonably intelligent sack of potatoes. For the sake of appearances, and because he felt like it, he now decided he was in a race, and started using his arms and legs. The colt responded immediately, lengthening his stride to win by what was officially described as fifteen lengths.

"I can stand any amount of that sort of embarrassment," Richard said smugly, and smiled at Caroline who was doing her best not to dance around.

"All right?" Edward asked Nancy as they walked towards the winner's enclosure.

"Was it! Do you know, Edward, that's the first time I've ever seen one of my horses after they've been sold."

"Really?" He was astonished.

"Yup! Boy, was that something!"

"That was quite moderate company he was in," Edward felt bound to point out. "In fact, they were all rather mediocre."

"Yes, but . . ."

"I know." He smiled. "I didn't actually expect him to do *that* well."

Richard gave James Henry to Caroline to lead in, and he received a substantial round of applause that had to be knowledgeable respect, for no one had won anything by backing him. Despite Edward's advance warning, Dooley had prowled off to investigate the market, returning ashen, an apparently broken man. The bookmakers had started James

Henry at four to one *on* with the rest at six to one and upwards. There had been virtually no betting on the race.

The journalist from Birmingham buttonholed Edward. "That's a good horse you've got there, Mr Manning."

"Thank you. Yes, he's very nice."

"This is the Northern Dancer colt that Sir Richard Stewart paid two hundred thousand for?"

"That's right."

"What are your plans for him?" Notebook and pencil were at the ready.

"He'll go to Ascot for the Coventry."

"And then?"

"We shall have to see how he gets on."

"He's entered for the Guineas and the Derby?"

"Oh yes – but I don't have to tell a chap of your experience that a lot can go wrong between now and then." Edward had no idea who the man was. It made no difference. He was beginning to enjoy talking to the press and TV. "I'll tell you this, though," he added confidentially. "We've already been working him over seven furlongs at home, so I'm very relaxed about him getting a good trip over a mile. I don't know whether he'll stay further, but the breeding looks good, doesn't it?"

'Nocker' Jarvis dashed back to Birmingham and wrote a fulsome piece for his paper. It raised eyebrows in London newspaper offices, as racing correspondents reached for their reference books.

Caroline and Edward stopped on the way home for a meal with Richard and Nancy, so they reached Saxon Court after James Henry. They went straight to the New Yard to see how he was.

"Grand," said Declan, who was looking him over with Robin Lane. "You wouldn't think he'd been in a race."

"Fifteen lengths!" Caroline said. She could still hardly believe it.

"I should think so against that lot!"

"Has he eaten up all right, Robin?"

"Yes sir, no problems. I think he enjoyed it."

Edward smiled. "I believe he did." He patted James Henry's neck. "We'll find you something a little more high class to enjoy next time," he said.

Siobhan had left a note. It was displayed prominently in the middle of the kitchen table.

"The Duke of Dorchester has bought 15 horses (2 & 3-y-o). Please ring him A.S.A.P."

"That's nice," Caroline said, reading it over his shoulder.

"The second piece of good news today. You know, darling, I think I might like it here after all!"

She laughed and tickled his ribs. Then she picked up the phone and handed it to him. "There you are, Manning, talk to Freddie!"

CHAPTER 10

Frank Manning's early retirement finally materialised the day after James Henry's winning debut. Edward was never entirely certain why it had taken so long. He came to the conclusion that his father had been far more dedicated to his career than he had ever admitted. However, on his sixty-first birthday, a splendid lunch was given in his honour, the speeches and presentations were made, and he left his office for the last time.

At home with Ann, he spent an hour poring over a well-thumbed specialist mail-order catalogue, and selected the two-thousand-pounds-worth of tools that were needed to elevate his lifelong interest in carpentry to professionalism. That evening they dined in style at a picturesque restaurant overlooking the River Severn above Worcester, and the following day they went to Saxon Court for a three-week stay. Knowing that Caroline and Edward were going racing, they timed their arrival for late afternoon.

Although only one horse was involved in a minor race at Bath, Caroline and Edward had gone to watch, in company with Imogen, Richard and Nancy Bloomfield. Frank was looking out of the office window as the van pulled in, and Caroline waved from the cab before extending both arms to give a thumbs-up gesture. Siobhan had known the result for over two hours: Parsifal had won.

"Only two lengths," she told Ann and Frank. "But he beat some good horses. Much better than Wolverhampton."

Frank watched the van drift slowly down to the entrance of the yard, and come to rest beneath the clock-tower. Parsifal, covered with a rug, looking slightly comical in travelling boots and knee-protectors, was brought out, fussed by Caroline and Edward, and taken away to his box by Declan. After Dooley had driven the van to the garage, Caroline and Edward remained in the archway, chatting animatedly. Suddenly they erupted into laughter, Caroline putting an arm round Edward's shoulders to hold herself up. Rosie Frost saw Frank's smile. "There's a lot of that, sir," she said. "This is a very happy place."

It was. Caroline and Edward generated joy quite naturally, at any time, under any circumstances. They seemed to sense that they were approaching a period of miraculous fulfilment, and there was an air of golden assurance about them.

Anxious that Ann and Frank should be fully at home, Caroline made sure they had breakfast in the kitchen with everyone else after the first lot.

"But for goodness' sake, don't say anything," she pretended to plead. "His Serene Importance requires absolute hush when he's evolving his strategies!"

Ann and Frank sat, listened, and were baffled. Frank was quick to spot the regard that everyone had for Edward's views, although it was usually concealed. Caroline pulled his leg mercilessly, often making a joke of his latest theory; Declan's reserve seemed to imply scepticism; Sean Gillespie was downright cynical; only Freezer displayed respect when Edward proposed something new. But they went away and did it, nine times out of ten it worked, and they were quick to say so before giving the next idea the same treatment.

When Freezer drove Ann and Frank out early one morning to see the first lot work, they were given further food for thought.

Their arrival at Saxon Court had coincided with a spell of glorious weather. The magical early mornings of approaching mid-summer heightened the pleasure that Edward always derived from going out with the horses. Beneath the Avenue's majestic poplars, there was a profusion of hedgerows and shrubs that he had never noticed until they blossomed into a colourful riot, and while the dew still lay heavy, the fragrances were intoxicating. After passage through this tunnel of delights, the champagne-like atmosphere of the Down had an invigorating effect on horses and riders as they emerged into the crystalline brightness. When the first of the thirty-six two-year-olds appeared, Ann caught her breath at a sight that was unexpectedly beautiful and thrilling.

"That's James Henry and Parsifal leading, ma'am," Freezer explained.

The two scions of the great Northern Dancer dynasty at the head of the string were a resounding proclamation of intent. James Henry, ridden by Caroline, was his customary insouciant self; Frank saw why the lads had taken to calling him 'The Toff'. Alongside him, Parsifal stepped out with a more obvious pride than was present in his normal amiable gait; he was responding to his feeling that something important was afoot because Sean Gillespie was riding him. Ann was very taken by Caroline's pink jump-suit and silk cap with the tassel, Frank by Sean Gillespie's tracksuit made up of two unmatched halves. Edward and Declan on their hacks were the last to emerge from the Avenue, and took up a position in the centre of a well-used circuit as James Henry led the string round at a trot. At once, Edward was talking to Declan, pointing things out, looking at him for confirmation of some point, asking questions. It was all done quietly, without any sense of haste. Even in the stillness of the morning, Ann and Frank were unable to hear what was said.

"All right, that's enough!" Edward called after ten minutes, and all

227

but two of the horses headed towards the sand-track on the New Ground with Declan in attendance. Caroline and Sean Gillespie rode up to Edward, and a long discussion ensued.

"What's happening now?" Ann asked Freezer.

"Most of them are going for an easy gallop over the sand. That pair are doing a hard six furlongs."

Caroline and Sean Gillespie finished their conversation with Edward, wheeled their mounts round, and set off at a canter down one of the straight seven-furlong strips in the centre of the big U-shaped gallop. As they went, Edward walked his horse over to his parents. "This ought to be worth watching," he said.

"Caroline and Mr Gillespie look funny," Ann said. "It's strange seeing jockeys dressed like that."

"They look all right to me," Frank said. "They're very . . ." he searched for the right word ". . . very professional."

Edward laughed. "We have been showing occasional signs of that," he said.

On the way to the start of their gallop, the two colts and their riders disappeared into a hollow formed by one of the great folds of Saxon Down.

"You'll only see the last two furlongs," Edward said. "I've got a better view from up here."

Nothing happened. Ann became impatient, then worried. "What are they doing?" she asked.

"Here they come now."

As Edward said it, they heard the noise, the harsh, rapid breathing and the beat of hooves. It was followed by the appearance of heads. Even before they breasted the hill and were fully visible, it was obvious that they were going at a tremendous gallop.

"That's fast," Edward said. "You won't find too many races run at that pace."

There was a white marker post at the furlong distance, and Caroline got to work as they passed it. Leaning forward along James Henry's neck and seeming to become an integral part of him, she used her arms and legs with skilful vigour. James Henry responded at once, lengthening his stride and pulling clear of Parsifal on whom Sean Gillespie was trying equally hard. At the finish, James Henry was three lengths clear.

"That's very good indeed," Edward said coolly, turning his hack to follow them. "Parsifal's nobody's fool and that looked a bit comprehensive."

"Goodness me, I enjoyed that!" Frank said. The two brilliant two-year-olds had passed within a few yards of them, and his face was flushed with excitement. "And my word, can't Caroline ride!"

"She's marvellous, sir," Freezer agreed. "I understand there's a possibility she may get an amateur licence and do a bit of race-riding next year."

James Henry and Parsifal were nearly at the Avenue entrance before they pulled up. Caroline and Sean Gillespie dismounted at once and Robin Lane emerged from the trees to lead the horses back to the yard. Edward paused in his discussion with Caroline and Sean Gillespie to look at the other horses filing back from the sand. He called out something to Alison Bairstow who was riding a filly of Mark Walgrave's. She laughed, and checked her mount for a moment to reply, then they all disappeared into the deep, sweet-scented shadow of the Avenue.

"It makes you think he was only playing at it at Avoca House," Frank said to Ann afterwards.

"It's very different here," she agreed.

"Much better facilities, of course."

"And he's got Caroline."

Over the next few days, Ann and Frank roamed at will over Saxon Court, making endless discoveries.

Ann was most impressed by the peace and quietness of the place. Four times a day, as each lot went out and came back, there were a few minutes of bustle, the noise of hooves on cobbles, Declan apparently everywhere, giving orders and checking the minutest detail. At all other times, silence reigned. Horses went out to race without fuss or ceremony. After lunch, most of them were taken to the paddock to enjoy the lush grass and sun or to swim; by four-thirty they were back in their boxes being prepared for evening stables. Anyone not actually there to see it would never know that a complex movement of over seventy mettlesome animals had taken place. Siobhan was the only constantly conspicuous sign of Saxon Court's efficiency. She was in the office by eight each morning, never leaving before six. Breakfast after the first lot was often her only break of the day, and even then she was usually required to take notes or provide advice from the wealth of information at her fingertips. Ann saw that Edward looked after the horses, Siobhan ran the business.

Frank's wanderings brought him into contact with Dooley, and to Edward's surprise, a friendship developed. When Frank started disappearing during the afternoon, and it was realised he was with Dooley, Ann disapproved. Imogen set her right.

"Frank's advising him about his investments."

"Investments?" Edward gaped at her.

"Oh yes. Dooley has a little nest-egg. Whenever he backs a winner, most of the proceeds get put away. It used to be a bank in Kildare. I understand he's changed to a building society since he came here. Frank's persuading him to be a touch more adventurous. They're great chums."

229

"How do you know all this?" Edward asked.

"Sean Gillespie told me. Oh, by the way, I've found out why he's always infesting the yard."

"Ah! Tell!" Caroline was agog.

"Julie Spencer." Imogen thought that was sufficient explanation. It was for Caroline and Ann. Edward was baffled. He failed to make any connection between his jockey and the pretty blonde girl who did two of the Duke of Dorchester's horses.

"Young Mr Gillespie has fallen in love with her," Imogen announced loftily, but with a twinkle in her eye.

"There you are, my boy," Caroline said triumphantly. "I told you there was more to it than my colt."

"Sean Gillespie's in love?" Edward's reaction would have been the same if Imogen had informed him that the first lot had been frightened by a squadron of pigs flying low over Saxon Down.

"Head over heels," she confirmed. "Needless to say, he didn't have the faintest idea what to do about it, so I've done a bit to help."

"What?" Caroline's interest was bubbling into excitement.

"I spoke to the gel. Very discreet of course."

Edward's look was eloquent.

"And?" Caroline asked eagerly.

"She seemed awfully pleased."

"Is she going to do anything about it?"

"Oh, I imagine so. She's a Catholic by the way, so that probably helps."

Frank took his whole-hearted embrace of retirement a stage further a few days later. As Edward left the house after breakfast, Dooley was easing the van away from the yard entrance. He was on his way to Salisbury with one of Mark Walgrave's horses. As usual, Freezer was in the cab, looking cheerfully expectant. Half-way through an automatic, almost unthinking wave, Edward froze. Sandwiched happily between Dooley and Freezer was Frank, grinning like a jackanapes.

The filly Hyacinth won her race cleverly, unfortunately in the absence of Mark and Sarah who were abroad on holiday. But there was plenty to talk about over dinner. To Dooley's delight, Hyacinth had obliged at the opulent odds of fourteen to one.

"Paddy and I each had a twenty-pound flutter," Frank said, and pushed the resultant bundle of notes across the table towards Ann. "And I put the bet on," he added proudly.

"Why?" Edward asked.

"Paddy said he was too well-known. If the bookies had seen him, they'd have decimated the odds."

Recognising an authentic Dooley word, Edward joined in Caroline's helpless laughter.

Ann was far from sure. She looked at the pile of twenty-eight ten-pound notes that Frank had left in front of her plate with mixed feelings.

"Go on, it won't bite you," Edward said.

"It might even pay for an Ascot dress," Caroline added. "Well – part of one!"

Frank was looking forward to Ascot with gleeful anticipation. He had a surprise to spring. Even Ann did not know about it. After all the measuring and fitting, he had smuggled it into their house, then into Saxon Court, where he had needed an accomplice. Caroline had been perfect, showing him a convenient spare bedroom, and helping to unpack it. When everyone gathered on the first day of Royal Ascot, he was a sensation.

"That's good, very good indeed," Edward said, walking round Frank on a mock tour of inspection, full of admiration for his morning suit. "Whatever possessed you to have one made?"

"I can never get one to fit me from these hire shops," Frank said, "and I didn't want to let you and Caroline down."

Edward was as touched as Caroline had been when she had received the same answer.

Richard had taken a box in the grandstand, and they arrived to find the table set for lunch.

"Totally wasted on that pair," Imogen said, setting about the smoked salmon. "They've got this utter obsession with horses!"

The moment they arrived on the course, Caroline and Edward had gone to the stables to check on their runner for the first day, James Henry. Delayed by a conversation with Bernard Dalrymple and Finoula, their lunch finally consisted of cheese sandwiches washed down with tepid mineral water.

The arrival of the Queen and her party in the carriage procession entranced Nancy Bloomfield. "Now that really is something," she said quietly. "They've nothing like that at Churchill Downs."

"They try," Richard said.

"Yeah, they do." Nancy smiled ruefully. "This is a whole new ball-game, though." She thought for a few moments, adding, "That outfit the Queen was wearing?"

"Yes?" Imogen was on her guard.

"I guess it's . . ." Nancy struggled for the word, and settled for ". . . old."

"Oh, it probably is. She has clothes for years. I expect she's had something *done* to it since she wore it last."

Nancy shook her head wonderingly. "But there ain't no doubt she's the Queen!" she said.

There were over two hours to wait for James Henry's race, which was fourth on the card. Not all that long ago, Edward would have fretted at the delay, seethed at the crowds of once-a-year race-goers whom he regarded as ill-informed, and thought of all the other things he might be doing. Now, he was perfectly content to enjoy the occasion with Caroline, and listen to Nancy's first impressions of a peculiarly British institution.

"Hardly anybody watched that," she said after the second race.

"Of course not!" Caroline seemed surprised at the idea that anyone should think an Ascot crowd would bother with horses. "They've mostly come here to be *seen*, not to watch."

However, those who did care stuck close to the paddock rails, and Edward sensed the strong current of interest as Robin Lane brought James Henry in when the time came.

"I believe they've made him joint favourite," Richard said.

"Who with?" Caroline asked.

"Bernard Dalrymple's."

Edward studied the horse that Finoula was leading round. "He seems a decent enough sort," he said.

Caroline picked up the whiff of faint praise. "He won a good race at Newmarket," she said. "He beat some good stuff."

"Possibly. But he isn't going to cause our boy any trouble." Edward's confidence sounded positively supercilious.

By the time the ten runners went to post, the betting market indicated that an overwhelming majority shared Edward's view. James Henry was favourite at six to four, Bernard Dalrymple's horse was three to one, and the rest were considered no-hopers.

Caroline and Richard exchanged comical looks behind his back.

No one derived greater pleasure from the Coventry Stakes than Nocker Jarvis, perched uncomfortably in the press box. He was always ambivalent about his annual trek to Ascot. His hard-bitten cynicism caused him to view the proceedings with extremely jaundiced eyes. Some of the things he saw and heard made him want to laugh or puke according to his mood. The compensations were the divorced lady in Camberley who was always miraculously glad to see him, and the times when the beautiful people got egg on their smooth faces, or his hunches were proved correct.

He didn't bother going down to the winner's enclosure afterwards. A grubby oik like him would never get near the action. Instead, he picked the phone up, and dictated the piece for his loyal readers in Birmingham to savour over breakfast the following morning:

James Henry's victory in the Coventry Stakes at Royal Ascot was achieved by seven lengths in thrilling style.

Three weeks ago, this handsome Northern Dancer colt destroyed the field in his debut race at Wolverhampton. I had no doubt then that he was something way out of the ordinary.

Then we got the 'experts' telling us he hadn't beaten anything.

They've got something to ponder this morning. James Henry was up against a classy bunch yesterday. Between them, they cost over six million pounds as yearlings and had won fifteen races.

They still got the same treatment as the Wolverhampton nags.

James Henry is destined for the very highest honours. He's going to be exciting to watch. The bad news is that you'll never get odds against him after this performance.

Bernard Dalrymple, whose horse had finished second, leaned across the dividing rail in the winner's enclosure to offer his congratulations.

"That's an outstanding animal you have there, Mr Manning."

"Thank you, Mr Dalrymple."

"My horse actually won, you know. The only trouble was, he got mixed up in the next race!"

Edward smiled at the generous compliment.

When James Henry had been taken away to the stables, one of Wesley Davies's henchmen grabbed Edward for a TV interview. Edward's insistence that Caroline should accompany him boosted media interest in Saxon Court.

"A very exciting win, Edward," Wesley Davies began.

"Yes." Amazingly relaxed, Edward took a little time to think of anything else to say. "He's quite good, isn't he?" he added eventually.

"What are your plans for him?"

"Nothing very definite at the moment. I want to see how he progresses after this one. I'm not going to force him. I'll be looking for a decent race some time in September."

"And next year?"

"We might think of the Classics. You'd better ask Caro about that . . . he's her horse."

Wesley Davies turned to Caroline. "Well, Caroline, the old man's put you on the spot!"

She laughed, completely at ease. "He's like that!" She was suddenly thoughtful. "We think he might have the makings of a Guineas horse . . . he should get a mile all right. Then it's the sixty-four-thousand-dollar question, isn't it?"

"What's that?"

"Will he get the trip at Epsom?"

"I'm supposed to ask *you* that," Wesley Davies protested good-naturedly.

"I know! But I haven't the faintest idea what the answer is, so I thought I'd ask you! It's far too early yet. Let's wait and see, shall we?"

"What about your other horses? I believe you've got several more promising two-year-olds."

233

When the interview ended, it was universally agreed that Caroline's first TV performance had been even more successful than Edward's. Her beauty and charming directness made a substantial impact. She was the answer to many a jaded sports-editor's prayer, and the racing pages of the popular press began to feature her. For them, she and Edward, with Richard and the still-mysterious Nancy Bloomfield in the background were the "exciting and glamorous new team who were going to put Saxon Court back on the map".

Pleased as he was with James Henry, and much as he was looking forward to seeing what Parsifal could do on the third day, Edward's special interest was with the Royal Hunt Cup. Murgatroyd was at the peak of fitness and condition, and seemed to know that he was expected to achieve an entry in the record books by winning the race for an unprecedented third time. He did. By means of stylish bloody-mindedness and courage, pushed on by Sean Gillespie at his most grim-faced and obdurate, he wore down three horses that were arguably much better than him, and got the verdict by a short head.

There were wonderful pictures to be had as Edward led him in, and Imogen caught one that duly found its way into the Colour Room when Siobhan had arranged the enlargement and framing. It showed quite clearly Edward's boundless affection for the horse who had taught him to be a trainer, and was his link with Avoca House and his grandfather. Recognising the self-evidence of this, Siobhan left the picture without a caption.

Shortly after getting back home that evening, Edward heard his mother say, "Oh dear, they're at it again!"

Joining her in the bow window of the office, he saw Dooley and his father under the clock-tower. Ten-pound notes were changing hands, then Dooley had a number of strategic points to make. He wagged a forefinger a good deal, actually prodding Frank's chest at one point.

"You mustn't worry about that, Ann," Caroline said, sliding an arm round Edward's waist as she came to see what was going on. "You're very lucky. Frank's going to enjoy his retirement. At this rate he won't have time to get bored and old. Ah . . . now then . . . look at this!"

Sean Gillespie and Julie Spencer appeared from the yard where they had been visiting Murgatroyd. They were hand-in-hand and looking very pleased with themselves. Pausing to exchange friendly abuse with Dooley, they got into Sean Gillespie's car, and headed for the village.

"You see, Imogen *did* sort it," Caroline said. "What's up, my boy? You thinking of having a nervous breakdown?"

Edward shook his head slowly. "No, I'm going to be all right. It's the sight of Sean Gillespie smiling."

On the third day of Ascot, Parsifal won the Norfolk Stakes. He was a length ahead of a very good horse who was three lengths clear of the rest.

"H'm. So now we know," Edward mused as he watched the video-recording in the evening with Caroline.

"What do we know, sweetheart?"

"Well, we know James Henry can do Parsifal by three lengths at a mile."

"And that was a fair bunch Parsifal beat."

"Yes." Edward drew her closer to him. "It's possible that horse of yours might be as good as you think he is."

"Hey, don't blame me! You've got a bit of a soft spot for him as well."

"Yes." Edward struggled to keep his face straight. "He's starting to look a bit useful." He squirmed as she attacked his ribs.

"We're not going tomorrow?" Caroline asked when they were serious again. They had no runner on the fourth and last day of Royal Ascot.

"No, we'll stay here and get on with something useful. I think even mother and Nancy have seen enough to be going on with."

"They both looked a bit frazzled today."

"People will never realise that it's damned hard work traipsing round and looking decorative. It's a shame your father and Elspeth couldn't come."

"Yes." Caroline looked a little sad. "To be honest, I don't think he'll ever bother with racing again."

"What about if we get your horse to Epsom?"

She smiled. It was the first time either of them had dared to say it aloud. "Oh yes. I think he might make an effort for *that*."

"I should jolly well think so! And what about Nigel? I thought he might look in."

"Yes . . . he sort of promised." Caroline's nose wrinkled. "He did come over. He went to see father."

"Oh Lord!"

"Yes, quite!"

They stared sombrely at one another, silently speculating on the probable wretchedness of the encounter.

"What are your plans for Murgatroyd?" she asked, making a conscious effort to move to more cheerful matters.

"Retirement. He's finished racing now."

"You're keeping him here?"

"Oh yes!" Edward's reply was firm, almost vehement.

"Will you do anything with him?"

"Yes, I've been wondering about that. Do you think he could carry me?"

"Don't see why not. He's a tough old bugger."

"Less of the 'old' . . . he's only seven. He's got twenty years ahead of him."

235

"Are you going to ride him out to work?"

"I've got an idea he might like that."

Before they went back home to Worcestershire, Ann and Frank saw the start of a most audacious project. After a lot of thought, obtuse hints at the breakfast meetings, and what Caroline called "sniffing at the runes", Edward decided that T. P. Malahide was going to win the Eclipse Stakes. Ten furlongs of the main gallop were marked so that they resembled the ground at Sandown Park, and two of the Duke of Dorchester's horses were selected to work with T. P. Malahide. For the first few days the trio did nothing more than walk together for an hour, yard gossip suggesting that Edward had invented yet another new theory.

"Actually," he confessed to Frank, "I just want them to get to know one another. This seems as good a way as any."

When they were given a stiff gallop, Frank was as impressed as he had been by watching James Henry and Parsifal, and told Dooley that T. P. Malahide was a good prospect.

Ten days later, Ann stopped gardening and Frank left his workshop to watch the race on TV. It was a desperately close thing. The last furlong, which seemed to go on forever, was dominated by an epic struggle between Bernard Dalrymple's Derby winner, Lord of the Isles, and T. P. Malahide. No other horse had a hope of getting anywhere near them. As they came to the line neck and neck, it was Lord of the Isles who finally cracked in the last few strides. He was a specialist at the slightly longer Derby distance, and achieved his results by running his opponents into the ground from the very start. On this occasion, he was not able to handle T. P. Malahide's final flourish.

"I'd say that was his best piece of training yet," Frank said as he and Ann watched a jubilant Edward and Valerie Malahide greet their champion.

"Better than Musetta?"

"Probably – not that I know much about it, of course. Edward picked this chap out in the sales himself . . . and he wasn't all that clever as a two-year-old."

Frank was right. It was the most brilliant feat that Edward had yet accomplished, and everyone knew it. While Wesley Davies was enthusing on TV, Edward was happy simply because he had given Valerie Malahide a top-class winner, and morale in the yard rocketed to new heights.

Richard spent an hour with Valerie Malahide after the race. Trying to set aside the excitement, they talked business: or rather, Richard talked, and Valerie listened. Afterwards, she went in search of Edward.

"Do you think there's any point keeping T.P. in training now?" she asked.

He looked at her quizzically. "What's Richard been saying?"

"He wonders whether it isn't best to think about retiring him . . . get him ready for stud."

Edward nodded. "Well, he's won a Group One, so his prestige is pretty high." He was unenthusiastic; he understood Richard's point of view, but had always thought it slightly cynical.

"What could you do with him if you kept him?" Valerie asked.

"Good question," he had to admit. "Bearing in mind his best distance is ten furlongs, there probably isn't a lot for him."

"And he is four."

"Yes." Edward thought it over and surrendered. "All right, you win! We'll let Richard have him."

A week later, T. P. Malahide was loaded into the van for the last time, and given a tumultuous send-off that he appeared to find rather puzzling. He was Saxon Court's first Group One winner, now he was on his way to a long holiday before becoming Widney Cheyne's first stallion.

Alison Bairstow went with him, staying for two weeks while he settled into his new, purpose-built home. Robin Lane was quite lost while she was away.

For the rest of that summer and a beautiful autumn, it often seemed that nothing else mattered apart from Moonlight Ring, the tree circle on Saxon Down, and the exploits of James Henry. These were the things that Edward knew he would always remember, not the never-ending stream of daily events.

The two horses that had been used in T. P. Malahide's preparation for the Eclipse Stakes both won at Goodwood. The Duke of Dorchester was inordinately pleased, and insisted on a substantial celebration. Even greater happiness surrounded the victory at Newbury of one of the Tornado two-year-olds belonging to Edwin Fforbes.

"*Such* a gentleman," Rosie Frost said to Caroline. "It's nice to see him do well."

Caroline smiled her agreement. Fortunately she had gone to Newbury with Edwin Fforbes. She had been able to lead his winner in while he was paralysed with shyness.

There were anxious times, too.

Alison Bairstow had an arm broken when a horse who was not used to her, wilfully threw her off his back. It happened inside the New Yard, and Alison landed very badly against a wall. The two lads with her when it happened naturally spent all their concern on her, thus incurring Declan's wrath. Unattended and wound up, the horse snatched his opportunity, escaped, and roamed Saxon Down for three hours before he could be recaptured. Less than a week later, Michael Doyle forgot

237

that Mark Walgrave's generally placid filly Heliotrope had flashes of inexplicable anger. Walking behind her in an unguarded moment, he caught the full force as she lashed out with both hind legs. He came out of it lightly; nothing more than two broken ribs was reckoned to be the best possible outcome of such an incident.

Yet whatever happened, Moonlight Ring and James Henry were pre-eminent.

The day after T. P. Malahide's Eclipse victory was a Sunday. There was no work, most of the lads had the day off, leaving only a skeleton staff to attend to feeds. Evening stables were suspended, but Declan and Freezer checked the horses in the morning and last thing at night.

The first luxury of the sabbath for Edward was breakfast alone with Caroline. They usually sat for at least an hour over the meal, then Edward went to the office. Undisturbed for three hours, he caught up on all the past week's racing news, looked at how other trainers' horses had been running, and reviewed the performance of his own. Caroline liked to spend the morning planning the coming week's meals for both the house and the hostel. When she went into the office around midday, she always found Edward surrounded by form books and pieces of paper covered with unintelligible notes. She had soon abandoned the notion that she ought to understand the Sunday-morning doodles that even he usually failed to explain with any conviction. The consequences were, however, plain for all to see on Siobhan's results board.

"And how do you see the world this morning?" she asked, settling on his knees.

"Not bad. We could be doing better."

"Really? Gosh! I've been labouring under a whatsit, then."

"How do you mean?"

"Well, I thought the Eclipse wasn't bad. You can see how we idiots pick these ideas up, can't you? I mean, we tend to get carried away if we win a Group One and beat two Derby winners."

"*Two* Derby winners?" Edward was surprised.

"Yes, two! That horse Avignon who came fourth won last year's Prix du Jockey Club, your actual French Derby, my boy."

"Good grief!"

"So there you are. We aren't doing so badly."

"No we aren't . . . but we can do better. I want to have a closer look at Edwin Fforbes's horses. One or two of them might be very useful indeed next year if they train on all right."

"That's why you're so good," Caroline said. "Most of us mere mortals would gloat about yesterday for weeks. You're already thinking about *next* year."

"Seems no more than common sense to me," he muttered.

"Ah . . . come on, admit it, you're brilliant!"

He laughed. "I wish I was. Do you know what I fancy?"

"Yes! Me!"

"Apart from that."

"Tell me."

"Let's take a picnic lunch up to Moonlight Ring. We haven't been there for ages."

Half an hour later they were walking along the Ridge Path. They found an ideal place inside the trees, and Caroline unpacked their small hamper while Edward admired the view.

"We really must come up here more often," he said. "It's rather nice being able to see one's acres from afar."

"I've always loved it," she replied. "And you can keep an eye on things. Look, Declan's taking some of them out to the paddock."

At a distance of nearly two miles she had to assume it was Declan, but the string of twenty or so horses was clearly visible.

"You know, I could still believe that this is all too good to be true," Edward said thoughtfully. "I'm sure I shall wake up one morning and find it was all a dream."

"Here!" She pushed a chicken leg at him. "Eat that and stop talking rubbish!"

When they had finished their meal, they lay quietly for a while, staring up at the myriad pinpricks of sunlight dancing through the dense vault of leaves above them. Once she had closed her eyes, Caroline was unaware of Edward's scrutiny. For five minutes he was motionless, admiring the beauty of her profile. His first kisses were very gentle, barely making contact with her eyelids, cheeks, nose, then lips.

Desire did not flare urgently, but enveloped them slowly like a warm glow. She sighed when his hand moved to her breasts, creating pleasure without disturbing the tranquillity. Between them they removed her skirt without causing the slightest interruption to their trance-like drift towards passion. When he went into her, there was no giving or taking; it was a serene act of unification. Caroline always regulated the tempo of their love-making. Normally she did it actively, thrillingly. Now, arms stretched out above her head in abandoned relaxation, she relied on him to draw his own conclusions from the responses of her body. Edward did so, becoming preoccupied with his mastery of her. When he finally permitted them to climax, the explosion sprang from sensations that had been skilfully elevated to the unendurable, not mere frenzy.

It was a very long time before either of them had the urge to speak. When Caroline did so, she sounded thoughtfully matter-of-fact. "That was nice." She mulled it over more thoroughly. "I'd say that was hedonistic. Yes. Definitely. What do you suppose the staff would say?"

"What about?"

"Mr Manning, His Lordly Immensity, the guv'nor, cavorting with a floozie in the open air."

"I think I'd sack anyone who called you a floozie," he said.

The laugh came all the way from her belly, and there were tears in her eyes when she finally managed to control it. "Oh, Edward, my dear," she gasped, "you get more wonderful every day, but you can still be a world-class stuffed shirt when you try."

He smiled sheepishly. "Yes," he agreed. "Odd, isn't it?"

"Not really." She sat up and threw her arms round him. "You're still the little boy in wonderland in some ways, aren't you?"

He nodded. He looked down the hill towards Saxon Court, then back to Caroline. She read his thoughts.

"Yes, it's all real. That is, and so am I . . . you might have noticed that a few minutes ago."

Later, when they were ready to go back, Caroline had a last look round, and swooped on her briefs that were almost hidden in a patch of long grass that they had not squashed.

"Ruined!" she said happily, stuffing them in her skirt pocket.

"You're not going to parade through my yard with no knickers on?" Edward asked in mock horror.

"Yes! See? I am a floozie. Tell you what, sweetheart, you were right. We must come up here more often."

By the end of the summer, the grass at their special spot was flattened and worn.

Caroline was not surprised when James Henry's next race turned out to be the Mill Reef Stakes at Newbury in September. There had been talk of sending him to York for the Gimcrack, a race which Mill Reef himself had won in spectacular fashion in 1970. After a great deal of mental to-ing and fro-ing, Parsifal went north to deal with the Gimcrack while James Henry was prepared for the local event named in honour of Edward's hero. Caroline and Edward naturally went to Newbury, but their view of the race was disrupted, and they had to wait until they got back to Siobhan's video-recording to savour the latest example of James Henry's supremacy.

Bernard Dalrymple had very nearly withdrawn his filly The Blessed Damozel. His Tewkesbury Lodge yard was ravaged by the worst bug in living memory, but it was humans, not horses, who were the victims. A vicious outbreak of gastroenteritis had brought all but the most essential work to a standstill, and it was questionable whether any sort of team could be assembled to get the filly to Newbury. However, she was fit, Dalrymple had a very high opinion of James Henry, and was eager to see how close The Blessed Damozel could get to him, so a special effort was made. She duly arrived at the course with Finoula, who was on the mend but looking very pale and drawn, and a fairly inexperienced girl who was not her regular custodian. Things were so chaotically bad at Tewkesbury Lodge that a freelance van driver had been hired.

Finoula told Caroline and Edward all about it when they met on the rails of the pre-parade ring. Although she was well below par, she was still able to give a gripping account of the last few days, and Edward had to suppress a smile at her use of the word 'drastic'. For once, the Oxford Dictionary would have agreed with her.

Sean Gillespie had been instructed to hold James Henry up in the early stages of the race.

"We know he can go like the clappers," Edward said, "now it's time to teach him how to pace himself. We're looking for a mile and a half next June."

A flicker of satisfaction crossed Sean Gillespie's face. It was the first time he had heard the Derby mentioned officially.

James Henry patently did not like the restraint, and gave Sean Gillespie a rough ride as he pulled for his head. With two furlongs to go, Sean decided that he'd both proved his point and had enough of a struggle for one day. The moment he let him off the bridle, an appreciative murmur ran through the crowd as he produced his vivid acceleration to draw clear. The Blessed Damozel's jockey shook her up and set off in pursuit. He knew that if he could finish within four lengths of James Henry, with the rest strung out behind him, Mr Dalrymple would be satisfied.

It took a long time to discover what happened next. No sooner had The Blessed Damozel appeared to move into top gear than she faltered, seemed to be on only three legs, recovered, then swerved across the track. When her jockey pulled her up, she was clearly in distress, and he was visibly shaken. The large Saturday-afternoon crowd gasped, first at the initial shock, then with relief. The Blessed Damozel had been on the wide outside of the field and had plunged away from her pursuers. Had she gone the other way, a pile-up would have been inevitable.

"Oh dear!" Caroline said quietly.

"I don't like the look of that." Edward's tone was grim.

"Broken leg?"

"Could be."

Sean Gillespie heard the crowd and was bemused. Surely another horse wasn't closing up on him? Stung by the effrontery of it, and without looking round, he urged James Henry on to a victory of almost Wolverhampton-like proportions. Edward hardly noticed it. He took command of the looming crisis.

"Finoula and that little girl can't handle this," he said. "You and Richard can look after our boy, can't you, Caro?"

"Yes."

"Right! Come on, Freezer. And you, Robin."

Checking that all the horses had finished and that the track was clear, Edward led the way on to the course. They set out towards the filly, now standing motionless, held by her jockey who had dismounted as soon as she had stopped.

The TV cameras spotted them. In Newmarket, Bernard Dalrymple, huddled in a dressing-gown, heaved a sigh of relief and muttered, "Thank God!"

"What's happening?" his wife asked.

"Edward Manning and his travelling head lad are going down to her."

Joe Hook, Tewkesbury Lodge's retained first jockey, knew Edward and Freezer, if only by sight, and was glad to see them. "It's not as bad as I thought, sir," he said. "She's cast a plate. It's made a mess of her, though."

After reassuring the filly, Edward ran a hand down her left foreleg, and lifted the foot, wincing at what he found.

"That didn't just drop off," he said. "It got wrenched off. Look at this!"

Freezer peered into the filly's hoof and nodded. "Pulled off from the front, sir. The back of the plate hung on for two or three strides. There's inside damage there."

"Jesus!" Finoula panted when she arrived. "What a mess!"

"What are you going to do about this?" Edward asked her.

"I've no idea!"

"Let's have the saddle off her, Freezer. You can clear off, Joe," Edward said to the jockey. "You need to weigh in anyway. We'll look after her. How long would it take you to get her home, Finoula?"

"At least four hours."

"What do you reckon to that, Freezer?"

"That won't do her any good at all, sir."

"That's what I thought. We'll take her home with us."

"But –"

Edward cut Finoula short. He was kind but very firm. "This filly needs urgent attention, not jolting round in a van for four hours. In any case, what if you did manage to get her there in one piece? The place is full of walking wounded, isn't it?"

Finoula smiled submissively.

"Right, go and find that poor girl you brought with you, and let's get cracking. Robin, go and find Dooley. We can get the van down here to save her walking back."

The Blessed Damozel was still frightened, but she was content to stay with Edward, and went calmly into the van with him when Dooley brought it down. Watching, Finoula realised that she had forgotten how very good Edward was with horses.

It was a thirty-minute drive from Newbury racecourse to Saxon Court. The Blessed Damozel and Edward's vet arrived at about the same time. As ever, Siobhan had been recording the race from TV, had deduced what Edward was doing, and made the necessary telephone call. The filly was immediately at home in a spare box and receiving attention. Finoula spent a few minutes talking to Bernard Dalrymple on the telephone, then waved frantically at Edward who was telling Declan all about it.

"He wants to speak to you," she mouthed.

"Good afternoon, Mr Dalrymple," he began in their customary style.

"Edward! This is extremely good of you. I really am most grateful."

When they had finished, Edward stood for a moment with an expression of mock, starstruck humility on his face. Caroline caught his mood in a flash.

"What? What is it?" she gasped breathlessly. "Tell me, O magnificent one!"

"He called me 'Edward'."

"He didn't!"

"He did!"

"Oh my Gawd!" Caroline clapped her hands to her face. "Whatever will become of us? Shall we cope? I'll need a new frock!"

"I'm not going to let it change my way of life," Edward declared resolutely.

Finoula watched, bewildered, and for once speechless, as Caroline and Edward collapsed into one of their giggling fits. It was the first time she had witnessed the sense of humour that was one of the foundations of their love. "He's ever such a nice man," she said at last.

"We know that," Caroline replied. "But he does make a point of being so awfully *proper*, doesn't he?"

The Blessed Damozel, her foot well on the way to recovery, went back to Newmarket five days later to a Tewkesbury Lodge that had a full complement of healthy staff. She travelled with two Saxon Court horses who were staying the night at Gordon Chapman's place before racing. When Bernard Dalrymple discovered the arrangements Edward had for overnight stabling before racing at Newmarket, he suggested that his own yard was always available, but understood Edward's loyalty in sticking to his grandfather's old friend.

Because of The Blessed Damozel, Finoula spent two days at Saxon Court with Mary and Declan. Later, Edward realised that this must have been the time when final plans were made for her mid-October wedding. What was decided then, produced the occasion that became enshrined in the folklore of the lads' hostel as 'the day Declan went to the races'.

Siobhan spotted it at once. "That's the day of the Dewhurst," she said when she was told the date of the ceremony to be held at a Catholic church in Newmarket.

First run in 1875, the Dewhurst Stakes was widely regarded as one of the pointers to next year's Classics, and was to be the culmination of James Henry's two-year-old campaign. Finoula shrugged and said there was no need to worry; the wedding was at eleven, the race at three-thirty, less than a mile from the venue for the reception.

When Edward had received official notification in the form of a splendidly printed invitation for himself and Caroline, he raised the matter with Declan, choosing his moment carefully. It was as they strolled back after evening stables. This was always the time when they were closest.

"This wedding looks as though it's going to be a bit of a do, Declan."

"It is that, sor."

"Many guests?"

"Over a hundred, I think."

"Posh reception?"

Declan stopped walking, eyeing Edward with determination. "I can afford it."

"I don't doubt it. I wouldn't dream of suggesting that you couldn't." They moved on in silence. "Do you know what I was thinking the other day?" Edward asked casually. Declan knew the question was rhetorical, and didn't bother to answer. "It occurred to me that you never got anything for thirty years of putting up with the Mannings. That's bad, isn't it? You'd think we could have run to a gold watch, or something."

"I didn't bother."

"No, of course you didn't. But it's time we rectified it. How does five per cent of Murgatroyd seem?"

Again they stopped, Declan thinking about it, the stare of his pale blue eyes disconcerting. "I'd have to pay five per cent of his keep."

"That's right – and entrance money, etcetera."

"All right."

"Good! That leaves you with one thousand seven hundred and twenty-nine pounds to come."

"Thank you, sor." Declan wondered how long Edward had been cooking it up, but said nothing.

"I'll get Siobhan to see to it in the morning. Now then, we've a problem with this wedding, haven't we? We're running his lordship that afternoon. I suppose you'll be on the way back here, so you won't be able to put your feet up and watch it on the telly."

"No." Declan looked very disappointed about that aspect of what was to be an otherwise exciting and memorable day.

"There is something we might do about it."

"Oh yes?"

"You could come with us and see the real thing."

"You mean go to the races?" Declan looked appalled.

"Yes."

Declan's initial alarm faded. He looked round furtively. "Could I just go with you and watch?"

"Of course. That's the whole idea."

"I wouldn't have to *do* anything?"

"Certainly not! Freezer and Robin will see to all the palaver."

"Right!" Declan's face cracked into a smile. "I'm your man."

It was a wonderful day, almost coinciding with Caroline and Edward's first wedding anniversary. The sun shone, Finoula and Declan arrived at the church in a carriage-and-four organised by Bernard Dalrymple, and Patrick Prendegast was suitably in awe of the whole business. Many of the non-Catholic guests had never attended a full nuptial Mass before, and were smitten by its thoroughgoing grandeur. Called to be a witness and sign the register, Edward had a word with the priest about it.

"I must say, Father, you make a real job of marrying them!"

The little Irishman smiled at him with twinkling eyes. "Ah, well, we have to, d'you see? It's on account of the fact that they're going to *stay* married when we've finished with them."

Five per cent of Murgatroyd had transformed the wedding breakfast from what would have been a very nice meal into a banquet. It was all pleasant and well organised, although Edward died a thousand deaths on behalf of poor Patrick Prendegast who so clearly found his speech a terrifying ordeal. There was no hurry, but when Caroline and Edward made their farewells and left at two o'clock, several people were starting to look at their watches. They included the bride. Before leaving for her honeymoon in Killarney, she was insistent upon seeing the brilliant namesake of the man she had worshipped carry out what was confidently expected to be a formality.

He did not disappoint.

With head high, ears pricked, and a style of which he was increasingly conscious and proud, James Henry romped home with the best two-year-olds of England, Ireland and France reduced to a toiling shambles somewhere between five and thirty lengths behind him. The manner of his victory was surpassing, and had a rakish exuberance that delighted the crowd. When Wesley Davies interviewed Caroline and Edward, everyone agreed that they had just seen the performance of the year. Nocker Jarvis's piece the following day, as effervescent as James Henry's triumphant gallop, appeared under the headline:

WHAT DID I TELL YOU?

Only Dooley could argue with the unanimous and instantaneous decision of the bookmaking fraternity to install James Henry as a very firm favourite for the following year's Two Thousand Guineas and Derby.

When Caroline escaped from Wesley Davies, she found Richard looking dazed. "You were right about him, weren't you?" he said. "You can certainly pick 'em!"

Smiling, Caroline went off to the racecourse stables. Nancy Bloomfield, who had been responsible for deciding the mating that had produced James Henry at Tornado Stud, went with her.

After the race, Imogen was deep in thought for a long time. Edward waited patiently for her pronouncement.

"I do believe," she said at last, "that he's starting to look like a *real* horse now."

Edward laughed. "He is. But this is where the *real* problems start. We've to get him through the winter and train him on."

"What exactly does that expression 'train on' mean?" Imogen asked.

"It means we can start next season where we leave off this year," Edward replied.

"Isn't that a formality?"

"God, I wish it were!"

"What's the problem?"

"There are two problems. First, the horse has to remain *physically* sound through the winter; then there's the *mental* thing. He must remember what he learned as a two-year-old and be willing to build on it. If he forgets or loses interest, you've had it."

"Oh." Imogen looked perplexed. "I see." Then she brightened. "Mind you, he seems to have a good start."

Although Edward agreed with her, he still had to fight the temptation to start reciting the endless list of promising two-year-olds who had failed to achieve a thing at three. It was one of the greatest mysteries, fascinations and frustrations of racing.

On the way home, Caroline reminded Edward that James Henry had been their last runner of the season, and sure enough, when they arrived, Siobhan produced the statistics. In their first full year at Saxon Court, they had sent out three hundred and forty-one runners, producing sixty-five winners and four hundred and twenty-five thousand pounds in prize-money. With a month of racing still to come, Siobhan estimated that Edward would be fourth in the list of winning trainers.

"Hey, that's not bad for beginners," Edward said, agreeably surprised at the figures.

"It'll be quite exciting when we get the hang of it," Caroline said.

"Next year?" Edward asked.

"Let's follow the advice we always give them when they interview us," Caroline said. "Wait and see."

Chapter 11

James Henry did train on.

In mid-April 1983, he went to Newmarket for the Craven Stakes, winning it without coming off the bit. Two weeks later, on the last Saturday of the month, he won the Two Thousand Guineas Stakes. His time was the fastest since My Babu in 1945, his odds the shortest since Nijinsky in 1971. Forty-eight hours earlier, The Blessed Damozel had won the One Thousand Guineas.

At eight o'clock on a perfect spring evening, James Henry was given a stupendous reception when he came home. Dooley's sang-froid was tested severely as he drove in to find that Saxon Court's seventy residents had been augmented by half the population of Compton Norris. They had come to celebrate the stable's first Classic victory for thirty-three years. Not many of the happy crowd doubted that they would be hailing the next triumph in little more than five weeks on the evening of Derby Day.

Frank Manning looked on genially, feeling proud of everyone in general and his son in particular. He was there because of his carpentry. Since Christmas, he had spent many hours in his workshop, and had brought the results in a hired van to assemble them. For the price of the timber, Rosie and Freezer were having a kitchen that would drive Mary wild with envy, and Dooley was getting the fitted wardrobes he had always wanted. For Frank, it had been a labour of love and discovery, yielding a satisfaction that he had never known in banking. Now, he viewed Edward's latest triumph with a sense of profound well-being.

Edward was having great difficulty drumming up support for Parsifal, who had finished second.

"Yes, he did well," Richard agreed. "He isn't as good as you said, though. You swore James Henry would only do him by three lengths over that distance if the race was run at a reasonable speed."

"Well, there you have it! It wasn't run at a reasonable speed, was it? That thing of yours was only half a cat's whisker off a record time."

"Damn it, that's why we ran Parsifal! You said he'd steady James Henry up. And look what happened! All that trouble and expense for nothing." Richard was grinning broadly.

"I know, the strategy was a failure. Never mind, you got an extra forty-five thousand for coming second as well."

Running Parsifal had stemmed from an observation by Edward that had triggered a theory from Alison Bairstow and Robin Lane. Although his temperament was mild and placid, James Henry refused to tolerate another horse alongside him when he was galloping. The only way he knew how to work or race was to be in front. The habit caused Edward concern. What was effective for a precocious two-year-old racing over no more than seven furlongs, was not bound to work over twelve furlongs at Epsom, where something had to be kept in reserve for the final assault on the hill.

"I think he can win it from the front," Caroline said. "Remember, sweetheart, you've never sat on him. He's capable of anything."

Half-believing her, Edward still worried, and looked for ways of teaching his star to adopt a more energy-conserving way of racing. It was Alison who spotted that James Henry was quite content to gallop beside Parsifal until asked to go ahead. So Parsifal went to Newmarket for the Two Thousand Guineas with the task of keeping his more brilliant companion company for the first six furlongs, and holding him to a more sedate pace.

It was the first time that Edward had ever run two horses in the same race, and he wanted a second jockey. Bernard Dalrymple had the answer. One of his ex-apprentices, John Dyer, was in his third season as a freelance. He rode for Tewkesbury Lodge when both Joe Hook and the second jockey were involved with other horses and a third was needed, but the engagements were usually in the unfashionable north, and amounted to no more than three or four a month. For the rest, John Dyer had to hope, and take what came.

"He's worthy of much better rides than I can give him," Bernard Dalrymple told Edward. "He'll do a thoroughly good job for you."

John Dyer visited Saxon Court twice before the race to do ride work on Parsifal.

"Gosh! Isn't he pale?" Caroline whispered to Edward when she saw him.

It was true: John Dyer had a perpetual, chalk-like pallor.

After he had ridden Parsifal, had breakfast and hurried off to Redcar where he had a ride that afternoon, Caroline had something to add. "I wonder if he's always that tense and worried."

"I expect he is," Edward replied. "But after what I saw out there, he can work for me any time."

The 'rehearsals' on Saxon Down went very well; however, no one had realised that James Henry had become an out-and-out showman, and responded to an occasion. Sean Gillespie had discovered that he was in one of his moods as they went down to the start, and had done nothing to cramp his style during the race. Nocker Jarvis's readers were addressed with tangible relish.

By common consent, this was not the most distinguished field ever assembled for the Two Thousand Guineas. But by the time James Henry had worked them over, they looked a mess.

Sir Richard Stewart's brilliant colt didn't waste a second of his near-record time. The instant they got going, he set about running them into the ground. At the furlong distance, I had visions of him beating Tudor Minstrel's 1948 record margin of eight lengths.

But stable-mate Parsifal, with John Dyer having his first ride for Saxon Court, came out of the pack to make a very courageous show of winning the race for second place.

Trainer Edward Manning said afterwards that he was very pleased with both his horses. "I only ran Parsifal to calm James Henry down a bit," he said. "It doesn't seem to have worked," he added with a rueful smile.

I'm glad it didn't. James Henry in action is a sight for sore eyes. If you can't get to Epsom, don't stray far from the TV.

It was a long time before everyone went home. Edward lost count of the number of times the video-recording of the race had to be played. Each time, there was extra excitement as a new facet of the race was spotted. The only thing that remained constant was Nancy Bloomfield's silent enthralment. She sat in a corner of the sitting room, well out of the way, with her eyes glued to the TV screen, and a half-smile on her face. At a point when quietness was finally descending, Siobhan caused excitement to rekindle.

"This is the first time since 1935 that the same person has owned both first and second in the Two Thousand Guineas," she announced. "That was His Highness The Aga Khan with Bahram and Theft. The only other occasion was . . ." she consulted her book ". . . 1888. The sixth Duke of Portland owned Ayrshire and Johnny Morgan – but there were only six runners that year."

At last they were all gone, and Edward was propped up comfortably in bed, with time to read the morning's newspapers. All the experts bar one had plumped for James Henry to win. The exception had chosen a French colt who had finished at least twenty lengths behind James Henry. Absorbed and amused by the verbose assassination of James Henry that was a preliminary to the bizarre selection, he did not notice Caroline come in from the bathroom.

"That must be riveting," she said.

"Yes. This buffoon reckons that . . ." He looked up. She had loosened her hair, and was brushing it out into a golden cascade over her shoulders, the way he liked it best. She was quite naked.

"Oh . . . perhaps it wasn't that interesting after all."

She had slipped into bed and was removing his pyjamas.

"I thought you said you were tired."

"I am. But first things first. You know Newmarket always makes me randy. What are you smiling at?"

"I know Newmarket makes you randy. So do Ascot, Goodwood, Sandown Park, Newbury . . ."

"Are you complaining?"

"Perish the thought! But be gentle with me, I've had a very hard day."

"All right. Just lie back and think beautiful thoughts."

Siobhan ensured that they had all the Sunday papers, and they were soon spread out all over the kitchen table. For once, two of the tabloids actually pleased Edward. Caroline had told a journalist that James Henry's stable nickname was 'The Toff', and the morsel had been eagerly accepted. Under the headline:

THE 2000 GUINEA TOFF

one carried a nice picture of the finish, showing James Henry steaming past the winning post, looking every inch a champion, while Parsifal battled along grittily in his wake. The other had a picture taken while Caroline was leading him in; the photographer had caught an instant when it looked as though he were about to kiss her proudly upturned face.

CAROLINE'S TOFF

was the bold caption.

"That's not at all bad, is it?" she said when he showed it to her.

"It's a jolly good picture of the horse," he replied, and received the expected assault on his ribs. He had already acknowledged it as an outstanding photograph of Caroline, and asked Siobhan to get several large prints of it.

"Wesley Davies has made his mind up at last," Caroline said, pointing out the column he wrote for a 'quality' paper each Sunday.

Edward read the first paragraph.

Yesterday afternoon on Newmarket Heath, James Henry gave general proof that he is an outstanding horse. The manner of his victory convinced some that he was the best since Nijinsky. I believe this to be a valid comparison in every sense. Like Nijinsky, James Henry is a son of Northern Dancer, and they both won the Guineas with exceptional style. Nijinsky's victory was merely a prelude. I am convinced that James Henry has similar epic delights in store for us.

"Just read that last bit," Caroline said, and stabbed a forefinger on the relevant passage.

Finally, if the horse and his form are not enough, I should remind you of Edward Manning's amazing record as a trainer. His first ever runner was a winner. His first entry at Royal Ascot won. His first attempt at a Classic was successful with Musetta in the 1980 One Thousand Guineas. Now he has captured the Two Thousand Guineas at the first try. If James Henry goes to Epsom, I fail to see what can stop him adding the Derby to this impressive list of firsts.

"Well, there you have it," Edward said. "What do we think of that?"
"He's got something right. It had to happen sooner or later."

Caroline and Edward went to Widney Cheyne for Sunday lunch. After the meal, Edward and Richard visited Musetta and her Mill Reef foal, Rhinemaiden, now a beautiful yearling. Then they strolled through the park. There was only one possible topic of conversation.
"How's the lad today?" Richard asked.
"Very good. You wouldn't think he'd been in a race. Parsifal's tired – but he's all right."
"What's the plan?"
"I'm going to give him some easy work on Wednesday. If that goes well, it's every Wednesday and Saturday until the race."
"Is he going to get the distance?"
"He's already done a mile and a half at home." Richard's eyebrows shot up in surprise. "Oh yes. He did it three times getting ready for yesterday."
"So we're home and dry?"
"No, we're not. We know he can do it on Saxon Down. We *don't* know whether he can do it at Epsom."
"Is it *really* that different?"
"Yes!"
"It's not just a con trick?"
"Absolutely not! There's only one way to find out if a horse gets the trip at Epsom."
"Run him?"
"That's what they've been doing since 1780."
"What's your gut feeling about it?"
"Well . . ." Edward halted, stared hard at the ground, and kicked at a pebble. "I think he's going to win it."
"You see no danger?"
"No, not really."

"What about Etienne du Pont's horse?"

The doyen of French trainers was expected to run a colt who had caused something of a stir in European circles.

"I've had a good look at him, of course. I know he won the Criterium at Maisons-Lafitte last year, but it wasn't all that impressive. I don't think he beat much."

"Has he been out yet this season?"

"No, I had Siobhan check on that the other day."

"So he might not be fit or working?"

"Quite."

After a few paces in silence, Edward stopped and gave Richard a most strange look. "Surely this can't be right," he said.

"What can't?"

"We're never going to win the damned thing first time, *and* with a horse named after him . . . are we?"

Richard considered it. "I don't see why not," he said at last. "Forget James Henry and his ambitions. Pretend he never existed. What are you left with?"

"I don't know. You tell me."

"A bloody good horse who's probably going to win the Derby."

"True. Difficult to ignore the old man, though. If he'd never existed . . ."

"*We* wouldn't be here." Richard finished it for him. "But that's got nothing to do with the horse. We've got Caroline to thank for him, haven't we?"

"Oh yes, absolutely. It's going to be her race. But it all seems to have been so easy."

"I imagine it always is with the right horse. The luck was getting him so soon. Mind you, what you've done with him hasn't been easy. And he's had no problems, has he?"

"Oh, I know. He could be lame or coughing tomorrow."

"He could. But I don't think he will. Your pessimism will have to take a back seat this time."

"Cautious prudence, not pessimism!"

Richard smiled his acceptance of the distinction. "What about Parsifal? Do you want to run him at Epsom?"

"I think so."

"You're sticking to the theory?"

"Yes. In any case, the second prize is worth having."

Neither James Henry nor Parsifal suffered any ill effects from the Two Thousand Guineas.

253

On the Wednesday after the race, they worked together over a mile. It was an easy-paced gallop with no finishing flourish.

"That's fine," was Edward's verdict. "We'll start going the full distance on Saturday."

That afternoon they re-measured and marked the main U-shaped gallop. Eventually, after Alison Bairstow and Robin Lane had walked several miles back and forth, they found a stretch that was a close resemblance to the course over which the Derby was run. It was left-handed, had a downhill approach to the final bend, and an uphill finish.

"That's the best we're going to do," Edward said to Declan after he had cantered over it on Murgatroyd. "The approach to that last bend isn't as steep as Epsom, but the rest isn't bad."

Edward decided that James Henry and Parsifal should have two work companions, and selected them with great care. After much deep thought and observation, a pair of four-year-olds were chosen. Alberta and Cheslyn Hay had not achieved anything as three-year-olds, but they had developed into steady, strong-galloping horses who were capable of setting a good pace for the first ten furlongs. It worked very well when they tried it. James Henry and Parsifal stayed with the pacemakers until they were about two furlongs from home, and were then encouraged to go on. Caroline held James Henry up for the first attempt so that he finished only fractionally in front of Parsifal.

Edward explained this to Richard who was watching.

"I know, I know," Richard said. "I'm not a complete idiot. You're going to build him up gradually so that he peaks on the day."

"Well, that's the idea."

"I'll come and watch every Saturday," Richard said. "Apart from sheer nosiness, it'll be good for me after a week stuck in the office."

James Henry and Parsifal worked each Wednesday and Saturday after the other horses had cleared the gallops and were on their way down the Avenue back to the yard. On Saturdays, Richard got to Saxon Court in time for breakfast, then watched the second lot go through their paces.

They were the two-year-olds, all unraced as yet, and they made a fascinating spectacle.

The yard had filled to capacity during the winter. Valerie Malahide, Edwin Fforbes, the Duke of Dorchester, Mark Walgrave and Richard himself had all bought yearlings the previous autumn, mostly at sales in Ireland and Newmarket. Although the prices paid had been moderate, Edward was confident that he had a great deal of good quality as a foundation for the future. There was nothing to match the class of James Henry or Parsifal, but it was already possible to pick out those who might win good races. The more advanced of the juveniles were ready to leave the sand-track, and graduate to the grass gallops where some of them began to display enthusiastic talent.

A full complement of horses meant that additional lads had been required. In March, Caroline, Edward, Declan and Freezer had picked the fourteen they needed from over a hundred applicants. The ratio of ten lads and four girls had been determined by the accommodation left in the two hostels. They were all fully experienced. Watching them at work, Richard felt that an important step forward had been made. He knew that Edward cared deeply about his staff, and wanted a strong team wedded to a common cause. The new arrivals seemed destined to meet his needs and repay his confidence as they became part of an enterprise founded on hard work, total competence, and old-fashioned *esprit de corps*.

But whatever happened, James Henry was the star.

Every morning, Caroline was in the yard with Declan on his six o'clock round. Whereas Declan was interested in ninety-nine horses, she had eyes for only one. Her obsession with the minutest details of his existence quickly spawned dozens of affectionate jokes among the lads.

"You're giving that horse a superiority complex," Edward said to her as they basked in the afterglow of love-making in Moonlight Ring on their first visit of the summer.

"He's far too sensible for that!"

"Is it true that you've been following him round with a spade and bucket?"

"What clown told you that?"

"Never you mind! I have it on the best authority that you're sending samples of his droppings for analysis every day."

"That's Liam Corrigan, isn't it? Eh? Isn't it?" She tickled his ribs until he admitted that it was.

"No, I'll tell you what it is." For a few seconds, she was convincingly serious. "I've discovered it has miraculous properties. It's true I tell you . . . so help me, as sure as I'm lying here with my knickers round my ankles! Haven't you noticed the roses in the front garden?"

"No, I haven't."

"Well, you have a good look. Dooley's been down on his knees, begging me to let him have some for his lupins. There were tears in his eyes."

The interest in the Wednesday and Saturday gallops among the lads was immense. When Robin Lane got back to the hostel for lunch after riding Parsifal in what had become known as 'Caroline's Flying Circus', he was cross-examined mercilessly. How far ahead had James Henry been? Was that the best he could do? Was Mrs Manning *really* holding him back? Could Parsifal maybe beat him? And even, when anxiety reached fever pitch, was Robin sure that the guv'nor knew what he was doing?

That overheated heresy reached Declan's scandalised ears. The offender was taken aside and spoken to. Apart from the Two Thousand Guineas and the Craven Stakes that had led up to it, they had already sent out over twenty winners. If this was considered below par, the doubter was informed, he was at liberty to seek employment with an establishment more to his liking. He decided not to bother.

When Richard arrived to watch the third of the Saturday-morning gallops, he found an ebullient atmosphere round the breakfast table. One of his own two-year-olds had won first time out the previous afternoon, and another was confidently expected to do the same at Thirsk in about six hours' time.

"And we're going to let James Henry rip this morning," Edward said. "He won't stand being held up any longer."

"Ten days to go," Richard said. "That sounds about right."

"It's exactly right!"

As usual on Saturdays, Edward left Murgatroyd behind and went out with Richard and Declan in the Land Rover. Keyed up with anticipation, Richard was almost bored by the business of the second lot, and was glad when they formed up to go back to the yard. As the leaders of the string approached the Avenue, James Henry and Parsifal, followed by Alberta and Cheslyn Hay appeared. The two lead horses were ridden by Liam Corrigan and Cathal O'Brien.

"Oho!" Richard said when he saw them. "No messing about, eh? The old guard."

"We're taking this fairly seriously, you know," Edward replied, trying to give the impression that he had only recently decided to do so.

"Complete with the latest jump-suit." Richard's tone was admiring. Caroline's pale-blue suit very nearly matched the azure of the silk cap with its golden tassel.

"Do you know, she's having the wretched things made to measure now," Edward confided.

"And very nice too! Brightens things up no end."

The horses, led by James Henry at a leisurely, poised canter converged with the Land Rover at the start of the measured mile and a half. Edward gave them their instructions as they circled round him.

"Give me a good strong gallop," he said. "That's you and Cathal, Liam. Keep your pair going as long and hard as you can." They nodded. "Caro and Robin, stay behind them until the home straight, then carry on and win."

"Any advice on how we should do that, chief?" Caroline asked mischievously.

"Yes! Murmur sweet nothings in his ear. If that fails get off and push!"

Richard was standing in a position to see the very special look that passed between them. He knew that he had no reason to consider himself anything other than a completely happy man, with a splendid wife and two marvellous children. Yet that two-way flash of love, respect and profound good-humour caused him a spasm of envy.

In the time it took to drive the Land Rover straight across the U-shaped replica of Epsom to a point near the finish, the horses had covered six furlongs at the cracking pace Edward wanted. Alberta and Cheslyn Hay pounded away resolutely in front, James Henry and Parsifal cruised along three lengths behind them.

"That must rate as quite an achievement," Richard muttered, more to himself than anyone else.

"What?" Edward asked.

"Getting him to stay behind and conserve himself like that."

"That's why we need Parsifal."

Caroline made her move as they were half-way through the final turn. There was no mistaking the point at which she started her run. Declan let out a grunt of approval, both for her timing, and the way James Henry responded.

"My word!" Richard said, and whistled softly.

Edward was watching every move through binoculars. "Yes," he said, "he's got it on him this morning. And just look at Parsifal! Robin's got him going beautifully."

James Henry, travelling with his usual stylish elegance, swept past Alberta and Cheslyn Hay as though they were standing still, while Parsifal moved smoothly into his slipstream. The rising ground of the final two furlongs made no difference to James Henry; as Caroline urged him on to his maximum effort, Parsifal was getting left behind.

When James Henry drew level with him, Edward assessed his superiority as five lengths.

Then he stumbled.

In that instant, Edward was certain he heard a crack.

For a fraction of a second it seemed that James Henry and Caroline between them were going to recover. She very nearly had him balanced again. But when he went a second time, the sheer impetus of his speed pitched him forward into a rolling somersault to his left. Caroline, with both feet still in the stirrup irons, was between him and the ground which he hit with a sickening thud that the three horrified onlookers actually felt. As Edward unfroze and rushed forward, he caught a fleeting glimpse of Parsifal swerving uncontrollably as Robin Lane pulled him up. The other two horses were a long way behind and were able to stop normally.

Caroline was lying on her back, clear of James Henry. The impact of hitting the ground and his subsequent struggles had torn the stirrups from the leathers.

She looked dreadful.

That a vibrantly healthy human being could assume such a ghastly pallor so quickly came as a terrifying shock. There was a roaring in Edward's ears, and he was doing things his mind knew nothing about. Looking up, he saw Robin Lane staring down in stunned incomprehension from a wild-eyed Parsifal.

"Ambulance!" Edward said. As Robin Lane set off for the Avenue, riding as though possessed, Edward was momentarily blinded by a vision. He was at the foot of the stairs in Avoca House, bending over James Henry, shouting at a frightened Kathleen Corrigan.

Shaking himself and looking round, he saw Richard, petrified and useless. "Richard! Rugs! Land Rover!" He hardly recognised his own voice, but was conscious of immense relief as Caroline squeezed his hand. Automaton-like, Richard came back with two horse rugs. Edward folded one and placed it under Caroline's head. He covered her body with the other.

Her eyes opened, and she whispered inaudibly. With an ear almost touching her lips, he heard her say, "It wasn't his fault. I think he broke a leg . . . left fore . . . I felt it go."

"Ssh. Don't worry." He stared at the trickle of blood at the corner of her mouth.

"She must have bitten her tongue," Richard said.

"Perhaps."

"She's badly hurt, isn't she?"

"Looks like it. All right, darling, we'll soon have you fixed up."

Edward turned as Declan touched him on the shoulder. When the grim look on Declan's face registered, he stood up, and they moved away together.

"Yes, Declan?"

"He has both forelegs broken, sor."

"*Both?*"

"Yes."

"You're sure?"

"I am. The near went while he was galloping. The fall did the off."

Edward looked at James Henry for the first time. There was no doubt about the off-side leg. It was a terrible mess. Splintered bone was sticking out of the skin below the knee.

There was blood in his mouth and nostrils.

"He's hurt inside as well."

"Yes, sor."

"Very badly, do you think?"

"It doesn't matter, does it?"

258

"No." Edward looked at Richard. It was pointless expecting guidance from him. "Do you know what to do?"

Declan nodded and walked over to Liam Corrigan on Alberta.

"I think she's fainted . . . or something," Richard said as Edward rejoined him and knelt down beside Caroline. "Her breathing doesn't seem too bad."

Edward set about unfastening Caroline's helmet. As he did so, he spoke quietly and carefully to Richard, but avoided looking at him. "Richard . . . both James Henry's forelegs are broken . . . they can't be put right. There's something wrong inside as well . . . he's bleeding."

There was a long pause. "I expect he's suffering?" Richard asked at last.

"Very much so, I imagine. He's done for, Richard."

"You're attending to it?"

"Declan is."

Edward eased the helmet off, and Caroline's hair fell loose over the rug beneath her head. The sun turned it to gold. Edward realised that he was quite calm, unreasonably, dreadfully calm.

It was suddenly very quiet.

In the silence, Edward became aware of the stricken James Henry's rasping breathing and groans. Declan was crouched at his head, murmuring what sounded like Irish endearments into his ear. Looking at the Avenue, Edward saw that a group of people were hurrying towards them on foot. Mary and Rosie were at the front, pursued by Alison Bairstow and Robin Lane. He couldn't identify any of the others. When he glanced at Caroline again she looked serene, but the colour of her face and the trickle of blood from her mouth chilled him.

"What do you think?" Richard whispered.

"She isn't very well."

"He rolled on her."

"I know."

Edward need not have worried about the prospect of being surrounded by people who might ask stupid questions or offer pointless advice. When they saw the scene, Mary and the others fell back, appalled and mute. Only Robin came forward. "The ambulance is coming, sir," he said. "Siobhan's waiting for them."

As Liam Corrigan came cantering back on Alberta, Declan walked to meet him, and took the nondescript canvas bag he was carrying across the horse's withers. He dumped it on the ground, and spoke to Mary. She nodded, and led her group well away. Declan stooped down and rummaged in the bag. Crouched at James Henry's head, he looked briefly at Edward before pulling the trigger. The explosion was dull, muffled. It sounded too contrived and distant to be real. The only manifestation of its effect was a brief convulsion in one of James Henry's back legs before he was finally still and silent. Declan returned the device to the bag, picked it up, and set off towards the Avenue without a glance to left or right. Edward saw that his face was so taut that it seemed to have shrunk. Some of the girls who had accompanied Mary and Rosie were crying; wanting to help with an accident, they had been confronted with a disaster. Mary shepherded them in pursuit of Declan.

They passed the ambulance at the mouth of the Avenue. The first thing that Edward noticed was a distraught-looking Siobhan sandwiched uncomfortably between the two men in the cab. He stood up as they manoeuvred the vehicle close to Caroline and brought the stretcher out.

"I think she may be quite poorly," he told the driver. "The horse rolled on her."

The man smiled reassuringly, and told him not to worry. When they pulled the rug off her to put her on the stretcher, Edward saw that it was one of his grandfather's from Avoca House. The initials JHM had been inside, across her breast. He also saw that Caroline's blue jump-suit was stained with blood between her legs.

As Edward climbed into the back of the ambulance and sat alongside the attendant who was going to ride with Caroline, it was eight minutes to twelve, forty-three minutes after it had happened.

Richard suddenly came to life.

"Where are you taking her?" he asked the driver.

"Royal Berkshire, Reading," the driver called out. Looking back, Edward saw Richard hurrying Siobhan towards the Land Rover.

He never noticed the bumpy ride over Saxon Down and along the Avenue, never saw the dozens of worried faces on either side as the driver took the short-cut through the arches in the yard. It was several minutes before he realised that they were on a main road, travelling very fast, and that the attendant had spoken to him.

"I'm sorry. I beg your pardon?"

"Who was the horse?"

"Oh . . . James Henry."

"What, the Derby favourite?"

"Er . . . yes . . . that's right."

"Christ almighty!"

Edward saw that the ambulanceman, a complete stranger, was totally shattered by the news. The man's reaction gave him his first real measure of the situation, and he began to feel light-headed and ill. Gazing aimlessly out of the rear window, he saw a familiar Rolls-Royce following the ambulance.

In Reading, the driver had to use the siren to ease a way through Saturday-lunchtime traffic. Caroline opened her eyes. She reached for his hand, and her grasp was frighteningly strong. She made no attempt to speak. The siren faded as they swung in through the hospital gates, and she let out a great sigh that was piercingly recognisable as a cry of broken-hearted disappointment. Looking closely at her, Edward saw that she was crying. It was a devastatingly gentle process. The only emotion, transmitted to him with searing force, was infinite sorrow. The look in her eyes was his first encounter with the ruination of their plans and dreams.

Caroline died in the operating theatre. Her grievously battered body could not stand the anaesthetic and the trauma of surgery.

"I'm terribly sorry, Mr Manning," the surgeon said. "I'm afraid there was nothing we could do. Your wife had massive internal injuries. Her spleen was ruptured, there was very extensive kidney damage, and . . ."

The man saw that Edward wasn't listening. That made it worse. He could only plough on with the horrific catalogue of injuries.

It was twenty-two minutes past one.

In the hour before they left the hospital, Richard was able to slip away for a few minutes and use a telephone. He made one call.

Siobhan had rung Widney Cheyne after Richard set off in pursuit of the ambulance. Assuming this, he thought that Imogen would have gone to Saxon Court at once. He was right. She answered the phone.

By the time Edward and Richard arrived, Imogen was fully composed and in command. She came to the car, helped Edward out, and guided him into the kitchen. Siobhan looked on impassively; she was never going to tell anyone that she had seen Lady Stewart break down and sob her heart out.

Sitting at the kitchen table with a cup of tea, Edward stared straight ahead, giving no sign that he recognised Imogen, Richard or Siobhan. The four of them were all alone. The silence in the house was absolute. It was the same outside. A fine, early-summer Saturday, and nothing stirred.

Imogen beckoned Richard into the office with her eyes.

"Has he said anything?" she whispered.

"Nothing."

"He looks awful."

"I don't think it's got to him yet. He seemed completely dazed even before we knew about Caroline."

"Shock. I'll get the doctor. Will you take him into the sitting room? Get him to put his feet up."

When Edward was out of the way, Imogen summoned a doctor. Then she sat tapping her teeth with a pencil for a while, thinking hard.

"Valerie Malahide," she said at last.

"Oh yes, she'll have to be told," Siobhan agreed.

"So will a lot of people," Imogen said grimly. "No, I was thinking of something else. You've got her number?"

Valerie was at home. She was spending a lazy afternoon in the sun on the terrace, pretending to read a book. Imogen's careful but inevitably shocking statement of the facts left her numb.

"Are you still there, Valerie?"

"Yes."

"I said I thought you should come over. At once. He's going to need you."

"Yes . . . I see that . . . I will."

"Ring me back when you're organised. I'll have you met at Heathrow. Be as quick as you can."

Imogen sat for a few moments. Siobhan could see that she was gathering strength to make the next call: she also saw her relax slightly when a man answered the phone.

"Hello Frank, it's Imogen Stewart. I'm afraid there's been an accident."

At four-fifteen, Freezer was feeling very pleased with himself; he had just finished parading his second winner in a busy twenty-four hours.

Yesterday afternoon, one of Richard's two-year-olds had won at Bath. They had got that one back home by six o'clock. There had been time only for a quick meal before setting out for Thirsk and an overnight stay with another. Now she too had won.

Freezer and Julie Spencer had the filly washed down, fed, and ready for the long journey back when one of the racecourse stablemen waved anxiously.

"Hey, Freezer, there's a message for you in the Clerk's office."

"What's it about, Alf?"

"No idea, mate. I heard it was urgent."

Dooley assumed his martyred expression. He knew that Freezer was far too conscientious to leave without checking. As usual, he was the only sufferer. Julie Spencer was already heading south with Sean Gillespie in his car.

The official in the Clerk of the Course's office was well-informed and friendly. "Oh yes, Mr Frost, your wife's been trying to get in touch with you. She wants you to ring her before you leave." He saw Freezer hesitate. "She said it was urgent . . . very urgent indeed. Here, use that phone."

Very soon after he made contact with Rosie, Freezer slumped into a chair. He made her say it all again, repeating the terrible details aloud, as if to make himself believe them. The official stopped filling in forms to stare at him, interest giving way to incredulity, then horror.

Dooley could see that something was dreadfully wrong as Freezer approached the van. He wept when he was told. So did Julie Spencer when they found her in a transport café near Doncaster. Sean Gillespie nearly fainted. Later, he had to stop the car to be sick.

Imogen telephoned Torquay. She was lucky again. Caroline's father was pottering around in the huge garden, and Elspeth answered the call. Siobhan sat rigid opposite Imogen as she went through it all for a third time. "I'll leave it to you to tell him, Elspeth," she said. "Yes . . . I thought it would be best. No, I'll let you know about the funeral. I think there'll have to be an inquest first. What? Oh, it's far too early . . . the full force of it hasn't got to him yet. Yes . . . believe me, Elspeth, I *do* know how close they were."

When Imogen put the phone down, her teeth were gritted.

"God! This is going to be bloody," she said.

The hot day helped Rosie and Kathleen Corrigan.

They wondered what to cook for the evening meal in the lads' hostel, and whether it would get eaten. A self-service salad buffet seemed appropriate. Exceptionally for a Saturday evening, everyone was in the dining room: usually, at least half the lads were out for the evening or away until Sunday night.

The buffet was barely touched. They sat in their customary groups, drinking mugs of tea or beer in tense, dejected silence.

"It's awful," a girl muttered. She was one of the new recruits, and had been at Saxon Court less than four months. "It's really awful."

"This'll finish the guv'nor," came from another table.

"Don't be so bloody silly!" Alison Bairstow snapped. Her face was drawn and pale. Beside her, Robin Lane held her hand tightly, and chewed his lower lip. He knew that for once, Alison's confidence was assumed. It was purely for show. She didn't really believe it. Neither did he.

Compton Norris got the news from Bert Coxon. He ran a knacker's yard at Steeple Norris, and was called in by Declan to remove the carcass from the gallop.

They had all seen the ambulance and Richard's hasty comings and goings, but they were not prepared for what Bert Coxon had to tell them when he called in the Fortescue for a pint at six o'clock.

The only real business done in the Fortescue Arms that night came from strangers passing through the village.

After Freezer's call, Rosie roamed their house ceaselessly. At frequent intervals, she looked anxiously through one of the front windows to see if anything was happening across at the big house. About seven o'clock, she found herself in the spare bedroom where Freezer did his painting. She had forgotten the three water-colours of Caroline and James Henry that he had been working on for several months.

Two were complete, and laid out on a trestle table; the other was on the makeshift easel waiting for finishing touches to the background. Intended for the post-Derby celebrations, they were the best pictures Freezer had ever done.

Trying to bite back another spate of tears, Rosie rolled them up, and put them in the battered old chest that was the only other furniture in the room.

Imogen's doctor left some sleeping pills for Edward. Without any idea what he was doing, he yielded to coaxing, and took two at eight o'clock. Imogen tucked him into bed and kissed him good night, but he did not react. Richard sat with him until he surrendered to deep, drugged oblivion.

Siobhan made up a bed for Imogen and Richard while Imogen telephoned her sons at Widney Cheyne. When she had spoken to them, she gave detailed instructions to their nanny. They were not to be told yet. She was especially concerned about Nicholas, who worshipped Caroline.

Nancy Bloomfield arrived at nine o'clock. She had spent the day shopping and sightseeing in London, and was still white-faced from the news she had been given on her return to Widney Cheyne.

Valerie Malahide called back: she was arriving at Heathrow at nine thirty the following morning.

Shortly after ten, Julie Spencer and Sean Gillespie, followed by Freezer and Dooley, arrived from Thirsk. They all needed the drink that Richard offered them.

Around midnight, as they were thinking of going to bed, Imogen remembered the manila envelope she had found Edward clutching when she put him to bed. Someone at the hospital had given it to him.

It contained the charm that Caroline always wore round her neck, her wedding ring, and the sapphires that matched her eyes.

Siobhan fetched Valerie Malahide from Heathrow. When she left Saxon Court, Edward was still asleep. When she came back two hours later, he was outside the office door, talking to Declan. From a distance, he looked almost normal. Valerie got out of the car, held out her arms, and he walked blindly into them. As he approached her, she was shocked at what she saw in his face. With all his resources stretched to near breaking-point, he was just holding desperation and panic at bay. Imogen was relieved, however; she had spotted a flicker of emotion from Edward that said he was glad to see Valerie.

He took her into the office and closed the door. Imogen pounced on her when she came out twenty minutes later.

"Has he said anything?" she asked.

"Oh yes."

"What about?"

"The funeral. It must be done *properly*. He wants to see George Roberts. I thought he was a builder."

"He's also the undertaker," Siobhan explained.

"Oh . . . I see. He says Caroline must be buried next to her mother, and he wants to talk to the vicar about the service."

"How does he seem?" Imogen asked.

Valerie thought about it. "Dreadfully businesslike," she replied at last.

"That's how he is with father and me," Siobhan said.

"At least he's *talking* to you three," Imogen said. "Come on then, let's get on with it. You find George Roberts, Siobhan. I'll go down to the vicarage and throw my weight about."

All the newspapers had the story on Monday. Richard had issued a statement, and embellished variants to cater for tastes in 'human interest' were printed. Siobhan made sure that Edward saw none of them.

The inquest was held on Tuesday, and, to Richard's immense relief, a post-mortem was not required. The Coroner enquired into the cause and nature of the accident. Edward provided the information with concise, icy calm. No, he stated, such incidents were unfortunately not rare. There were many known cases of horses breaking a leg while galloping each year.

A verdict of death by misadventure was recorded.

Back at Saxon Court, Edward accompanied Declan at evening stables. Most of the lads were distressed by his demeanour.

Afterwards, he spoke to Richard for the first time since they had left the hospital seventy-five hours ago.

"We can't run Parsifal at Epsom. It's out of the question. He's badly shocked and disturbed. He'll never come right in time."

Valerie helped Edward make the decision. He knew exactly what he wanted, but needed someone to agree with him before putting it into operation. Once she had given the scheme her blessing, it happened within the hour.

At Edward's request, George Roberts drove the hearse to Saxon Court himself. Declan and the five lads who had been pall-bearers at James Henry's funeral carried the coffin into the Colour Room, where it was placed on a massive oak table that had been there since the days of Ollie Derwent.

The lid was not screwed down. When everyone except he and Valerie had gone, Edward lifted it off.

They both gasped.

In the alabaster stillness of death, Caroline's beauty was breathtaking. Valerie wanted to say something, but Edward gripped her hand tightly, willing her to keep silent.

When they returned to the office, he sat in the window-seat with Valerie and Siobhan to read through the letters of sympathy. There were eighty-six in the first batch, many from complete strangers who were lovers of racing. "I saw you and your wife at Newmarket the day James Henry won the Dewhurst," a retired solicitor had written from Nottingham. "I was very upset to hear . . ."

The racing establishment was shaken by the news:

Tewkesbury Lodge
Newmarket

Dear Edward,

Judith and I offer our deepest sympathy on your shocking and tragic bereavement. If there is anything I can do to help, big or small, please let me or Finoula know.

Yours sincerely,
Bernard Dalrymple.

And there was one from a cynic who had been moved to tears. Identifying himself as "The scruffy hack who spoke to you at

Wolverhampton", Nocker Jarvis had written what he felt was a rather clumsy letter. Edward, however, put it carefully on one side.

After dinner, Edward slipped away to the Colour Room. Because Freezer used the place as a sort of office when he was at home, there was a single seat. Edward placed it three feet from the table, near Caroline's right shoulder, and sat down.

Half an hour later, Alison Bairstow peeped through the door, hesitated, then went away. When she came back, she was carrying a chair from the hostel dining room. She set it at the foot of the coffin and sat down.

With the dusk at nine-thirty, Mary arrived with a bundle of candles. She put one at each corner of the coffin, lit them, and knelt down to pray. Shortly after she left, Cathal O'Brien tiptoed in, touched Alison on the shoulder, and took her place. At eleven, Valerie relieved Edward; just past midnight, Michael Doyle took over from Cathal O'Brien, and Nancy Bloomfield replaced Valerie.

No one ever spoke in the Colour Room. Outside, there was no formal arrangement. But everyone sensed when it was their turn, and precisely when they should go.

Between Wednesday evening until Friday afternoon when they took her to church, there were always two people watching over Caroline.

The re-enactment of the primordial Lykewake ritual sprang spontaneously from sorrowing love.

Edward walked behind the lads as they carried the coffin into the Church of St Matthew and All Saints. Valerie had offered to be at his side as she had for most of the week.

"No, thank you," he said. "I shall have to do this on my own. I'm sure it's what Caro would have wanted." He spoke very quietly, but with implacable conviction.

He halted momentarily inside the door, bewildered by the size of the congregation. Imogen, Siobhan and Valerie had answered countless telephone calls, and most of those who had asked about the funeral had come. They had begun arriving an hour before the service, filling all but the first three rows of pews, then standing in the side aisles. Old Grace Fisher, who had cooked for Joshua Fielding, been present at Caroline's birth, and nursed her mother through her last illness, was there in her wheelchair. Behind Bernard Dalrymple and his wife, Edward recognised two stewards of the Jockey Club, a trainer from Yorkshire, and another from Newmarket. The Duke of Dorchester and his Duchess, Arabella, were squeezed between Dooley and the caretaker of the village school. Edwin Fforbes was nodding serious-faced responses to the whispered comments of Clarrie Edwards from one of the village shops, Rosie was explaining something to a courteously attentive Rear-Admiral.

After prayers, Psalm 121 was sung, then Edward mounted the lectern to read from the Bible. He stood for a long time, looking first at the coffin. He thought how appallingly unhappy his mother looked, and felt sorry for her. The daughter-in-law for whom she had waited for so long had gone, and the future was more bleakly uncertain than if Caroline had never existed. Caroline's father seemed not only exhausted, but positively ill with shock and grief. Elspeth sat very close to him, insulating him from his son. Caroline's brother had no real alternative to sitting close to his father, and was grateful for the barrier she provided. Cyril Brookes-Smith's contempt for Nigel had been heightened by the tragedy; with Caroline snatched away from him, he had nothing left of his original family. This much had been made brutally plain when he and Nigel had met unexpectedly outside the church.

Edward studied the coffin with what seemed to be an air of disdainful detachment. It was on a trolley in exactly the same place that Caroline and he had stood for their marriage, little more than eighteen months ago. Only Valerie's sudden unease brought him back to reality. His inactivity had lasted long enough to cause her physical discomfort. Her distressed movement caught his eye, and he began to read Chapter 21 of The Revelation of St John the Divine:

"And I saw a new heaven and a new earth . . . And I John saw the holy city, new Jerusalem, coming down from God out of heaven, prepared as a bride adorned for her husband . . ."

The burial was a small, private gathering. The lads carried the coffin to the grave followed by Edward, now with Valerie at his side. Then came Caroline's father and Elspeth, Frank and Ann, Richard and Imogen flanking a trembling Nicholas who was determined to be brave, and finally Nigel, deliberately keeping distance between himself and the others. The other four hundred mourners either stayed in the church, or formed groups on the yew-lined path outside.

Afterwards, Edward tried to speak to as many of them as possible. There was to be no gathering at Saxon Court; Elspeth wanted to get Caroline's father back to Torquay as quickly as possible, and although Ann would have liked to talk to Edward, Frank appreciated that it had to be avoided. Only Nigel Brookes-Smith was in no hurry to leave; both Edward and Valerie had the idea that he was hanging around for some imperfectly defined purpose. Eventually, his half-hearted resolve snapped, and he too left, much to Valerie's relief.

Edward shook his head as she tried to steer him towards the car. Instead, he set off back to the grave. For the first time since the accident, he was moving at his normal brisk pace, and she had to run to catch up with him. George Roberts was checking on his men's progress. They had filled in the grave and piled up the earth, and were now covering the mound with the wreaths and flowers that had taken all morning to deliver.

"Thank you, George," Edward said quietly after he had taken in the scene. "You did her proud."

George Roberts nodded, and stared down at his brightly-polished funeral shoes.

"Had to, didn't we?" he said. "Her was the nearest to royalty us'll ever have round here."

For a second or two, Valerie thought they had reached the breaking point. But no, Edward hung on, the strain of the effort showing on his face as he turned and hurried to the car. Once he was safely home, and had collapsed on the window-seat in the office, she saw what getting through the funeral had cost him, although she was still no nearer his true feelings, which were now hidden by the additional cloak of weariness.

When Declan came in an hour later, he was carrying a large vase, which Edward immediately recognised as one of Richard's proudest and most cherished possessions. It was a copy of the Portland vase that had been in the Stewart family since Josiah Wedgwood made it in 1766. When Imogen moved to Declan's side, there was no doubting the importance of the event.

"Richard's colt has been cremated," she said, and was pleased by the flash of relief that crossed Edward's face. The alternatives had been unthinkable. "This vase has got some of his ashes in it. We thought it should be here somewhere."

"The Colour Room," Edward said, standing up, and appearing to lose much of his tiredness.

They took it across at once. The big table had been pushed back against the wall that Siobhan had started using for pictures of Caroline and Edward's stewardship of Saxon Court. After Declan had placed the vase on the table, Edward positioned it beneath the biggest and best picture of James Henry. Siobhan's caption was:

Sir Richard Stewart's colt James Henry and Mrs Caroline Manning at Saxon Court after winning the Two Thousand Guineas Stakes.

Stepping back to study the effect, Edward looked satisfied.

"We have the rest of the ashes," Imogen said quietly, in a matter-of-fact voice. "Maybe you'll think of something to do with them."

Edward turned to Imogen and nodded. It was the first time he had communicated directly with her in nearly a week.

For the next few days, he came close to terrifying Valerie and Siobhan, and alarmed Imogen who was now spending only the days at Saxon Court. He did this by his attempts to carry on in a manner that he perceived as normal. He started riding out in the mornings again, worked furiously hard in the office during the afternoon, and conducted evening stables. All the time, the dreadful calm lay insurmountably between him and the rest of the world, and the only people he ever spoke to were Valerie, Siobhan and Declan.

"He's like a drunkard," Valerie said to Siobhan. "Have you ever seen someone who's completely blotto trying to act as though there's nothing wrong? The drunk's totally convinced he's doing everything perfectly, whereas everyone else is either amused or embarrassed."

"Except we're frightened," Siobhan said.

The culmination came on Derby Day.

To widespread disbelief, Edward insisted on watching the race, and gathered a group of seven together in front of the big TV in the sitting room. They hardly dared breathe as Wesley Davies spoke sombrely of the tragedy that had inflicted such a dreadful loss on Edward Manning and the sport. However, he was scrupulously unemotional, and Edward remained impassive. Valerie and the others thought that the worst was over.

But then, as the jockeys came out, Wesley Davies drew attention to the fact that they were all wearing black armbands as a token of respect to Caroline. Valerie and Mary exchanged a panic-stricken look.

A fraction of a second before the atmosphere in the sitting-room became totally unbearable, Edward stumbled off, upsetting a coffee table as he went. Imogen turned the set off.

Eventually, it was Valerie who went in search of him.

Having established that he wasn't in the house, she went to the Colour Room first. It was deserted. Unsure of what to do next, she headed towards the yard. At the sound of her heels on the cobbles, Declan emerged from the feed room in the Old Yard, touching his cap when he saw her.

"Have you seen Mr Manning, Declan?" she asked.

"Yes, ma'am. He's up in the tack room." Seeing that she didn't know where it was, he led the way into the New Yard. "Up there," he said, indicating a flight of worn stairs up to a loft.

As she climbed, the smell of leather and preservative came to her. The light was dim in the loft, and it took a little time for her eyes to adjust. Edward was sitting on a pile of rugs in the midst of the wooden racks from which over a hundred saddles and bridles hung. He was staring blindly at the picture of 'Caroline's Toff' that he had snatched from the office wall.

"How am I supposed to manage without her?" he asked Valerie, apparently calm and in control of himself.

"I don't know," she said, "but we'll all do our best to help you."

"Yes." He looked at her wildly. "I expect you all will . . ." She saw that his shoulders had started to shake. ". . . it won't be your fault, there's nothing you can do. Nothing!"

Valerie moved swiftly to his side as the sobs came. She felt almost relieved now that it had finally happened, but a desperate time lay ahead of her. Edward's feelings finally boiled over into a cataclysm of grief. She thought about Declan: if he was still pottering about, he must surely have been able to hear. He would understand.

It was two hours before exhaustion finally got the better of misery, then Valerie waited while Declan dealt with evening stables before she took Edward back to the house.

She was determined that no one except her would see him in this state, now or in the wretched days ahead.

CHAPTER 12

Three months later, in early September, Parsifal went to Doncaster and won the St Leger.

His victory cheered the yard staff and the racing press. Although no one said so, it was assumed that it marked the turning of the tide: things would get better now.

In terms of races won, Caroline's death had not had a disastrous effect. Most of the horses had been fit and working well at the end of May and, whether Edward was playing a part or not, Declan had maintained the routines necessary to produce winners. Richard had supported Edward's frozen inability to have anything to do with Royal Ascot, scarcely three weeks after the tragedy. However, the runners had started going out soon afterwards, and the winners followed.

They tended to be unexciting, workmanlike events; Edward's experimentation, intuition and inspiration were missing. His often uncanny knack of seeing something new in a horse at exercise had gone, largely because he no longer took a close interest in what was happening on the gallops, and his conduct of evening stables reduced the occasion to a formality. Races which ought to have been won were lost due to lack of polish in preparation, and the season's new intake of two-year-olds seemed to hold scant hope for the future. Potentially, there were some very good animals among them, including a colt for which the Duke of Dorchester had paid three hundred and fifty thousand pounds as a yearling. Edward's final line of defence against grief became detachment, and the juvenile horses did no more than keep reasonably fit without learning to race.

Parsifal was the exception.

It was as though Edward regarded him as a companion in affliction and bereavement.

Parsifal had been a close witness of the accident, and was deeply disturbed by it. He went off his food, and lost condition, convincing Edward that he knew all about the terrible aftermath of what he had seen. The endless hours that Edward had once devoted to Murgatroyd were now spent with Parsifal. Almost all other things were ignored, left to someone else, but Declan often found Edward in Parsifal's box when he did his last round at nine o'clock. Much sooner than anyone expected, Edward coaxed him back to eating. For two weeks they walked miles across Saxon Down together. Watching from her bedroom with powerful binoculars, Valerie saw that Edward had a very great deal to say to the colt on their long treks, and Parsifal gave every sign of understanding. The improvement in his condition and spirit soon reached the stage where Robin Lane was able to start working him again.

Edward made a special point of watching him, and spotted something almost immediately.

"That horse has changed," he said to Declan, who waited to hear more. "He's using himself differently. He's more economical." There was a pause while Parsifal was studied with great care as he worked over another half-mile. "He's acting like a four-year-old. He's grown up." The final judgement was delivered quietly and grimly. Edward seemed to be implying that Parsifal had struggled through the same painful process as he himself had; he was also suggesting that Parsifal had handled it more successfully.

A few days later, it was discovered that Parsifal was capable of a steady gallop over a mile and three-quarters, and could then produce a finishing burst that looked most impressive. The decision to run him in the St Leger was taken on the spot.

Edward, who had not been near a racecourse since Caroline's death, watched the race on TV and derived little pleasure from it. The moment Parsifal passed the winning post, Edward set about denigrating his achievement.

"He hasn't beaten very much," he said to Siobhan, who had watched the race with him.

"The second and third horses have a lot of good form," she protested. "They've both won Group races."

"Oh . . . I didn't know that." Edward was suddenly respectful. His own recent carelessness had made him notice that Siobhan kept herself very well informed. "Where? When?"

"In France. Last month."

"What, at Deauville?" The respect was gone.

"Yes."

"That doesn't mean a thing! They're only running against donkeys off the sands!"

"I think you're wrong," Siobhan said defiantly. "He's won a Classic fair and square, and you ought to be pleased."

He almost took issue with her, but thought better of it. She could see what was passing through his mind. "To hell with it! It's not worth the effort," was the end. At that, he got up and walked out of the room.

Siobhan reminded herself that this was an improvement. Edward had at least taken the trouble to prepare Parsifal and watch the race. It might be a turning point.

On the TV screen, Freezer and Robin Lane were piloting Parsifal

273

through the crowd towards the winner's enclosure where Richard waited, looking relieved rather than happy. At Richard's side, Edward's new assistant, not sure what to do, was trying to cope with his first big occasion. They would be coming home with the hope that the afternoon's work would make a difference to Edward.

Siobhan felt sorry for them.

Fifteen weeks had passed since Edward had broken down in the tack room on Derby Day. Valerie Malahide had divided her time almost equally between Saxon Court and Dublin.

The first onslaught of anguish lasted three days, and made Edward physically ill. He retched violently whenever he attempted to eat or drink anything, his hands shook, and his face acquired a gaunt hollowness that was to last for a long time. Only when Imogen's doctor gave him sedative injections was he able to relax sufficiently to be able to handle food and regain some strength.

He ignored most people. For him, they simply did not exist. When forced to do so, he held robotic conversations with Siobhan, Imogen, Richard and Declan; he spoke only to Valerie. She found herself following paths that started by being bewildering or painful before becoming frightening.

"Do you know how long it was before they even took any X-rays of Caro?" he asked one day.

"Immediately, wasn't it? Richard said they took her straight in."

"No. I mean the time between it happening, and getting her to hospital."

"Oh. No, I don't know."

"It was an hour and twenty minutes."

He looked at her, expecting a comment. She had nothing to say.

"Do you think that's right? An hour and a half to reach hospital?"

"It's quite a long time," she admitted.

"Long time? It's a disgrace! That's what comes of being stuck in a God-forsaken hole like this. We're miles from anywhere and nobody gives a damn."

"Everyone did their best."

"Well their best wasn't good enough, was it? She died."

Valerie struggled to find the right words. "Caroline was very badly injured, Edward. It's more than likely that a few minutes wouldn't have made any difference."

"A few minutes! Damn it, Valerie, we're talking about an hour. This bloody place cost an hour! What could they have done with that?"

She didn't know.

A few days later, he came at it from a different angle.

"The problem is quite simple. It's horses." He seemed calm, almost resigned.

"Whatever do you mean?" Valerie asked.

"These awful accidents happen . . . quite often . . . horses often break legs galloping."

"I saw it happen at the races once. It was the first time T.P. took me to the Curragh after we were married."

"The results aren't always as bad, of course."

"No."

Edward was silent for a long while. "It was a mistake ever getting mixed up with them," he said at last.

"That can't be true, my dear."

"Why not? It was a horse that killed her." Edward's voice rose dangerously.

"Yes . . . but she knew the risks."

"And accepted them?"

"Presumably so. She'd been involved with them for long enough. What happened to her must have been a million-to-one chance."

"Oh, I see. That's all right then. It's a hell of a shame we can't produce winners at that price. Dooley would like that!"

Valerie did her best not to show how hurt she was at being sneered at. His mood shifted. Suddenly he was sorry for himself.

"Actually, I think it was all my fault."

"How?"

"I should have stopped her riding him."

"That wouldn't have been easy."

"I know. She was besotted with that damned horse. But she shouldn't have done all his ride work. We've got people to do that."

"People to get killed?"

"Yes, if need be!" He glared at her defiantly.

She refused to be intimidated. "Robin Lane is dispensable, is he?"

"More so than Caro!"

During the ensuing ugly silence, his eyes fell to the floor as she stared him into submission.

"We should have done something else," he muttered sullenly.

"I don't understand."

"We should have left this place and found another way of earning a living."

"What?"

"I don't know! There are plenty of things."

"Caroline wouldn't have wanted a life without horses."

"Nonsense!"

"No it isn't, and well you know it."

275

"She'd never known anything else. There are lots of other jobs she'd have liked."

"Such as?"

"I've never thought about it."

"Doesn't that show you what an absurd idea it is. It's never occurred to you until now."

"Of course it has! If we'd been able to sit down and talk about it properly we'd soon have come up with something."

Valerie looked at him hard and took a deep breath. "Edward, you are wrong," she said quietly, but with great force. "Absolutely wrong! You and Caroline would never have met if it hadn't been for horses, and she wouldn't have considered any other way of life for a second."

"Ah! This is the latest version of the theory that Caroline only married me so that she could stay in this place."

"Don't be ridiculous!"

"It's what everybody thinks."

"Who?"

Edward glowered. "Everybody!" he repeated. "But it wasn't true. We were very happy."

"Yes, you were. Everyone knew that and talked about it."

"Did they? Really?"

"Yes, really. You were a remarkable couple. You radiated happiness, and it spread to other people. But it was all bound up with horses. You can't stick two people in a vacuum and tell them to be happy. There has to be an environment, something for them to *do*. With you and Caroline it was horses."

"And it killed her."

Occasionally, Valerie spent an afternoon with Imogen at Widney Cheyne. It was a chance for her to relax, and bring Imogen up-to-date on Edward's state of mind.

"That's about it," Valerie concluded on her next visit. "He holds Saxon Court and horses responsible for Caroline's death."

"Actually, it isn't easy to argue with that," Imogen said after she had mulled it over. "That's going to be difficult to come to terms with."

"I sometimes don't think he'll bother," Valerie said.

"Oh? Why?" Imogen's interest became acute.

"His latest idea is simply to walk away and leave it all."

"Is it, by God!" Imogen concentrated, looking fierce in the process. "Do you know, Valerie, I reckon he's just about capable of that in one of his worse moments."

"The way he's been this last week, I'd say he was more than capable. He's even talked about going back to teaching."

"He doesn't need to work. His grandfather left him more than enough to be going on with."

"So he could clear off and do nothing?"

"Oh yes."

"What do you think the chances are?"

Imogen shrugged. "Fifty-fifty? I don't know. He seems to be getting really carved up about it."

Valerie nodded. "It's getting worse the more he thinks about it. He's started to doubt if he can actually run that place without Caroline – whether he *wants* to is another matter."

"Is he still carrying on normally with Siobhan and Declan?"

"Yes . . . well, what passes for normal these days. He goes through all the motions with them, and pretends to take an interest. I'm not sure he takes all that much in . . . he gets bored very easily. This morning, Siobhan was in the middle of telling him about next week's plans, and he just walked away."

"Declan and Siobhan are running the show?"

"Yes. And Freezer's helping as well. They don't like doing it, but they can see there isn't any alternative."

"What about the yard staff?"

"All right – so far."

"What does that mean?"

"No problem with the old guard from Avoca House, and the ones that were left over after Caroline's father are probably going to be all right. But there's a new batch of about a dozen that came in this year. They're very worried."

"Think the place is going to fold up?"

"Something like that."

"I take it this information comes from Alison Bairstow?"

"Yes." Valerie smiled.

"Very good girl. She's going to be one of those that help us pull through."

"What *do* you think will happen?" Valerie asked anxiously.

Imogen smiled ruefully, and reached for her cigarettes. "What wouldn't I give for a crystal ball that good," she said. "I believe that if Edward *is* going to clear off, he'll do it sooner rather than later. The longer he stays, the more he'll think about things and be able to straighten them out. The high-risk period is going to be the next six months – especially after racing stops."

"What can we do?"

"Hold his hand as much as possible and hope for the best."

"If only we could make sure he doesn't do anything silly," Valerie said.

"Like what?"

"Leave Saxon Court. I'm sure he'd regret it bitterly afterwards."

"I wouldn't bank on that actually. He only ever went there because of

Caroline. Now she's gone . . ." Imogen waved a hand. "There is one thing," she said optimistically.

"Yes?"

"He wouldn't want to let Richard down. I'm pretty sure he'd think several times before he did that."

While Valerie was at Saxon Court, she and Siobhan kept a constant, unobtrusive eye on Edward, charting the progress of his moods, providing support when it was needed. There were several occasions when Edward got into a car and drove away, leaving them half-convinced that he would never come back. Once he was away all day from eight in the morning until late evening. He returned tired and hungry and listened undemonstratively to Siobhan's mild censure of his unexplained absence, wolfing the makeshift supper she had prepared for him. No one asked him where he had been, and he did not volunteer the information.

During Valerie's absences in Dublin, Imogen persuaded Nancy Bloomfield to help Siobhan. Nancy loved going to Saxon Court, always looked forward eagerly to a visit, but was usually baffled at the end of it.

"I can't make it out," she told Imogen. "He always seems glad to see me."

"He likes you."

"Yeah, I think he does. But he always gets uptight if we get on too well. Kinda stuffy. All very British and proper."

"That's fairly typical. He was like that with all women before Caroline."

"What's it about?"

"If I could answer questions like that, I should set myself up as a psychiatric guru. He's always been the same. Apart from Caroline, Valerie is the only woman he's ever been comfortable with on a personal basis."

Nancy shook her head. "He's a funny guy."

"Recent events have made things extremely difficult for him," Imogen said, in what Nancy recognised at once as protective justification of almost anything Edward chose to do or say.

"Oh sure. He's having a tough time."

"Tell me, Nancy, what do you talk about?"

"Parsifal mostly. He's really into that horse. He says he's going to win the St Leger."

"Does he now?" Imogen's eyebrows rose in a rare display of surprise.

"He seems quite confident. He's going to prove me wrong."

"How come?"

"I always thought he wouldn't be much good on a racetrack, but he might be brilliant at stud. I told Richard that before he bought him."

"I thought he'd lost interest in the horses."

"Yeah, he has. It's only Parsifal he's got a thing about."

"Does he ever mention Caroline?"

"Not to me."

Imogen sat and pondered. As might have been expected, Edward appeared to be conducting his mourning and grief within the constraints of rigid protocols. Only Valerie was allowed to see his real feelings. He participated in formal, uninformative conversations with a small select group, and virtually ignored everyone else.

———

Coming back from Dublin towards the end of July, Valerie was pleased to discover that she unexpectedly triggered an enthusiasm other than Parsifal in Edward. They were having dinner at a restaurant near Wallingford, and she was telling him about a concert she had attended, when she saw that he had become distracted.

"What are you thinking?" she asked cautiously.

"I've just realised that I can't listen to music at home," Edward replied. "There isn't a decent radio, no gramophone – nothing! And I left most of my records with mother and father when I went to Avoca House."

It was something that Valerie had never appreciated, and it now seemed a strange omission. She presumed that the hectic activity involved in mastering a difficult new career followed by marriage to Caroline had made music superfluous.

"Perhaps you ought to do something about that," she suggested.

"I will. Tomorrow!"

Because Parsifal was only cantering that morning, there was nothing to interest Edward on the gallops, and he was in Reading soon after the shops opened. Valerie had to go with him.

"You can help me choose," he said.

"I don't know the first thing about it."

"I'd still like you to come with me."

She was used to his reliance on her. While she was at Saxon Court, he always wanted her with him, except when he chose to disappear, worrying everyone in the process.

They spent an hour with a knowledgeable dealer who demonstrated various pieces of equipment, and then guided Edward into a final choice that struck Valerie as being fiendishly complex and hideously expensive. Nevertheless, she felt sorry for Edward when the transaction was complete. He had been expecting to walk out of the shop with his purchase, take it home, and have it working within the hour.

"Oh no, sir, that won't do at all," the dealer said. "Equipment of this quality needs installing and testing properly." He went on to explain that he would deliver the kit and connect it all together in three days.

"You are funny," Valerie said to Edward as they headed back to Saxon Court.

"Why?"

"You've waited goodness knows how long for this stuff, now you get steamed up over a few days' delay."

"But I didn't *know* I was waiting, did I?" he replied with irrefutable logic. She smiled wryly, and did not argue. It occurred to her that the expenditure of nearly three thousand pounds on what T.P. would have called a 'record player' might augur well for the future. Perhaps this lavish home comfort meant that he had decided to stay.

They reached Saxon Court to find Caroline's brother in the office with Siobhan. Valerie had met him only once, in the unhappy circumstances of the funeral. He was eighteen months younger than Caroline, and Valerie now saw the likeness: he was handsome in a way that suggested his sister. Edward greeted him warmly, with an animation that surprised Valerie.

"Actually, I was wondering if you could spare time for a chat, Edward," Nigel said, once the initial greetings were over.

"Of course. Come through." Edward led the way into the sitting-room.

As they disappeared, Siobhan saw Valerie's look of curiosity, and offered an explanation. "I think Edward has a soft spot for him. He's always been very welcome here."

Fleetingly, and with nothing more than intuition fired by the merest suggestion of a look on Siobhan's face, Valerie formed the impression that Siobhan herself was by no means averse to seeing Nigel Brookes-Smith.

In the sitting-room, Nigel studied Edward sympathetically, and asked, "How's it going?"

"Bloody awful!" Edward waved him to a chair. "I still haven't been able to accept that she's gone ... really gone for good. I often think she'll be back tomorrow ... or the day after."

"I feel like that about her."

"You two were quite close, weren't you?"

"Very – especially when we were kids. She always tried to protect me from father."

"Have you seen him since the funeral?"

"No way! I had a fair basinful from him that day."

"I thought something had been going on."

"He gave me a right earful! I know he was badly cut up about Beetle, but even so ... he went over the top." Nigel almost invariably referred to Caroline by her childhood nickname.

"I haven't been in touch at all," Edward said. "He looked damned ill that day. I thought he could use some time to get over it without me making a nuisance of myself. I take it you're on leave?"

"Er . . . no. As a matter of fact, I'm not." Nigel's mood switched from one form of gravity to another in which there was a strong element of awkwardness. "Actually, I've left the Army."

"Good grief!" Edward was very surprised. "Whose idea was that, yours or theirs?"

"Bit of both. I'd been getting fed up with it for a couple of years . . . then I had a few rows with my C.O. Last one was a real bust-up. It was made very plain afterwards that I could wave goodbye to promotion."

"What was the problem?"

"I'd fallen out of sympathy with the whole bag. You know, it's something you either swallow hook, line and sinker, or go mad. I'd come to the conclusion they were nothing but a gang of dangerous juveniles playing at soldiers."

"God! That must have made life difficult."

"It did. Then I found out I was due for another posting to Northern Ireland. After the last lot I couldn't face it, Edward. I was shit-scared, so help me!"

"I wouldn't know where to begin facing up to that."

"Neither did I this time round, so I resigned my commission. The powers-that-be heaved a bloody great sigh of relief, and gave me a chit to say how sorry they were to lose such a splendid chap."

"What do you do now?"

"Find a job."

"You haven't got one?"

"Not yet."

"Any prospects?"

"No." Nigel paused. "I want to work with horses. Always did. Could you offer me something, Edward? Anything. You must want a lot of fetching and carrying doing. And I managed to pick up a fair bit about the business despite the old man. He refused to teach me anything. Said I was useless."

"So I understand," Edward said. "I don't necessarily subscribe to your father's ideas and opinions, Nigel. In fact, to be perfectly straight with you, I think he made a mess of running this place." The severity of his look was exacerbated by the gauntness of his face caused by loss of weight.

"I've often wondered if his heart was in it," Nigel said.

"I question if he ever knew the first thing about horses," Edward replied with a scathing edge to his voice. "Caro was always very evasive on the subject." He looked speculatively at Nigel for a few minutes. "You want a job?"

"Yes, please. I'm keen as mustard, and I'd work like stink."

Edward thought about it, and made up his mind. "Right, you can be my assistant. There *is* a hell of a lot that needs doing, and I expect I'm making a mess of most things."

"That's very decent of you, Edward."

"When can you start?"

"How about tomorrow? No, hang on . . . I'll have to find somewhere to live first."

"Where are you at the moment?"

"With an Army pal near Aldershot. Decent bloke, but his wife's getting fed up with me."

"I'll find you a place here. There must be something."

Although Edward failed to notice it, Siobhan looked pleased when she learned that Nigel was coming to work at Saxon Court. "We must find him somewhere to live," Edward told her. "Any ideas?"

"Here, or in the village?" she asked.

Edward looked at Nigel. "It would be jolly nice to be here," he said.

"There's the place next to us," Siobhan pointed out. What had been the second head lad's house in Cyril Brookes-Smith's day had never been used since Edward took over.

"What sort of state is it in?" Edward asked.

"It should be all right. Let's go and have a look."

While Nigel and Siobhan went to inspect the house, Edward told Valerie what had happened.

"That's good," she said. "You need help."

"Every bit I can get," he replied sourly. For an instant, he gave a glimpse of the immense bitterness that was building up inside him.

Nigel acquired enough furniture from a sale to make the house habitable, and started work a week later. He was an instant success, and one thing was immediately apparent. Whatever else had put him out of favour with his Army superiors, it ought not to have been his ability to motivate and manage staff. His natural authority was backed up by a pleasant manner, and he made no secret of all he had to learn. His good fortune was assured once Liam Corrigan and Alison Bairstow decided that he would do; as usual, yard opinion followed them. Great importance was attached to the fact that he was Caroline's brother. He was accorded the status of a talisman. Perhaps he would bring a little style back to Saxon Court and have a beneficial effect on the guv'nor.

Richard was intrigued by Edward's decision to have an assistant.

Since Caroline's death, he had been following a difficult course that had often called for great patience. His basic role was that of comforter and supporter to a good friend who had suffered a sudden and dreadful loss. But as the owner of Saxon Court, he had a strong interest in its well-being and success, and, in the final analysis, he had an investment to protect as well as an ambition to cherish. Richard had never heard Edward say that he was sick of the place and was going to leave it, yet he had to take Valerie's reports seriously.

"I refuse to worry about the investment," he told Imogen. "If the worst happens, I have two choices. I can find another trainer, or I can sell the whole lot to a Middle-Eastern gentleman for much more than we paid for it."

"You wouldn't like either of those options," Imogen said firmly.

"No, I wouldn't."

"Is there nothing you can do to stop it coming to that?"

"What would you suggest?"

"Talk to him."

"Tell him to get a grip on himself?"

"Something along those lines."

"Give him the James Henry treatment?"

"If need be!"

Richard smiled sadly. "You're forgetting one thing, my dear. Edward's far more like the old man than I am . . . he's virtually an exact replica. I'm just an imitation. If I try giving him a lecture, he'd probably eat me for breakfast."

Imogen gaped at him. "You're frightened of him!"

"Don't be silly, darling. I'm frightened of the *consequences*."

"Go on." Imogen was unconvinced.

"If I start talking to him like a Dutch uncle, he'll almost certainly feel threatened, and there'll be a row . . . right?" Imogen nodded. "And what does he do after he's bitten my head off and we're not speaking to one another? How does he react to his best friend turning against him?"

Imogen was in no hurry to answer.

"He clears off, doesn't he?" Richard said.

"All right. So what do we do?"

"Keep our fingers crossed."

Imogen's acceptance of the inevitable was a long way from being whole-hearted.

After Nigel had been at Saxon Court for two weeks, Richard drove over to watch the horses work on Saturday morning. It was the first time he had done so since the day of the accident, and was motivated by a telephone call from Edward.

"Parsifal's going to Newbury next Thursday. I want to see how he handles the longer distance under race conditions. He'll do his final gallop on Saturday after the second lot."

It was the nearest that Richard was going to get to an invitation, and he accepted it.

The morning was full of interest and surprise.

When Richard arrived in time for breakfast, Nigel greeted him with affable respect. His Army background had instilled hierarchy into him, and he showed that he considered Richard to be one of the more deserving members of the upper echelons. Secretly amused, Richard reminded himself that Caroline must have told her brother a great deal about life at Saxon Court.

After breakfast, Nigel went down to the yard to organise the second lot. Following him, Richard found Siobhan waiting by the lads' hostel.

"Nigel's learning all about stable management," she explained eagerly. "Father's very glad to have him. He's not too keen on ordering people about," she confided. "Nigel's very good at it."

He was indeed, Richard discovered. There were forty-two horses in the second lot. Handling that number of thoroughbreds in a confined space could all too easily become fraught and chaotic. The lad whose mind was not fully on the job, and failed to control a fractious horse in time, could scatter the whole string with disastrous consequences. Although there had never been any problems under Edward or Declan, Nigel had made up his mind that there was room for improvement. The business of saddling, mounting and moving out was performed with a rapid precision that caused Richard to smile.

"He thinks he's running a cavalry troop," he said.

Richard was half-way down the Avenue, striding after the horses, before he became aware of the first big surprise. Still chattering away, Siobhan was trotting along at his side. He could not recall her ever going out on the gallops before. Possibly she was doing it to support Edward: whatever the reason, it would surely interest Imogen.

After the majority of the horses had gone through their paces, and it was time to work Parsifal, Richard received the second surprise. Edward appeared in the Land Rover with Sean Gillespie beside him. In the back of the vehicle were Robin Lane and John Dyer, the permanently worried-looking jockey who had done so well on Parsifal in the Two Thousand Guineas. Alison Bairstow had been walking Parsifal, and when she got off him, Edward gave John Dyer a leg-up, while Robin mounted Parsifal's pacemaker. As the two horses set off towards the start of their gallop, Richard strolled over to Sean Gillespie.

"What's this, Sean?" he asked. "Aren't you riding him?"

"No, sir." Sean touched his cap, and shook his head sadly. "He won't go for me."

"Really?"

"No, sir! We've tried everything, and he won't have it. Robin, or your man Dyer, that's a different matter now. But he'll do nothing for me."

"Is John Dyer going to ride him in the Leger?" Sean nodded. "That's a hell of a disappointment for you."

"It is, sir. Never mind. He's got to win this race. It's *very* important."

Richard understood what he meant. "John Dyer can't be too happy with the situation," he said.

"Pah!" Sean waved a hand derisively. "That fellah worries about everything. I've never known such a case. Still . . ." a roguish gleam appeared in his eyes ". . . he benefits from it. The only thing he'll never have to worry about is his weight!"

It was the first evidence Richard had seen of Julie Spencer's mellowing influence. If Sean Gillespie was going to be denied a third Classic victory, he was taking it philosophically.

Parsifal won his race at Newbury. He did it comfortably, giving John Dyer the sort of ride that almost made him smile. Satisfied with the outcome, Edward set about preparing the colt for the St Leger. His enthusiasm for the task included taking Nigel completely into his confidence, explaining every nuance of the programme, discussing its successes and failures, debating new ways of holding the horse's interest.

By the time Parsifal won the St Leger, Nigel was telling Siobhan that he had learned more and achieved a greater sense of satisfaction in six weeks than in the previous twenty-six years. "Your father and I could make a fair show of running this place if we had to," he told her. It seemed almost arrogant until he smiled self-deprecatingly and added, "There's only one snag."

"What's that?"

"I wouldn't have the faintest idea where to look for the next winner!"

"I think father's the same," Siobhan said. "He can do all the right things with them once Edward's picked them out and said what he wants. But he could never decide what might be possible."

"Funny, isn't it? We need him to say things like, 'That one can win over a mile in two months.' Then it's easy!"

"That's why Edward's name is on the licence," Siobhan said. "He used to be very good at it . . . perhaps he will be again."

"Yes." Nigel was slightly embarrassed by her sudden sadness. "I'm sure things will come right."

A week after winning the St Leger, Parsifal went to Widney Cheyne to be prepared for the start of his stud career which would commence with the next breeding season in mid-February. Ahead of him were five months of being pampered in luxurious surroundings while his diet and exercise regime were gradually adjusted to change him from a racehorse into a stallion. Edward travelled in the back of the van with him, chatting constantly, explaining what was happening. In public, he still belittled his second Classic win of the season on the dubious grounds that the opposition had lacked class, but had given Nigel a memorable savaging when he caught him echoing the sentiment to Dooley.

The following day, Edward belatedly turned his attention to the two-year-olds. He pointed out seven to Nigel, and told him what to do with them. Before the month was out, six of them had won races. The seventh was outrageously exceptional.

Benvenuto Cellini was a very good-looking brown colt for whom the Duke of Dorchester, advised by Richard, had paid three hundred and fifty thousand pounds at the previous autumn's Keeneland sales. His impeccable breeding suggested that he should be very effective at the Derby distance. On days when he felt like it, he moved and performed extravagantly well; at other times he behaved abominably. Only Julie Spencer and Sean Gillespie could stay on him and make him work. The long list of those he had flung on the ground included Liam Corrigan, Declan and Freezer. It was not altogether unexpected. The report that had come from Caroline's friends Hugh and Celia Massingham after schooling had suggested that his temperament might prohibit training and racing.

To everyone's surprise, Edward took to the horse, and gave him special attention. Knowing looks were exchanged when he went to Wolverhampton for his debut, with Murgatroyd's lucky rug, and the sheepskin noseband worn by Parsifal in the St Leger. It was not one of his days for running. After behaving so badly at the stalls that the starter was on the verge of asking for his withdrawal, Benvenuto Cellini dropped himself out of the race after the first furlong, and finished last by a very, very long way.

"I thought he was going to delay the start of the next race," Freezer told Rosie on his return home. Three hours after the event, he was still mortified.

When Edward insisted on running him again only six days later, Siobhan almost told him not to be so silly. This time, however, Benvenuto Cellini did not disgrace himself. He ran consistently, if lazily, to finish fourth, four lengths behind a horse who was winning his fourth race in a row.

Afterwards, Edward underwent a complete change of mood that lasted for a worrying two weeks. He talked to Julie Spencer and Sean Gillespie for hours on end about Benvenuto Cellini, without giving them a hint of what he had in mind. Declan, Siobhan and Nigel were kept completely in the dark until the end of the first week in October. Siobhan was checking the entries for the last few runners of the season, and found that the colt was down for the Dewhurst Stakes; she remembered doing it some months ago, before they had discovered how wayward he was.

"It's the four-day stage for this," she said to Edward. "Presumably you want him taking out?"

"Certainly not! He'll run." To Siobhan's astonishment, his determination was reinforced by anger.

It was the most bizarre end to the season that anyone could have imagined.

On the day of the Dewhurst Stakes, Benvenuto Cellini *did* feel like running. More than that, he ran superbly well, realised his full potential, and won it. Even Edward had difficulty keeping a straight face, and no one else could be bothered to make the effort. After his brief moment of glory in the winner's enclosure, the colt was taken to the racecourse stables, and given a 'routine test for artificial stimulants'. Following the negative findings, one of the Stewards of the meeting 'accidentally' bumped into Edward, and asked several jocular but probing questions. He went away satisfied by the explanation of the colt's performance, but worried by Edward's attitude.

Many Saxon Court staff were overcome by amused disbelief. Dooley was an exception; he had not considered Benvenuto Cellini worth a bet. His starting price was twenty to one.

Siobhan was another exception. She heard what Edward said to the Duke of Dorchester.

"Well, there you are, Freddie. If you sent him to stud now you might earn a shilling or two."

"My dear chap, I wouldn't dream of entertaining such squalid thoughts!"

"That's all right then, because he'll make a fool of himself next time. You can bet on it."

Siobhan knew it was almost certainly true. She just wished they hadn't been so breezily uncaring. It sounded an altogether wrong way of greeting a Group One victory.

———————————

Imogen went to Dublin in late November. Since moving to Widney Cheyne, she had continued to go back occasionally, especially to buy her more important Christmas presents. "I know where everything is," she explained to Richard. "Makes it much easier."

Usually she went there and back in a day. This time she stayed overnight at Howth with Valerie.

Over dinner, Imogen's first task was to recount the main events at Saxon Court since Valerie's last visit in August. Parsifal's St Leger performance, and telephone conversations with Siobhan had encouraged her to believe that all was as well as could be expected. At first, nothing that Imogen said dispelled that view.

"So it was quite a good season as far as *racing* was concerned," Valerie said.

"Yes. Ironically, it was better than last year. Richard thinks that Edward would have been champion trainer but for the accident. We can assume that James Henry would have won the Derby, and the King George VI and Queen Elizabeth was on the cards as well."

"Edward never talks about James Henry?"

"Never! I think he's decided that he'll never have another horse that good, and he's given up worrying about it."

"Perhaps that's a good thing."

"In theory, yes. In practice I'm afraid his whole attitude may have changed – and it's not an improvement. Siobhan says he was downright cynical over that Benvenuto Cellini creature."

"Yes, that seemed a funny business."

"That's putting it mildly. The gutter press said that getting him to win the Dewhurst was an incredible feat of training."

"That's what I thought."

"You won't find many people in the know who believe that. It was pure fluke. He could just as easily have finished tailed off last – or even stayed in the stalls. And Edward knew that when he ran him."

"Good gracious!" Valerie looked concerned.

"That horse is an utter wrong 'un. Edward and Freddie Dorchester thought it was a great joke. *And* the Stewards had the wretched animal dope-tested."

"With no result, of course?"

"Of course. In the end everyone accepted that it's what you'd expect from such an erratic animal. He's brilliant on paper – bloody awful in the flesh. To cap it all, Edward's already said that he won't win a thing next season. He actually gave that morsel to a journalist!" Imogen looked horrified at the memory.

"What about Nigel?" Valerie asked.

"He's all right – seems useful." Imogen's reply was a fraction late appearing, and too carefully enunciated to carry total conviction.

"Come on, tell me," Valerie demanded.

Imogen toyed with her coffee cup as she collected her thoughts. "He really *is* useful," she said. "He's very good with the staff, and he virtually runs the yard. Unfortunately, he seems to be helping a deplorable trend . . . unconsciously I might say."

"What's that?" Valerie asked apprehensively.

"The beatification of Caroline."

Valerie looked perplexed.

"This is the notion that there is absolutely no problem that Caroline wouldn't have sorted out in thirty seconds flat," Imogen explained. "You can imagine the sort of thing – there was only one Caroline, and we shall never see her like again."

"How does Nigel come into it?"

"He was very fond of her. It seems she stuck up for him and looked after him when they were children. Since the season ended, and things have quietened down, Edward and Nigel have been spending a lot of time together. They chew the rag, get thoroughly maudlin, and start gilding the lily."

"And this always was a bad time of the year for Edward."

"Absolutely! When the clocks go back, and the nights stretch out, he gets as miserable as sin. We had two years off the agony routine because of Caroline. It's worse than ever now."

"Things sound bad."

"I think they are. Richard isn't all that bothered. He takes the view that Edward hasn't walked out, it's looking less likely that he will, therefore we're all right. I can't agree. Something wants doing."

"What?"

"God knows! The blunt fact of the matter is that Edward seems in danger of turning into a rather peculiar and useless person. He needs dragging out of it."

"Any ideas?"

"No! I'll give a prize to anyone who can come up with the answer."

Valerie allowed three days to pass before telephoning Edward. After listening to what he had to say about his current problems, she mentioned that she was thinking of going to London. She did it casually, using Christmas shopping as an excuse. The invitation to spend a few days at Saxon Court was immediate.

"I've wanted to see you for ages," he said when he met her at Heathrow. "But I know you've got better things to do than listen to me moaning."

"Don't be silly," she replied. "You only had to ask."

Immensely pleased to see her, he prolonged their customary greeting embrace. Looking at him closely, she could see that he had changed, although she was unable to put a finger on what had happened to him.

The chance to do so soon came.

Valerie had used a flight that reached London at six-thirty. After Edward had extricated the car from the airport, he suggested they stop for a meal on the way. "We shan't get anything at home unless we cook it ourselves," he said. "Everyone's having the night off." The statement was a complaint, suggesting that Mary, Rosie and Kathleen Corrigan had no right to be spending the evening by their own firesides.

Edward turned the meal into a disaster. Valerie admitted to herself that the service *was* slack; the waitress *did* bring him melon after he had ordered soup; no, the potatoes weren't cooked terribly well; the bill was incorrectly totalled. In the past, he had always handled such things with quiet good humour. Now, the young waitress was browbeaten with a cold anger that seemed calculated. The intense relief of escape from the restaurant was short-lived. He drove the last ten miles in grim silence. The car was now equipped with stereo; the tape he rammed into the playing mechanism was of Schubert's 'Death and the Maiden' quartet. The first movement's harshly angular struggle, without hope of ever achieving peace, matched Edward's present mood, and suggested a baleful portent.

Saxon Court was unrecognisable.

Standing by the car, Valerie was disorientated. She had never been there in winter, and the pitch-blackness of the night came as a shock. There were no lights on in the house. There were lamps behind tightly closed curtains in the lads' hostel, and the houses of Declan and Freezer, yet their warm glow emphasised the dark rather than alleviated it. The yard did not exist. Perhaps on a clear night the outline of the long roof and the clock-tower would be visible; tonight, the sky was full of storm-cloud. A south-westerly gale, strengthening by the minute, was roaring through the bare trees, creating eerie sighing and groaning noises.

It was unnerving. Valerie almost commented on it. Startled and blinking in the sudden glare of light outside the office, she remembered Edward's remarks about a God-forsaken hole, and remained silent.

She slept badly. At first, she was troubled by Edward's foul mood, and the incessant creaking as the house reconciled itself to the gale. Then the rain came, driving on to the bedroom windows with needle-like ferocity. During the small hours, Valerie's fitful sleep was disturbed by a great tearing sound followed by an earth-shaking crash. After that, the rain stopped, the wind eased slightly, and she had a few hours sleep.

Downstairs at eight o'clock, the office was in a cheerful uproar. Nigel, who had obviously been up and about for some time, was telling Declan, Freezer and Dooley about the elm tree that had come down in the night, and what they were going to do about it. The fallen tree was blocking a side entrance used for feed deliveries and the removal of stable waste. George Roberts had already been contacted, and was on his way with a chainsaw; Nigel was laying plans for a military-style clearance operation while Dooley promised to have the fifty-year-old tractor in action within the hour, and made gleeful comments about firewood.

There was tremendous relief about a crisis that they could actually resolve by action while enlivening a few days that had threatened to be boring. It was so interesting listening to them that Valerie took some time to realise that Edward was not present. Then she became aware of the noises in the kitchen. She found him raking through the refrigerator, upsetting the contents, muttering to himself, and moving rapidly from irritability to bad temper.

"Good morning," she said, waiting in vain for a reply. "What's wrong?"

"There's no bloody bacon!" He still didn't look at her.

"Not to worry. We'll get some."

"We're virtually out of tea, as well."

"All right, leave it to me."

"It's not good enough! Caro wouldn't have allowed this!" Now he did face her, and Valerie found herself confronted with the problem that had worried Imogen so badly.

Edward spent the morning in the yard. During his brief appearance for a hurried lunch, he was irascible about a number of horses he had discovered with minor ailments, and the slowness of the vet in responding to his call. Having moaned for fifteen minutes, mentioning Caroline incessantly, he went back to the yard to wait for the vet. Valerie spent most of the afternoon helping Rosie prepare dinner.

Later, Edward was in a better mood; all the sick horses had been attended to, and the smell of roasting beef in the kitchen made him rub his hands in appreciative expectation. Nigel ate with them, and Valerie enjoyed basking in their comments on the excellence of the meal.

Over coffee she mentioned Benvenuto Cellini, and was rewarded with a flash of the old Edward. "He's a hell of a horse when he puts his mind to it," he said. "The way he won the Dewhurst was brilliant. Here, come and look at the tape."

They went to the sitting room and watched the video-recording that Siobhan had dutifully made of the race. At the time, she had anticipated obtaining evidence to convince Edward that the horse was not worth bothering with; instead, it was a performance almost as good as James Henry's a year ago.

"Isn't he another Radames?" Valerie asked.

"Good point," Edward replied. "But no! He's much better for a start, and he's got a lot more brain, so he isn't so easy to con. Hardly anyone can ride him."

"We haven't tried with John Dyer," Nigel pointed out.

"No, we haven't." Edward scribbled himself a note. "Of course, you know what he really wants, don't you?"

"What?"

"Caro. She'd have had him right in no time."

Valerie was dismayed to see that Nigel, exactly as Imogen had said, agreed with him. Much worse, Nigel began developing fanciful ideas about precisely how his sister would have coped with the colt, and transformed him into the horse of the decade.

The conversation was unstoppable, and Valerie made no attempt to intervene. When she could stand it no longer, she went to bed.

After an excellent night's sleep, it was nine o'clock by the time she went downstairs the following morning. Edward had gone.

"He's away to the Massinghams," Mary said.

"Who are they?"

"They do the schooling. They've got the little girl Rhinemaiden there now."

"Ah yes, of course."

Musetta's first foal, the Mill Reef filly, was only a few weeks off her second birthday, and was being prepared for training. Valerie would have liked to have gone with him to see how she was progressing; for a few minutes she felt piqued at not being asked. She quickly shrugged it off and decided to go for a much-needed walk now that the weather had finally settled down.

It was past one o'clock when she came back after an exploration of Compton Norris's two neighbouring villages, only to find that the house was deserted, and the yard shut up for the afternoon. Assuming that Edward was probably staying out all day, Valerie made herself a snack lunch and took it into the sitting-room, where afternoon sunlight made her aware of the new gramophone cabinet and its impressive contents. Edward had been very busy buying records: there were over two hundred. Taking a closer look, she discovered a book partly concealed among them.

It was the one Caroline had bought at Miami Airport.

After a quick scan through it, Valerie found a note between the pages towards the end of the book. It was written on Saxon Court notepaper in Caroline's bold, instantly recognisable hand. There was no date. It said:

"Sweetheart, back at 1.30. Have a look at page 76. That's the sort of mood I shall be in. Be prepared!"

Valerie turned to page 76 and studied the photograph.

It was a long time before she finished contemplating this revealing insight, and replaced the book carefully.

Edward was in a rare good humour when he returned as darkness fell. The daughter of his beloved Musetta, by the horse he revered above all others, had captivated him. When Nigel joined them for dinner again, Rhinemaiden dominated the conversation.

"Do you know what Nancy Bloomfield thinks?" Edward asked after he had given a lengthy account of the filly's virtues. Nigel shook his head. "She swears she'll make a good brood-mare! Aren't these breeders incredible? The poor woman was quite put out when I said we might want to win a race or two with her first!"

Edward and Nigel became so deeply and keenly embroiled in discussion that they hardly noticed Valerie. They did not see her preoccupation, they missed the point at which she seemed to reach some sort of decision, and her announcement that she was going to have a bath and an early night caused nothing more than a slight pause in the conversation.

Valerie lingered in the bath, deliberately allowing plenty of time for her resolve to weaken. It did not.

She heard Edward come upstairs shortly after she had gone back to her bedroom. She sat at the dressing-table, brushed her hair until it shone, then applied make-up to her face with great care, pausing frequently to study the results in the mirror. At last, she was satisfied; the effect was slightly more striking than her usual style, but not so much as to be blatantly obvious. Shrugging off the bathrobe, she stood naked in front of the full-length wardrobe mirror and appraised herself. "You're a bloody fine-looking woman, Val," dear old T.P. had always said. That had been a few years ago. In three months' time she would be forty. Head cocked critically, turning this way and that, she came to the conclusion that he would still be justified in saying it. Her careful diet and exercise regime were repaying the effort and occasional sacrifice.

A last moment of doubt came and went; Valerie wafted a lightly perfumed spray across her breasts and stomach, replaced the bathrobe, and went quietly into the corridor.

Edward was propped up in bed, reading a book. He looked mildly surprised to see her. "What's wrong? Can't you sleep?" he asked.

"No, I'm all right."

She knew there was not a second to spare. He had to be taken by surprise.

When she cast the bathrobe aside, he looked shocked, trying to persuade himself that it had happened by accident. Disbelief followed. Then she saw that his eyes were roving with startled interest over her body.

"What on earth are you doing?" he asked.

"Teaching you an important lesson," she replied, and slid into bed beside him.

Predictably, he froze. "This is silly, Valerie," he said. He sounded bewildered and unconvincing.

"We'll see about that."

"We talked about this. I thought we agreed . . ."

She stopped him with a kiss. At first, he remained unyielding, but once her tongue found his, he sighed, and she felt the tension begin to ebb from him.

Although he relaxed, his mind was in a turmoil. He had known Valerie for fifteen years; over the last five years they had achieved the companionable warmth of close friendship. He would have sworn that he knew all about her, yet it had never occurred to him that she was capable of such wanton behaviour. She set about arousing him with a skilful determination that his body found irresistible even though his mind tried to blot it out.

When she finally guided one of his hands between her legs, he discovered that beyond the silky smoothness of her inner thighs, she was ready for him.

"This isn't happening," he mumbled. "It isn't . . . it can't be."

"Shut up," she whispered. "Stop moaning and make love to me."

Valerie felt the precise instant at which he became governed by genuine pleasure rather than mechanistic obedience to what he imagined was expected of him. Briefly, she too enjoyed it, but he was unable to control his climax, and wallowed helplessly in its throes before subsiding. She knew that his subsequent inactivity was the product of humiliation, not exhaustion.

"Don't worry," she soothed, stroking his neck and shoulders.

"I used you," he muttered. "That's all it was. I used you . . . and I made a mess of it."

"Shush! It's all right."

Valerie put her arms round him and waited, knowing that her action would have made things infinitely worse for Edward unless the situation could be retrieved. She watched the second hand on the bedside clock sweep out the minutes, her breathing made shallow by anxiety. At last, after she had endured nine minutes, he stirred, and she saw that his face had brightened.

"I'm sorry," he said, and smiled contritely.

"No, don't be . . . I shouldn't have such clever ideas."

Drawing back slightly, he studied her with the sort of interest he hadn't displayed for months. As if suddenly aware of her breasts, he stroked his fingertips over them. "Amazing. Absolutely amazing," he said.

"What is?"

"You're very attractive, Valerie. Mind you, I've always known that . . . I didn't realise you were *this* attractive."

When he kissed her, it was her turn to respond to passion. This time, his penetration of her body had assurance and purpose.

"That's very good," she gasped. "Very good indeed."

Valerie's response acted like a tonic on Edward. His indulgence in her was adroit and caring, taking her to levels of pleasure then ecstasy that she had never expected from the adventure. For a gratifyingly long time they moved with harmonious power, as though they had a wealth of experience of each other's needs.

She smiled lustrously when they were finally sated. "We both seem to have needed that rather badly," she whispered.

They slept for several hours. When she felt it was time to go back to her own room, Valerie woke him.

"I hope you learned something," she said.

"Yes. Yes, I did."

"What? Tell me."

"There *are* other women."

"Right. Remember that."

"God knows what I'm going to do about it."

"You don't have to *do* anything. Just be aware of it. Stop crucifying yourself."

He stared hard at her. She was convinced he had taken the point.

"I don't suppose we shall do that again?" he asked quietly as she moved towards the door.

"Wait and see. Leave the future where it is."

He thought she had gone, but she turned, and smiled wistfully. "I've half-wanted to do that for a long time," she said. "I'm glad we did. You're nice."

Valerie looked hard at Edward. "Are you going to be all right now?" she asked.

"Yes."

"Promise?"

"Yes."

They were saying goodbye at Heathrow Airport three days later. She had not returned to his bed. He doubted if she ever would.

"You know what James Henry asked you to do?" Valerie asked.

"Yes."

"Do it for Caroline as well. Win the Derby for her. But don't turn her into a saint while you're doing it. And don't shut yourself away. There are people who need you every bit as much as you need them. Just remember that."

He nodded.

"She would approve of that, Edward. That's what she'd want, not the way you've been."

CHAPTER 13

Valerie resumed the pattern of her life. Although she had never begrudged the burden and disruption placed upon her, it was a relief to slip back into normality. Her sponsorship of music had gradually involved her in a large number of activities. She was much in demand as a festival organiser, and she was increasingly asked to do work for the Irish Government's Ministry of Arts.

Hidden away in a secret corner of the routine was her relationship with Eammon Pearce.

Pearce was the son of the accountant whom T.P. had advised Valerie to depend on. He had taken over the family practice a year after T.P.'s death, and managed Valerie's increasingly complex financial affairs. He was the same age as her, completely trustworthy professionally, good-looking and disastrously under the thumb of his strong-willed, rather unattractive wife. Even though they were not Catholics, there was no question of divorce or separation since she controlled the purse strings. Eammon Pearce had married the daughter of his father's partner, begun to regret it almost at once, and lacked the strength of character to throw it all in and begin again on his own.

Every month he had to spend two days at a sawmill in the heart of County Wicklow. The long-standing contract to do all the accountancy for the place was lucrative, and offered a chance to spend three nights away from home in congenial surroundings. Eighteen months after T.P.'s death, Valerie began to accompany him on these visits, sharing the suite he took in an hotel on the shore of the Upper Lake at Glendalough. When they were there, Eammon Pearce left at eight o'clock, and drove to the isolated sawmill in the hills. Valerie spent the day reading, walking, or catching up on her correspondence. He returned at six, they chatted, had dinner at seven, and went to bed.

During an afternoon on which Pearce had delivered some important papers to her house, Valerie had discovered that they were strongly attracted sexually. They were both in a restive, reckless mood that day, had given in to impulse, and discovered a satisfying compatibility. With just enough in common to give a workable semblance of friendship, they began going to Glendalough each month to indulge in sex: Valerie never thought of it as making love.

Much to Eammon Pearce's annoyance, events at Saxon Court had played havoc with the Glendalough arrangements. He greeted their reinstatement with great ardour, blissfully ignorant of Valerie's thoughts about Edward. They ranged from guilt at what she had done, to semi-serious notions that perhaps she held the key to Edward's long-term happiness and success. For a while, the latter was a beguiling prospect, which faded during a busy January. There was the perennial prohibition that if anything lasting were to spring up between her and Edward, it would have happened long ago, before Caroline. Now, she saw Saxon Court as another barrier: even setting aside her lack of detailed knowledge of horses, she knew that she could never *give* herself to the place as Caroline had done, and as anyone who followed her must.

Valerie travelled to England at the end of April to see her filly Jane Eyre run in the One Thousand Guineas. Jane Eyre had done nothing of note as a two-year-old because of persistent sore shins; however, the problem had cleared up, and Edward agreed that she was worth the entrance fee.

Not until the horses were on the way down to the start, and Edward was chatting to Bernard Dalrymple, did Valerie have a chance to talk privately to Imogen.

"How's he been?" she asked.

"Up and down ... *very* up and down. His best time was after you were here. He was pretty good for two or three weeks. Then it was bloody. It looks as though poor Ann made a bit of a mess of Christmas."

"How?"

"Going on rotten about Caroline, I suppose. He was in a bad way when he came back ... didn't start pulling round until he got cracking with the horses."

Jane Eyre finished fourth. Sponsorship, becoming more popular every season, had now spread to the Classics, and in the richest ever One Thousand Guineas, Valerie's prize-money came to nearly seven thousand pounds.

Two days later, Benvenuto Cellini finished spectacularly last in the Two Thousand Guineas, causing Sean Gillespie to plunge into a murderous mood, and giving Edward grounds for grim satisfaction at the realisation of his prophecy. Between Jane Eyre's creditable performance, and Benvenuto Cellini's disgraceful apology for an effort, one of Mark Walgrave's horses unexpectedly won a Group Three event.

"We're going to have a funny season," Valerie heard Edward say to Nigel. "A very funny season indeed!" He seemed almost to be looking forward to it with sardonic relish.

So it proved. Horses who had shown signs of promise, were disappointing; some failed in their work at home, others when they got on the racecourse. On the other hand, animals that Edward had openly dismissed as mediocre or worse, had no difficulty in winning the modest class of race for which they were first entered, and carried on winning when Siobhan insisted on running them against better opposition. From her unique position in the office, Siobhan was the first to suspect that in addition to his careless approach to work on the gallops, Edward was far less interested in finding the right race for a horse. The danger signals came after the breakfast meetings when she saw that he appeared not to have heard the advice he had been given.

Her solution was to start entering horses for races without consulting Edward. She listened carefully to the discussions over breakfast, sometimes spoke to Nigel to check her understanding of the situation, telephoned the owner, and made the entry.

The consequences could be ludicrous.

One evening in May, Edward was lounging in the office window-seat when the van came back, Dooley pausing to drop Nigel outside his house before going down to the yard.

"Hello, what's going on?" Edward asked.

"That's Luisa Miller coming back from Salisbury," Siobhan replied.

"Oh. I didn't know she was going." He was quite unconcerned.

Siobhan imposed a slight delay before saying, "She won."

"That's good!" Edward smiled vacantly, and returned to the magazine he had been reading.

"You're going to be late for evening stables if you don't get a move on," Siobhan said. An edge in her voice betrayed irritation.

"Not to worry . . . Nigel said he'd do it."

Edward was perfectly pleasant and relaxed.

But two days later, when he was a guest at the wedding of Sean Gillespie and Julie Spencer, his mood had changed completely. His detachment and indifference came close to giving offence to several people. Imogen, casting a benign eye over the happiness she had helped to initiate, was very annoyed.

"So help me, I am going to strangle him if this goes on much longer," she whispered through clenched teeth to Nancy Bloomfield. Nancy sympathised with the idea. Completely settled at Widney Cheyne, she was delighted with her work and the agreeable environment. Her only difficulty was that since Caroline's death, Edward's attitude towards her had become wildly erratic. Mostly he was friendly, treating her as a respected colleague. Then, just as she was beginning to feel that he had accepted her, the bomb would explode and it became worse with the passage of time. Arriving at church that morning, he had responded to her greeting with a cold stare of non-recognition.

Edward took Siobhan aside at the reception. "Are they going away?" he asked.

"Who?"

"Sean and Julie."

"Only for a week. To Ireland."

"What the hell are we supposed to do?"

"I told you this weeks ago," Siobhan said. "I've arranged for John Dyer to ride for us."

"Is he up to it?"

"He won the St Leger for you!" She had never been angry with him before.

"All right," he muttered, and walked away.

Siobhan felt light-headed. By implication, he had condoned her status as a self-appointed decision-maker.

Throughout the entire season, Edward devoted his reduced attention and energy to two horses, Benvenuto Cellini and Rhinemaiden, although his approach to them was very different.

A week before Rhinemaiden left schooling at the Massinghams' at the end of January, Edward had called Cathal O'Brien into the office. "I'm giving you Musetta's filly, Cathal," he said.

"I'm already doing two for Mr Fforbes, sir."

"We'll change that!" The lad looked uncomfortable. The allocation of yard duties was Declan's responsibility. "I want you to look after her as if she was your own."

"I didn't do very well with her dam, sir," Cathal reminded him unhappily.

"That was no fault of yours, and this one's going to be different. She's a little bit shy, so she'll need plenty of love."

Declan was unruffled by the changes he had to make; as he told Mary, he should have anticipated that Edward would want the filly in Cathal's gentle care.

Benvenuto Cellini was a very different matter. Edward's interest in the colt sprang from the strange rapport that had grown between them. "Well, what's it to be today, you bastard?" he would often ask the horse, and be rewarded with a knowing look that seemed to say, "Wait and see. I haven't quite decided yet."

After a day's deliberation with the Duke of Dorchester, it was decided to run the colt in the Derby, but not to bother with a prep race.

"The fact is, Freddie, I don't want to look *too* much of a fool," Edward confessed. "The more we run him, the more funny looks I'm starting to get."

The Duke roared with laughter. "That horse is great sport," he said. "Mind you, I can see your point. You always seem to be keeping an eye open for the men with white coats when we take him out."

Edward made a tremendous fuss about Benvenuto Cellini's appearance at Epsom. This was not because he had any serious hope of winning, but for the simple reason that it was his first ever Derby runner. For only the third time since Caroline's death, he went to the races, and, complete with morning suit, found himself standing in the paddock before the world's greatest race. He was thankful that Richard had left the bank to fend for itself to come and support him.

"What's it feel like?" the Duke asked in a whisper that was audible thirty feet away.

Edward looked and felt sick.

Once the interminable preliminaries were over, and the race was actually under way, everything went according to expectations. At Tattenham Corner, Benvenuto Cellini was last, and experiencing difficulty handling the steeply downhill bend. In the straight, the ultimate winner, well placed on the rails, began his run for home with Benvenuto Cellini something like thirty lengths behind him. About thirty-six seconds later, Benvenuto Cellini finished fifth, two lengths behind the winner, only a neck away from the photo-finish for second, third and fourth. In three furlongs, he had swept past sixteen horses, made the crowd seethe with excitement, and caused most of Sean Gillespie's life to flash before him.

"My God, Manning!" the Duke said to an ashen-faced Edward. "What would have happened if that race had been a touch further?"

"I'd rather not think about it, Freddie!"

Edward was badly shaken. Benvenuto Cellini's astounding performance in the closing stages of the race had taken his breath away. It seemed certain that if the Derby course had been half a furlong longer, he would have won it. The realisation came as a shock. The greatest, most coveted prize in racing could have dropped into his lap by accident, without planning or preparation. It was a profoundly disturbing thought that left him on edge for weeks.

Two months later, the colt had another of his good days, and made a convincing show of winning a Group Two race at York. After consultation with the Duke of Dorchester, Richard took steps to remove Saxon Court's most disruptive influence by opening negotiations with an Irish stud farm. The owners were prepared to believe that Benvenuto Cellini would be capable of producing excellent progeny without his temperamental flaws, and he was soon on his way.

Rhinemaiden made her debut at Windsor in August. She had a thoroughly miserable race. The start was a chaotic affair; three of the runners were over-excited by their first race, and ran inwards when the gates opened, causing a great deal of jostling and bumping during which Rhinemaiden was all but knocked over. When Sean Gillespie got her settled, she ran very well, only to end up being forced to drop back against the rails as another horse swerved in front of her. Edward lodged an objection, but the Stewards were unconvinced that Rhinemaiden would have gained a place without the interference, and took no action.

To give her the best possible chance of recovering from the experience by building her confidence, Edward ran her again a week later. This time, at Newbury, things were very different. Rhinemaiden took command of the race two furlongs out, and finished the job in a style that had the aficionados smiling at they reached for their notebooks.

For her final race of the season, she received the most meticulous preparation given to any horse at Saxon Court that year. Throughout September, Edward was on the gallops every morning, without once delegating responsibility to Nigel as he had done for much of the summer. Rhinemaiden's walking, trotting and cantering were the subject of hawk-eyed scrutiny, and her galloping partners were chosen with a fastidious care that was reminiscent of the early days at Avoca House.

She repaid the effort with unstinting largesse by winning the Cheveley Park Stakes at Newmarket, the only Group One race in the Calendar exclusively for two-year-old fillies. In getting the better of two other very good animals in the last furlong, she showed considerable courage, earning glowing praise from all quarters, and a short-priced quotation from bookmakers for the 1985 One Thousand Guineas. Accompanying Edward at Newmarket, Richard saw a great deal to cheer him; Edward was very proud of Rhinemaiden and it showed.

"That's one of the best races I've ever won," he said as they drove back to Saxon Court. "T. P. Malahide's Eclipse was the best," he added after a few moments thought, "but she wasn't far behind him."

Siobhan was very pleased because it was obvious that Edward had given his heart to Rhinemaiden, and she hoped that it was a sign of better times to come. The Cheveley Park Stakes had given belated brightness to an otherwise indifferent season. The number of winners had been only thirty-one, with prize-money of barely two hundred thousand pounds. The result was not very bad when seen against Bernard Dalrymple's tally of eighty-seven races and six hundred and fifty thousand pounds, but it needed improvement, especially in terms of the class of race won.

There was one aspect of the season that particularly concerned Siobhan. For the second year running, Saxon Court had sent no horses to Royal Ascot. There was a perfectly good explanation for last year: it was unthinkable so soon after Caroline's death. This year had been a different matter. Five horses had got as far as the four-day declaration stage, but all had been taken out when it was decided that Rhinemaiden was not ready to make her debut. No one had dared to question Edward's logic. As the owner most involved, Richard had been glad to be safely past the first anniversary of the accident, without asking awkward questions. The blunt fact of the matter was that none of the five horses was anywhere near ready for a race, and Rhinemaiden's genuine backward-ness had been used as a blanket excuse.

As it happened, Siobhan's worries on that score were unnecessary: Edward *did* realise that things would have to get better.

"It's been a bloody terrible year," he said to Mark Walgrave.

"These things go in cycles though, don't they? There's a lot of luck involved."

Edward looked unconvinced.

He was spending Sunday at The Elms, a habit that had grown as the strain of seven days a week at Saxon Court became unbearable. Mark and Sarah, always closely attuned to him, had been a consistent comfort after Caroline, and within the last few months, Edward had become a godparent to their twin sons Christopher and Martin.

"It's damned hard work," Edward said. "Soul-destroying sometimes. I wonder whether it's worth it without Caro."

Mark gazed at him sombrely, and felt helpless. These days, Edward was nearly always in control of himself, but beneath the veneer, the quiet desperation was always there.

Fred Bird appalled Imogen, and she made no secret of the fact.

She called him a spiv and a barrow-boy to his face, and Fred was delighted, knowing that she would be saying even worse behind his back. For him, Imogen's aristocratic disdain was very nearly the last staging post on the long road to success. Ragged-arsed kids in Bethnal Green didn't even get noticed by the Lady Stewarts of this world; now he was big enough and close enough to get right up her nose. He loved it, and thought the world of Imogen.

Fred was fifty-five, tall, lean, and permanently looking for action, pleasant or otherwise. He was a marvellous friend, but a terrible enemy. His public face had precious few moments of repose. Those who did business with him were always conscious of and often felt threatened by his continual movement and change, both physical and mental. He was a brilliantly successful wheeler-dealer who, in the past two years, had crowned nearly forty years of living on his wits by becoming a millionaire.

Fred had left school in the summer of 1945, and promptly carved a niche for himself in the black-market world of nylon stockings. He had made a profit of never less than two hundred per cent on an outlay that soon reached a hundred pounds a week without falling foul of the law. Working sixteen hours a day, and trusting no one, least of all his brothers and sisters, he emerged from the alleys in 1949 with thirty thousand pounds stashed away, and became a bona fide street-trader.

It was 1959 before Fred finally gave up his barrow, having learned that there was limitless money to be made in lingerie, and developed a taste for the most ostentatious life-style that he could reasonably afford.

For nearly twenty years, Fred had bought and sold. He made himself the middle-man between the underwear manufacturers of the East

302

Midlands, and virtually every street market in London. In the early 1960s, he became a regular user of the newly-opened M1 motorway, transporting over a thousand dozen pairs of knickers each week to his small warehouse in Bermondsey where queues of customers formed at six each morning. It was lucrative, had unlimited growth potential, and afforded Fred ample excitement and pleasure. In 1955 he had married a girl from Hackney; they had been happy enough for a while, but she had been unable to share his big business vision, was inclined to be painful about the finer points of some of Fred's deals, and had aged far more quickly than was good for her. Somewhere along the line, she had been paid off and divorced.

The final chance came in 1980, when Jeff Riggs, one of Fred's few long-time cronies, was made redundant by the Leicester knitwear group for whom he had been a production manager. Within a month the business in his back garden had produced the first samples of a range of exotic lingerie. Fred took one look at it and saw the potential. Jeff Riggs got an immediate injection of much-needed capital, Fred became a company director and, in the same week, opened a shop in London to sell everything that the cutters and machinists of Melton Mowbray could produce.

'Fred Bird's' in Tottenham Court Road was a runaway success, as was a second shop just off Oxford Street. When he tried to implement his plan for twelve shops in major cities, Fred was confronted by a barrier. Wanting a loan for the first time in his life, he was rejected by the bank he had used for twenty-five years.

So, thinking big, as ever, he decided to try merchant banks.

The first two kept him in the waiting room for half an hour, then said they were too busy.

The third produced an arrogant youngster to tell him that the idea was laughable.

At the fourth, he was given a careful interview by a man he took to be a time-serving fuddy-duddy who asked a few apparently innocuous questions, and then disappeared, looking inscrutable.

Ten minutes later, Fred was ushered into an immense, oak-panelled office to be greeted by the Chairman, Sir Richard Stewart, Bart.

Fred opened fifteen shops with the two million, repaid the loan in eighteen months rather than the agreed five years, and caught a glimpse of the thing he had wanted above all else since he was a kid. He had first encountered it in Miss Millership, a teacher at Essex Street Junior School: she had carried it with the regal ease of a God-given gift, and he had never forgotten her.

It was *quality*.

"He's a very nice bloke, actually," Richard persistently told Imogen.

"He's a guttersnipe!"

"Very possibly – but he's *all right*. Heart of gold. And does he know how to make money!"

"A tradesman! And look at his ridiculous airs and graces. What does he call it?"

"Quality."

"Pah! The man's a mountebank!"

"I think that business about quality is rather charming."

Imogen gazed at her husband as though he had taken leave of his senses. "And all from knickers," she said in a hollow voice.

"He makes no secret of it." Richard smiled with admiration. "As a matter of fact, he's rather proud of it."

"I know," Imogen replied icily.

Fred had dined at Widney Cheyne the previous week, and his life's work had dominated the meal. The Duke of Dorchester had made matters worse by being vastly entertained. Emboldened by the approval of a peer of the realm, Fred had, Richard admitted, rather gone over the top with his stories of what some women had been prepared to pay for a decent pair of stockings in the 'good old days'.

"Anyway," Imogen said, in her firm, 'official' tone, "this latest idea of his is completely beyond the pale."

"I don't think it's that bad, darling," Richard said with deliberate mildness. "It seems only sensible to me."

"Really? I imagine Edward's reaction is going to be pretty spectacular."

Richard had the uneasy feeling that she was right.

A year ago, Fred had decided that his chances of finding the elusive 'quality' would be enhanced by owning racehorses. He had fancied the idea for some time, in any case. Accordingly he had bought eight yearlings at the Doncaster sales, and placed them with a northern trainer. They had pursued persistently undistinguished two-year-old careers. None of them had ever come close to winning. Even worse, since they were based, and mostly competed in races two hundred miles away from Fred's busy orbit, the status they conferred on their owner was small. It was inevitable that Fred should ask Richard if he could help get his eight horses into Saxon Court.

"Certainly not!" Edward snapped when the subject was broached. "The owner who gets fed up with one trainer soon starts being a downright nuisance with any other stable."

It was more or less what Richard had expected. Edward was fiercely loyal to his perception of a trainers' 'club'.

"He's not fed up," Richard explained. "It's just that his horses are at the wrong end of the country." Seeing Edward soften a little, he added an important point. "Aren't you going to be a little below strength next season?"

"So Siobhan tells me."

"Well, can I at least bring Fred Bird to see you?" Richard asked. "You might be able to do each other a bit of good."

Edward agreed, with little enthusiasm.

It was a fine, crystal-clear morning in early December when Richard drove into Saxon Court, with Fred beside him, and his heart in his mouth. The place looked at its winter best, thus laying the foundation for what followed. As so many others had done before him, Fred could do nothing more than goggle in wonder at his surroundings. Advancing to meet him, Edward saw his expression, and felt an immediate sympathy for him. Whatever he sometimes said about Saxon Court, he was proud of it, and liked people to admire it. And there was a breezy optimism about Fred that struck a chord in Edward: he wanted cheering up, and here was the man to do it. Fred was in paradise from the moment he arrived, and once he had seen the two halves of the yard from the arches beneath the clock-tower, he was almost speechless.

"That's *quality*," he breathed.

Edward correctly took it to mean the same as James Henry's 'class', and they began to get on like a house on fire, while Richard stood back and watched in amazement.

There were two conditions. Edward insisted that he would not take Fred's horses until he was satisfied that all fees due to their present trainer had been paid.

Fred agreed readily, then walked straight into the second condition. "I take it we can do all our business with notes, Mr Manning?" he said.

"I beg your pardon?" Edward gave him a look that would have warmed Imogen.

"Cash. Readies. No messing about with VAT."

"Oh no, Mr Bird, that won't do at all." Edward rather laid it on. "Even if I could be persuaded to work like that, my secretary would never tolerate it. You will receive an account on the first Friday of every month, and it will comply with tax regulations."

"Any discount for quantity or prompt payment?" Fred asked cheekily.

"No. There is, however, a penalty of five per cent per week for payments delayed longer than seventeen days."

Thunderstruck, Fred looked at Richard, hoping for denial.

"Quite right," Richard confirmed. "I get a bill every month, and I own the blasted place!"

The 1985 work programme was delayed by severe weather. Heavy snow fell during the second half of February, and the all-weather gallop was under snowdrifts for ten bitterly cold days. When it cleared, and cantering started, Edward stated his first priority quite clearly: Rhinemaiden would follow in her dam's footsteps and go for the Nell Gwyn Stakes in mid-April as a prelude to the One Thousand Guineas two weeks later. Watching and listening anxiously, Siobhan hoped that this was not his *only* priority.

Still far from keen on going racing if it could be avoided, Edward stayed at home, and watched the Nell Gwyn on TV. Rhinemaiden did what was expected of her, and won it in precisely the way that had been decided in advance. As soon as the race was under way, Sean Gillespie took her into a lead that none of the other contestants could quite erode, although two of them finished very strongly, and got to within a length of her.

To Siobhan's dismay, Edward seemed distinctly unimpressed.

"Let's see that again," he said after he had thought about it.

She rewound the tape and replayed it.

"H'm. Once more," he muttered afterwards.

He watched the race five times.

"That's not too good," he said at last, but refused to elaborate.

Sean Gillespie found himself buttonholed the moment he and Julie arrived for work at six thirty the following morning.

"How was it?" Edward asked.

"All right." Sean was uneasy.

"She looked very one-paced to me."

"She was."

"You didn't push her, though."

"You told me not to."

"Yes. That pair behind you would have done you in another furlong."

"Probably."

The extra furlong would have made the race as long as the Thousand Guineas.

"How long could she have kept that pace up?" Edward asked.

"Forever, I reckon."

"Yes. That's what I thought."

Edward had a busy morning on the gallops, after which he asked Siobhan and Nigel to join him for lunch in the kitchen. They sensed that his silence was due to preoccupation with a problem rather than a bad mood, and respected it.

"I'm going over to Widney Cheyne," he announced when they had finished eating. "I want to talk to Miss Bloomfield."

Widney Cheyne had a back entrance that enabled Edward to reach the stud and Nancy's cottage without coming in view of the house. He found her in the garden. Although she concealed it well, Nancy was horrified to see him. She looked like a scarecrow. A pair of faded dungarees at least two sizes too big for her, and a pretty dreadful check shirt had seemed the most appropriate dress for destroying nettles, and her hair was a windblown mess.

As so often, his attitude amazed her.

"Hi, Nancy! I'm sorry to barge in on you like this," he said. "I need some advice." He was friendly, almost deferential.

"Sure," she said, casting the spade aside, and doing her best to adjust. "What's the trouble?"

"Rhinemaiden. Did you see the Nell Gwyn yesterday?"

"Yeah. To be honest, I thought she was lucky to win it."

"So do I. That's why I'm here."

"OK. Come on in."

Edward put his cards on the table once they were settled in her pretty sitting-room with its view of one of the paddocks. "She's changed a lot over the winter. She's come on much more than I expected. I don't think she's going to be any good at a mile, and she'll get knocked up if we try to win the Guineas with her. What do you think about going further?"

"Well, I don't have to tell *you* that Mill Reef's a big influence for stamina," Nancy said.

"No." Edward smiled. He was well aware that his admiration for Rhinemaiden's sire could become boring. "The snag is, I know virtually nothing about Musetta's breeding . . . never bothered to find out."

Nancy pulled a big, stiff-backed notebook from under a coffee table. "There," she said, flicking through the pages to find it. Musetta's family tree was laid out for five generations in beautiful italic script. Her maternal grandsire, underlined in red, caught Edward's eye at once.

"Majestic Prince . . . I don't know him," he said. "Was he good?"

"He won the Kentucky Derby and Preakness Stakes in 'sixty-nine."

"Two legs of the American Triple Crown?"

"That's right."

"Both a mile and a half?"

"Yup!"

They talked for over two hours, Nancy increasingly conscious of a heavy responsibility. Edward was hanging on her every word, and she knew what the outcome was going to be long before it happened.

"Right! I'm taking her out of the Guineas. We'll run her in the Oaks instead."

After he had gone, Nancy sat in bemused inactivity for a long time. Tomorrow, Edward might well ignore her if they met; today, he had been in desperate need of her advice, and had listened to her with respect. "Hell!" she said, and shook her head.

———————

Edward's decision not to run Rhinemaiden in the One Thousand Guineas was unpopular. Richard questioned it very closely indeed, and came close to using his owner's right to overrule it. During the discussion, Edward became over-sensitive to Richard's comments, an argument developed, and Edward became angry.

"You think you know better? Fine! *You* train her then! And you can look after the others while you're at it!"

After that, they avoided each other for two weeks.

Tempers also flared in the lads' hostel.

"It's a bloody funny way of running a railway," a relative newcomer said.

"No, it isn't," Alison Bairstow insisted. "She's better suited by twelve furlongs."

"Don't be daft! The guv'nor's losing his bottle!"

Robin Lane had to restrain Alison from hitting him.

As if unaware of the controversy and criticism, Edward drew up a new training schedule for Rhinemaiden and supervised it himself. At the end of the first week in May, she went to Lingfield for the Oaks Trial Stakes, and gave Sean Gillespie a peach of a ride round the twisting, rolling course that so closely resembled Epsom. None of the other contestants were ever really on terms with her, she dictated the tactics of the race from the off, and when she lengthened her stride at the end, they faded away.

Siobhan switched off the video-recorder and looked at Edward. "All right?" she asked.

"She'll do," he said, keeping a grip on his satisfaction. "*That* should shut them up, don't you think?"

Siobhan had not realised he knew about the disparaging comments that had been flying round; it was interesting to discover that he had been indifferent to them rather than unaware of them.

Richard, who had been to Lingfield, rang Edward when he got back to Widney Cheyne.

"I owe you a bit of an apology," he began.

"That's all right. She did well, didn't she?"

"She did indeed. You won't have heard, of course," Richard said, "they've made her red-hot favourite for the Oaks after that."

"Have they? My goodness!" Edward's attempt to appear interested failed. He sounded flippant, mildly sarcastic.

Dooley was one of the few people who believed that Edward knew what he was doing at Lingfield. Following Rhinemaiden's unexplained withdrawal from the Guineas, there had been a riot of ill-informed speculation in the press. As a consequence, her starting price in the Oaks Trial was a generous twelve to one, and Dooley wagered his maximum stake of two hundred pounds.

During the four weeks between Lingfield and Epsom, Nigel was given an object lesson in the single-minded preparation of a horse for a specific objective. Edward devoted all his time to Rhinemaiden, watching over her exercise and work, varying the routine constantly to keep her interest, building her condition day by day towards the target he had marked on the office calendar. The filly did everything – except one thing which Declan noticed but never mentioned. On days when she worked hard, she was not taken anywhere near the measured gallop that had been used for James Henry's pre-Derby exercise.

Edward went to Epsom on the day, having decided that he could not get out of it. He made his presence conditional upon a favour from Richard.

"You'll have to handle the TV interview when she wins," he said.

"*When?*" Richard asked, surprised at the confidence.

"Oh yes. She'll destroy that lot!"

"But you don't feel up to facing Wesley Davies?"

"No – or his blasted research assistant. They might want to mention Caro."

"Yes, I'll do that for you." Richard smiled gently. He was acutely conscious that the second anniversary of her death had just passed; Edward had not mentioned it. Although not operating in the style that Richard would have liked, they were still in business, and apparently about to win a Classic.

The Oaks, inaugurated a year before the Derby in 1779, was an occasion for ladies as well as high-class fillies. Imogen jumping at the chance to wear a 'posh frock', was eagerly to the fore, with Nancy at her side. Nancy's unease at Edward's likely attitude towards her was fully justified; after a swift assessment of her elegantly attractive turn-out, he lapsed into a civility that was rather dull and lifeless. There was nothing to indicate the approaching fruition of a scheme in which they had been partners.

Some time before Rhinemaiden went into the paddock for the start of the build-up to the race, Freezer was about to saddle her when he found Edward at his side.

"All right, Freezer, I'll do that," he said quietly. After pulling the girths tight and making a fuss of her, he whispered something in her ear and went away.

"Well I'm blowed," Freezer said. "I've never known him do that before."

"He always did it at Avoca House," Cathal O'Brien replied.

Over twenty minutes passed between Rhinemaiden leaving the paddock and arriving at the start. The runners had to parade past the grandstand, led by their lads, then they walked across Epsom Downs between the two extremities of the horseshoe-shaped course. Unlike many of the other eleven runners, Rhinemaiden remained perfectly calm throughout this hazardous period, and set off with a purpose that seemed deceptively casual once the race began. Nevertheless, after the first half-mile, when they came to the level ground after the uphill start, Rhinemaiden had a lead of two lengths.

Turning left all the time, they began the long descent to Tattenham Corner, and once Sean Gillespie was confident that she had found her legs for the slope, he encouraged her to go on more strongly. Entering the final straight, she was four lengths clear, and everyone except a handful of bookmakers believed that the race was as good as over.

Sean Gillespie would never forget his third ride to victory in a Classic. He told Julie afterwards that Rhinemaiden came up the hill like a Rolls-Royce; he was so preoccupied with the powerful smoothness of her progress, that he never heard the happy roar of the crowd.

"I don't believe it," Richard said, looking through his binoculars.

"What?" Imogen asked.

"Sean Gillespie is smiling. He is . . . he's actually smiling."

"Nonsense!"

"It's true," Nancy confirmed. "As a matter of fact, he looks a bit silly and soft about it all."

Rhinemaiden's winning margin was six lengths, her time only a fraction of a second outside the record for the race. As she passed the post, she won a hundred and thirty thousand pounds in prize-money for which Edward felt a momentary flicker of gratitude; winnings of that magnitude helped ease the strain.

Imogen's camera went to work on the happiest event for a long time. She caught one beautiful moment in the winner's enclosure as Edward and Rhinemaiden seemed to be exchanging the most affectionate confidences. When it was framed and hung in the Colour Room, Imogen herself provided the caption:

"How was that then, guv'nor? All right?"
"Perfect, darling, absolutely perfect!"

Back at Saxon Court, Richard shook Edward's hand and congratulated him.

"Very well done, Edward. You were right about her."

"It's what I'm paid for."

Richard laughed at the false modesty. "Two important things to remember," he said, suddenly very earnest.

"Yes?"

"We bred her ourselves."

Edward nodded. "I suppose you'll take her back soon?"

"Yes. Nancy wants a foal out of her at the first opportunity."

"All right . . . but I reckon she'd make a marvellous four-year-old."

"So do I actually, but Nancy insists."

After what had happened, Edward was not going to argue with Nancy's views on breeding. "What's the other thing?"

"You've got a horse round Epsom. You picked her out and prepared her, and she's won over the Derby course. The old man would have liked that."

They looked at each other long and hard. Edward took the point.

Edward participated in Royal Ascot that year only because he felt he must, there was no alternative. He had no expectations of any of his four runners because they lacked proper preparation. Siobhan's fear had been realised: Rhinemaiden was his sole priority. Nigel had been left to look after the rest, struggling with inexperience, and whatever disjointed, grudging advice he could wring out of Edward.

Three of the horses finished nowhere. The other came second in the Norfolk Stakes, pleasantly surprising Edward, but causing his owner to behave badly. What happened confirmed Imogen's low opinion of Victor Macleod, and made her forget the outrage she felt when Edward had invited Fred Bird to share their box for the meeting.

A year ago, Richard had engaged a firm of management consultants to carry out a review of the bank. Their report identified the need for a General Manager to take charge of the more mundane day-to-day activities and computer operations. Richard had accepted the recommendation, and hired the man who made it. Victor Macleod was thirty-five, humourless, over-anxious to make an impression, and regarded by virtually everyone except Richard as disruptive and dangerous.

Despite Richard's benign, protective stance, Macleod found life at Stewart's far from easy. There were countless ways in which staff at all levels could be obstructive, and the impenetrable urbanity of senior members conspired to make him unacceptable in any social sense. At first, merciless use was made of his bachelor status, but once a clumsy attempt at an affair with his secretary had established his heterosexuality, it was widely agreed that no woman in her right mind would have him.

Macleod's answer was simple and carefully calculated. He convinced Richard that he had an interest in racing, and enlisted his help in buying two yearling colts. He thus obtained the possibility of privileged entry to Widney Cheyne via Saxon Court.

He chose to do nothing about it until one of his horses made his debut in the Norfolk Stakes. Run against Edward's advice, the horse finished second, well-beaten along with the rest of the field by an outstanding individual called Harbinger from Bernard Dalrymple's stable.

Edward was chatting to Sean Gillespie before he went to weigh in, when Macleod appeared.

"Look here, Manning," he said, "I want that horse ridden properly next time. If that means getting a decent jockey, then so be it!" His tone and manner were both extremely unpleasant.

In the immediate dreadful silence, Sean Gillespie had the sense to disappear. Bernard Dalrymple who was talking to Harbinger's owner, turned and stared coldly at Macleod.

Edward froze, his mouth half-open, his mind blank once the initial surge of fury had ebbed away.

Two journalists edged closer, their faces keen.

Richard whispered something to Macleod who scowled, turned on his heel and walked away.

Ten minutes later in the comparative privacy of the racecourse stable, Edward and Macleod had a blazing row, while Richard tried to calm them down.

Fred Bird saw it all. He remained silent.

Imogen waited until she and Richard were at home.

"Your man Macleod did exceptionally well today, don't you think?" she said, her voice glittering with cold anger. "I thought he showed a truly masterly grasp of life's subtleties."

She stared at Richard, making no attempt to ameliorate his mute discomfort.

"I imagine Edward will derive enormous benefit from that," she went on. "What are you going to find for him next? A hole in the head? Perhaps a wooden leg would suit him!"

———

Fred's opinion, delivered soon after his unexpected arrival at Saxon Court on Saturday afternoon was tersely unequivocal.

"That geezer Macleod. He's a shit!"

Edward looked away, and stared out of the office window, pretending to look at the clock-tower. When he turned back, he nodded wearily. "Yes, you're quite right, Fred."

Fred pulled up a chair, and looked at Edward with close, friendly interest. "Look here, son," he said, "this ain't good enough, you know. You're pushing yourself too hard. Do you know, I've never seen you relax. Not once!"

Edward made no response. As he always did when tackling a difficult issue head-on, Fred hunched forward earnestly.

"Things have been bloody awful for you since your missus died. Oh yes, I've heard all the talk. They're all very sorry for you, but they haven't got the faintest bleedin' idea what to do about it. Well let me tell you, my son, you need to sort yourself out, or they'll be carting you out of here feet first. You'll be down the bone-yard with your missus if you don't watch it."

Taking Edward's silence as acceptance, he pressed on.

"What you doing for the rest of today and tomorrow?"

"Er . . . nothing . . . I might pop over and see Richard tomorrow."

"You stay clear of him for a bit. Give him time to have a good ponder about that bastard Macleod. What you need is a clean pair of underpants and your toothbrush."

"Why?" Edward asked blankly.

"Because we're going to my place. We'll get on the boat, sod off down the river, make right prats of ourselves, and have a bloody good time! You can start learning how to let your hair down."

A confused jumble of emotions flitted across Edward's face. Then he nodded, grinned, and jumped to his feet. "That sounds like the best idea I've heard for a long time!" he said.

———————

What Fred habitually called his 'little place' was at Goring, only seven miles from Saxon Court. Edward smiled when he saw it; the 'little place' was a beautifully renovated late-Victorian country house in five acres. At the bottom of the meticulously maintained garden there was eighty yards of private River Thames frontage with a landing-stage. Against it, a hundred-thousand-pounds-worth of luxury motor cruiser was moored.

Edward was given a quick conducted tour, throughout which Fred drew attention to the salient features with high-spirited pride, often putting a price-tag on an item. The refurbishing had been carried out in a riotous mixture of styles that was made successful by the immense scale of the house. There was a huge kitchen with every conceivable appliance and gadget for which the bill had been twelve thousand pounds. The dining-room was straight out of the eighteenth century; the sitting-room, big enough to hide thirty people, might well have won an avant-garde design award. Fred drew particular attention to his office, all leather and weighty sobriety; it was more like the nerve-centre of an old-established City enterprise than an essentially upstart racket. It reeked of 'quality'.

The old coach-house had been connected to the house and partitioned; one half was a gym, the other a billiard room.

Fred laughed when he saw how impressed Edward was by the latter. "I never had time for a mis-spent youth, but I always promised myself one of them when I made it. Mind you, I can't play for toffee!"

Upstairs, everything was light and airy in soft pastels. Fred looked in several rooms until he found what he was looking for.

"Here we are, son," he said. "This is all right. You'll be comfortable in here."

Edward agreed. It was the most luxurious, well-appointed spare bedroom imaginable, complete with its own bathroom. There were full-length windows on to a balcony, and a view of the garden and river. Below the balcony, just far enough away to be comfortably visible, a stunning-looking girl was sunbathing.

"That's Steph," Fred said casually.

She called herself Stephanie Jones, but her real name was Covington-Sykes. She was twenty-three, and earned a very lucrative living by displaying her body in minimal dress.

Stephanie had been educated at a well-known private school, and completed the first year of a History degree course before realising that there were more profitable and potentially pleasant things in life than pursuing an education that led to uncertain employment prospects.

It had started when she became Rag Queen in her only summer term at University. Over a two-week period, the local newspaper had printed a series of glamorous pictures of her, and the offers of photographic modelling work had appeared. With no need of professional advice, Stephanie had immediately displayed great shrewdness. The tabloid newspapers were ignored while she did a sumptuous spread for a glossy men's magazine that liked to think of itself as being rather up-market. The pictures showed her in moods of arrogance, boredom, warm friendliness, and even complete astonishment at finding herself naked in front of a camera. Accompanied by an almost-accurate potted biography that made much of the fact that her father was a Deputy Lord Lieutenant of his county and a Master of Foxhounds, the portfolio was a quiet but complete success.

Colonel and Mrs Covington-Sykes had been rather tickled by their daughter's achievement. They lodged a mild objection only when she began using the name Jones in order to shed an élitist image that had served its purpose. Once Stephanie had deigned to appear in a tabloid newspaper for a fee of ten times the initial offer, her career was fully launched and prospered.

Although the best-paid of her work was for advertising and selling, she had always rejected the idea of appearing in a mail-order catalogue, and had carried on doing so until she found herself face to face with Fred Bird at his most persuasive. Fred's determination to spread his underwear gospel, and to do it with the best possible model, had won the day. Little more than a year after its launch, the forty-eight-page catalogue, presented with the style of a prestige company prospectus, had become a sought-after collector's item, as well as providing impetus to Fred's sales figures.

Stephanie now spent most of her time with Fred, although she still maintained a flat in London. She was debating whether to set up a model agency, or let her savings and investments do the work.

Edward learned or deduced all this as they sat under the awning of the cruiser on its progress in the general direction of Oxford. Fred was absurdly happy in the wheelhouse, sporting a yachting-cap he knew to be ridiculous, and behaving as though he were in command of a hundred-gun ship of the line.

Stephanie had come as a revelation to Edward.

Possibly because of the carnival atmosphere generated by Fred, Edward found that he was completely at ease with her from the moment she smiled up at him as he stood by the sun-lounger and was introduced. She still wore the bikini when they went aboard the cruiser, and settled down to answer Edward's questions about her career as though they had always been friends. When he displayed frank interest in, and admiration of her body, she was unconcerned. That, she seemed to be saying, was what it was for.

After eight miles or so, Fred decided they had gone far enough, and it was high time the pubs opened, so they stopped at Wallingford. Stephanie produced a tracksuit from a locker, and it was perfectly natural that Edward should help to rearrange her long, blonde hair after she had pulled the top over her head.

They found an inn that served good, simple food, and over the meal, Stephanie cross-examined Edward gently about his work. Her interest and discerning comments encouraged him to unwind and talk much more freely than was customary nowadays, even with his friends at Saxon Court. In the two hours during which they talked, she learned a great deal.

"I've never known anyone so dedicated to their work," Stephanie said when they were on the boat again, and heading back through the half-light of a perfect midsummer dusk.

"Fred is, surely," Edward replied.

"Oh yes." She laughed softly. "But I meant dedicated to something *nice*."

"Maybe I'm very lucky."

"You were. I understand the last two years have been pretty tough."

"Yes." He leaned towards her. As he did so, he caught her scent. There was no perfume, just her hair, the faintest trace of soap, and the intrinsic fragrance of her flesh. He drew back sharply, dismayed at the effect it had on him. "Yes . . . I . . ."

Stephanie knew that for a few seconds, he had teetered on the brink of saying something important and revealing. She was equally certain that he would have felt foolish afterwards.

Edwin Fforbes was a guest at Widney Cheyne that weekend, and on Sunday morning he and Richard were busy with bank affairs, enabling Imogen to slip away unnoticed. She drove to Saxon Court with the intention of telling Edward not to worry about Victor Macleod: something would be done about him. Her reaction to Siobhan's news that Edward had gone off suddenly with Fred the previous day, and was not expected back until Monday morning was one of dismay.

"Oh Lord!" She sank into a chair and reached for her cigarettes.

"What's wrong?" Siobhan asked. "Is it that bad?"

"Yes . . . I think it may well be." Imogen was weighing her words very carefully.

"Why?"

"That man Bird has some very bad habits!" She sounded severely old-fashioned.

Siobhan almost smiled; she quite liked Fred.

"Such as?"

"I don't know, thank God! A man like that is bound to have unsavoury proclivities."

"Perhaps – but Edward can look after himself," Siobhan said with loyal firmness.

Imogen looked at her. It was a while before she spoke, and she seemed to have deflated. "I do hope you're right, my dear," she said. "Oh, I *do* hope so."

In the weeks that followed, Edward divided his free time between Fred, and Mark and Sarah Walgrave. Watching him closely, Siobhan found no cause for concern. Edward said very little about the time he spent at Goring, and never mentioned Stephanie; Siobhan sensed the element of secrecy, but also saw that he was benefiting from interests away from the yard. She had always known that there were times when he found life in an essentially closed community stifling, and his time with Fred also acted as a counter-balance to the disappointments surrounding Rhinemaiden.

Following her Oaks victory, Richard wanted her to win at least one more good race. At first, Edward was puzzled by this; the filly was earmarked for stud and had already done enough to enjoy a first-class reputation. Richard's frank statement of motives came as a surprise.

"I could use the prize-money," he said. "There are things I'd like to do with the stud, and I want my racing interests to be self-financing. At the end of the day, I'm running a business."

To himself, Edward admitted his inclination to lose sight of this objective, and selected the St Leger as a possible target. With its sponsorship-boosted prize of over a hundred thousand pounds, it was one of the few English races worthy of Rhinemaiden, and fillies had a good record in it.

After the Oaks, Rhinemaiden went to Widney Cheyne for three weeks holiday. The rest had the added advantage of introducing her to Nancy Bloomfield and the surroundings that would be her home for twenty years or more. No sooner had she returned to Saxon Court, than she pulled a muscle in one of her hind legs while cantering, and was off all work for ten days. The day before she was due to start trotting, she evidenced the first symptoms of a stomach bug that was to cost another two weeks and left her with no zest for work. Finally, a damaged foot led to a succession of abscesses that defied even Declan's healing skills and necessitated daily attention from the vet. When she was finally healthy the St Leger was only two weeks away; Richard admitted that there was no hope of getting her ready in time, and she went to Widney Cheyne for good.

While Edward devoted July and most of August to Rhinemaiden and little else, Nigel and Siobhan had a hand in producing a trickle of winners. One that pleased Edward very much indeed, was a horse of Fred's who captured a handicap at Bath.

"Nice piece of placing, Nigel," Edward said.

"That was Siobhan's idea actually," Nigel replied, modestly gratified with his success and Edward's praise. "She spotted that all the others were a load of rubbish."

"You make a good team," Edward said. "Next time we do that we must make sure that Mr Bird is there to see it."

Ironically, after moving his horses south, Fred had gone north that day on business.

Edward had developed a fondness for the mid-October meeting at Newmarket in general, and the Dewhurst Stakes in particular. For no apparent reason, he decided that it was a race for which he *ought* to have a runner, and after Benvenuto Cellini, he was prepared to believe and try anything. For 1985, he had two runners, with Sean Gillespie riding for Richard, and John Dyer for Edwin Fforbes. Neither of the horses had shown any great promise, and duly finished well down the field.

It was of no consequence. Edward was determined to have an enjoyable day, and he did. After lunch with Bernard Dalrymple and his wife at Tewkesbury Lodge, he spent an hour with Finoula and Patrick Prendegast, about to celebrate their third wedding anniversary and the first birthday of young Patrick who seemed destined to be the tallest, fattest jockey in the history of racing. Finoula was back at work in the two-year-old yard, and was enthusiastic about Harbinger, the horse who had upset Victor Macleod at Royal Ascot. For Finoula, next year's Derby was already a one-horse race.

On the Heath, it was a perfect October afternoon, still and golden. With an air of detachment, Edward watched a precocious Irish colt storm home in the Dewhurst, almost unaware of his two contenders in the middle of a bunch of mediocrities fifteen lengths away. He stayed until the last race, long after Dooley and the others had gone, then headed back to Saxon Court at a leisurely pace, improvising a new route.

Towards the end of his dilatory journey, Edward realised that he would pass close to Fred's place, and made the necessary detour in search of the sort of company that he felt he needed.

It was nearly eight o'clock, and dark when he got there. The only light in the house was illuminating the wide-open front door. Stephanie had just arrived, and was reading a note on the telephone table. She was frowning, but smiled when she saw Edward. "Hello, you're a welcome sight," she said. "Fred's shot off to Manchester."

"Oh." Edward dithered on the threshold.

"Come in, come in!" She waved him towards her. After four months, they seemed like very old friends. "He's gone to sack the manager of the shop," she announced as she finished reading the note. "It seems he's a crook as well as a bum."

"When will he be back?" Edward asked lamely.

"Don't know. The heir apparent is a very pleasant young lady who could take two or three days to induce." Edward was given no time to be shocked; Stephanie found the prospect of Fred's adventure mildly amusing, and she was hungry. "Have you eaten?" she asked.

"Er . . . no . . . I'm on my way back from Newmarket. I just looked in to . . ."

Stephanie was going to the kitchen, and he followed her. "Let's get this show on the road," she said briskly. She dumped her tweed jacket across a chair, and rolled up the long sleeves of her blouse. "Get the kettle on," she told him. "And I could do with a gin and tonic. Large. Go easy on the tonic."

He took some time to find the gin, and when he finally handed the glass to her, she had the grill pan in action.

"Does Fred often go off like this?" he asked.

She laughed at his earnest concern. "Quite often," she replied, and smiled at his expression. "No, I don't care," she volunteered. "Fred and I suit each other's convenience for the time being. He used to think I was 'quality'." She laughed fondly at the memory. "But of course, *real* quality would *never* live with him!"

Pleased with her logic, she concentrated on cooking.

The meal was a mixed-grill made up of everything she could lay her hands on, and was a triumph.

"Just like mummy makes," Stephanie laughed, and began to eat lustily. "God, I'm famished!"

"What have you been doing today?" Edward asked.

"London . . . talking to some people about a scheme I have."

"What happened?"

"Oh, it was all right . . . I think! I was very keen, but it's starting to look like a lot of hassle for not very much."

"Your agency idea?"

"Yes. What about you?"

"I've been racing."

"Do any good?"

"No, but I didn't expect to. It was just a day out. I saw some friends . . . quite nice."

Some minutes later, he realised that he was telling her about the problems and frustrations surrounding Rhinemaiden, revealing the way the disappointment had affected his work.

"But presumably another really good horse could make it all worth-while again?"

"Oh yes."

She sensed the lack of warmth in his reply.

After they had eaten, Stephanie made coffee, and they remained at the kitchen table until Edward became uneasy with their conversation. Largely at his instigation, the talk had taken a depressingly negative turn.

"I'd better be going," he said, looking first at the clock, then his watch.

"Oh!" Stephanie was more than simply startled by his sudden decision. Exasperation flitted across her face. "Aren't you staying the night?" she asked.

"No . . . I'd better get back. There are things to do in the morning."

He was standing up now with the table between them. It was as if he sensed danger.

"You can get up early. It isn't far is it? Fifteen minutes?"

They stared at one another. Stephanie saw that his face was registering a conflict of some sort, but it was impossible to deduce what was passing through his mind.

"Don't you want me?" she asked.

Something seemed to snap inside him.

"Yes, Stephanie, as a matter of fact, I do! You're bloody attractive, and it's a hell of a long time since I've had a woman! It's two years . . . and that was only for one night. But it isn't a good idea, is it?"

"Why?"

"Because of Fred." He was regaining his composure.

"There's no need to worry about him. Even if he ever found out, he'd probably laugh about it. He's totally amoral."

"You may well be right. But he and I have a business arrangement, remember. That means I shouldn't appropriate his girl friend. It's not done in the best circles."

319

Stephanie understood that his abrupt, self-mocking aloofness was a shelter and defence mechanism. She went with him to the front door.

"Feel free to change your mind," she said quietly. "No strings attached. We might as well enjoy ourselves, don't you think?"

Then she kissed his cheek lightly. Even that merest touch of her lips had a vibrant promise that made him flinch.

Ten minutes later, Edward stopped his car on the high ground a mile from home, and got out.

He was moved to do so by the view. A full moon in a cloudless sky suffused everything with a scarcely-real silver glow. Virtually every detail of Saxon Court's buildings was discernible in a theatrical blend of light and shade.

It was cold. Dressed only for the autumnal warmth of the day, he shivered. As a consequence of the involuntary movement, he was looking directly at Moonlight Ring, eerily beautiful in the mysterious haze.

At once, he was reminded of Caroline.

Summer. Long, long ago.

It was one of the most powerful remembrances ever to come to him. He closed his eyes against tears.

As the cost of his refusal of Stephanie asserted itself and embittered him, a thought of such malevolent power came to him, that he spoke it aloud.

"It's going to be an awful winter."

Looking back to the stable only deepened the conviction. He said it again with sour emphasis.

"It is going to be *the* most bloody awful winter."

CHAPTER 14

Edward clung to the idea, and turned it into a self-fulfilling prophecy.

It started the morning after.

Having slept badly, Edward was in the office before Siobhan. His attention was caught by her scoreboard. He was well aware of what it showed, and he had no wish to see the summary of the season that she would produce within the next few days.

The basic facts were simple, and bad enough: twenty-three winners, a hundred and ninety-one thousand pounds in prize-money. With twice as many horses in his yard, Bernard Dalrymple had just become the first trainer to pass the magic million pounds mark, and one of his Newmarket neighbours had earned seven hundred and fifty thousand pounds.

Rhinemaiden's two races had brought in a hundred and forty-two thousand pounds, and when she was taken out of the reckoning, the picture was bleak. Forty-nine thousand pounds from twenty-one winners was far worse than the first season at Avoca House, even accepting the figures at face value. Allowing for inflation and sponsorship, the results were lamentable.

Theoretically, there was no immediate danger. As long as horses stayed in the yard, and the bills were paid, Saxon Court would survive. In that, Edward was better placed than many trainers, since his owners had a strong commitment to him. Victor Macleod was the exception, but his two horses amounted to next to nothing, so he could go to hell. Yet the great loyalty of his supporters increased the pressure to produce adequate rewards.

"Must do better," Edward said to himself, echoing the direst form of words he had ever written on a school report.

There was a problem with the yard staff. Morale had been precarious all season, and those who cared about it had been hard-pressed to keep things moving. Once the statistics were known to be final, Liam Corrigan, Alison Bairstow and Robin Lane could not stop the inevitable. The kitty broke down to shares of around seventy pounds, about a third of what many had expected after Rhinemaiden won the Oaks. Only the original Avoca House contingent were immune to the chronic dissatisfaction that caused avid enquiries to be made for jobs in other stables.

Knowing about it, Edward withdrew behind his defences.

He rarely left Saxon Court, and stopped going to Fred's, even when invited. He went through the motions of the winter routine in the yard, speaking to no one except Declan and Siobhan, and then only about business matters. When darkness fell each shortening day, he shut himself in the sitting room and listened to music. He found a complete set of Walter Scott's *Waverley* novels left behind over thirty years ago by Joshua Fielding, and began to read them with laborious attention to detail. At seven, he went into the kitchen and ate whatever Mary or Rosie had left in the oven, never taking more than ten minutes over it before hurrying back to the sanctuary of the sitting room.

Fred's birthday at the beginning of December was an event that could not be avoided.

When Edward arrived, he was dismayed to find over fifty people already the worse for drink, and all doing their best to talk loudest. For nearly an hour, he had to be the focus of attention after Fred had told everyone that they had a famous racehorse trainer among them. When the ordeal finally petered out, Fred took him aside for a quiet word.

"You're looking peaky, son. Dead off-colour."

"I'm all right."

"You arranged a holiday?"

"Not yet. I may not bother."

"Why don't you come with me and Steph? We're off on a cruise. Three weeks in January. Just the job! It's only four grand. I'll pay if you're pushed!" Fred roared with laughter at his own joke.

"No thanks. Where are you going?"

"The good old Caribbean, my son. Limbo dancing and dusky maidens! Can't beat it."

Edward's face froze. "Oh no! Definitely not that!"

With the noise getting louder all the time, Edward was on the point of slipping away when he found Stephanie in the kitchen. She had her feet up on a chair, and was squinting at the light through the rich amber contents of a brandy glass. She was not entirely sober.

"Hi! Long time, no see," she said. "Have you been avoiding me? Can't say I blame you. You don't look too good."

"There's nothing wrong with me."

She shrugged and indicated the party. "Hardly your scene, is it?" she said.

"No. Nor yours?"

She shook her head emphatically. "Fred's friends are tolerable in minutely small numbers and doses. That lot, I can do without. Drink?"

She held her glass out facetiously. Edward's aversion to alcohol was legendary. Apart from the very best champagne on special occasions, he simply did not like the stuff.

But instead of the usual dismissive wave of the hand, he moved closer and sniffed at her glass.

"Mmm . . . that smells rather nice," he said.

"Tastes even better. Try some."

He took the glass from her hand and sipped, treating the smooth, glowing spirit with great respect before swallowing it. He nodded. "Good . . . very good indeed. What is it?"

"Armagnac. Nothing but the best. Help yourself."

Edward poured slightly more than a double measure, and they chatted inconsequentially for ten minutes while he savoured it.

"That really is very nice," he said.

"More?"

"No!" He laughed, already a fraction light-headed. "I have to drive."

"Ha! Tell that lot in there!" She waved towards the noise. "You haven't changed your mind?"

"Er . . . no."

"No, I didn't think you would. Shame. Here, take the bottle. It's all right, there's another eleven in the garage. Birthday present from an admirer. Or it might be guilt-ridden gratitude for the latest deal."

Edward's hesitation was a mere token gesture. He picked the bottle up.

"Enjoy it," she said.

"I probably will. I feel better already."

"That's the way! Think of me while you drink it."

"I might just do that."

"Well try and come up with something sensible."

"Like?"

"Changing your silly mind!"

Edward had a good measure of Armagnac when he went to bed, and found that he slept better than he had done for months.

Two days later, he visited Reading to buy gramophone records and books. Returning to the car, he passed a good wine shop, walked on a few paces, then turned back. They sold Armagnac. While the bottle was being carefully wrapped, he changed his mind.

"Actually, I'd better have three," he said. It qualified him for a free carrier-bag.

Anxious to avoid comment, Edward left the three bottles in his car until Siobhan went home, then took them up to his bedroom, putting them in the bottom of the wardrobe.

The three bottles lasted until the end of the first week in January. Edward never drank until after his evening meal, although the nightcaps became more generous; the pleasant feelings induced while he was still awake began to be more important than the soporific effect. He spent Christmas uneasily with his parents, and saw 1986 in at Widney Cheyne where Nancy found him more unnerving than ever. She and Richard had decided that Rhinemaiden's first foal should be sired by Parsifal, and that Musetta would be one of the mares in T. P. Malahide's

323

increasingly busy schedule. Nancy had thought Edward would be delighted with the news. Instead, he greeted it with cold indifference.

Serious problems began with the second batch of Armagnac.

One evening in mid-January, Edward telephoned Valerie at about eight o'clock. He intended trying to get himself invited to stay with her in Dublin for a week or more. To his annoyance, there was no reply. She *ought* to be there, he decided, and tried again ten minutes later. He kept on doing it for over two hours. Between each attempt he had a drink, and became more angry. At ten o'clock, when he found that he was no longer capable of dialling the number, he had a last stiff drink, and collapsed into bed.

When he woke up, Edward thought at first that he was seriously ill. It was some time before he realised that he was experiencing his first bad hangover.

He was in the yard at his usual time for the winter-morning inspection routine. He imagined that he did well; only once did he have to steady himself against a wall as a wave of dreadful nausea swept over him. "I feel awful," he muttered to Declan. "I think I must be sickening for flu."

Declan was sympathetic. He had noticed Edward's very deliberate, carefully calculated movements. "You need to lie down, sor," he said.

"Yes, I think I might do that."

At nine-thirty, while Siobhan was involved in a long telephone call, Edward slipped out of the office and into the kitchen where he made himself a cup of strong black coffee.

It tasted awful. He was on the verge of tipping it down the sink, and reverting to his customary tea, when he recalled the myth of the hair of the dog. Moving quickly and silently, he went upstairs. In his bedroom, he poured a stiff measure of Armagnac into the coffee and tried again. It was much more palatable. Magically, the worst effects of the hangover began to fade almost at once. After two more mugs of fortified coffee, Edward felt on top of the world.

That night, Edward felt very tired after his meal, and went straight up to bed. He grimaced at the bottle on the dressing-table; it had been full when he had laced his first coffee, now three-quarters of it had gone.

"Not very good, old lad," he muttered as he stumbled into the bathroom. "Not very good at all . . . must do better. Tell you what . . ." he was addressing his reflection in the mirror ". . . now this is a good idea . . . wouldn't it be the statesmanlike thing to give Stephanie a ring in the morning?"

He woke feeling reasonably clear-headed and full of resolve to do better. Downstairs at seven o'clock with the house still to himself, he made a pot of tea, and settled down with the morning paper, spending several minutes looking at ordinary, everyday news before turning to the racing pages, with no expectation that there would be anything to interest him. Steeplechasing had never held any attractions.

At the head of the page in heavy type, spread across four columns eight inches deep, was a report on the death of Mill Reef. Apparently, a heart condition had deteriorated, and he had been put down. Most of the piece was effectively an obituary, listing the great horse's racing exploits in 1970 and 1971, then discussing the more notable of his progeny.

Mill Reef had been only eighteen, no age at all.

With tears in his eyes, and his hands trembling, Edward made a cup of coffee and took it upstairs.

After that, he bought Armagnac by the crate.

He organised coffee-making facilities in his bedroom, and began collecting breath-freshening sprays and mouthwashes.

Shortly after Saxon Court threw off its winter torpor, and the horses began cantering on the all-weather gallop, Imogen arrived for breakfast, and spent most of the day there. She wanted to look at the horses, and discuss curtains with Siobhan. There was also something she had to tell Edward.

"Siobhan and Nigel are getting on extremely well together," she said as soon as they were alone.

"Of course they are!" Edward looked at her as though she had made a statement that was so obvious as to be stupid.

A thought came to Imogen. "Don't you know?" she asked.

"Know what?"

"There's a strong romance going on."

"Don't be ridiculous! There can't be. Siobhan isn't old enough."

Imogen laughed. "She's twenty-three, Edward."

He blinked. He still thought of her as sixteen, and too young to drive a car. "Are you sure?" he asked.

"Quite sure. Apart from the way they've been behaving for the last six months or so – under your very nose, I might say – Richard and I ran into them in the Plough and Harrow at Hatchetts Green the other evening."

"What were they doing?"

"Same as us, having a meal. We chatted to them, and they confessed all."

"Well, there's no law against it, I suppose." Edward sounded as though he wished there was.

"From what I can gather, it's only the question of religion that's delaying a marriage. Bit tricky apparently."

Edward looked at her morosely. "Typical!" he muttered, leaving her wondering what, if anything, he meant.

Imogen spoke to Richard about it that evening.

"Edward didn't know about Siobhan and Nigel."

"That doesn't surprise me. He never was very bothered about things like that. How did he react?"

"Badly. He was downright crabby about it." She stopped to think. "Actually, he was in a very funny mood. No . . . that's not right. *Condition* . . . that's it! He was in a strange condition."

"What do you mean?"

"He was sort of weary . . . everything seemed far too much trouble. And bad-tempered. Very bad-tempered."

"How odd!" Richard frowned with concentration, trying to envisage what was wrong with Edward. He gave up. "I hope Siobhan and Nigel will be happy," he said. "She deserves it. Still, Nigel seems a very decent bloke."

"Ye . . . es." Imogen drew it out, injecting a good deal of doubt.

Richard looked at her questioningly. "All right. Tell me."

"There's nothing to tell. At least, there isn't a shred of evidence."

"But?"

Imogen tapped her nose. "This tells me he isn't completely *sound*."

"In what way?"

"I imagine he could be very weak under pressure – hence his problems with the Army. There might be circumstances in which our Nigel could squirm his way into all sorts of trouble."

"H'm." Richard looked unhappy. "You have been known to be wrong," he said.

"Oh yes! There was that business with Winnie Cartwright and Bertie Farnes-Barnes or whatever his silly name was. I was *utterly* wrong about that!"

Richard nodded, remembering it well. He couldn't quite recall whether it had been ten, or eleven years ago.

What Imogen had seen in Edward was one of the two states imposed on him by drink dependence. He drank on alternate days. Then, his mood was buoyant but volatile until he was alone for the evening, when he became over-emotional and befuddled. The following day, he was recovering from the after-effects and trying to conceal them. Energy had to be conserved, and he was usually painstakingly nice to everyone, although self-disgust could produce a descent into the churlishness that Imogen had experienced.

A dramatic example of Edward's other state came a few days later in full view of nearly all the staff.

Terry Dawson was unpopular in the lads' hostel, and a disruptive influence on the yard. He had been at Saxon Court less than a year, with his mean-mindedness and spiteful tongue in evidence from the start. Aged about thirty, with pinched, unprepossessing features, he claimed to have been in some very distinguished stables, adopting a supercilious attitude on the strength of it. Declan had always felt that Edward had been passing through one of his periods of indifference the day he set Dawson on; any proper investigation into his history or references must surely have sent him away without a job.

Dawson had been allocated Victor Macleod's two horses, and he complained incessantly about their inability to win anything, thus depriving him of his two per cent.

It was midday. The second lot were coming back in. An argument developed between Dawson and another lad who had bumped against him in the bustle. Dawson's horse, already edgy, reacted to the angry voice and foul mood of his handler by rearing up on his hind legs in an attempt to break loose.

At that moment, Edward appeared in the arches. Having been out with the first lot on Murgatroyd, he had drunk enough since to brighten his eyes, and give him a feeling of elation about the season ahead.

Dawson had his back to Edward as he lashed out with his whip. The blow was aimed at the horse's face, but caught him across the neck instead.

All but three of the forty or so people scattered round the New Yard froze in disbelief.

Declan and Robin Lane rushed to get hold of Dawson's horse.

Moving like lightning, with a look on his face that would be talked about in the hostel for a long time to come, Edward went for Dawson.

It was Nigel and Liam Corrigan who finally got between them. Taken by surprise, and weighing only nine stones, Dawson was no match for Edward's appalling fury. Edward had wrenched the whip from Dawson's hand, and was about to start using it on him when Nigel and Liam intervened.

"You mindless, vicious little bastard!" Edward snarled. There were flecks of spittle at the corners of his mouth.

Dawson was trembling. It had started as anger, now there was fear in his eyes. "I'll have the law on you for this," he gasped. "It's assault, that's what it is, assault!"

"You do that," Edward shouted. "And I . . ." he prodded Dawson's chest to hammer home each word ". . . will . . . make . . . bloody . . . certain . . . you . . . never . . . work . . . again! Now get out!"

Nigel and Liam marched Dawson away, acting as both custodians and protectors. Edward stood glaring after him, his shoulders heaving. When he turned to look at the yard, it was deserted. Declan had restored order.

Dawson left the hostel ten minutes later with his bags. There were faces at every window, and a group of lads watching from beneath the clock-tower.

He was heading towards the main gate, but stopped as he drew level with the office, and took a step towards it.

"What the hell do you want?" Edward demanded, appearing suddenly and frighteningly at the office door.

"My money! You owe me a week's wages."

Edward strode towards him, a hand in the back pocket of his trousers. He pulled out Dawson's crumpled insurance card, selected a few bank notes from a wad, and rammed them into the top pocket of Dawson's anorak. Nothing was said, but Dawson blenched under Edward's corrosive stare.

When he was sure that Dawson had gone, Edward went back into the office. He felt absolutely splendid, pulsating with excitement. Stephanie came into his mind. Was she at home, he wondered. Briefly, his hand hovered over the telephone before he rejected the idea. No. He had work to do. But it was nice to have had such a daring thought while he was more or less sober.

Lunch in the lads' hostel was a time of simmering tension. Kathleen Corrigan in the serving-hatch strained her ears to pick up opinions, but found it very difficult. When conversation did surface, it was garbled, with everyone trying to speak at once.

"What a carry-on, eh?"

"Did you see the way the guv'nor looked?"

". . . I thought he was going to kill him."

"Terry had it coming, ever since . . ."

". . . he did, he damned nearly hit him, you know."

"I told you Terry would end up like that."

"He was a pig!"

"Well I reckon the guv'nor did the right thing."

". . . he lost control of himself . . ."

"You're right!"

". . . fancy getting in that state."

"You know what he's like about cruelty."

"I didn't . . . but I bloody-well do now!"

By evening stables, things were calmer, and slipping into perspective. Edward was much more his old self, chatting as he visited each box, thinking aloud about plans for winning races. He had spent most of the afternoon with the horse that Dawson had abused. The animal seemed to be recovering well, and Edward had drunk no more since the incident. As he walked back towards the house with Nigel, he changed abruptly from a discussion of the horses to a friendly personal enquiry.

"You seeing Siobhan this evening?"

"Er, yes." Nigel was caught off-balance by Edward's first mention of the relationship. Approval seemed to be going hand-in-hand with recognition. "We're going to have a meal at the Fortescue."

"Are you? Good! Here . . ." Edward produced a twenty pound note ". . . have it on me. Go on. You've earned it."

Later, when Nigel told Siobhan about Edward's generosity, she looked puzzled and shook her head.

"He's been in a very funny mood today," she said.

"No more than usual."

"Oh no . . . this is different."

"That was because of the business with Dawson."

"That was only the start of it. He was in a really odd frame of mind when I came back from lunch."

"How?"

"Sort of full of himself."

Nigel thought about it. "Yes. 'Lord-of-all-I-survey' stuff." Siobhan nodded. "Yes, he was like that at evening stables. Very grand and gracious."

Terry Dawson trudged several miles after he left Saxon Court, before getting a lift to a railway station. After a wait of over an hour, he caught a slow train to London, then a tube to Epping.

"Oh Terry, not again!" his long-suffering sister wailed as she opened the door to him.

"Don't worry, sis, this is different," he said, and marched upstairs to dump his bags in the bedroom to which he considered he had a God-given right.

Later, while his sister and her husband watched the Nine O'clock News, Dawson slipped out to a phone box.

Victor Macleod bided his time. It was nearly two weeks before a suitable opportunity arose as he and Richard finished a routine operational review. They were having lunch together in Stewart's own dining room, and there was a little time to kill before they went down.

"I believe there's been a spot of bother at Saxon Court," Macleod began.

"Oh?" The jangle of alarm bells in Richard's head did not disturb his bland exterior.

"A member of staff got slung out on his ear. Very nasty business from what I can gather."

"You mean Dawson?"

"Yes, that's the chap." Macleod masked his disappointment.

"Yes." Richard paused. "I didn't realise his dismissal was such common knowledge, Victor. Was it in the papers?"

Macleod took the point and feigned embarrassment. "Oh no, good gracious, no! As a matter of fact, Dawson rang me up about it."

"Really?" Richard's eyebrows moved a carefully-calculated fraction.

"Yes! Silly, of course, but he was worried about my two horses. He looked after them."

Richard knew that no stable lad, not even Dawson, would dare ring Stewart's; he also knew that Victor Macleod's home telephone number was ex-directory.

"Victor, Edward Manning fired Dawson because he maltreated one of your horses," Richard said. "It's perfectly standard practice in any decent stable."

"Ah . . . Dawson mentioned that. He thought some such story would be trumped up."

"It isn't a story, Victor. There were forty witnesses to what happened, and I've spoken to some of them. It was purely fortuitous that Dawson didn't do lasting damage to your horse."

"Oh dear. I see." Macleod assumed a grave look that was designed to cast aspersions on Dawson. "Dear me! Tell me, wasn't Manning a touch heavy-handed about it?" he asked, as though seeking to dispel a rumour.

"I wouldn't have thought so," Richard replied. "What Dawson did was extremely serious. Edward Manning would be perfectly entitled to act as he saw fit. That's the way things are in racing stables."

"Ah, yes. Good. I was sure there was nothing to worry about." Macleod waited, changing his mood to one of scheming confidentiality. "By the way, Manning doesn't drink, does he?"

"No. Not at all."

"That's what I thought. There was a suggestion that he was drunk when this row with Dawson blew up."

"Dawson again?"

Macleod nodded. "I seem to have been taken in by him. I suspected *that* was untrue, but I thought I should let you know. If there *were* anything in it, you'd need to know. It might not be too good for your investment in the place."

"Thank you, Victor. I appreciate your concern." Richard's tone betrayed nothing of his real feelings. He was discovering the hard way that Macleod thrived on the creation of stress and discord.

"I can't understand it," he said to Imogen. "It's completely without motive as far as I can see. What on earth does he expect to gain from it?"

"Oldest trick in the book," she replied. "Get the whole place in an uproar with everybody at everybody else's throat, and something to one's advantage might come of it. That's how Lenin operated. Bet you didn't know that!"

Richard said nothing to her about the suggestion that Edward was drinking heavily. That worried him. It might account for the persistent reports of uncharacteristic behaviour.

The next time Richard went to watch the horses work, Edward was quietly efficient. On his third day without drink after an especially bad bout, he gave the impression that he was starting from scratch in an attempt to rebuild his career. The truth was that a clock was running in his head: he hadn't had a drink for sixty-two hours. When it got to seventy, he would have deserved one.

"That blasted man Dawson rang Victor Macleod up," Richard told Edward.

"You're joking!"

"I'm not. Dear Victor delivered the poison the other day. He was awfully disappointed that I knew all about it."

"Well I'm damned!" Edward was annoyed, but it was well-controlled.

"He even had some cock-and-bull yarn about you having taken to the demon drink," Richard said, making light of it.

"Good gracious!" Edward said mildly. "Tell me something, Richard. Would it make things awkward for you if I told Macleod to take his two hacks to another stable?"

"No, I don't think it would. It might even be a good thing. Imogen swears he only bought them to ingratiate himself."

"There's every chance she's right! I won't do it just yet. I've a feeling there's going to be a very good opportunity before too long."

Edward was showing a lot of interest in the Duke of Dorchester's three-year-old colt, Frescobaldi. Impeccably bred from a successful son of Northern Dancer, the animal had cost three hundred and twenty-five thousand pounds as a yearling, only to show every indication of following in Benvenuto Cellini's infamous footsteps. It had been fairly obvious from the start.

"Well, Manning, what do you think of him?" the Duke had asked when Edward first saw his latest purchase.

"He's a handsome enough fellow," was the cautious reply.

"And?"

Edward had studied the colt carefully, noting the way the animal stared back at him. "I think you may have done it again, Freddie," he said. "This looks like another stumer. He might be a bit simple as well. At least Benvenuto Cellini had brains."

So it had proved. Frescobaldi did not seem capable of understanding what he was supposed to do. As a two-year-old the previous year, he had been entered for over fifty races, and been taken out of all but one. After it, Sean Gillespie had not spoken for two days.

331

Now, after a winter during which Robin Lane had spent a great deal of time with him, he seemed to have acquired a smattering of sense, and the Duke wanted to run him in the Derby.

"Surely not!" Richard said when he found out.

"No reason why not," Edward replied. "He's working very well indeed. I don't think he'll make a *complete* fool of himself."

Frescobaldi duly went to Lingfield for the Derby Trial, and finished second, three lengths behind Harbinger, Bernard Dalrymple's horse. There were two lengths between Frescobaldi and the rest.

Afterwards, it was obvious that Frescobaldi had had a hard race, and he was rested for a week before an attempt was made to bring him up to readiness for the Derby. When he did start galloping, Edward was uneasy.

"What's wrong?" Nigel asked.

"I don't know," Edward muttered.

"He looks all right to me."

"He's fit enough . . . there's no doubt about that. It's his mind that worries me."

"I thought we'd agreed he hasn't got one," Nigel joked.

"Oh, he's got one all right. I can't get on to the right wavelength for it, though. That animal has definite plans, and I can't work them out."

Nigel was at a loss. In many respects, he was as good as, if not better than, Edward in the day-to-day running of the stable. Nigel could keep a string of horses fit and healthy, but their psychology was a closed book to him. Despite the successes he had seen Edward produce when he was in the right mood, Nigel was uncertain whether all this talk about understanding horses wasn't really claptrap.

Edward's disquiet about Frescobaldi never left him, and as the horses walked round the paddock before the Derby, Nigel saw that he had become gloweringly suspicious.

"You'll put the poor creature off if you stare at him like that," Nigel whispered.

"He's up to something," Edward said. "Mark my words, he is up to something."

When the horses eventually reached the start after the parade and traverse of Epsom Downs, Frescobaldi deposited Sean Gillespie on the ground while the roll was being called. He did it in the nicest possible way, and made no attempt to bolt for freedom, but trotted round upsetting the other horses, many of whom were already highly-strung by the preliminaries. After two more jockeys had been thrown off, and the rest had dismounted, Edward turned to Nigel.

"See what I mean," he said grimly.

The starter and his assistants were under no illusions about Frescobaldi's willingness to enter the stalls, so he was held back until last. What no one had bargained for, was his unwillingness to let any of the other runners be installed. As he pranced around causing mayhem in a rather polite fashion, Edward became very tense, his mouth a hard line below the binoculars. It seemed an age before he heaved a sigh of relief as Sean Gillespie carried out the secret orders he had been given, and withdrew from the race.

The Duke of Dorchester thought it was a huge joke. "Let's face it, Manning, he'd never have won the bugger," he laughed. "Delaying the start for twenty minutes was the only way he was going to get his name in the papers!"

Edward smiled bleakly. He was watching Frescobaldi walking back across the centre of the course. Sean Gillespie was obviously livid, but for the first time in several weeks, Frescobaldi looked as though he didn't have a care in the world. Nigel glanced apprehensively at Edward, and went to talk to Freezer.

With the race finally under way, Edward slipped into a toilet. Producing a hip-flask, he drank from it with greedy desperation. Timing himself by the second hand on his watch, he downed the equivalent of three double measures, used a mouth spray, and re-emerged in time to be deafened by the crowd as the popular Harbinger came up the hill like an express train with a place in the hall of fame and a ten-million-pound price tag on his bridle.

Edward was blinking tears away. He was always stirred by the sight of a good horse triumphing in such thrilling circumstances. Yet he was a mere onlooker. Three years on from Caroline and James Henry he was no nearer achieving it himself. It was like the day at Newmarket with Musetta, when he had first seen Bernard Dalrymple's horses at exercise, and felt like an upstart.

There was a consolation. In response to Edward's urgent request, Richard had brought Victor Macleod along. After the race, Edward took him quietly aside.

"That Harbinger is a good horse," Edward began. He made it sound like a piece of irrelevant small-talk.

"Yes." Macleod was wary.

"In fact, he's quite outstanding," Edward continued. "Quite a few people spotted that the day he won the Norfolk at Ascot." Edward's tone changed as he fixed Macleod with a stare like a razor. "But you didn't, did you?"

"No . . . well . . . I was wrong there." Macleod made the admission with grudging bad grace.

Edward appeared to be mulling the matter over. "I like my owners to know about things like that," he said. "There's never any disgrace in being beaten by a very good horse."

"Yes. Quite so. I shall have to learn."

"I've got a much better idea. Take your two horses out of my yard,

Macleod. Try to find another poor devil to put up with your bombastic, ill-informed arrogance. I'll send you a letter."

"You can't do this!" Macleod was furious, barely able to control himself.

"Oh yes I can."

Edward smiled, and walked away.

He found Richard looking as though someone had given him a million pounds. "I've just heard that Chandler has won at Carlisle," he said happily.

Edward looked at him blankly. "Who's Chandler?" he asked.

"One of T. P. Malahide's first crop," Richard replied. "Mrs Priest bought him, and Bill Elsdon's got him at Malton."

"Ah!" Edward recognised the names of a much-respected owner and trainer who operated mostly in the north. "So, you've got a stallion who can produce winners."

"*Winner*," Richard corrected, grinning from ear to ear. "And it was only worth fifteen hundred pounds."

"Even so . . ." Edward waved a hand to sketch a brilliant future.

"Are you coming back to Widney Cheyne?" Richard asked. "We could celebrate. Nancy will be very pleased."

"I promised Fred Bird I'd look in to tell him about the latest attempt on the Derby," Edward replied. T. P. Malahide was forgotten, and an air of dejection enveloped him. "I'll come over at the weekend."

Knowing what traffic conditions would be like as the huge Derby-day crowds dispersed, Edward made no attempt to leave the course until after six o'clock. When he left, he failed to notice Nigel and Victor Macleod at the other end of the car park. Nor did they see him. They were in Macleod's car, deep in a conversation that was simultaneously shocking and exciting Nigel.

It was nearly eight o'clock when Edward reached Fred's house after a tedious journey that had given him time to become thoroughly depressed. His spirits lifted when Fred met him at the front door. Fred had heard all about Frescobaldi, and was sizzling with fun about him.

"Cat's meat, son, that's what you want to do with that bleedin' article," Fred advised. "You tell your mate, His Grace, that I know a geezer down Shoreditch who'll give him a fair price. You never know, he might fetch as much as two hundred quid."

Edward was still laughing thirty seconds later when he met Angela Maitland.

———

It was a week since Stephanie had received the panic telephone call from Los Angeles. She had to consult Fred and ring back.

"I've a very good friend who's been in America for two years. She's had enough and wants out in a hurry. Can she stay here until she can find somewhere decent?"

"What's she like?" Fred asked.

"All right. You'll like her."

When Stephanie had collected her from Heathrow at six-thirty on Friday morning, Angela Maitland was a wreck. Jet lag after a long flight on top of a debilitating week had left her virtually incapable of coherent speech and thought. Stephanie bundled her upstairs to bed before Fred could do more than open his mouth, and make a pointless gesture. All he saw was a tousled head of raven hair, and a wickedly expensive crimson coat that was draped over her shoulders.

She stayed in her room for thirty hours, sleeping for most of the time. Stephanie took her some breakfast up after lunch on Saturday, and an hour later she came down to meet Fred. Stephanie had been right. He did like her.

With her dark hair, green eyes, deep tan and shapely body, Angela Maitland was devastatingly attractive. There was no subtlety or modesty about her; the impact was immediate and spectacular. Fully aware of her formidable natural assets, she enhanced and emphasised them with every move and gesture, every look and word. Like Stephanie, she also had the aura of 'quality', although, in her case, it was more worldly, purposeful and occasionally blatant. When she chose, she could be demure and ladylike, lost, needing help through a world that was all too much for her. But at all times, in all moods, she was utterly carnal.

Stephanie and Angela had been exact contemporaries at school. Their looks and distaste for the system had set them apart, and more or less forced them to be friends. Angela was by far the more outrageous of the two. She had done her first nude modelling assignment while still at school, been expelled, turned into a martyr, and brought the wrath of the tabloid press down on the headmistress and governors. Unlike Stephanie, she was then on her own: her parents disowned her.

Angela was consumed by the ambition to get into films. She had broken into TV with a succession of minor, purely decorative roles, and done work for commercials, but she soon came to the conclusion that there was no real prospect of a career in England. Against Stephanie's advice, she had gone to Hollywood.

Even a mediocre agent had no difficulty in opening doors with her looks and nationality. The first letter to Stephanie relayed the excitement of capturing a part in a soap opera. Dotted about in only three episodes, the sum total of the role was trivial. However, the money was unbelievably good, the opportunities immense. After that, there was always something about to happen. It never did, and Stephanie knew that it never would. The hard fact of the matter was that no one really trusted Angela. If

335

she'd been an established star they wouldn't have had much choice, but as one newcomer among hundreds, they could afford to ignore her.

A letter, followed two weeks later by the phone call, indicated that something had gone seriously wrong. It was no longer possible to hang on, hoping for the best. Stephanie concentrated on picking up the pieces, without asking questions or sermonising. Before she flaked out after her long flight, Angela had outlined a new objective. All she wanted now was someone to look after her. The only qualifications were that he had to be wealthy and reasonably personable.

Angela went to the kitchen on the pretext of helping Stephanie prepare supper.

"He's nice," she said enthusiastically. "Really dishy!"

"Yes, he is." Stephanie kept her smile and voice pleasantly neutral.

"And he trains racehorses?"

"Yes. He's been to the Derby today."

"Aha! Hence the morning suit?" Stephanie nodded. "He looks great in that."

"Tails do something for a man," Stephanie said, quoting her mother.

"How thrilling!" Angela said. "Even *I've* heard of the Derby. I'll get him to tell me all about it."

"That may not be a very good idea," Stephanie warned. "From what Fred was saying, there seems to have been a fearful cock-up. Edward's horse refused to have anything to do with it, and nearly fouled it up for all the others."

They both glanced in the direction of the sitting-room as Fred roared with laughter yet again. Edward, now seeing the funny side of it himself, was giving a humorously dramatised account of the afternoon's fiasco. He had his feet up on a coffee table, and a drink in his hand: it was sheer luxury to be able to do it openly. But enjoyable though he was finding the Frescobaldi saga, he wanted to get it over so that he could ask Fred about Angela.

"I suppose he's married?" Angela asked Stephanie.

"No, he's a widower." The look on her friend's face made Stephanie present the full facts. "His wife was killed in a riding accident three years ago – I think it was just before the Derby, actually. They were very close, by all accounts . . . very close indeed. She helped him with the horses. He took it badly. I don't think he's got over it yet."

Angela appeared thoughtfully sympathetic, concealing the fact that something in Stephanie's tone had alerted her. "Have you had a go at him, Steph?" she asked.

"Yes." Stephanie wished that she didn't always have to be so honest.

"And failed?"

"Yes! He seemed to think that Fred should be respected."

"My word!" Angela was vastly impressed. "What's he made of, for Christ's sake?"

"He's a very decent bloke. He's got principles. They may not be very good for him, but he's got them."

Baffled, Angela looked for positive points. "He seemed to like me."

"Yes."

Stephanie was accustomed to the way men reacted to Angela. She had hoped Edward would be different. He had not been totally disappointing; unlike most men, he had not goggled at Angela and wasn't licking his lips. But he had given very clear signs that he liked what he saw.

"I think . . ." Angela stretched her legs, studied them, and appeared to find them to her liking ". . . I think that Mr Manning needs cheering up."

"Possibly. Just be careful, Angela. Like I said, he's decent."

Although he stayed until midnight, Edward alarmed Angela by leaving without making an arrangement to see her.

"What's wrong?" she asked Stephanie over breakfast the following morning. "Am I losing my grip?"

"Relax. If he's not racing today, he'll telephone after lunch."

The call came at two-thirty. Stephanie listened impassively.

"Hello, Edward . . . yes . . . that would be nice . . . love to! . . . fine . . . seven o'clock then." Angela replaced the phone and beamed. "Dinner on Saturday night," she said.

Stephanie kept quiet.

A heatwave prompted Angela to wear a simple, white, full-skirted summer dress. With no need of stockings, she added colour and accentuated her legs with a pair of emerald-green stiletto-heeled sandals. She recognised the approval on his face when he collected her. As they drove to a restaurant by the river, and sipped apéritifs while studying the menu, she embraced him with her presence. It was, she signalled to him, a pleasure and something of an honour to be asked to dine with him.

When the head waiter conducted them to their table, Edward was suddenly aware of a vivid new experience. Angela caused heads to turn. Two men in a party of eight, their wives safely distracted by the others, looked at her with hungry yearning, then gave Edward looks of covetous envy. For the first time in his life, he felt a thrill of *male* pride.

The meal was perfect, beautifully cooked, served with no nonsense at precisely the right tempo. As they set about the first course of smoked

337

salmon, Angela said, "I'm afraid I don't know the first thing about horses."

"Thank God for that!" Edward smiled, and she saw that he was genuinely pleased. "Tell me about America."

She interested and amused him for the duration of the meal. What she related was a carefully selected and embellished version of her experiences. When she flirted with the scandalous and sensational, she saw at once that he was quite excited, despite his half-hearted expressions of amazed disapproval. He wanted to know about the mechanics of film-making, and seemed fascinated by the Californian lifestyle. She told it all in a low-key manner, slowly and quietly, maintaining a firm grip on his attention. When they moved into a conservatory for coffee, she explained why she had thrown it all in and come back to England.

"It's very superficial. The moment you dig beneath the surface, you find there's nothing there. And I must confess I didn't get on too well with the men."

"Good Lord! Whyever not?"

"They're basic . . . very, very basic. Actually, I thought they were complete oiks . . . totally uncouth. Maybe I met all the wrong ones. I suppose the truth is that I'm hooked on Englishmen."

And her manner left Edward in no doubt that she was currently totally happy in that respect.

Outside, she thanked him as he searched for his car keys. "That was lovely, Edward. Thank you."

"I enjoyed it very much indeed," he replied.

She had placed a hand on his shoulder, and showed no inclination to move it. He looked at her earnestly. She was something absolutely new in his experience, and he knew that a novel approach was called for. He was encouraged by the hand on his shoulder.

"There's something I have to ask you, Angela."

"Go on."

"I hope I'm not being too uncouth."

"You couldn't if you tried."

"Your place, or mine?"

She smiled. It was slow and sensuous. "Yours, I think. Let's not bother Fred and Steph."

It was past sunset when they reached Saxon Court, but the light was good enough for Angela to take the place in. A fleeting impression was enough for her.

"Nice," she said. "How many horses do you have?"

"A hundred."

There was more she wanted to know, but it could wait; it was big and obviously worth a fortune. She was perfectly content to let Edward hurry her inside.

He stopped at the foot of the stairs to kiss her. She had been half-afraid that he would be timid, and need leading, but the way he kissed her swept that doubt aside in an instant. His hands underlined the urgency of his mouth, roaming all over her. It was a voyage of discovery, not a mauling, and she let him know she liked it.

"You've got nothing on under this dress," he said, agitation overruling his intention of mock-reproof.

She laughed throatily, and broke away from him. "Let's go and find out," she said, and ran lightly up the stairs.

Stepping out of the dress with careless ease, she placed it over the back of a chair.

"See! You were wrong," she said. She was wearing a pair of briefs. Nothing else. Just the briefs and the sandals. Feet apart, hands on hips, she faced him with total confidence.

"Not Fred Bird's rubbish," she said, smiling knowingly.

"No." Edward had studied the catalogue because of Stephanie. He knew that Angela was wearing something much more classily expensive. He sat on the foot of the bed to take his shoes off, his eyes never leaving her.

"You look bloody marvellous," he said. The tightness of his voice was, she knew, caused by lust, not nervousness. There was no need for her to say anything until he was naked.

"Ah!" She smiled voluptuously at his rampant arousal. "The best compliment of all."

Kicking off the sandals, Angela pulled the briefs down her thighs in a tight skein, watching his face tauten as he saw what he had only suspected so far – the black triangle of her exceptionally luxuriant pubic hair.

She had judged his mood and state perfectly. When she moved towards him, he seized her, and they fell on the bed.

His passion left her breathless, yet she had a crystal-clear perception of the tangled web of pent-up emotions impelling Edward, and the gratitude he would feel for their release and exorcism. She also knew that she was going to enjoy it. Joe Weissman had been a long time ago, and none of the others had ever bothered much about her feelings.

After a rapturous struggle during which Edward repeatedly tried to enter her, she got him flat on his back, and swung herself astride his hips.

"Now then," she gasped, "I might not know much about horses, but I think I know how to ride you!"

As he tried to protest and struggle, she impaled herself on him. She smiled at the look on his face, a mixture of bewildered distress and ecstatic pleasure.

"Poor Edward!" she murmured. "You thought *you* were going to fuck *me*, didn't you? Oh dear!"

"Is that your wife?" she asked gently.

She stood bathed in morning sunlight, sipping coffee and looking at the photograph on the dressing-table.

This was a different world. They had just made love in the big bath. Looking at her profile in the soft, revealing light, Edward could see the lingering prominence of her nipples. The look on her face reminded him of the question.

"Yes."

"She's very lovely." Angela studied him. "It must have been tough for you."

He nodded. He was standing in the bathroom door, drying his hair.

"Well, hopefully things get better from now on," she said.

"If I have you . . ." He was suddenly insecure.

"You have."

"Then I'm all right."

"Good." She held up her dress ruefully. "I'm going to look a sight," she said.

He moved to a wardrobe. "You seem about the same size as Caro," he said. "Is there anything here you could wear?"

• "You didn't get rid of them?"

"No. At first I couldn't bring myself to . . . then I never got round to it."

Angela liked the idea. It had the symbolism of possession.

She was the same size as Caroline, and found a roll-neck sweater and pair of slacks that fitted her. It was while she was searching for shoes more suitable than the green sandals that she found the cache of empty bottles.

"Jesus, Edward! Have things been this bad?" she asked.

"Yes." He flushed at the embarrassment of her discovery. "Yes . . . I'm afraid they have."

"What the hell are they doing here?"

"I never bothered to chuck them out."

"God, there's fifty or more!"

He looked, and nodded miserably.

"Right, this lot's going, and we start now."

She found a large carrier bag into which she pushed her dress and three of the bottles.

"You must have a cleaning woman," Angela said, "and I'll bet she's as nosey as sin – they always are. We'll smuggle them out gradually. And don't put any more in there. Right?" She kissed him.

"Right!" He smiled gratefully.

"You need looking after," she said.

"Are you volunteering?"

"Oh yes." Angela was quite certain about it.

It was Sunday, and Siobhan was not yet in the office. Edward felt sure they had left Saxon Court without being seen by anyone.

He was relieved at the unexpected bonus of finding Fred alone. Stephanie had left early to visit her parents in Somerset. While Angela was changing into some of her own clothes, Edward told a delighted Fred all about it.

"Just the job, son, just the job!" Fred said. "I thought she might bring a glow to your cheeks as soon as I clapped eyes on her. Knows what it's all about, does she?"

"Oh yes!" Edward nodded furiously.

They spent the day on the river. After lunch, Angela spread herself out on the foredeck to improve her suntan, and Edward spent an hour studying the body that had occupied him with such satisfying vigour for much of the night. She watched him through half-closed eyes, reading his thoughts perfectly. As Fred joined the queue of boats waiting at Benson Lock, she sat up, smiling.

"You're getting horny again," she said accusingly.

"Yes, I am!" He was proud of his new confidence.

She took him down to the saloon.

Edward forgot the promise he had half-made to go to Widney Cheyne. Nancy was especially disappointed by his non-appearance. The previous day she had received confirmation that Rhinemaiden was in foal to Parsifal. T. P. Malahide's mating with Musetta was also known to have been successful.

Ten days later, Royal Ascot was a strange business.

The contingent of nine Saxon Court horses achieved five second places and three thirds. With prize-money creeping up, albeit not fast enough for most owners, Edward was credited with place money of over fifty thousand pounds. Ever-anxious for a new angle, the press wondered if any trainer had ever produced such a record at the meeting. On eight occasions, Edward and his horses were one side or other of the winner's enclosure, but never in it.

He was completely unconcerned.

Angela was with him for all four days of the meeting, and with her at his side, it was difficult to interest him in anything else.

Imogen was outraged. She knew that Edward's introduction of Angela the day before the Royal meeting was a deliberate ploy to avoid criticism. She had unhesitatingly dubbed Angela 'that Maitland creature', and that was that; Edward shrugged and left Imogen to it.

Instead, he set great store by the opinion of Mark and Sarah Walgrave, who had welcomed Angela with open arms to the extent that she and Edward were staying at The Elms for the duration of Ascot. Seeing how cheerful and assured Edward had become, they regarded Angela as something of a saviour.

Towards the end of the last day, Edward and Angela were leaning on the rail of an empty paddock. Angela's dress was white and crimson. Like the outfits of the previous three days, it was successfully intended to be dramatic and sexy rather than pretty or elegant. Imogen glared at them from a distance.

"And he met her at Bird's place?" she asked Richard.

He nodded.

"There you are then! What have I been saying about Bird?"

Edward's affair with Angela, all the more astounding because of its unexpected suddenness and blatant sexuality, had put Richard in a quandary. He rather liked Angela, admiring the style with which she deployed her powerful resources, and the effect she was having on Edward seemed beneficial. Nevertheless, Richard uneasily admitted to himself that Imogen's opinion could not be disregarded lightly.

"Miss Maitland seems very determined – about something," Edwin Fforbes had said after watching her in action. That about summed it up, Richard thought.

"It's a damned shame Valerie Malahide didn't come over this time," Imogen said. "She'd soon have done something about this."

Looking at Edward and Angela, Richard was inclined to doubt it. He was distracted by Edwin Fforbes.

"I thought Miss Covington-Sykes might be here today."

"Who?" Richard was baffled.

"Stephanie," Edwin explained. "Fred Bird's ... er ... young woman."

"Oh, yes, of course!" It took Richard several seconds to wonder what had prompted Edwin's remark. He thought of seeking clarification, then decided against it; Edwin had obviously been making idle conversation.

On the paddock rail, Angela looked round with speculation and censure mixed in her expression.

"What's the matter?" Edward asked.

"Has all this never struck you as boring?" she asked.

"Not *boring* exactly ... it's a hell of a pain sometimes when you can't get it right."

"Like this week, for instance ... so near, and yet so far."

"That's the way it goes sometimes."

"Well, I think it's boring, and I'll tell you something else."

"What?"

"Most of this lot know even less about horses than I do."

Edward looked round at the crowd, thinning rapidly as the last day drew to a close. "You're quite right," he said. "I've never had much time for them, to tell you the truth."

"Don't get me wrong," Angela said. "I've enjoyed it – or most of it. I can't help feeling we could have been doing better things."

"Such as?"

She moved closer to him and smiled. "How about screwing? Wouldn't that be better?"

As Alison Bairstow approached the paddock with a horse for the last race, she saw Edward's hand slip from Angela Maitland's waist to fondle her buttocks.

Alison frowned. Talk in the yard had suggested that the guv'nor's new woman might liven things up a bit. But no one had envisaged this sort of thing.

CHAPTER 15

Imogen paused briefly to scowl at her surroundings. With the October evening closing in under a low sky full of rain, even Widney Cheyne looked depressing.

"Bloody weather!" she muttered, and hurried on towards Nancy's cottage, her wellingtons squelching through piles of sodden leaves.

As she took off her boots and oilskin in the porch, she shouted a greeting through the deserted kitchen, and Nancy appeared.

"Still raining?" Nancy asked, reaching for the kettle.

"Chucking it down!" Imogen collapsed into a comfortable old chair by the boiler, and pulled her cigarettes out of a cardigan pocket. Her face fell as she saw the packet and the state of its contents. "They've gone soggy!" she complained, rooting around until she found one that looked almost smokable. "How long's this been going on?"

"Two days. I hear there's a guy building an ark up at Hatchetts Green."

Imogen ignored the quip, and sank into deep thought, peering with disdainful suspicion at her cigarette from time to time.

"Was that Siobhan I saw leaving a while ago?" Nancy asked.

"Yes."

Nancy studied Imogen as she made coffee; she was not in the best of moods.

"Did Siobhan come to see you about the wedding?" Nancy asked eventually.

"Yes . . . well, sort of. They've named the date."

"Great! When?"

"A week before Christmas."

"Does that mean they've got the religion thing cracked?"

"Don't know." Imogen shook her head. "We didn't talk about it. My impression is that it's been swept under the carpet . . . along with a lot of other things."

Nancy sat down, and looked patiently at Imogen who had lapsed back into furious thought.

"It looks very much as though we have a problem coming up," Imogen said at last. "Siobhan came to tell me that she and Nigel will be leaving Saxon Court after they're married."

"What on earth for?"

"Nigel's setting up on his own at a stable in Epsom. It's a small place

– about twenty boxes, and rather run down from what I can gather."

"Hell's teeth!" Nancy thought about it. "Will Nigel be able to make a go of it?"

"No, he won't. You'd have to be a James Henry Manning for that. I didn't say anything to Siobhan, of course."

"Where's the money coming from? His father?"

"Good God, no! Quite apart from anything else, Cyril Brookes-Smith hasn't *got* any money."

"What! I thought he had tons of the stuff."

"Oh dear, I didn't tell you, did I?" Imogen looked apologetic. "Things have changed. I ran into Elspeth the other day . . . well, it was back in the summer, actually."

Nancy laughed. "Ah, c'mon, Imogen, what do you mean, you ran into her? Where was this? I know! The subway at Piccadilly Circus!"

"No, as a matter of fact, it was Paddington. Elspeth was on her way home after a few days in town, and I found her in the tea rooms. We had a good chin-wag before her train left. Cyril doesn't have any money because he's given it all away."

"Jesus!"

"Quite. It seems he really does have it in for Nigel in a big way. He was rather upset when he finally realised that he was a very rich, fairly old man with a dodgy heart. He could go on forever, he might pop off tomorrow. Whatever he put in his will, Nigel could contest it, and almost certainly win a sizeable chunk, if not the lot. Elspeth's got enough in her own name to keep them comfortable, so he gave it away. Well over four million with the interest that had accumulated."

"What did Nigel say?"

"He doesn't know. The two charities concerned were ordered to keep quiet, and Nigel didn't bother going to papa for this venture."

"So who is backing him?"

"I don't imagine that it needs any backing. He's renting the yard from an appalling individual called Julian Sparshott, and it's the sort of operation you could run on a hand-to-mouth basis. However . . ." Imogen paused to bid farewell to her cigarette ". . . Siobhan mentioned Victor Macleod. It looks very much as though he's mixed up in it somehow."

"Edward will like that!"

"Won't he just! Siobhan isn't exactly dancing with joy. You see, Nancy, the difficulty is that she's awfully fond of Nigel. I think he's been doing things she doesn't like, but she's turning a blind eye for the sake of true love and all that hogwash."

"What does Edward have to say?"

"Aha!" Imogen sat back, wiggled her toes, and assumed a portentous expression. "Well may you ask! Edward doesn't know yet."

"Hell! Why not?"

"They haven't been able to tell him ... at least, Siobhan hasn't. I imagine Nigel isn't keen to face up to it. Edward is far too busy. Siobhan thinks she might have to send him a letter to book an appointment."

"What's he doing? The horses aren't working, are they?"

"No, but he is. Very hard, one suspects."

"What at?"

"The Maitland creature."

"Oh."

Nancy had seen Angela Maitland only once, and that had been no more than a glimpse at Newbury races in August. It had been enough to form an opinion.

"I mean, what is one supposed to make of *that*?" Imogen asked.

Nancy shrugged. "Not much. I guess it won't last."

"He seems positively enslaved by the wretched woman."

"She's probably a good lay."

For a moment or two, Imogen looked as if she were going to explode. The crisis passed, and she fumbled morosely at the sodden cigarette packet again. "The fact is that Siobhan's departure presents us with a problem. It might be the last straw. Siobhan told me that she's been making most of the race entries for some time. I don't mean she was just doing as Edward told her ... *she's* actually been deciding which race to put a horse in."

"What's Edward been doing?"

"Going through the motions of training them. Well, that's the theory. In practice, he's been concentrating on one or two that he finds interesting."

"Like Rhinemaiden?"

"Yes, and that dreadful pair Benvenuto Cellini and Frescobaldi. So, what are we going to do about Siobhan?"

"Get someone else to do her job?" Nancy suggested, knowing that the idea was painfully obvious and uselessly vague.

"Well of course! But who? That's a very testing job even if Edward were pulling his weight. The way he is, the whole thing could end up a shambles if we get the wrong person." Imogen shuddered at the memory of Mrs O'Keefe, the tyrannical incompetent who had wrecked the office at Avoca House before Siobhan had taken it over.

"Don't you think Edward might want to sort it out for himself?"

"My dear girl, he'll bury his head in the sand."

"So what do we do?"

"Siobhan and Nigel will be clearing off almost at once. That gives us three months to find someone before the place gets busy for the season. I can hold the fort."

"You?"

"Yes! I know my typing isn't up to much these days, and Richard constantly tells me that I'm diabolical on the telephone, but I'm very determined, Nancy . . . and I *care* about Saxon Court."

They chatted for another half-hour, Imogen mostly thinking aloud about the best way to tell Edward. As she was leaving, lured back home by the prospect of undamaged cigarettes, Imogen hesitated, as if a thought had suddenly come to her.

"Was that you I saw giving Parsifal a spin across the park the other day?" she asked.

"Yes. He loves a gallop. He'd still go at a fair clip if I let him."

"Funny, isn't it?" Imogen seemed to be talking to herself. "I'd never thought of you as a rider."

Nancy laughed. "I've been doing it since I was four."

"I thought you'd got the hang of it." Imogen had actually observed Parsifal's exercise through binoculars, and been surprised by Nancy's consummate skill as a horsewoman. "Very good," she said absentmindedly. "By the way, how heavy are you?"

"A hundred and twenty-three pounds – that's eight stone eleven in English," Nancy replied. "I can do a bit less when I'm properly in shape."

"Just goes to show, doesn't it?" Imogen said, and stomped off into the rain.

Edward was told three days later. He never knew how carefully planned it was.

During the previous afternoon, Siobhan spoke to Edward, establishing that he was going to be in the following day. She relayed the news to Imogen.

On the day, Siobhan dragged Nigel into the office at ten-thirty. At precisely the same time, Imogen left Widney Cheyne.

Edward was ill at ease from the start. Angela was away visiting friends for a few days, and he was bored without her. Sensing the nervous formality of Siobhan's manner, he prepared for bad news.

She did most of the talking while Nigel looked uncomfortable. From time to time he reinforced a point that Siobhan had made, but he did it by simple repetition, without adding to what she had said. Edward sat quite still, paying careful attention, showing no feelings.

"I'm sorry about that, Siobhan," he said when she had finished. "You'll be missed."

"I shall be sorry to go," she said, and hurriedly added, "in lots of ways."

"Yes . . . well . . ." Edward sighed helplessly and glanced round the

347

office. Siobhan had a powerful impression that he was looking at all she had created, and realising how much he would miss her. He returned to the present with a jolt, smiling bravely. "I said you'd make a good team, didn't I?" he asked, and nodded, answering his own question. "Well, good luck!" He paused.

Siobhan sensed that he had nothing more to say. Fearing the onset of embarrassment, she was suddenly faced with the most absurd end to their conversation. Edward stood up and shook hands, first with her, then with Nigel, and walked out of the office, leaving them staring at each other in speechless amazement.

When he got outside, Edward had no idea where he was going. Watching apprehensively from one of her front windows, Mary saw him scratch the back of his head, look round as though completely unsure of his surroundings, and finally head toward the Colour Room. There was no evidence of a blazing row, and on balance, Mary felt glad. If Edward had been angry and unpleasant, it might have made Siobhan think again, although the most probable outcome would have been a hardening of attitudes.

Inside the Colour Room, Edward wandered aimlessly. He studied the pictures from the Ollie Derwent period, suddenly feeling a new rapport with the ethereal detachment that permeated every portrait of his great predecessor. It was said that in an age when training regimes were usually harsh, he used to charm his horses into winning races. Edward smiled acknowledgement to the man whom many had dismissed as a dilettante, and wished that he possessed some of his powers. Moving on to the infinitely less sympathetic Joshua Fielding, it was a relief to be distracted by the sound of the door opening.

Since Caroline, Declan always removed his cap in the Colour Room, and he did so now, holding it self-consciously in front of him.

"I don't like this business, sor," he said.

Edward pulled a face and spread his hands. "It can't be helped, Declan. I hope she's happy. Have you seen this place they're going to?"

"I have. It's not too good."

"Can they get a living out of it?"

Declan considered the point that had been exercising his mind for two weeks. "I don't know. We'll have to see."

"Don't worry. I expect they'll get some help."

Understanding where it would come from, Declan nodded his gratitude.

Edward's eyes flickered briefly over the pictures of Caroline, and he took a step towards the door. "How's my friend Frescobaldi today?" he asked.

"His temperature's down." Declan allowed a moment to pass before asking, "Are we keeping him?"

348

"Well, nobody else wants him, and His Grace is prepared to keep paying."

Declan shook his head, and pursed his lips, a sign of profound disapproval.

As they emerged from the Colour Room, Imogen arrived. Edward was instantly transformed.

"That's a piece of luck," he said. "She's just the lady I need. I'll see you later, Declan."

Imogen barely had time to collect her thoughts and get out of the car before Edward was at her side. Cutting short the greetings and small-talk by which she implied that her visit was a casual coincidence, he hurried her into the office.

"The most bloody awful thing's happened," he told her. "Siobhan's leaving."

"What on earth for?"

"She's marrying Nigel."

"I know that. It doesn't mean she has to leave . . . does it? What have you said to her?"

Imogen's ploy produced the desired effect.

"I didn't! Good God, Imogen, I'm not a complete idiot! I want Siobhan to go like I need a hole in the head. Nigel's setting up on his own at some hick place in Epsom, and she's going with him."

"Oh, I say!" Imogen's act was totally convincing.

Edward collapsed into the chair behind his desk. "It's a hell of a shaker," he said. "The fact of the matter is, she's been running this place. Oh yes . . ." he waved Imogen's protest aside before she could make it ". . . Siobhan's been doing *much* more than her fair share. What the devil am I going to do?"

"Keeping calm is a good place to start."

"All right." He stared at her expectantly. "How do we replace Siobhan?"

"Eventually, and with difficulty," Imogen said. "I expect it's going to take some time to find the right person."

"The right person is buggering off to a clapped-out dump at Epsom!"

"Well, someone suitable . . . and it could take time. We've got one thing on our side. It's the quietest time of the year."

"But I still need help."

"Of course. Will I do?"

He blinked at her, and Imogen saw that he was very pleased with the idea, could scarcely believe his good fortune. "I say, Imogen, would you?"

"Naturally." She gave him her warmest smile. "I won't be perfect, but I know more or less everybody, and I can soon find out where everything is."

349

"That's very good of you, Imogen."

"Not at all. Seems the sensible thing to do. Don't worry about it. I'll get together with Siobhan to work out the best way of getting into the run of things." She looked at the stack of brochures on his desk. "Thinking of going on holiday?"

"Yes." Edward's demeanour turned to a mixture of defence and defiance.

"Good! A proper break will pep you up." Having achieved her objective with far greater ease than she had thought likely, Imogen was not prepared to risk a slanging match over what she was certain was the prime purpose of the holiday.

After Imogen's successful foray, Richard went to Saxon Court with the vague idea of consolidating her efforts. It was two months since he and Edward had enjoyed a good chat, and the time seemed ripe for a repair of that omission. All went well at first. They strolled round the yard, looked at some of the horses, and talked about everything from the international money scene and Stewart's view of the Stock Exchange 'big bang', to their boyhood memories of Belfields. Not until they were back in the kitchen did the topic of Siobhan and Nigel crop up.

"I can't see how he's going to make it work," Edward said. "I haven't seen the place yet, but Declan doesn't rate it. And where's he going to get his owners from?"

"That may not be as tricky as you imagine," Richard said. "He's only got twenty boxes to fill, and I believe a dozen are already promised."

"Oh, that's good." Edward was genuinely pleased. "They've been tremendously busy . . . I think they've gone there this morning."

"It's all done with luck of course. Alec Stedding's packing it in, and one of his owners didn't want to move his horses too far, so he's giving Nigel a chance."

Alec Stedding, one of racing's most colourful characters, had trained at Epsom for thirty-five years. Edward knew that he was handing in his licence and retiring because, as Alec had told the world at Royal Ascot, he was "broken down by age, poverty, sex and drink".

"Nigel will have his work cut out trying to follow Alec," Edward laughed.

"No chance at all," Richard said. "Especially with Siobhan to keep him in line." He then made the mistake of assuming that Edward knew everything. "And he's got to put up with Victor as well."

"Eh?" Still smiling at memories of Alec Stedding, Edward almost missed the point.

"Nigel's getting Victor Macleod's horses," Richard said. "So there's going to be no bed of roses."

"Nigel is taking Macleod's horses?" Edward's voice was ominously quiet. Richard saw that he had blundered.

"Yes . . . he is."

"After what happened here?"

"He's got to make a living, Edward."

"Damn it, man . . ." Edward's fist came down on the table with enough violence to upset the coffee cups ". . . he's got a living here!"

"All right, all right. But you can't blame him for wanting to have a go himself."

"And getting mixed up with Macleod? Did you know this was going on?"

"I suspected something," Richard admitted. "Edwin Fforbes heard whispers."

"Did you try to stop it?"

"Of course not! What could I have done? What *should* I have done? You'd finished with Macleod, and Nigel's a free agent."

"Free to steal Siobhan?"

"Don't be ridiculous, Edward! He's not stealing anything. Siobhan knows what's she doing."

"Does she, by God! So she knows that her precious Nigel couldn't train our cat, does she?"

"That's unfair! He's done all right here."

"Richard, *nobody's* done all right here since Caro went. A mentally defective baboon could pull a few winners out of that yard with the quality of horseflesh in it, and Declan doing his bit."

"You're being grossly unjust," Richard snapped. "Let's give him a chance to show what he can do."

"Balls!" Edward sneered. "That's sanctimonious crap, Richard! Thank God Imogen's got some sense. She's going to *help* me instead of talking pious rot." Glaring at Richard with blazing eyes, he added, "You could do with her at the bank. She'd soon have Macleod sorted out!"

Two days before Siobhan's wedding, Edward and Angela Maitland flew to the Seychelles.

He made no attempt to prevent uncharitable conclusions being drawn about both the timing and the length of the prodigiously expensive holiday in the very best hotel that the island of Mahé could provide.

The departure date was deliberately chosen to conflict with the marriage ceremony. In addition to avoiding an English Christmas and New Year, which Edward had come to detest, the three-week duration meant that Siobhan and Nigel would be gone from Saxon Court by the time he returned.

He left behind a magnificent canteen of cutlery that had cost nearly two thousand pounds. It inevitably became the centrepiece of the

351

wedding-present display that Mary arranged in the parlour, but both she and Siobhan viewed it with silent dismay. A bouquet of flowers, given in love and thanks for the last seven years, would have meant much more.

Within an hour of arriving on Mahé, Angela decided that she was in paradise. As soon as she saw the Renaissance International Hotel with its thirty acres of tropical gardens and private Indian Ocean beach, she stopped worrying about Edward's moods of the past weeks.

Eight days later, at the mid-point of the holiday, the subject she wanted to discuss emerged quite naturally.

It was early evening, time to think about getting ready for dinner. Edward stretched out so that every fibre of his body was drawn into tension, then relaxed slowly into sybaritic languor.

"There isn't much wrong with this life," he said. Thinking about it, he decided that he was entitled to feel pleased with himself, and smiled. "Actually, there's *nothing* wrong with it, nothing at all."

"Quite happy, are we?"

"Yes . . . reasonably so. No grounds for complacency, though."

"Oh dear!"

He smiled again, recognising the tone of mock-alarm. Angela was lying on her side, her head on his chest. He was admiring the perfect curving sweep of her hips and thighs.

"I think I'm just getting nicely into my stride now," Edward said smugly.

She raised her face to him, and he saw that the persistent heat of passion seemed to have softened her striking bone structure to make her even more attractive.

"You need a little rest now?" She smiled, giving the impression that she herself was anxious for a period of respite.

"Yes, that's not a bad idea." He looked at his watch. "We've had four hours of unmitigated lust, and I'm hungry."

"It wasn't quite that long," she corrected him. "You dozed off for nearly an hour."

"Is that a complaint?"

"Yes! I was deprived. No . . . seriously, you were bloody marvellous. I feel fabulous."

"You look it." Edward was confident that after dinner, they would start where they had left off.

"We could live like this all the time, couldn't we?" Angela suggested.

He thought about it. "Yes, I suppose we could."

"Maybe it's worth considering. It would be good for you."

"Do you think so?"

"Yes. Do you realise you haven't had a drink since we got here?"

He took her point. She never nagged him about it; she got rid of the empty bottles, and tried to motivate him to stay off it for at least three days a week. "I haven't even wanted one," he said. "That's your good influence."

"And this place."

"Yes . . . I've known worse. As a matter of fact I love it here."

"I know. Tell me something, Edward."

"Of course."

"Don't bite my head off for asking."

"I promise . . . I might bite something else."

"Do you think Saxon Court is right for you? You don't seem to get a minute's pleasure out of it, and most of the time it looks like a terrible strain."

To her relief, he nodded seriously and gave it some thought. "Yes, you're right," he said. "It hasn't been too good."

"What's it all about? Why do you do it?"

"Well, I've always liked horses, and there was my grandfather."

Angela knew nothing about James Henry. Edward told her the whole story. He began as they showered together, carried on while they were dressing, and kept going until they were drinking coffee after dinner. Angela's initial fear of boredom soon passed. Much of what she heard caused wide-eyed disbelief or gasps of admiration. Although she had no interest in what James Henry had set out to do, she was forced to admire the élan with which he had done it.

"So there you are," Edward said as they sauntered round the garden before returning to their suite. "I promised him I'd win the Derby."

"All right, Edward, I understand that, and why you did it. But is it possible? Can you simply go out and win the Derby?"

"No, and I never for a moment thought I could. You need the right horse, followed by several tons of the best luck in the world."

"Where do you find the right horse?"

"You don't. If it ever gets to be your turn, *he* finds you. I think I had him . . . I'm becoming convinced I did. But he was killed with Caro."

"And will you find another?"

He shrugged. "It's possible."

"Do you *really* believe that?"

"I have to, don't I?"

"You need to think about that. There's something else, too. You'll probably never be happy at Saxon Court because of Caroline. The place is littered with memories."

He stopped walking and looked out to sea. "What would we do if I packed it in?" he asked.

Angela clamped down on her excitement.

"You can afford to do nothing, can't you?" she asked casually.

"Oh yes. I gave that some *very* serious thought after Caro died."

"In that case, the only thing to do is decide *where* we do it."

Putting an arm round her in a gesture that Angela interpreted as at least partial acceptance of the idea, Edward led her back to bed.

Then, and in the perfect days that followed, he found it impossible to think objectively about Saxon Court. From the moment he had left it to pick up Angela, and drive to Gatwick Airport, it had seemed incredibly remote, unreal. Reality was here, in exquisite surroundings with an exciting, pleasure-loving friend.

What he could sometimes be objective about, was his enjoyment of Angela. At no time had he doubted the wealth of experience that had turned her into such an erotic virtuoso. Far from disapproving of her past, he found that he was thrilled by it. Now, when she introduced some alluring new trick, he would ask her how she had come to acquire it, listening avidly to her explanation. Time and time again, as she roused him to new feats, her body often glistening with sweat in the equatorial night, he added a little more to the masculine conceit that she had created in him.

For her part, Angela was well content. Edward was an entertaining and courteous companion, and was fast developing into her best-ever lover. He had started by being considerate but ordinary; now he was vividly enterprising, but still always thought of her. Whenever an opportunity presented itself, she followed a gentle line of conversation that assumed Edward would be leaving Saxon Court.

When they flew back to England, Angela had persuaded herself that there was no reason to doubt this assumption.

The only thing that prevented Angela moving into Saxon Court was her dislike of the place.

She had fallen into the habit of spending two or three nights a week there, but always felt a slight sense of relief when she left. There was nothing she could put her finger on to explain her antipathy. The house itself was very pleasant although she would have liked a more modern approach to décor and furnishings, and the complete collection of buildings would have looked very nice on a calendar or chocolate box. It was, of course, a closed, esoteric community. Angela was largely successful in having nothing to do with it, but when contact was inevitable, she always felt very much the outsider: and the house seemed far too steeped in the past for her taste. Angela's interests revolved around the present, and how it might shape the future. The vehicle for this was the

354

large bed in the master bedroom. That was her natural habitat where she was completely at ease.

Fred was happy to let her stay on at his place. He assumed that she and Edward would eventually decide to marry or live together, and until that happened, he was anxious not to do anything that might spoil things for Edward. Fred also had the feeling that when Angela left, Stephanie would follow her, and he wasn't ready for that yet. Apart from his fondness for Stephanie, he had it in mind to produce a new catalogue using *both* of them.

On the long flight home from the Seychelles, Edward began to adjust to what lay ahead. For two hours he felt desperately sad at leaving the Garden of Eden for God-knows-what in an English winter. Then he began to put the past few weeks behind him. Yes, it had been very nice. What was it they said about that sort of thing? Sun, sea, sand and sex. It *was* an attractive lifestyle, and perhaps one day . . .

Angela slept soundly all the way. When he woke her over the Channel, she was too drowsy and befuddled to notice the change in his attitude. All she wanted to do was get home and tell Stephanie about it.

If she had gone to Saxon Court, she would have seen that as soon as Edward arrived, he collected Declan, and went to the yard to see how the horses were. He did that before taking his luggage out of the car, or going into the house.

When the Duke of Dorchester paid one of his flying visits a week later, the first person he saw was Imogen.

"Egad, Imogen, you look a sight," he said, recoiling with shock.

The fact that she was well aware of it made her look of displeasure even more virulent. It would have stopped most men dead in their tracks.

"What's going on?" the Duke asked, sublimely unmoved.

"We have a crisis," she announced stiffly.

"I'm not surprised with you looking like that! I hope you're not going near the horses."

"Frozen pipes, Freddie, frozen pipes," Imogen explained through tightly clenched teeth.

"Right! Yes! All is made clear." A sudden thaw following several days of harsh frost had created chaos everywhere. Given an explanation for the bucket and mop that Imogen was carrying, the Duke felt a lot happier. "Where's the trouble?" he asked. "Not in HQ I hope?"

"No, it's in Mr Frost's house." Imogen's look declared that she was resigned to the inevitable.

"Oh, that's good! Freezer's frozen, what?" After an immoderate outburst of laughter, the Duke appeared to become serious. "Now look here, Imogen, I'm not going to say anything about those trousers, or that damned awful thing you've got round your head. But there is one question I'd like answered."

"Yes, Freddie?"

"Why are you wearing odd wellingtons?"

"They're not in the least odd!"

"What? One's green, and the other's black. I call that bloody odd, I don't mind telling you!"

"Tchah!" Imogen said, and marched towards Freezer's house with as much dignity as she could muster.

The Duke was still grinning broadly as he came into the office. "She's a corker when she's roused," he said to Edward. "Well, well, well! My goodness, look at that tan!"

"It's fading quite a lot now," Edward replied.

"Have a good time?"

"Marvellous, thanks."

"Did Miss Maitland enjoy it?" The Duke had a twinkle in his eye.

"Oh yes. It's a wonderful place."

"So I believe. Incidentally, I've been trying to wangle an invite to dinner for you two, but the memsahib's put the kibosh on it. She doesn't seem to like your friend."

Edward nodded understandingly. It had never occurred to him that Arabella, Duchess of Dorchester would be pleased by Angela. Although she had not met her, Imogen's briefing would have rendered the formality unnecessary.

"How's Lady Macbeth coping with the paperwork?" the Duke asked.

"Pretty well . . . mind you, things are very slack now. She won't be able to manage when we start racing. I'll need a proper replacement for Siobhan by then."

"Any joy in that direction?"

"No, but I haven't tried yet. I'm not looking forward to it."

"What about young Brookes-Smith? Is he any loss?"

"Yes. I hate to admit it, but he was quite useful."

"He was a sort of errand-boy, wasn't he?"

"That's what I took him on for. He turned into a very good yard manager."

"Are you going to get someone else?"

"I'd like to . . . well, actually, I've been giving it a bit of thought. I don't *need* anyone who's good with horses . . . I've got plenty of expertise in that department. What I could *really* do with is a chap to look after the business side of things, and make the right sort of noises on the racecourse. I've gone off that!"

The Duke sat down. "I wonder if I could help you," he said.

"Oh? What did you have in mind?"

"I'm looking for a billet for my boy Monty . . . he's the youngest. He's all right, but he turns into a complete pain in the arse when he's idle, and he's just 'become available' as they say."

"What's he been doing?"

"He's been up in Scotland, helping Gerald."

"Ah yes." Edward tried to recall what Imogen and Richard had told him about the Dorchesters. Gerald, Marquess of Saxmundham was the Duke's heir, and looked after his Scottish estates. Another son, Lionel, was in charge of the East Anglian farming interests.

"Didn't stay long," the Duke said airily. "About twelve months."

"Didn't he like it up there?"

The Duke looked mildly surprised, as though he had never considered the matter. "He did go on blind about the weather now I come to think about it. No, I fear that Monty's problem is the ladies. He's somewhat fond of them. As a matter of fact, he's permanently in rut!" The Duke of Dorchester was rather proud of his youngest son.

"I see." Edward smiled. "What was the problem, a shortage?"

"Oh no! Some damned handsome gals up there. No, you see the thing is, Monty started having it off with Percy."

"Percy?" Edward looked startled.

"Gerald's wife. The Marchioness. Persephone."

"Ah!" Edward was both enlightened and relieved. Without thinking, he said, "Ariadne Baverstock's dreadful daughter!"

The Duke roared with laughter. "That's Imogen," he said. "You can spot her style anywhere, can't you? She's quite wrong. Percy's all right. Don't know what she ever saw in Gerald. Between you and me, Manning, I have the impression that Gerald isn't one hundred per cent committed to the conjugal caper . . . don't get me wrong, he's basically sound. It's just that he lacks enthusiasm . . . Monty's quite the reverse, of course!"

"So Monty had to go?" Edward asked, managing to keep a fairly straight face.

"Absolutely. Gerald played merry hell. Never heard anything like it! Pity he can't rouse himself to other things."

"What was Monty doing before that?"

"Ah, now this is the bit you're going to like. When he left Oxford, he cleared off to America. We lost track of him for a while, then he turns up on a stud farm in Kentucky. He was there for five years. Ended up virtually running the show from what I can gather."

"Where was he?" Edward asked eagerly.

"Oh Lor' . . . I can never remember these funny names." The Duke scratched his head and frowned. Suddenly, his face lit up. "I know! The owner was called Colorado Hartigan."

"High Eaves!" Edward's voice rose in excitement. "Is that what the farm was called?"

"Yes, that's right, it was!"

"Good grief!" Edward gaped at the Duke. "I tell you what, Freddie, I wish I'd known about this before."

"Good stuff, is it?"

"It is! Why did Monty pack it in?"

"Had no choice as far as I can see. This chap Hartigan went and got himself killed in a road accident." Edward nodded: the tragedy was well-known in racehorse circles. "It seems he'd got no relatives . . . not an heir in sight. Next thing you know, there's lawyers and executors climbing all over the place, and Monty didn't think much of it. I say, Manning, 'Colorado' surely can't have been his real name – can it?"

"I have no idea, Freddie, and it doesn't much matter. Have you any idea what that place turned out?"

"No, 'fraid I haven't."

"The very, very best. High Eaves yearlings have won the Derby twice since I've been training – Harbinger was one." The Duke looked suitably impressed. "Last year's French Derby winner was High Eaves, and the year before that, they had the American Triple Crown winner. Now do you see?"

"Yes, by Jove! I thought Monty knew a thing or two. He can't muck the things out, or feed them, but I believe he knows a good one when he sees it. Might he be some use to you?"

Edward made an effort to remain calm. "Would you please ask him to get in touch with me," he said.

As the Duke left, Imogen and Rosie were entering the house vacated by Nigel to see if it had suffered frost damage. After listening to the Duke and Imogen trading insults, Edward went back to the office, and telephoned Nancy.

"What do you know about a chap called Monty de Vere Lawson-Grey?" he asked.

"Never heard of him," she replied. "Hell, you'd remember a name like that!"

"I've been told he used to be with Colorado Hartigan at High Eaves."

"Oh, *that* guy! He called himself Monty Dorchester."

"That's reasonable. He's the Duke of Dorchester's youngest son."

"No kidding!"

"Was he any good?"

"Supposed to be. They said he knew the business. How come you're asking?"

"He's looking for a job."

"With you?"

"If I want him."

"I guess he could be good if you use him right. He ran the business side of High Eaves."

"I'm going to talk to him. I'll let you know what happens."

Later that afternoon, when Mary came across to cook his supper, Edward decided that it was high time he spoke to her about Siobhan.

"Yes, it was a good do," she said in response to his opening question about the wedding. "She looked lovely."

"You must let me see some photographs," Edward said. "Did they have a nice honeymoon?"

"Great!" Mary came to life, and her eyes sparkled. "They had a wonderful time."

Edward decided to admit the full extent of his ignorance. "Er . . . where did they go?" he asked.

"Enniskeale Castle." He knew it was an ancient fortress in County Clare, part of which had been converted into a palatial hotel. "They had the traditional Christmas and New Year package."

"And they're settling in at Epsom?"

"Trying to. There's a lot needs doing. The kitchen's a disgrace."

"I must go and see them when they've had time to get it right. They won't want me snooping around while it's still a mess."

"Siobhan would like you to go," Mary said. Then, with a brave flourish, "Sure, he's not so bad! She'll put him straight."

It was both an admission and a confident hope.

Monty came to lunch three days later.

Lord Montague Albert de Vere Lawson-Grey, or Monty Dorchester as he liked to be known, was twenty-nine. There was Spanish blood in his mother's family, and it showed in Monty; with his dark hair which he wore long, and expressive eyes, there was something of the gipsy about him. He affected a languid approach to life, keeping his face in brooding repose, but when he was entertained or angered, emotion crackled from him. It was not difficult to appreciate what the bored Marchioness of Saxmundham – and many other women – saw in him.

Like his brothers Gerald and Lionel, Monty had been packed off to prep school, then Winchester. Unlike them, he had proved both willing to learn and intelligent, and had gone on to Oxford to take a First in Classics. Monty explained what had happened to him after Oxford.

"There was quite a bit of talk about me going to the Foreign Office," he said, making Edward smile. It sounded as though the Prime Minister had asked Monty to take the whole thing over and make a proper job of running it. "But I couldn't face being a civil servant – even in the fast stream with a silver spoon in my mouth. Her Grace, my mother, thought I should have a go at being Something in the City." He heaped mock-grandeur on the phrase, and smiled at the memory.

359

"But you went to America?" Edward prompted.

"Yes!" Monty became animated. "Have you ever been? Amazing place, quite *a-mazing*! I like it. I didn't make it to washing dishes in New York, but I got damned close."

"How on earth did you get involved with Colorado Hartigan?"

"Easy! I walked up to him on Churchill Downs one day, and offered to make myself available."

"What did he say to that?"

Monty chuckled fondly at the memory. "If I recall the incident correctly, I was told to take a running jump while stuffing myself," he replied. "However, I managed to prevail."

"How?"

"Quite simply . . . bear in mind this was 1980 – nearly seven years ago. A horse he'd bred had just won the Kentucky Derby. Old Colorado was looking pretty pleased with himself until I pointed out what the animal was worth *now*. He'd sold it for ten thousand dollars as a yearling. I said I could do better and he set me on. Six months later we put the first million-dollar yearling through the ring at Keeneland, and we never looked back."

Monty's account of the next five years wasn't quite as deadpan as he would have liked; the triumphs and failures, and his reactions to them stood out quite plainly. It was apparent that something close to a father –son relationship had sprung up between Hartigan, grandson of a penniless Irish immigrant, and the English aristocrat who had to earn his own living. Well over a year after Colorado's sudden death, Monty was still upset over the event, and bitter about its consequences.

"A bloody great lorry jack-knifed into his car." Pausing to think about it, Monty looked suddenly sad. "He was less than a mile from home," he said, and Edward saw a depth of affection that he sensed Monty Dorchester felt for very few people. It passed as quickly as it had come. "He had a sleeping partner in Chicago, and he thought he was going to get the whole estate because Colorado didn't have any relatives." Monty laughed mirthlessly. "Imagine thinking that an Irishman didn't have any relatives! There were no brothers or sisters, and he'd never married, but my God, you should have seen them crawling out of the woodwork! I was laying on coaches to bring them out from Lexington Airport. We even had one gang from *Tasmania*. And, of course, they brought their lawyers with them." The memory of it depressed and deflated him. "You won't have seen a pack of American lawyers in action?"

Edward shook his head.

"Lucky you! I was the only thing they agreed about. They made me public enemy number one. I lived in, you see, and it was assumed I was hanging around to grab anything that was going. I stuck it for a couple of weeks, then I walked out and left them to it."

360

"And they turned it into a terrible carve-up, didn't they?" Edward asked.

"Absolutely! And it's still going on. One of the best of the younger stallions went to New Zealand only last month. A fat lot of good he'll do there!"

"Then it was Scotland?"

"Yes." Monty laughed. "Not the brightest idea."

Edward thought quickly. "My only reservation about offering you a job, Monty, is that you seem too well qualified."

"Kind of you, but not true. I can spout the lingo like an expert, and I do know a good horse when I see one, but I hardly know the first thing about what you get up to."

"That wouldn't be necessary," Edward assured him.

"I'd like to pick up a bit of experience." Monty paused, clearly thinking hard. "Look, let me be frank with you, Edward. Ultimately, I've a fancy to be somebody's racing manager . . . one of those Sheikhs with horses all over the place. Ahmed al-Jabr is the sort of fellow I had in mind."

"I believe he's got over two hundred in training," Edward said.

"He has indeed. How would you feel about having me for, say, a couple of years before I have a go at getting a job like that?"

"That's fine. No problem there at all," Edward said, and they shook hands on it. "Do you want fixing up with somewhere to live?"

"There's no need for that, thanks. I've just picked up a nice flat in Newbury. Had to! Her Grace, my mother isn't keen on having me under the same roof as her good self."

"Start when you like," Edward told him. "There's no panic for a month yet."

"Fine. Father mentioned that you needed someone to run the office."

"Very much so! Imogen Stewart's doing a grand job as a stand-in, but I must have a good permanent secretary soon."

"Is it essential to have a person who knows about racing?" Monty asked.

"Not really. I want a first-class administrator. She'd soon pick up enough to be useful."

"I think I may be able to help you."

"Really?"

"Leave it with me."

Monty smiled happily. He knew that he had taken his first step into Edward's favour.

Edward was not in the least surprised to find that Imogen did not particularly like Monty. Whereas Mary, Rosie and Kathleen Corrigan were charmed senseless the minute Monty got to work on them, Imogen's disapproval was massive and tangible. Monty was as unconcerned as Edward, but for a different reason. He had seen it all before. Women like Imogen usually reacted in that way. It was unease, brought on by the disturbing feelings he produced in them. Those unable to handle the unexpected thrill of sexual desire tended to become hostile. It never occurred to Monty that there might be another reason for Imogen's hostility.

However, not even Imogen raised any objection when Monty produced Elaine Mayhew, and Edward was delighted.

Mrs Mayhew was, Edward judged, in her late thirties, a tall, elegantly attractive woman with sad eyes and a slight air of weariness about her. She was softly spoken and nervous, yet was totally frank about herself, and her need for a change of job. She had worked in the Duke of Dorchester's estate office for nearly ten years. Recently, the Duchess had started to take an active interest in things, and life had become much less pleasant. Following the retirement of the estate manager, an autocrat of dubious competence had been appointed as his successor. Mrs Mayhew and he clashed on his first day, and had been at daggers drawn ever since.

Work was a necessity for her. Her husband used to commute to London every day; two years ago, he had telephoned from his office to say that he would not be coming home again because of his involvement with an attractive young colleague. Elaine Mayhew had been able to buy a small cottage with what she had salvaged from the subsequent shambles. It was in a pretty village ten miles from Saxon Court, she had a small car, there were no children for her to worry about, and she seemed ideal.

After fifteen minutes of nervous social chit-chat, Edward offered her the job, and she accepted.

"I think you've probably been lucky there," Imogen said after Mrs Mayhew had left.

"She'll be very good," Edward declared confidently. "She'll never be up to Siobhan's standard, of course, but she'll do."

"Make sure you help her," Imogen said. "It's largely up to you to see that she makes a go of it."

When he was alone for the evening, Edward surveyed his prospects, and came to the conclusion that they were the best they had been for a long time. Monty Dorchester and Elaine Mayhew would take care of the administration, he would try to do something with the horses, and there was Angela to enjoy. In a mood of optimistic expansiveness, he started drinking.

For Angela, almost everything since the Seychelles had been a baffling disappointment.

362

Her wildest dream had been that Edward would be out of Saxon Court within the month; realism made her think of early spring as a likely target. She watched anxiously for the first signs that he was preparing for the move, each day an agony of suspense that brought her patience nearer and nearer to breaking point. The advent of Monty Dorchester and Elaine Mayhew came as a near-mortal blow to her hopes. For as long as Edward was worried sick about how he was going to run his business, Angela believed that the chances of him walking out were high. His new acquisitions seemed to be the answer to all his prayers and a death-knell to hers.

Adhering rigidly to her policy of avoiding Edward's professional life, Angela never saw Monty and Elaine, but she heard all about them. To her, the conclusions were obvious: Edward had no intention of leaving. When she finally tackled him about it, choosing her time carefully, she discovered that the state of his mind was far more complex than she had supposed.

"No, Angela, the fact is, I don't know what I want," he admitted.

"I thought you'd made your mind up when we were in Mahé. You seemed pretty sure about it."

"Maybe I was *then*. Things have changed since. I must give this place one more go. If this year's no better, I promise you I'll quit."

"All right, darling."

Her agreement was totally convincing because she had no alternative to Edward. If she were to abandon their relationship, Fred might throw her out of his house, she would lose what promised to be a good modelling opportunity, and be back where she had started. She told herself that she must hang on, but work hard exploring new openings.

As ever, confiding in Stephanie proved to be useful.

"Perhaps you've been pushing him too hard," Stephanie said.

"Could be." Angela shrugged, and smiled in a way that suggested mock-repentance. "You know what I'm like."

"I do indeed . . . and I'm sure Edward has been feeling the benefit! But it's like I told you, he's a funny bloke. I think he has difficulty making up his mind . . . with people, at any rate. I'm told he's marvellous with horses. If you try pushing him into things, it will only make him worse."

"That sounds about right. I think I have been a bit over-enthusiastic."

"Oh dear! You've done it again, haven't you, Angela?"

"Done what?"

"Gone off the deep end with all your eggs in one basket."

"Stephanie, how could you! That is a mixed metaphor,"Angela cried, echoing the horror of an oversensitive English mistress they had terrorised at school.

"Is it? Well it's no more than you deserve. Look, go easy on him. If necessary, go and tantalise someone else for a while."

"Who?"

"I don't know! Hang on, I might. It looks as though we're going to do that catalogue, so you're bound to get a chance."

"Has Fred made his mind up?"

"I think so. He was talking about it yesterday."

"Oh goodie!" Angela rubbed her hands with glee, and Stephanie smiled indulgently.

Fred confirmed this the following day, offering Angela over five thousand pounds for what was expected to be three, albeit quite taxing, days' work. Cheered by that, and the prospects it would offer, she settled down to curb her impatience with Edward.

She did not pester him again, and made a small effort to take an interest in what went on at Saxon Court. Having listened to Edward's eulogies of Elaine Mayhew based on how quickly she was learning, and how invaluable she was going to be, Angela made a point of meeting her. After only a minute with her, Angela decided that Elaine was riddled with hang-ups, was almost certainly a complete failure as a woman, and made herself comfortable in the office window-seat. While she waited for Edward to finish work for the day, she resigned herself to boredom as he reached for a ledger to explain something else to his eager new helper.

In fact, what she heard was so exciting that she found it extremely hard work pretending uninterest. Edward was going through the accounts for January. Still working part-time to ensure a smooth transition, Imogen had compiled the figures from bills she had sent out and payments made. Income for the month was a little under eighty thousand pounds.

"That's the standard figure," Edward told Elaine. "That's what we get for looking after a hundred horses. You'll find it goes much higher in the season when we have to start charging owners for racing fees and things like that. Now, over here . . ." he turned a page ". . . here's what we paid out."

"Good heavens! Nearly forty thousand pounds on wages," Elaine said.

"We're a big outfit," Edward replied. "There are over sixty people on the payroll. Then there's another twenty thousand pounds for various things . . . there, you see . . . we paid a big feed bill in January."

"That's an awful lot of hay!"

Edward laughed. "Most of what they eat is a good deal more exotic than that," he said. "Especially at this time of year. And it looks as though Imogen has set something aside for the heavy fuel bills we're expecting . . ."

Angela was staggered by the sums of money being bandied around by Edward. She had never bothered to try forming an estimate of the income the stable might yield. She knew that he had paid well over seven thousand pounds for the Seychelles holiday without turning a hair, and now she began to see how this was possible. It was, she decided, most definitely worth being nice to Edward for the time being.

Nothing went wrong with this idea until the end of February.

Angela arrived at Saxon Court on a Friday afternoon for what she intended turning into a very special occasion. Declan was heading towards his house as she got out of the car she had borrowed from Stephanie. Their eyes met. Declan wondered whether he ought to touch his cap. They had never been introduced, but perhaps it was time to accept the inevitable. Then he saw the small suitcase she was carrying, and turned away to conceal his contempt. When Edward had first arrived from Avoca House, he had used Declan and Mary's spare bedroom rather than spend a night in the Big House with Miss Brookes-Smith before they were married. Now this woman, who didn't seem to give a damn about what the place stood for, came and went as she pleased.

Some of Declan's feelings transmitted themselves to Angela, and she felt a tremor of unease. "Sod him!" she thought furiously. "I'll show the lot of them!"

It was nearly eleven o'clock when she and Edward returned after dinner in Reading. An hour later, as they prepared for a second session of love-making, the bedside telephone shrilled.

Edward was exasperated as he snatched at the receiver, but his mood soon changed.

"Edward, it's Nancy. Sorry to bother you at this hour, but you asked me to let you know when Rhinemaiden was ready to foal."

"Is she?"

"Yup! Any time now."

"Does it look all right?"

"Sure. No problems at all."

There was a pause as Edward thought about it. "All the same, I think I'll come over."

"Better be quick."

"I will."

"This mare's not going to hang around."

"I'm on my way!"

As Edward jumped out of bed and made for his clothes, Angela protested. "Hey! Where are you going?"

"Widney Cheyne. Rhinemaiden's about to foal."

"Who the hell's Rhinemaiden?" Angela demanded.

Her tone jarred on him, and for the first time, she was on the receiving end of one of his blighting looks. It was unpleasant. "She's a very special lady," he said coldly. "A very special lady indeed."

Angela looked at the bedside clock. It had turned midnight. "But it's your birthday, Edward," she said, trying to redeem the situation.

He smiled happily. "Yes, quite a coincidence, isn't it? Worry not, my dear. I shall return for my present." He kissed her perfunctorily. "Go to sleep. I shan't be all that long."

It was mid-morning when he got back. Rhinemaiden had become perverse at the last moment, and delayed the production of her foal for eight hours beyond the time forecast by Nancy. Edward had not bothered to telephone Angela, and she had left, annoyed and frustrated.

Ironically, the woman she had written off as a failure enjoyed a much more satisfying night. At about the time Edward arrived at Widney Cheyne, Monty Dorchester left Elaine Mayhew's cottage. As he tested the iciness of the lane, he reflected that she wasn't up to his normal standard, but she did her best, and was very grateful for his efforts.

She would do until something better turned up.

CHAPTER 16

The photographs for Fred's new catalogue were taken during the first week in April.

Fred was launching an enhanced collection of lingerie and introducing a new range of swimwear designed to be more suitable for the bedroom than the beach. Sales were projected at over four million pounds in the first year, and a substantial budget had been allocated to the catalogue. The location selected was a new luxury hotel in Brighton where a 'Regency' master suite and the indoor swimming pool provided ideal photographic backdrops.

Angela, Stephanie and Fred arrived at the hotel on Sunday evening so that the girls could relax, and become accustomed to the atmosphere. When shooting started on Tuesday morning, Angela realised that her fee was going to cost three days of extremely hard work, especially since they had to use the pool before six-thirty in the morning to avoid the pre-breakfast swim of the more energetic guests.

But the hopes of diversion that Stephanie had promised were stillborn; the men involved were a great disappointment. The only one that Angela considered a potentially worthy bedmate was the director of the public relations firm who were supposedly masterminding the project. Unfortunately, after a brief appearance on Tuesday morning, he hurtled off to London, never to be seen again. The photographer, already quite famous, and supposedly destined for great things, was pleasant enough, but fiercely dedicated to his work.

With faultless intuitive skill, Fred himself organised the sessions, deciding what each girl wore, and how they should be posed. This time, the catalogue was to be sixty-four pages, and he was looking for a hundred pictures. As soon as he saw the first proofs, he knew that there were no problems. Anything with dramatic colour, such as crimson, black, emerald green or electric blue was worn by Angela, who had taken it into her head to entertain herself by playing up to the wretched assistant. Fred chuckled over most of the pictures; her blatant pelvis-thrusting, and smouldering stares were precisely what he wanted. Alongside her, Stephanie in white or soft pastels looked positively vestal.

Angela felt torn between elation and depression when it was all over, and she had caught up on her sleep. At the end, the photographer had taken her on one side to tell her that she was very good, and that he felt

367

sure he would be asking for her again before long. Belatedly discovering that he was a very shy man, Angela was touched. Exhausting though it had been, she had enjoyed showing herself off, and Fred had paid her in cash. But she also felt empty and lonely. It was ten days since she had seen Edward.

To remedy this, she got up earlier than usual on Saturday morning, and drove to Saxon Court. Confident that Edward would share her desire for a pleasant day, she did not bother letting him know that she was coming. In the highest of spirits, she walked jauntily into the biggest breakfast meeting since the days of Caroline.

For the past two weeks, the horses had been working hard, and a number of them were showing exceptional condition. Determined to make the best of this good fortune by capturing a few early-season prizes, Edward had organised several final pre-race gallops that morning. When Angela entered the kitchen, there were ten people sitting round the table. Four of them were strangers to her.

As well as Edward and Declan, Richard, and Mark and Sarah Walgrave had come to watch their horses. A worried-looking Elaine Mayhew was doing her best to keep up with the conversation. Those that Angela did not know or recognise were Sean Gillespie, John Dyer, Robin Lane, recently promoted to the new post of chief ride-worker, and sitting close to Edward, Nancy Bloomfield. Monty Dorchester and Freezer had gone to Thirsk the previous afternoon for an overnight stay with two horses.

Conversation did not stop instantly; it was a second or two before everyone except Edward was aware of the poisonous look that Nancy was receiving. Who, Angela wondered, was this wholesomely good-looking woman to whom Edward had been talking with such animation?

Edward looked mildly surprised, too preoccupied to register stronger emotion.

"Angela ... how nice!" he said. "Come and sit down. Have some breakfast. You've got some more of that bacon, haven't you, Rosie?"

"Oh yes, sir."

Squeezing in between Edward and Richard, Angela flashed a quick look at Rosie. It came as a shock to discover that Edward's staff called him 'sir'.

"I won't have anything to eat, thank you," she said hurriedly. "Just coffee, please."

"Now, who don't you know?" Edward asked. "This is Nancy Bloomfield from the stud at Widney Cheyne. That miserable-looking devil is Sean Gillespie, our number one jockey, and that's John Dyer who's about to go to Thirsk to ride a couple this afternoon ...

368

oh, and Robin Lane who's doing all the important ride-work these days."

Angela nodded to each of them in turn, noticing that Robin Lane and John Dyer were in awe of her, Sean Gillespie looked as if he didn't give a damn, while Nancy's face displayed open friendliness. Angela felt uncomfortable as they all studied her. She had no idea what she had walked into, and wished to hell she hadn't.

To her intense relief, the moment passed. Richard asked a question about a horse, and the arcane jargon began to fly. Angela sipped awkwardly at the huge mug of coffee that Rosie had placed in front of her, and tried to appear interested in what was being said.

"That's all right, Richard, don't worry. We haven't let her down yet this year."

"She's still got a bit to learn, sir," Robin Lane chipped in. "She only had that one race last year, and she ran very green. What we need to do is . . ."

While Robin explained a point to Richard, Edward turned to Mark Walgrave to tell him about one of his horses. "Yes, next Thursday at Newmarket. He'll have his two-furlong pipe-opener on Wednesday, and I think he'll be all right this time."

"Who's riding him?"

"Whoever you want."

"He went well for John at Salisbury last back end."

"OK. Let's try that again."

Edward nodded at Elaine, who wrote something down. Angela had the impression that it was most likely meaningless; the poor woman had no more idea than herself what was going on.

But suddenly, the conversation stopped, chairs were pushed back, and everyone was moving. Edward smiled at the puzzled look on Angela's face.

"Time for the second lot," he said. "Come and watch. You'll be fine in the Land Rover with Mark and Sarah."

"What's the second lot?"

He stared at her in disbelief. Angela saw what he was thinking, and her insides cringed.

"The second lot of *horses*," he said. "We're taking them out on to the Down for exercise and work."

"No. I'll give that a miss, if you don't mind. How about this afternoon?"

They were moving towards the door, Edward impatient to be away. "Fine!" he said. "If you get here about one o'clock you can come with us."

"What on earth are you talking about, Edward?"

"Newbury. We're going to Newbury. I wouldn't bother as a rule, but

369

with Monty and Freezer up at Thirsk, Alison and I will have to do our share."

"It's racing, is it?"

"Yes, of course." There was a suggestion of long-suffering patience in his voice.

Angela's temper flared at the suspicion that she was being treated like an idiot.

"No, Edward, I do not want to go to the bloody races," she said, keeping her voice discreetly low, despite her anger. "I rather fancied spending the afternoon in bed with you. Give me a ring if you ever have any time to spare!"

Astonished, Edward turned towards the yard without bothering to watch her dramatic departure.

Although he succeeded in concealing it, Dooley was ill at ease on his first trip with Monty Dorchester. Freezer, who had dealt with all sorts during his career, was quite comfortable with the son of a Duke, and Dooley envied him for it. Hoping for the best, Dooley stuck to his natural gnomic obscurantism, and found that they got along without any difficulty.

About half-way to Thirsk, they stopped at a transport café where Dooley became very impressed by Monty. The way he dealt with a pair of queue-jumping lorry drivers, each about twice his size, won widespread admiration. The men were notoriously disruptive, but by the time Monty had finished with them, all they wanted to do was sit quietly in a corner, nursing the uneasy feeling that they had been made to look very foolish.

Then, towards the end of their break, Monty offered to drive the rest of the way.

"It's perfectly all right, Paddy," he said reassuringly. "I'm qualified for big stuff." He produced his driving licence to prove it.

Dooley agreed. His enthusiasm for long trips was waning.

"I drove bloody great lorry loads of trees in Scotland," Monty said, by way of explanation. "I had to do something to relieve the boredom."

Without having the faintest idea what Monty was talking about, Dooley looked as though this was the most reasonable idea he'd heard for a long time.

The two horses they had taken were The Godfather belonging to Fred Bird, and Valerie Malahide's filly Gadfly. Both were three-year-olds with nothing to their credit so far. When he looked them over in the racecourse stables, Monty decided that Fred's horse was not yet ready to improve on his record.

Freezer agreed. "He needs the race, sir," he said. "The guv'nor thought this would be an easy one for him."

"Not very distinguished company?"

"No, sir."

"But that filly looks a very different kettle of fish."

"Nice, isn't she, sir?"

"Yes. There's a touch of the real stuff there. Is she ready to win?"

"I believe the guv'nor thinks so, sir."

"What do *you* think, Freezer?"

"I'd say she'll do it. There isn't all that much for her to beat."

Monty nodded, giving no indication of what was passing through his mind.

The Godfather raced first, and finished well down the field. Sean Gillespie, perfectly prepared to accept Monty as Edward's representative, reported that he had given the colt a taste of pressure over the last two furlongs, and he would be better for it.

While Gadfly was being led round the paddock before her race, Monty made a careful study of the other horses. Although he feigned bored indifference, Freezer saw the hard, calculating intensity in his eyes, and felt apprehensive. He had no idea what Monty was trying to do, but he was certain of one thing: there was much more to it than a simple, professional assessment of the runners. Obviously decided upon something, Monty turned sharply to stride off towards Tattersalls', merging with the crowd.

Passing swiftly down the line of bookmakers, he saw that there was reasonable business for Gadfly at six to one, the odds taken by Dooley ten minutes previously for his modest twenty-pound flutter. As soon as Monty's stake of two thousand pounds had been accepted, the tremors started running up and down the line, and when the race began, Gadfly was joint-favourite at five to two.

If Edward had paid proper attention to Gadfly's two-year-old career, she might well have been a prospect for the One Thousand Guineas. As it was, like so many of Saxon Court's young horses in recent years, she had come to hand late, and learned next to nothing about racing as a juvenile. Today, she gave a convincing display of what might have been possible. Half-way through the mile race, she was cruising effortlessly on the bit, three lengths behind the leaders who were making hard work of it. When Sean Gillespie let her go, a smile of satisfaction flitted briefly across Monty's face.

He took part in the formalities connected with Gadfly's effortless victory before collecting his winnings. He locked himself in a toilet cubicle to distribute the twelve thousand pounds plus his original two thousand around several pockets, including two special ones inside the lining of his mackintosh.

When he paid it in to his bank in Newbury, he gave instructions that it was to be transferred immediately to another bank in Switzerland.

Fifteen minutes after Gadfly won the three-fifteen race at Thirsk, one of Mark Walgrave's horses was first past the post at Newbury. Nancy brought Edward the news about Gadfly while the three-thirty at Newbury was in progress. He was sufficiently affected by it to confide in her.

"I hope this is a sign of good luck," he said. "I really need to do better this year. It's been pretty awful, you know . . . very worrying."

Nancy looked sympathetic, forbearing to point out that if he applied himself more conscientiously to his job, the luck would have a far better chance of materialising. Encouraged by Imogen to do so, she intended going to Saxon Court whenever possible to watch the horses at work. Something good might come of it.

She had first done it three days ago, arriving unexpectedly, yet reasonably sure of a warm welcome in view of Edward's more consistent attitude towards her over the past months. He was indeed glad to see her, and they spent a long time studying and talking about Frescobaldi. Edward was becoming more convinced by the day that he was a good horse, and that something could be done with him. Alison Bairstow and Robin Lane had already discovered that, as in the old days, Edward was open to any suggestion, especially the far-fetched ones.

After her first visit, Nancy went back to Widney Cheyne for lunch without making further arrangements: there seemed to be no need for them. The second time, she triggered Angela's anger, and accompanied Edward to the races.

"Shall I see you on Monday?" he asked as they prepared to go their separate ways at the end of the afternoon.

"No, I can't make it Monday." It was a small lie which achieved its hoped-for result. She was pleased to see that he looked disappointed. "Tuesday's OK, though."

That evening, as the elation of the day's successes began to ebb, Edward telephoned Angela. She made no secret of her joy at his call. Fred and Stephanie had gone to Paris for the weekend, leaving a lonely void in which the suspicion that she had behaved badly and over-reacted that morning flourished demoralisingly. Edward was soon driving towards Goring with fierce urgency. Within minutes of his arrival, they were engaged in love-making that had an element of savagery about it. Afterwards, they left the sitting-room where the first encounter had been played out on the floor, and went up to Angela's bedroom.

When Edward left on Sunday morning, he was astonished by how little food and sleep they had needed. For reasons that he came close to understanding, Angela's time in Brighton had given her an enormous sexual appetite, the quenching of which left him exhausted but ludicrously proud.

On Tuesday morning, Nancy arrived ready to work, not merely to pass helpful comments. When the second lot went out, she rode Frescobaldi for the first time.

By the end of April, Edward knew that he could postpone it no longer. He would have to visit Siobhan and Nigel at Epsom. His chagrin over what he now saw as the silly business of Victor Macleod's horses had evaporated, and he was keen to find out how they were getting on, and whether there was anything he could do to help. The only thing that worried him was Declan's attitude. He had spent several days helping his son-in-law, and the experience had left him grimly tight-lipped. Something was wrong.

Imogen, still keeping an eye on Elaine Mayhew and the office, had noticed something else. Siobhan visited her mother once a week. She had tended to come to Saxon Court at times when the place was deserted, times with which she would be very familiar. If she saw Imogen, she waved, then hurried on, removing any chance of conversation. After Siobhan's appearances, even Mary was tense and uncommunicative.

"Something's up," Imogen told Edward, "and I want to know what it is."

"I've been getting that feeling, too," Edward agreed. "I'm going to see them soon."

"Good! Take me with you. I can talk to Siobhan while you find out what Nigel's up to."

"Fair enough. I'll ring Siobhan and fix something."

"No! Don't do that." Imogen paused briefly to think. "Let's just go. I know it sounds awful, but catching them on the hop may be the best way of finding out what's going on."

"Are you sure?" Edward asked, looking unhappy.

"No, I'm not. It's what we're going to do, though."

They went a few days later.

Nigel's place was at the end of a deeply rutted lane, on the edge of the Downs with easy access to the public gallops. It consisted of a vast barn of a house in which Siobhan and Nigel must have been completely lost, with the yard, made up of wooden boxes, behind it. While Imogen and Edward were still sitting in the car, gazing in dismay at the house, Siobhan appeared at the front door. She had a paintbrush in one hand, and a saucepan in the other. Dropping both, she hurried to Imogen's side of the car.

373

"Oh dear! This is a nice surprise," she said. "Very nice! We're in a terrible mess. Not quite straight yet."

"Worry not, my dear," Imogen said. "We just happened to be passing, and we thought it was high time we came and saw you."

"Yes. That's nice. Come in, come in."

Siobhan often seemed flustered, so Edward attached no importance to that. What *was* worrying, was the sense of tension underneath it all, and the lines on her face. He noticed the jerky anxiety in her walk as she led them into the house.

"Watch out for the paint! The last lot took ages to dry."

The smell made the warning superfluous. They passed along a dingy, high-ceilinged passageway where paper was peeling off the walls into a kitchen-cum-dining-room that was a haven of light and spacious comfort.

"My word, you have been busy!" Imogen said, taking it all in. Much was obviously new: redecoration had not yet concealed the scars of installing a double sink, a washing-machine and solid-fuel stove. New window frames awaited the first coat of paint, and the plaster on the walls was still drying out; there were cupboards to be fixed in position.

"This is going to look marvellous before too long," Edward said. "As soon as you get some paint on this, you'll have a palace."

Looking a little easier, Siobhan moved towards the kettle simmering on the stove, just as it always had done at Avoca House. "You'll have some tea?" she said.

"Of course!" Edward grinned, rubbing his hands in anticipation. Imogen was aware of his resolve to be friendly and helpful. "And how is everything? How's it going with the horses?"

"Not bad. We're nearly full up. There are only two empty boxes now. Mr Stedding has been very helpful."

"Yes, he would be," Edward said. "He's a funny old stick, but everyone says he's got a heart of gold." He looked out of one of the windows at the yard, an L-shaped arrangement of boxes, only one arm of which was fully visible.

"There used to be ten more boxes," Siobhan said. "They fell down two years ago. Mr Sparshott didn't bother doing anything about it." She made it sound like an apology.

"Make sure that none of the others go the same way," Edward urged. "You've only to ask if you need help. Give me the word and I'll have a dozen lads here before you can say Jack Robinson. What you need is . . ."

Imogen was horrified when she saw what had seized Edward's attention. Nigel had emerged from a shed that served as both tack room and feed store; his companion was Terry Dawson.

"Edward!" she cried, urgency making her voice harsh. It was too late. He had wrenched the door open, and was moving across the yard with dreadful purpose.

Nigel and Dawson stopped in their tracks when they saw him. Dawson's initial look of surprise gave way to hatred and fear.

"What the bloody hell is he doing here?" Edward demanded of Nigel, pointing at Dawson as though he were a distasteful inanimate object.

When he thought about it afterwards, Edward realised how weak Nigel had been. He would have been fully entitled to retaliate with a similar question. Instead, he looked positively guilty.

"He's working for me," he said. "He's my head lad."

Edward refused to believe him. He stood glaring at him, until it finally sank in.

"Nigel, you are out of your mind," he said. "You know the rules as well as I do. Or do you? Have you bothered to find out?"

"What rules?" Nigel was developing a blustering truculence.

"All your staff have to be registered with the Jockey Club, and you cannot hire without a reference from the previous employer. Do you know that, Nigel?"

Dawson did, and made himself scarce with accomplished shiftiness.

"He *is* registered," Nigel said. "I checked."

"Yes!" Edward retorted bitterly. "And you know why, don't you? I was too idle to let them know what had happened."

"Victor Macleod more or less insisted I use him," Nigel said miserably.

"Macleod! What right has he got to insist on *anything*?" Edward roared. "Damn it, man, he doesn't own the place, does he?"

"Well, yes, he does . . . more or less," Nigel admitted. "He's done some sort of deal with Sparshott."

"What sort of deal?"

"I don't know. I think he's taken a half share in it . . . Sparshott needed the capital."

Edward gave him a look of scathing mock-pity. "If I were you, Nigel, I'd find out what was going on," he said. "But, for God's sake, Dawson! You've actually got the horse he abused, haven't you?" Nigel nodded. "What the hell are you using for principles?"

"I can't afford principles," Nigel shouted. "We're not all as lucky as you! We can't all walk into one of the best stables in England!"

Edward was suddenly staring into a pit of rancour whose existence he had never suspected. Nigel was convinced that Saxon Court should have been his.

"I wanted to help you," Edward said quietly. "But you get nothing from me until you've sorted this mess out."

Turning on his heel, he headed towards the side of the house. For a few dreadful moments, Imogen thought he was going without a word to

Siobhan. At the very last minute, Edward saw her, stopped, and hurried over to her. He spoke with great intensity. Imogen did not hear what he said, she only saw a wretched-looking Siobhan try to cheer up, nodding her head repeatedly.

Edward went over to Mary and Declan as soon as he got back to Saxon Court.

"I've been to see Siobhan," he told them.

"And Nigel?" Mary asked.

"Yes, I spoke to him."

"So you know?" Declan asked.

"About Dawson? Yes."

"What do you think?" Mary wanted to know.

"I think it's appalling," Edward said. "I told him so, of course. Do you know anything about this business of Macleod taking a share in the place?"

"No, sor." Declan shook his head dejectedly.

"Is it very bad?" Now that it was out in the open, Mary could show her true feelings. She looked worried sick.

"It isn't good, Mary," Edward told her. "If Nigel gets a grip on himself, it could turn out all right. I don't like the look of the place, but that doesn't stop it being a success if it's run properly."

"What about Terry Dawson?"

"*That* is bad. Nigel could lose his licence over that. I've told him what's right, the rest is up to him. I'm not going to do anything about it."

Declan looked infinitely grateful.

"But look here . . ." Edward gave them both a stern look ". . . make sure you keep me informed. I know Siobhan comes to see you, Mary. If things get very bad, we might have to act to protect her. Do you understand that?"

They nodded unhappily.

Throughout May, Edward worked hard, enjoyed Angela and drank nothing. During the month, ten winners went out. Nine of them were looked after by Monty Dorchester and Freezer. Twice, Monty's behaviour made Freezer uncomfortable, as it had at Thirsk. At Bath and Newmarket, Monty relieved the bookmakers of very substantial sums of money with big bets at generous odds.

The tenth winner gave Edward a great deal of satisfaction.

Ridden at exercise by Nancy, Frescobaldi had become a reformed character. His objection to starting stalls vanished, and when asked to exert himself, he did so with genuine vigour. No one was more pleased than Declan.

"Miss Bloomfield has a way with her," he said approvingly.

"Yes, isn't she good?" Edward was brimming with enthusiasm. "Fancy not knowing she could ride like that!"

"Reminds me of Finoula," Declan said.

The acid test came when it was time for Robin Lane to give Frescobaldi a final stiff piece of work in preparation for a race. Would he behave well for Robin, or was it only Nancy who could make him act sensibly? The night before, Edward lay awake worrying about it, but the following morning, all his misgivings were swept aside. Frescobaldi had learned.

"He's starting to look fairly useful," Edward said to Nancy as they watched him dispose of his four galloping companions with ease. "You've done wonders with him."

"No, I haven't. It's just the way the cookie crumbles. He's probably grown up a lot . . . they sometimes do between three and four. And remember, every horse teaches."

"All right. What have we learned from this one?"

She laughed. "Hanged if I know, but there's got to be a lesson in there somewhere."

Five days later, Frescobaldi won a five-thousand-pound race at Newbury, leaving the rest of the field completely outclassed. Dooley got odds of twelve to one about him, and allowed himself to look as pleased as Edward.

"Well, there you go," Nancy said a little sadly. "I've done something useful."

"What do you mean, *done*?" Edward asked. "You don't think you've finished with him, do you?"

"There's nothing I can do for him now . . . whatever it was!"

"Oh yes, there is. Look, Nancy, I've got plans for that fellow. This is only the start. I *need* you to keep working with him so that he stays right. Can you come over at least two mornings a week?"

"What are you planning for him next?"

Edward looked round conspiratorially. "Royal Ascot . . . the Hardwicke Stakes."

Nancy whistled.

"Will you keep working with him?"

"Sure. Make it first lot, though. That way I can be back at Widney Cheyne in time to do some work for Richard."

There was another element in the strengthening friendship between Nancy and Edward. Quietly, without any obvious display of emotion, Edward had fallen head-over-heels in love with Rhinemaiden's foal, a chestnut colt, who, at three months, gave every promise of growing into a very handsome horse.

On the Sunday afternoon following Frescobaldi's win, Imogen and Richard were out for a stroll with their sons when they found Edward and Nancy looking at the foal. Nancy was leaning on the fence, Edward was sitting inside the paddock, playing with Rhinemaiden's baby while she munched grass contentedly, hardly bothering to keep an eye on them. His attention caught by the sound of Imogen's camera, Edward got up and walked to the fence, the foal trotting at his side.

"Ah!" Richard assumed an attitude of sickly, mock-sentimentality, then felt guilty at the embarrassment that momentarily overcame Edward. He was surprisingly sensitive to leg-pulling on the subject of the extraordinary relationship that had sprung up between him and the foal.

"Having a love-in?" Imogen asked.

"I think he's smashing," Edward said, simply, like a boy with his first puppy.

"Actually, I'm not all that struck by him," Richard said.

"What on earth do you mean?" Edward was suddenly almost aggressive.

"Well, he's a chestnut, isn't he? They rarely amount to much."

"Where did you get that rubbish from?"

"Oh . . . nowhere in particular. It tends to be the received wisdom, doesn't it?"

"Hyperion was a chestnut," Edward reminded him.

"Yes indeed . . . you always get the odd exception."

"Hey, steady on there, Richard," Nancy said. "Hyperion was one heck of an exception!"

"Then there are the markings," Richard went on, apparently ignoring her. "White socks mean weak legs – and this little chap's got four of the wretched things, and the blaze often denotes lack of courage." The foal had a prominent white stripe down his face from forehead to muzzle; it would be a striking feature once he was fully grown.

"What absolute bunkum!" Edward scoffed, unconsciously using one of his grandfather's favourite expressions of disapproval. "Sea Bird and The Minstrel were chestnuts with socks and blazes. There was nothing wrong with their legs, and you can't say they were short of courage!"

"Oh!" Richard seemed surprised. "Well, I take the point, of course, Edward, but I still have reservations. I've been wondering if I ought to sell him."

"If you insist on being that daft, will you give me first refusal?" Edward asked.

"Yes, if you like. Do you think he's *that* good?"

"I haven't the faintest idea," Edward replied. "But one thing I am sure of . . . he'll be a beautiful horse to train."

Richard nodded. "Right, I'll bear that in mind," he said. "Now there's the one I fancy."

He pointed to the adjoining paddock where Musetta and her T. P. Malahide foal were eyeing them with great interest. Musetta had foaled ten days after Rhinemaiden, and the bay colt she had produced seemed to be Richard's favourite.

"Yes, he's not bad," Edward said, still fondling the ears and neck of *his* foal.

"He's going to be called Cavaradossi," Richard said.

"That's a chap in *Tosca*," Imogen explained to Nancy. "Decent enough fellow, I understand, but he went and got himself shot in rather silly circumstances."

"I imagine you'll be able to do something with him, Edward?" Richard asked.

"I wouldn't be a bit surprised. Let me know about this one, won't you?"

"Yes, I will." Richard sounded indifferent, and Edward went away far from satisfied.

Having spotted Nancy's concern, Imogen had a quiet word with her.

"Don't worry about that chestnut," she said. "I'm pretty sure Richard doesn't mean what he says. He's playing games."

"What for?" Nancy asked.

"No idea! Whatever he's doing, he's certainly got Edward worked up. That's an achievement!"

Still doubtful, Nancy nodded.

"Tell me," Imogen said as they began to walk towards Nancy's cottage, "how are you getting on at Saxon Court?"

"Fine!"

"You seem to have done a good job with that Frescobaldi."

Nancy laughed. "That was sheer luck," she replied. "I think he was ready to start behaving himself, and Robin Lane had done a lot with him. Edward seems to think I worked some sort of miracle."

"Does he, now? I take it that means you're getting on well?"

"Sure. No problems."

"Do you see much of La Maitland?"

"No. I don't think she's there during the week."

"But they're still at it?"

"I imagine so."

Imogen decided to say no more.

For the first time in four years, Royal Ascot offered the promise of success and enjoyment. Edward declared five horses to run, and had every confidence that they would yield additions to his healthy tally of winners.

On the Monday before the first day, Richard gave a dinner party at Widney Cheyne. To Edward's astonishment, Imogen had asked him to bring Angela, but he did not bother to relay the invitation. Horses were bound to be the major topic of conversation, and he was no longer prepared to tolerate her hostile boredom.

There were twelve round the dinner table, the women in long dresses, the men in dinner-jackets, and Imogen surveyed the gathering pleasurably. Fred Bird looked presentable, despite the indefinable aura of the spiv, and Imogen had decided that Stephanie was 'all right'. Monty Dorchester, very elegant and as sexually predatory as ever, showed restraint in the presence of his father, and Mark and Sarah Walgrave bubbled with their usual good humour. Over cocktails before the meal, their gaiety had affected even Edwin Fforbes who was taking a week's holiday for the Royal meeting.

Edward was late arriving. One of the lads had been kicked by a horse that morning, and he was spending a couple of days in hospital for observation. The fact that Edward had been to visit him, and insisted on telling everyone that there was no cause for concern, was carefully noted by Imogen. It looked much more like the Edward of old.

As they ate, Edward chatted to Valerie Malahide who was seated next to him. She had flown over from Dublin that morning, and was staying at Widney Cheyne for the week. While Edward was listening to news of her musical activities, he was distracted and amused by Fred, sitting opposite them. Valerie looked wonderful: for her, it seemed life really had begun at forty. There was a vital bloom on her that took at least ten years off her age. Meeting her for the first time that evening, Fred had immediately assumed a slightly dazed, awestruck expression, much as when he had caught his first glimpse of Saxon Court. Fred struggled *not* to look at Valerie, and his largely unsuccessful efforts diverted Edward.

No serious topic of conversation to involve the whole group cropped up until they were drinking coffee in the drawing room afterwards, and it was Fred who set it off.

"I've been thinking it's about time I got myself a really good horse," he said. "Something with *quality*."

Edward's heart leaped into his mouth as he imagined Richard offering Rhinemaiden's foal to Fred. His relief at Richard's reply was visible.

"I had much the same idea myself. The stud's coming along very nicely, but I'd like some new blood."

"Me too," the Duke of Dorchester said. "I know you fancy your chances with Frescobaldi, Manning, but it's time I started thinking about finding you another problem. Can't have you getting complacent!"

"What sort of animal are you talking about?" Edward asked.

"A Derby winner!" the Duke and Fred said in unison.

Edward laughed. "Get me half a dozen while you're about it! Where do you propose going to find him?"

"No idea, son," Fred said. "That's for you to tell us."

"There is only one place," Richard said.

"Where's that?" Fred asked.

"Keeneland . . . Kentucky. They've usually got some pretty good stock there, and my spies tell me that this year's crop of yearlings is likely to be above average."

"Are you thinking of going to Elmer Drury's?" Edward asked.

"No point. All his stuff goes through the ring these days. In any case, I'm told he hasn't got much this time. We'd have to go and bid alongside the world and his brother."

A feeling close to fear began to envelop Edward. Richard saw his discomfort and looked at him questioningly.

"I don't want to go over," Edward muttered. "I couldn't face it."

For a moment, Richard's face was blank, then he nodded sympathetically. "Yes, of course," he said quietly, realising that for Edward, Kentucky meant Caroline, and the first discovery of their happiness.

"When is the sale?" Fred asked.

"They're on more or less all the time from October through to Christmas," Richard replied. "But the best time is early November."

"How long would you want to stay?"

"At least a week. It takes a few days to find your way around and pick up the grapevine."

"That's no good to me," Fred said. "November's a busy time – boosting sales for Christmas. That's when I do forty per cent of my business. I couldn't be away for a week . . . longer, I suppose, if you count the time there and back."

"You and Nancy could do it, Richard," Edward suggested. "With her judgement and your luck you should be able to find two or three good ones."

Richard was considering this when Edwin Fforbes cleared his throat anxiously. Edwin was consulting a pocket diary. "You've asked for the whole of November to be kept free, Richard," he pointed out. "We have to think about Wilcox and Dempster, and Koestlers."

"Damn! Thank you, Edwin, I'd forgotten." Richard was both irritated and grateful to be reminded of two important pieces of potential business for Stewart's that were expected to become available for tender in November. "That's that, then! It was a nice idea."

"Hey! Wait a minute, Richard," the Duke of Dorchester said. "Just remember we've got an expert here before you write the idea off."

All eyes turned to Monty, to whom the Duke was pointing.

Monty was sitting slightly outside the circle. He had been still and undemonstrative, following the conversation attentively. The men had virtually ignored him, but all the women except Imogen were very aware of him. Valerie Malahide was amused: perfectly used to being stripped naked by men's minds and eyes, she placed Monty in a class of his own for conveying ruthlessly potent intent. Sarah Walgrave's feelings were rather different. Half-afraid of Monty, she nevertheless saw circumstances in which she would surrender to a few hours of what he had in mind, and suspected that she would enjoy it enormously. In their different ways, Nancy and Stephanie regarded Monty as a confounded nuisance; Nancy thought he was a poseur, Stephanie was convinced he was dangerous.

He was idly assessing their opinions of him when he suddenly became the focus of attention.

"Monty could do that for us," the Duke went on. "Child's play for a chap with his experience and contacts. About time he did something useful!"

Richard clearly liked the idea. "What do you think, Monty?" he asked. "*Could* you do that?"

"Yes, and I'd be pleased to. We'd have to agree exactly what you wanted, and fix a price range. You know what it's like out there, Richard." Monty looked round the others, and addressed them. "Most of the auctions are pretty hectic affairs. There are exceptions, but they're the very big ones, like that Seattle Slew colt who fetched nine million last year . . . I take it we're not in that league?" He smiled at the nods of agreement. "As a general rule, you've got about two minutes of hassle while the bidding's in progress, then you have to slap your money down. It's bad enough doing it for yourself. For someone else . . . well . . . it's a hell of a responsibility."

"It's being done all the time, though," Edward pointed out.

"How's it work?" Fred asked.

"It's quite simple," Edward told him. "We get a catalogue. Monty and I would go through it and pick out the interesting lots."

"That doesn't mean those that are obviously good," Monty said. "They'll get fought over for millions. We'd be looking for the stuff that hasn't become fashionable yet."

"And we've got our own bloodstock expert," Edward added. "You'd help, wouldn't you, Nancy?"

"Sure."

Edward continued. "Then we agree a price limit. Fred, you might say something like, 'Lot Ninety is my first priority, and my limit is two hundred thousand. Failing that, Lot a hundred and twenty at three hundred thousand . . .' and so on."

"Sounds all right to me," Fred said.

"Bang on!" the Duke agreed. "D'you know, Monty, I might come with you. A trip like that should be quite a hoot."

Monty smiled indulgently. "I'm sure we could persuade Her Grace, my mother that you *needed* to."

Everyone was amused at the Duke's discomfort.

"It seems a good idea to me," Richard said. "Let's leave it at that, and think about it."

The weather was extremely unkind. It was the wettest and windiest Royal Ascot for twenty years. Cherished outfits were ruined, elaborate coiffures became bedraggled, and the popular press enjoyed itself enormously.

A RIGHT ROYAL WASH-OUT!

and

YOU NEED YOUR WELLIES, MA'AM!

screamed the headlines in an attempt to encapsulate the discomfort of the crowds.

None of it dampened Saxon Court spirits. Despite heavy rain immediately before the meeting, and during the first two days, the course stayed reasonably firm, allowing horses far greater freedom of movement than the spectators could enjoy.

On the first day, Richard's two-year-old colt, Amonasro, made his debut in the Coventry Stakes, and came within half a length of winning it. Edward's two runners the following day performed bravely to be beaten without being disgraced. Day three saw the end of the rain, and the onset of a strong wind that dried out the ground, while ruining hats. In rapidly improving conditions, Edwin Fforbes's three-year-old filly, Suzuki, swept her previous obscurity aside, winning the Group Two Ribblesdale Stakes after a thrilling battle that left her owner gibbering with excitement.

Suzuki was Edward's first winner at Royal Ascot for five long, miserable years. After the filly had been taken from the winner's enclosure back to the stables, Nancy saw him close his eyes for a few moments. She imagined that he was praying that the next one would come soon. It was the first time that she read his thoughts correctly.

On the last day, Frescobaldi certainly looked the part. He strolled round the paddock appearing to be worth every penny of the three hundred and fifty thousand pounds he had cost as a yearling. Everyone appreciated his condition and class, and when he went down to the start for the Hardwicke Stakes, another shroud over the past had been drawn back, although Edward did not know it at the time. A Saxon Court horse was the firm favourite for a Group Race.

Afterwards, Sean Gillespie actually volunteered an opinion. Neither Edward nor the Duke of Dorchester said anything to him other than, "Well done," and "Beautiful!" But after Sean had dismounted, he

383

paused before launching into his crouching scuttle towards the weighing room, and gave Frescobaldi a hard, quizzical look.

"You know, if he'd done that at Epsom last year," he said, then stopped. Edward and the Duke knew exactly what he meant, and nodded. Frescobaldi had performed brilliantly, leaving the trainers of many of the other horses in the race wondering why they had bothered.

When Nancy joined them, Edward dropped his bombshell. "Right, so far, so good," he said. "Now we can get him ready for the main event."

"Which is?" Nancy asked.

"The King George VI and Queen Elizabeth. We're going to run him in that!"

Watching TV in a break from decorating the kitchen, Siobhan saw Nancy gape at Edward in amazement, while the Duke of Dorchester started to chuckle. Edward's success went some way to brightening her gloom.

Angela had done more than merely keep out of the way during Ascot. Fred's catalogue photographer had been as good as his word, and found her two days of lucrative work. The same hotel in Brighton wanted a better brochure, and Angela was cast in the role of businesswoman enjoying the facilities, while taking part in a high-powered conference. She dutifully went through all the motions of registering, expressing satisfaction with her room, ordering a meal in the restaurant, being the driving force of the conference, playing squash, and taking a satisfying dip in the jacuzzi. Without Stephanie, it was even more boring than the last time. There were several attractive men around, but they all lacked the courage to approach her, despite the signals she sent.

There was an arrangement for her to go to Saxon Court on Friday evening at about seven o'clock. Confident that everyone would have had enough of racing for at least one week, she went early. It was not quite six o'clock when she arrived, and was dismayed to find a dozen cars still parked outside the Big House. When she heard the cheerfulness associated with Frescobaldi, she hesitated, not knowing whether to go or stay. At the exact moment that she decided to go rather than face another situation in which she was bound to upset Edward, Monty Dorchester came out of the office door.

It was the first time they had ever seen one another.

"Ah! Now then, this is going to be interesting," Imogen said with quiet intensity. She and Nancy saw the encounter from the kitchen window. "That pair have never met. Amazing, isn't it? I've tried to do something about it, but I was thwarted."

Monty was on his way home. He had done his duty throughout a long, hard week, impressing most people, charming some. Now he was bored with Frescobaldi's famous victory, and had the prospect of a tedious night satisfying Elaine Mayhew's tiresomely cloying desires.

When he saw Angela, he stopped in mid-stride. He had the same effect on her. She returned his look of entranced, sensual speculation. What passed between them, without a single word or gesture, was vividly palpable in the kitchen.

"Holy cow!" Nancy whispered.

"Lust at first sight," Imogen added. She, too, kept her voice low, although there was no possibility of being overheard.

When Monty finally spoke to Angela, he held her hand for much longer than was necessary for the purpose of introduction. As they gazed into each other's eyes, their body language became eloquent, causing Imogen to stiffen indignantly.

"Bloody hell, we're going to need a bucket of cold water," she fumed.

As it was bound to, the delirium between Monty and Angela subsided, and they turned towards the office door. He had persuaded her to stay, and was escorting her to ensure that she survived the gathering.

"More or less as I thought," Imogen said. "That pair were made for one another."

"What happens now?" Nancy said.

"I haven't the faintest idea," Imogen replied. "But I imagine we ought to batten down the hatches and prepare for ructions. One presumes that Edward will object when young Lochinvar pinches his bit of stuff!"

Two hours later, Monty left Angela and Edward. As they prepared to go in search of dinner, he headed belatedly towards Elaine Mayhew with less enthusiasm than ever.

The King George VI and Queen Elizabeth Diamond Stakes was run over a mile and a half at Ascot on the last Saturday of July. After Longchamp's Prix de l'Arc de Triomphe, it was Europe's most prestigious middle-distance race for horses of all ages, and carried the coveted Group One cachet. Edward had five weeks in which to get Frescobaldi ready for his sternest test.

This time, he did not repeat the common mistake of the past few years; while preparing one horse for a major race, he made sure that the other ninety-nine received attention. Consequently, there was a steady flow of winners. Eight came during the five weeks. One of them belonged to Fred, who made a point of going to Salisbury to watch the race. Or so everyone thought. Fred's main purpose was to spend an afternoon with Monty.

When racing was over, Fred insisted on giving Monty a lift back to his flat in Newbury, and invited himself in for a drink. Aware that he was being scrutinised, Monty produced mementoes of his time with Colorado Hartigan as evidence. Fred was satisfied and interested. The only thing that bothered him was the flat itself. It was half of the first floor of a spacious house built around 1900 with views over a pretty stretch of the Kennet and Avon Canal. It was very pleasant, but Monty was renting it, and that seemed all wrong to Fred.

"You should have bought something," he said. "Put your money to work. Paying rent's a mug's game."

"I couldn't be bothered with all the aggro of buying," Monty said. "I agreed I'd do two years with Edward, and then move on, so it didn't seem worth it. In any case . . ." he smiled disarmingly ". . . I like this place very much. It reminds me of the rooms I had in Oxford. That and High Eaves were the only times I've ever felt really at home."

Fred went away baffled, almost believing it, but reserving the right to be uneasy. Recognising the need to satisfy Fred's natural curiosity about his credentials, Monty was still glad to see the back of him, and poured himself another stiff drink. He was finding life difficult. Going through the motions of working for Edward was proving much more irksome than he had imagined, and the existence of Angela now imposed extra strain.

After their much-delayed first meeting, she and Monty bumped into each other at least once a week. However fleeting, such meetings were enough to intensify the excitement that crackled between them like a powerful electric discharge. For once, Monty had no idea how to pursue his desire. Angela seemed firmly attached to Edward. At Royal Ascot, he had heard Richard, Edwin Fforbes and Valerie Malahide discussing the possibility of their marriage. What, in God's name, Monty asked himself, did such a magnificent woman see in a fool like Manning? By no stretch of the imagination would she be attracted to lame ducks unless there was something in it for her. It had to be his money. There was no other explanation.

Things looked better once he had reached that conclusion. Such an attraction was negotiable.

Monty would have felt even happier had he known how easy it was going to be.

The day of the race was fine and warm. Angela and Stephanie spent the morning sunbathing while Fred messed about on the boat. He was contemplating a trip up-river, but not until he had watched the race on TV. Stephanie seemed to have caught some of his enthusiasm, and Angela realised that it would seem suspiciously churlish of her if she failed to join them. Because it was a Saturday afternoon, coverage of other sports restricted the time that could be devoted to racing, so Angela was spared

386

the preliminaries. When the programme tore itself away from cricket and moved over to Ascot, the horses were being loaded into the stalls.

Frescobaldi had developed into a strong-galloping horse, and had made all the running in his two previous races, winning from the front. Fred saw at once that this tactic was to be used again. Within the first furlong, Frescobaldi had taken a firm grip, with a pace that soon had the rest off the bridle as their leaders sought to restrict his lead to something they hoped would be challengeable in the final furlong.

Turning into the home straight, with a little over three furlongs to run, Frescobaldi lengthened his stride, and most of the rest looked run off their legs. But as Fred chortled, and rubbed his hands gleefully, the redoubtable French mare Charlotte Corday burst from the pack to mount an assault.

She was five years old, and in her fourth season of racing. The winner of nearly a million pounds in prize-money, including no less than six Group One races, she was as keen and zestful as a youngster. Exciting the large crowd on the course, and putting the fear of God into Fred, she closed the gap between herself and Frescobaldi to half a length, while Sean Gillespie looked on with disdainful detachment. His coolness under pressure had never been greater; in the last hundred yards, he asked Frescobaldi for the supreme effort, and took him away from Charlotte Corday to win by a length.

Angela did not need Fred's whoops of joy, and Stephanie's happy smile to tell her that Frescobaldi, Edward, and that blasted American woman from Widney Cheyne had achieved something quite outstanding: nor was the significance of the hundred and eighty thousand pounds first prize lost on her. Things had been going well for Edward *before* this; now, she knew there wasn't a snowball in hell's chance of him giving up training.

"You'll be having a right old time tonight, gal," Fred said, knowing that she was going to Saxon Court. "That should brighten our Edward up a bit."

Angela tried to look cheerful as Fred and Stephanie set off on the boat. They said they might stay out all night.

She spent two hours deciding not to go. At five o'clock, she went as far as to telephone, but unlike the days of Siobhan, there was no one there, and Elaine Mayhew had forgotten to switch the office phone through to Freezer's line. At six o'clock, Angela changed her mind and went. Inasmuch as she had anything remotely like a clear idea of what she was going to do, it consisted of telling Edward what she thought, and having done with it.

Reaching Saxon Court only ten minutes after Frescobaldi and his entourage, she was unnerved by what she found confronting her. Frescobaldi was outside the hostel, being petted and admired by the twenty-five lads and girls who were on duty that weekend. Nearby, Edward and Nancy were surrounded by a cheerful crowd.

387

Standing partly screened by the car, about fifty yards from the merriment, she was wondering what on earth to do when Monty appeared at her side.

"There's going to be a bit of a celebration tonight," he said quietly. Angela noticed a trace of sardonic disapproval in his voice. "You're welcome to it!" There was no mistaking the censure now.

"Oh no, I'm not!" Angela's voice was low but firm. "I'm not having anything to do with it. I want a drink, Monty."

His dark eyes flickered from her, to his car, to Edward, engulfed in congratulations and oblivious of them, back to Angela.

"Do we need both cars?" he asked.

"I don't intend coming back here," she snapped.

Only Imogen saw them go. She was in the kitchen, washing champagne glasses that had not been used since the day James Henry won the Two Thousand Guineas. She nodded with grim satisfaction.

Angela followed Monty to a pub just outside Newbury. They made themselves comfortable in a corner of the almost deserted lounge bar, and Angela downed the whole of her first drink at one gulp. While Monty was gazing at her, working out how to start the conversation to his own advantage, she did it for him.

"Horses, I have had to the back teeth," she said. "I'll scream if anyone so much as mentions one of the bloody things again!"

Monty exaggerated his display of surprise. "I assumed you must be very fond of them," he said.

"No way! They're beastly creatures."

"Oh dear." Monty sipped his drink and studied her. "There is a credit side . . . sometimes. Frescobaldi's probably earned my father three or four million this afternoon."

She stared at him incredulously. "I never knew the prize-money was that much," she said.

Monty laughed. "No, no, it isn't. That's my estimate of the animal's stud value."

"Good God!" Angela was shaken.

"The galling thing is that the old boy's already got sackfuls of the stuff, and none of it will ever come my way."

Angela opened her eyes wide at the rancour of his tone. "Why not?" she asked innocently.

"Primogeniture, my sweet. I'm the third son, so I have to make do with the crumbs from the table. If father had a free hand, he'd probably see me right . . . sadly Her Grace, my mother doesn't agree with hand-outs – *especially* in my case!"

Monty fetched more drinks, and explained his position. Their conversation wandered into the past, and was not interrupted when they moved into the grill room for a meal.

What most fascinated Angela, was the acrid bitterness underlying most of what he had to tell her. She learned that Monty's elder brothers Gerald and Lionel, apples of their mother's eye, unable to do wrong in her sight, were complete idiots. Gerald apparently compounded this by being totally humourless, whereas Lionel had the mentality of a prep-school boy, playing pranks on guests, such as leaving plastic spiders in their beds. Monty dredged up bad memories of his brothers going back over twenty years, and Angela listened sympathetically.

Changing completely, Monty spent half an hour talking about Colorado Hartigan with genuine respect and affection. Angela was intrigued to hear about the Swiss bank account that Monty had opened during his time in Lexington.

"I managed to find a hundred thousand to put in it," he said. "I've added to it since I've been with Edward . . . there have been some nice bets. It isn't a great deal . . . yet. It's very important to have an account like that, though . . . you never know when it might be handy."

The subject of Edward and Saxon Court returned as they finished eating their meal, and Monty was contemptuous again.

"I don't know what things were like when this marvellous wife of his was around," he said. "At the moment, he's just playing with it. And the sickening thing is the amount of money swilling round the place . . . all wasted on people who don't need it, and have no idea what to do with it."

"There's something like eighty thousand pounds a month going through," Angela said, remembering Edward explaining the accounts to Elaine Mayhew.

Monty waved the figure away dismissively. "That's only the petty cash they put in the books," he said. "The *real* money starts when you talk about bloodstock values . . . and remember, there's a merchant bank mixed up in that." He paused, eyeing her with frank speculation. "Between you and me, Angela, I think I may have a scheme to get my hands on some of that."

"How much?" she asked.

"It's a little early to say . . . but at least a million."

Angela placed her empty wine glass slowly and carefully in the dead centre of the table, choosing the spot with precision. Then she gave him a look that was full of surmise. "I think it's time we stopped pissing about, Monty," she said. "Let's find a nice comfortable bed, and you can tell me all about your scheme."

It was past eight o'clock before Saxon Court returned to normal, with only Imogen, Richard and Nancy still talking to Edward.

"Let's go out and eat," he suggested. "I wonder if the Fortescue could fix us up."

A phone call ascertained that there would be a good table waiting for them in fifteen minutes, and they set off at once. Entering the Fortescue Arms, Edward was surprised to be greeted with a burst of applause and good wishes. He had forgotten how much the well-being and success of his stable meant to a local community that had almost given up hope of a cause for celebration. Watching Edward closely, Imogen saw that he was touched by the reception. Not until they were seated in the dining room, and had ordered their meal, did he raise the topic for which she had been waiting.

"I say, I've just remembered. Angela was supposed to be coming over this evening."

"Oh?" Imogen managed a perfect blend of mild surprise and disinterest.

"Yes . . . I'm sure she said she was."

"Probably got tied up with something else," Imogen said, withholding information without a qualm.

"Yes, that's probably it." Edward was puzzled rather than concerned.

Although Richard had no idea what was going on, he sensed that this was the moment to introduce a distraction.

"I've made my mind up about Rhinemaiden's foal," he said. "I'm going to keep him."

All thoughts of Angela gone, Edward smiled. "That *is* good news," he said.

"Moreover," Richard continued, "as a special favour because of your interest and obvious faith in him, I've decided to offer you a half share."

"How much?"

"What would you say to a hundred thousand?"

"Done!"

Richard and Edward shook hands across the table.

"He'll have to run in your colours, of course," Edward said. "What are you going to call him?"

"I'm very much afraid that the poor creature is going to be saddled with Wagner again," Imogen declared mournfully. "It's a great shame! Just as things seemed to be looking up."

"That's not strictly true, my dear," Richard said. "There were several medieval poets mixed up in it long before Wagner decided to have a go."

Edward smiled, and nodded, understanding what Richard had in mind. "Wolfram von Eschenbach, for example," he said.

"Quite . . . not to mention good old Chrétien de Troyes," Richard added.

"And all the chaps who dreamed up that business about King Arthur and the Round Table."

"Absolutely! By the way, did you know that Walther von der Vogelweide was involved, as well?"

"No, I didn't. That's fascinating."

"So what are we going to call this horse?" a bewildered Nancy demanded.

"Lohengrin, of course," Edward said. "What else would you call the son of Parsifal?"

"As I understand it," Imogen said to Nancy, "Lohengrin was the idiot who lost his girl friend, and trundled around on the back of a swan to look for her. *Now* do you see what I have to put up with?"

When Angela had breakfast with Monty the following morning, she was satisfied and exhilarated. Even without her encouragement, Monty was a sexual athlete of the highest class: together they had surpassed all their previous experiences and expectations. And the plan he had revealed during the intervals in their frenetic activity had set her imagination aflame.

"Why don't I move in here with you," she suggested. "I'm sure Fred's getting sick of me, and the feeling's mutual."

Monty's mood changed instantly. "No! That won't do at all," he said forcefully.

"Why not?"

"I don't want them to have the slightest whiff of suspicion," he replied. "The whole thing could be dead the minute anyone asks a question."

"So what do we do?"

"Make everything look completely normal."

"Everything?" Angela asked doubtfully.

"Yes."

"Does that mean I'll have to carry on screwing with Edward?"

"Yes, unless you can find a way of stopping it without upsetting him."

Angela looked at Monty's face; it was implacable. "All right," she said. She liked Edward. Sleeping with him was the least of the things she would do for a million pounds.

Fred and Stephanie did spend the night on the boat, and returned after lunch, asking no questions. By that time, Angela had telephoned Edward, had a pack of lies accepted as an explanation for her non-appearance the previous evening, and was getting ready to go to Saxon Court, prepared to stay overnight.

For two or three hours on a warm July Sunday, the embryonic web of deception was vulnerable; if Edward, Fred or Stephanie had taken the trouble to ask one question, and treat the answer with scepticism, the plan might have been stillborn. If Imogen's younger son, Richard, hadn't given her a hectic morning by falling off a paddock gate and breaking an arm, she would certainly have considered what had become of Monty and Angela. Indeed, she might well have gone further, and discovered that from mid-afternoon, Angela was with Edward, behaving as though the previous night had never existed. Instead, she spent several hours fretting in a hospital casualty department.

Once Angela had survived that Sunday, she felt invincible.

She and Monty were very careful. On the few occasions when they met in public, they behaved as though they were no more than acquaintances, without interest in each other. Imogen assumed that the Saturday evening had misfired, and thought of devising new ways of bringing them together. Conscious that she was being devious, and feeling slightly guilty, she said nothing to anyone, not even Nancy, who had become her confidante in most things. Stephanie was preoccupied with problems of her own, spent a lot of time at her London flat, and never bothered to question Angela's comings and goings.

There was one indication of the change that had taken place, but it was obscure, and no one had a chance of interpreting the tenuous evidence. Angela kept each weekend free for Edward, while spending every available minute during the week with Monty. Consequently, he had much less time for Elaine Mayhew. He went to her cottage on Saturdays simply to keep her quiet, fearing neurotic disruption if he did not. Often, the strain of concealing the fact that he could hardly stand the sight of her made him less than effective as a lover. Elaine's manner in the office became extremely tense, but Edward paid no attention to it. She frightened him. He had realised that what he had thought of as nervousness was something far more serious; she was, he decided, the sort of woman who might slash her wrists in an attention-grabbing cry for help.

When she started making mistakes, he turned a blind eye at first. An order for feed was not placed; an embarrassed George Roberts had to mention that he had not been paid for some repair work to part of the New Yard roof; Mark Walgrave received a bill that contained charges for some of Edwin Fforbes's horses. Edward smoothed over and rectified these incidents without mentioning them to Elaine. Then she began to get race entries wrong.

Twice she omitted to remove horses at the four-day stage. These were irritants rather than disasters, but an event took place at the end of

August that could not be overlooked. Two horses had been entered for a good-class handicap at Newbury; one belonged to Mark Walgrave, the other to Fred. At the four-day stage, Edward told Elaine to take Mark's horse out, leaving Fred's to stand as an almost definite runner. It was a perfectly normal procedure that he had gone through countless times with Siobhan. When Edward himself made the ten o'clock phone call on the day before the race to declare Fred's horse as a runner, he discovered that Elaine had taken it out, leaving Mark's horse in.

Edward was furious. Although Fred had fortunately not been told, his horse would have had a very strong chance of winning the race. Elaine met his reprimand with floods of tears, and hysterical ramblings about having far too much to think about. Edward's intention had been to dismiss her on the spot, but he was intimidated by her distraught outburst, and went out to take refuge with the second lot. When he came back, Monty seemed to have exerted some sort of stabilising influence to restore a tense calm.

Following this incident, Angela had to endure three consecutive nights of loneliness while Monty did his best to soothe Elaine, who never suspected the ulterior motives behind his apparent kindness. His plan was not coming to fruition as quickly as he would have liked; indeed, for much of the time, he feared that it might have died completely. He was, however, certain of one thing: if Elaine Mayhew were allowed to create chaos at Saxon Court, the ramifications could only be to his disadvantage. In addition to his private endeavours in her bed, Monty spent much more time in the office in order to help Elaine.

His reward came on a Saturday morning at the end of September, when he had all but given up hope, and Angela's impatience was wearing him down. Richard was at Saxon Court to watch two of his horses work, and was pleased to run into Monty.

"Ah, the very man!" he said breezily. "I've got the catalogues, and we're having a council of war at my place next Sunday."

"Catalogues?" Monty simulated incomprehension.

"From Keeneland. Remember . . . the sales. You said you'd go and buy for us. I hope you haven't changed your mind."

"No, of course not. I'll do all I can."

"Lovely. You can come to Widney Cheyne next Sunday?"

"I'll be there!"

The discussions began over what Richard called 'a late breakfast' at nine o'clock. Valerie Malahide had come from Dublin to join the Duke of Dorchester, Edwin Fforbes and Fred. With great regret, Mark Walgrave had ruled himself out, having decided to plough his available money into his company rather than horses this year. Edward and Nancy were there to give advice, and everyone began the day equipped with

393

photo-copies of the catalogue, annotated with their thoughts on possible best buys.

It was nearly nine o'clock in the evening before Monty went painstakingly through the list for the last time to triple-check what they wanted, and Richard laughed at Fred's demeanour.

"You look spiflicated, Fred!"

"I feel it! I thought I knew a thing or two about business and money, but this is something else!"

Hell-bent on acquiring another colt to follow Benvenuto Cellini and Frescobaldi, the Duke of Dorchester had specified a lot for which he was prepared to pay up to five hundred thousand pounds. Richard had matched the figure, although Edward had told him that the animal in which he was interested was likely to fetch at least four times that amount. Edwin Fforbes's two potential purchases had been estimated at a more modest three hundred thousand pounds for the pair, while Valerie and Fred were in for four hundred thousand pounds each. The total was two million, one hundred thousand pounds, or around three million dollars.

"I need to be thinking of fixing you up with facilities, Monty," Richard said. "I believe that the thing to do is organise a draft with Fraunhofer Mackenzie in Lexington."

Monty smiled. "The studman's bank! Colorado was a customer for thirty years. I wonder if Ned Golanski still runs that branch."

"That's the name I have," Richard said, consulting a file. "Do you know him?"

"Very well indeed. We used to go fishing together." It was turning out better than Monty had dared hope.

"Marvellous!" Richard beamed. "That saves on the introductions." He looked round the table. "Everybody happy? Speak now, or forever hold your peace!"

There was no dissent. It was agreed.

Angela was very calm about it. She spent an evening with Monty, making plans for herself based around his journey to Lexington on 1 November.

There was little danger of Monty being accompanied. After an incident nearly thirty years ago, the Duchess of Dorchester was not prepared to let the Duke out of her sight for more than two days, and that dispensation was granted only if he stayed in England. Nevertheless, it was agreed that Angela should fly out the day before Monty in case Richard or Edward should change his mind at the last minute. To avoid the risks of a journey from Fred's home direct to London Airport, she planned to go to an hotel two days before her flight.

The biggest problem was thinking of a story to tell Stephanie, of whom Angela was apprehensive. Angela had long ago accepted the fact that her friend was intrinsically honest, and learned to adapt to this constraint when they were together. Now, she felt that additional forces were at work. Fred and Stephanie were almost certainly nearing the end of their relationship; their mutual usefulness had run its course, leaving nothing but a dwindling physical attraction to patch over the substantial differences in their personalities and attitudes. Angela had come to believe that Stephanie had a soft spot for Edward, and would soon make a play for him. What better beginning could she have than to discover the plan and expose it?

In the event, it was all very simple. Angela told both Edward and Stephanie that she was going to visit her parents in York. It was, she said, time that she tried to make friends with them again. Stephanie embraced the idea; devoted to her own parents, she had never liked the rift between Angela and hers. She also chose to assume that the visit might be connected with plans for a wedding, and Angela did nothing to discourage the belief.

"I'll only be a few days," Angela said. It was all she needed; four or five days after she left Fred's house, Monty's scheme would have been implemented, and they could all do what the hell they liked.

"Give me a ring and let me know how it's going," Stephanie said eagerly.

"I will."

With that out of the way, Angela spent a day in London. She visited a travel agent, where, using money supplied by Monty, she bought a single ticket from London to Lexington for herself, and two singles from Lexington to Geneva. Richard was taking care of Monty's ticket to America. Perhaps they could send the unused portion back to him so that he could claim a refund. The idea amused her.

Afterwards, she went to her bank, where she had arranged to see the manager. He admired her legs while they had coffee and biscuits in his office, and she told him about a number of fabulously exciting modelling assignments that were coming up. In theory, Angela had no need to worry about spending-money, but when she left the bank, she had five thousand pounds' worth of traveller's cheques in US dollars. Mr Ponsonby promised to take good care of the forty-five thousand pounds she had in a deposit account, and would, of course, act promptly and with discretion on any instructions she gave for its disposition.

Due to set out for York on a Monday morning, Angela spent what only she and Monty knew was her last weekend in England at Saxon Court. She arrived at lunchtime on Saturday to find Rosie talking to a group of lads outside the office.

"Mr Manning's down in the yard, Miss Maitland," Rosie said in her usual pleasant manner. "He shouldn't be too long."

Angela smiled her thanks, made a move to go into the house, but stopped. She looked towards the arches and the clock-tower. What *did* go on down there, she wondered? For nearly eighteen months, she had been in and out of Edward's house and bed, yet she had never visited his workshop, the heart of Saxon Court, the very reason for its existence. Gripped by a sudden, last-minute urge to see it, she set off.

They were in the Old Yard. Edward was down on hands and knees, examining the lower forelegs of a chestnut filly. Robin Lane was holding her head collar while Declan and Freezer looked on. Alerted by the sound of Angela's stiletto heels on the cobbles they turned in her direction.

Edward stood up, smiling at her over the filly's back. "Hello, darling," he said. "Shan't be a minute. All right, Robin, give her a turn."

Robin walked the filly round in a circle while Edward, Declan and Freezer studied her. Angela could see that she was moving awkwardly, rather as if she had sore feet. She was also impressed by the beauty of the animal and the grandeur of her surroundings.

"What do you think, Declan?" Edward asked.

"She's on the mend, sor."

"Freezer?"

"I agree, sir."

"And she's eating properly again, Robin?"

"Yes, sir."

"Good. Give her another dressing tonight." Edward put an arm round the horse's neck, and rubbed his face against her muzzle. "You'll soon be all right, sweetie," he said. "Just stay patient with me, will you?"

If Angela had not seen the look that passed between Edward and the filly, she would never have believed it possible. The exchange of love and trust was piercing in its powerful simplicity. She thought about it all afternoon, and it helped to give their subsequent love-making an elegiac quality.

The memory of a few moments of near-magic stayed fresh with Angela, and came to haunt her in the months ahead. She knew that she had never been part of such a relationship, and began to fear that she was incapable of inspiring such feelings.

CHAPTER 17

When Imogen was a little girl of eight, she had stumbled across one of her father's outside men in the act of making love to the maid. Although it often suited her to pretend otherwise, very little had surprised her since. What quickly became known as the Hallowe'en Miracle, once retrospective calm had descended, was a spectacular exception. Years later, Imogen still felt a malignant chill at the thought of what would have happened if Fred Bird hadn't been the man he was, with a deplorable business, the morals of an alley-cat, and thirty years hard experience of living by his wits.

October 29th began early for Imogen. Richard had to be at London Airport at seven-thirty to catch a flight to Frankfurt, and she decided to drive him. She chatted briefly to Edwin Fforbes who was already waiting when they arrived, wished them luck for their important, week-long visit to Koestler's, then went to Saxon Court. Racing was over for another season, she knew that Edward was worried about the state of things in the office, and she intended giving Elaine Mayhew a hand to clear everything up. But first, she surrendered to hunger, and allowed Mary to cook her a huge breakfast.

When Edward came back from the yard at one o'clock, she had lunch with him, reporting that she had found little wrong.

"Edwin and Valerie were overcharged in September," she said. "And there's something wrong with the vet's bill. Apart from that, things don't look too bad."

"Thank God for that! And thank *you*, Imogen."

"I can see why you're worried about Mrs Mayhew," Imogen said. "She's not the most relaxed – or relaxing – person one's come across."

Edward nodded despondently. He had seen enough of Elaine that morning to know that she was more wound up than usual, and ascribed her attitude to resentment at what she saw as interference from Imogen. The truth was that Monty's impending two-week absence in America was well on the way to destroying the remnants of her control. He had made it worse by taking a few days' holiday before the trip, supposedly to visit friends in Northumberland and the Lake District. She had spent a miserable, lonely weekend, and there were at least two more before she saw him again.

"I'm probably going to have to get rid of her," Edward told Imogen. "I don't think she's ever been on top of the job."

"Well, this is the time of year to do it," Imogen replied. "But be careful how you set about it. We don't want anything happening here."

Edward took her meaning.

Angela enjoyed the way her journey to York began.

Stephanie had people to see in London, and was spending most of the week at her flat. Fred drove them both to Reading railway station, and they caught the train together. Over-solicitous that Angela should reinstate normal relations with her parents, Stephanie fussed like a mother-hen with last-minute advice. The very fast, twenty-minute journey gave her time for nothing more than the recitation of platitudes before they said goodbye at Paddington station. Hoping to hear good news within the week, Stephanie headed towards the taxis while Angela went to the underground. She travelled to Knightsbridge and Harrods.

She had left virtually all her belongings at Fred's house as a token of her intention to return. None of it was any loss: she had grown bored with all her clothes. She bought a suitcase, and spent a pleasant three hours filling it. After a leisurely late lunch in the store restaurant, Angela was assisted ceremoniously into a taxi, telling the driver to take her to Marylebone railway station.

The journey to High Wycombe was tedious. It took over an hour for the stopping train to cover the thirty-six miles, and Angela had time to think. Suddenly, the excitement of what lay ahead acquired an element of uncertainty, and with it came misgivings. What happened after the money was safely deposited in Switzerland? With a diligence that she now saw as sinister, Monty had avoided committing himself. A bad few minutes ended when she persuaded herself that he *had* to stick with her: she knew enough to send him to prison. It was a cheering thought.

Another taxi took her to the hotel on the north-eastern outskirts of High Wycombe. It was brashly stylish, deliberately impersonal and busy, and once inside the room that Monty had booked, Angela felt safely at home. She had something like twenty-four hours before Monty returned from whatever mysterious assignment had taken him north; with a hairdresser, beauty salon and sauna on the premises, that would be no problem.

She enjoyed a good dinner. As every unaccompanied man in the dining room wondered whether he dared join her, she had completely forgotten Stephanie. It never occurred to Angela that she had walked out of the life of her only true friend.

After dropping the girls in Reading, Fred returned home to spend a busy morning in his office. At one-thirty, a little later than planned, Vanessa Blandford arrived.

"I'm sorry," she said. "Terrible hold-ups the other side of Bristol, and again at Swindon."

"Don't worry about it, love. You're here safe and sound. That's what matters." Fred helped her with her bags, one small and relatively light, the other big and heavy. He correctly assumed it contained a full range of samples. Even before he offered her refreshment after her long drive, he had the case open on the kitchen floor, and was rummaging through the contents.

"You're right," he said, holding up a pair of French knickers admiringly, "this looks like good gear."

"We do our best."

"The only snag is . . . and it didn't dawn on me until this morning . . . we haven't got anybody to model them. They've both cleared off and left me."

"The two girls in your catalogue?"

"Yes."

"I'm not in their league, but I can show you anything you want to see."

Fred looked up, and saw that she was perfectly serious.

Five years ago, Vanessa Blandford had started her own business in an almost-derelict farmhouse on the Lizard in Cornwall. With a few thousand pounds from a legacy, she had launched an enterprise that was a mixture of country-arty-crafty and specialist dressmaking. Carefully advertised, it had survived, making a living for Vanessa and six others, without ever looking like flourishing. In response to the tastes of a small but gratifyingly loyal clientéle, the emphasis had swung completely to clothes, and after two years, pots of honey and handcrafted tablemats had been phased out.

The design and small-scale production of lingerie had started as a shamefaced joke to please the wife of an industrialist who maintained an estate in Devon while concentrating his time and energy on his business life in the West Midlands. His lady, who advocated a beauty treatment based on "plenty of fresh air and orange juice during the day, and young men at night", reported great success with the prototypes, which gradually became part of the product range. They sold well, but not nearly well enough to satisfy Vanessa's new aspirations. When she had set out, she wanted nothing more than to earn an adequate living doing something she enjoyed in pleasant surroundings. Now, she wanted enough money to retire when she was thirty: she thought she might take up painting.

People told her that the lingerie was a potential winner; all that it needed was the breakthrough into a bigger market. Vanessa did the calculations over and over again. With twenty thousand customers a year instead of only two thousand, she would be sufficiently wealthy in two years. It looked beguilingly simple, yet as time passed, she realised that the extra nought, nothing at all on paper, was an impossibility in practice.

Fred had become aware of Vanessa Blandford's range a year ago. At the time, he had admired it, but thought it too up-market for him. Her stuff was expensive. She had also managed to give what should have been a perfectly ordinary pair of knickers an élitist twist, appealing to the sort of woman who wouldn't be seen dead in one of his shops. They had met at a trade federation exhibition, and she floated the idea that he should take some of her stuff on a no-risk, sale-or-return basis.

When she had telephoned him two weeks ago to repeat the offer, things had changed. Perhaps there really was a posh niche in the market to be exploited. Much more pressingly, Jeff Riggs in Melton Mowbray was running out of steam, unable to cope with the growth called for by new shops and rising demand. Showing every sign of wanting to take life easy, Jeff was recovering from a serious illness, and could only produce excuses. Expansion was out: the Council would never agree to planning permission – not that it mattered, because new hands were unavailable. People wouldn't travel more than a couple of miles to work.

Fred needed a new source of supply.

As he carried out a thorough inspection of her merchandise after she'd had a cup of coffee and a sandwich, Fred let Vanessa know nothing other than that he might be interested in buying a small selection.

"Have you got spare capacity?" he asked.

"Yes, I'm afraid I have," she admitted.

"So you could cope with an order?"

"Like a flash!" she promised.

"Have you got space? Could you move extra people in?"

"Oh yes." She thought about it. "There's room for another half a dozen."

"What about the locals? Are they interested in work, or do they want to sit on their backsides and draw social security?"

"They want work," Vanessa replied firmly. "I've got people queuing up for it."

The conversation developed, going into great detail. Vanessa answered the questions frankly; realising that she was being investigated, she saw no point in withholding the information Fred sought. The latter part of the afternoon was enlivened by Vanessa's discovery of the billiard room, and Fred's amusement when he suffered persistent defeat at her skilled hands.

"Where the devil did you learn to play like this?" he asked.

"My uncle Jim. He stood me on a pile of books and got me started when I was five. Mother didn't approve!"

"That makes no odds, does it? Everybody should have an uncle like that."

Towards the end of dinner in a local steakhouse, Fred had an idea.

"All my stuff's made in Melton Mowbray," he said. "It's a very interesting operation . . . run by a good mate. Would you like to have a look at it?"

"Why not?"

"We could all learn something. We'll go tomorrow."

When they left Jeff Riggs's small factory at four o'clock the following afternoon, Vanessa was intrigued by what she had seen, and had formed the opinion that Fred would have to give her an order. The only doubt in her mind was the extent to which he was ready to accept that.

"Well, what do you think?" Fred asked, as he began to pick his way through the Leicestershire by-ways towards the M1 motorway.

"Interesting. Very interesting." Vanessa was noncommittal. She had half-sensed that Fred's main purpose in taking her had been to introduce Jeff Riggs to a sense of urgency; if that were so, he had failed. The affably lethargic Riggs had either not recognised the threat, or relegated it to insignificance.

"Come off it," Fred chided. "You must fancy your chances of competing with that lot." He had been very disappointed in what he had seen. Things were slipping downhill.

"All right, yes. I do!"

"That's the ticket! We'll get something fixed up."

Fred drove fast down the motorway, chatting all the time. However, his mood changed when he came off it at an exit roughly half-way between Luton and Watford. Although he would never have admitted it, he hated the journey from north to west round London, especially after dark when he was never completely confident of finding his way. Tonight, he was also preoccupied with Jeff Riggs, who seemed to have reached the stage where he had stopped caring. Intending to pick up the westbound M4 at Slough, Fred saw that he had taken a wrong turning some minutes after passing Amersham.

"I'm making a right cock-up of this," he told Vanessa. "But I'll keep going. We can get back this way, and it might be best to give the M4 a miss at this time of day."

"Is there any chance of finding a meal down here?" Vanessa asked. Any benefit of the meagre snack that had done service as lunch had long since disappeared.

"Yes, I think there's a hotel coming up. It's a pretty crap place if I remember right, but the restaurant's not bad."

As so often, the original estimate of two miles turned out to be nearer five, and Fred was becoming quite worried when the shape of the hotel, picked out by lights, eventually loomed up.

"Thank God for that," he muttered as he drew into the spacious forecourt, and saw that his luck had changed back to normal. There was a good parking space within easy reach of the main door.

Something occurred to Fred after he had switched the engine off. "What did you reckon to that new basque Jeff had on the go?"

"To be honest, I thought it looked a bit tatty, and that's daft when you think of the effort that goes into it. It's going to take a first-rate machinist two hours to do one of those things. And I didn't go much on the colours. What he should have done was . . ." She stopped when she saw that Fred was taking no notice of her.

The front bumper of his car was only feet away from a tinted plate-glass window that gave a view of the hotel's vast reception area in which dozens of people were milling around at a busy time for arrivals. Fred was gaping at Monty Dorchester who was standing by a luggage trolley. Angela, dressed and made-up to kill, was greeting him with great enthusiasm.

"Something wrong?" Vanessa asked.

"Dead bloody right there is," Fred said quietly.

She waited, hoping for an explanation. There wasn't one.

"Now what the bleedin' hell are that pair up to?" Fred asked. His tone was made up of suspicion and tension.

"Which pair?"

"To the left of that pillar."

"Crimson dress?"

"That's right."

"H'm. They make quite a couple, don't they?" Vanessa studied them hard, frowning with the effort. "Isn't that one of the girls in your latest catalogue?"

"Yes."

"And you know the bloke?"

"I do."

"So? What's the problem?"

"They shouldn't be here, and they shouldn't be together. She said she was going to see her mum and dad in York, and he's supposed to be in the Lake District."

Vanessa shrugged. "They just wanted a few days together. No harm in that."

Fred ignored her. "What have we here?" he asked himself. "What *do* we have here?"

Vanessa gave up. She could see that Fred was very disturbed. She assumed that he thought he had some sort of right to the girl, who was

402

obviously playing around. With a man that dishy, Vanessa wasn't going to blame her.

Fred watched the scene in reception with hawklike concentration. Monty eventually detached himself from Angela and went to register. When he rejoined her, she asked him a question which he was unable to answer. After looking around for inspiration, he led Angela towards the hall porter's desk. Whatever information they wanted was forthcoming immediately. Angela was satisfied, they crossed the foyer, collected Monty's luggage, and disappeared into a lift.

Fred was galvanised into action. "Sit tight, love," he said, getting out of the car. "Shan't be a minute."

He knew exactly how he was going to set about it, and made it look totally convincing. Having gone in through the doors like an express train, Fred halted, looked bewildered, then allowed his eyes to meet the mildly interested stare of the hall porter. What Fred lacked in 'quality', he made up for with authority. The hall porter recognised it instantly, and prepared to be of service.

"What a piece of luck!" Fred began. "Thought we'd lost 'em."

"Who might that be, sir?"

"Mate of mine . . . slipped off and got married quietly on Saturday. Then he does a disappearing act with his missus, so we haven't had a chance to give them their present. Anyway, they're here! I saw them go into that lift, and you were talking to them."

"How can I help you, sir?" As well as warming to Fred's personality, the man was conscious of the ten-pound note that had materialised.

"I'd like to know when they're leaving. We can get something fixed up about this present then." Fred leaned on the counter and became conspiratorial. "It's a motor car, you see. You need to lay on a bit of a do for a thing like that."

"What name is it, sir?"

"Dorchester." Fred said it without thinking, and prayed that Monty hadn't been too elaborate. When the hall porter nodded and went to talk to the girls on the reception desk, the ten-pound note vanished with him.

Because of the activity caused by a group of eight arrivals, it took nearly two minutes. Unable to see exactly what was going on behind the reception desk, Fred suffered agonies of impatience. At last, the man came back. He was holding two registration slips, and looking puzzled.

"What's up?" Fred asked.

"Ah yes . . . that figures," the hall porter said, more to himself than Fred. "The lady's going tomorrow morning, and Mr Dorchester's going on Thursday."

"Typical! That's bloody typical of that pair!" Fred fumed. Another

403

ten-pound note appeared. "Knowing them, it's going to be somewhere really exotic like Outer Mongolia!"

"No, I'm pretty sure it's America. The lady wanted to know if we had courtesy coaches to the airport."

"You do?"

"Yes, sir. She's catching the one at eight o'clock in the morning. The gentleman said that would do for him on Thursday. He's catching the same flight I think . . . only twenty-four hours later, if you see what I mean."

Fred nodded. "I'll bet I know what's happened here. She's a model, you know." The man looked as though he had thought as much. "She's got herself lined up with a job, and they're getting the honeymoon on some poor sod's expenses. All right for some, ain't it? Well, it looks as though we shall have to catch them when they come back. Shame! Thanks for your help, son." The second ten-pound note slid across the counter. "Not a word, eh? Don't spoil the surprise."

"Rely on me, sir."

Fred knew that he could. This was how he had operated all his life. Bullshit and palm-greasing: pick the right man and it worked every time.

He had started the car's engine before he remembered Vanessa. "Sorry, love," he said. "You're going to have to wait for that meal. Shouldn't be too long."

"Where are we going?"

"Newbury!"

Vanessa sat still and silent while Fred drove the thirty-five miles in forty minutes, mercifully through easy traffic. Although he had been to Monty's flat only once, he found it unerringly, without hesitation or wrong turn.

"Great!" he said when he saw the lights in one of the ground-floor flats, and was out of the car like a jack-in-the-box.

The doorbells were so arranged that he was able to make the correct choice first time. He adapted instantly to the youthful sixty-year-old woman of taste and refinement who opened the door.

"I'm dreadfully sorry to bother you, but I've got an urgent message for Mr Dorchester. Do you happen to know what time he might be back?"

"He won't be back. He left last week . . . Thursday it was."

"Left?" Fred acted dumb.

"Oh yes. I think he said he was going to live with his parents . . . or it may have been his brother."

"Ah!" Fred smiled. "I know where I can find him."

"I believe the new people are coming in tomorrow. These flats are never empty for long. They're *much* sought-after, you know."

"I'm sure! Thank you very much for your help."

When Fred got back into the car, Vanessa saw that his face was taut with grim satisfaction.

"Do you want to tell me about it?" she asked an hour later when they were, at long last, comfortably settled in a restaurant.

He mulled it over. "You'll probably find out all about it tomorrow," he said, and smiled at her disappointment. "I'll tell you this much, though. Our two friends are up to no good. I'd guess it's about two million quid's worth of no good."

"Really?" Vanessa's eyes were saucer-wide.

"I'm ninety per cent certain. There's one more thing I'd like to know."

"Which is?"

Fred eyed her calculatingly. "I could use your help," he said.

"Will it get me an order?" Vanessa asked.

"Don't worry about that, love. It's in the bag." He admired her nerve.

Vanessa hardly hesitated; the talk in the trade was that Fred's word was good. "What do you want me to do?" she asked.

"Would you recognise that woman again?"

"I think so . . . she's not exactly inconspicuous, is she?"

Fred made sure of being in good time. He dropped Vanessa outside the international departure terminal at Heathrow Airport at eight o'clock the following morning. While she went inside to mingle with the crowd, he drove into the car park, and found a place from which he could watch coaches and taxis arriving.

The bus on which Angela was travelling got there a few minutes after nine o'clock. The name of the hotel was displayed prominently on the side, and both Fred and Vanessa spotted it before it reached the terminal. They watched Angela get off. She was alone. After collecting her case from the luggage compartment at the side of the coach, she entered the terminal. Once he had lost sight of her, Fred's fingers began to drum fretfully on the steering wheel.

Vanessa had spent the hour preparing for the moment when Angela came in through the automatic doors. She had watched hundreds of people do the same thing, making a careful analysis of their movement patterns as they made their way to the desks of the various airlines. Consequently, as Angela began her walk down the long hall, Vanessa was no more than five yards away from her, slightly behind her, and travelling on a parallel path. When Angela moved towards Pan American, Vanessa followed her, making it look perfectly natural.

There were only one or two people waiting at each of the check-in positions. Vanessa noticed that Angela chose the one presided over by a good-looking man, and started a queue behind her. As Angela handed in her ticket, Vanessa dropped her handbag, making sure that it was open before letting it go. The prepared collection of keys, small change, old shopping-lists, diaries, and cosmetics fell round Angela's feet. She made as if to help the grovelling, apologetic Vanessa, but the young airline official was having none of it. Angela Maitland was the most exciting thing that was going to happen to him today, and he intended making the most of every second of their conversation. After verbose attention to detail about allocating her just the right seat on the flight to New York, he went to great pains to explain the arrangements for her connecting flight. Scrabbling around with her ear close to the baggage conveyor, Vanessa heard it all. When she scuttled away, still apologising, neither Angela, nor her besotted admirer took any notice of her.

Fred had left his car, and was waiting outside the main doors.

"Well?" he demanded. "What do you know?"

"She's definitely going to America. She's leaving on a flight to New York in an hour. Then she's got a two-hour wait, and she's going to a place called Lexington."

"Are you sure?"

"Yes. I couldn't make it out at first. She found a young bloke who went gaga over her, and I thought he was going on about Lexicon."

Fred allowed himself a few moments of quiescence; he was quite still, with a gleam of triumph in his eyes. "Gotcha!" he said softly. Then he grabbed Vanessa's hand, and dragged her across the road towards the car park.

"Where are we going?" she gasped.

"Little place called Compton Norris. Know it?"

"Never heard of it."

"It's not far. Berkshire."

"As long as it's not Lexicon!"

Fred had known times when it took an hour or more to cover the two miles from the airport to the motorway. This morning, however, the gods who had deserted Monty and Angela were smiling on him; after only ten minutes, he was travelling west with a disregard for the speed limit that made Vanessa wonder whether she ought to say something. She decided not to. It was Fred's licence, and she had come to the conclusion that he was a very good driver. Her only utterances were: "Nice!" when they passed through Compton Norris, and, "Good gracious!" as Fred swung the car into Saxon Court.

Fred wound his window down to speak to Alison Bairstow who was standing outside the office with another girl.

"Where's the guv'nor?" he asked.

Alison moved swiftly towards the car. "I'm afraid he's not here, sir. He went over to Widney Cheyne first thing to see Miss Bloomfield."

"Right. Thanks." Fred was reversing when he thought of something.

"Give him a ring, love. Let him know I'm on my way. Tell him it's dead-bloody-serious, will you? And make sure Lady Stewart knows about it."

"Yes, sir!"

Vanessa cleared her throat and looked hard at Fred as they headed back towards the village. "That was a racing stable, wasn't it?"

"Yes."

"Quite a smart outfit, I'd say. Uncle Jim was into horses as well as snooker. Do you own it?"

Fred roared with laughter. "No! To tell you the truth, that place is a bit beyond me. There's a shade too much quality there for a lad from the back streets."

Vanessa smiled. "I don't think I believe that, Fred," she told him. "And where to now? Widney Cheyne, wherever or whatever that is?"

"That's right."

"Will I be able to go to the loo and have a cup of coffee there?"

Fred felt a mild twinge of guilt at Vanessa's plaintive tone. "Yes. It's not all that far," he promised her, and applied his foot to the accelerator.

He went in through the main, front gates, and down the long, winding road that gave a splendid view of the house and the park. Sunshine after squally showers set the scene off to perfection.

"You don't do too badly, despite the back streets," Vanessa said. "What goes on here?"

"It's the home of Sir Richard Stewart, Bart," Fred announced with mock-grandeur.

"And what's he do when he's at home?"

"He runs a stud farm. Look, you can see it . . . over there to the left. When he's *not* at home, he's Chairman of a merchant bank. What are you laughing at?"

"I was thinking of the doors you can open with knickers."

"That's what I've always said, love, that's just what I've always said."

As Fred's car approached the front of the house, Edward and Nancy came hurrying towards it.

"What on earth's the matter, Fred?" Edward asked. "Alison made it sound like life or death."

"She's a good girl," Fred said approvingly. "Where's her ladyship?"

"There." Edward pointed at one of the ground-floor windows.

"Right. Come on!" Fred put a protective arm round Vanessa's shoulders, and piloted her to the front door, while Edward and Nancy stared at her with unconcealed curiosity.

Meeting them in the hall, Imogen's attitude to Vanessa was incomprehension laced with hostility. It was written on her face. Correctly interpreting her thoughts, Fred attacked.

"You can come off your high horse, Imogen. This is Vanessa. She's a business associate. First thing Vanessa wants is a lavatory, then we'll have a cup of coffee while we tell you about it."

"About what?" Imogen demanded.

"Wait and see. Look after Vanessa and be nice to her. That girl has played a blinder. Come on, chop-chop!" Fred gave Vanessa a gentle push towards Imogen, and set off to the ground-floor sitting-room. Edward and Nancy trailed along behind him, exchanging baffled looks, and Imogen joined them as soon as she had shown Vanessa to a cloakroom and ordered coffee.

"Now then, what *is* going on?" she asked.

"Wait for Vanessa," Fred said wearily. "The poor kid's been dashing around like a blue-arsed fly and *she* deserves to know all about it."

Imogen bottled her exasperation. *This* was a very different Fred, radiating the sort of powerful energy that Richard, like his natural father, James Henry, sometimes produced.

When Fred was ready to begin, he went off in what his small audience found a surprising direction.

"Are you a director of Stewart's?" he asked Imogen.

"Yes."

"A proper director? You can get things done?"

"Yes, if need be. Why?"

Fred ignored both the question and her mounting impatience. "What exactly are the arrangements with Monty over buying these nags? How does he pay for them?"

"We have draft arrangements with Fraunhofer Mackenzie in Lexington," Imogen said, noticing Vanessa's surge of interest in the place-name.

"I know that," Fred said. "How *negotiable* is that loot?"

"What exactly do you mean?" Imogen asked. Her eyes had narrowed, and she seemed to be looking at Fred down her nose.

"Can friend Monty spend it on anything he likes? What if he decided he wanted to pay cash on the nail for these horses?" The room was deathly quiet as Fred and Imogen stared at each other. Fred went on. "Monty's got the full backing of Stewart's, he's good for over two million, and the manager of this bank in Lexington is an old buddy of his. Is that the position?"

Vanessa could see that while Edward had no idea what Fred was talking about, Nancy's mind seemed to be attuned to Imogen's; much of the colour had drained from her face.

"You'd better tell us all about it," Imogen said to Fred.

He kept the preliminaries as brief as possible. Even so, Imogen showed signs of restlessness at the explanation of Vanessa's visit, and their trip to Melton Mowbray. News of the chance sighting of Angela and Monty in the hotel at High Wycombe produced a strong reaction; Imogen was leaning forward in her seat, Nancy was very tense, and Edward looked annoyed. Imogen listened to the account of the dash to Newbury, and the discovery that Monty had given up his flat with mounting excitement.

"That was good thinking," she said, congratulating Fred on his action. "What's been going on this morning?"

"We went to the airport to see Maitland off," Fred said. "She didn't know, of course. Come on, Vanessa, let's hear about it."

Because she was terribly nervous, she started off as though giving evidence in a court of law, but Imogen's admiration for what she had done soon had her behaving normally and enjoying herself.

"God knows I've caused enough trouble with a handbag in my time," Imogen declared. "I have to admit I've never thought of doing it *deliberately*. What a wheeze!"

"I never imagined it would work that well," Vanessa confessed. "I heard everything."

"She was going to Lexington?"

"Definitely. On a single ticket."

"I must say, this is all a bit thick!" Edward burst out. "What the devil does Angela think she's doing? She and I have a ... er ... an understanding."

Imogen came close to laughing at him before unleashing her anger. "Really, Edward! Shut up! There are more important things at stake here than the loss of your fancy woman."

Vanessa saw that he was deeply hurt. He paid no attention to Nancy's comforting grip on his wrist. She wondered if Nancy *knew* she'd done it; the gesture seemed instinctive.

Imogen turned to Fred. "Let us be sure we have this perfectly straight," she said. "There is every reason to suppose that Maitland and Dorchester are very intimately acquainted ... and have been for some time?" she asked Fred. He nodded. "She, having told everyone that she was going to visit her parents is currently en route to New York, and will then go on to Lexington. Monty is travelling to Lexington tomorrow, and has given up his flat."

"That's it," Fred confirmed.

Imogen was thoughtful. "I wonder why they travelled separately?" she said.

"Could Monty have been absolutely sure that one of us wouldn't decide to go with him at the last moment?" Fred asked.

"No ... no, I don't suppose he could," Imogen replied. "*That* proves they're up to no good, doesn't it?"

"I reckon so."

Imogen was deep in thought for a while, staring at Fred. "It looks very much like it, wouldn't you say?"

"At least ninety-five per cent certain."

"Looks like what?" Edward asked.

"Fred and I are of the opinion that Monty is about to help himself to our money and disappear," Imogen said, as though addressing a mental defective. "As a by-product, I imagine we've seen the last of the Maitland creature."

Vanessa felt sorry for Edward. He looked incapable of taking it all in.

"With Richard away, he must have thought he'd got it all stitched up," Fred said.

"Ha! We'll soon see about that!" Imogen looked at her watch. "H'm ... eleven-fifteen. We've tons of time. When does America open?"

"Two o'clock our time," Nancy said. "What are you going to do?"

"Stop the draft, of course," Imogen replied.

"What about Monty?" Edward asked.

"What about him?" Imogen stared at him. "*If* I've made a dreadful mistake, then Monty will no doubt get in touch. I shall heap shame on myself, and do everything I possibly can to recover the situation. Somehow, I don't see that happening."

"Nor me," Fred said.

"Right, I could do it all from here," Imogen said, "but I think I'll run up to town and use the office ... I should get a real grip on it that way. Fred, do you think you could drive me to Didcot to catch a train?"

"With pleasure!"

"In fact, you might as well come to London with me ... in case I need a heavy man." She beamed at him.

Fred was speechless. He knew he deserved a prize, but this was beyond his wildest dreams.

"And what about you, my dear?" Imogen smiled at Vanessa. "I expect you've done enough dashing about for a while?"

"I have really ... and I've a long drive home to Cornwall tomorrow."

"No matter. Stay here, put your feet up. Get Nancy to show you the horses."

"Oh yes, I'd like that."

"Splendid! Fred's coming to dinner this evening, so you'll be handy for that. What about you, Edward?"

"Eh?" He was miles away.

"Are you coming to dinner tonight?"

"Er ... no. Father's arriving this afternoon. I expect he'll want to talk."

"Shame. Come, Fred, the game is afoot! I tell you what, it's a damned good day for it."

"How do you mean?"

"It's Hallowe'en, my dear man. I can use my broomstick officially without any observations from you!"

Fred actually blushed.

Monty received a rapturous welcome in Lexington from Angela, who took a cab out to the airport to meet him. Sensing her mood, he looked forward to a good evening, and was not disappointed; rather than waste time getting dressed and going to the hotel dining-room, they used room service.

"Tell me again," Angela said as they ate dinner propped up in bed. "What's the schedule for tomorrow?"

"I go to Fraunhofer Mackenzie, see Ned Golanski, get some money, take it round to my old bank, and have it transferred to Zürich. That should take an hour. The rest of the day is ours."

"And we fly to Geneva on Saturday?"

"Correct. We'll have a few days there, then toddle over to Zürich and talk to a *real* bank."

"How much are you taking out of Fraunhofer Mackenzie?"

"Just over a million. It's the sort of money people wave around at sales, and it might be all I can carry. It's a pity about the rest."

"What's to stop you going back for some more after lunch?"

"The sales don't start until Saturday. What am I supposed to have spent a million on in a few hours?"

Angela sadly took the point.

Five hours earlier, during the evening of November 1st in England, Richard telephoned Imogen, and she told him what had happened.

"I always said Fred was all right," he said, when he had recovered from the shock, taken it all in and congratulated Imogen on her swift action.

"Yes, you did. I might have to consider changing my mind about him."

From the way she had told the story, Richard knew she already had.

At Saxon Court, Frank Manning spent the latter part of the evening watching TV after a hard but satisfying day. The main purpose of his visit was to provide Kathleen Corrigan with some new cupboards for her kitchen, and it had all gone extremely well; his prefabrication technique was now faultless. He was slightly concerned about Edward, who seemed tense and withdrawn. On the pretext of needing an early night, Edward had gone up to his room where he was alternately cursing Angela and desperately missing her. He drank a great deal.

Vanessa Blandford sat in front of a log fire in her flat above the workshop, and mused on an incredible three days. She wondered if Fred would remember his promise of an order.

––––––––––

Fraunhofer Mackenzie's magnificent Lexington branch had been open nearly an hour on Friday morning before Monty sauntered in. Two of the front-office staff who knew him well greeted him effusively.

"Good to see you again, Mr Dorchester."

"Are you coming back, or is it just the sales, sir?"

"Hi, Steve, Bill! You're both looking well. I'm only over for the sales I'm afraid."

"But you're staying two weeks?"

"Sure."

"You'll have to come out and see Sharon and the kids."

"Love to!"

"What can we do for you?"

"I'd like to see Ned Golanski, please."

"Sure thing. Just one moment, sir."

One of the men hurried away and held a conversation via an inter-office telephone. The watchful Monty had the impression that it was very animated.

"Come right this way, sir."

Monty smiled at several pretty girls as he trod the familiar path between the desks. Ned Golanski came to meet him, right hand held out, a broad smile on his face.

"Hiya, Monty. Good to see you."

"Hello, Ned. How's tricks?"

"Great, just great. Come on in."

Ned Golanski stood aside to let Monty into his office, and followed him in. Monty noticed the handsome new trophy on the bookcase, and walked over to admire it.

"This is nice," he said. "Where did you get it?"

"Paris tournament last fall," Golanski replied proudly. "You wouldn't believe the fish there were in the river that day. Have a seat. I'll get some coffee." He used the intercom on his desk. "Hey, this is great! I didn't think you'd be coming after the other day."

"Why, what happened?" Monty sounded perfectly calm.

"Stewart's cancelled the draft."

"Really?" Monty's eyebrows rose in astonishment.

"Yes. It's the darnedest thing I've seen. Wednesday, it was. We got a telex."

"Do you think I could see it?"

"Sure." Golanski took it from a folder and passed it across. Monty's face remained impassive as he read it.

OUR ARRANGEMENTS FOR DRAWING FACILITIES UP TO $3.4 MILLION FOR MR M DORCHESTER [REF: G31/ 11:15.10.87] ARE HEREBY CANCELLED REPEAT CANCELLED. PLEASE ACKNOWLEDGE.
STEWART'S – LONDON

"I do wish people would tell me these things!" Monty allowed himself a spark of irritation as he passed the paper back.
"It gets worse!" Golanski said. "When I acknowledged, I asked if this meant we wouldn't be seeing you. Look at this!"

WE ARE UNAWARE OF MR DORCHESTER'S PLANS OR MOVEMENTS.
STEWART'S – LONDON

Monty suppressed a sardonic smile. Of course! Imogen Stewart. Only she could have sent that.
"I don't have the faintest idea what this is all about, Ned," he said. "When I left London yesterday morning, my instructions were quite clear. I was going out to Barn Nine for a preview this afternoon."
Golanski shook his head. "It's weird," he said. "Presumably you want to ring these guys and find out what the hell's going on?"
"Er . . . yes . . ." Monty temporised. "I'll get in touch from the hotel," he said. "It's Friday afternoon in England, Ned . . . there's probably no one in the office. You know what they're like. I may have to get hold of people at their homes."
"Well you come right back to me, Monty. Let's have this thing straight for you to do business on Monday."
For the sake of old times, Monty had to sit and chat for ten minutes, during which he agreed to spend Sunday with Ned Golanski and his family on their ranch. When he left Fraunhofer Mackenzie, the effort of responding to the cheerful friendliness of the staff was very nearly too much for him.
As soon as Angela saw his face, her stomach contracted sickeningly. She was waiting in the hotel foyer. He told her about it when they got to their bedroom. He was unemotional, apparently accepting defeat with philosophical resignation. When he had finished, and she asked, "What do we do now?" she saw that, far from being calm, he was deathly white, and shaking with fury.
"Manning!" he spat out. "That bastard Manning! What did you tell him?"

413

"Nothing. I never said a word."

"You must have done! You let something slip." For a second, she thought he was going to hit her, and she took a pace backwards, away from him. Forcing herself to stare into his eyes, she saw they were black with a terrible anger. The deep danger passed as quickly as it had come, and he was roaming round the room like a caged beast.

"It was that bitch Imogen Stewart who did it," he said. "She stopped the draft . . . I'm sure it was her. She and Manning are as thick as thieves . . . he'll have gone running to her, and she did the rest. God! I wanted that money . . . damn it, I *deserved* it! Look at them! Every stupid, uncouth idiot has got money . . . piles of it . . . and they don't even know what to do with it. I would! By God, I'd show them how to live! I . . ."

He stopped, looked surprised at the vehemence of his outburst, and quietened down. Angela said nothing, but she never took her eyes off him.

Monty sank down on to the edge of the bed. "I wonder how he found out," he said. Shaking his head, he looked fleetingly sad and lost. Then he was on his feet again, pulsating with dangerous vigour. "I must try to see Hubert Pearson at Spalding Grafton's," he said. "I'll be about an hour."

It was only after he had slammed out of the bedroom that Angela realised how dreadfully frightened she was. For a time, she had caught a glimpse of something bad and manic in Monty.

Monty was away for nearly two hours. When he re-entered the bedroom, he knew at once that there was no need to check. She had gone.

Next day, he flew to Geneva as planned. He found a room in a moderate, anonymous hotel and rested for two days. Then he telephoned Madeleine de Courcy. She was delighted to hear from him, and sent a car at once to fetch him to her lakeside villa at Lucerne. She had always promised that he would be made very welcome, and she was as good as her word. Appalled to hear of the bad luck that had dogged him since the death of Colorado Hartigan, she used all her considerable resources to cheer him up.

The design of the hotel made it easy. The guest rooms were in chalets, set in an ornamental garden. Once she had made up her mind and flung everything she had into the new suitcase, Angela went into the garden, and hurried towards the gate to a side-street she had discovered during the twenty-four hours before Monty had arrived from England. Fifteen minutes later, she left Lexington on the first escape she could find, a Greyhound bus bound for St Louis, Missouri.

For the first hour of the journey, she stared bitterly at mile after mile of lush grassland and white fencing. It was the kingdom of the thoroughbred horse. Almost everything that happened in this rolling landscape was somehow connected with the breeding of potential champions, horses that went all over the world. Some had gone to Saxon Court. Edward had told her about Parsifal, others sometimes mentioned the legendary James Henry.

Edward!

How *could* he have known about her and Monty? She was convinced he hadn't. Monty's plan was obviously exposed, but surely there was nothing to implicate her in it? For a long time, she considered returning to England: she forced herself to envisage likely airline timetables and time differences. She could be back in London on Saturday afternoon.

The illusion faded with the sunset and gloomy dusk in downtown St Louis. Angela couldn't face it, her nerve had broken. Edward would never be *allowed* to believe her innocence. Imogen, Richard, Fred, Stephanie and all those who worked for Edward would erect a protective screen round him so that people like her and Monty never again got close enough to cause trouble. She took a cab to the airport and bought a seat on a night flight to Los Angeles. Maybe not even Joe Weissman would still care enough to forgive her, but she had to try. He was her only hope.

When the aircraft was airborne, sheer exhaustion closed Angela's eyes. She thought of Stephanie, and the full realisation of what she had done finally hit her. Her mind squirmed away from that torment, only to come to rest on Edward. The vision of him with that chestnut filly flooded back to her, and she wept, the tears marking her travel-stained face.

Vanessa Blandford used Saturday mornings to catch up on her paperwork, and think out new designs. On 7 November, Harry Woodcock brought the post at about nine o'clock as usual, and Vanessa flicked through the thirty or so items. Her curiosity was aroused by an expensive-looking envelope, addressed in a handwriting she did not recognise. She opened it at once.

The briefest glimpse of its contents made her gasp, with shock rather than disbelief. It was Fred's order. She had a fair idea of the value before taking pencil and paper to it, nevertheless, the final figure of a hundred and eighty-five thousand pounds was staggering. She picked up the telephone.

"Fred, it's Vanessa Blandford. I've got your order."

"Good! Have you started work on it yet?"

"It's Saturday!"

"I thought you said you'd got people crying out for work."

"So I have. We'll start on Monday. I thought I'd better talk to you first."

"Talk away."

"You do mean it, don't you, Fred? It's not a joke?"

"I never joke about business, love. Can you handle it?"

"Yes!"

"Get on with it then. I want a sixth of that lot every month for the next six months. Can you finance the first month?"

"Hell! I hadn't thought of that."

"How about ten thousand on account?"

"Are you sure?"

"Positive. I'll put it in the post now."

"This is all very good of you, Fred."

"No, it isn't. Your gear's good, and the price is right. Don't let me down, and there'll be plenty more where that came from."

Their frantic time earlier in the week was never mentioned, but Vanessa had no doubt that it had played a major part in securing the order. She wondered what would become of Monty and Angela. They could be grateful for one thing: the drastic course of action outlined by Imogen was unlikely to be implemented.

Edward would have been content to hide in uncertainty. For as long as nothing was heard of Monty and Angela, a slender case might be made out for their innocence. As yet, there was nothing to suggest that they had been to the bank in Lexington, and tried to get hold of the money. He was not permitted the luxury of ambiguity for long. If only out of courtesy, Richard *had* to speak to Fraunhofer Mackenzie, and he did so at the first opportunity, two o'clock on Monday afternoon.

He relayed the results to Edward immediately.

"Monty was at the bank early on Friday morning," Richard said. "Golanski – he's the manager – told him the draft had been stopped. He took it very well apparently, and said he was going to talk to us."

"Oh." Edward's voice was leaden.

Sensing that it was up to him to continue the conversation, Richard did so.

"It's seventy-two hours since that happened, and he hasn't been in touch."

"All right, I take your point," Edward said irritably. "We've seen the

416

last of Monty." He was in the office, standing with his back to Elaine Mayhew, and so missed her look of anguish.

"Looks like it," Richard replied. "Golanski was very concerned that Monty hadn't been back to him. They really were close friends, it seems, and he was thinking Monty might have had an accident or something. I decided to put him out of his misery and tell him why we stopped the draft. He was shattered, of course."

Edward was indifferent to the point. "What about Angela?" he asked. "Any news of her?"

"No, I'm afraid not, Edward, and I *did* enquire. She certainly didn't go to Fraunhofer Mackenzie with Monty."

There was no need for Elaine Mayhew to ask. Anger drove Edward to tell her.

"Monty-bloody-Dorchester won't be coming back," he said. "It looks as though he was trying to fiddle God-knows-how-much out of us!" Elaine saw the significance of the frenzied activity the previous week, although this did nothing to soften her horrific sense of loss. Without noticing the look on her face, Edward strode towards the door. "And to cap it all," he added furiously, "he's got my friend Miss Maitland with him!"

At lunchtime the following day, Elaine Mayhew telephoned Edward, purportedly to explain her absence. She had barely begun to elaborate on her trumped-up illness when she stopped, changed her mind, and said she was giving up her job with immediate effect. With no more civility than was strictly necessary, Edward accepted her resignation and terminated the conversation.

"That's something to be thankful for, at any rate," he said to his father. "She's packed it in."

Frank, sitting at Edward's desk, greeted the news without sign of emotion.

He had gone home to Worcestershire on Friday evening knowing all about Monty. And there were other things to worry him. For Ann's benefit, he had fabricated a story about Kathleen Corrigan's cupboards not being quite right, and had returned to Saxon Court that morning. In under an hour, he had confirmed his fears. Edward and Imogen's idea that they had the office in good shape was misguided. Bills had been paid, and accounts rendered, but the financial records behind it all were a shambles. Elaine Mayhew had no idea of book-keeping, and the Tax Inspectors would never accept her records.

And, despite his son's elaborate camouflage tactics, Frank also knew that Edward was drinking heavily.

417

Chapter 18

Within days of its exposure and defeat, there was a divergence of opinion over Monty's escapade. Imogen, Richard and Fred came to treat it almost as a joke, especially in the light of Fred's fortuitous intervention, which acquired heroic overtones in the repeated retelling that was inevitable. Edward, the Duke of Dorchester and Stephanie saw it very differently.

Edward was disgusted by Monty's actions, but his outrage was watered down by humiliation at the loss of Angela, producing an insidious alloy of emotions. Monty had shown that he was treacherous and audacious, characteristics that Angela almost certainly admired; doubtless he had also demonstrated supreme skill and endurance as a lover. Jealousy, and the ache of sexual deprivation drove Edward to spend hours speculating about the precise nature of the bond between Monty and Angela, and wondering what had become of them after the failure of the scheme to grab wealth. His self-pitying tendency to blame himself for the whole sorry affair was nurtured by the deleterious effects of alcohol.

Dismayed by the behaviour of his favourite son, the Duke of Dorchester seemed to age overnight. His sprightliness and healthy glow disappeared, to be replaced by a grey melancholy.

"Damn it, Manning, I knew Monty was a bit of a lad," he said, "but I never imagined he was an out and out wrong 'un. I'd never have recommended him, you know. Never!"

"It's quite all right, Freddie," Edward replied. "I should have spotted it myself. And there was the business with Angela."

The Duke shook his head miserably. "That was a dashed bad show. No woman's safe when he's around, but he might have had the decency to stay away from her."

"I was a fool for not seeing *that*."

Minor variants of this conversation took place with a monotonous regularity that neither of them noticed. Monty's scheme had finally breached the floodgates of his mother's wrath, and the Duke took refuge at Saxon Court at least three times a week, joining in Edward's drinking bouts.

Stephanie was appalled by Angela's apparent complicity in the conspiracy. The main part of the drama was played out while she was in London; Fred did not bother to telephone the news to her, a lack of action she soon saw as significant. When she did know, her immediate reaction was to apologise.

"What for?" Fred asked.

"Bringing her here. Letting her get involved with Edward."

"Forget it! It's not your fault. I could have thrown her out . . . Edward didn't have to get mixed up with her. It's the luck of the game."

Fred was cheerful enough, but he made little attempt to be totally convincing. They both knew it was the end. Stephanie sensed that he had someone else in mind, and she had found a small business she wanted to buy. Fred made no comment when she began taking her clothes away.

When Frank decided that he simply must tell Edward about the mess the accounts were in, he took the precaution of doing it in Imogen's presence. He knew that she would not allow the problem to be swept under the carpet.

Imogen grasped the seriousness of the situation at once. "How do we sort this out?" she asked. "Do we need to get an accountant in?"

"That's one way," Frank agreed. "The other, is to let me do it."

"You?" Imogen's surprise came close to implying doubt as to Frank's ability.

"It is a long time since I've done anything like this," Frank said mildly. "But it's like riding a bike . . . you never forget how to do it."

"No, I'm sorry, Frank. I meant that you must have better things to do."

"I haven't – and this is rather important. I'd like to have a go at it."

"That's wonderful, isn't it, Edward?"

"Yes." Edward felt compelled to show interest. "How long will it take you?" he asked.

"Five or six days. If I start now, I should have it finished by next week."

Frank stayed until Friday afternoon, and made good progress on the accounts, but, working in the office all day, he found many other things to do. The most important was the need to pay the yard staff on Thursday. This came as a shock to Edward; however indifferently slipshod he became about affairs at Saxon Court, he still attached a high priority to the well-being of the staff. Siobhan had always dealt efficiently with pay-day, leaving behind a system that Elaine Mayhew had been able to operate. Now, without Frank, there would have been a severe problem.

By Tuesday of the following week, the accounts had been put in order, and Frank explained some of the things he had found. "The biggest mistake was including nearly two hundred thousand pounds of prize-money in stable income," he said. "At least, I think that's what it was. I must say, I can't imagine what Mrs Mayhew was thinking of to do a thing like that."

"So I'd have paid too much tax?" Edward said.

"Yes . . . but nearly half that two hundred thousand pounds was cancelled out by random errors the other way. The Revenue wouldn't have liked it."

"Good God! I'm going to ring the bloody woman up and tell her what I think about her!" It was one of Edward's drinking days. He was bright-eyed and aggressive.

"You'll do no such thing!" Imogen snapped. "She's out of our hair, let's keep it that way." One of her most telling looks stopped Edward dead.

Frank happily spent two or three days each week in the office. As well as officiating over the payroll and maintenance of the accounts, he picked up any administrative work that needed doing, and became quite indispensable. He went to the Fortescue Arms with Dooley at lunchtime, and began work on a project to renew the doors on the boxes in the Old Yard. After over a hundred years of use, some of them were starting to fall apart, and Edward agreed to the replacement of them all. A production line was set up in the workshop near the barn, two of the lads joined in, and eight of the half-doors were turned out each week, enabling four boxes to be re-equipped.

At first, Ann was concerned that it might be too much for Frank, especially with the car journeys on Tuesday mornings and Thursday evenings. She soon accepted that he was thriving on his new career with all its interest and novelty, and decided against putting pressure on him to stop unless winter weather made driving hazardous. Frank knew this, and was grateful. He enjoyed the work, but he also felt a compulsion to keep an eye on Edward that he thought had gone forever when his son ceased to be a small boy twenty-five years ago.

Once Edward had adjusted to the new routine, he normally drank very little during the days that Frank was at Saxon Court. He went to Widney Cheyne regularly, spending a great deal of time with Nancy. They took long walks round the park, looked at the foals Cavaradossi and Lohengrin, and, as dusk fell, could usually be seen through the uncurtained windows having tea in Nancy's cottage. But every Tuesday, when Frank arrived, Edward looked tired and ill as he recovered from the excessive alcohol consumption of the period from Friday to Monday. This was the time when maudlin raking over of the Monty débâcle with the Duke of Dorchester often ran riot. The Duke courted disaster each time he left to drive home, and after his departure at five-thirty or six o'clock, Edward drank fiercely, and alone.

Siobhan was shocked by his condition one Sunday morning when she looked in to see him while visiting Declan and Mary. Her initial impression was that he was ill, until something in his manner, and the watery, slightly glazed appearance of his eyes suggested that he was suffering from a very bad hangover. He moaned peevishly about the mess that Elaine Mayhew had made of the office work; when he eventually condescended to ask how things were going with her, it was evident that he paid no attention to her careful camouflage of life at Epsom. During his first season, none of Nigel's horses had ever looked remotely like winning a race, Victor Macleod had made no secret of his disappointed impatience, and Siobhan was very worried indeed.

In mid-December, as Frank was considering how best to approach Edward about his drink problem, Nancy went to America for a month. She had done in each of the six years she had been in England to spend Christmas and New Year with her father in Vermont. Her departure caused Edward's drinking to escalate. He had now reached the stage of imagining he needed over a bottle of Armagnac a day.

The crisis came within seventy-two hours.

It was a Wednesday afternoon. As yet unaware that there had been a change for the worse, Frank was busy in the office. Richard, having a day away from London, had been visiting an important client in Guildford. His business was satisfactorily concluded over lunch, so he set out for home, and the attractive prospect of a long evening with Imogen and his sons. Half-way through his journey, he realised that he would pass within two miles of Saxon Court, and made the slight detour without hesitation.

Edward had been drinking since eleven o'clock. He had started secretly with laced coffee, then, when Frank went to lunch with Dooley, he took the bottle down to the kitchen, returning to his bedroom a few minutes before he knew they would return. He stayed there, still drinking, trying to do a crossword puzzle. When he put the empty bottle in the wardrobe, he saw that the shameful pile was getting out of hand again: without Angela's efforts, it had grown. His father never left the office before five-thirty and always kept the door closed to avoid disturbance from the kitchen. Confident that he could slip out to his car unnoticed, Edward loaded six bottles into the big plastic carrier-bag that Angela had always returned after each trip.

For some time afterwards, Edward blamed the carpet that had worn slack on the stair treads; he also believed it would have been better to have put shoes on rather than slippers.

When he lost his footing, he had to grab the banister with both hands to stop himself pitching headlong down the stairs.

The carrier, packed with bottles, hit three steps on the way down. The noise, echoing through the hall, seemed to Edward to be magnified a hundredfold. At the bottom, the bag burst, spilling its contents with an horrendous clatter. In the midst of fabricating a story to tell his father,

Edward gaped stupidly. Richard was the last person he had expected to come dashing out of the office.

Richard stared at the bottles, clearly unable to believe his eyes. Edward was fascinated by the fact that none of them had broken. Richard picked one up and studied the label. Then his gaze went up the stairs to Edward, still hanging on to the rail.

"I think you and I had better have a chat about this," Richard said quietly.

Edward made the effort to pull himself together, regained the landing with the exaggerated dignity of intoxication, and went back into his bedroom, slamming the door behind him.

Frank, looking grave, remained at the foot of the stairs as Richard went up, knocked on the door, and went into Edward's room without waiting for an answer.

At first, Frank could hear nothing other than the murmur of voices, Richard's insistent and reasonable, Edward speaking jerkily and sullenly.

After a few minutes, Richard's voice rose. "No, Edward! I don't sympathise with you. It's utter lunacy. It's got to stop. At once!"

Edward's reply was unintelligible, but the anger was clear enough.

"Don't be ridiculous, Edward! Nothing's been ruined – but if you carry on like this, *you* soon will be. Have you *seen* yourself? You're in a shocking state. Come and have a look!"

There were sounds of ineffectual protest from Edward, a dull thud as a chair was knocked over, then silence. Frank assumed that Richard had taken Edward into the bathroom. For a moment or two he felt hopelessly lost. Moving slightly, his foot struck one of the bottles; he was bending down to pick it up when Mary came in to begin work on the evening meal. There was a wealth of knowledge and understanding in the look with which she assessed the situation.

"I'm glad it's happened," she said after Frank had told her all about it. "Sir Richard will get something done."

Frank was acutely aware of what her statement implied. "Has this been going on long?" he asked.

"At least two years," she told him. "That's only my opinion, mind. Declan doesn't agree – but he always sticks up for him, come hell or high water."

The saddest thing, Frank thought, was that Edward was probably convinced that no one had noticed.

Mary made a pot of tea, and they waited in the kitchen for Richard. It was nearly half an hour before he appeared, carrying two unopened bottles of Armagnac.

"It's all right," Frank assured him. "Mary knows. She has done for some time."

"I wish you'd said something, Mary." Richard paused, and shook his head. "No, you couldn't, could you? What a miserable business!" He put the two bottles on the table. "That's all there is, as far as I can see. I've looked more or less everywhere." He sat down, reaching for the cup of tea that Mary poured. "There's a wardrobe full of empty bottles." He shook his head.

"How is he?" Frank asked.

"Flaked out. I've undressed him, and shoved him into bed. I think he's in a bad way."

"What do we do now?"

"Can I make a suggestion?" Mary asked Richard, who clearly had no idea what to say to Frank.

"Of course, Mary. Please do."

"Tell Lady Imogen. She'll fix it."

Richard nodded. "What do you think, Frank?" he asked.

"Yes. Mary's right. We must get him straight . . . and presumably you want him to carry on here? He's no good to you in this state."

"Absolutely!" Richard smiled forlornly. "As one banker to another, Frank, I have an investment in this place, and Edward is the best person to look after it. What's the matter?" Frank was looking very thoughtful.

"I don't see any need to let Ann know about this," Frank said carefully. "She'd be very upset, and that means she'd start fussing. I could envisage her putting pressure on Edward to pull out. The only time she's ever been fully convinced about this place was when Caroline was here."

"All right, we won't breathe a word," Richard agreed. "It's up to you what you tell Ann."

When he left Saxon Court, Richard shuddered at the memory of what he had said to Frank about protecting his investment. However convincing it might have seemed, it was such a prosaic reduction of the truth as to be an aberration. But Frank knew nothing of the promise made to the dying James Henry. And he thought he was the old man's only living son.

That evening, Imogen and Frank spoke for a long time on the telephone.

Slumped at the kitchen table, Edward looked dreadful when Imogen marched in at eight-thirty the following morning. He winced at the effort of lifting his head to look at her.

"I suppose you've come to tell me what an idiot I am," he said. Despite everything, there was a flicker of defiance.

"No, I have not," she replied. To his surprise, she came to his side, and put an arm round his shoulders. "I've come to take you to Widney Cheyne. A few weeks there will do you the world of good."

"Do I have any alternative?" he asked.

"I'd prefer it if you didn't think in those terms."

"Do I?"

"No, you don't."

He thought about it. Imogen watched a succession of emotions cross his face. Truculence was followed by petulance, then resignation was overtaken by what seemed like relief.

"It might be a good thing," he said, and struggled to his feet.

Imogen had it all organised. Rosie was to deal with the office phone when Frank wasn't there, Declan and Freezer were more than capable of maintaining the winter routine of the yard. While Edward was still packing the clothes he needed, Freezer went round telling all the lads and girls something very close to the truth. This was perfectly normal: Freezer was always the communicator. The guv'nor wasn't very well, he said, and was going to Widney Cheyne for a time so that he could be properly looked after. There was nothing to worry about, and he would soon be back, as good as new. As Imogen drove Edward away, a group of the lads waved sympathetically.

Stephanie marked the advent of 1988 by moving into her new home and business. It had all been finalised before Christmas, but the inertia of the holidays prohibited action until 4 January. This enforced delay was the only hitch in an incredibly smooth sequence of events.

She had been staggered by the price an estate agent had placed on her flat in London. He suggested that in five years, it had appreciated from the sixty thousand pounds she had paid for it, to over two hundred thousand pounds. Disbelief had vanished when, within hours of the flat going on the market, she was faced by three potential buyers who were eager to start an auction. Totally bemused, Stephanie had left them to it, and slipped out to the shops, returning fifteen minutes later to accept the winning bid of two hundred and forty-five thousand pounds.

Booming London property prices meant that she could buy the antique shop in the pleasant Sussex town of Lewes with a degree of confidence that had seemed pie in the sky at the venture's inception. Well-situated in a busy thoroughfare, the shop had originally been a Georgian town house. Apart from a tiny office in the old pantry, the whole of the ground floor was dedicated to the shop, the five rooms forming a rabbit-warren that was a browser's paradise. Upstairs, the living accommodation needed only a coat of paint to make it very homely.

After spending four days getting the flat more or less how she wanted it, Stephanie turned her attention to the shop, in which the stock she had taken over was still in the haphazard disarray left by the valuers.

Selecting half a dozen pieces that were eye-catching, she arranged them in the window, and went outside to see how they looked. It was Saturday, the pavement was busy, and as Stephanie studied her display, moving to different viewpoints without regard for the people hurrying past, it was inevitable that a collision would take place.

When she did back into someone, the automatic apologies began before she turned to look at the man she had pushed into the gutter. "I say, I'm awfully sorry, I . . ."

Recognition brought amazement.

"Edwin, what are you doing here?" she asked.

"I live here," Edwin Fforbes replied. "Well, my house is a few miles away actually, but I usually come into town on Saturday. What about you? What brings you here?"

"My shop!" Stephanie waved an arm with grandiose pride, nearly removing the hat of a passer-by.

"Good gracious! I noticed it had been sold. Are you living here?"

"Yes. Come and have a coffee. Let's get out of this awful wind."

She took him up to the flat, where he gave vent to his surprise at literally bumping into her, and said complimentary things about both the flat and the shop. Ten minutes of inconsequential chat emboldened him to ask, "How does this fit in with Fred?"

"It doesn't," she replied briskly. "That is over. Kaput! Finito! All washed up. No, don't worry, it was all very civilised and mutual. It had been conking out for some time. Our usefulness had expired. That dreadful business with Monty and Angela was sort of the last straw. She was my friend after all."

"Yes . . . but surely no blame attaches to you over that?"

Stephanie smiled to herself; she could envisage him using such a slightly quaint mode of expression at the bank.

"Not really," she said. "Fred didn't hold it against me – he's not that sort of bloke. I felt pretty guilty, though. I dread to think what Edward made of it all. I meant to ring him up, but I never got round to it."

"I understand he hasn't been too well," Edwin told her gravely. "Getting better now, I'm told."

"Oh dear. More coffee? Was he very upset, do you know?"

The conversation meandered on for another fifteen minutes, with Edwin Fforbes devoting most of his efforts to wondering at his incredibly good luck in finding Stephanie, and gathering his courage. When it finally came, his suggestion had an air of cheerful casualness completely at odds with the state of his nerves.

"We're almost neighbours. Perhaps we ought to have dinner to celebrate."

She thought about it for what seemed like a very long time. She was, he thought, looking for a polite way of telling him not to be such a silly old fool, thus dashing the dreams he had cherished for such a long time. But when the reply came, accompanied by a glowing smile, he experienced an almost adolescent elation. "Yes. That's a nice idea, Edwin. I'd like that very much indeed."

Edward was agreeably surprised by what happened to him at Widney Cheyne. He had gone passively, expecting nothing – apart from the uneasy notion that Imogen might put him under some sort of restraint. She did no such thing. He was free to come and go as he pleased, and the huge drinks cabinet in the dining room was there if he wanted it. After three days of physical misery, shivering one minute, sweating the next, and with hallucinatory defects of vision, he began to feel better. Regular meals and vast quantities of fruit juice soon brought him to the point at which he saw that he could not let Imogen and Richard down. When part of his mind reasoned that a drink, just one small one, would do no harm, would make him feel even better in fact, he was able to appreciate that he owed it to himself not to practise such self-deceit.

Richard was glad to talk to him about it.

"There *must* have been something visible between Monty and Angela," Edward said. "I'd have seen it if I hadn't been drunk most of the time."

"You might have done," Richard agreed. "So what?"

"Then I'd have known what they were up to."

"You mean the stunt Monty was trying to pull? I doubt it, you know. You'd have been too busy being annoyed."

"I'd have known!"

"What, that they were going to rob us of two million quid? Oh come on, Edward, I doubt if even Fred would have suspected *that* of them . . . although, I don't know." Richard smiled. "Fred's a wily old devil."

"Whereas I'm naïve?"

"To an extent. But remember, you've led something of a charmed life. That school was hardly a cut-and-thrust job, was it? And since you've been training, you've been surrounded by trustworthy, honest people. Monty was a five-star rogue, and Angela . . . well . . . she was just downright amoral."

"I might have seen some of that if I'd had my wits about me instead of being addled with booze."

"You might have done."

"I could have wrecked everything," Edward muttered. "I'll make damned sure it never happens again."

"We *all* must," Richard said.

The key to success in Edward's struggle was company. He had failed to notice what a lonely place he had made Saxon Court, especially after work, and in the winter. Now he had Imogen and Richard in the evenings, and Richard's mother during the day.

Since coming to Widney Cheyne to occupy what she referred to as "the most palatial granny flat north of Biarritz", Julia had been occupying herself by writing a history of Stewart's. Richard had promised to have it published, if only as a private limited edition, for the bank's bicentenary. Edward frequently joined Julia in her workroom, crammed full of archive material, and listened to some of the more hair-raising adventures she had uncovered, and which were definitely not for publication. They also walked miles round the park, and she told him the full story of James Henry's early days at Avoca House, with details and anecdotes that were new to him, giving him much food for thought.

"What's the matter?" Julia asked, when she saw him particularly pensive one day.

"I know it sounds an awful thing to say at this stage, but I never knew the old man had such a hard time."

"Oh yes! The first few years were very dodgy indeed. There were times when sheer bloody-mindedness and the thought of you were the only things that kept him going."

"Me?"

"Yes, you. He was determined to leave something you could build on."

Edward felt very small. "Could do a hell of a sight better," the voice of the school report said to him yet again, and Julia saw that she had made a successful point.

Christmas passed quietly, a triumph for Frank, who distracted Ann from visiting Widney Cheyne to find out precisely what was wrong with Edward, by whisking her off on the Mediterranean cruise she had always wanted. As Edward toasted the New Year with a glass of mineral water, he realised that he had forgotten when he had last calculated, to the hour, how long it was since he had drunk alcohol.

When she came back from America, Nancy saw the change in him. His eyes and complexion had improved, and at long last, he had started to lose the gauntness that had come on him after Caroline. When she had slept off the effects of her journey, he told her all about it.

"Drink's bad," she said, after she had heard him out with an increasingly stern face. "It did for a cousin of mine."

"What, you mean killed him?" Edward was horrified.

"Yup!" Nancy frowned at him. "You've got to stop it."

"I have done," he said triumphantly.

"Tell me that in a year's time . . . then another year . . . and then another."

"God! Is it that bad?"

"It is. Still, Brewster had nothing to do but drink, you've got plenty of work waiting. There's a good season coming up."

"You think so?"

"I know so."

On a Friday evening at the end of February, Edwin Fforbes took Stephanie to Covent Garden to see Borodin's rarely performed opera *Prince Igor*. He knew and loved the work from a set of 1950s vintage gramophone records, but there was another reason why he thought they should go. The most expensive horse he had yet bought was named after the opera's hero. Stephanie left the shop in charge of Mrs Cartwright, her reliable part-time assistant, and caught a late-afternoon train to London, where Edwin met her at Victoria Station.

It was only the second time that Stephanie had ever seen an opera, the first being a mediocre touring production of *The Marriage of Figaro* when she was sixteen. Approaching the experience with some trepidation, she became entranced the moment the lights went down, and the overture began. It was a sumptuous production, emphasising the barbaric splendour of medieval life in a remote part of the vast Russian empire, and she found it absolutely thrilling from start to finish. When they had supper afterwards, her head was still reeling with the music and spectacle of the Polovtsian Dances.

On their last train, which left Victoria at a minute to midnight, Stephanie fell asleep almost immediately. When she awoke nearly an hour later, her head was on Edwin's shoulder, and he, too, was dozing. He had actually put his feet up on the seat opposite, but had carefully spread the *Financial Times* on it first.

At Lewes, they found that it was a bitterly cold night, with snow gusting in the strong wind, and treacherous conditions underfoot.

"Oh Lord!" Edwin muttered, peering up into the eddies of snow round a street light.

"You can't go home in this," Stephanie said. When he looked at her doubtfully, she added, "You might not get up that hill past Broadbridge. What happens if you get stuck? You'd better come with me."

They were both rather surprised when he agreed with her.

The heavy belt of snow that swept across the southern counties of England that night caused Edward delay and frustration. Now back at Saxon Court, and in full command of himself, he had used the previous week's mild weather to start the horses on light work. They had all

428

cantered a few furlongs, and he was well pleased with most of them. For the five days that the snow hung around, even the all-weather gallop was unusable, so he had to be content with trotting in the covered ride.

Edward did not have Nancy to help him. This was the breeding season, and for the next two months she would be fully occupied supervising the stallion duties of T. P. Malahide and Parsifal. She also had to make arrangements for the eighty brood-mares who would be visiting them. She promised to come to see him on Saturday mornings whenever possible, and Edward went to Widney Cheyne one afternoon a week to talk over his ideas and spend time with Cavaradossi and Lohengrin who were now strapping yearlings. They both had a lot more growing to do, but they were safely well on the way to becoming very fine horses.

The closing date for entry to the first four Classic races of the season was 24 February, Edward's birthday. Two days prior to this, Frank learned a new facet of work in the office when he entered Edwin Fforbes's Prince Igor for the Two Thousand Guineas and the Derby.

"Has he got a chance?" Frank asked.

"Yes, for the Guineas. I'm not so sure about the Derby. He isn't really bred for much more than a mile. I fancy him to do well in the Guineas if I can get him right."

"That's exactly what Dooley said."

Edward laughed. "In that case, we're home and dry!"

Frank felt sure that he would be visiting a bookmaker before the week was out.

Prince Igor had cost Edwin Fforbes two hundred thousand pounds as a yearling at the Dublin sales. He was a rather wilful individual who had already demonstrated the need for a team of many temperaments and talents in a successful stable. When he had first come to Saxon Court, a number of the lads and girls had tried, in vain, to do something with him. After three months of sometimes painful and anguished frustration, Edward had handed the colt over to 'Greaser' O'Malley. Greaser, whose nickname stemmed from his penchant for immense quantities of butter on bread or toast, was one of the original Avoca House contingent. He was a happy-go-lucky, completely charming bachelor of thirty-five, who always did his horses right, and had produced his share of honest winners. But nothing potentially brilliant had ever come his way until Prince Igor, who needed a subtle blend of strength and sorcery to make him work. Whatever the mixture was, Greaser had it, and Prince Igor had made good progress as a two-year-old the previous season. He won his three races, and then became the only real disappointment of Frescobaldi's great year. A week before the Dewhurst

Stakes, he pulled a muscle while galloping and had to be withdrawn, thus ending the season undefeated but still something of an unknown quantity.

Despite his awkwardness, Edward believed in the colt and wanted to see him do well. By the middle of March, conditions on the gallops were close to ideal, and Greaser soon had him covering the ground in fine style. Very encouragingly, the two horses with whom he did his early work both went out to win races in mid-April. After that, Prince Igor galloped with Fred Bird's colt, The Pedlar, also entered for the Derby, but whose prime target was a race at York in May. Edward made sure that he set the highest standards by example; he rode out on Murgatroyd with both lots each morning, and evening stables was once more a searching examination of the smallest detail.

Five days before the Two Thousand Guineas, he came back from watching Prince Igor's last gallop with a feeling of quiet confidence, to be confronted with an unexpected test of his new-found control. His father pointed out an airmail letter, just arrived with the morning post. Because the envelope was marked 'Strictly Personal', Frank had not opened it. Edward kept it by his plate during the breakfast conference, shooting frequent uneasy glances at it. When he went out with the second lot, Frank found it on the floor under the kitchen table, still sealed.

Edward eventually opened it when he was alone, eating the lunch that Mary had prepared. According to the postmark, the letter had left Santa Ana, California a week ago. He stared at the contents for some time before starting to read. He had never seen Angela's handwriting before. What an extraordinary relationship it must have been, he thought, as though he had not been part of it. The writing was neat and somehow formal, not at all what he would have expected. There was no address, and it was undated.

Dear Edward,

I'm sorry. I really am. It's no good pretending I didn't want a share in the money, but it wasn't my idea in the first place. Monty and I got on very well, and I knew that we (you and me) had no future, so I went along with him.

I haven't seen Monty since he came back from the bank with the news that it had all gone wrong. As soon as he went to see somebody, I just ran. I came back to the West Coast to look for a chap I used to know, and we're getting married next month. Although he doesn't earn much money, he's a lot better than I maybe deserve!

I cleared out of Lexington because I was scared stiff of Monty. He took it very badly. He's a frightening character sometimes. I'm sure he can't do you any harm, but look out all the same.

Good luck, and be happy. Give my love to Stephanie, and tell her I'm very sorry. I miss you both.
Angela.

Edward read it three times, then tossed it aside. He finished his lunch and went to Widney Cheyne to talk to Nancy.

Later that afternoon, Frank found the letter. He studied it, shook his head sadly, and put it in a safe place.

The Two Thousand Guineas proved to be the most exciting running of the race for several years. On a Rowley Mile that was unusually firm and fast for the time of year, two of the eleven runners were clearly unable to handle the ground and the pace. Passing the bushes, Bernard Dalrymple's Hereward the Wake and a French challenger went for home at a tremendous clip, opening up a three-length gap between them and the rest. As they tore past the furlong marker, Edward shrugged, and waved farewell to what had been a nice idea while it lasted.

He had turned his back on the race to speak to Nancy when the noise of the crowd, and her sudden vice-like grip on his arm made him whip round. Sean Gillespie had kept Prince Igor well covered up at the back, last, apart from the two stragglers who weren't coping with the ground. But now, they were scorching down the centre of the track, Sean looking for all the world like the avenging angel, his face set in a fiendish grimace of determination. Edward held his breath. Prince Igor was undoubtedly gaining on the leaders at a spectacular rate: would it be enough? From where Edward was standing he was unable to judge the relative positions of the three horses with any accuracy.

On the line, he thought Prince Igor hadn't quite made it, but the voice of a shrewd bookmaker cut through the din. "Manning's horse has got it," he yelled, and he was right. Although the judge called for a photograph, Sean Gillespie was adamant.

"The man's blind!" he said scornfully. "He won by a mile."

The official verdict of a head – about twelve inches – confirmed the judge's prudence, especially since only the same narrow margin separated second and third.

Bernard Dalrymple was as generous as ever. "Well done, Edward. Very nice piece of work. That jockey of yours is getting good!"

Edward smiled weakly. "I thought he'd left that one a bit late."

"No, just right. That fellow won't go much more than a mile, will he?"

"I don't think so. He's very questionable for Epsom."

"No matter. He did you proud today." Bernard Dalrymple moved

431

closer, lowering his voice. "I say, I've heard whispers about young Dorchester. Is there any truth in them?"

"Probably!" Edward replied dourly. He correctly assumed that the sad ramblings of the Duke himself had been the origin of the rumour.

"Good God!" Momentarily they were both grim, then Bernard Dalrymple brightened. "Ah! There's Mrs Prendegast pulling faces at you," he said. "She thinks you robbed us."

Edward waved at Finoula who was leading the second-placed Hereward the Wake away, and glowering comically in his direction.

Imogen and Richard who had travelled to Newmarket for the race were naturally overjoyed by Edwin's success, yet it was almost insignificant compared to the presence of Stephanie.

Before that memorable Saturday at the end of April, Edwin had not breathed a word to anyone about his burgeoning romance. This reticence was mostly the product of his inherent bashfulness, but there was a tiny element of harmless mischief. He wanted to see the reaction of his friends when they found out. The Two Thousand Guineas seemed an ideal occasion to proclaim their relationship, Stephanie was eager to see the race, so Mrs Cartwright looked after the shop for the day.

Edwin was not disappointed.

He and Stephanie stopped for lunch in Cambridge, and did not arrive on the course until half an hour before the Guineas was due to be run. Both Imogen and Richard were struck dumb when Stephanie and Edwin approached them; Edward was busy with Prince Igor, and so missed the initial shock. Edwin was doing his best to look nonchalant, but achieving only limited success; to make quite certain that no one misunderstood the situation, Stephanie linked arms with him. She looked superb in a burgundy-coloured cloak and matching fedora hat.

Imogen was pleased. Her only complaint, which she made with vigour, was that she had known nothing about it. When Edward appeared, he, too, was surprised and happy, if a little sad. Edwin Fforbes, unassuming and sometimes painfully shy, had become a partner in a deeply-felt love that charmed all who saw it. Stephanie, who could so easily have appeared to be his daughter, or even a disreputable passing fancy, had gained stature and serenity in the symmetry of their relationship. As the three of them stood together in the paddock while the horses walked round, Edward felt like an intruder. For the first time, he appreciated something of what he and Caroline had generated.

Stephanie's influence was powerfully evident when the race was over, and Edwin had to take his place in the winner's enclosure. Simply by being at his side, Stephanie transformed a potential ordeal into a triumph. When she raised her left hand to pat Prince Igor's neck, the spring sunlight was turned abruptly to fire by a magnificent cluster of diamonds. Imogen had failed to spot the ring until that moment; while she advanced

432

on Stephanie in search of further details, Edward spoke to Bernard Dalrymple, waved to Finoula, pulled faces back at her, and agreed to give Wesley Davies a TV interview.

It was five years to the day since he had last appeared before the cameras. Mary and Rosie, watching in the lads' hostel, remembered James Henry's great victory in the Two Thousand Guineas. For a few seconds, they were quiet and tense in the midst of jubilation.

Without Siobhan, Imogen had appointed herself official photographer. Technically, she was almost as good, but took substantially longer. When they all arrived back at Saxon Court, only Prince Igor was unmoved by the forty-five minutes of posing beneath the clock-tower. The final group consisted of Edwin, Stephanie, Greaser and Frank. Edward lodged a facetious protest with Imogen.

"You didn't get me in!"

"Quite right! We don't want the Colour Room cluttered up with pictures of you."

"How did father get in on the act?"

"He's a very deserving case."

"Why?"

Imogen gave him a hard stare. "Because he's running the place. He's here five or six days a week now. Or hadn't you noticed?"

Edward hadn't. He looked suitably chastened.

The decision as to whether to run Prince Igor in the Derby had to be taken without the assistance of a video-recording of the Two Thousand Guineas. Recordings were sometimes made these days, but there was no consistent substitute for Siobhan. On this occasion, Rosie had forgotten, and gone to the lads' hostel to watch the race; Frank had no idea that a recording was so desirable. In any case, he had yet to master the intricacies of the recorder, and was rather in awe of it.

Sean Gillespie swore that Prince Igor would get a mile and a half, Edward and Greaser were undecided, Nancy was sure that he wouldn't. In the end, it was Freezer who had the casting vote.

"No, sir. Another furlong, and he'd have been going backwards."

Edwin Fforbes was advised to take his colt out of the Epsom Classic in favour of Royal Ascot two weeks later. He agreed at once.

The Pedlar did well at York, finishing second in the Dante Stakes after being boxed in for most of the run for home, and there was a strong feeling that he would stay the Derby distance. Fred was so tickled pink to have a runner in the premier Classic, that the question of The Pedlar actually winning the race never arose. They had a wonderful day out, Fred was at the peak of his form, and The Pedlar ran well. But like the

433

other fifteen horses, he was unable to offer very much resistance to Hereward the Wake, who handled the supreme test with consummate ease to become Bernard Dalrymple's third Derby winner.

At Royal Ascot, Prince Igor confirmed his class by winning the St James's Palace Stakes in style, and Edward looked on approvingly as Stephanie, dressed with impeccable taste, helped Edwin with the formalities.

"Edwin's having a very good year," Edward said to Richard.

"Isn't he just! Very well deserved, though. And what do you think of this little lot?"

Richard was looking towards Valerie Malahide and Fred Bird, who were deep in a conversation that seemed to be most serious. Valerie was at Widney Cheyne for Ascot, and had been greeted on her arrival by vast quantities of flowers from Fred, accompanied by an invitation to dinner that she had unhesitatingly accepted.

Edward smiled. "Fred's got a thing about Valerie," he said. "Do you remember that get-together we had to decide what we wanted Monty to buy in Kentucky? I saw something then. He was almost mesmerised by her."

"Really? I suppose it's 'quality', is it?"

"Yes. I say! Look at Stephanie! See the way she's watching them?"

Richard smiled at the expression on Stephanie's face as she looked at Valerie and Fred. With her own happiness secured, Stephanie seemed almost beatifically indulgent, willing Fred to be successful.

"I can see Fred's point," Richard said. "Valerie's a sweetie, and she's very grateful to Fred for settling Monty's hash."

"Naturally."

"I can also reveal . . ." Richard sidled closer with an air of mock-conspiracy ". . . that Fred reminds her of old T.P."

"Good grief! I always thought he was a gentleman."

"Don't be ridiculous! That was only after he sold out and discovered Beethoven. You don't build a haulage empire by being a softie – especially in Ireland in the fifties."

"I see. It's like being a merchant banker, is it?"

Richard laughed, and went to look for Imogen.

There seemed to be developments between Valerie and Fred over the four days of the Royal meeting, but not even Imogen was able to deduce what they were, and for some obscure reason she drew the line at asking Valerie. When Valerie flew back to Dublin at the end of the week, she left an air of mystery and a strangely subdued Fred.

The entertainment they provided did much to soften the disappointment that followed Prince Igor's victory. Edward had decided to bring some of his two-year-old hopefuls out, despite uncharacteristic pessimism from Declan, Freezer and Robin Lane, all of whom insisted that

434

the juveniles were backward. They proved to be right. Eight horses competed in the five available races; they all moved down to the start like budding champions, but came back with nothing better than a fourth place, and a list of excuses that threatened to stretch to Windsor Castle. Light relief was provided by John Dyer, who rode what was deemed to be the weaker animal in the three races where Edward had duplicate entries. He finished well ahead of the increasingly disgusted Sean Gillespie each time.

Nancy, now free of the most onerous of her duties at the stud, agreed with Declan. The two-year-olds were all fit and full of condition: for whatever reasons, they had not learned to race, and had no idea what to do with themselves once battle was joined.

"I've never had this problem before," Edward said. "At least, not on this scale. The whole lot of them are duffers."

"That's horses for you," Nancy replied. "You never stop learning. Shall I come and have a look at them?"

"Yes, please."

Edward worked the two-year-olds on Tuesdays and Fridays as the second lot. Riding Prospero, a retired gelding from the original batch of horses that Mark Walgrave had bought, Nancy went out on to Saxon Down with Edward to watch them. Careful not to make heavy demands too early, Edward galloped them in pairs along the sand, about twenty yards between each pair. It was a routine that had become something of a ritual, and after watching it for the third time, Nancy realised how rigid it was. The same two horses, ridden by two girls, always led the procession.

"That's the trouble," she said, pulling a stopwatch from the pocket of her breeches. "That front pair aren't doing anything. What sort of time is this for five furlongs?"

She passed the watch across, and Edward's eyebrows arched in surprise when he saw the time it registered. "One minute eighteen seconds," he said. "That's ridiculous!"

"You can see it now, look." Nancy pointed at the last few pairs, still to complete the gallop. "They're going at no pace at all. The lead pair are crawling, and the rest are following. They can't do much else, can they?"

"Right! Well done, Nancy. I'll soon get this sorted out."

Next time the two-year-olds worked, Alison Bairstow and Robin Lane were at the front. Alison rode the Duke of Dorchester's filly Santuzza, Edward's favourite, and Robin was on Valerie Malahide's Prometheus, a fine-looking T. P. Malahide colt. Carefully briefed by Edward, they set a slightly faster tempo, increasing it again the following Tuesday. By the end of July, the gallop was being run at a cracking pace, and the better horses were ready to move from the sand to grass.

Two weeks later, they started winning.

Observers wondered whether Bernard Dalrymple's famous purple patch at the back end of the 1980 season was in danger of losing its place in the record books. Between the middle of August and the first week in October, Saxon Court two-year-olds competed in seventy-three races. There were forty-two winners. One of Richard's colts won three times in the seven-week period, and Santuzza pleased Edward enormously by capturing the Mill Reef Stakes at Newbury. Punters and bookmakers waged a war of attrition of which Frank and Dooley became increasingly aware as the odds available to them shrank by the day. Frank, inclined to be far more daring than Dooley, finally had to admit defeat at Kempton Park. He took an afternoon off, and went with Dooley, Freezer and Liam Corrigan to see one of Fred's horses make her debut. When betting opened, the filly was quoted at the outrageous price of seven to one *on*, despite her moderate breeding and heavily bandaged forelegs. She duly finished last but one, and the bookmakers were not surprised; but after the experiences of the past few weeks, they were not prepared to take the smallest chance.

Edward laughed at it all. He was partly moved by amused incredulity. "Let's send a donkey to Newmarket tomorrow," he said to Frank one morning over breakfast. "I bet it would win!"

However, most of his motivation came from happiness.

Throughout a glorious late summer, he worked closely with Nancy, whom everyone at Saxon Court was starting to think of as Edward's unofficial assistant. Every time Frank went to the end of the Avenue to watch work, he instinctively looked for them; they were always in the same place, still and attentive, Murgatroyd and Prospero like statues against the sunrise.

It was perfectly natural that Edward and Nancy should drive to Sussex together for the wedding, leaving Imogen and Richard to make their own arrangements. Edwin and Stephanie had decided not to wait any longer. Although flattered by Stephanie's assurances about his youthfulness, Edwin was anxious to grasp as much as possible of his unexpected happiness while he still had time. Perhaps Stephanie would keep going with the shop for a while; it depended on when the children arrived.

It was the first English wedding that Nancy had attended, and she enjoyed it immensely. To no one's surprise, Stephanie, in a breathtaking dress, made a wonderful bride, and her distinguished-looking groom was clearly unable to believe his good fortune. Yet Nancy's greatest thrill came at the reception. What had once been Edward's favourite champagne was served. She saw him refuse it and ask for mineral water.

Many men would have questioned Monty's assessment of his year in Lucerne. At the very least, they would have thought him difficult to please.

Madeleine de Courcy was forty-four, looked thirty, and had a highly-developed appetite for epicurean eroticism. Four years ago, she and Monty had become lovers within hours of meeting each other, forging a bond that neither of them could forget. She was in Kentucky with her husband's agent who had been sent to buy bloodstock.

Rolfe de Courcy, then aged seventy-two, was a shadowy figure. He left his study only to sit on the verandah overlooking the lake, where his hooded eyes were ever-watchful. His life had been spent on the fringes of European finance; never visible in any business transaction, he took a half or one per cent of vast sums of money for 'arranging' matters. There were those who suspected that the launching of his nebulous career owed much to collaboration with the Nazis in his native Dijon between 1941 and 1944. The fraud divisions of three national police forces kept files on him, but had never been able to obtain hard evidence. When he died intestate, leaving Madeleine and a daughter who had always hated the sight of him, his widow inherited a fortune she could not comprehend. Well over one hundred million Swiss francs were deposited in fourteen banks under a variety of pseudonyms.

Madeleine asked Monty to unravel her convoluted financial affairs, and empowered him to act on her behalf through an astonishing web of banks and lawyers. Taking his time, so that he always had something to do when boredom threatened, Monty consolidated the fourteen bank accounts into two. He shifted twenty-five million pounds through deliberately obscure channels, and took only one per cent for himself, adding two hundred and fifty thousand pounds to his own cache.

He satisfied Madeleine de Courcy by night, and robbed her by day, and was still soured by discontent.

Almost every weekday, Madeleine held a coffee morning which was attended by women in a similar position to herself, bored, living on money that made them uneasy, not at all sure whether it was wise or safe to display their wealth. After being the showpiece of two such gatherings, Monty escaped the tedium either by visiting banks, or the Café Bertrand.

A feature of the café was its comprehensive selection of English

437

newspapers, and Monty followed Edward's progress through the best season he had enjoyed since Caroline's death. The canker took a firm hold on him when he read of Prince Igor's Two Thousand Guineas victory. For a few moments, until he became aware of the startled scrutiny of a pretty waitress, his face was white with anger. That was still more money for Manning and his clique to gloat over! The colt's earning capability at stud was something like half a million a year while he had to grub around for petty cash.

Madeleine was too self-centred and silly to bother looking far for an explanation of Monty's moods. She countered his black depressions with an extravagant present, or an extra effort in bed. He let her believe that it worked.

When it came, the phenomenal run of success enjoyed by Edward's two-year-olds was an almost daily threat to Monty's presence of mind. Twice he flung the paper down and fled from the Café Bertrand to shout his bile at trees and mountains.

A dreadful calm enveloped him after he finally snapped. He told Madeleine that he had to go to England for a few days to deal with family business. She accepted it, thinking that he would be his old self again once he was rid of whatever was worrying him. Complacently involved in preparations for an elaborate dinner party, she never bothered to question his curious method of travelling.

Monty went by train to Stuttgart, and thence to the Hook of Holland where he caught a ferry to Harwich. He liked that type of journey when he needed time to think. At Harwich he hired a car, and went round the estuaries of the Rivers Stour and Orwell to Ipswich where he booked into a small hotel, and rested until nightfall. After dark, he drove the twenty-five miles into the sparsely-populated remoteness of East Anglia confident that he would find what he wanted.

At the end of a season that left him with eighty-six winners and four hundred and eighty thousand pounds in prize-money, Edward immediately turned his attention to the future instead of lapsing into winter despondency. Assured of what appeared to be a promising intake of two-year-olds, he made the customary arrangements with Hugh and Celia Massingham for schooling and preparing them for training. However, this year, there was an innovation. After thinking long and hard about Cavaradossi and Lohengrin, Edward had a question for Nancy.

"Do you think we could do that pair ourselves?"

"Why?"

"No particular reason, I just want to."

438

"I used to do it at Tornado. There's no reason why we shouldn't. What gives?"

"Nothing. I'm interested, that's all."

Nancy fell in with him, although his professed lack of motive failed to convince her. They started at the end of October, gradually increasing the time they devoted to the task each day as the two young colts began to understand what was expected of them. The differences in their temperaments, already fairly clear, now emerged strongly. Cavaradossi was an exuberant extrovert, very free-moving, often to the extent of having legs everywhere, and not knowing what to do with them. He usually found the answer, treating the whole thing as a huge joke. Lohengrin was his direct opposite. Contradicting his flashy good looks, he was a most serious-minded character, always moving with care, seeming to calculate every pace in advance.

Edward and Nancy talked about their two charges endlessly. On an afternoon in November, they were returning from one of their walks round the park, and were discussing Cavaradossi. They were on the private road that led from what Imogen called 'the tradesmen's entrance' to the back of the house, and were half-way down a very narrow hundred-yard stretch. At this point, the road was barely eight feet wide with banks on either side rising into thickets of hawthorn, and was known as the 'Khyber Pass'.

"I suppose it's too early to have any definite ideas on what you're going to do with Lohengrin?" Nancy asked.

"No, as a matter of fact, I don't think it is," Edward replied. "I've decided that . . ."

He stopped and turned, his attention caught by the faint sound of the car behind them. It had just come over the brow of the hill, and was travelling almost noiselessly at no more than five miles an hour. Despite the deep gloom of dusk, it was showing no lights.

Monty had come to Widney Cheyne for Imogen. He had never forgotten the second telex to Ned Golanski at Fraunhofer Mackenzie. *She* had sent it. *She* had been responsible for all his problems.

He had timed his arrival carefully, knowing the winter routine at Widney Cheyne. Imogen would be in the study at the back of the house. All he had to do was make her come to the window. Then he would use the shotgun at point-blank range.

At first, Monty was dismayed to see the two figures in front of him; the plan depended on getting in and out without being seen. But there was still enough light in the sky behind them for him to recognise Edward. Without even wondering who the woman was, Monty saw the chance of an added bonus, and acted with venomous decision.

439

His foot stabbed at the accelerator. As the car surged forward, he turned the headlights full on.

Blinded and stupefied by the lights, Edward wasted valuable seconds before realising that the car was being driven deliberately straight at them. He leaped swiftly to the nearest bank, and was several feet up it when he saw that Nancy had not moved; she was standing in the middle of the narrow track, staring into the lights like a frightened rabbit. Instinct told him that shouting was a waste of time and desperately-needed breath. Jerking himself away from safety, he flung himself at her. She hit the bank with a violence that knocked all the breath from her. Edward heard Nancy gasp above the devilish racket of the engine, only yards away from them, as he landed on top of her.

Removed from the baleful influence of the lights, Nancy's mind was working again. She could feel Edward slipping. Digging her heels into the soft ground of the bank, she hung on to his shoulders. For a fraction of a second, as the lights hurtled past them, she thought he was safe.

It was the rear wing of the car that struck Edward's left leg. He made no sound, but she felt the pain ricochet convulsively through him before he spun into the road.

As the car careered away, Nancy scrambled down to kneel at Edward's side. He was lying flat on his face, and with her eyes still reeling from the lights, she could see nothing more than a shape in the near-darkness.

He did not move or answer her frantic questions.

The receding noise of the car's engine rose suddenly to a wild crescendo. Horrified, Nancy imagined that the killer had somehow managed to turn round, and was coming back. Then, in the instant before the fearful crash, Nancy was certain she heard a gunshot.

She got up and started running. Her legs were shaking abominably, but she had to find Imogen.

Monty knew that he had hit something. The bump was quite pronounced. He thought it was probably the woman. He turned his head to look back. There was nothing except the darkness, yet he kept looking.

At the bottom of the Khyber Pass, the road widened, and curved to the right across a field that was kept mown closely enough to resemble a lawn. There were no banks.

When he felt the slight lurch as the car left the road and mounted the grass, Monty abandoned his futile scan behind him and turned to look ahead. The oak tree was directly in front of him, twenty yards away. It was

440

nearly two hundred years old. Monty did nothing. In the three-quarters of a second left to him, he wondered if it had been wise to jettison the plan of a stealthy approach to the house.

The violence of the impact fired the cocked shotgun lying across the back seat of the car. The forensic experts later came to the conclusion that this explained why one of the back doors was a long way from the main bulk of the wreckage.

———

Imogen's routine had been disrupted since breakfast, and she was running very late. She was among the outbuildings, feeding the dogs when she heard the car. The noise was quite clear in the still evening. Her questioning frown was returned by the two men who had been helping her clear out an implement store, and were awaiting further instructions.

"What the hell's going on?" she demanded rhetorically.

Neither of the men offered an answer. Instead, they listened to the noise of Monty's manic rampage down the Khyber Pass.

When the collision with the oak tree rent the air, Imogen moved like lightning. She had seized a flashlight, and was on her old bicycle, pedalling furiously, while the men stood and gaped.

She met Nancy as she drew level with the wreck.

Nancy was keeping to the road, intent on getting to the house and help. "He tried to kill us!" she gasped. "He did! He drove right at us! He hit Edward . . ." Nancy was sobbing hysterically ". . . I think he's dead! He's killed Edward!"

Imogen let her bike clatter to the ground as she put an arm round Nancy. "Here, steady on now, steady on," she said.

"We were walking down the Khyber Pass, and this car . . . it came up behind us . . . just crawling . . . as soon as the guy saw us, he put his foot down . . ." Nancy suddenly seemed calm. "He saved my life," she said.

"Who did?" Imogen asked quietly.

"Edward! He saved my life."

Imogen could feel Nancy shaking. With her free hand, she was pointing the beam of the flashlight at the mangled car against the oak tree. By now, Bennett and Tyson had caught up with her, and they, too, had brought lamps. One thing was certain: the driver had not been wearing a seat belt. His body was sprawled across what was left of the car's bonnet.

"Where's Edward?" Imogen asked gently. Getting no reply, she shook Nancy quite fiercely. "Nancy! Where is Edward?"

"Back there." Nancy made a futile gesture into the darkness. "Couple of hundred yards."

Imogen turned to her men. "Bennett! Will you go with Miss Bloomfield, please. Find Mr Manning. It seems that he's been hurt."

"Yes, ma'am!"

Nancy was regaining control. Some of Imogen's strength had transmitted itself to her, and she set off at a resolute trot with her escort.

Imogen walked towards the car, Tyson hovering protectively at her side. They went right up to it. Wisps of steam or smoke from the engine swirled around in the light of their torches.

She recognised him from the undamaged back of his head.

"Monty Dorchester!" Imogen spat the words out with such virulence that Tyson was distracted from the horrendous spectacle. Better still, she had something for him to do.

"Do we have a fire extinguisher, Tyson?"

"Yes, ma'am."

"Get it! I'm not having this lot going up in flames and destroying evidence!"

Edward was struck down at nine minutes to five. The impact of being hurled into the road knocked him unconscious. When he came round, pain made him faint. At six minutes past five Nancy found out that he was still alive. It had been the longest and worst quarter-hour of her life.

While she was making the necessary telephone calls, Imogen sent a maid to rout the five stud grooms from their cottages. Some of them stood guard over the shambles at the oak tree, others took blankets to keep Edward warm until the ambulance arrived. His left leg was a mess. The ankle was broken, and the knee smashed. He was in terrible pain.

Nancy told him the identity and fate of their attacker as she gave him tea from a thermos. He seemed almost relieved.

"I've often wondered what became of him," he said weakly. "What's happening?"

"I don't know. Imogen's sent for the police, of course. And poor old Freddie."

"Oh dear! This will finish him."

"And she's as mad as a wet hen about what Monty might have done to her oak tree. They can't get a good look at it yet. I don't think she minds too much about him trying to kill us . . . what does get to her, is that he did it *here* . . . on her property."

Edward smiled. He could readily imagine the chatelaine of Widney Cheyne giving that impression. Nancy and the others would probably never realise how skilfully it had been calculated to steer their thoughts away from the horror.

Nancy went with him to the hospital in Oxford. When Richard arrived at seven-thirty after a busy day in London, doctors and surgeons were still pondering over the X-rays. Richard insisted that the best possible job was to be made of repairing Edward's knee, and that it was to be done immediately.

Edward was in the operating theatre until midnight, and Nancy was still waiting when he came out.

Imogen was far too busy to go to the hospital. In any case, she hated sitting around, doing nothing.

———— ————————

In the middle of the following afternoon, a meeting that had started over lunch came to an end in Imogen's sitting-room. As well as herself, those present were the Duke of Dorchester, his middle son, Lionel, Frank and the Assistant Chief Constable of the County. During the previous evening, determined attempts had been made to fob Imogen off with a mere Chief Superintendent; it had taken her all of ten minutes to convey the full force of her requirements. Nancy was back at the hospital, and had been joined there by Ann. Richard was at Saxon Court.

Despite the hectic activity of the last twenty hours, they were all conscious of how little they had been able to discover.

The question of the firearms was easy.

In addition to the shotgun on the back seat of the car, the police found a rifle and another shotgun in the boot together with a frightening quantity of ammunition. Lionel had identified the weapons easily enough; they had been stolen from a store-shed on one of the estate farms in Suffolk during the night before Monty's appearance at Widney Cheyne. Lionel was abject. An officer of the Suffolk police had been disdainful and reproachful about the unsuitability of the shed as an armoury, pointing out that the break-in had been carried out with casual ease.

Beyond that, they knew nothing.

Monty's wallet contained only ninety pounds in notes, his driving licence and passport. The driving licence still gave his address in Newbury, and a succession of negligent officials had stamped nothing in the visa pages of the passport since his entry to America a little more than a year ago. The lining of Monty's fairly new French-made jacket had another six hundred pounds in English banknotes concealed in it. There was no indication of where he had come from, or spent the last year.

After looking at two sheets of paper that summarised what his officers had pieced together, the Assistant Chief Constable glanced at Imogen.

"You said that Mr Dorchester – as he called himself – would have had a fair idea of the routine here, Lady Stewart?" he asked.

"Yes."

"He had no reason to expect that Mr Manning would be here?"

"Not at that precise time, no."

"And there's nothing to suggest that he tried to find out where Mr Manning was."

"Apparently not."

"Who *would* he have expected to find here at that time of day?"

Imogen gazed at him calmly, and said, "Me . . . apart from the staff, of course."

The policeman nodded. "You told Superintendent Norrington that Mr Dorchester may have considered that he had grounds for a grudge against you."

"In response to a direct, leading question, yes, I said that. I did not volunteer the information."

"Quite, Lady Stewart."

The Assistant Chief Constable saw that it was pointless to pursue the matter in search of detail. The shutters were down, the ranks closed. "That seems to be it," he said. "We still have a few ends to tie up for the inquest, but you shouldn't be troubled any more."

"Thank you, Chief Constable." Imogen showed absolutely no sign of the strain she was feeling. "There is one more point. May I take it that you see no need to involve the *media* in this." She bestowed profound distaste upon the word with almost loving care.

"No, Lady Stewart."

"Excellent."

"There is the question of the inquest."

"Leave that to me! Mr Dorchester was, of course, a frequent and welcome visitor here. The only possible explanation I can think of for the tragic accident was his unfamiliarity with that particular road."

"Thanks, Imogen," the Duke muttered when the Assistant Chief Constable had departed.

"Not at all, Freddie. We can do without the gutter press. Hello, what's this?" She took the sheet of paper that Frank was offering her. It was the letter Angela had sent Edward. After reading it, Imogen looked at the Duke.

"This is from the Maitland creature, Freddie," she said. "It was apparently written after she and Monty had gone their separate ways. She says that Monty was a pretty frightening character, and advances the view that he might try something nasty."

"Bloody cheek!" the Duke growled.

Lionel, who had been looking most uncomfortable, felt the time had come to speak.

"There was the Warburton business, dad."

Imogen peered questioningly through the smoke of the cigarette she felt she had deserved.

444

"Chap at school with Monty," the Duke explained. "Monty gave him a bit of a going-over."

"He damned near killed him!" Lionel said. "And there was Clarke."

"Another murder attempt?" Imogen asked sweetly.

"Well . . . yes . . . I suppose you could say that," the Duke admitted. "But that was over a girl at Oxford. Fine-looking wench!"

"Ah! That makes all the difference, does it?"

The Duke of Dorchester had been cherishing a single crumb of comfort: Monty's final appalling gesture had stunned the Duchess into silence. Imogen's devastatingly acid smile removed even that puny consolation.

———————

Five days later, Edward rose gingerly from the chair beside his hospital bed, and groped tentatively for the crutches. Imogen and Nancy held him steady while the physiotherapist looked on; she already sensed her redundancy. The two women whose lives Edward had saved intended to play a very full part in his recovery.

Madeleine de Courcy resigned herself to the fact that Monty was not coming back.

The three hundred and fifty thousand pounds that Monty had stolen from her and Colorado Hartigan began to moulder in a Zürich bank which was so securely discreet, that another ten years would pass before anyone wondered what had become of number 5031961.

A tree surgeon pronounced the oak sound and virtually unscathed. He coated the damaged bark with a sticky black substance.

CHAPTER 19

Edward did not mind being in hospital.

Imogen spotted this after the first forty-eight hours when he had recovered from the effects of shock and the operation. She had an intuitive grasp of his state of mind, and decided that he must be shaken out of it at the first opportunity.

An unfortunately clear perception of how close he had been to death left Edward demoralised and frightened. He blamed Saxon Court and his lack of judgement for his vulnerability. As with Caroline, it would never have happened but for the stable; to this, he added his own stupidity in hiring and tolerating an employee whom everyone now regarded as an unbalanced, homicidal maniac. Less than a second had stood between him and oblivion. In hospital, there were no decisions to make and no danger; he was surrounded by people dedicated to saving life and reducing pain.

Four days after Edward's first attempts with the crutches, Imogen's relentless badgering of his consultant triumphed, and he was moved to Widney Cheyne. In addition to a refusal to allow Edward to withdraw from the world, Imogen's purpose was to make the best use of Nancy's time.

On the morning of Monty's murderous attempt, Nancy had mentioned that it was time she booked a flight to America for the annual visit to her father. She made 14 December sound fairly definite as her departure date. Once it had been determined that the operation on Edward's knee appeared to have been successful, Imogen made a point of raising the topic.

"Don't forget your ticket, Nancy."

"What ticket?"

"To America! You were about to get it when we were so rudely interrupted."

"Well . . . I dunno. Maybe I should stay here. Edward's going to need help."

"Yes, he is. But I'm not having you giving up your holiday."

Nancy saw the futility of argument at once; Imogen was at her most intransigent.

Nancy's father was a widower. Her mother had died when she was six, leaving Joseph Bloomfield to raise his daughter and three-year-old son, Martin. Joseph, nearly twenty years older than his adored wife, never contemplated remarriage, and made a splendid job of rearing his children. From snippets that she had accumulated, Imogen had a comprehensive picture of the close-knit relationship between Nancy and her father, and the younger brother to whom she had been mother as well as sister. Nancy spoke of Martin often, usually as a consequence of the weekly letters they exchanged. From the earliest age, Martin had shown substantial musical talent, and now, happily married and settled not far from Joseph, he was a violinist in the Boston Symphony Orchestra. Nancy was immensely proud of him.

No, Imogen had decided, there was absolutely no question of Nancy sacrificing her annual reunion, particularly since she had recently become an aunt. The plan for extricating Edward from hospital gave him two weeks of Nancy's support before she left, and Imogen ordered him to make the most of it.

"Remember, when she's gone, you've got me to contend with!"

Nancy drove him hard, and the first two days were purgatory.

"Look, I know it's a bastard," she said when Edward clearly wanted to give up, "but what did that doctor say?"

"Plenty of exercise," he replied grimly.

"Right! Otherwise you're probably gonna be stuck with a gammy leg, OK? What's funny?"

"You."

"How's that?"

"You've lost a lot of your accent, but you always get very American when you're worked up about something."

"Cut the crap and let's have some action round here!"

She almost succeeded in sounding abrasively dynamic; yet as she hoisted him out of the chair into which he had collapsed to feel sorry for himself, there was a twinkle in her eyes.

From then on, progress became measurable. As Edward's knee became less stiff and painful, it was the broken ankle that stopped him graduating from crutches to sticks. Still encased in plaster, and capable of producing an unpleasant array of aches and pains, it inhibited the confidence needed to throw away the crutches. Although Nancy's slightly unwilling departure to America had no obviously detrimental effect on him, Imogen saw that Edward missed her.

He had come to rely on her strength, which had two distinct components. Physically, Nancy was strong enough to lift Edward out of a chair or support his unsure attempts at walking. Additionally, and even more valuably, he discovered that she had a spiritual fortitude that was all-encompassing. In happy ignorance of how badly she had gone to pieces during the preceding fifteen minutes, he was first aware of it when she had climbed into the ambulance and accompanied him to hospital. Thereafter she buoyed him up; there was always a gesture, look or quiet word to dispel his fears and depressions.

It was left to Imogen to tackle the most difficult problem, and she approached it in her customary way, head-on. On Christmas Eve, she put Edward into the Rolls, and drove him to Saxon Court for the first time in five weeks.

Barely able to conceal his apprehension, he seemed utterly nonplussed when they arrived. While they were still sitting in the car in front of Declan's house, he stared round in bewilderment.

"Do you know, I'd forgotten how *big* this place is," he said.

Imogen understood. "It *is* big," she agreed. "It needs to be. You've got a hundred horses here, and what . . . sixty, seventy souls?"

Edward nodded. "That makes it even more bloody daunting," he muttered.

Imogen was watching the gathering starting to form. Frank, busy in the office as usual, was first. For him, Edward's injuries had given rise to a happy byproduct in that he and Ann were spending Christmas at Widney Cheyne. Rosie and Freezer were coming down the path of their garden, and from Declan's house, a procession was emerging. Mary and Finoula were eagerly at the front, followed by Finoula's two Patricks, husband and son; Declan was some way behind with Siobhan, who had also come home for Christmas. Edward had eyes only for Siobhan, looking more pale and drawn than ever; he was sure that she had lost weight. Imogen noticed a group of lads beneath the clock-tower. They had just come out of the yard, and now, with Robin Lane and Alison Bairstow leading, were coming to greet Edward. As Mary and Finoula helped him from the car, the conversation was chaotic.

"Ah . . . you haven't got crutches. I wanted to see that!"

While Edward was trying to explain that he had at last moved on to sticks several days ago, Finoula gave him a huge kiss. "If you'd had the crutches, I was going to get you a black eye-patch and a parrot," she said. "You'd have looked drastic!"

Ignoring his wife's peals of laughter, Patrick Prendegast smiled gravely, and asked, "How are you, sir?"

"A damned sight better than I was, thank you, Patrick." Edward was cheering up in response to the goodwill surrounding him. "Yes, thank you, Mary, I'm all right. Hello, you lot! Merry Christmas."

Robin, Alison and the rest of the lads had arrived.

"How's the leg, sir?" Alison asked.

"So far, so good."

"You'll be able to ride again?"

"Lady Stewart and Miss Bloomfield will skin me alive if I don't . . . Hello, Liam . . . how's Kathleen?"

"She's very well, sir."

"Will you be back after Christmas, sir?"

"I don't think it's going to be too long now, Robin."

Imogen led a move towards the Big House. "Come on, Mary. Let's get the kettle on."

Almost everyone followed them: Siobhan hung back. It was quite deliberate, but only Edward noticed.

"How are things?" he asked.

"I'm all right." He did not miss the brave weariness with which she avoided the question. "What about you?"

"Fine."

"Mother says you could easily have been killed."

"I think that's what Monty Dorchester had in mind."

"That's all my fault, isn't it?"

"What in God's name are you talking about, Siobhan?"

"He would never have come here if I'd stayed." Seeing the depth of her sincerity, Edward did not attempt to interrupt her. "And I should have done. I'm not doing any good where I am."

"Oh! Isn't it any good?"

"No." She said it quietly, without the slightest emphasis, yet it was utterly final.

"Do your mother and father know that?"

"I haven't actually told them so."

"But they know?"

"I expect so."

"What are you going to do?"

"I've no idea. I'm married to him, aren't I?"

He knew what she meant. He remembered what the priest had said after the wedding of Finoula and Patrick: ". . . they're going to *stay* married when we've finished with them." Whatever Nigel thought about it, he and Siobhan had been joined according to the full rites of the Catholic Church. For her, that was irrevocable.

They started to move towards the house. Edward was managing with one stick, and took Siobhan's arm with his free hand. "Can I do anything?" he asked.

"No." Suddenly she seemed unsure. "At least, I don't know . . ."

They halted for a very private chat, companions in misfortune. Watching them from her kitchen window, Mary thought of the persistent well-intentioned undercurrent of opinion in the yard after the first shock of Caroline's death had passed. Edward and Siobhan had always been so closely attuned to each other that some had thought they would marry. The realisation that a vital component was missing from their relationship and the arrival of Nigel had saddened Mary a little. Would they, she wondered, ever get a second chance?

Inside, the atmosphere in the pleasantly overcrowded kitchen rapidly became very convivial. Frank brought in a bottle of sherry from the office to supplement the cups of tea and coffee that Imogen and Mary had distributed, but the mood of light-headed gaiety came from the season and the relief of seeing Edward, making obvious progress, although he was still badly incapacitated. Imogen saw that her idea was working out; despite the seriousness of the intermittent mumbled exchanges with Siobhan, Edward did relax and start to enjoy himself. Everyone, especially the lads, treated him with respect, yet the subtle air of authority and natural leadership that deserved such treatment was missing. It was as though Edward was an amiable outsider, an owner perhaps, who had dropped in to be pleasant at Christmas-tide. Imogen noticed the defect, and hoped that time would cure it.

"That wasn't too bad, was it?" she asked when they were on their way back to Widney Cheyne.

"No. Not really."

"You'll soon get used to it all again."

"Yes . . . I suppose so."

Imogen concealed her irritated disappointment at the lack of conviction in his voice. "How's Siobhan?" she asked. "I thought she wasn't looking too good."

"Bad. Very bad indeed." Edward was starting to come to life. "Something will have to be done about that mess before long."

Imogen felt much happier. Edward's voice and face were vehement.

On the day after Boxing Day, Declan went over to Widney Cheyne after breakfast. Edward was delighted to see him, and when they had chatted for fifteen minutes over a cup of coffee, he suggested a visit to the two colts Cavaradossi and Lohengrin, whom Declan had not yet seen.

There was no doubt of Declan's opinion of Cavaradossi. His face lit up the moment he saw the horse.

"You like him?" Edward asked.

"Oh yes, sor." Declan walked straight into Cavaradossi's box and began making friends with him. "He's very nice." He bent down to feel the colt's legs, looking well-satisfied with the results of his investigation. "He's a good eye . . . nice and bold . . . genuine . . . plenty of character and spirit."

"Sir Richard will be pleased to hear you say that," Edward said. "He thinks an awful lot of him."

"Don't you?"

"Oh yes! He's good – no doubt about that. He's still a bit of an idiot."

"He'll grow out of that once we've had him for a month. What's his best distance going to be?"

"In *theory*, no more than ten furlongs."

"That's a shame . . . if you're right."

450

"You know what his father was like, Declan. He wasn't any good at more than a mile until he was four. What did you have in mind?"

"He's got the look of a Derby horse."

Edward was astonished; such immediate enthusiasm from Declan was unknown, and therefore seemed almost foolhardy. "You haven't even seen him walk," he protested.

The pale blue eyes stared back at Edward, unblinking, confident, disturbing. "This horse will do well. He looks like a champion to me."

"I hope you're right, Declan. We could do with one. Now . . ." they went to the next box ". . . what about this chap?"

Declan's face fell when he saw Lohengrin. "He's a chestnut, then," he said dourly.

"Not you as well!" There was a trace of amusement about Edward's exasperation. "Why does everyone have it in for chestnuts?"

"They never do much good."

"And don't tell me – the white socks and blaze really finish it off?"

"They're not a good sign."

"You do realise that he's bred to stay for ever?"

Declan nodded. "That's the *theory*," he replied, and his eyes almost twinkled. "In *practice* I can't see him exerting himself that much."

"No courage?"

"That would be my guess."

"Right!" Edward laughed. "Now we know where we are!"

He was fully aware that any aspirations for the two colts were nothing more than wild optimism. One or both of them might do very well; they could both be dismal failures; there was no guarantee that they could even be got on to a racecourse and pointed in the right direction.

"Siobhan didn't seem very bright the other day," Edward said as they moved away from the stables.

Declan shook his head. "No, it's not good," he said sadly.

A new idea came to Edward, making him start angrily. "He's not treating her badly, is he?"

"I don't think so. He seems fond enough of her in his own way."

"It's all to do with the horses and the way he's running the show?"

"Yes."

They continued to pick at the subject of Siobhan and her miserable life with Nigel until Declan went home for lunch. They achieved nothing other than to increase their unease.

"Everything all right?" Imogen asked. She had been pleased to see Declan, thinking that he, too, had come to the conclusion that Edward must be kept in touch with Saxon Court. The way they had parted made her fear that something had gone badly wrong.

"Oh yes . . . we were talking about Siobhan."

"Declan isn't happy either?"

"No." Edward looked grim.

Four days later, on New Year's Eve, Declan came again. Whereas his first visit had been largely for social purposes, it was definitely business this time. During the next two weeks, the new intake of two-year-olds would be coming into the yard, and Declan was eager to allocate them to the lads who would be doing them so that they could begin settling down in preparation for training. It was a job he was perfectly capable of doing himself, but he always liked to check with Edward in case he had already formed preferences.

The list of fifty-two horses had been painstakingly compiled by Frank from the mass of correspondence and hurried notes on scraps of paper that were always the tenuous guide to the future at this time of year. Although mistakes were a commonplace occupational hazard, Edward had complete confidence in his father's thoroughness, and smiled sympathetically at the two omissions; they had always been so obvious to him that there was no official record of them in the office.

"Let's have Cavaradossi and Lohengrin in," he said, reaching for Declan's pencil. "What about Cavaradossi? Come on, you're the expert on this one . . . What shall we say? Alison Bairstow?"

Declan considered it. "No," he said at last. "They wouldn't get on. Too much temperament. Elegant Hawkins is the man for him."

John Hawkins was a comparative newcomer, but Edward was not surprised at Declan's nomination for the horse of whom he thought so highly. Hawkins, aged twenty-seven or -eight, had spent eight years with Alec Stedding at Epsom. When Alec retired, all his staff had to look for jobs since the stable was closing down, and two of them considered themselves lucky to be offered vacant places at Saxon Court. Hawkins's nickname was transparently obvious; his appearance was always absolutely immaculate. Even when the first lot were out in pouring rain, he contrived to look elegant in a dark-green waterproof suit that must have cost him a small fortune. And his style was inherent, not a mere affectation of dress; he rode with a calm grace that concealed his strength.

"Right, that could be a very useful combination," Edward agreed, and wrote 'Elegant H' against Cavaradossi. "I want Cathal O'Brien to do Lohengrin." As he marked the list, he was conscious of Declan's intense look. Declan knew that a great deal of thought had gone into the choice; Cathal always got the horses that Edward wanted treating with special care and tenderness. Lohengrin's dam, Rhinemaiden, was a case in point: back in the Avoca House days, Musetta had been another, although that hadn't worked.

"There you are, you can use your own judgement on the rest," Edward said, and pushed the list across the table.

Declan nodded. Then, without any warning, he launched into a new, vitally important topic. "I shall be due for retirement in two years," he announced.

Edward was taken completely by surprise. "Surely not?" he said.

"I was sixty-three in November."

"Good Lord! I forgot your birthday!"

"It was while you were in hospital."

Edward's face showed his appreciation of Declan's masterly understatement.

"You need to be thinking about it," Declan pointed out. "There's a new man to be found."

Edward looked dismayed. "How the devil do I set about that?"

"Pick him out now, and get him ready."

"One of our own?"

"Definitely . . . no need for outsiders."

"Who? Liam Corrigan?"

"No!" Declan came very close to scorn. "In any case, he wouldn't thank you for the job. He's happy as he is."

Having made the suggestion without thinking, Edward felt slightly foolish, and appreciated that Declan was right to reject it out of hand. He racked his brains. "How about Freezer?"

This time, Declan shook his head only after careful consideration. "No . . . the job would worry him. He's all right with what he's got."

Edward gave up. "So who would you suggest?"

"Robin Lane."

Declan felt rather pleased with himself as he watched the rightness of his proposal dawn on Edward.

"Yes . . . he'd be good, wouldn't he? All the lads respect him."

"They do. He's full of ideas, and he's got a feeling for horses. He'd suit you . . ." Declan smiled ". . . and he'd see you out nicely."

Edward took the point; Robin was twenty-five, fourteen years younger than himself. All being well, he would never have to worry about finding another head lad. "How ought I to set about it?" he asked.

"Make him second head lad. That gives him and everybody else time to get used to it."

"I'll do it as soon as I come back," Edward said. "Thanks for telling me about your retirement. I should have realised, but . . ." He looked helpless.

"You've been busy," Declan said resolutely.

"I suppose that's a good excuse . . . and we always think things will go on forever, don't we?"

Declan nodded, then pulled himself together before he picked up the nostalgic sadness that was threatening Edward. "There's a long way to go yet," he said. "And we've got some good horses this year."

"Yes, we have." Apart from the newcomers, there were last season's two-year-olds. They had done very well, and it would soon be time to start thinking of taking them a stage further. "What will you do, Declan, go back to Ireland?"

"I don't think so. Mary wants to stay here. She won't put up with the water between her and the girls. And there's all her friends in the village."

"I wouldn't have thought she had the time to make friends," Edward said.

"She does. It's the Women's Institute, d'you see?" Declan himself looked bemused at how she fitted it all in.

"So you'll be looking for a place in Compton Norris?"

"Yes, we'll get something nice."

You will indeed, Edward thought after Declan had gone, but *I'll* do the getting.

Two days after Nancy came back from America, she and Imogen decided that Edward was fit to return home; he decided not to disagree with them. His only grounds for objection were based on unease to which Imogen's reaction was predictable and daunting. Progress on his knee and ankle had been good; both felt peculiar sometimes, but he was mobile enough with only one stick, and the hospital physiotherapist said there was no further point in him coming to see her. His only two constraints were that he did not yet feel confident enough to drive a car or get on a horse.

Fully aware of his misgivings, Nancy arranged for him to travel back to Saxon Court in style with Cavaradossi and Lohengrin. Dooley brought the van to Widney Cheyne accompanied by Cathal O'Brien and Elegant Hawkins. While the two lads made the acquaintance of their new charges, Edward limped round the house collecting the vast number of his possessions that had found their way to him during the seven weeks of his convalescence. Nancy watched his increasingly laborious progress with amused tolerance.

"You don't want to go, do you?" she asked.

Edward looked round to make sure that Imogen was nowhere to be seen. "To be absolutely honest, I'm dreading it," he admitted.

"You'll soon get back into the swing."

"Will you be able to come over and help?"

"Sure. Remember we've got the breeding season coming up, though."

"Yes. Do what you can."

"I will."

At last, long after Cavaradossi and Lohengrin had been loaded safely

454

into the van, Edward was satisfied that all his things were in the rear cab, and he climbed up beside Dooley in front. As they moved off, it was comforting to look in the mirror and see Nancy preparing to follow in her car.

Conscious of the two young horses making their first trip, Dooley drove very steadily. To Edward's relief, he made no attempt at conversation after the initial greeting; it was, Dooley seemed to be suggesting, no more than an ordinary day's work. The silence, the gentle motion of the van, and the nondescript panorama of the apparently dead winter landscape lulled Edward into soporific near-oblivion. As they cruised gently down the main street of Compton Norris, recognition of his surroundings came slowly, and the fact that passers-by were waving cheerily took a long time to dawn on him.

"What do they know?" Edward asked.

Dooley pulled one of the amazing faces that suggested he was employing supernatural powers to conjure mysteries from thin air. "I expect they know yourself's coming home with a couple of good horses," he vouchsafed eventually.

"And how might they know that, Paddy?"

"Ah . . . yes . . . who's to tell? These things always get around."

"*Two* good horses, you say?" Edward asked.

"That's the story."

"Declan didn't think much of the chestnut."

Dooley shook his head, shaping his lips as though to whistle. "That's not at all what I heard," he said. "One might be just a little bit better than the other, but they're both very decent animals. Oh yes, very decent."

Smiling to himself, Edward gave up.

He had actually entertained the foolish notion that it would be possible to slip into Saxon Court unnoticed. When the van passed the gates, there was not a soul in sight; by the time Dooley pulled up beneath the clock-tower, virtually everyone was either surrounding the van or hurrying towards it. The only exceptions were Frank and Kathleen Corrigan, one busy in the office, the other preparing lunch in the lads' hostel.

It was immediately apparent to Edward that there had been a great deal of talk about Cavaradossi and Lohengrin, for, as they were brought out of the van and walked round, all eyes were on them.

"It's only natural," Nancy said when she saw the expression on Edward's face. "The breeding of this pair make them very interesting. You trained both sires and both dams."

"Yes . . . I see what you mean. I *knew* that, of course, but I hadn't appreciated the full significance of it."

Nancy smiled mischievously. "I also think that a lot of them believe Cavaradossi is likely to do very well."

"What do you think?"

455

"I agree . . . but then I bred him, so I'm biased."

"And Lohengrin?"

"I bred him as well, didn't I?"

They had lunch with Mary and Declan, then Nancy set off back to Widney Cheyne. When Edward went down to the yard, he found the person he was looking for straightaway; Robin Lane was with Freezer and a group of lads, taking a good look at the two new colts. Having called him away from the others, Edward wasted no time in getting down to business.

"Robin, I'm going to introduce the post of second head lad. I think a place this size needs one anyway, but I'm mainly thinking about the future. Declan will be retiring at the end of next season, and I have to be getting someone ready to take over from him. I'd like you to do the job."

"Me, sir?" Robin looked stunned.

"That's right."

"I don't know what to say."

"How about, 'yes'?"

"You're thinking of making me head lad of this place?"

Edward sympathised with the way Robin looked round; he, too, felt overawed. "Yes, I am," he said.

"I'm not sure whether I could do it."

"Do you want to?"

"Of course!"

"Declan and I think you're up to it."

"Very well! Thank you very much, sir."

"Come up to the office at three o'clock. We'll have a chat with Declan about it."

The conversation lasted nearly three hours. At the end, when Robin's duties had been agreed, Edward went with him to the hostel, and made the announcement in the dining-room during the evening meal. He was glad to see that there was no sign of dissent, indeed, most people seemed pleased; they took Robin's promotion as an indication that Edward was planning for the future, a good omen to add to the expectation surrounding the arrival of Cavaradossi and Lohengrin.

The following morning, Edward and Frank had just made a start in the office when Robin and Alison came in. "Hello, you two," Edward said cheerfully. "What can I do for you?"

"We'd like to talk to you please, sir," Robin said. He was nervous and looked dreadfully serious.

Edward was alarmed. "Er . . . yes," he said. He saw that, whatever it was they had to say, they were unwilling to say it in the office where there was the constant risk of interruption as folk trooped in and out. "Shall we go into the kitchen?"

Robin was still in no hurry to start when they got there and Edward had closed the door. He had to be prompted. "Come on, Robin. Spit it out."

"We're going to get married."

"That's wonderful! Sit down. When?"

"Well, we had been thinking of the autumn, but we've decided to make it sooner . . . before you start the full training schedule, so we don't upset things."

"That's fine." A horrible thought struck Edward. "You aren't going to give up work, are you, Alison?"

"No, sir, not for two years at any rate. It might be best if I stopped then."

"Yes." Edward thought about it: maybe the head lad's wife shouldn't work in the yard; there would be other things for her to do.

"We've got a favour to ask you," Robin said.

"Go on."

Robin turned to Alison. "We'd like a posh do at the church," she said. "My parents won't be coming. They split up years ago, and we've lost touch . . . I don't really know where they are. To tell you the truth, I don't much care." Alison made the statement defiantly, and Edward assumed that trouble at home had been one of the factors that had driven her away to work for Cyril Brookes-Smith and Caroline. "So we wondered if you'd give me away."

Edward was taken completely by surprise, almost giving Alison the wrong impression. He pulled himself together quickly, telling himself that he must not gape like an idiot. "Yes, Alison, I'll be pleased to do that for you," he said. "And thank you for asking . . . it's a great honour for me."

"Thank *you*, sir," she smiled. "We should look all right together, although you're nowhere near old enough."

Edward laughed. "You want a top hat and all the trimmings?"

"Yes, please."

"I take it your parents won't be there either, Robin?" Edward asked.

"No, sir."

They exchanged a look that summed up their memories of Robin's mother's attitude when he had run away from home to ask for a job at Avoca House. That had been nine years ago.

"Where are you going to live?" Edward asked.

"We haven't thought of that," Robin replied. "We had plenty of time when we were thinking of autumn. We'll have to look around and find out what's going in the village."

"Do you want to live out?"

"Not particularly . . ." Robin looked at his partner ". . . do we, Ali?"

"No."

457

"There's a house for the second head lad," Edward pointed out. "It's the one that Mr Brookes-Smith used. What do you think of that?"

Robin and Alison looked at each other; like all couples with a deep bond, they had their own telegraphic system.

"That would be marvellous," Robin said.

"All right, go and have a look at it – Mary's got the keys. See what you think. I'll have it done up for you . . . it was never sorted out properly when I came here. Don't be afraid to ask for alterations. George Roberts and his merry men will soon fix it."

"Thank you very much."

"Go and look at it *now*, then come and tell me what you think. And we'd better fix the date while we're at it, we shall need to talk to the vicar."

When they had gone, Edward collected his thoughts and went back into the office. His father, engrossed in the accounts, scarcely noticed him. Edward walked to the big bow-window and looked out. The yard and surrounding buildings were as big as ever, but this morning, with the sun shining, and winter's end in sight, it all seemed far less forbidding.

"What was all that about?" Frank asked without looking up.

"Alison and Robin are getting married."

"That's nice. They've been fond of one another for a long time, haven't they?"

"Ever since I moved here."

"Imogen will be pleased. She often talks about them."

"Alison wants me to give her away."

"Does she, by Jove!" Frank looked up. Thoughtfully, he tapped his pencil against his teeth. "You know, on top of all this lot . . ." he waved a hand over the accounts ". . . that's quite a family you've got out there."

A smile started to form on Edward's face. Alison's request, which had come close to flooring him when she made it, was already providing a radically new perspective of his responsibilities.

At the beginning of February, the horses began trotting in the covered ride, and the two Classic entries, Santuzza and Prometheus, made use of the all-weather gallop for easy cantering practice. Edward moved around reasonably well, always carrying a stick, but finding that he needed to use it less and less. Several days of sharp frost in the middle of the month showed that his knee was susceptible to extreme cold, and the odd-looking gait he developed during this period produced facetious comments from Imogen.

She was taking no chances. With both her sons away, Nicholas at Eton and Richard at a prep school in Windsor, she reduced the effort she expended on what she called 'good works around the parish', and visited Saxon Court almost every weekday. Muffled in cardigans, and using a shooting-stick so ancient and disreputable that it must have been a minor heirloom, she accompanied Edward to the covered ride and all-weather gallop, often startling him with the perspicacity of her observations. "That animal's lazy . . . that one's nice . . . the girl on that big bay colt isn't happy . . . in fact she's frightened to death of him."

The wedding of Alison and Robin, arranged for the last Saturday in February, was a godsend for Imogen. Everyone expected that she would take a great interest in it, and she duly did, absolutely thrilled at the union between two of her favourites: but it also gave her the perfect vehicle for keeping an eye on Edward without him being conscious of her scrutiny. She was pleased by what she saw, and realised, yet again, what a remarkable character Edward was. Away from his horses, he often floundered, making life very difficult for himself; with them, he became a dramatically different person, master of every situation. Imogen noticed that even in the confines of the covered ride, Edward acquired an air of authority; as the horses went round, their riders always kept one eye on him, waiting for a signal or instruction. On the gallop his command was supreme.

Whenever possible, Edward did his best to make light of the lingering effects of his injury, and knowing his earlier fears, Imogen admired his spirit. After one visit to the covered ride, they found George Roberts at the back of the yard, to one side of the arch; he was taking measurements and looking speculative. Edward halted, and looked at him quizzically. George returned the stare with bland affability, as though there was no earthly reason why he should not be here rather than in the house his men were getting ready for Alison and Robin.

"What's going on, George?" Edward asked.

"I'm measuring up."

"What for?"

"Your podium . . . it's been decided you ought to have one."

"Podium?" Edward was mystified.

"Ar . . . you know, about this high . . ." George held a hand out at waist height ". . . with some steps." Seeing Edward's continuing bafflement, George made it completely plain. "So's you can climb on your horse with that leg."

"Oh, you mean a mounting block."

"If you like. 'Podium' has more about it."

"Who's been doing all this deciding?" Edward asked.

George pushed his cap to the back of his head and looked flummoxed. "Well, 'tis all sorts, really."

"All right, who told you to build the thing?"

459

"I wouldn't say it happened like that. You see, we had a confabulation and the general consensus was that you'd got to have a podium."

Edward surrendered. "Very well, George, but let me make a suggestion. It should be over there." He pointed to the other side of the track from the yard to the covered ride and gallops. "I shall want to get on Murgatroyd from his left-hand side – that way it's my good leg I have to swing over him."

"Right you are!"

"George?"

"Yes?"

"Oughtn't there to be some sort of lifting tackle as well?"

"Oh no . . . be unsightly that would. In any case, we'd need planning permission if you want to erect free-standing apparatus."

Making an effort to keep straight faces, Imogen and Edward went through the arch, where Edward paused to look into the Old Yard. A group of two-year-olds were being unsaddled and put back in their boxes; although Cavaradossi and Lohengrin were among them, it was a brown filly who caught Edward's eye.

"Look, there's Aphrodite," he said. "Isn't she a beauty? Fred's probably coming to see her tomorrow."

Aphrodite, daughter of a Derby winner out of a much-respected mare, was Fred Bird's first attempt at a 'quality' horse to compensate for the failure of Monty Dorchester's mission to Keeneland. Acting on Richard's advice, Fred had paid nearly two hundred thousand pounds for the filly at the previous October's Newmarket sales.

"Fred won't be here tomorrow," Imogen said firmly.

"Why not?"

"He's in Dublin."

"What for?"

"Market research."

"How do you know that?"

"Valerie told me."

"Aha!"

"I'm perfectly certain it's purely business," Imogen said, squashing his assumptions with a look.

It was. Nevertheless, the week that Valerie spent showing Fred round Dublin, introducing him to people who might be useful, did have an important bearing on the future. Over dinner each evening, Fred fell a little more under her spell, and Valerie finally decided that he really was remarkably like dear old T.P. It was also a week when, according to the habit and custom of the past, she should have gone to Glendalough with Eammon Pearce. Because of a meeting of a European Arts Committee which Valerie had attended in Rome, their January assignation had gone by the board. When Pearce's disappointment at another cancellation boiled over into bad temper, Valerie terminated their relationship. Fred's discovery that she needed a new accountant gave him an opportunity to display his powers of organisational acumen, and he grasped it with both hands.

The mounting block was ready two days before the wedding. Edward was full of admiration for the finished product. George Roberts had unearthed a supply of the original bricks used to build the yard, and they had been put together by his apprentice as a celebration of the bricklayer's art. When Edward went to try it out, he was confronted by an almost terrifying sight. As well as Liam Corrigan and Murgatroyd, almost everyone else had turned up; including George Roberts and his men, there were nearly seventy of them, neatly lined up in four rows, all looking as though they were expecting a grand ceremony. Worst of all, Imogen was standing by the new structure. She was wearing one of her church-fête-opening hats. Taking his place alongside her, Edward felt happier when he saw Nancy smiling at him from the crowd, and had to strangle a grin when she gave him a gigantic wink.

Imogen's speech was lofty, inspirational, and magnificently irrelevant. Ignoring the interest that Murgatroyd was taking in her hat, she delivered a stirring homily on man's responsibility to the environment, made brief mention of the revised bus service from Compton Norris to Reading, and asked for contributions to the village hall roof fund. Doing his best to avoid catching Nancy's eye, but suddenly finding Sean Gillespie's expression an equal threat to seriousness, Edward realised that Imogen was finishing.

". . . and so, ladies and gentlemen, it gives me very great pleasure to declare this podium well and truly open."

As cheering and clapping broke out, Edward mounted the four steps, bowed, and stepped effortlessly astride Murgatroyd, who, in no doubt that the applause was intended for him, set off for the covered ride.

They all followed, and watched as Murgatroyd trotted round twice. When he broke into his loping canter, still strongly reminiscent of the way he used to move down to the start of a race, everyone could see how pleased Edward was; he was smiling at the joy of being on a free-moving horse again. His knee felt slightly stiff, and he suspected that there would be complaint from it later, but it was a small price to pay for such elation.

Alison spent the night before her wedding with Mary and Declan. On the morning of the ceremony, which dawned fine and mild, Edward was looking out of the kitchen window from seven-thirty onwards. Frank, who always cooked himself a substantial breakfast, watched with amusement.

"It's the bridegroom who's supposed to get in that state," he said. "For heaven's sake, sit down and have some breakfast."

"Julie hasn't arrived yet," Edward muttered. Sean Gillespie's wife was helping Alison to get ready.

"There are three hours to go," Frank pointed out. "Rosie's already gone in, hasn't she?"

"Yes."

"Well, relax!"

Edward did his best. After tea and toast, he went round the yard with Declan, who seemed completely unmoved by the chaos building up in his house.

"Leave it to the ladies," he counselled. "They know what they're doing."

When Edward finally went across at eleven o'clock, the time he had been ordered to present himself, he found complete serenity. Everyone was having a cup of tea; Alison was standing up so as not to crease her dress, the others were all sitting down, and Mary actually had her feet on a stool.

"My word, Alison, you look smashing," Edward said, and took another look at her as she smiled her thanks. Today, she looked very young – eighteen at most – whereas she was a year older than Robin.

The only slight cause for concern was the late arrival of seven-year-old Penelope Gifford from the village. Penelope, daughter of the local police sergeant, was to be one of the bridesmaids, the other being Deborah Williams who had come straight from school to work at Saxon Court less than six months ago. All was well, however; Penelope's father delivered her only a few minutes behind schedule, the chauffeur-driven Rolls-Royce was waiting, and they set off.

Lurking outside St Matthew and All Saints with her camera, Imogen obtained a picture that was destined to be much admired, and eventually found its way into the Colour Room. Pausing at the church door to check that all was well with her bridesmaids, Alison noticed that Edward's tie was crooked. She handed her bouquet to Deborah, and reached out to straighten it, the camera clicking at precisely the right moment.

As they went in, a congregation of well over a hundred rose to their feet. Alison paused to smile at Greaser O'Malley and Elegant Hawkins who had been acting as ushers, and were still standing near the last row of pews. Although he looked splendid in his morning suit, Greaser was awkwardly self-conscious; alongside him, Elegant was at the zenith of his sartorial career. At the other end of the aisle, Robin and his best man, Cathal O'Brien, prepared themselves. They had spent the night in the Fortescue Arms, and although nervous, seemed none the worse for the experience.

Robin and Alison had asked for the original 1549 service of marriage, the form used at Edward and Caroline's wedding. This time, Edward was able to enjoy the resonant cadences of Thomas Cranmer's magnificent language, relished by the vicar, who clearly preferred it to modern versions. Edward became so enthralled by the beauty of the ceremony that he seemed unaware that it was over, and Alison had to nudge him to indicate that they were going to the vestry to sign the register. Imogen and Richard, Robin's parents for the day, joined in, as did Nancy.

The wedding breakfast was a great success. After an outstanding speech from a relaxed and happy Edward, Robin showed what he was made of, doing almost as well, despite his nerves. For some reason that no one could understand, Imogen then stood up and began to hold forth; she punctuated a rambling but entertaining discourse on the joys of matrimony by reading out the messages of greeting that had arrived for Alison and Robin. Robbed of a duty he had been dreading, Cathal O'Brien sat back in his chair and stopped looking worried. Edward studied the guests, all hanging on Imogen's every word; they constituted what Frank had called his family, and he reflected that Alison had a firm grasp of that idea, as well as the bond between stable and village. Her choice of bridesmaids had forged new links between the younger representatives of both halves of the relationship.

"A very good do, Robin," Edward said as the guests began to disperse.

"It was. Thank you very much, sir." In keeping with his role of father of the bride, Edward had insisted on paying for the day. Robin smiled. It was a semi-private gesture. "I'm doing all right for a chap who ran away from home at sixteen with no qualifications or prospects," he said, adding in a much more serious vein, "that's all down to you, of course."

Edward could think of nothing to say.

That afternoon, Alison and Robin set off for their honeymoon in the Canary Islands. They had wanted to be away for only a week, but Imogen, who was making them a present of the trip, insisted on two weeks when she discovered it would take Frank that long to complete the fitted kitchen and wardrobes in their house.

The 1989 racing season got under way in the last week of March, and as usual, Edward took no notice of it. Another three weeks would pass before his first runner went out, and he was completely engrossed in the preparation of two horses for the first Classic races. He was determined that the Duke of Dorchester's Santuzza should go in the One Thousand Guineas, and Valerie Malahide's Prometheus seemed well worth a crack at the Two Thousand Guineas. As well as this pair who received special attention from Alison and Robin, all last year's two-year-olds had wintered well, and were making extensive use of the all-weather gallop.

Without Nancy, who was busy at Widney Cheyne as T. P. Malahide and Parsifal performed their annual stallion duties, Edward had no time for anything other than his horses.

One afternoon Edward was busy in the kitchen with Declan and Robin. They were deciding the work programme for the next week when Frank wandered in from the office. He was holding a racing newspaper.

"Nigel had his first winner yesterday," he said.

Edward looked up from the papers and notebooks that were spread on the table, and extended a hand. "Let's have a look," he said.

A horse called Caley's Pleasure had won an eight-hundred-pound Handicap at Nottingham. After a brief glance at the details of the result Edward passed the paper back. "Six lengths seems fairly convincing," he said. "Mind you, it's about time."

Declan's face remained expressionless, and Frank went back to the office, disappointed that there had not been more reaction. The following day's news produced a much more marked effect.

"The Stewards seem to be having a real go at Ernie Marshall," Frank announced.

Edward did not recognise the name for a moment; when he did, his eyes narrowed. Ernie Marshall was one of the many jockeys who had to make a living away from racing's glamorous centre-stage. In a good year he might expect to ride twenty winners, hardly ever getting a mount in the south. He it was who had ridden Caley's Pleasure for Nigel at Nottingham.

"What do they reckon was wrong?" Edward asked.

"He was supposed to have had a bet on that horse."

"Did he, by God!"

Seeing the extent of Edward's interest, Frank provided more detail. "The bet was alleged to have been five hundred pounds at twelve to one."

Edward's face was grim. He got up, and went across to discuss it with Declan.

"What's the problem, do you think?" Frank asked when he came back half an hour later.

"That's a hell of a big bet for a bloke like Ernie Marshall to make," Edward said.

"I can understand the temptation if he thought the horse was going to win."

"How about if he *knew* the horse was going to win?" Edward said. He refused to say any more, and Frank had to wait a week for the answers to all the questions he wanted to ask.

The Stewards dealt severely with Ernie Marshall, suspending him for six months, so it was another jockey who rode two horses for Nigel at Warwick three days later. They both won at long odds. Without hesitation, the local Stewards called for a test in search of drugs to be carried out on the horses, both of whom belonged to Victor Macleod. The two blood tests revealed the presence of Xanthine in massive quantities. The caffeine-like substance, occurring naturally in cocoa beans, was a powerful stimulant. Disqualification of the two horses was immediate, and Nigel was told that he would be required to appear before the disciplinary committee of the Jockey Club to explain the findings of the tests.

"Well that's the end of that," Edward told Frank. "They'll tear his licence up and set fire to the pieces. The stupid bastard!"

"That stuff couldn't have got into them by accident, could it?" Frank asked. Within the past month he had read two articles describing how prohibited chemicals might sometimes find their way into a horse's system from contaminated food, or some antiseptic creams used on open wounds.

"Not a chance," Edward replied. "Certainly not in the dosages they seem to be talking about. They'll do tests on the feed and the other horses to make sure."

Nigel was surprised and embarrassed when Caley's Pleasure won at Nottingham. The gelding had been working reasonably well, but had done nothing to suggest he was capable of the performance that won the race. When he got home to the celebration that Siobhan had organised for their desperately-needed first winner, his less than convincing attempt at happiness made her nervous.

Within twenty-four hours, the Stewards had suspended Ernie Marshall, and Siobhan was worried. An obvious stigma had been placed over them, but when she questioned him, Nigel seemed genuinely ignorant of what had happened. Significantly, he had no idea of how Marshall's contravention of the laws of racing had been discovered. The illicit wager had been made in a city-centre betting office in Manchester by Ernie Marshall's wife, and it was reasonable to assume that she was not responsible for the nasty little whisper that brought the affair into the open so quickly. Someone with a grudge, a vindictive nature, and considerable know-how had made the necessary phone calls.

As well as being apprehensive, Siobhan felt unclean at her involvement, however tenuous, with something patently shady. It was as if she had found the house ransacked, with nothing missing, but the horrible feeling that a malevolent stranger had rummaged through everything. Unsure of what to do, hoping for an explanation in the fullness of time, she avoided contact with her parents.

465

What happened at Warwick left no room for doubt. When an ashen-faced Nigel got back at six o'clock, with two horses that were showing signs of being very unwell, Siobhan had known the appalling truth for two hours.

"Well?" she demanded. "What have you got to say?"

"Siobhan, I don't know. As God's my judge, I never touched those horses. Truly, I swear it!"

She looked at him. For a full fifteen seconds, she stared at Nigel, frightening him with the intensity in her eyes. He had never imagined her to be capable of such anger.

"What are you doing?" he asked as she picked up the telephone. There was panic in his voice.

"I'm getting the vet," she said. When he looked at her with stupid incomprehension, her voice rose dangerously. "Those horses are sick, Nigel. They need attention."

When she had finished the call, she stared at him again.

"You know, I believe you," she said quietly. "I don't think you did have anything to do with this." When he looked relieved, the return of anger was instantaneous. "And that's every bit as bad as being involved yourself. Let's go and talk to the man who *will* know!"

Nigel had to run to keep up with her as she hurried across the yard. Three of the seven lads were in a huddle outside the box of one of the drugged horses; Siobhan ignored them, making her way to the gap at the corner of the L-shaped line of boxes. Behind it was the caravan in which Terry Dawson lived. Siobhan had never set foot inside it: now, she wrenched the door open and went straight in. Stepping round the items of clothing lying on the floor, she pulled the wardrobe doors open. It was empty. So was the chest-of-drawers.

"Gone!" she said, and Nigel nodded miserably.

Siobhan was about to leave when an impulse drove her to pull open the big drawer underneath the bunk bed. It contained the cash-box from the tiny office that she had tried to run as though it were part of Saxon Court. The box had been forced open.

"There was over four hundred pounds in that," she said. "It's pay-day tomorrow."

Siobhan called the police. Nigel stood by ineffectually while she gave details of the theft to a young detective constable. "And there's another thing," she said when the question of the money was out of the way. "This man Dawson doped two of our horses today."

"Can you prove that, madam?"

"No, I cannot," she replied. "But he did it all right. You find him, and we'll soon get to the bottom of it."

"Do you have any sort of address? It might show us where to start looking."

Siobhan insisted on knowing the next of kin of every member of staff in case of an accident. The detective constable copied down the address of Terry Dawson's sister in Essex, and went on his way.

"What was the point of all that?" Nigel asked peevishly.

"Protection!" Siobhan snapped at him. "We don't know what Dawson is going to do next, do we?"

For the rest of the evening, Siobhan forced herself to be calm; she prepared a meal, and gave Nigel the impression that she was trying to put a terrible day behind her. The telephone did not ring; in one respect she was grateful for that. She took it as a sign that no one at Saxon Court had yet heard the news. There was another, potentially sinister implication in the silence, which she raised as they got ready for bed.

"It's funny that Mr Macleod hasn't rung."

"I don't suppose he knows yet," Nigel said. "I shall have to talk to him tomorrow."

"Do you *really* think he's *that* indifferent?" Siobhan asked. "He knows what's happened."

Nigel looked miserable.

"What are you going to do?" Siobhan asked him after breakfast.

"What do you mean – today?" He resented her question.

"No, I do not. The Jockey Club will take your licence away. What do we do then?"

"I think that's a very negative and pessimistic attitude, Siobhan. They're bound to be sympathetic when they hear about Terry Dawson. What's the matter *now*?" Siobhan had sighed wearily.

"Nigel, you should never have had Terry Dawson here in the first place," Siobhan said. "Everyone told you that, but you wouldn't listen. You're going to be *made* to understand that now. You also have a very clear responsibility to see that your horses come to no harm. That's the first duty of a trainer. You haven't done that. You might not have stuck the needle in or put the stuff in their feed, but you let Terry Dawson do as he pleased."

He scowled at her. "All right, I'll probably lose my licence. I can reapply in a year."

"And start all over again?"

"Yes."

"Where?"

"I don't know, do I?" Her insistence was bringing out his temper, weak and blustering. "We shall have to see what's available when the time comes."

467

"And in the meantime? What do we do while we're waiting to see what turns up?"

"I've no idea! For God's sake, Siobhan, give me time to think, will you?" A thought occured to him, and he smiled sardonically. "We could always ask Edward for a job . . . well, *you* could. He'd always listen to you. He thinks the sun shines out of your backside."

The look that Siobhan gave him was scathingly contemptuous; it was the first time in her entire life that she had felt and exhibited such emotion. Nigel's reaction to it was interrupted by the arrival of two men, sent by the Jockey Club. One was a vet who had to take blood samples from every horse in the yard, the other was to carry out an analysis of all the feed in stock. Nigel was forced to accompany them, and as soon as he was out of the way, Siobhan telephoned Saxon Court. Her mind was made up. The position was hopeless, and Nigel was incapable of change.

Her call was timed to perfection. It was breakfast time between the first and second lots, and Declan had just finished eating when Frank called him into the office.

"It's Siobhan," Frank whispered to Edward.

Declan was not long, but an atmosphere built up in the kitchen during his short absence. When he came back, Edward, Frank, Freezer, Robin and Sean Gillespie were all looking at him with tense expectation.

"She's had enough," he said, sitting down to finish his mug of tea. "She's coming home. She wants me to go and fetch her."

"When?" Edward asked eagerly.

"Now. Straightaway. Can I borrow the Land Rover?"

"Of course. Would you like me to come with you?"

"No."

Edward could see what Declan was thinking, and he was right. Edward's presence might make an already bad situation worse. "Maybe you could do with company, though. Just in case."

Declan nodded. "Liam and Cathal might be handy," he said.

"Right! Robin, will you go and get hold of them? Let them know what's happening."

Robin was gone in a flash.

"What does she know about this fiasco at Warwick?" Edward asked Declan.

"The horses were given Xanthine. She thinks it was Dawson did it. He's skipped."

Edward derived no satisfaction from the news, in fact he felt ill for a few moments. Abusing horses was the most heinous crime, and doping was abuse with the squalid motivation of avarice.

The Jockey Club vet and analyst were thorough; they were hindered by Nigel. Originally going out to them for the sake of appearances, he soon began to inundate them with long-winded explanations and excuses for all manner of things. They half-listened to what he had to say while collecting their samples. Nigel was still hovering round them, delaying their attempts at departure when Declan arrived.

Declan got out of the Land Rover, looking at the two men trying to edge away from Nigel; he had a fair idea of what they had been doing. Liam Corrigan and Cathal O'Brien obeyed the instructions they had been given, and stayed out of sight in the tarpaulin-covered back of the vehicle.

The sight of Declan finally broke Nigel's nerve. "What the hell have you come for?" he shouted.

Siobhan answered the question by coming out of the back door with a suitcase. Declan took it for her, and Nigel saw that she had another two cases ready.

"Here! What's going on? What are you doing?" Nigel hurried towards Siobhan. Left alone, the two men sent by the Jockey Club took the opportunity of escape.

"I'm leaving you," Siobhan told Nigel. Her voice was steady, her face paler than ever, the tenacity of her resolution beyond doubt.

He failed to take it in at first; he stood stock-still while Declan put the suitcases and two cardboard boxes in the back of the Land Rover.

"Siobhan, you don't mean this," Nigel said at last.

"I do!"

He sneered as the extent of her determination dawned on him. "Oh! So that's it . . . the rats leaving the sinking ship, eh? Thank you very much for your loyal support."

Siobhan's chin rose angrily. "This particular rat is disgusted with itself," she said.

"What does that mean?"

"I'm sick with myself on account of what I've put up with. You've done things wrong since the day we got here. I should have put my foot down."

"I suppose your beloved Edward would have done it all much better . . . even in a clapped-out hole like this."

"There's no need to drag him into it," Siobhan retorted coldly. "But it does seem to me that he's got more feeling for horses in his little finger than you have in the whole of your body."

"So, it's the end, is it?"

"I don't know, Nigel. That depends entirely on you."

"What can I do?"

"Plenty! Start facing up to facts, and you might see what needs doing."

Siobhan climbed into the Land Rover's cab, and Declan relaxed. He saw now that Nigel wouldn't have tried to hurt her; he was weak, not cruel. He moved towards Nigel.

"Do you want any help with these horses?" he asked.

"No, thank you, father-in-law. I shall manage." Nigel's mocking tone vanished after he had thought about what he had said. "It looks as though that may not be true much longer," he said sadly. "By the look of things, she'll want a divorce."

"Divorce isn't for her," Declan pointed out. "You should know that."

"Oh! Yes. Perhaps there's some hope, then."

"I don't know. This is very bad." The stare from Declan's pale blue eyes had unnerved stronger men than Nigel. "She'd never have complained for herself, but she won't stand for having the horses messed around."

Nigel waved as they drove off, and out of kindness, Declan returned the gesture. Siobhan looked straight ahead, her face rigid. When she discovered Liam Corrigan and Cathal O'Brien slumped grimly in the back of the Land Rover, she started to weep.

She was in control of herself by the time they got back to Saxon Court. It didn't last long. Edward had been waiting, unable to concentrate on anything else until she was safely back where she belonged. He dashed from the office door to meet her, not bothering with his stick, forgetting all about the knee that he was still supposed to be treating with care. After no more than half a dozen paces, he stopped, frustration and pain on his face. Hurrying towards him, Siobhan was afraid that he was going to fall over.

"My God!" he said through clenched teeth as she held him up until Frank could reach them with the sticks. "What a pair we are. For Christ's sake, Siobhan, don't you dare start crying, or we shall all be at it."

At three o'clock that afternoon, Imogen telephoned Richard at his office.

"Have you seen the racing pages?" she asked.

"I have indeed."

"Bloody, isn't it?"

"Yes. I presume you know a bit more than the press?"

"Of course. The lamentable Dawson is almost certainly responsible. He did a bunk some time yesterday afternoon. Siobhan called the police in because he walked off with a fair dollop of money. The interesting facts are these: as of this morning, Macleod hadn't been in touch with Nigel. Secondly, the police have made an attempt to find Dawson, and he doesn't appear to be in his usual funk-hole, which is his sister's place in Essex. The boys in blue are anxious to talk to him because of the Ernie Marshall affair. It seems that Marshall was supposed to hand over twenty per cent of his winnings from that horse at Nottingham. When he didn't, Dawson shopped him. Marshall's wife threatened to tell all, and Dawson responded with some fairly horrific promises concerning a razor."

"How do you know all this?" Richard asked.

"I spoke to my friend the Chief Constable," Imogen said, as though stating the obvious to a retarded intellect.

"Silly of me," Richard murmured. "Right, thank you for that, my dear."

"Hang on, I nearly forgot. Siobhan's left Nigel."

Richard whistled. "She's with Declan and Mary?"

"She is."

"You were right about Nigel, weren't you?" Richard said.

"Was I? How?"

"You said he was feeble enough to get himself into trouble."

"Oh, that!" Imogen was scornful. "Any fool could see it."

Before carrying on with drafting a proposal to provide fifteen million pounds of finance to a Swedish engineering firm, Richard spent five minutes mulling over what Imogen had told him, paying particular attention to Victor Macleod's amazing inactivity following the positive dope-testing of his horses.

Towards five o'clock, Edwin Fforbes poked his head round the door to ask, "Do you have a minute, Richard?"

"Yes, come in, Edwin."

"I've just been with Macleod, and a pretty rum thing happened as I was leaving his office."

"Really?" Richard's gaze was very alert.

"I was chatting to his secretary in the outer office, and a call came in from Nigel Brookes-Smith. Macleod didn't want to know. Katherine had to tell Brookes-Smith that his lordship was in an important meeting and couldn't be disturbed."

"I see." Richard thought about it. "There's something bloody funny going on here, Edwin. Imogen tells me that Macleod made no attempt to get in touch with Nigel yesterday."

"Good gracious!"

"Something else. You remember that awful chap Dawson? The one that Edward booted out for ill-treating a horse . . . Nigel gave him a job, made him head lad, if you please. It seems that he was the one with the needle or whatever. He's disappeared, and the police want to talk to him about all sorts of nasty things. Tell me, Edwin, do you have Victor Macleod's home telephone number?"

"Certainly not!" Edwin Fforbes seemed scandalised by the idea. "What on earth would I ever want to talk to him at home for? I suppose I could look him up in the book if the world was coming to an end."

"No, you couldn't, Edwin. He's ex-directory. I know the number . . . Macleod insisted on giving it to me. I believe Dawson has that number." Edwin Fforbes gazed at Richard in puzzlement. Richard's next question made it quite plain that his mind was working along very dramatic lines.

"Tell me, Edwin, have we ever had to use the services of a private investigator? Do we know of someone who's reliable?"

After Siobhan's departure, Nigel rallied. He organised the lads to muck-out the horses, and give them a good grooming. While they were busy with that, he went to the bank, drew cash, and returned to pay them. After he had made himself eat a little lunch, he spoke to all his owners, leaving Victor Macleod until last. He was brutally honest with the five to whom he did speak. It was, he told them, almost certain that he would lose his licence, so their horses would have to be transferred to other stables; he promised to do all he could to make the transition smooth, and they seemed grateful. On the whole, they were sympathetic to his plight, tending to accept that he had not been directly involved in administering the stimulant to the horses at Warwick.

He was disappointed by his failure to make contact with Victor Macleod, suspecting that he had been fobbed off, that there was no important meeting in progress. Before going out for an evening meal, he began to write a letter to the Jockey Club, admitting his culpability in employing Terry Dawson, but going on to explain how he had been forced into it. When he came back from an Indian restaurant, Nigel continued to work on the letter until midnight. He was dissatisfied with what he had written; the essence of what he wanted to say was there, but determination to drag Victor Macleod into the mire had given rise to a rambling, highly emotive account of his troubles. He thought he would be able to lick it into shape the following day.

When Nigel woke up at five o'clock, it was with a new perception of the future; he had to have money, and there needed to be enough of it to enable him to ride out the next year, or however long it took him to get his licence and Siobhan back. The time had come for his father to stop playing idiotic games and help his only living relative to a new, proper start. He set off for Torquay at a few minutes past six.

The meeting between Nigel and Cyril Brookes-Smith was a fearsome affair. When Imogen heard Elspeth's watered-down version of it eight days later, her face registered a range of emotions that were normally alien to her.

Cyril Brookes-Smith kept in touch with racing, and knew what had happened. His reaction to his son's unexpected arrival was to gloat over his predicament. His sentiments were, "I've always said you were no good, and this proves it to the hilt. You wanted me to give you Saxon Court, and look at you! You can't even run a miserable whelk-stall of a place without landing in it up to your neck."

Ignoring this, and a welter of similar taunts, Nigel insisted on his innocence of doping the horses, and demanded money. He named two hundred and fifty-thousand pounds as the sum he wanted, something less than seven per cent of what he supposed his father's personal fortune to be.

Brookes-Smith waited nearly thirty minutes before he told his son the truth. In that time, Nigel explained what he would do with the money, began to think that the absence of any form of refusal meant that he was going to get it, and finally resorted to pleading.

When he learned that his father had given all his money to charity with the specific purpose of ensuring that there was nothing for him to inherit, Nigel was calm, stunned into silent defeat. That could well have been the end of the matter; Elspeth was convinced that Nigel would have gone quietly away if her husband had said no more. But Cyril Brookes-Smith was a sick old man, living on what he knew to be borrowed time, and he wanted to make the most of his triumph. He crowed over his final gesture, deriding his son mercilessly, raking up everything that he considered Nigel had ever done wrong.

"My God," Nigel shouted, "It's a damned good job Beetle didn't live to see you in this state."

"Don't you dare mention your sister! You weren't fit to clean her shoes . . . in fact you always made a mess of that as well!"

As the air thickened with insults of increasing vileness, Elspeth took hold of Nigel and dragged him from the room.

"Please . . . think of me," she gasped. "He'll have another of his attacks if you carry on like this."

"Yes. I'm sorry, Elspeth." He still looked distraught, but the venom had drained away. "I suppose I shouldn't have come."

"Look here, Nigel, I've got money . . . more than he knows about. Let me help you."

"No. It's very, very kind of you, but no. I'll think of something."

Nigel wandered round Torquay for an hour, and had lunch before setting off back to Epsom. During the afternoon he stopped for petrol and a cup of coffee at a motorway service station where he also bought a packet of cigarettes. It was over two years since he had given up smoking, and the first one made his head reel. When he unlocked his car, he found that his hands were shaking. He drove the remaining eighty miles with great care; to the exclusion of all other thoughts, he concentrated on not causing an accident.

It was nearly seven o'clock when he reached the place he had to think of as home. He poured himself a liberal measure of whisky, and drank it with rampant desperation. Then he went to look at his horses.

They all seemed clean and comfortable, settling down for the night. The lads had obviously been very busy. The exception to the well-ordered tranquillity was that one of the horses that had been doped was lying dead in his box. Protected by a thick layer of fresh bedding, the animal's body was still warm. Nigel guessed that the lads had finished off around five o'clock, and that death, probably from heart failure, had occurred soon after.

The first lad was in the yard at six-fifteen. He called the police at once. There was so much to interest them that it was over seven hours before they asked their colleagues in the Thames Valley force to contact Siobhan.

A few years ago, the mean little shed that had to serve as tack room and feed store had shown signs of collapse after an autumn gale. Someone with an engineering bent had solved the problem with a massive baulk of timber bolted diagonally across the shed, just beneath the pitched roof. It was from this beam that Nigel had hanged himself.

Edward went with Siobhan to identify him in the mortuary. Afterwards, he accompanied her back to the house in which she had never been happy.

"I'm the dead man's brother-in-law," he told the Chief Inspector in charge of the investigation.

"Yes, of course! Your late wife . . . yes, I remember the accident. Do you think you might know anything about all this?"

"I imagine so."

"I'd be very glad of your help, sir. This looks a funny business. We aren't too happy about that dead horse."

"Yes, I'm going to organise a post-mortem on that poor creature. My guess is that we shall find he died as a result of being doped up to the eyeballs the other day."

"'Strewth! Do you reckon your late brother-in-law did that, sir?"

"No, definitely not. That was almost certainly the handiwork of a right bastard called Dawson."

"Terry Dawson?"

"That's him."

"We're looking for him. We're getting very nasty reports about him . . . demanding money with menaces, threats to cause bodily harm."

"Up north?"

"And locally."

The letter that Nigel had been trying to write was still scattered on the dining-room table. Edward went through it, made sense of it, and explained it to the Chief Inspector.

"Dear me!" the policeman said. "This does look a wretched business. Can I trouble you for a statement later on, sir?"

"Of course. I'll be glad to. I want to do everything I can to help the widow."

Siobhan had a bundle of mail that had come that morning. Edward was attracted to the letter with the Torquay postmark. Opening it, he found nothing but a cheque. Payable to Nigel, it was for fifty thousand pounds to be drawn on the account that Elspeth had kept hidden from her husband.

Edward's telephone conversation with Elspeth lasted nearly an hour. The Chief Inspector was glad to know how Nigel had spent his last day alive, and the knowledge dispelled some of the guilt that had gripped Siobhan when the police had come with the ghastly news. Edward saw no point in telling them that after Nigel had left Torquay, Cyril Brookes-Smith suffered a stroke, and was now very poorly in hospital.

CHAPTER 20

They talked about it endlessly.

"Poor old Siobhan."

"What a bloody shambles."

"Never ending, is it?"

"I know. Gorblimey, it's only four months since that sod Dorchester tried to kill the guv'nor."

"I heard there was more to it than that."

"What, more than murder?"

Dozens of such conversations took place in the lads' hostel. The events of that catastrophic week had a profound effect on morale, even though they were not directly connected with Saxon Court. The run of persistent bad luck was diligently traced back six years to the death of Caroline, and the gloom was deepened by the fact that the robustly-healthy Mary had been made ill by the latest avalanche of misfortune. Suffering from blinding, crippling headaches, she was housebound for over a week.

Edward worked fiendishly hard, especially in the period leading up to Nigel's funeral. He was loyally supported by Declan, Freezer and Robin Lane, while Frank performed prodigies in the office. Everyone else went through the motions, hoping that something would turn up. The possibility that a filly who was really rather unprepossessing would soon provide cause for celebration was nothing more than a gleam in Nancy Bloomfield's eye.

The day after Nigel committed suicide, the private investigator hired by Richard to watch Victor Macleod's flat reported that a person answering Terry Dawson's description was in residence there.

Richard telephoned Edward that evening.

"I believe you have a tame chief inspector who wants to talk to Dawson."

"That's right."

"I know where he is. Would you like to pass the message on?"

"Absolutely!"

"He's in Victor Macleod's flat."

"You're kidding!"

"I am not."

"How do you know?"

"I hired a private eye to confirm a hunch." After a long silence, Richard had to ask, "Are you still there, dear boy?"

"Yes." Edward's voice sounded strangled. "I'm boggling."

"Do it quietly, there's a good fellow. Now your Chief Inspector is going to have to ask the Metropolitan Police to go and feel Dawson's collar, but I'd like to know when they've done it."

"All right. Any particular reason?"

"I feel the need for a chat with Victor about it. Let me give you his address."

After Edward had written it down, Richard changed the subject abruptly. "Any joy yet with placing Nigel's horses?"

"I'm going to Epsom to see the owners tomorrow."

"Let me know if there's anything I can do to help."

When Richard put the telephone down, he found Imogen looking at him with wide, shining eyes. "I say, darling, this is rather epoch-making," she said.

"What is, my dear?" Richard asked innocently.

"Macleod harbouring Dawson. And the way you found out about it. My word, isn't life full of surprises!"

"You're surely not going to tell me that you didn't think I was capable of getting up to that sort of thing?"

"Well . . . I . . . that is . . ."

Richard roared with laughter. "You're at a loss for words," he said. "Damn it, you really are. What a turn-up for the book!"

"I tell you what," Imogen said, recovering very quickly. "I'd give absolutely anything to be a fly on the wall when you have your 'chat' with that blighter Macleod."

"Ah yes." Richard looked blissful. "I really do feel that I've earned that!"

Siobhan insisted on going to Epsom with Edward, and attempting to play a part in finding homes for the nineteen horses that she and Nigel had looked after. Edward agreed, knowing that it would be far better for her to have something to do. He was aware that the emotions assailing her were not those that a young woman in her position might normally experience. Her one-time love for Nigel had taken a mortal battering during their short marriage, and lack of respect for him had forced her to leave. She was shocked by his death, for which she held herself partly responsible; yet in the very act of a tragic waste of life, Nigel had given her cause for mortification: the faith she held so strongly regarded suicide as a dreadful sin.

During a long day, they succeeded in making arrangements for all but three of the horses. Alec Stedding was on hand to mobilise support from the twelve trainers operating in the Epsom area, who said they would take the lads as well as the horses. One owner, for whom the experience had been traumatic, wanted to move his three horses away from Epsom altogether. Disappointed that there was no room for them at Saxon Court, he agreed to Edward's suggestion of Newmarket.

"I'll talk to Gordon Chapman about them," he said to Siobhan when they were alone. "It's about time I did him a favour."

"Yes." Siobhan was vague. She was looking round her ex-home to see if there was anything else she should take away. For the moment, she was unable to link the name with James Henry's friend who always provided overnight stabling at Newmarket when Edward needed it.

"Are you hungry?" Edward asked.

"I am actually."

He nodded, suspecting that she hadn't eaten a great deal over the last two days. "We'll stop for a meal on the way back," he said.

They found a quiet restaurant near Wokingham.

"We must talk about Nigel's funeral," Edward said after they had made themselves comfortable and ordered. "Once the inquest is out of the way tomorrow we shall presumably be able to go ahead and make arrangements."

Siobhan's face clouded over. "You will come to the inquest with me?" she asked.

"Of course I will."

"I'll stop being a nuisance soon." She tried to smile. "What do you think I should do about his funeral, Edward? I haven't a clue."

"You don't want him to have a Catholic burial?"

"No!" It was a long wait for her to elaborate on the stark, vehement statement. "I don't know whether I could persuade a priest to do it . . . and in any case, it would be hypocritical. Nigel wasn't a Catholic. He only pretended to be to keep me and mother happy when we got married."

Edward was silent for a while. "Very difficult," he said.

"You must be really fed up with him. His father was right all along, you see. He wasn't much good."

"Oh no, I'm not having that!" The fierceness of Edward's response startled her. "I've even less time for Nigel's father now than I did before. As far as I can see, he always did Nigel down . . . and this business with the money was a bloody disgrace. He's nothing but a vindictive old has-been . . . that is if he ever *was* anything, and I've always doubted that, to be frank."

"Have *you* no idea what Nigel would have liked?"

Edward's immediate reaction was to shake his head and look blank.

Then he had an idea. "He thought the world of Caro," he said. "We could put him near her. There are still some empty plots around her. I'll get George Roberts to look into it first thing tomorrow morning."

Siobhan brightened. "That sounds like a good idea." Then she was despondent again. "Do you think we'll get many people there?"

"Enough. I'll make sure of that."

He was so busy attempting to take all the bones out of a trout at one go that he missed the look she flashed at him. It was partly relief at his taking charge of the situation, and part curiosity at his authoritative tone. Edward was very much in control.

On Sunday afternoon, two officers of the Metropolitan Police went to Victor Macleod's flat with a warrant for Terry Dawson's arrest. He was hysterically abusive, and, thinking that Macleod had turned him in, made the sort of threats that he had used against Ernie Marshall's wife. Dawson was taken to Guildford where he was handed over to the Surrey police who charged him, and locked him up in cells pending an appearance before a magistrate the following morning.

After Dawson's precipitate departure, a badly unnerved Macleod spent the rest of the day and a sleepless night wondering how Dawson had been traced to his flat.

On Monday morning, Richard wasted no time. When Macleod reached his office, his secretary was dithering nervously. "Sir Richard wants to see you at once, Mr Macleod," she blurted out as soon as he stepped across the threshold. "That was fifteen minutes ago."

The atmosphere in Richard's office was quite distinctive.

Victor Macleod had always been of the opinion that his Chairman and Managing Director was a rather ineffectual character. It was a notion based on his own arrogant conception of what constituted an effective performance. Within seconds of him sitting down, Richard's steely gaze had destroyed all illusions. The quiet disinterest in Richard's voice made it seem all the more menacing.

"There are a number of things I don't know or haven't been able to work out yet," he began. "The most important is whether you put Dawson up to interfere with those horses."

Macleod's reaction was entirely predictable. "Good heavens above, Richard, what *are* you talking about?"

Richard smiled. It was not the sort of smile that Macleod would remember with any pleasure. "Dawson was arrested at your flat yesterday afternoon." Macleod's face drained of all colour, and his eyes showed fear. Richard paused for a long time before adding, "For your information, the police knew where to find him because *I* told them."

479

There was a look on Macleod's face that Richard was sure Imogen would have enjoyed. He showed no inclination to speak.

"Let me tell you what I think." Richard's tone had a flavour of mock-confidentiality. "I haven't the faintest idea why you decided to become involved with racing. It's been suggested that it was to butter me up, and I suppose that's the only possible explanation, although it sounds absurd to me. I believe your original intention in setting Brookes-Smith up in that dreadful place at Epsom was to show Edward Manning and me a thing or two. When you discovered that it wasn't that easy, you decided that you had to make some quick money out of it. And you knew all along what a charming character Dawson was, didn't you? He rang you up when Edward quite properly slung him out of Saxon Court – do you remember telling me? Fancy a chap like that knowing your ex-directory number."

The two men stared at each other, Macleod determined to say nothing, wondering how he could scheme his way out of it, Richard concealing his enjoyment of the situation.

"I can't prove a thing," Richard said with bland indifference. "But I don't have to. Dawson has been charged with a number of offences, one of which is very serious indeed. This morning, the magistrates will remand him for a Crown Court, and bail will be refused. What do you suppose will happen when he comes to trial? He doped three horses, one of whom died as a consequence. He threatened Ernie Marshall's wife with a razor. I understand there are other people prepared to testify to his winsome ways. Nigel Brookes-Smith is dead, albeit by his own hand, but it all adds to the picture. I imagine Dawson will have a lot to say for himself . . . 'sing like a canary' . . . isn't that the expression?"

Macleod flicked his tongue across his lips. Apart from that one sign of nervousness, he remained defiant. And silent.

"I know you haven't been connected with the mainstream of our business," Richard said with cool contempt, "but I expect you realise that Stewart's has a reputation for being involved with the Turf. We have a number of highly-valued clients who use us purely because of our knowledge and sympathetic understanding of the sport. I have to watch our reputation extremely carefully, and you've been a great worry to me, Victor. You let the side down rather badly that day at Ascot . . . raised a few eyebrows in high places, that did. And what are people to think when they discover that I have a general manager who's been getting himself mixed up with at least one highly dubious character? To be honest with you, it occurred to me that I might have to ask for your resignation."

Richard paused, giving the impression that he had rejected the idea completely. Still wary, Macleod showed faint signs of relaxation: he shifted to a more comfortable position in his chair.

"But I decided that wouldn't do at all . . ." Richard leaned forward slightly ". . . someone might expect me to provide you with a reference, and I would be deprived of the very great pleasure of sacking you." Richard stiffened. "Mr Macleod, you are dismissed from the service of Stewart's!"

"You can't do that!"

The look on Macleod's face indicated that he knew it was an idiotic thing to say.

"Yes, I can, and I've just done it," Richard said.

"I'll sue you."

"Splendid! A piece of advice, though. Start this afternoon. At the moment, the only justification I have is that you harboured a wanted criminal in your home in the full knowledge of what you were doing. Give me a few more days, and I'm sure I shall be able to do much better."

Richard pressed a button on his desk. Immediately, the door to the outer office opened, and the bank's head of security came in.

"Mr Jordan and one of his assistants will go with you to your office, Macleod, and supervise the removal of your personal belongings. You will surrender all keys. When Mr Jordan is fully satisfied that the proper procedures have been completed, you will be escorted from the building."

Macleod had stood up when they were interrupted. Conscious, as he was meant to be, that he was being treated like a criminal, his face flushed with chagrin. Watching him with disdainful detachment, Richard chose the precise moment at which the surge of hot-headed bravado began to ebb, and said, "Carry on, please, Mr Jordan."

"Very well, Sir Richard."

After they had gone, Richard turned slightly in his chair, and stared at the wall. Sir Nick had installed a very private bathroom during his period as Chairman. A superb job had been made of the connecting door in the panelling; many visitors were unaware of its existence, and Macleod had not noticed that it was fractionally ajar.

Nothing happened.

Smiling to himself, Richard said, "You can come out now, my dear."

A chair scraped on the floor, and Imogen emerged.

"All right?" Richard asked quietly.

"My goodness!" Her smile broadened. "You enjoyed that, didn't you?"

"Yes!"

"So did I." She sat on the edge of his desk, swinging the long, shapely legs of which, secretly, she was very proud. "What do you suppose he'll do?"

"Make himself very scarce. My guess is that he'll grab what he can from his share in that place in Epsom, and clear off somewhere."

"Good riddance! Yes, that was super . . . almost worth catching that awful train for. Is it always that crowded?"

"I thought this morning was quieter than usual."

"It was pandemonium! And I refuse to believe that *all* that crowd had first-class tickets!"

There were twenty-five people at Nigel's funeral. All but Imogen and Elspeth came from Saxon Court. Although not a member of the official guest-list, George Roberts hovered helpfully in the background during the short service and burial in a plot adjacent to Caroline's grave. He also went back to the buffet lunch that Edward had organised in the Big House.

"Thanks, George," Edward said. "I'm glad we could put on a bit of a show for him."

"Poor bugger," George replied. "Do you know, I was doing some work here twenty years ago – young Nigel would be seven or eight I suppose. He'd done summat wrong, and you should have heard that dad of his! Down in the yard, they thought the war had started. Not good enough, is it?"

"No, George, it bloody well isn't. We can see where it's ended up."

"Ar!" George ruminated for a while. "Terrible time that family's had," he said. "There was Miss Caroline, of course, and her mother before her. That was a shocking business. Wasted away to nothing in six months, she did. And my word, she'd been a fine-looking woman."

Later, Elspeth, who looked very tired, made a point of thanking Edward for what he had done.

"Someone had to make the effort," he said. "Poor old Nigel lived here for a damned sight longer than me . . . so far."

"You're staying put, are you?" Elspeth asked.

"Most definitely!"

"Good. There was some talk of you leaving."

"Yes. That was after Caro, of course. I think I'm just about over it by now."

She nodded. "It takes a long time. I know."

"How's Cyril?"

"Very ill." Elspeth sighed. "They don't seem all that optimistic about him at the hospital . . . and they always try to be, don't they?"

"And this happened after Nigel dashed down to see you?"

"Yes. It was completely self-inflicted, there's absolutely no doubt

482

about that. He got far too excited. Over the wrong sort of thing, too. He really was so very *spiteful* about Nigel. The Lord alone knows what the poor boy had done to offend him."

Seeing no point in rushing back to Devon to visit a man who couldn't recognise her, Elspeth was staying with Imogen and Richard at Widney Cheyne for at least one night. Edward hoped she would get some sorely-needed sleep.

When everyone had gone, Edward sensed that his father had something to say.

"What are you going to do about Siobhan?" Frank wanted to know.

"Ah yes . . . I was meaning to talk to you about that. If she's willing, I'd like her to start running the office again."

Frank smiled. "She's willing, all right. She was looking round yesterday, and I could tell what she was thinking. She belongs here. You mustn't let her go again."

"I can hardly stop her if she wants to go."

"I don't think you'll have that problem. So I'm to have the old heave-ho, then?"

"Not necessarily." Edward looked intently at his father. "Depends on you."

"As a matter of fact, I'd like to stay around. There's plenty for me to do, Paddy can't cope with a lot of the odd jobs during the summer when he's driving to the races almost every day."

"That's fine by me. What about mother?"

"Ah, now this is the interesting thing! She's decided she'd like to move down here. Apparently she's always had a hankering to live in the south. The things you can find out about folk after forty years!"

Edward frowned. "Are you thinking of selling up?"

"Oh yes. We could do with a smaller house – providing it's got a big garden. There are a couple of suitable properties for sale in the village at the moment. Why, what's the matter?"

Something was troubling Edward. "Do you know, I don't like the idea of you selling that house," he said.

"Why?"

"Well . . ." Edward was far from sure what he was trying to say ". . . I've always loved the place, but I think the main thing is that it was James Henry's. Avoca House was the same. I hated leaving that."

"So what do you think we should do?" Frank asked. "We can't keep it on as a sort of museum piece, can we? And what would you do with it when it's yours?"

Edward nodded. "I know it's ridiculous and impractical . . . I just don't like to think of the Mannings giving that house up."

"You've jolly well *got* to be practical about these things. None of us is getting any younger, and that house is much too big for your mother . . .

she's suffering quite a bit with arthritis. In any case, we want to be near you."

There was nothing Edward could do except agree. "It would be lovely having you down here," he said. "You go ahead, and I'll make sure you're kept busy."

"Isn't it funny?" Frank said. "Here I am, utterly hooked on stable life, yet for years I thought the old man was off his head. I even dreamed about it the other night."

"I hope it wasn't a nightmare."

"No, it was all very nice. I dreamed that this is going to be the best year you've had so far."

"Good! It's my tenth, you know."

"Then it's time you were getting good."

"I've learned a thing or two, but it's a never-ending process."

"When do you think Siobhan will be ready to start?"

"Not yet. She's not showing much at the moment because she's very tough, but that's an awful experience she's been through. Let's see how she is in a month."

To Robin Lane, getting to grips with his new responsibilities, it was a month that seemed to go on for ever. For Edward, the month flew past; at its memorable end, he had no idea where it had gone.

In many ways, the greatest success of April was the way his left knee stood up to a punishing regime. Edward's routine was that of seven years ago, when he and Caroline were embarking upon what was to be their only full season at Saxon Court. He rode out with both lots each day, and worked hard in the office every afternoon, poring endlessly over race entries and training plans, usually with Declan or Robin on hand for consultation. For the final duty of the day, evening stables, Edward found it necessary to use a stick; after nearly twelve hours, the knee could become troublesome as ligaments tired.

Morale among the lads took a tentative step forward when their first runner turned into a winner. This was often more than a single, isolated piece of good news, since it was believed to indicate that a stable was 'in form', with its horses healthy and working well, and lady luck ready to offer every assistance. So it proved. Five more winners followed in rapid succession, and mealtimes in the lads' hostel became riotous again.

Edward's major preoccupation was with Santuzza and Prometheus, possibles for the One and Two Thousand Guineas respectively. Prometheus presented no problems; at the first sign of work, he set to willingly, and won the Craven Stakes as part of his preparation for the Classic. However, Santuzza, winner of the previous year's Mill Reef Stakes, simply could not get going to any purpose. Always a somewhat awkward-looking and ungainly mover, she seemed unable to find the synchronisation necessary for a good gallop: in the jargon of the yard, she had 'lost her action'.

Every experiment that Edward and Robin could devise was tried, all without success. Nearing the end of her busiest time at the stud, Nancy came over to ride her, achieving no more than her regular lad or Sean Gillespie. Nancy had tremendous faith in Santuzza, and was bitterly disappointed. The answer came the following day.

After Santuzza's lot had finished their warm-up canter, Alison, who was watching with Edward, suddenly said, "I haven't had a go on her yet, sir. Shall I try?"

"Anything you like, Alison. If we can't get her moving today or tomorrow, she'll have to come out of the Guineas."

The change-over of riders went wrong.

Afterwards – not that it mattered – Edward thought that Alison's possibly over-brisk, businesslike approach must have made the filly nervous. For whatever reason, Alison was no sooner mounted, than she was on the ground, flat on her back, with Santuzza taking off in the general direction of Reading. Quickly satisfied that only Alison's pride was hurt, Edward focussed his attention on Santuzza. There was nothing hectic about her; she wasn't actually bolting. She had decided that it was time she tried to sort things out for herself and was perfectly calm about it. Her progress was erratic at first. She pursued a zigzag course, lashing out repeatedly with her back legs. When she had covered about two furlongs, and knew she was free to do as she pleased, she halted to take a long look round. Then she set off down the main gallop, devouring the ground. Most of the fifty horses that watched her go were capable of greater elegance, but none was more effective.

"Well, there's nothing wrong with the way she's moving now," Edward said to Declan who had come up alongside him on his hack.

"There is not. Do you want her fetching back?"

"No. She won't like it if we go chasing after her. She's all right. Leave her to get on with it. Let's have the others on the all-weather."

For the next few minutes, Edward watched the second lot start the routine of working in pairs while keeping an eye on Santuzza, smiling when he saw that his assumption had been correct. As she disappeared into the dip, he had to stand in the stirrups, looking high over Murgatroyd's head to see what became of her. She covered seven furlongs, exactly the trip over which he had wanted to work her, pulled up, and moved to the unmown edge of the gallop to crop at the succulent spring grass. After that, Edward concentrated all his attention on what was happening on the all-weather track.

When he rode down to collect her, she watched his advance until he was within a hundred yards of her, then came to meet him. Once Edward had hold of her rein, she accompanied Murgatroyd back to the yard as docilely as a pet out for a stroll with its master. At evening stables, Edward gave her a thorough inspection, found she had come to no harm, and decided to give her a stiff work-out two days later with Sean Gillespie on board. It was a great success: Santuzza had resolved her problems, and would have left her three work-companions for dead if Sean had let her.

"That's it, then," Edward said. "She can go in the Guineas. I don't think she'll disgrace us."

"She's every chance," Declan said, and Robin nodded agreement.

"I'd like to get the Duke to go and see her run," Edward said, thinking aloud rather than making a definite statement. "He could do with cheering up, he's been very down in the dumps these last few months. The trouble is, I believe he hardly ever goes out nowadays."

"I wonder if I could persuade him."

Unsurprised by her intervention, Edward glanced thoughtfully at Siobhan. This was the third consecutive day on which she had appeared in the middle of the afternoon to make tea and listen to what was being said.

"That might not be a bad idea," he said. "He's always had a soft spot for you." It was an over-simplification. The Duke of Dorchester invariably listened to what Siobhan had to say with careful respect, abandoning his habitual facetiousness. "Would you like to give him a ring?"

She shook her head. "I'll go and see him." With the ghost of a smile, she added, "I've plenty of news for him. If I can borrow a car, I'll go tomorrow."

"Fine," Edward replied.

As she left the office, Edward, Frank and Declan exchanged knowing looks.

The Duke of Dorchester not only went to Newmarket on the last Thursday of April for the One Thousand Guineas, he was astonishingly close to his old form. Edward's spirits lifted the moment he saw him, looking as chirpy as he had done before the double blow dealt by Monty.

"Now then, Manning, do you think my nag's going to make a fist of this?" was his greeting.

"I live in hope, Freddie. You're looking pretty sprightly."

"Clean air and good living, old cock. I'm told you've been having fun and games with the filly."

"She lost her action."

"Siobhan told me all about it. Good of her to come and see me. Here, I say, what a time she's been having, eh?"

"Dreadful."

"She seemed very fed up. I got the impression the whole lot of you were . . . that's why I came today. Don't mind telling you, Manning, I've been a bit down myself since Monty, but when that poor gal told me what a state you were all in, I thought I'd better come and cheer you up. I say, it seems to me that her husband wasn't much good."

"Weak," Edward said. "He allowed himself to be pushed around by a pair of right villains."

"There are some real bad hats about," the Duke said. "Still, we must look on the bright side. She's a widow now. She can start again. She deserves that."

There was a hard set to the Duke's mouth and chin, and Edward was surprised by the harshness of his sentiments. But he was right.

A field of twelve fillies, only one of which was obviously hopelessly out of her class, gave rise to a curiously fluid, indecisive betting market. An Irish contender, Inis Diomain, who had won two Group races at the Curragh as a two-year-old, was a fairly firm favourite, but her relatively long odds of five to one reflected the general lack of confidence in previous achievements. It was to be a race for establishing form, not confirming it. Santuzza had been trading at six and seven to one, but drifted out to ten to one once everyone had seen her set off for the start in an ungainly fashion. That was the point at which Dooley pounced and placed the bet he and Frank had agreed on.

"Would you say that she was a creature of outstanding natural beauty?" the Duke asked as he watched his filly go by.

"No, Freddie, I'm afraid I wouldn't," Edward said. "And she doesn't look much better when she gets going, but she covers the ground all right."

When the race started, La Rondine, a French filly, immediately set a blistering pace which took her three lengths clear in the first half-furlong until Inis Diomain and several others went after her. Sean Gillespie was having nothing to do with the headlong dash at the front, and kept Santuzza at the back, letting her settle and find her legs.

"Do you suppose they're going to keep this up?" Imogen asked as the leaders passed the four furlong post, the mid-point of the race.

"I don't see how they can," Edward replied. "That pace is ridiculous. Wait till they get past the dip and on to the hill. We should see some fun and games then."

"Ours is a heck of a long way behind," the Duke said doubtfully.

"Don't worry, Sean's getting her going," Edward said quietly.

"My word, Manning, I see what you mean. She can shift a bit, can't she?"

487

"Still not a pretty sight, but she's getting there," Edward said.

Once they met the rising ground at the bushes, the horses at the front began to flag. "Ah! Right!" Imogen said in her official voice. "I can see what's going to happen here. It's going to be another of those back-stabbing jobs. Sean will do them on the line by three-quarters of a nostril."

"Those were the sort of tactics we were thinking of," Edward admitted.

"Very sound," Imogen said approvingly. "Sean's frightfully good at that caper . . . oh, I say . . . look at this!"

Most of the front-runners were tiring very quickly indeed; relative to Santuzza, they really did seem to be going backwards. Inis Diomain was a much tougher nut to crack, and Sean had to show Santuzza the whip in order to get the momentum for the final assault. At the line, she was the winner by two lengths.

The Duke was delighted. "Well done, Manning. Good show! That's a damned fine piece of training when you consider that she couldn't put one foot in front of the other a couple of weeks ago."

"Did Siobhan tell you how we got her straight?" Edward asked.

"Oh no . . . and I wouldn't expect her to. Trade secrets and all that, what?"

Edward smiled. "I think you're going to like this, Freddie. What happened was . . ."

"Oi!" Imogen shouted at them. "There's work to be done before we get down to the droll reminiscences. Here comes Freezer with your horse, Freddie. You're supposed to pretend to lead her into the winner's enclosure. And Edward, my dear, I can see nice Wesley Davies advancing on you with a purposeful look in his eye."

It was a perfect evening when they got back to Saxon Court at a little before seven o'clock. Newmarket Heath had been beset by blustery showers. Now the wind had dropped to a light breeze, and the only clouds were like widely-dispersed balls of cottonwool in the bluest sky that Edward had seen for a long time. Imogen had travelled to and from Newmarket with him, and she smiled as they cruised in through the gate, Dooley and the van close behind. Three lads were hanging around expectantly outside the hostel, and one of them dashed off excitedly as they appeared.

"They'll be quite pleased about this," Imogen said.

Although happy to be a part of it, Edward was always surprised by the commotion generated on these occasions. This evening, he wanted to do nothing more than collapse into a comfortable chair and rest his knee which was playing up after a day that had included two long spells of driving. He would, but not yet. Most of the lads were out of the hostel and hurrying to greet the heroine of the hour at the traditional place beneath the clock-tower. They seemed more enthusiastic than usual;

488

Edward understood that Santuzza's performance must have seemed a miracle to them after an abysmal six months.

He was about to make the effort to join in the celebration when Siobhan appeared at the side door of the Big House. She had a camera in one hand, and his walking-stick in the other. As she hurried towards the car, Edward looked surprised, whereas an expression of satisfaction spread over Imogen's face.

"You shouldn't have gone without this," Siobhan said, thrusting the stick at him. "You looked quite uncomfortable while Wesley Davies was interviewing you. There's a pot of tea in the kitchen. Your father's left a note. I'll just go and do the photographs."

Imogen laughed at Edward's bemusement, and went into the house ahead of him while he paused to exercise his knee before following her. She poured tea for both of them, smacked her lips over the first sip, kicked her shoes off and lit a cigarette while Edward read Frank's note.

Well done! Siobhan tells me that she has now taken over the office, so I've gone home. I'm putting the house up for sale. Will be in touch early next week. Good luck for Saturday.

"What's happening on Saturday?" a dazed Edward asked Imogen who had already read the note.

"Aren't you running Prometheus in the Two Thousand Guineas?" she suggested.

He grinned foolishly. "This is all a bit too much," he said. "I'd spoken to dad about Siobhan, of course. I didn't think she'd wade in and start . . . just like that."

"Can't think of a better way," Imogen said.

Edward wandered into the office. The white board caught his attention at once. Eight feet by four, it dominated one wall. That morning, it had been a mess, covered with felt-tip pen jottings that had accumulated over a year or more. Before leaving for Newmarket, Edward himself had added to the jumble with a note to order special feed for ten of the two-year-olds. The board had been cleaned and returned to the use for which it was originally acquired. Now, there was very little on it. To the right, the season's seven 'ordinary' winners were listed; on the left of the board, three columns for Groups One, Two and Three had been drawn. It was bang up-to-date with Santuzza's winnings of £125,641 underlined in blue.

"She's made a start already," Edward said to Imogen when she came into the office to see what he was doing.

"So I see. And this was on the kitchen table."

She handed Edward a video cassette. It was labelled: '1000 Guineas, 1989: Santuzza'.

489

Siobhan was back, and he could rely on everything being precisely as he liked it.

Prometheus finished second in the Two Thousand Guineas. For reasons that Imogen appeared to know, but treated as highly confidential, Valerie was unable to go to Newmarket to see the race, and it fell to Nancy Bloomfield to play the part of owner. Richard, who was there to lend support and watch one of his horses in the race following the Guineas, was impressed by Prometheus whom he had never seen in action before.

"Are you running him at Epsom?" he asked Edward.

"Valerie's keen to have a go."

"I would. You know what they say."

"'Second in the Guineas, first in the Derby,'" Edward quoted.

"Exactly. I can see you don't think much of the idea."

"It isn't impossible. Mill Reef did it."

Richard laughed. "But Prometheus is no Mill Reef?"

"He certainly isn't. No horse is. Our problem is The Yeoman."

"Do you think he's that good?" Richard asked sceptically, having another look at the colt who had won the Two Thousand Guineas.

"He's just proved he's no slouch, hasn't he?"

"They say he won't get the trip at Epsom."

"*They* always do," Edward replied sourly. "If Giles Hawksworth runs him in the Derby, my guess is that he's the one they'll all have to beat."

Richard decided to shut up, knowing that Edward would have looked very closely at The Yeoman. He also knew that Edward had a healthy regard for the colt's trainer. The Hawksworths had been turning fine horses out of Latimer's Barn in Wiltshire for more than a century. Giles, the fourth generation of the family, had taken over when he was only twenty-two, and now, at forty-five, was universally held in the highest esteem. Edward always kept an eye on him; Richard had often heard Edward mutter, "I wonder what Latimer's Barn will do about this," when he was assessing the form of an important race.

Throughout the five weeks between the Guineas and the Derby, Edward prepared Prometheus for the Epsom Classic, and was gratified by the horse's progress. There was every indication that he would stay the gruelling mile and a half, his condition held up well, and it was decided to run him. While this was going on, Siobhan's scoreboard showed that there had been no neglect of other horses; on average, three winners a week were being sent out.

Valerie Malahide appeared at Saxon Court with Fred Bird on the day before the Derby. Edward had not even known she was in England,

490

although she had told him by telephone that she was hoping to see her horse run. He accepted that she and Fred were developing a life that had its own motivation and priorities that were nothing to do with him.

"How are things?" Edward asked Fred when they were alone.

"All right . . . yes, not bad at all," Fred said, causing Edward to be curious at the lack of conviction.

"What's up, Fred? You look positively hunted."

"I've got a lot on my mind."

"Tell me about it."

"Well . . . the fact is, me and Mrs Malahide are thinking of getting spliced."

"That's terrific! Can I be best man?"

"Shush!" Fred looked round furtively. "This is on the secret list. We haven't quite been able to make our minds up yet."

"Good grief, Fred, how long have you been at it?"

"It's not easy, son, not easy at all. However, you could say we're at an advanced stage of negotiation."

Edward kept a very straight face. "Any particular problems?" he asked.

"No, not really," Fred replied a fraction too airily. "Well, there is one," he added, after thinking about it. "But keep this under your hat . . . I don't want this leaking out."

"Cross my heart and hope to die."

"She wants me to get rid of the business."

"And do what?"

"Nothing. I'd have to go to concerts and things . . . you know, sort of take an interest."

"That's good for the soul, Fred."

"You reckon?"

"Most definitely."

"Do you know anything about this chamber music lark?"

"Yes. It's terrific. What you want to get stuck into are the late quartets of Beethoven . . . opus 131 is the stuff to give the troops. That's the one in C sharp minor, by the way."

Fred looked horrified.

Edward had a chance of talking to Valerie after the following day's Derby in which Prometheus finished a creditable fourth behind The Yeoman, who won it in fine style.

"Fred tells me you're making him sell his business," he said, leaping in with both feet.

"That isn't strictly accurate," she said.

"What is, then?"

"I don't want him mixed up in it on a day-to-day basis."

"Why?"

"Would you want to be married to him while he was still up to his neck in knickers?" Valerie asked with a smile.

"You're thinking of all the opportunities?"

"I am indeed!"

"He'd never trust anyone else to run it."

"I know. Therefore, he'll have to sell it. There's another problem as well."

"What's that?"

She looked round, and Edward laughed.

"Don't worry, I won't breathe a word to a living soul," he promised.

"We can't agree where to live."

"What's the problem?"

"Sheer bloody-mindedness," she replied.

Edward did not ask her to elaborate.

When October came, Frank's dream was proved to have been justified. It *was* Edward's best-ever season, with ninety-one winners and prize-money of nearly seven hundred thousand pounds, a performance that put him third in the trainers' table behind Giles Hawksworth and Bernard Dalrymple. Such a successful year had many high points, yet from the middle of June onwards, Cavaradossi was pre-eminent. Following a most convincing victory in the Coventry Stakes at Royal Ascot, he was rarely out of the public eye or headlines. After Ascot, he won the Champagne Stakes at Doncaster, a relatively minor race at Sandown that was really no more than a public piece of work, and finished his two-year-old career by dominating the field from start to finish in the Dewhurst Stakes. His subsequent winter ante-post favouritism for the 1990 Two Thousand Guineas seemed well justified. Inevitably, comparisons were made between Cavaradossi and James Henry, with many thinking that Cavaradossi was every bit as good as his now-legendary precursor.

Nocker Jarvis was highly dubious about it all.

Cavaradossi made his debut at Wolverhampton in May, a week before Prometheus went in the Derby. In search of an easy race that would give him a gentle introduction to the serious work that lay ahead, and help in the preparation for Royal Ascot, Edward was surprised to discover what had more or less chosen itself. It was the Wheaton Aston Stakes, the modest event in which James Henry had made his debut.

Nocker, accompanied as usual by Charlie Onions, self-appointed official seer of Wolverhampton, watched the proceedings before the race with a jaundiced eye.

"It's been a long time," Charlie said.

Nocker agreed. "Seven years."

"And this looks another good 'un."

"Yes."

Charlie detected Nocker's scepticism. "What's up, our kid?"

"I'm not convinced."

"He's class, Nocker, you can see that with half an eye."

"No argument, Charlie, no argument. But the thing is, nobody's come with him. Remember that time when he run James Henry? We had half the nobs in Berkshire here, didn't we? And what have we got today? Just Freezer Frost."

"Manning doesn't go racing very often these days."

"He didn't, but he's been out and about a lot this season. Alf Witherspoon saw him at Leicester the other day."

"Oh." Charlie Onions realised that he had some thinking to do. "Who's the lad?" he asked. "Never seen him before."

"They call him Elegant Hawkins. Used to be with Alec Stedding at Epsom. I think it's the first time he's condescended to come this far north."

"They look a right pair, don't they?"

Cavaradossi, with Elegant, who was dressed up to the nines, paraded round the paddock as though they owned it, making the other horses and their lads look rather ordinary.

Charlie Onions winced when Sean Gillespie appeared with the other jockeys. "I'd forgotten about that bloody tassel," he said. "It never looks right at a place like this."

Nocker Jarvis laughed. "No soul, Charlie, that's your trouble. That get-up looks a treat at Ascot."

Head high, ears pricked, and with a definite air of "Have a good look at me while you've got the chance," Cavaradossi moved down to the start like a smoothly-flowing animation from a textbook. He came back even better; with Sean Gillespie determined that he should learn as much as possible from his first race, none of the others ever stood the remotest chance. Cavaradossi won by ten lengths, actually making his short starting price of six to four on look generous.

"Well, what do we think of that?" Charlie Onions asked.

"Very nice," Nocker replied. "He could be the best horse anybody's seen this year. But what I want to know is this, Charlie . . ." and he stabbed a finger repeatedly against his crony's shoulder ". . . why didn't Manning come to watch him?"

"He's got two going at Newbury. He'll be there."

"Pah! They're rubbish compared to this boy. This is potential Classic material we're looking at here, Charlie. Who's he got riding that pair at Newbury?"

"Dyer."

"Exactly! His number one jockey's here. So why ain't he?"

Charlie Onions shook his head in sorrow rather than anger. "You're making too much out of it, Nocker. Harry Messenger always said you was a mountains and molehills merchant."

Edward *was* present at Cavaradossi's subsequent racecourse appearances. But Charlie Onions was never allowed to forget Nocker's hunch, and at the beginning of August he saw something that he had to admit was probably significant.

The popular press began to cast Cavaradossi in the role of potential world-beater after his Royal Ascot victory. One of the reasons for this had nothing to do with Cavaradossi himself: Edward had four other winners at the Royal meeting, giving him the accolade of top trainer over the highly publicised four days. "It's beyond me," Edward complained to Richard. "Why *do* they jump to these absurd conclusions? All that's happened is that the luck's run for us *here*. We could be right up the creek this time next week, never mind next year."

"Don't be such a spoil-sport," Richard laughed. "Let them have their fun." He had just turned down an offer of a million pounds for Cavaradossi, and was feeling very benign. "This is the only time they ever get to talk about racing – when they've finished with the hats, of course. They feel duty-bound to try and make an earth-shattering pronouncement or two."

"Well, I wish they'd get it right," Edward grumbled, and dropped the subject. Quietly, he was pleased with the way things were going, and played up to Wesley Davies in a TV interview.

"This is looking like a pretty good year, Edward."

"Not bad, is it?"

"Tell me, how highly do you rate Cavaradossi?"

"He looks good, doesn't he? He's a bit lazy at home, you know. Never does any more than he has to."

"Is he a Guineas horse?"

"Should be. We think he might get the mile all right. Actually, Paddy Dooley believes he'll be very effective at a mile."

"I see." Wesley Davies looked impressed. Then he realised that the name was unfamiliar to him; Saxon Court clearly had a vital new member of staff. "Who's Paddy Dooley?" he asked.

Edward smiled blandly at him. "My van driver," he said.

Edward was gladdened by one aspect of Royal Ascot that he knew would have given his grandfather a great deal of pleasure. Two of his bag of five winners belonged to Mark Walgrave, who tasted top-quality success for the first time. The Elms at Bagshot, for over thirty years the base of the Avoca House visit to Ascot, thus became the scene of a celebration that would have cheered the old man.

After Ascot, the winners kept coming; if Siobhan's scoreboard went more than three days without further addition, eyebrows were raised. The steady flow of successes gave Edward a freedom from pressure that he had not known since Caroline, and he used it to good advantage, most especially in the preparation and planning associated with the two-year-olds.

His unwillingness to put juveniles on a racecourse until he felt they were absolutely ready was turning into something of a fetish. Cavaradossi and one of Richard's fillies, together with Mark Walgrave's Ascot pair, were very forward, and grasped their early chances. The others were watched during their daily exercise, and sent off to race as and when they became ready. Edward's almost constant decision-making companions on Saxon Down were Nancy and Robin Lane.

One morning in July as their horses were ambling back down the Avenue with the second lot, Edward said, "I think Oscar's ready to have a gentle go at something."

"Yup, I agree," Nancy said.

Among themselves, the three invariably used the nickname that Robin Lane had helped to coin. While they were watching Lohengrin canter round the covered ride soon after he arrived from Widney Cheyne, they had all commented on the studious seriousness of the way he went about what should have been the perfectly automatic process of picking his legs up and moving.

"I've never seen anything like it," Nancy said. "When this guy gets his action the way he wants it, he's gonna be worth watching."

Smiling, Edward shook his head in a mixture of admiration and puzzlement. "He's the most earnest horse I've ever seen."

"*The Importance of Being Earnest*," Robin said.

"That's good, Robin, we'll call him Oscar," Edward laughed, and the name stuck.

Back in the office, Edward looked at the list of five races for which Siobhan had Lohengrin entered over the next two weeks.

"That one," he said, marking it.

"Wolverhampton again," Siobhan said.

"Yes, that's a nice easy five furlongs for him."

Siobhan consulted one of her immaculately-kept files. "There's Newmarket the same day," she told him. "I think you'll want to be there as well."

"What's the programme?"

She showed him, and he nodded. "Yes, we'll be sending two there, so you'll need to hire a van and driver."

"For Wolverhampton?" she asked, pencil poised.

"Oh no, Siobhan, for Newmarket. *We'll* take Oscar."

Nocker Jarvis had a field-day.

"Now then, Charlie, what about this lot, then?"

Charlie Onions looked uncomfortable.

"He's got two horses at Newmarket, and the number one jockey's gone there to ride them. *But . . .*" and Nocker wanted to be certain that the point was taken ". . . but Manning's here himself, in person, that woman with him is Nancy Bloomfield who I reckon did the breeding, and have you seen how they got here?"

"No."

"They brought him up in their own van. If I know anything, they'll have hired one to go to Newmarket."

Charlie Onions shuffled and said nothing.

Nocker took a close interest in the events that followed the appearance of the jockeys. Sean Gillespie was not renowned for his paddock conversations, and received any last-minute instructions with a nod that was undetectable at a range of more than five paces. With John Dyer, things were very different; he took part in an animated three-way conversation with Edward and Nancy, always maintaining his worried-to-death expression. When he was mounted, it was Edward not Elegant who led the horse to the racecourse gate. At that stage, Nocker couldn't tell whether he was talking to John Dyer or the horse.

For much of the race, the punters who had backed the joint second favourites entertained hopes of a famous coup; certainly the two horses appeared to have it all stitched up at the furlong distance, and were settling down to a ding-dong struggle to determine which of them would win it. Most of the crowd were so taken with what was happening at the front, that they failed to notice Lohengrin's advance. Charlie Onions would have missed it if it hadn't been for Nocker's grunt and nudge. Still seeming to measure every stride with fastidious care, Lohengrin was making amazing progress. Because of the steadiness of his gait, and the fact that John Dyer was undemonstratively motionless, it was completely unspectacular compared to the furious battle raging ahead of him. Most people were astounded when he cruised fluently into the lead and won it.

"Well?" Nocker asked.

"He only just made it," Charlie Onions said sourly. "Three-parts of a length ain't much against that load of rubbish."

"Only just made it!" Nocker exploded. "Only just made it . . . God give me strength! He was never off the bit, you bloody fool. That jockey

496

had a word with him a furlong out, then he just sat there while he got on with it."

"Get out of it! You'm getting fanciful, Nocker. It's senility."

"I had the glasses on him. I saw his lips move."

"He was saying his prayers, you daft bugger, not talking to the horse."

Nocker turned his back on Charlie Onions's scorn, and made his way to the winner's enclosure.

"Hello, Mr Manning," he said at a suitable moment. "Nocker Jarvis."

Startled, Edward looked at him blankly. Then he smiled in recognition. "You wrote to me after my wife died."

"Yes, I did." Nocker suddenly felt like a fish out of water. He had forgotten about that.

"That was very good of you. It was much appreciated. I'm afraid I never replied to all the letters."

"This is a nice horse," Nocker said abruptly to change the subject.

"I think so," Edward said. "Some don't like him because he's a chestnut with all this white."

"Old wives' tale," Nocker said dismissively. "Got any plans for him?"

"No, it's too early. He seems to have come through this one all right. I might start thinking about the future when he's got a couple more races under his belt."

"He's bred to stay, isn't he?"

"Forever – or so Miss Bloomfield thinks."

Nocker studied Nancy, who smiled at his frank curiosity. She was, Nocker decided, quite a looker when you got close to her. These outdoor, horsey types were often very deceptive; they could look a right mess, but get some decent clothes and a dab of make-up on them and the result was surprising. This one had smashing brown eyes, and a pretty good bone structure. Her hair was all right, too; it wouldn't take all that much tinting to make it the colour of the handsome horse of which she and Manning were clearly very fond.

"I've heard a story that you only bought his sire for his breeding potential," Nocker said. "You never thought he'd make much of a racehorse. Is that true?"

Edward laughed. "That was the idea," he admitted. "He didn't do too badly racing, did he?"

"Do you think he'll produce some good 'uns?"

"We'll have to wait and see. At least he's had his first winner now. I think I'm right in saying this was only his second attempt . . . a Parsifal filly ran at Haydock Park last week, I believe."

"That's right. She finished third."

When he walked away after another five minutes, Nocker was very tempted to write about Lohengrin in much the same way as he had done

497

with James Henry. Then he thought again. The piece he submitted for publication at the end of the day was all about a popular local horse who won the race after Lohengrin's for the third year in succession.

Lohengrin raced twice more that season, winning both times.

Before his next appearance, Edward and Siobhan had the unpleasant task of attending Terry Dawson's trial at which they both gave evidence. Edward was staggered at what had come to light about Dawson. In addition to his demanding money with menaces in connection with Caley's Pleasure and the two horses at Warwick, he had made serious attempts to corrupt staff at two other stables in the Epsom area. Money, it seemed, was never enough for him; as an additional motivation to his accomplices, he always found it necessary to issue threats. One of the procession of witnesses told a harrowing tale of a pet dog that Dawson had killed to demonstrate his ruthlessness. From the dock, Dawson made a fairly comprehensive job of blackening Victor Macleod, who, Edward knew, had disappeared as predicted by Richard. Dawson was sent to prison for three years, and Edward made a note to be alert when he was released.

A month after Wolverhampton, Lohengrin overcame stronger opposition at Newbury to win a race worth five thousand pounds. Acting on Edward's instructions, Sean Gillespie gave him a harder ride than John Dyer had done, and the result was impressive. However, the race took place on a Thursday, without TV coverage, and none of the journalists present wrote about it.

At the end of September, he competed in the Royal Lodge Stakes at Ascot. Only Nancy knew how anxious Edward was to run Lohengrin in this event, which was over a course of one mile, the longest distance which two-year-olds were allowed to race. A good performance would be a strong intimation that a horse might be capable of tackling middle distances as a three-year-old. Lohengrin put up a very good performance. At six furlongs, he had all but one of the opposition run off their legs; over the last two furlongs, he battled it out with Bernard Dalrymple's talented Vasco da Gama, already a winner of two Group races. It was Lohengrin who got the upper hand, and in the last fifty yards, both Edward and Nancy thought he was going away easily. Sean Gillespie, an unashamed and surprisingly ardent admirer of Cavaradossi, grudgingly admitted that Lohengrin might make a good horse.

The race should have been televised as part of the Saturday afternoon sports compendium, but technical problems prevented this, and the five-minute slot allocated was easily filled with the athletics that were the mainstay of the programme. For some curious reason, none of the newspapermen thought that Lohengrin had done all that well, and those who did write about the race did so in muted terms.

In the press, Lohengrin was completely overshadowed by Cavaradossi, the hottest 'talking' horse for some years. The season had been dominated by Giles Hawksworth's brilliant colt The Yeoman from Latimer's Barn in Wiltshire; in September he followed his Two Thousand Guineas and Derby triumphs with victory in the St Leger and a place in the list of all-time greats as the winner of the Triple Crown. A month later, he added the ultimate jewel to his achievements by carrying off the Prix de l'Arc de Triomphe at Longchamp. Once the newspaper eulogies for The Yeoman had subsided, sports editors looked for his successor, and the way Cavaradossi dealt with a high-class international field in the Dewhurst Stakes made him the obvious contender. Edward gave no indication of his thoughts; he was simply glad to have won one of his favourite races for the third time, Cavaradossi following in the footsteps of James Henry and the outrageous Benvenuto Cellini.

Nowhere were the strengths and weaknesses of every horse in the yard debated more keenly than in Robin Lane's house on Saturday evenings. Soon after they had returned from honeymoon and become established in their new home, Robin and Alison started inviting a few friends in for drinks and supper. The usual gathering consisted of Liam and Kathleen Corrigan, Greaser O'Malley, Elegant Hawkins and Cathal O'Brien. When they met as usual on the evening after the Dewhurst Stakes, Alison had some news not directly connected with the yard.

"I was in the office this morning, and the guv'nor was very chuffed," she said. "He'd just heard he's got planning permission for the bungalow."

"Which bungalow?" Robin asked.

"The one on the Avenue – opposite the cottages, but a bit further down, nearer the gallops."

"What's that for?" Greaser asked, and Alison saw that all the others were mystified, too.

"It's for Declan and Mary when they retire."

"That's a nice idea," Elegant said. "Do they know about it or is it a surprise?"

"Of course they know!" Alison said. "The guv'nor had to talk to them about it, didn't he?"

"I don't know. Nobody tells me anything."

"Right, pin your ears back and listen. Declan and Mary said they didn't want to go back to Ireland, and they'd look for a cottage in the village. Then the guv'nor and Declan got talking, and they agreed that a bungalow down the Avenue would be nice, so George Roberts comes in to draw the plans up . . . Mary's over the moon about it. She was able to say just what she wanted, and George drew it like that. The only trouble was when Declan wanted to pay for it."

"Oh dear, the guv'nor wouldn't like that. Oh dear!" Liam Corrigan shook his head.

"He definitely did not! Siobhan told me all about it . . . she was there while they were at it. The guv'nor put his foot down and said they'd got to have it as a retirement present. He told Declan that his grandfather would have insisted on it, and that was the end of that."

Liam nodded. "Yes, himself *would* have done that."

"It will be lovely to have them there," Kathleen said. "They'll be able to watch the horses go past."

"And God help us if we start looking sloppy," Robin said. "He'll be out in a flash. Now then, Elegant, tell us how Cavaradossi did yesterday."

"He won it. He was quite impressive."

"We know that. We saw the tape. How was he afterwards?"

"All right. He ate up pretty quickly and slept most of the way back."

"What did Sean think?"

"He was pretty enthusiastic – well, by his standards. He said he was the second best ride he'd ever had."

"James Henry being the first?"

"I presume so. He fancies him for the Guineas next year. I heard him tell the guv'nor so."

"And the Derby?" Robin asked.

"I don't think he's got that far yet."

"H'm." Robin was deeply thoughtful.

"What's up, love?" Alison asked him.

"I'm sure the guv'nor's got plans."

Alison laughed. "That's his job, you twerp."

"I know, but I like to work out what he's thinking. I'm certain he's got some cards that he's keeping very close to his chest."

"What cards?" Elegant asked.

"I don't know." Robin smiled ruefully. "Has he said anything to you, Cathal?"

"No. Should he have done?"

"You do Lohengrin."

"All he's said is that he wants him treating gentle."

"I think I can see what Robin means," Elegant said. "The guv'nor and Miss Bloomfield have got a thing about that horse."

"They spend a devil of a lot of time with him," Greaser agreed.

"Miss Bloomfield rode him out this afternoon," Kathleen said.

They all gaped at her in amazement.

"I was cleaning the front windows when she went down the Avenue. She was with the guv'nor, of course. He was on Murgatroyd."

"What did they do?" Cathal asked.

"Nothing much as far as I could see. They were out for an hour."

"I never knew that horse was out," Cathal said. As usual, he had gone to the yard at four o'clock to prepare for evening stables. There was no sign that Lohengrin's afternoon had been exceptional in any way.

"Paddy Dooley told me a funny story this morning," Greaser said. Although not a betting man himself, he liked to keep up-to-date with Dooley's vast knowledge of the subject. "Somebody's had a five-thousand-pound bet on Lohengrin for the Derby."

"Who?" Alison asked, her eyes wide.

"Don't know. It was in one of the big betting offices in the Midlands. Birmingham or Coventry, somewhere like that."

"What odds did he get?"

"Thirty-three to one."

"He was quoted at fifty after the Royal Lodge."

"That wasn't serious," Robin said. "In any case, the bookies would soon change their tune when a punter turns up with that sort of money."

"Is Lohengrin even entered for the Derby?" Elegant asked.

"I doubt it," Alison said. "The guv'nor normally wouldn't bother until the end of January. He likes to see them through the worst of the winter first."

Two hours later, when Cathal O'Brien was helping Alison to wash up the supper things, she asked him a question that reduced him to total confusion, despite the quiet, innocent way in which she launched it. "Cathal, when are you going to do something about Siobhan?"

"What do you mean?" But it was too late for an attempt at denial; he had already blushed to the roots of his hair, and nearly dropped the plate he was wiping.

"You're very fond of her, aren't you?" Alison took the plate away from him; it was part of a dinner set that was a much-loved wedding present.

"It's true, I am," he confessed forlornly.

"And you have been for as long as I've known you – ever since you came over from Avoca House, and I bet it was going on before that. You weren't at all pleased when she married Nigel Brookes-Smith."

"No, I wasn't."

"Well, she's free now, and a decent time has gone past."

Cathal twisted the tea-towel into a knot and gazed at his feet. "I'm not good enough for her."

"What utter rubbish! Of course you are."

"In any case, there's the guv'nor."

"What about him?"

"He likes her a lot."

"So he does, Cathal, but not *that* way."

"They're saying he'll marry her."

"Who are?"

"Some of the fellahs. It's been going on for a long time. Ever since Miss Caroline died."

"Look, Cathal, I'm not going into any details, but you can take it from me that the guv'nor's got no intention of marrying Siobhan. Now believe that, it's the God's honest truth."

"How do you make that out?" Cathal asked stubbornly.

"If he was going to marry her, don't you think he'd have done it ages ago? He's known her long enough."

"Well, there was Miss Caroline."

"Yes . . . but what about *after* her? He had all the time in the world, and what did he do? He got involved with that Maitland disaster."

Cathal blinked. It was the first time he had heard the official Imogen line on a topic that had provoked endless talk in the hostel. "So what should I do?"

"Ask her out for a meal. She likes Chinese food. Take her to that place by the river in Newbury . . . The Dragon Gate . . . you know, we went there with Greaser after Prince Igor won the Guineas."

When Cathal went back to his room in the hostel, still looking far from certain, Alison had not bothered to give him a piece of advice that she knew was totally unnecessary: there was no need to tell him to go gently.

Later, Edward cursed himself for being so slow on the uptake.

Cathal O'Brien was thirty-three, and had never asked a girl to go out with him. After Alison had told him what to do, it took him a week to decide when and how to do it, and another three days to pluck up the courage. When he finally went into the office one afternoon, he was horrified to find Edward there as well as Siobhan. While Cathal had been marshalling his forces, Edward was away at yearling sales in Dublin and Newmarket, and the coast had been beautifully clear. Now he was back.

"Yes, Cathal, what can we do for you?" Edward asked.

Cathal took root, tongue-tied.

"Is it Oscar?" Edward asked. "Is anything wrong?"

"No, sir. He's fine."

"You gave him a good walk this morning?"

"I did. Yes, I did."

"We'll keep that up all winter, Cathal. This new feed should be here tomorrow. I shall be very interested to see how he takes to that."

"I'll keep a good eye on him, sir."

"I know you will, Cathal. That's why I gave him to you."

Cathal shuffled out of the office without ever noticing the smile of welcome that Siobhan had given him.

More or less the same thing happened the following day, and again three days later, leaving Cathal at his wits' end. Thereafter, he looked for times when the guv'nor was out of the office, but to all intents and purposes there weren't any. If Edward was in the yard, Cathal had to be with him. Edward never seemed to visit Widney Cheyne except in the evenings; when Nancy Bloomfield came to Saxon Court, it was principally to look at Lohengrin, and Cathal had to be on hand to report.

He abandoned hope.

The village of Compton Norris had a Catholic church tucked away at the end of one of its pleasant side streets, and Cathal always attended one of its three Sunday Masses. Two weeks before Christmas, he went to the earliest service, a departure from his normal routine. Shortly after he had taken his place, Siobhan came into the church, smiled, and sat down beside him.

They walked back to Saxon Court together. When Cathal blurted out his question, Siobhan was careful about the order in which her reactions emerged.

"That's good of you, Cathal," she said. "Yes, I'd like that."

While he was coming to grips with this, she asked, "Is this what you've been trying to ask me for the last few weeks?"

He nodded. "It's more like ten years, actually," he said.

She laughed. It was gentle and affectionate, and her face lit up in a way that no one had seen for a long time.

Edward was compensated for Nancy's annual absence in America by spending Christmas with his parents at the house in the village that was starting to look and feel like home after their October move.

But before Nancy went to see her father and brother, she and Edward were guests at one of Imogen's happiest dinner parties. It was a celebration of the tenth anniversary of Edward becoming a trainer, premature by ten days so that Nancy could be present. The other guests were Ann and Frank, Mary and Declan, and Alison and Robin. Edward was half-surprised at Declan's ready acceptance of the invitation, and was astonished when he turned up in a superbly cut dinner-jacket, with Mary looking quite lovely in a dress that Siobhan had made for her.

"By the way, where is Siobhan?" Imogen asked after she had finished admiring the dress, and learned of its origins. "Why isn't she here?"

Edward exchanged looks with Mary, and was given permission to make the announcement. "She's got a date," he said breezily.

"Eh? Who with?" Imogen asked suspiciously.

"Cathal O'Brien."

"Wonderful! It's about time he got a grip on himself. They'll do well together."

"Steady on, Imogen," Edward laughed. "Give the poor souls a chance."

As the evening unfolded, Alison and Robin sat entranced by reminiscences of Avoca House and James Henry, whom neither of them had known. After two glasses of wine, Declan became more expansive than anyone other than Mary had ever seen, and told the full story of what had happened the day O'Gorman's mare got loose at the Phoenix Park. The exploits of a character called O'Leary from Ballymurphy reduced everyone to tears; in the later stages of the saga that had been spread over two days, one Seamus Dooley, father of Paddy, made an appearance, and Edward noticed Imogen's lack of surprise.

When Richard began to talk of the past season's successes and the prospects for 1990, it was inevitable that Cavaradossi should dominate the conversation. Edward and Declan exchanged knowing smiles across the table.

"Come on, you two, what's the joke?" Richard asked.

"Declan took a terrific shine to that horse the minute he clapped eyes on him," Edward explained. "He said he'd be a champion . . . yes he did. I was pretty surprised, too."

Everyone turned to Declan, who nodded and looked smug.

"Whereas you don't think he's all that good," Imogen said provocatively.

"I really can't imagine where that story's come from," Edward replied. "He's done very well so far."

"And you trained him," Richard pointed out.

"Precisely. So I must have faith in him."

"And next year?"

"I don't know. We shall have to see if he trains on."

They knew it was true, nevertheless they all groaned at the standard avoidance of the question. "I'd like him to win a decent race or two, then you can all say 'I told you so'," Edward said.

"But you don't think he will," Imogen probed.

"I never said anything remotely like that!" Edward protested. "Tell me, did anyone hear me say anything against that very gifted animal?" he asked, looking round with an air of injured innocence.

Frank was intrigued. He was fully aware that he was no judge of a horse. Also, he had missed many of the important events of the year because of involvement in the time-consuming business of buying and selling houses, and moving to Compton Norris. However, he sensed that Edward was masking his true feelings about Cavaradossi, and waited for an opportunity to tackle him. It came during the Christmas period when they went for a tramp across Saxon Down, leaving Ann falling asleep by the fire.

"I'd love to know what you *really* think about Cavaradossi," Frank said.

Edward stopped walking to lean on his stick. "All right," he said at last. "I'll tell you. He's a damned good horse – there's no question about that. But he isn't going to be anywhere near as good as Richard and the press think."

Frank stepped back in surprise. "They've got it all wrong?" he asked.

"The press certainly have . . . not for the first time, mind you. It's what racing's all about."

"What about his performance at Newmarket? That was pretty impressive, wasn't it?"

"The Dewhurst? Well, yes . . . it's a decent race, and I like winning it. But I didn't rate the opposition."

"I thought it was good."

"No!" Edward shook his head forcefully. "The two best horses weren't in it. Vasco da Gama had pulled a muscle, and Giles Hawksworth took Caer Caradoc out because of the state of the ground. Now if our chap had beaten *that* pair, I'd be very happy."

"Oh dear! Richard may be thinking in terms of the Derby."

"He'll have to think again," Edward said. "Whatever else Cavaradossi does, he will not stay a mile and a half round Epsom."

Frank was flattered by the confidence. Later, he began to develop the feeling that Edward had not told him everything.

CHAPTER 21

Four months later, Cavaradossi's victory in the Two Thousand Guineas was greeted with much less than rapturous acclaim, and focussed attention on Edward's true aspirations.

A remarkably mild and dry March, in which the first day of spring was a genuinely pleasant landmark rather than an occasion for donning extra clothing, brought many of the horses to a peak of condition that was unusual so early in the year. Cavaradossi was only one of twenty who relished the fine weather and set about their work with gusto. Before the colt's stiffest test so far, Edward decided to give him a prep race, and he went to Newmarket in mid-April for the Craven Stakes. He won it easily without exerting himself, and was confirmed as a very firm favourite for the Guineas, to be run two weeks later.

He became the seventh winner of a Classic race to be trained by Edward, the fifth at the Guineas meeting, a fact duly brought out by Wesley Davies in the subsequent TV interview. But the manner of his victory failed to inspire his supporters, and came perilously close to giving many of them heart failure. With a furlong to run, he had what appeared to be an unassailable three-length lead. For reasons that were unclear, Bernard Dalrymple had taken Vasco da Gama out of the race, and none of the other contestants had handled the sharp pace with any obvious degree of confidence or comfort. Then, as Cavaradossi tackled the last furlong, further than he had ever been asked to go before, Caer Caradoc mounted an assault. At first, he was impeded by a horse who was weaving badly under pressure; when he eventually got going, there was no doubting that something desperately serious was in hand.

Cavaradossi's lead was evaporating, and there was nothing to be done about it. Only too well aware of what was going on, Sean Gillespie rode like a demon, all to no avail. Cavaradossi had nothing left, and was barely maintaining his rhythm under the pressure. Caer Caradoc was second because the winning post came too soon for him; another fifty yards and the race would have been his.

Richard remained impassive during the formalities which involved the presentation of trophies by the sponsors, but as soon as he and Edward were out of the public eye, the mask fell away.

"God! I wouldn't go through that again for anything," he said. "He wasn't up to it, was he? There was absolutely nothing in the tank after seven furlongs."

"Hang on, let's not jump to conclusions," Edward replied. "I'll talk to Sean and have a good look at the video. There might have been something wrong."

Richard shook his head. "You won't find anything. He had every chance. Damn it, he had the lot of them in his pocket at the distance."

"We did win, you know," Edward reminded him. "I know he seemed to be going backwards at the end, but he was still first past the post."

"H'm . . . yes, all right." Richard was far from convinced. "What did Giles Hawksworth have to say?" He had seen Edward chatting to Caer Caradoc's trainer.

"He was quite happy. He promised to get his revenge at Epsom . . . if we bothered running Cavaradossi, that is."

"What did you say?"

"The usual, that we'd have to think about it."

Richard was giving up the struggle to control his disappointment. "Second in the Guineas, first in the Derby," he muttered. "This could be the year for it. Caer Caradoc was going on well, wasn't he?"

"Oh yes. It still depends on a great deal of other things, though." Edward's tone was quite unremarkable. He might have been asking the time.

"Such as?"

"On all the horses who *weren't* here today."

"Such as?"

"Vasco da Gama. He's good. Bernard Dalrymple must fancy his chances with him."

"Oh Lord! I'd forgotten all about that fellow." Richard looked more despondent than ever.

Investigation revealed that there were no excuses for Cavaradossi: he had run out of steam, a mile was too far for him. As dozens of racing journalists and commentators scraped egg off their faces and cast around for another super-horse, Edward kept an open mind. He allowed Cavaradossi's entry for the Dante Stakes at York to stand, even though it was run over a distance more than two furlongs longer than the Guineas.

"Don't worry," he told Siobhan when she questioned the decision, "I shan't be forcing him. *If* he runs, it will only be to measure the opposition."

"You think Mr Dalrymple will send Vasco da Gama to York."

Edward smiled and nodded. Siobhan had made a statement, not asked a question. Edward thought she had probably deduced his plans in conjunction with Cathal O'Brien with whom she had become very close since the evening of the Chinese meal. They were not secret;

Imogen and Robin Lane already had a fair idea of the way his mind was working.

Nearly three weeks before the Two Thousand Guineas, the first runner of the season had gone to Newbury. Lohengrin almost literally strolled to victory in a race for three-year-olds worth a comparatively meagre seventeen hundred and fifty pounds. Dooley, accompanied by Frank, had been appalled by the degree of reality that the bookmakers had brought to bear on the situation. Certainly Lohengrin did stand head and shoulders above the rest in terms of class; even so, the miserable odds of three to one on came as a profound shock.

"I went to Newbury this afternoon," Imogen told Richard when he got home that evening.

"What for?" he asked absently, most of his attention on a bulky sheaf of papers from the office.

"The races, of course!"

"Oh . . . did Edward have something running?"

"Yes. At least, I suppose you could call it running . . . it was more like a saunter, actually. Lohengrin."

Richard looked up from the report he was reading. "What happened?"

"He won. Very comfortably."

"That's good. Was he the first runner?"

"Yes."

"Have you noticed how many times Edward does that? Right from the beginning for Murgatroyd."

Imogen looked at him hard and said, "It was a mile and a half," very deliberately.

"Oh. I see." Richard gave up the idea of an early return to the report.

"Quite. I thought that might make you sit up and take notice."

Richard stared at her thoughtfully for a few moments before he asked, "Whatever made you go? You don't normally bother, especially at this time of year."

"I thought it was high time we found out what Edward and Nancy have been up to with 'Oscar'."

"Who's Oscar?" Richard asked.

"That's what they call Lohengrin." Imogen paused. "Tell me, what other horses have had nicknames?"

"There was 'The Toff', of course."

"Yes. Go on."

Frowning, Richard shook his head. "I can't think of any more."

"Precisely!"

"So how did the race go?"

"Bit of a non-event really. Oscar went along with the field until two furlongs out, then John Dyer seemed to have a word with him, and off he went. Left the others looking rather sorry for themselves."

"John Dyer?" Richard asked.

"Sean Gillespie had five rides up at Thirsk for various people."

Now regarded as one of the top ten jockeys, Sean's busy schedule included regular work for several other trainers. Edward had obviously released him from his retained obligation for the afternoon.

"That *is* interesting," Richard said pensively.

"Isn't it just! Perhaps you should find out what's going on."

Until Cavaradossi's fortuitous Two Thousand Guineas win, Richard had been far too preoccupied with affairs at the bank to pursue the issue. When he did start asking questions, he discovered that Lohengrin had indeed been entered for the Derby; as a joint-owner, Edward had done it on his own initiative a few days before their shared birthday, his own fortieth, Oscar's third.

A week after the Guineas, Richard went to Saxon Court, timing his arrival to coincide with breakfast. His intention was to go out with the second lot and discover as much as possible about Edward's plans. To his surprise, everything was revealed in five minutes, before he had a chance to start his meal. As he drove in through the gates, he saw the big horse van down at the yard, beneath the clock-tower. The main side loading-door was open, and Dooley was standing alongside it. But instead of his customary long-suffering demeanour, there seemed to be an air of alert expectancy about him. This impression was underlined by a group of lads who were hanging around instead of hurrying off for breakfast.

Lohengrin's white blaze stood out unmistakably in the shadow of the arches. When he came out, clad in rug and leg-protectors for the journey ahead, Cathal O'Brien was leading him, with Robin Lane and Freezer in close attendance. The colt looked at the van, and walked up the ramp without any urging. Cathal went in to travel with him while Dooley closed the doors, and Freezer and Robin exchanged last-minute thoughts. Finally, in response to Dooley's impatient gesture from the cab, Freezer climbed up beside him. Richard watched the van crawl past, Freezer waving respectfully, before it turned towards the village and gathered speed.

Inside the house, nothing was quite as it should have been. Only Declan and Sean Gillespie were at the kitchen table, although the usual eight places had been laid. Siobhan was busy at the cooker, so Richard assumed that Mary and Rosie were working in the dining room of the hostel. Looking into the office, Richard found Nancy applying a little make-up to her face with the aid of a mirror propped up on a filing cabinet. She had left Widney Cheyne two hours ahead of him, dressed for riding out with the first lot; now she had changed into clothes suitable for a day at the races.

"What's going on?" Richard asked.

"Hi! We're taking Oscar to Lingfield."

"For the Derby Trial?"

"That's right."

"Good Lord! Is that today?"

"It is . . . and haven't we got the weather for it?"

Richard looked out of the window to remind himself what a beautiful morning it was. He noticed that the huge lawn stretching towards the yard was in exceptionally fine condition, and realised that Frank had been busy.

"Er . . . this is all a bit serious, is it, this business with Oscar?" he asked.

"The guv'nor thinks so!" Nancy smiled at her affectionate parody of the language of the yard.

Richard shook his head sadly. "I haven't had a chance to get to grips with things round here this year," he said. "Life's been pretty hectic at the bank."

From conversations with Imogen, Nancy knew that Richard had been dreadfully busy, working the most punishing hours. She had feared that there might be trouble, but two days ago, a deal had been announced that had stunned the financial world by its scope and brilliance: photographs of Richard and Edwin Fforbes had been in all the news-papers.

"I don't think that Edward's been *deliberately* secretive," Nancy said. "It's just that he wanted to give the horse a quiet time. We decided it was the best way to handle him."

"Did you, now?" Richard said. "Imogen's been trying to tell me for ages that you two were up to something. How's he going to do today?"

"Wait and see like the rest of us," Edward said, still fiddling with his tie as he bustled in. He, too, had changed, and was wearing one of his special suits for racing; it gave him the air of a businessman with a faint suggestion of the county show.

"Is he going to do well?" Richard asked.

Edward considered the question carefully. While he did so, Nancy picked up the clothes-brush that always lay on the window-sill, and used it on the back of his jacket; Richard saw that it was a perfectly natural, automatic action.

"Yes, I'm hoping he will do quite well," Edward said. "If he does, I think he should go to Epsom."

"You know best," Richard replied.

"You keep believing that, Richard," Edward replied. "But don't *ever* bet on it! Come on, let's have some breakfast."

The kitchen had filled up. Frank, Robin, Alison and Elegant Hawkins were now at the table, and Rosie was back from the hostel, anxiously checking that there were enough places.

"I suppose you've come to see some work," Edward said to Richard.

"Yes, I did."

"You'll be able to watch Cavaradossi do his final spin. He's going to York for the Dante next Wednesday."

"He'll never do that distance," Richard protested. "What's the point of sending him?"

"I want to find out what Vasco da Gama's made of," Edward explained. "Our boy is going to run the first seven furlongs as though it's the Dewhurst. Some interesting things should happen once he's spread them all over the shop."

Richard noticed that Sean Gillespie viewed the prospect with sardonic relish, while Elegant Hawkins was faintly amused that his horse was to be used as a maverick.

"Once we've got that out of the way, we'll find a couple of nice races at six or seven furlongs for him to win," Edward went on. "Declan's in charge of the second lot. If you're polite to him he'll let you watch, and Robin might drive you down in the Land Rover."

Each year, in the period between the Two Thousand Guineas and Derby, the press indulged in feverish speculation and dissection of mostly useless information in their quest for the winner of the world's greatest race. It was a time for burying earlier misguided predictions in a welter of irrelevant 'facts' that annoyed or amused the trainers and staff of the stables concerned. Owners had blazing rows with jockeys; horses were reported as having done training gallops at speeds far in excess of what any trainer in his right mind would permit; a little-known stable had a dark horse that had cost only seven thousand pounds, yet was poised to produce the greatest upset since 1913 when Aboyeur's winning odds had been a hundred to one.

What happened that afternoon at Lingfield in the Derby Trial Stakes, a Group Three race worth fifty-two thousand four hundred pounds, gave the pundits plenty to think about, particularly since none of them had considered the possibility that Saxon Court might have a better horse than the semi-disgraced Cavaradossi.

There were nine runners, all of them entered for the Derby. This was normal, although everyone had come to accept the well-established pattern that few if any of them would take part in the Epsom Classic: this year there were to be only two.

Sforzando, a colt from Bernard Dalrymple's stable, took a strong-paced grip on the race from the start, and made all the running for nearly the whole of the first mile round the triangular-shaped course. Four or five lengths behind him, Sean Gillespie sat on Lohengrin with corpse-like patience, showing no sign of the frantic fifty-mile dash from Saxon Court after working Cavaradossi in the second lot.

Rounding the final turn, Lohengrin began to advance. As usual, his progress was completely unspectacular. Acting on instructions from Edward, Sean Gillespie remained uncharacteristically placid, merely urging him along gently with barely-detectable movements of hands and knees. Lohengrin's impeccable, studious style of moving concealed the pace of his gallop until he had passed Sforzando, and was starting to put daylight between himself and the rest. It was only then that Richard, watching the race on TV with Imogen, had a proper appreciation of what was happening.

"Do you know, that's a really good horse we've got there," Richard said. He sounded surprised, agreeably so. "He doesn't seem as though he's doing anything exceptional, but just look at the way that gap's opening up. He's walking away from them."

"Mmm." Imogen was watching Richard rather than the race.

Lohengrin took absolute command a little more than two furlongs from home; thereafter, the only point at issue was the margin by which he would win it. It was a long time since Richard had seen a horse who was so obviously master of the situation, yet he never lost his slightly comical seriousness as he surged on. The official verdict was six lengths: it could have been much more. Sean Gillespie, who had appeared to do nothing to produce the relentless gallop that had left the rest toiling like hacks, was easing his horse over the last hundred yards. Passing the post, he stood in the stirrups and looked back, giving the impression that he was rather worried about the stragglers.

"Well now, what do we think of that?" Richard asked, turning the TV off.

"Two things," Imogen replied. "I think we ought to get off our bums and trundle over to Saxon Court. It's a beautiful day, we could join in the fun and take Edward out for a slap-up feed."

"Yes." Richard liked the idea. "Let's go to that place at Hatchetts Green. What's the other thing?"

"You need a holiday." This was her 'official' voice.

Richard sank deeper into the armchair and thought about it. Pleased that he had not rejected the suggestion immediately, Imogen asked, "How long have you been at it non-stop?"

"Several months," Richard conceded.

"You've had one day off since Christmas – and that was to go to Newmarket and be frightened out of your wits by that useless Cavaradossi – and it's now the ninth of May," Imogen told him. "You've pulled off the most whopping wheeze, and I'm very proud of you. But it's time for a rest. Edwin can mind the shop for a bit."

"He's been mixed up with it, too, darling!"

"Not as much as you. In any case, didn't you say he was taking September off?"

"Yes."

"Presumably that's when Stephanie's expecting the baby?"

Richard laughed. "Why do you think that?"

"True or false?"

"True!"

"Right, this is what we do: give Edwin a few days off next week so that he gets his strength up, then have a holiday yourself. Three weeks is what you want."

"All right. Where shall we go?"

"Saxon Court."

"Saxon Court?" he echoed, and stared at her.

"Yes."

"Not Antibes or Bermuda?"

"No, Saxon Court."

"Explain."

"I rather think there are going to be some fairly stirring things happening there over the next few weeks. You wouldn't want to miss them."

"Wouldn't I?"

"Definitely not! In fact you'd never forgive yourself if you did."

"You're assuming Edward won't mind?"

Imogen smiled. She had won. "Why on earth should he? If he does, we can always evict him."

When Imogen and Richard reached Saxon Court an hour later, they found the customary weekend calm. The lads seemed to be taking advantage of the splendid weather and the fact that there were no evening stables on Saturdays. Once inside the Big House, however, they found that the appearance was deceptive. Ann, Frank, Mary, Rosie, Siobhan and Robin Lane were in the kitchen, their excitement controlled but tangible.

"Join the party," Frank said when he saw Richard. "They should be here soon. Edward said they weren't going to hang about."

"What's your opinion of this Lohengrin character, Frank?" Imogen asked, sitting down beside him, looking very intense.

He laughed. "I don't know enough to have a proper opinion," he said. "There are one or two things, though."

"Go on."

"Edward and Nancy have spent an enormous amount of time with him." Imogen nodded. "They take him for walks, and they talk to him.

That's a fact, I've seen it. Edward goes to his box to tell him things. Then you have the two expert Edward-watchers. They've got quite a lot to say for themselves lately."

"Who are they?"

"Paddy Dooley and Robin."

"Well, Robin?"

"The guv'nor thinks very highly of Oscar, ma'am."

"Any fool knows that!" Imogen's smile wiped out the severity of her tone. "Come on, Robin, this is fascinating. Let's have all the details."

They all became so deeply absorbed in the ensuing conversation that they stopped worrying about the time. Fifteen minutes passed before Imogen, herself startled, made everyone jump with a sudden, "Good Lord!"

Edward and Nancy were in the corridor. Their intention to go into the office had been diverted by the unexpected crowd in the kitchen.

"I knew it," Edward said. "The minute my back's turned you all start talking about me."

"How the devil did you get here?" Imogen demanded.

"We came in the back way."

"Why were you skulking about like that?"

"I didn't want Oscar upset," Edward said. "He's had enough excitement for one day."

"He didn't look all that excited on the telly," Imogen said. "I thought he was half-asleep."

Edward laughed. "Cathal tells me that he *did* fall asleep on the way back."

"He's a nice horse," Richard said.

"Yes, he's a thoroughly good sort," Edward replied. It was the highest praise he ever gave a horse; Richard could only remember two others who had received the accolade, James Henry and Parsifal. "Be with you in a minute," Edward went on. "There's something in the office I want to show Nancy. Any chance of a cuppa, Siobhan, I'm dying!"

Imogen was left open-mouthed, and Siobhan hurried to the kettle as Edward and Nancy disappeared into the office.

Nancy sat in the window-seat while Edward went to a filing cabinet. He selected a large notebook, and sat down beside her. "I've got a system of working out a horse's performance," he told her. "It's a sort of rating figure. Lots of people do it . . . my recipe's a bit different."

"Is it any good?" she asked.

"Yes, it's quite handy. I often use it for getting a horse into the right race so that he's got the best possible chance. The snag is the time it takes to do all the calculations."

He opened the notebook. Caroline was the only other person to have seen inside it. Flicking through the pages, he came to one headed: DERBY – 1990. Twelve horses, including Lohengrin, were listed, each accompanied by a figure ranging from a hundred to a hundred and twenty-nine.

"Those are the ones that matter," Edward said. "The others either won't run or don't stand a chance."

Nancy scanned the list. "You've got Oscar down for a hundred and seventeen," she said. "That doesn't look good enough."

"It isn't . . . but that was based on what he did a month ago at Newbury, and that wasn't a very fast time."

"What about today?"

"It was very nearly a course record. Sforzando went off at a hell of a lick."

"What *was* he doing?" Nancy asked. "He blew up on the home turn and finished last. What was all that about?"

"My guess is that he's Vasco da Gama's pacemaker. He was having a practice run *and* finding out what Oscar's made of. We should get the same thing at Epsom."

"OK. Got you. What about our fellah? How did he do today?"

"A hundred and thirty-six."

"That puts him out front."

"At the moment. We shall have to see what Vasco da Gama does at York next week."

"And you're gonna push him hard with Cavaradossi?"

"That's right."

Edward closed the notebook and put it aside.

They gazed at each other.

It began as silent speculation about Lohengrin's chances at Epsom. Edward was conscious of the change when he realised that he had stopped thinking about an imponderable complex of factors and was more concerned with the beauty of Nancy's eyes. At exactly the moment that he reached out to her, Nancy was moving towards him. She greeted the fusion of their lips with a soft grunt of satisfaction and flung an arm round his neck to draw him closer. It was a long kiss that left them breathless. After the initial, incredibly sweet contact, a powerful flame of need, of nascent desire flickered through them. They had just yielded to the necessity to breathe, and were blinking at one another in happy bewilderment when Siobhan brought the tea-tray in. Both Nancy and Edward were completely unaware of her.

"I've just had a good idea," Edward said.

"What's that?" Nancy asked.

"Will you marry me?"

"Yup! Sure thing!"

515

Siobhan put the tray on one of the desks and fled.

"What on earth is the matter, Siobhan?" Imogen asked as Siobhan shot into the kitchen in an obvious state of high excitement.

"Edward's just asked Nancy to marry him," Siobhan gasped, so carried away that she forgot her own rigid code governing the way in which people's names were used.

With one exception, everyone looked flabbergasted.

"What did she say?" Imogen asked calmly.

"She said, yes, she would."

"Thank God for that!" Imogen looked round, finding herself surrounded by faces that were beginning to acquire the glow of happiness as the surprise faded. "My word, it's taken him long enough, hasn't it?" Imogen said. She was smiling broadly, but there was a hint of exasperation below the surface.

"Oh dear, this is good news," Ann said excitedly. She was hovering on the brink of tears.

"More new dresses," Frank said to Richard with an air of mock-misery.

"Eh?" Richard was miles away. Still coming to terms with Lohengrin's performance at Lingfield, he had hardly begun to grasp a piece of news that was, to him at least, completely unexpected.

"The wedding," Frank explained. "We shall have to buy new frocks and things for the wedding."

"Oh yes, of course."

Bursting to tell Alison, Robin slipped away almost immediately and sprinted across the road to his house. "The guv'nor's done it at last," he cried as he rushed in through the kitchen door.

"Done what?" Alison was weighing out the ingredients of a cake, and almost resented his exuberant intrusion.

"Asked Miss Bloomfield to marry him. She accepted, of course."

"When?"

"Just now . . . not long after they got back from Lingfield."

"Were you there? Did you hear him do it?"

"No, but Siobhan was."

"Yippee!" Alison knocked two eggs on the floor in her excitement.

"Hey! Where are you going?" Robin asked.

"The hostel. They'll all be thrilled."

"I'm coming with you."

Imogen waited ten minutes before marching into the office. Nancy and Edward were still in the window-seat; Nancy's head was on his shoulder, and they looked ridiculously pleased with themselves.

"We're going to get married," Edward said.

"I know," Imogen said, as though she had been given a piece of rather stale, totally unremarkable information.

"How?"

"Siobhan was in here when you popped the question. Don't suppose you noticed her." Nancy and Edward exchanged amused glances. "Anyway, jolly well done. I'm absolutely thrilled. When's it to be?"

"End of the season," Edward said. "There are important things to be sorted out first."

"Quite right! Now then, Richard and I were going to take you out for a meal tonight in any case, but this is an excuse for a real beano."

"Wonderful," Edward agreed. "Where are we going?"

"Hatchetts Green."

"In that case, we'd better get cracking if we want a decent table. I must have a quick rinse first, I'm a bit filthy. Some of us have been at work since six this morning."

"Good point. That reminds me," Imogen said. "Richard's been overdoing it, so he's starting a holiday towards the end of next week. We're coming here."

"Here!"

"That's right. There's no need to look like that, we shan't be any trouble. I've already spoken to Mary about getting a room ready. You won't know we're around."

Shaking his head, Edward made for the bathroom.

"Well, well!" Imogen said after he had gone. "What on earth brought this on?"

"No idea. It just happened . . . wham!"

"You're pleased, I take it?"

"Am I!"

"Been a bloody long time, though, hasn't it?"

Nancy shrugged. "He had to work things out his own way."

"And everything seems to be going very well in the yard," Imogen said. "Especially in one particular department, eh?"

Nancy remained impassive, and Imogen walked over to the scoreboard. "Twenty-one winners, two hundred and five thousand pounds prize-money," she said. "Pretty healthy."

"He'll be champion trainer this year," Nancy declared. She said it with such complete assurance that Imogen turned round with raised eyebrows. "Oh yes," Nancy added. "Depend on it! There's a wonderful filly in that yard. No one knows anything about her yet, but they will!"

"Aphrodite," Imogen said. "Belongs to Fred Bird."

"Sure, that's right. How come you know that?"

"Edward pointed her out to me when she first came here. I could see he thought she was special."

Imogen noticed how the filly had been brought in to avoid the possibility of a mention of Lohengrin. It was the same during dinner; Nancy and Edward talked freely and happily about every topic except one. Richard made several attempts to steer the conversation round to the horse he owned jointly with Edward, but each time he was deftly headed off.

———————

Edward woke as Nancy brought him a cup of tea. For a few moments, his surroundings baffled him; there was even a different pattern to the bird-song flooding in through the open window.

"Hi!" she said, and smiled at his bewilderment. "That's right, buster, you're in a strange woman's bedroom."

"A woman's strange bedroom," he corrected.

"What's the difference?"

"You're not a strange woman, are you?"

"I'll never understand your language."

"You will. You're coming along in leaps and bounds."

"Like?"

"Well, you now say 'Darby' instead of 'Durby'."

"And 'Ascot' instead of 'Ass-cart'."

"That's right." Edward sipped eagerly at the tea, and nodded his approval. "Yes, very decent early-morning tea." He looked round the room appreciatively. "It's a good place altogether. The service is excellent."

"You made full use of it last night."

"Is that a complaint?"

"Nope!" She smiled. "You're pretty active for an old guy of forty with a useless leg!"

"And how old are you?"

"Younger."

"How much?"

"A hell of a lot!" Nancy was laughing, but as she stared at him, her face became serious. "Will you tell me something, Edward?"

"Of course."

"You were very funny with me for a long time after Caroline died."

"How?"

"Some days you were as nice as pie, others you were awful."

"No, I wasn't. You're imagining it."

"I'm not. It was always happening. Nearly every time I went to the races . . . especially Ascot."

"I expect I was worried about something. I usually was in those days."

"What about Sean Gillespie's wedding? Do you remember that? Let me tell you, sir, you gave me one look that day, just one . . . and I felt like a lump of dog-shit."

Edward looked uncomfortable.

"Well?" Nancy insisted. "What was it about?"

"I suppose it was a sort of defence mechanism," he replied wretchedly.

"Defence? What was I doing, attacking you?"

"No. Defence against me."

"Come on, tell. And, oh boy, this had better be good."

"I always found you attractive . . . very attractive indeed. I suppose I fancied you. I mean, I liked you and everything . . . thought you were a nice person . . . but the fact is, Nancy, I was sexually attracted to you as well. So the way I stopped it was to ignore you."

"Why did you want to stop it?"

"I thought it wasn't at all the right thing to do. Affairs with colleagues can cause all sorts of problems."

"So what's changed?"

"I love you."

"And you didn't before?"

"I don't know."

Nancy was unsure whether to laugh or cry, and it showed on her face. "You're saying you deliberately avoided having a relationship with me because of some frightfully British stiff-upper-lip idea that it wasn't the right thing to do?"

He nodded. "That's about it, I suppose."

Edward thought that she was going to be very angry. So did Nancy. But she calmed down. "And it caused one hell of a mess, didn't it?" she said softly.

"I'm afraid it did." Edward thought about all the things that would never have happened if he and Nancy had recognised their love earlier.

"You might have been killed," she said, reading his thoughts perfectly.

"We both could."

They stared sombrely at each other for a few moments before Nancy began to smile and said, "We're gonna be all right now."

"We are indeed! We've a lot of time to make up."

"No trouble! Tell me, did I live up to your expectations?"

"In what way?"

"You said you used to find me attractive."

"I still do! And yes, you're all right." He attempted to embrace her, but she eluded him with a mischievous grin.

"Wait! I need a shower first."

Left alone, Edward recalled the events of the previous evening. The subtle transition from being Nancy's close friend to future husband had taken place quite effortlessly over dinner. Richard had watched it with amazement, Imogen acted as though it was the most natural thing in the world, and had spoken to Nancy as if she were already mistress of Saxon Court. Not until they got back to Widney Cheyne, and Richard had paused to drop Nancy and Edward off outside her cottage, did Edward realise that he had no way of getting home unless he took Nancy's car or she drove him.

The question of him going home never arose.

Nancy made hot drinks, and they stood in the kitchen to debate Lohengrin's training schedule. One moment they were trying to decide his galloping partners, the next they were in each other's arms. After that, the progression to their love-making had been unhurried and deliciously inevitable.

Edward smiled at the memory and wondered how much longer she was going to be in the shower.

One of the first things that Imogen and Richard did after starting their holiday at Saxon Court was to watch a video-recording of the Dante Stakes, in which Cavaradossi had played his part to perfection. Urged on by a demented-looking Sean Gillespie, he came out of the stalls like a rocket, and scorched off down the course as though he intended making all the running in a five- or six-furlong sprint.

For a while, the rest were content to let him get on with it, moving along in a compact bunch five, ten, fifteen, then twenty lengths behind the flying Cavaradossi. Signs of nervousness appeared when they had covered four and a half furlongs with six to go.

"They daren't let him get away with it," Edward chuckled as three jockeys took their horses clear of the pack and set off in pursuit of the tearaway.

Nancy rubbed her hands gleefully; she had already watched the tape a dozen times, but her excitement was undiminished. "They *think* ours is going to blow up at seven furlongs or a mile," she said. "But right now, none of them are betting on it!"

As he had done in the Guineas, Cavaradossi shot his bolt at seven furlongs. Sean Gillespie tucked him neatly out of the way on the rails, and settled down to canter him home with an air of philosophical and entirely innocent resignation. At that point, Vasco da Gama was over forty lengths behind the new leader, and Joe Hook, Bernard Dalrymple's first jockey, had a daunting task. He had remained cool, keeping his horse going smoothly and isolated from the panic induced by Cavaradossi. As a consequence, there was only one horse behind him, while some of those in front were going ominously well.

"Now, watch this," Edward instructed. "You'll see how very good he is."

Once clear of the final turn, Vasco da Gama's run for home was brilliant, and became justly famous as one of the finest performances seen that season. He mopped up the tail-enders and mid-division as though they had been standing still, then set about the four leaders, two of whom showed unexpected tenacity. In the ensuing struggle, which Vasco da Gama won by a length, the outstanding rapport between him and Joe Hook was very apparent.

"H'm. Very good," Richard said, much impressed.

"Very good indeed," Edward said.

"What's the verdict?" Richard asked.

"He's a shade better than Caer Caradoc," Edward replied. "I think he's the one we've got to beat. We have to bear in mind that's a relatively easy track, and he was going a furlong and a half less than Epsom. But I don't want to take anything away from him. He's a bloody good horse."

Richard nodded. He was unaware of Edward's rating system. Even if he had known about it, he would have learned nothing: Nancy was still attempting to discover how Vasco da Gama's performance had been assessed.

·"I wonder what Bernard Dalrymple thought of the tactics," Richard said.

"Oh, he knew exactly what we were up to," Nancy smiled. She had gone to York with Cavaradossi. "I saw him afterwards and he gave me a look!"

"It's up to you, then," Richard said to Edward.

"Yup!" he replied happily, smiling at Nancy.

Richard never for a moment regretted falling in with Imogen's suggestion of a holiday at Saxon Court. They spent most afternoons exploring Berkshire. They looked at village churches and stately homes, and went to every vantage point on the Downs, constantly delighted at what they saw. Like so many people who led very busy lives and took their holidays abroad, they were astonished at what only one relatively small part of their own country had to offer. On Imogen's fortieth birthday they had lunch in a pub by the Thames, then drifted through the next two hours in a rowing boat on the river.

"Do you know how long it is since we last did this?" Imogen asked.

"Yes. Almost exactly nineteen years to the day," Richard replied. "I rowed you down the Backs after a May Ball. If I remember correctly, we then went to Ely for an incredibly dirty weekend, and you proposed for the first time."

Laughing, Imogen scooped up a handful of water and threw it at him. "You liked Cambridge, didn't you?" she asked. "You were always making a nuisance of yourself at weekends."

"There was nowhere else to go," he replied. "Belfields was too far away for an ordinary weekend."

"Wasn't that the year you and Edward went to the Derby with James Henry?" Imogen asked.

"It was indeed. Mill Reef won it."

But the aspect of the holiday that set it quite apart from any other experience were the mornings on Saxon Down. Richard got up at his usual time of six o'clock. However, instead of dressing in a city suit and hurrying off to Didcot to catch the seven forty-four train to London, he wore slightly scruffy clothes, went round the yard with Declan, and then drank tea with Edward until it was time to go out with the first lot. For the first few mornings he walked, setting off before the horses, and taking up the best vantage point, about two hundred yards from the end of the Avenue. Then Edward, recalling that Richard had done a bit of riding in the distant past, got him mounted on a placid old gelding who was spending his retirement at Saxon Court after ten years of hunting with the Duchess of Dorchester. For the first three days, Richard suffered excruciating protests from muscles he had forgotten existed; but the extra height of a horse enabled him to see much more, and being mounted somehow made him an integral member of the team.

He discovered that watching work every day was very different from seeing the occasional Saturday morning. Patterns quickly emerged. The progress, or lack of it, of individual horses was apparent. He soon learned to spot the animal who would be ready for a race in two or three weeks. Above all, Richard saw how totally happy and in his element Edward was. An air of quiet confidence enveloped everything that he did. Partly this was due to the sustained success of the previous season, which had done wonders for his self-esteem, as well as lifting the morale of the yard to heights not seen since Caroline.

There was also Nancy, whose love produced a marked change in Edward. In some ways, there were clear similarities with Caroline: it was obvious that Edward thought the world of her. Whenever she came to Saxon Court, he always interrupted what he was doing to greet her and spend a few minutes in affectionate private conversation. But the differences were equally plain. Edward had matured and gained assurance in the difficult years since Caroline, and his need for Nancy was somehow more human and recognisable, more down-to-earth than his all-embracing dependence on Caroline.

Then there was Lohengrin.

Richard was constantly reminded of the affinity that had sprung up between Edward and the colt within hours of his birth. When he was anywhere near Lohengrin, Edward became charged with even greater confidence and warmth, and it was impossible not to notice the very special way he treated the horse.

Lohengrin always went out with the first lot, leading the string down the Avenue, alongside Edward on Murgatroyd, but always slightly in front. He never used the cantering circuit with the others; as soon as they reached Saxon Down, Cathal O'Brien wheeled him away towards the back-straight of the main gallop. Accompanied by Moss Close, one of Mark Walgrave's horses that Edward was hoping to run in the Royal Hunt Cup at Ascot, Lohengrin walked and trotted until there was a mile to go, then cantered the remainder of the way. On Wednesdays and Saturdays he was encouraged to gallop the last five furlongs. The moment they finished, Lohengrin and Moss Close went back to the yard, leaving the other forty-odd horses to use the gallop.

After watching this procedure for a week, Richard decided to comment on the unusual approach. He was riding back down the Avenue with Edward, looking forward to breakfast with ravenous anticipation. "You'll give that horse a superiority complex the way you're carrying on," he said.

Edward smiled. "Oh, I *do* hope so," he replied. "He must be an utter élitist. Look . . ." he pointed through the tree screen on the right ". . . George Roberts and his crew are getting on famously with Declan's bungalow. This weather's doing us all good."

On the Sunday before the Derby, it rained all day. The weather forecast indicated that Monday would be similarly unpleasant before the remainder of the week was fine, albeit cool for early June.

Imogen was disgusted. "This is all a bit poor," she complained, staring out of the sitting-room windows at the grey murk over the Downs. "We ought to get a refund for this!"

"You've done jolly well," Edward told her. "In any case, we need this for Wednesday. Oscar likes a bit of give in the ground, and Epsom must be pretty parched after the last three weeks."

"Pah!" Imogen continued to glare at the rain, while Edward went back to his scrutiny of the newspapers with Nancy and Richard. They had them all, including some that had inspired Imogen's wrath.

"They're fairly evenly split," Edward said, casting the last paper aside a few minutes later. "Five votes for Vasco da Gama, and four each for Caer Caradoc and ours."

"A lot of people seem to have been very impressed by what Vasco da Gama did at York," Richard said. "Do you think . . ."

"Hang on," Edward said, getting up as the phone started ringing. After a great deal of argument, Siobhan had been persuaded to have Sundays off: today, there had been half-hearted talk of a trip to the south coast, but the weather had probably put a stop to that, even assuming that Cathal O'Brien could have been dragged away from Lohengrin for more than an hour.

Edward was out of the sitting-room for a long time, and when he returned, he made no attempt to join in or interrupt the conversation that had carried on without him. It was Nancy who detected his abstraction.

"What's up?" she asked.

"That was Julie Gillespie on the phone," Edward replied. "Sean's been taken into hospital. It's appendicitis. They're operating now."

"Hell!" Nancy said.

Richard looked stunned, and Imogen said, "This is a bit thick!"

"What's the matter?" Edward asked them blandly.

"What are you going to do for Wednesday?" Richard asked.

Edward appeared to be having difficulty in recalling the significance of Wednesday. "John Dyer can ride him," he said.

"Is he up to it?" Imogen asked, and regretted it at once. Edward's casualness disappeared instantly, and she received a look that was severe enough to be intimidating.

"John's ridden him twice," Edward reminded her. "He won both times. Comfortably."

"Yes ... but ..." Imogen shut up.

"Let's hope Sean's all right," Edward said. "It sounds as if there was a bit of a panic. I'd better get in touch with John Dyer." He stood up, extending a hand to Nancy. "Come on, darling, let's ring him."

"I think this is all very careless of Sean Gillespie," Imogen said as Nancy and Edward moved towards the door.

"What *do* you mean?" Edward asked.

"Wouldn't you have thought that a man in his position would have had his appendix seen to before now?"

Edward raised an eyebrow at Nancy, and they headed for the office.

Nancy marvelled at Edward's coolness, and the way he handled John Dyer.

"Hello, John, it's Edward Manning ... yes, very well, thank you. How are you fixed this week? ... That's good, can you do some rides for me? ... Quite a few actually, Sean's in hospital ... appendicitis ... I don't know, I'll go and see him tomorrow ..." Edward was silent for a long time; Nancy could hear John Dyer's voice and the anxiety without being able to make out what he was saying. "No, John," Edward said firmly. "I want *you* to do the Derby ... Don't be silly! You know the horse, and he's very happy with you ... Absolutely not! I won't hear of it ... No, there isn't any need for that, John. Be here first thing in the morning. Just take it easy and get a good night's sleep."

Edward shook his head and smiled as he replaced the receiver. "He wanted me to get a 'proper' jockey," he said. "Imagine that!"

"I can understand how he feels," Nancy replied.

"Oh yes, of course. It must be ..." Edward's tone changed abruptly as he saw the car pull up outside. Fred Bird was at the wheel with Valerie beside him. "Ah! At last!"

He failed to hear what Nancy said as he bounded towards the door. It was, "Hey! Look at those suntans!"

Fred was getting out of the car, grimacing at the rain as Edward opened the side door and gave vent to his feelings. "Where the hell have you been, Fred? We've been scouring the country for you."

There was some truth in it. For three weeks, Edward had telephoned Fred's house at least once a day. Imogen and Richard had called in several times on their afternoon travels, but Fred had disappeared without trace.

"Hold your horses a minute, son," Fred called out cheerily. He was helping Valerie out of the car, making sure that his umbrella covered her. "Now then," he said when they were inside. "What's the panic? Has the cat had kittens?"

"I'm running that filly of yours in the Oaks."

"What, Aphrodite? That's nice. Saturday, ain't it?"

"Yes."

"Be a good day out, my love," Fred said to Valerie, who smiled her agreement. "How is she?" Fred asked. "Does she stand any chance?"

"She's got every chance of winning it," Edward said. "*That's* why I've been trying to get hold of you for God knows how long."

"Only three weeks, son. No time at all. We've been tied up . . . hello, here's me old mate Imogen!"

Possibly because she was looking for it, Imogen spotted Valerie's new wedding ring within a fraction of a second. Although she gave them a severe telling off for getting married in secret, there was no doubt that she was delighted. It was a long time before she had extracted all the information she wanted from Valerie, including details of the honeymoon cruise. Richard joined in the happy chaos which stayed anchored in the corridor between office and kitchen, with never less than two people talking at once. Eventually, Imogen told Valerie about Nancy and Edward.

"There's been an outbreak of sense and reason round here. Edward asked Nancy to marry him. I'm immensely relieved to be able to report that she accepted him."

Smiling bashfully, and standing very close together, Nancy and Edward did their best to accept the flood of congratulations from Valerie and Fred.

There was a queue to see Sean Gillespie on Monday afternoon. As busy as ever at organising, Imogen had flown his mother over from Ireland, and Mrs Gillespie, a sixty-five-year-old dynamo, added a great deal to the hubbub in the waiting room. Edward was quick to notice something that he knew he should have seen the day Sean got married: Elizabeth Gillespie had a close friendship with both Richard and Declan that

525

obviously went back a long way. He wondered if he would ever discover the reason for the very special regard Imogen had for her.

Nancy and Edward found Sean Gillespie sitting up in bed with Julie at his side, and looking rather more healthy than he did normally.

"My goodness, Sean, do you feel as well as you look?" Edward asked.

"I'm not too bad at all. A bit sore, you know." Sean waved a hand round the room. "Thanks for this." On Edward's instructions, he had been taken to a private ward after his operation. "You've got John Dyer riding him, then?" Sean said, making no secret of his main concern.

"Yes. I'm going to keep it in the family. John thought I should try for someone else."

"Who?"

"They say Sammy Shore's looking for a ride."

"Pooh! That dose!" If anything, Sean's post-operative contempt had the edge on his efforts in more usual circumstances. "You're better off with Dyer. He might make a go of it . . . Sammy Shore wouldn't. Are you taking him up to the course tomorrow?"

"Yes. I've come to the conclusion that the traffic's impossible on the day. You can't keep a horse cooped up in a traffic jam for hours on end then expect him to run for his life."

When they left after their allotted thirty minutes, Nancy shook her head sadly.

"What's wrong?" Edward asked.

"Poor old Sean. He really is cheesed."

"I know. It's so ironic. He was president of the 'Cavaradossi-for-king' club for a long time. I don't think he rated Oscar at all."

"He didn't," Nancy said. "He was very surprised after Lingfield. He said he'd never had a ride like it. The best ever, he called it."

"Sean told you that?" Edward was amazed.

"Sure. What's the matter?"

"'Strewth! You must be even more special than I thought."

———

Lohengrin's visit to Saxon Down on Tuesday morning was extremely brief. John Dyer walked him four furlongs down the main gallop, then cantered back, allowing him to gallop the last two furlongs. This was the pre-race blow-out, the last check that all was well with his breathing and action. Reporting that there were no problems, John Dyer changed to Aphrodite who was to have her last hard piece of work before Saturday's Oaks, and Cathal O'Brien took Lohengrin back to the yard.

By three o'clock that afternoon, he was making himself at home in the stables on Epsom racecourse. Dooley parked the van, and was turning the front part of it into a mobile home in which he and Cathal would spend the night. While Edward was watching Nancy help Cathal groom Lohengrin as if for evening stables, Patrick Prendegast arrived with Vasco da Gama and Sforzando. He smiled when he saw Edward.

"Mr Dalrymple said you'd be taking this very seriously, sir," he said.

"I'm just having an afternoon out, Patrick," Edward said nonchalantly. "How's Finoula?"

"She's very well. She'll be here tomorrow. Let's have a look at your fellow." Patrick peered into Lohengrin's box. "Ah yes . . . he's very nice."

"Yours looks good," Edward replied. Whereas Lohengrin was flashily handsome, yet had a demeanour of amiable docility, Vasco da Gama's bearing was that of a proud, arrogant aristocrat. He was a big bay horse, the only marking being the white star on his forehead with which his great sire Nijinsky hallmarked all his progeny.

Nancy and Edward chatted to Patrick until John Dyer arrived, at which point Edward said, "Excuse us, Patrick. We're going for a walk."

John Dyer had never ridden at Epsom. He had spent much of the past twenty-four hours watching every video of the Derby that Siobhan could find. Now they were going to walk the course.

As they crossed the Downs towards the start, Nancy was fascinated by the gangs of men erecting the contraptions that would make up the Derby Day fair.

"Something for everyone," she said.

"Not what it used to be apparently," Edward replied. "In the old days Barnum and Bailey's circus was on the rails, all the way from Tattenham Corner to the winning post. I believe Phineas T. Barnum used to come here himself to supervise it. The crowd would have been absolutely immense . . . half a million."

"How many now?"

"There should be well over a hundred thousand out here tomorrow if the weather holds."

"Times change!"

"The big difference is that a lot of people actually want to *see* the race nowadays," Edward said. "So they stay at home and watch the telly."

When they had completed the traverse of the Downs and were standing at the point where the Derby would start, Nancy gaped at the hill that confronted her.

"They cannot be serious!" she said in a low voice.

"I'm afraid they are, darling. Our boy will have to get himself up there a bit sharpish. Now, John, what do we think of this?" He was prodding the turf with the stick that Siobhan had insisted he took with him.

"It seems a bit soft to me, sir."

"Yes, it is. I think there's been more rain up here than we had. Not

527

to worry. The drainage is first-class, and this wind will soon dry the worst out."

The weather forecast was proving accurate. The rain had stopped during the night. After a cloudy morning, the sky was now clearing from the south-east, and no more rain was expected for several days. They set off up the hill, climbing steadily for the first half-mile through two gradual sweeping bends, first to the left, then the right. Level ground was reached at a point where the first of three spurs came into the main horseshoe-shaped course from the right. An ascent of a hundred and fifty feet from the start had brought them to the highest point on the course. Nancy looked round at the magnificent views.

"Is that London?" she asked, pointing to the massive conurbation sprawling towards the horizon.

"Sort of," Edward replied. "That's Croydon over there. All that to the north is Kingston and Richmond-upon-Thames."

As they moved on the track was level, curving to the left, and they passed the six-furlong post. "Half-way," Edward said. "Now, John, this is where you'll need to have him well balanced."

John Dyer nodded, his face clouding with apprehension as he saw what lay ahead. The start of the descent to Tattenham Corner took Nancy's breath away.

"I'm not saying anything," was her response to Edward's look. "Not a word!" She took another look at the hill and changed her mind. "You're gonna tell me that horses can gallop down that without breaking their necks?"

"They all manage it. Some better than others, of course."

"OK. I hear what you say. I don't *believe* you, but I hear what you say."

Edward talked to John Dyer all the way down the hill. They tested the ground at frequent intervals, and debated the best approach to take. Nancy was startled as a train appeared almost alongside the course; she had not realised they were close to a railway line. When she recovered, Edward was saying, "I think Sforzando's the problem you'll have to look out for down here, John. He's going to fade away about now. Let's hope he doesn't get in the way."

Suddenly, the great bend was over, and they were in the straight. "There you are," Edward said with a grand gesture. "Impressive, isn't it? This is where it all happens, John."

It was nearly six o'clock by the time Nancy and Edward had finished chatting to friends in the stables and were ready to leave. John Dyer was staying for a while to spend time with Lohengrin; Edward sensed that he wanted to try to build on his already good empathy with the colt. Dooley had performed his famous disappearing act. As Edward was unlocking the car, he was arrested by the look on Nancy's face.

"What is it, darling?" he asked.

"Can I stay with you tonight? I don't want to be on my own. It'ud be kinda spooky."

"Of course." He put his arms round her. It would be the first night she had spent at Saxon Court. "What about your glad rags for tomorrow? How do we get hold of those?"

"Let's go and pick them up now."

After calling at Widney Cheyne, they stopped for a meal at a steak house. To calm her nerves, Nancy began to delve into the history of the great race that was first run two years before George Washington finally forced King George III and his Ministers to accept American Independence. It was something they had never discussed before, and seeing the soothing effect it had on her, Edward pulled out all the facts and anecdotes he could recall. Principally, they were concerned with the more famous winners and the larger than life characters associated with many of them.

He took her back to Saxon Court and they made love in the pretty bedroom where the wardrobes were no longer full of Caroline's clothes and empty bottles.

Cathal O'Brien looked up at John Dyer. "Relax," he said. "You'll upset the horse. He's calm enough. So's the guv'nor."

John Dyer wished he could relax. If only there weren't so many people.

They were in the parade past the grandstand. The horses were being led down by their lads so that all the people who had not been able to look them over in the paddock got a chance to see them. It was the rule for all Group One races for three-year-olds and above. Many horses found it an ordeal, and responded by sweating up or misbehaving. The sixteen runners for the two hundred and eleventh renewal of the Derby Stakes were in race-card order, Lohengrin being number six. The horse directly in front of him was already showing signs of stress.

John Dyer averted his eyes from the grandstand. Someone had told him there were fifty thousand people in it, and the noise of their excited chatter was frightening. Beyond the grandstand, the crowd stretched as far as the eye could see, and it was the same on the other side where the hundred thousand that Edward had predicted were picnicking and enjoying the fair.

Conditions were ideal. The sun was shining, although it was only pleasantly warm rather than hot; the wind was light, from the south-east, and the jockeys in the earlier races had reported that the course was riding perfectly. Lohengrin was cool, calm and collected. His night in strange stables had been restful, he had eaten all the hay that Cathal had left for him, and he looked magnificent. As they approached the end of the parade with the leaders already turning to go back, the loudspeakers announced that the prize for the best turned-out horse went to the lad of Lohengrin. In the sitting-room at Saxon Court, with the video-recorder running, Siobhan felt a surge of pride for Cathal and moved nearer the edge of her seat.

"Right, there you go!" Cathal said, unclipping the leading-rein from the bridle. As he turned Lohengrin to the right, John Dyer glanced down the course to the five-furlong start. Tattenham Corner was discernible only as a break in the mass of humanity lining the rails.

Breaking into a canter, Lohengrin's head went high, and his ears pricked. Before he settled, he permitted himself a long look into the grandstand. What he saw seemed to impress him. The feeling was mutual. A murmur of appreciation rippled through the crowd, following him down.

It was a pity Charlie Onions wasn't here, Nocker Jarvis thought. He could have no complaints about the tassel today: like Lohengrin, it looked just right. Nocker watched the market closely. Vasco da Gama was firm at two to one. Caer Caradoc was attracting attention and moved in from five to one to nine to two. But it looked very much as though the clever money was going on Lohengrin; he went seven to two, three to one, eleven to four and finished at five to two.

Approaching the paddock, John Dyer saw Edward. He looked totally unconcerned. What was it he had said to Lohengrin as they were leaving? "Go on, my boy, you'll be all right. Your mother found her way round here." Rhinemaiden, of course, the Mill Reef filly who'd won the Oaks. John Dyer also saw that Nancy and Richard were still tense. They were soon lost from view, and he concentrated on pulling his horse up in preparation for the long walk across the Downs to the start.

Edward watched all the runners go past. Nancy noticed that his face remained quite expressionless until the last one, Vasco da Gama, who was sweating. "H'm . . . he's not taking too kindly to this," Edward said, and turned away in search of something to interest him. It was likely to be fifteen minutes before they got their next proper view of the horses.

Imogen was talking to Valerie and Fred twenty yards away, and he moved towards them. Responding to his quizzical glance, Valerie came to meet him. Before she had a chance to say anything about the occasion, Edward broached a topic that he had been forced to ignore since Sunday afternoon.

"So how did you and Fred manage it?" he asked. "Who surrendered?"

"No one," she replied, smiling. "Happy compromises all round. We're going to live here *and* in Dublin. We shall spend summer in England for the racing, then we'll go to Ireland in the winter when this place gets boring."

"Very good. What about the business? Has he sold it?"

"No. A miracle! We've found someone to run it. Fred's going to be a sort of demi-semi-executive chairman . . . two or three days a month of high-powered decision-making. I'm terribly pleased. He'd have been lost without it, you know."

"You don't have to tell me that. Who's the multi-talented paragon? Do I know him?"

"Vanessa Blandford."

"Who?" Edward's face was blank.

"The knicker-lady from Cornwall. Do you remember, she helped Fred find out what Monty Dorchester was up to?"

"Oh yes. I did meet her." Edward's face briefly showed his unease at the memory of that appalling day.

"Apparently she was thinking of opting out to concentrate on beautiful thoughts," Valerie said. "But she did have a secret yen for the old cut-and-thrust, and we made her an offer she couldn't refuse."

"And Fred trusts her?"

"Implicitly! She's his second favourite woman." Valerie paused and looked across at Nancy, now laughing at one of Fred's observations. "And things have come right for you, too."

"Haven't they just! She's bloody wonderful."

"Imogen says it took you long enough."

"She's quite right, I suppose. Still, better late than never, eh? Come on, we ought to watch this race."

John Dyer got no respite from the crowds. There were hundreds of them strung out along the path over Epsom Downs, and the rails at the start were packed two and three deep. Normally this was a quiet, almost secret business: today, there were thousands of spectators, as well as the obtrusive clutter of television for worldwide live coverage. Lohengrin paused briefly to study it all, then ambled round in a circle with the other horses, four of whom were now sweating and fretting badly, although Vasco da Gama seemed to have quietened down.

Captain Anthony Ayres, the Jockey Club's chief starter of races, was in charge, impeccably attired in morning suit and gleaming black top hat. He called the roll, with the name of each runner and the number allocated in the draw. Vasco da Gama was in stall number two, near the rails; Caer Caradoc was five; Sforzando, the pacemaker, was in the middle of the field at eight and Lohengrin almost on the outside at fifteen. The handlers went to work with their customary caring efficiency, having a last look at saddle-girths, and putting the horses into their stalls. Only Caer Caradoc was difficult, taking a couple of minutes to agree to

531

go in. John Dyer pulled his goggles down, took a deep breath, stroked Lohengrin's neck and felt very sick.

"All in, sir," someone shouted.

Then: "Ready?"

Briefly, the white flag showed and the gates burst open.

In the split-second as the horses launched themselves on the great adventure and trial, the noise inside the stalls was thunderous as the hollow tubular structure resonated to the kinetic energy being unleashed from it. John Dyer closed his eyes. He opened them again as he felt the rush of air on his face. Lohengrin had jumped off perfectly and found his legs within three strides. Ahead, the official with the red flag who had the unenviable task of halting them if there was anything wrong with the start, hurried to the rails and ducked out of sight. The ambulance and the car carrying the video patrol equipment emerged from behind the stalls and set off in pursuit at thirty-five miles an hour.

At Saxon Court Mary saw that Siobhan was chewing her handkerchief.

Sean Gillespie's knuckles were white as he sat in the chair by the side of his hospital bed, his eyes fixed on the TV screen.

Sforzando did exactly what Edward had expected. Within the first furlong he moved strongly into the lead, with the field following in a V-shaped formation, like a flight of geese. John Dyer kept a firm grip on Lohengrin, holding him on the bit so that they were last but one on their side of the V, level with Vasco da Gama on the other side. There was little change for the next two furlongs; to minimise the effects of the long, gradual bends, the jockeys kept their horses spread out across the width of the course, and the V formation held remarkably well.

John Dyer felt better. He was comfortable in his favourite position, with all his weight in the stirrups, his torso almost parallel to the ground, and his backside clear of the saddle. Lohengrin was galloping smoothly, well within himself; his breathing was good and the ground was to his liking. Although he was a long way from enjoying himself, John Dyer had stopped feeling sick.

Approaching the top of the hill, the V began to close up on the near-side rails, and Vasco da Gama moved forward, passing four horses until he was third, two lengths behind Sforzando who now seemed to be accelerating. Guiding Lohengrin in towards the rails, John Dyer had the first inkling that his horse was developing his own ideas on the race; Lohengrin actually lost ground, ending up last, but well clear of the rails so that there was a clear way ahead.

On the level at the top of the course, John Dyer was astonished to see a TV camera being towed along a track outside the rails. Fortunately, it was twenty lengths away, concentrating on the leaders. Lohengrin either didn't see it or failed to react.

When they reached it, the descent to Tattenham Corner looked even more terrifying from the back of a horse. There was trouble at the front immediately. Sforzando couldn't handle it, and slowed abruptly, the confusion shunting down the line. Momentarily, disaster threatened as two horses in the middle bumped together; somehow it was averted, but John Dyer never saw how because he was preoccupied by the change in motion as Lohengrin adjusted to the gradient.

And he did it superbly.

This was where his studious, stride-measuring method of moving came into its own. Within fifty yards John Dyer felt completely relaxed and safe. For another fifty yards, he imagined he was on Saxon Down, doing no more than a routine piece of ride-work. Everything else ceased to exist. Then he realised that they were passing other horses. Four or five were already behind them, and two more were falling back now. Going the long way round the bend, and clear of all possible trouble, Lohengrin was sailing past the opposition without the slightest sign of haste or urgency.

Concentrating hard on the bend that went on and on forever, John Dyer was vaguely aware of the excitement in the crowd to his right. It never occurred to him that he and Lohengrin were causing it. The gradient was easing now, the rails on the far side disappeared as the final spur joined the circuit, and there it was, the end of Tattenham Corner and the home straight. From his position on wide outside, John Dyer could see the winning post, three and a half furlongs, thirty-eight seconds away. There were three horses inside him. Ahead, on the rails, Caer Caradoc was leading Vasco da Gama by a length.

As Caer Caradoc's jockey went for his whip, John Dyer gave Lohengrin his head and began to use his knees, closing up on Vasco da Gama. Caer Caradoc held them for nearly a furlong, then he began to fade; it was too far for him. Vasco da Gama was in command when they came to the two-furlong marker, but Lohengrin was on terms with him as they went beyond it, and came into the cauldron of noise from the densest of the crowds. Looking across at his adversary, John Dyer saw Joe Hook working away with his usual stylish and fierce determination. Vasco da Gama was going well, drawing away again. He was half a length in front.

That was when Lohengrin stopped being studious.

John Dyer shook at the surge of power and courage under him. There was a frightening moment of hesitation, then Lohengrin gave his all, and started to gallop as he had never galloped before. Joe Hook's expression of alarm coincided with a great roar from the grandstand. One word stood out from the cacophony. It was on the public address system, too.

Lohengrin!

He took the race by the neck two hundred yards from the line, and the cheers were deafening. His pricked ears waved around, apparently with a will of their own, and he lengthened his stride. John Dyer was torn between the thrill of travelling faster than ever before on a horse and disbelief that there were people in the grandstand throwing top hats in the air.

Nancy and Richard were standing close on either side of Edward, each gripping one of his hands tightly. In the instant at which Lohengrin passed the post to become Edward's first Derby winner, he looked up to the sky, and they knew exactly what he was thinking. It was a time to believe in a heaven whose angels could see all that happened on earth.

"James Henry and Caroline will be on their way to the party now," Richard said, so quietly that only Edward heard him.

"What was it he said?" Edward asked.

"'I want you to win it with a decent, honest horse, a brave horse,'" Richard quoted exactly.

"I reckon we've done that."

"Yes. My God, that last furlong! I've never seen anything like it." Richard looked drained.

"I know."

"Come on, darling." Nancy gave Edward's hand an extra squeeze before releasing it. "Let's go!"

Beyond the winning post, John Dyer pulled Lohengrin up in a quiet, almost deserted world. He was joined by Vasco da Gama who had been on terms at the distance but beaten by four lengths an incredible furlong later. Joe Hook nodded acknowledgement of defeat at the hands of a much better horse, and they set off back to the grandstand. Neither of them had any idea what had happened behind them. A twenty-five to one outsider finished third, then the rest had been spread out over more than three hundred yards, hopelessly outclassed and beaten by Lohengrin's masterly handling of the descent to Tattenham Corner and glorious run up the straight.

Edward and Richard went to the gate together to meet their horse. At the last moment, as Lohengrin approached them, Richard pushed Edward forward, and said, "Yours!"

Taking the rein from Cathal, Edward stroked Lohengrin's muzzle, and noted that he seemed to have come through it splendidly. He looked up. "Well, John?" he asked.

John Dyer shook his head. He was smiling, but his eyes were very bright, and he was blinking rapidly. He shrugged. There were no words.

All Derby winners receive acclaim, and that given to Lohengrin as Edward led him through the crowd to the most famous and coveted winner's enclosure in the world was tumultuous. The lads in the TV room of the hostel were struck silent as they watched the progress of their Oscar, his passage cleared and eased by a mounted police officer. None of them were in any doubt that this was exactly what the guv'nor had intended ever since he had held the new-born foal in his arms. They were witnessing the culmination of three years of love, trust and faith.

While Cathal walked Lohengrin round the ring after John Dyer had gone to weigh in, Richard nudged a rather po-faced Edward, and whispered, "Look at him, the cynosure of all eyes!"

Edward stared at him. "You've been saving that up," he said accusingly.

"Yes, I have," Richard admitted, and they both laughed. It made a good picture.

Bernard Dalrymple was first with the congratulations, leaving Patrick Prendegast to look after Vasco da Gama. "Very well done, Edward. That was a marvellous performance."

"Thank you, Bernard. I'm only sorry your horse had to get beaten. As a matter of fact, my reckoning was that he'd probably win it based on his performance at York."

Bernard Dalrymple laughed. "You didn't know your own strength."

"I thought he might find a bit extra, but that was outstanding."

"It was indeed. Well done."

After Lohengrin had been taken away to the stables, Edward was grabbed by Wesley Davies, then by a reporter for an American TV station. The next race was being run before he was able to free himself from interviews, providing quotes for the press, the sponsor's trophy presentations and a deluge of congratulations. When he walked into the stables, he stopped dead, smiling and shaking his head at a most comical sight. Freezer was holding Lohengrin's head collar while Cathal washed him down with a hose. The Derby winner had a stupidly blissful expression on his face, and was untroubled by any sense of occasion.

The reality was brought home to Edward by Nancy. She ran to him, wrapped her arms round him very tightly, and burst into tears.

At five-thirty, when the bulk of the crowd had dispersed, Nocker Jarvis watched them go. Nancy and Edward were in the cab of the van with Dooley; Freezer followed, driving the car they had used to come to Epsom that morning. Edward had loosened his tie and was without his morning dress coat, and Cathal, acting on Siobhan's instructions had tied blue ribbons on the van's door handles.

Nocker was the first person to be aware of how he would be affected by Lohengrin's victory. Weeks were to pass before Edward appreciated that as well as the consummation of a dream, he had a half-share in a horse worth fifteen million pounds; John Dyer hadn't begun to think about his future; at least two per cent of the three hundred thousand pounds prize-money would eventually influence Siobhan and Cathal. But not yet. First, they had the simple joy to experience.

Dooley had been right, back in October. A bet of five thousand pounds at odds of thirty-three to one *had* been made in a Midlands betting office on Lohengrin to win the Derby. Nocker thought long and hard before risking most of his life's savings, but knew that he had no choice. What he saw that day at Wolverhampton convinced him that a once-in-a-lifetime opportunity was there for the taking. It wasn't so much what Lohengrin did on the track, impressive though that had been: it was how the horse and his trainer had behaved towards one another. Nocker had never seen anything like it in thirty years. Now he was the richer by a hundred and sixty-five thousand pounds, enough for a cottage in the Shropshire hills and the book he wanted to write.

Edward recognised Nocker and leaned out of the cab to shout, "Hello, Mr Jarvis. Did you have a bet?"

"Yes, thank you, Mr Manning, I did."

Edward laughed. "I thought you might. I saw that you'd rumbled me that day at Wolverhampton."

"My warmest congratulations, Mr Manning."

"Thank you. Here, I say, wasn't he good?"

"He was brilliant, Mr Manning. Absolutely bloody brilliant!"

The village began gathering far too early. It was barely five o'clock when the first groups formed in the High Street, the older folk, and mothers who had seen their children home from school and given them tea. William Fairbrother, hale and hearty at eighty-two, had vivid memories, of Joshua Fielding's six Derby winners, the last exactly forty years ago, the year Edward was born. He pottered the length of the High Street, pausing to tell of the good old days, and making sure that everyone realised that, "Young Mr Manning and that smashing Miss Bloomfield" had brought them back again. "'Twas her as set it up," William insisted. "Her bred 'im, and that's what does it. Nobody's ever won the bugger without a good horse! And remember, this y'ere's the tenth time we've done it. Oh yes! That Ollie Derwent had three."

When the men began returning from work, the Fortescue Arms became the focal point as tables and chairs were fetched out into the garden. There was an atmosphere of festivity and good-natured patience. No one bothered about the time. Instead, eager debate about the forthcoming midsummer fête sprang up; the exploits of Herbert Sutton, the village's opening batsman were discussed enthusiastically, and William Fairbrother carried on telling the tale.

Once free of the traffic in the vicinity of the racecourse, Dooley drove his special cross-country route, avoiding all but the smallest towns.

"Isn't that nice," Nancy said. "People are waving at us."

"That's highly debatable," Edward told her. "It's most likely that they're *really* waving at Dooley."

"Why?"

"I don't know. They always have done, and I suppose they always will."

Dooley remained impassive, and Nancy eventually stopped staring at him.

It was nearly seven o'clock when they reached Compton Norris, and Nancy said, "Heck! Who are they expecting? Royalty?"

"Yes," Edward said. "And we've got him in the back."

They were at the Fortescue Arms for ten minutes, Edward receiving congratulations, Nancy dazed by the knowledge of what they had done and the happy crowd surging round the blue-ribbon bedecked horse van.

"It means a lot to them," Edward explained as they eased away from the well-wishers. "There's always been a close link between stable and village."

"I sure am taking on something," Nancy said, as though the full enormity of her future had only just hit her.

"You are indeed," Edward agreed. He put an arm round her. "And you'll cope wonderfully well."

As they drew into Saxon Court, scores of people spilled out of the Colour Room where they had been watching a recording of the race on an immense forty-eight inch television set provided by George Roberts. Declan broke away from them, and hurried to Edward as he got down from the van.

"I might have been a bit wrong about that horse, sor," he said.

Edward nodded gravely. "The legs? Nothing wrong with them, you think?"

"No, sor."

"And his courage?"

"No complaints!"

They grinned at one another.

"It's wonderful," Declan said, and Edward was astonished to see that he was close to tears.

Nancy and Edward joined the party in the Colour Room. They drank tea and ate smoked salmon sandwiches while watching Siobhan's video-recording of the race over and over again. John Dyer and his pretty wife arrived in time to hear Edward's final judgement. "That's where he won it, coming down the hill. John gave him a lovely run down there."

"I beg your pardon, sir," John Dyer said. "*He* gave *me* a lovely run!"

Edward laughed, then gesticulated at the screen. "Here, look at this, John. Just watch the way he comes up the straight."

John Dyer's expression indicated that he could not believe he had been part of Lohengrin's all-conquering gallop. And he must have dreamed that business about the top hats in the air; there was no sign of it on TV. But then the cameras had been looking at his magnificent horse, not into the grandstand.

"I must ring Sean Gillespie," Edward said when it was over.

"He's been in touch," Siobhan said.

"How was he?"

"Very pleased. He . . ." Siobhan hesitated. "He said he didn't think John took a very good line round Tattenham Corner. Sean seemed to think he would have done much better if he'd gone tighter."

Everyone, including John Dyer, roared with laughter.

"What about the photographs?" Siobhan asked Edward.

"Tomorrow," he replied. "We've all done enough for one day – especially Oscar. I might take him to Widney Cheyne, then we could get a picture of him with Parsifal and Rhinemaiden."

"And Murgatroyd," Siobhan said.

Edward considered the significance of the suggestion. "That's a jolly good idea," he said. "One for the family album."

In fact, the photograph of him with the first winner he ever trained and his first Derby winner was to be given the greatest place of honour in the Colour Room.

"Now then, there's something I want to know," Imogen said, fixing Richard with a purposeful eye.

"Yes, my dear?"

"Did you have the vaguest idea how good this animal was when you sold Edward a half-share?"

Richard laughed. "We shall never know the answer to that," he replied.

"Why not?"

"Because I'm not too sure myself, darling. Sometimes I thought he might be all right . . . then I got convinced he'd be a wash-out."

"But you knew, didn't you?" Imogen said to Edward. "Right from the start."

"I had a bit of a hunch," he admitted eventually.

"What are you going to do with him now?"

"The King George VI and Queen Elizabeth," Edward replied.

"And then?"

"We'll see how he is." The standard reply, even at his greatest moment.

"Presumably he goes to stud at the end of the season?" Imogen asked.

"Yes."

"Where?"

"Widney Cheyne, of course!" Edward and Richard said in unison.

"Oh good!" Imogen beamed. "We shall be moving up in the world with a Derby winner on the staff. Although I must say, that fellow Parsifal isn't doing too badly, is he?"

"Nancy always said he wouldn't be bad," Edward reminded them.

At nine o'clock they went down to the yard to see Lohengrin. To the surprise of everyone except Frank, Dooley was promenading through the gates with a pleasantly attractive lady of about forty on his arm.

"Good grief!" Edward gasped. "Who on earth is she?"

"That's Polly," Frank said. "Extremely nice person. She works for a building society. She and Paddy have developed an understanding."

"I don't believe it," Edward said at last. "This is turning into a madhouse. I mean, how old is Dooley?"

"Fifty-one next month," Imogen replied unhesitatingly. "No age at all. It's about time he settled down."

"Tell me, Imogen," Edward said. "Do you know everything?"

She took her time to think about it. "Yes, I suppose I do, really," was her considered opinion. She sounded surprised.

They found that Mary, Rosie, Alison, Kathleen Corrigan and several others had been busy in the Old Yard, where all the boxes but one were closed up for the night. Lohengrin was looking out, studying the buckets of flowers on trestle tables in front of him. And the brickwork above him was festooned with royal blue ribbons.

"Ah!" Edward stopped and smiled. "The Blue Riband."

Nancy detected the catch in his voice. "How'd it get that name?" she asked.

"Disraeli, 1848," he replied.

"What, Prime Minister Benjamin?"

"Yes . . . but it was before he became Prime Minister."

Edward pushed his beloved Oscar away from the door, and went into the box to check his ankles. Satisfied, he leaned on the half-door, nodding to Declan who had come through from the New Yard.

"Do you remember what else James Henry said, Richard?" Edward asked, rubbing his face against Lohengrin's. "He said, 'Win it with a horse that will restore people's faith in their dreams.'"

There were a few moments of profound silence. Then Declan spoke.

"Yes, sor. You've done that. Definitely."

POSTSCRIPT

Cathal O'Brien surprised everyone, especially his bride, by enjoying his wedding day enormously. Siobhan had feared that the ceremony and reception they shared with Nancy and Edward at the end of October might be too much for him. There were, after all, nearly four hundred guests, and George Roberts had to do a quick job on the Garden Suite of the Fortescue Arms to get them all in.

But, in addition to gaining the woman he had always loved, Cathal's confidence had improved to the point where Edward had no hesitation in making him second head lad now that Robin Lane was taking over from Declan. What had set the seal on Cathal's self-possession was his trip to France with Lohengrin, returning with Le Prix de l'Arc de Triomphe in their luggage. And, like everyone else, he had received a tremendous boost from Edward's standing. Nancy's belief that he would be champion trainer had come true.

For their honeymoon, Nancy and Edward went to New England to tell her father and brother all about it. Flying across the Atlantic, Edward talked at great length about Manrico, a two-year-old colt belonging to Stephanie and Edwin Fforbes. Manrico was widely regarded as a strong contender for the highest honours.

Edward had been very pleased by the way he won the Dewhurst Stakes.

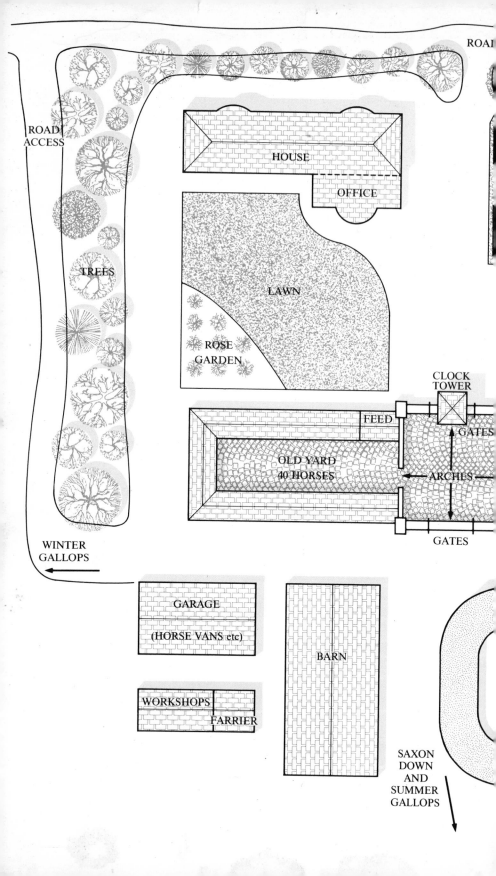

ROAD

ROAD
ACCESS

TREES

HOUSE

OFFICE

LAWN

ROSE
GARDEN

CLOCK
TOWER

FEED

GATES

OLD YARD
40 HORSES

ARCHES

GATES

WINTER
GALLOPS

GARAGE

(HORSE VANS etc)

BARN

WORKSHOPS

FARRIER

SAXON
DOWN
AND
SUMMER
GALLOPS